1 MONTH OF
FREE
READING

at

www.ForgottenBooks.com

By purchasing this book you are
eligible for one month membership to
ForgottenBooks.com, giving you
unlimited access to our entire
collection of over 1,000,000 titles via
our web site and mobile apps.

To claim your free month visit:

www.forgottenbooks.com/free519535

ISBN 978-0-267-55082-1
PIBN 10519535

Preface

A GREAT deal may be expected from a Dickens Dictionary
which has no legitimate place in it. One writer looks to it
to define the term "waterman"; as well as to explain what
Dickens intended by a "cab." I have the hope that some
day I may complete a Dickens Encyclopaedia which would
appropriately contain all such matters. But my aim in
the compilation of this Dictionary has been to present a
concise guide to the characters and the scenes in the works
of our great novelist in a form as complete as possible. I
have kept these two points consistently before me, but I
am well aware that many errors both of omission and commission exist in the work. I am comforted, however, by the
knowledge that the work has been only partially attempted
before, and even then with many imperfections. At the
same time, I shall be grateful for information or any suggestions that will enable me to improve any future edition
of the "Dictionary."

One of the greatest difficulties in the compilation of
the work has been the separation of the characters and
places from the casual comparative allusions with which
the novels and, more particularly, the Miscellaneous Papers
abound. Nothing germane has been intentionally omitted,
but the Dictionary does not pretend to be an index or a
concordance.

It was originally intended that the "Dictionary" should
contain a large amount of descriptive topography. But

while the places mentioned in the works are undergoing constant change (in fact many of them are even now quite unrecognisable), the works themselves are always the same, and it seemed advisable therefore to limit the scope of the " Dictionary " to the works themselves rather than to render it prematurely out-of-date by the inclusion of temporary information.

The explanation is necessary to understand the arrangement of the " Dictionary," but a short description may save some time in the case of occasional references. The entries are arranged as far as possible in alphabetical order. I say as far as possible, because numerous entries under words such as " Boy " make it impossible to select an alphabetical order that will commend itself to every reader. The descriptive passage beneath the entry is taken from the novel or work. The note descriptive of the place of the character, or of the place, as the book progresses, follows in smaller type preceded by the word " note." Following this, in a different style of type, is the original where a prototype is known. These are due sometimes to my own investigation, but in the majority of cases they are collected from a variety of sources. Even if they are unlikely they are mentioned, but with a caution as to their reliability. The works I have drawn upon are too numerous for individual mention, and include a very large number of miscellaneous cuttings from periodicals of all kinds.

I have endeavoured to include the whole of Dickens' works except the Letters, and " A Child's History of England." The former were not written for publication, and the latter is obviously unsuited for dissection. I have not included " To be Read at Dusk," but have adopted the standard of " Miscellaneous Papers "—that valuable collection of fugitive pieces gathered together on the authority of the " Household Words ' contributors' book,' " etc.

A Bibliography of Dickens would have been a valuable feature no doubt, but it would have been too extensive for inclusion in the present compilation. I hope, however, to be able to produce it at no very distant date.

I have to offer my most sincere thanks to Mr. B. W. Matz for his great kindness, and for his assistance in reading through the whole of the proof sheets, as well as for the many valuable suggestions he has made during the course of the work.

ALEX J. PHILIP.

GRAVESEND,
    December, 1908.

Synopses of the Various Works

Ⳇ **Sketches by Boz.** (Published in volume form 1836.)

A series of papers of a humorous character dealing with life and scenes, chiefly in the Metropolis, as they were, for the most part, at the time of publication and the earlier part of the nineteenth century. They first appeared in the *Monthly Magazine* and the *Morning and Evening Chronicle*. They are arranged in sections, opening with Our Parish and continuing successively with Scenes, Characters, and Tales.

Sunday under three Heads. (Published 1836.)

Sunday—As it is : As Sabbath Bills would make it : As it might be made.

Ⳇ **Posthumous Papers of the Pickwick Club.** (Published in volume form 1837.)

After the first chapter the Club scarcely reappears until its interment at the end of the book. The narrative has no plot, and chronicles the doings of the Corresponding Members of the Club, the central figure of which is Mr. Pickwick. Mr. Pickwick, accompanied by Tupman, Snodgrass and Winkle, makes an excursion, in the interests of research, into Kent. They meet Jingle, and through this chance acquaintanceship they encounter the first " real " adventure to the party. On this occasion they encounter Mr. Wardle, and accept his invitation to the Manor Farm, Dingley Dell. During their too great enthusiasm for sport, rather greater than their skill, Winkle wings Tupman. Tupman retires and is nursed by Miss Wardle, when he falls under the spell of her charms. Jingle again turns up and cleverly puts Tupman out of court and elopes with Miss Wardle. They are pursued by Mr. Wardle, who is accompanied by Mr. Pickwick. They elude their pursuers on the road, but are discovered at the *White Hart Inn* in the Borough, where Jingle is induced to relinquish his claims on the lady for a monetary consideration. Here Mr. Pickwick finds Sam Weller and attaches him to his service. In announcing the change to his landlady, Mr. Pickwick falls into the greatest adventure in the book, viz., the breach of promise case Bardell *v.* Pickwick. During the progress of the preliminaries of the case Mr. Pickwick and his friends make other excursions : to Eatanswill ; to Bury St. Edmunds ; to Dingley Dell again ; to Ipswich ; and back again to Dingley Dell. Mr. Pickwick loses his case and Mrs. Bardell is awarded £750 damages. Mr. Pickwick refuses to pay, and in the interval that elapses between the finding of the jury and his commitment to prison he and his friends visit Bath. The Bath visit is full of interest, the most important event being Mr. Winkle's adventure with Mrs. Dowler in the sedan-chair. Mr. Pickwick enters the Fleet Prison and Sam arranges for his own arrest so that he may still attend his master. Jingle and Trotter

xiii

are found in a state of destitution in the prison. Mr. Pickwick befriends them and assists them to emigrate. As Messrs. Dodson and Fogg are unable to get their costs from Mr. Pickwick they imprison Mrs. Bardell. Mr. Pickwick is prevailed upon by the plight of his late landlady to pay the costs in the case and in return obtains a release. During this time Winkle has succeeded in marrying Arabella Allen. Snodgrass and Emily Wardle are married at the house at Dulwich, to which Mr. Pickwick retires. Sam and Mary accompany him.

Mudfog Papers. (Published **1837.**)
   Public Life of Mr. Tulrumble. First Meeting of the Mudfog Association for the Advancement of Everything.
   Second meeting of the Mudfog Association for the Advancement of Everything. **(1838.)**

Pantomime of Life. **(1838).**
   Mr. Robert Bolton. **(1838.)** Some particulars concerning a lion. **(1838.)** Familiar epistle from a parent to a child. **(1838.)**

⋏ **Adventures of Oliver Twist.** (Published in volume form **1838.**)
   The object of this book was to show " the principle of good surviving through every adverse circumstance." Oliver is born in a workhouse and named Oliver Twist by the Parish Beadle. His mother dies without revealing anything of her history, and Oliver becomes a workhouse brat, at first farmed out and then returned to the workhouse. He is apprenticed to an undertaker named Sowerberry. He fights, and beats, Noah Claypole, the other apprentice ; this calls down the wrath of the powers and Oliver runs away to London. On the road he falls in with the Artful Dodger, who shares his food with him and then takes him to Fagin. The first time Oliver goes out with Fagin's boys on the " pinching lay " he is arrested for a theft he did not commit. He is only released on the testimony of the Bookstall Keeper. Mr. Brownlow, the old gentleman whose pocket had been picked, takes him home with him and has him cared for. When on an errand for his benefactor he is recaptured by Fagin's gang. He is then forced to take part in the housebreaking expedition to Mrs. Maylie's house at Chertsey. He raises the alarm, however, but is wounded, and is found next morning at the Maylies' house. His story is credited, and with the assistance of Dr. Losberne the Bow Street runners are deceived. Fagin and Monks hunt out Oliver's sanctuary and plan his recapture. But Nancy, who has been stricken with remorse, reveals everything to Rose Maylie. Nancy is murdered by Bill Sikes for this. Sikes accidentally hangs himself over the Folly Ditch in his attempt to escape, and the gang is broken up. Fagin is executed. Charlie Bates turns over a new leaf and becomes a farmer. Claypole turns evidence and becomes a paid informer with the assistance of Charlotte. It transpires that Monks and Oliver are half-brothers, and the former has been endeavouring to make the boy a criminal, to prevent his inheriting under their father's will. Rose Maylie turns out to be the sister of Oliver's mother. Monks goes abroad with the portion that has been given him, but dies in prison in a state of poverty. Rose marries Harry Maylie, who takes a country parish. Mr. Brownlow again takes Oliver under his protection. Bumble and his wife are left inmates of the workhouse, where they had so long lorded it over the former inmates.

Sketches of Young Gentlemen. (Published 1838.)

The Bashful Young Gentleman—The Out-and-out Young Gentleman—The Very Friendly Young Gentleman—The Military Young Gentleman—The Political Young Gentleman—The Domestic Young Gentleman—The Censorious Young Gentleman—The Funny Young Gentleman—The Theatrical Young Gentleman—The Poetical Young Gentleman—The Throwing-off Young Gentleman—The Young Ladies' Young Gentleman.

Life and Adventures of Nicholas Nickleby. (Published in volume form 1839.)

Like *Oliver Twist*, *Nicholas Nickleby* contains a purpose, viz., the exposure of " farming " schools where young children were taken for a small fee and were underfed and cruelly treated, which at that time were remarkably common in Yorkshire. Nicholas, his mother, and his sister Kate, come to London relying on the assistance of Ralph Nickleby, when the death of Nicholas' father leaves them almost penniless. Ralph is a miserable miser, but he secures the post of usher in one of the Yorkshire schools for Nicholas ; and places Kate with Madame Mantalini. Nicholas is unable to adapt himself to the conditions of the school and leaves the place, accompanied by the poor drudge Smike, after soundly thrashing Squeers the schoolmaster. Nicholas and Smike travel to London, assisted by John Browdie. There they are befriended by Newman Noggs and Nicholas becomes tutor to the Kenwigses children. As Ralph Nickleby threatens to do nothing more for Kate and her mother unless Nicholas leaves London, he and Smike go to Portsmouth. They there meet Mr. Vincent Crummles, the head of a mediocre theatrical company, " and go on the stage " with some success. An urgent letter from Newman Noggs recalls them to London. In the meantime Kate has gone from the Mantalini establishment and entered the household of the Wititterly's. She is molested by Hawk and Verisopht, clients of Ralph Nickleby. Nicholas overhears a conversation in a public place in which Lord Hawk disparages Kate, and thrashes him. Nicholas, Kate, and their mother then decline to have anything more to do with Ralph, and Nicholas secures a berth with the Cheeryble brothers. Squeers recaptures Smike, but John Browdie again befriends him and he escapes. Ralph and Squeers concoct a plot to get Smike from his protectors by putting forward Snawley as Smike's father, but they are frustrated. Nicholas falls in love with Madeline Bray, and Frank Cheeryble with Kate Nickleby. Ralph and Gride endeavour to ruin Madeline by forcing her to marry Gride, who wants her property. At the last moment Nicholas prevents this. Smike dies. Ralph discovers that he has been persecuting his own son, and this, together with the failure of his other schemes and monetary losses, preys on his mind until he hangs himself. Gride's old woman servant robs him and is in turn robbed by Squeers, who is eventually landed in prison. Through the intercession of the Cheeryble brothers Frank marries Kate, and Nicholas weds Madeline.. The end of the story, so far as the other characters are concerned, is quickly told. Dotheboys' Hall School is broken up. Newman Noggs recovers himself. Lord Verisopht dies at the hands of Hawk, who flies to the Continent. Vincent Crummles has come to London and then goes to America. Lillyvick returns to the bosom of the Kenwigses family ; his wife, formerly Miss Petowker, leaves him in favour of a half-pay captain.

✗ **The Old Curiosity Shop.** (Published in volume form **1841**.)

This, Dickens's fourth novel, first appeared in *Master Humphrey's Clock* (1840–1.) The central figure is that of *Little Nell*. She is first seen in her Uncle's shop—the Old Curiosity Shop—where she appears to be responsible for the whole household management, although she is only a child. Her uncle, with a feverish desire to accumulate a fortune for his little niece, is secretly visiting the gaming tables. He loses more than he wins and borrows money from Quilp, the evil dwarf. Quilp eventually " closes down " and sells up the shop. Nell and her grandfather leave secretly, to escape the dwarf, and in their long and wearisome journey meet many people and experience strange adventures. They are being searched for by the brother of Nell's grandfather, but, as they are being hunted by Quilp, and the fear of him is constantly before them, they are always moving on and endeavouring to cover their traces. They are ultimately discovered in a little village where they have been befriended by the schoolmaster they had met on their travels, who had then become the parish clerk. When they are found Nell has just died broken in health, but not in spirit. Her death shatters what remains of her grandfather, and shortly after he, too, is found lying dead on her grave. Running parallel with this, the central theme of the story, is another thread of less importance. Kit Nubbles was shop boy at the Old Curiosity Shop, and when that is disposed of he enters the service of the Garlands. A false charge is proffered against him by Sampson *Brass*, but he is liberated from prison through the instrumentality of the Marchioness, the maid-of-all-work at, the Brass's, and Dick Swiveller, who was the friend of Nell's brother and had been employed by Sampson at the instance of Quilp. Dick Swiveller marries the Marchioness. Kit marries Barbara. Quilp is found dead on the river bank and his wife marries again on the strength of his money. Sampson and Sally Brass become outcasts.

Pic Nic Papers. (By various writers. Edited by *D*ickens) (Published **1841**.)

Sketches of Young Couples. (Published **1840**.)

The Young Couple—The Formal Couple—The Loving Couple—The Contradictory Couple—The Couple who dote on their Children—The Cool Couple—The Plausible Couple—The Nice little Couple—The Egotistical Couple—The Couple who coddle themselves—The Old Couple.

⌐ **Barnaby Rudge.** (Published in volume form **1841**.)

This also appeared first in *Master Humphrey's Clock*. The story opens some five years before the Gordon Riots in 1788 at the *Maypole* Inn. The circumstance, embracing the murder of Reuben Haredale and the missing gardener and steward, leading up to the main theme of the story are here related. Mrs. Rudge and Barnaby leave the neighbourhood of Chigwell to escape a mysterious stranger. Geoffrey Haredale, brother of Reuben, who succeeds to the estates, is suspected of the murder. His daughter Emma falls in love with Edward Chester, the son of Sir John Chester, the villain of the story. The respective fathers, although enemies, unite in an attempt to prevent the lovers marrying. Joe Willet, son of the landlord of the *Maypole*, is in love with Dolly Varden, daughter of Gabriel Varden, the locksmith, but the machinations of Sir John Chester ruin this love affair also. Joe " takes the shilling " and leaves the country. Just before the riots Barnaby and his mother enter London in the hope of being lost sight of, but the stranger discovers them. Barnaby, a half-witted but harmless boy, is drawn into the excitement without any clear understanding of what it is all about. The effects of the riots are disastrous for some of the characters of the story. Mr. Haredale's home, the " Warren," is burnt down. And eventually Sir John Chester is killed in a duel by Geoffrey Haredale, who then enters a convent. The mysterious visitor to Mrs. Rudge is discovered to be her husband, who had murdered not only Reuben Haredale but also the gardener. He is afterwards executed. Maypole Hugh, the illegitimate son of Sir J. Chester ; Simon Tappertit, Gabriel Varden's apprentice ; Dennis the hangman and others all take a part in the riots. Hugh and Dennis are hanged. Barnaby is released by the efforts of his friends. Simon loses his legs, becomes a shoeblack and marries. Miggs, who had been an undesired admirer of Simon, leaves the service of Mrs. Varden and becomes a wardress. Mrs. Varden herself becomes somewhat more of a model wife when she was no longer under the domination of Miggs. Joe Willet returns from the American Revolution with the loss of an arm in time to assist in the discovery of Emma Haredale and Dolly Varden. Emma and Edward are married, and Joe and Dolly make another couple. Joe succeeds his father in the *Maypole* Inn near by where Barnaby and his mother spend the rest of their lives on the farm with the animals Barnaby loves so much.

American Notes. (Published in volume form **1842.**)
A discursive account of the author's first visit to the States.

A Christmas Carol in Prose. (Published **1843.** Now included in Christmas Books.)
Depicts the change wrought in the nature of Ebenezer Scrooge, a hardhearted miser, by the revelations of the spirits in a dream.

Life and Adventures of Martin Chuzzlewit. (Published in volume form **1844.**)
Mr. Pecksniff was an architect living near Salisbury. He makes his living by taking pupils at a premium of £500. To him comes Martin Chuzzlewit Junior, who has quarrelled with his uncle of the same name. The immediate cause of the rupture is Mary Graham, a sweet girl companion and attendant to Old Martin, with whom young Martin, has fallen in love. Pecksniff is a canting hypocrite believing that by sheltering the young man he will advance his own ends. Old Martin, however, causes his nephew to be turned out, and in turn becomes an inmate of Pecksniff's house ; the architect, thinking in this way to do still better for himself with regard to the old man's money. Pecksniff has two daughters, Mercy and Charity, and a devoted attendant, Tom Pinch. When young Martin leaves the house he goes to London in company with Mark Tapley ; from there they go to America, where they meet with all sorts of adventures and nearly die of fever at Eden, where they have bought a plot of land. During their absence Pecksniff appears to have obtained complete control of Old Martin. Jonas Chuzzlewit, son of Anthony Chuzzlewit, a brother of old Martin, marries Mercy Pecksniff. Desiring his father's death he attempts to poison him. His design is frustrated, however, though Anthony dies and Jonas believes his scheme has been successful. Jonas invests his money in the

Anglo-Bengalee *Life* Insurance Company and becomes a director. The company is a fraudulent one, and the promoter, Montague Tigg, in the interest of his own pocket, obtains a hold upon Jonas by discovering through the instrumentality of a spy, the suspicious circumstances of An- thony's death. Pecksniff is persuaded by Jonas to put his money into the concern. Jonas murders Montague Tigg and hopes to bury all knowledge of his former attempted crime. While these events have been going or in London, affairs have been rapidly nearing a head in Pecksniff's home Pecksniff proposes to marry Mary Graham. Tom Pinch at last discovers his employer's baseness and is dismissed. He also goes to London, where he visits John Westlock, who had been one of Pecksniff's pupils immediately before young Martin went to his kinsman. Tom and his sister, who had been a governess, set up housekeeping ; and Tom obtains the appoint ment of librarian to some one whose identity is hidden from him. The threads of the story are unravelled as follows : Martin (the uncle) reveals himself as the benefactor of Tom Pinch, and denounces Pecksniff as a scoundrel. The revelation takes place in the room where Tom has been at work on his books, and the result is a general reconciliation. Martin is taken back to favour and marries Mary Graham ; John Westlock marries Ruth Pinch ; Mark Tapley marries the landlady of the *Blue Dragon*. Tom Pinch is attached to Old Martin. Mercy, whose husband (Jonas) poisoned himself on the way to prison after the exposure of his villanies, is watched over by old Martin who becomes the *deus ex machina*. Charity is deserted at the foot of the altar and returns to her father. Pecksniff, after the loss of his money, becomes an outcast and lives as much as possible on the money he can squeeze from Tom Pinch. Throughout the story Bailey Poll Sweedlepipe, Mrs. Gamp, and Betsey Prig, with Mould the undertaker make frequent spasmodic appearances, but they are not essential to the plot.

The Chimes. (Published **1844.** Now included in Christmas Books.)
   The Chimes has a somewhat similar moral to that of the Christmas Carol. Toby Veck takes the place of Scrooge, and in a dream is taken up to the belfry, where the bells take facial expression, and the goblin of the great *Bell* appoints the Spirit of the Chimes to show him pictures of the future. These are, however, only pictures, although Toby profits by their lessons.

Cricket on the Hearth. (Published **1845.** Now included in Christmas
   Books.)
   Edward Plummer is engaged to May Fielding, but goes to South America. In his absence May is to marry old Tackleton, but with the assistance of Mrs. Peerybingle matters are rearranged and May and Edward are married Bertha Plummer, a blind girl, is in love with old Tackleton and is terribly disappointed when she learns he is about to marry May, but her father confesses to having deceived her, and everything ends happily more or less

Pictures from Italy. (Published **1846.**)
   Letters of travel first appearing in *The Daily News.*

Battle of Life. (Published **1846.** Now included in Christmas Books.
   The central figures are Alfred Heathfield, Marion Jeddler, and her sister Grace. Heathfield is a ward of Dr. Jeddler. He is engaged to Marion

On his return from a Continental tour Marion disappears—it is supposed she elopes. Eventually Alfred marries Grace, when it transpires that Marion had not eloped, but had taken refuge with an aunt, as she had discovered that her sister loved Alfred, until the time when Grace's happiness should be complete. She afterwards marries Michael Warden, with whom she is supposed to have eloped earlier in the story.

Dealings with the Firm of Dombey and Son. (Published in volume form 1848.)

Paul Dombey is the head of the firm Dombey and Son. He has a daughter whose existence he practically ignored because she was not a boy. At length a son is born. But when little Paul sees the light his mother dies. The boy, of a sweet and lovable, but old-fashioned disposition, is not strong. He is placed in charge of Mrs. Pipchin, but although he grows older he grows no stronger. In spite of this, however, he must be fitted for his place as " son " in the business, and is placed in Dr. Blimber's school. The natural consequence follows and little Paul dies. His sister Florence is now more distasteful than ever before to her father. She is lost in London, robbed by Good Mrs. Brown and brought home by Walter Gay. She makes the acquaintance of Walter's uncle, Solomon Gills, and his friend Captain Cuttle. Walter is engaged in the office, but is sent by James Carker to the Indies, ostensibly as a promotion. On the voyage the ship is wrecked. Edith Granger, a proud, high-spirited woman, is married to Mr. Dombey. There is no love between them, but Dombey wants her " presence," whilst she marries him for his money and position. Misfortunes then begin. Affection springs up between the second Mrs. Dombey and Florence : this displeases Mr. Dombey, and he annoys her by conveying messages of displeasure by his manager, Carker. She elopes with Carker to revenge herself on her husband, and immediately leaves him, both as a punishment for his presumption and because she has no love for him. Carker follows her, however, and on his return is killed on the railway. Walter, who had been supposed lost with the ship, returns home, as also does his uncle Solomon Gills. Florence leaves home after being still further ill-treated by her father. Walter and Florence are married. After Carker's defection it is found that the business requires the utmost care. This the head of the firm does not give, and bankruptcy follows. When the smash comes Florence returns to her father and persuades him to make his home with them. He is broken in health. His wealth has vanished, and he instinctively turns to the daughter he had spurned. Toots, the friend of little Paul at Dr. Blimber's, marries Susan Nipper. Harriet Carker, sister of John and James Carker, marries Mr. Morfin. Miss Tox remains Miss Tox and undertakes the reformation of Robin Toodle.

The Haunted Man. (Published 1848. Now included in Christmas Books.)

The burden of the story is " Lord keep my memory green." Redlaw is visited by an evil spirit which wipes out his recollections of the sufferings he had experienced. He finds, however, that he is in an unfortunate state and communicates the evil to others. He is restored by the influence of Milly Swidger.

The Personal History of David Copperfield. (Published in volume form in 1850.)

David is a posthumous child born at the Rookery, Blunderstone. He is brought up by his mother and Peggotty for several years. Then Mr. Murdstone lays siege to his mother. He is sent to Yarmouth with Peggotty, where he meets Daniel and Ham Peggotty and Little Emily. On his return he finds that his mother is married to Mr. Murdstone. Then begins a period of repression and persecution by Murdstone and his sister that results in David being sent away to school. His mother's spirit is broken and she dies, when David is called home again from Salem House, where he has experienced a great deal of ill-treatment, but has made friends with Steerforth and Traddles, who become important characters in the book. Peggotty marries Barkis, and David is sent into the Murdstone and Grinby factory, where he cleans bottles for a few shillings weekly. His lodgings are with the Micawbers, who now first appear in the story and reveal a new phase of life to the small boy. This does not continue very long, however, as David runs away and takes refuge with his aunt, Betsey Trotwood, at Dover. He is placed at Dr. Strong's School at Canterbury, and lodges with the Wickfields in the same town, where he meets Uriah Heep, then Mr. Wickfield's clerk. After leaving school David looks about him, and while doing so spends a short time at Yarmouth with the Peggottys. He met Steerforth in London, who accompanied him. Steerforth betrays little Emily and they elope, leaving England for the continent. David is articled to Spenlow and Jorkins and falls in love with Dora Spenlow. Uriah Heep has gained a complete ascendency over his employer, and is largely feathering his own nest. Betsey Trotwood loses her money, which is in the care of Mr. Wickfield ; she comes up to London and surprises David by announcing her loss in her characteristically abrupt way. Peggotty's husband dies leaving her provided for. Daniel Peggotty sets out on foot in search of Little Emily. David obtains a post as secretary to Dr. Strong, assisting him on the Dictionary, and studies shorthand with a view to reporting. He eventually masters the mystery of the art and turns it to good account. Mr. Spenlow dies leaving Dora almost unprovided for, and she and David are married. Dora knows nothing of household duties and they have many unpleasant experiences. Daniel Peggotty succeeds in tracing Emily through the instrumentality of Martha Endell, and they all emigrate to Australia. Micawber has been employed by Uriah Heep, who designs to make a tool of him by advancing small sums of money. But Micawber has been able to collect evidence of Heep's malpractice, which he reveals to Traddles, with the result that Uriah is unmasked. His designs to marry Agnes Wickfield are frustrated and he is compelled to refund the money he has appropriated, part of it being Betsey Trotwood's five thousand pounds. The Micawbers also emigrate to Australia, where something " turns up " and they prosper David's child-wife dies and he travels for some time, during which he continues his literary work and becomes famous. He afterwards marries Agnes Steerforth is drowned off Yarmouth ; and Ham is drowned while attempting to rescue him. Peggotty and Betsey Trotwood live together. Tommy Traddles marries the " dearest girl in the world " and rises to the top of his profession. Steerforth's man, Littimer, finds himself next cell neighbour to Uriah Heep in prison. And Mr. Dick attaches himself to David's children.

The Child's History of England. (Published in volume form in 1853.
   For obvious reasons this work is not included in the present Dickens Dictionary.

Bleak House. (Published in volume form **1853.**)

Bleak House is the story of a long-drawn-out suit in Chancery, or rather, the Chancery suit is the peg on which the very human story is hung. John Jarndyce refuses to take any part in the fight for the Jarndyce money, but he has as his wards Ada Clare and Richard Carstone, both interested in the settlement of the suit. To them comes Esther Summerson, who has been brought up by her aunt Miss Barbary, and afterwards at Greenleaf, a school at Windsor kept by Miss Donny. Esther is companion to Ada, but she soon becomes housekeeper, and confidant of them all. The two wards fall in love one with the other. Richard finds one path in life would suit him just as well as another, and so tries several, with the like result each time of finding something that would suit him better. The suit brings them all into touch with people many and curious, among them Miss Flite, Krook, Snagsby and Jo. Caddy Jellyby is the daughter of a woman with a " mission." Caddy has no liking for the " mission," or the work it entails. She becomes the friend of Esther Summerson. Lawrence Boythorn is a friend of John Jarndyce, and his neighbours are Sir Leicester and Lady Dedlock. Tulkinghorn is the family lawyer of the Dedlocks, and he discovers a " past" of Lady Dedlock, using the information to terrorise his victim. Lady Dedlock is interested in the death of Captain Hawdon, who, as Nemo, had executed law copying for Snagsby. George Rouncewell, Mr. George, had been his orderly. The secret, which is not revealed in the book till much later, is that Esther Summerson was the illegitimate daughter of Captain Hawdon and Lady Dedlock before she married. Lady Dedlock only became aware of Esther's relationship by the revelation of Guppy, who had secured some papers from Krook's shop. Harold Skimpole is a weak but cunning man who preys on John Jarndyce. At one time a broker, Coavinses, as Skimpole calls him, is in possession. Later the man dies, and Esther has Charlotte as her maid, John Jarndyce befriending the other children, who are left. Jo, the street sweeper, is " moved on " so effectively that he is hounded out of London. He is found at Bleak House, ill and half-starved and is taken in. He moves on again, but has communicated smallpox to Charlotte. Esther nurses Charlotte and in turn catches the disease. Richard follows his usual practice and throws up the Army. Returning home he settles down to watch the progress of the suit in Chancery in company with Vholes. Ada thinks she can better assist Richard as his wife, so she marries him. Esther receives a proposal from John Jarndyce, and from a sense of duty, as well as for other reasons, attempts to stifle her affection for Allan Woodcourt. Tulkinghorn threatens to reveal Lady Dedlock's secret on the morrow, but he is found dead. Suspicion falls on George Rouncewell, who had visited him earlier, and those who know something of Lady Dedlock's circumstances suspect her. But the crime is traced by Inspector Bucket to Mademoiselle, Lady Dedlock's maid. Lady Dedlock has left home, however, and Inspector Bucket, accompanied by Esther, endeavour to trace her ; they find her—dead at the gate of the cemetery where Captain Hawdon lies buried. John Jarndyce finds that although Esther will marry him her heart has been given to Allan. Secretly he prepares a home for them and they are married. Richard Carstone dies leaving Ada with a little son. The suit has consumed the estate in costs, and the case was never settled, but the shock was more than Richard could stand, broken as his health was. Caddy Jellyby marries

Prince Turveydrop. Phil Squod and Mr George are installed at Chesney Wold in the service of Sir Leicester Dedlock.

Hard Times for these Times. (Published in volume form **1854.**)

Hard Times draws a picture showing the futility of eliminating love, and kindness from human life and intercourse. Thomas Gradgrind professes to rule his life and those dependent upon him according to fact and logical calculation. He has a friend, Josiah Bounderby, millowner and banker. Cissy Jupe is left by her father friendless in Coketown and is taken into the home of the Gradgrinds. Gradgrind's son, of the same name, is a selfish and cunning rascal; when he is old enough he has a stool in Bounderby's Bank. Louisa, his sister, marries Bounderby, but without affection. Tom uses his sister both before and after her marriage without scruple to further his own ends. Even this is not sufficient, however, to cover his needs, and he appropriates the Bank money, arranging matters so that it appears a robbery has been committed. Suspicion is directed against Stephen Blackpool. Louisa arranges to elope with Harthouse, who has come to Coketown on political business; instead of doing so she flies to her father. But the arrangements have been overheard by Bounderby's housekeeper, Mrs. Sparsit, who eagerly embraces the opportunity of doing some mischief to Louisa by carrying the tale to her husband. Bounderby hurries in turn to tell the tale to Gradgrind, but finds not only that Louisa has been before him, but that she is sheltered there. He refuses to listen to any one and offers Louisa a choice; the result is that she remains with her father. A reward is offered for the arrest of Blackpool, who has left the town in search of work. His friend Rachael endeavours to clear his name, and ultimately she and Cissy find him injured at the bottom of a disused shaft. He dies. Tom leaves Coketown. His father follows him, and is in turn followed by Bitzer, who secures Tom; but with the assistance of Sleary and his company Gradgrind is able to effect his son's escape. Bounderby dies in a fit. Cissy Jupe marries; and Gradgrind sorts his ideas afresh.

Little Dorrit. (Published in volume form **1857.**)

William Dorrit, a prisoner in the Marshalsea. He has been there for so many years that he has become the "Father of the Marshalsea." Little Dorrit, his daughter Amy, is engaged casually by Mrs. Clennam, While there she is seen by Arthur Clennam, who has just returned to this country. Clennam attempts to assist the family, but the circumlocution of the Circumlocution Office renders it impossible. He enters into partnership with Daniel Doyce and almost falls in love with "Pet" Meagles. She however marries Henry Gowan, an artist without much steadiness of character. Flora Finching, a widow, and daughter of Mr. Casby, was a former sweetheart of Clennam's, but he has lost whatever love he may have had for her, although she is still arch and coy in an elephantine way. Little Dorrit's father inherits a large fortune. He leaves the prison and travels on the Continent. His wealth makes him proud and condescending it has a similar effect on Fanny and Edward, his son and elder daughter; only Amy and his brother William are unaffected by the sudden accession of wealth. Fanny marries Edward Sparkler, the son of Mrs. Merdle by a former husband. Mr. Merdle is a financial magnate of the first water with whom Clennam and *Dorrit*, as well as many others, are persuaded to invest their money. The inevitable crash follows. The Dorrits are ruined ; Clennam is ruined. Fortunately Mr. *Dorrit* himself died before the disclosure. Clennam relinquishes everything to the creditors and becomes an inmate of the Marshalsea. *Little Dorrit* finds him and nurses him through an illness. His partner Doyce returns and reinstates him in the firm, and he and *Litte Dorrit* are married. This is the warp of the story. Crossing it at intervals is the dark shadow of Rigaud, the villain adventurer, who blackmails Mrs. Clennam on the strength of his knowledge of her secret. He is buried in the ruins of Mrs. Clennam's house.

Reprinted Pieces. (Published in volume form **1858.**)
    1850. *Begging-Letter* Writer.
        Child's *Dream* of a Star.
        Christmas Tree.
        Detective Police.
        Ghost of Art.
        Poor Man's Tale of a Patent.
        Three *Detective* Anecdotes.
        Walk in a Workhouse.
    1851. *Bill* Sticking.
        Births. Mrs. Meek, of a son.
        Flight.
        Monument of French Folly.
        On *Duty* with Inspector Field.
        Our English Watering-Place.
        Our School.
    1852. Child's Story.
        Lying Awake.
        Our *Bore.*
        Our Honourable Friend.
        Our Vestry.
        Plated Article.
        Poor Relation's Story.
    1853. *Down* with the Tide.
        Long Voyage.
        Noble Savage.
        Nobody's Story
        Schoolboy's Story.
    1854. Our French Watering-Place.
    1855. Prince Bull : a Fairy Tale.
    1856. Out of the Season.
        Out of Town.

⋆A Tale of Two Cities. (Published in volume form **1859.**)
    Dr. Manette has been incarcerated in the Bastille for many years. His daughter Lucie and Mr. *Lorry* from Tellson's *Bank* repair to Paris to bring the released prisoner to London. His reason has suffered, but under the fostering care of his daughter his mind and body both improve. Charles *Darnay*, who has relinquished his title and all claim on the French estates of the family, is tried at the Old Bailey on a charge of treason—a serious one at this period of the French Revolution : he is acquitted largely through

a resemblance he bears to Sydney Carton, a lawyer in the court. Carton
a dissolute genius, Stryver, and Darnay all aspire to the hand of Lucie
Manette. Darnay is accepted and marries Lucie : Carton has too good
a knowledge of his own shortcomings, but he is ready to do anything for
Lucie's happiness. Darnay goes to Paris to secure the liberation of Gabelle
and is himself imprisoned as an aristocrat. Lucie and Dr. Manette go
to Paris to his relief and secure his release ; but he is rearrested at once
on another charge and sentenced by the Tribunal. Sydney Carton under
takes the work at this point. By his knowledge of the antecedents o
the spy, who has become a turnkey, he obtains admission to the prison
where he impersonates Darnay. Darnay and his friends all succeed in
escaping from France—Miss Pross with the greatest difficulty, leaving
Madame Defarge dead behind her. Jerry Cruncher relinquishes his trade
of body-snatcher. And Sydney Carton dies beneath the blade of the guillo
tine.

Lazy Tour of Two Idle Apprentices. (With Wilkie Collins.) (Published
   1857.)
     A series of articles written by Dickens and Wilkie Collins, describing a
holiday tour.

Hunted Down. (Published **1860.**)
     The story of the pursuit of Mr. Julius Slinkton by Mr. Meltham, and
his ultimate detection. Slinkton poisons his niece, who was married to
Meltham, and attempts to poison Meltham, who had assumed anothe
name.

The Uncommercial Traveller. (Published in volume form **1861.**)
     Travel papers from home and abroad dealing with many subject
grave and gay.

⅄ **Great Expectations.** (Published in volume form **1861.**)
     Pip is introduced as a very small orphan boy, being " brought up
by hand " by his sister, wife of Joe Gargery, blacksmith in a village in
the Kentish marshes. He falls in with a convict escaped from the marshes
who terrifies him into purloining food and a file. Pip sees his convict cap
tured with another by the soldiers, and his petty theft is not discovered
Things go on in their quiet way, Pip meantime being educated at the villag
dame-school, until he is taken by Uncle Pumbleehook to play with Miss
Havisham. Miss Havisham is a demented lady who was deserted o
the eve of her wedding. Miss Havisham's only companion is Estella, whom
she is bringing up to break men's hearts. The girl begins early and prac
tises on Pip. His visits to Miss Havisham cease, however, and he is appren
ticed to Joe Gargery, Miss Havisham paying for his indentures. Joe'
" man," Orlick, entertains a deadly hatred for Pip, and almost murder
Mrs. Joe, although the perpetrator of the crime is not discovered until lon
afterwards. The Great Expectations enter into the story when Mr. Jagger
takes Pip to London to make a gentleman of him. The secret benefactor
is believed to be Miss Havisham. Pip quickly adapts himself to his ne
circumstances, spending money at a great rate. He shares chambe
with Herbert Pocket, and is tutored by his friend's father. This continu
for some years until the return of Provis reveals to Pip that he does n

owe his rise to Miss Havisham, but to the convict whom he had assisted whilst a little boy in the marshes. The great business then is to secure the safety of Provis, who is in instant danger of capture. Their plans are all laid, and the boat from which they are to board the steamer far down the river. But on the very brink of success Provis is recaptured through the instrumentality of Compeyson, a fellow convict, and the man who had so cruelly wrecked Miss Havisham's life. Provis is sentenced to death, but the injuries he received in his endeavour to escape prove fatal, and he dies before his execution takes place. Pip now finds himself penniless, and soon after he passes through a serious illness. He recovers to find that Joe has nursed him and has paid his debts. He goes down home, intending to propose to Biddy, the homely friend of his childhood, but learns that she has married Joe, whose wife died as a result of the injuries inflicted by *Orlick*. Miss Havisham dies, and Estella marries *Bentley Drummle*, who leads her an unhappy life until his death. Pip becomes a clerk in Herbert's firm and ultimately becomes a partner. He pays a visit to England, and accidentally meets Estella, whom he marries.

Our Mutual Friend. (Published in volume form in **1865**.)

Old Harmon has made an enormous fortune as a dust contractor, which he leaves to his son on condition that he marries *Bella* Wilfer. The son on his return to England is supposed to be drowned and the money is inherited by Mr. Boffin. Young John Harmon is not drowned, however, but adopts the names first of Julius Handford and then of John Rokesmith, and becomes the private secretary of Mr. Boffin. The Boffins take a large mansion and adopt *Bella*. John falls in love with *Bella*, but she repulses him as only the secretary. Mrs. Boffin discovers Rokesmith's identity, and they all concoct a plot by which Bella's interest and love are to be aroused. Boffin feigns to be a miser and abuses his secretary in season and out of season until the end is attained and John and *Bella* are married. The simple deception is continued, however, for some time, until Rokesmith is arrested by the police for his own murder. The revelation is then made. Side by side with this are at least two other stories : Gaffer Hexam is a questionable riverside character who is accused by his former accomplice, Rogue Riderhood, of the murder of Harmon, but on the evening of his arrest he is found drowned. His son and daughter, Lizzie and Charley, separate. Charley has been secretly educated and becomes a pupil-teacher and, later on, a full-fledged schoolmaster. Lizzie supports herself and meets Eugene Wrayburn, the friend of Mortimer Lightwood, the lawyer entrusted with Mr. Boffin's affairs. Eugene does not know whether he is serious or not in his intentions, but he arouses the intense jealousy of *Bradley Headstone*, the superior of Charley Hexam. Headstone attempts to murder Eugene up the river, where he has pursued Lizzie. Rogue Riderhood has become a deputy lockkeeper, and discovers Headstone's dark secret. He uses it to obtain hush-money from his victim, but Headstone is driven mad by his thoughts and his jealousy, and commits suicide, drowning Rogue at the same time. Eugene recovers and marries Lizzie. A friend of Lizzie's is the girl Cleaver, Jenny Wren. She is a dolls' dressmaker and obtains her pieces from Riah the Jew, who is ostensibly Pudsey and Co. In reality Pudsey and Co. are Fascination Fledgeby. Fascination enters into an agreement with Alfred Lammle to pay him a sum of money on Lammle bringing about his (Fledgeby's) marriage with Georgina Podsnap.   Lammle is a fortune hunter who has married Miss Akersham, only to discover that she also is a fortune hunter.   Having no fortune between them they are obliged to live by their wits.   The marriage scheme falls through, and Fledgeby ruins Lammle by buying up bills against him.   Lammle discovers his duplicity and administers a sound thrashing before leaving England.   When Boffin comes into his fortune he employs Silas Wegg, a man " *with* a wooden leg " to read to him.   Wegg is a precious rascal who thinks he has discovered a will that will dispossess his employer, and threatens him with absolute ruin.   He takes a man named Venus into his confidence, but Venus has no liking for the part, and informs Mr. Boffin of the plot.   The will turns out to be valueless, having been invalidated by one of a later date.   The grand climax is reached when Wegg is unmasked and turned out, and the real state of affairs is revealed to *Bella*. Venus marries Pleasant Riderhood.

Christmas Stories. (Published **1854-1867.**)
   Seven Poor Travellers. (1854.)
   Holly Tree. (1855.)
   Wreck of the *Golden Mary*. (1856.)
   Perils of Certain English Prisoners. (1857.)
   Going into Society. (A House to Let.) (1858.)
   Haunted House. (1859.)
   Message from the Sea. (1860.)
   Tom Tiddler's ground. (1861.)
   Somebody's Luggage. (1862.)
   Mrs. Lirriper's Lodgings. (1863.)
   Mrs. Lirriper's Legacy. (1864.)
   Dr. Marigold. (1865.)
   Two Ghost Stories. (Dr. Marigold's Prescriptions.) (1865–6.)
   Mugby Junction. (1866.)
   No Thoroughfare. (1867.)

George Silverman's Explanation. (Published **1868.**)
   The story of an orphan who is befriended and educated.   By his exertions he secures a scholarship at Cambridge, and is eventually presented with a " living " by Lady Fareway.   Lady Fareway's daughter studies under his direction, and an affection grows up between them.   He perceives the disparity between them, however, and endeavours to transfer her affection to Granville Wharton.   He succeeds, and the two young people are married.   George Silverman is dismissed from his living by Lady Fareway, but he secures a college living through the assistance of the young couple.

Holiday Romance. (Published **1868.**)
   King Watkins the First has many children, but his eldest child is Alicia who is mother to her brothers and sisters and housewife as well.   Her godmother gives her a magic fishbone, which for one occasion only will bring her what she wishes for.   She keeps the fishbone until the King's money is all gone and he is unable to get any more anywhere, when she wishes for Quarter Day.   It is Quarter Day and the King's salary falls down the chimney.   The Princess Alicia is married by her godmother to Prince Certainpersonio.

⁊Mystery of Edwin Drood. (Published in volume form 1870.)

This, the last novel, was never completed, and various guesses have been made from time to time of the conclusion. The scene is laid in Cloisterham. John Jasper is the choirmaster of Cloisterham Cathedral and uncle and guardian of Edwin Drood, but secretly he is addicted to the opium habit. Edwin Drood is a young engineer who has been betrothed by his late father to Rosa Bud. Edwin and Rosa do not feel that they love one another sufficiently to marry. Neville and Helena Landless come to Cloisterham, the latter to the Nun's House, the former to study under the Rev. Crisparkle. They make the acquaintance of Edwin and Rosa. A quarrel arises between the two young men, and this John Jasper fans and magnifies. Jasper is in love with Rosa, although ignorant that she and Edwin have proposed to be brother and sister only in their affections. Crisparkle intervenes and the young men become reconciled. They both visit Jasper on Christmas Eve. After the event Edwin disappears and Neville is arrested on the charge of having murdered him. He is released, however, but leaves Cloisterham and takes up his residence in London. Rosa flies to London to her guardian on account of Jasper's unwelcome attentions; and Helena joins her brother. Two new characters enter the story at this point, Lieutenant Tarter, and Datchery. The latter is a mysterious old man generally believed to be one of the other characters disguised. What place he had to fill can only be guessed, nor can the murderer of Edwin be singled out with any certainty.

Miscellaneous Papers, Plays and Poems. (Published in volume form **1908.**)

These miscellaneous essays and tracts are gathered from several periodicals and spread over a period from 1838 to 1869. They do not warrant a minute analysis here, but a list of the contents will be found under the abbreviations.

List of Abbreviations

Abbreviation.	Title.
M. P., B. . . .	Miscellaneous Papers, Blacksmith.
M. P., B. A. . .	Miscellaneous Papers, Best Authority.
M. P., B. L. . .	Miscellaneous Papers, British Lion.
M. P., B. S. . .	Miscellaneous Papers, Betting Shops.
M. P., C. . . .	Miscellaneous Papers, Chips.
M. P., C. C. . .	Miscellaneous Papers, Court Ceremonies.
M. P., C. E. . .	Miscellaneous Papers, Crime and Education.
M. P., C. H . .	Miscellaneous Papers, Child's Hymn.
M. P., C. H. T. .	Miscellaneous Papers, Chauncy Hare Townshend.
M. P., C. J. . .	Miscellaneous Papers, Chinese Junk.
M. P., C. M. B. .	Miscellaneous Papers, Card from Mr. Booley.
M. P., C. P. . .	Miscellaneous Papers, Capital Punishment.
M. P., C. Pat. . .	Miscellaneous Papers, Cheap Patriotism.
M. P., D. M. . .	Miscellaneous Papers, Demeanour of Murderers.
M. P., D. V. . .	Miscellaneous Papers, December Vision.
M. P., Dr. C. . .	Miscellaneous Papers, Cruikshank's Drunkard's Children.
M. P., E. A. S. .	Miscellaneous Papers, Edinburgh Apprentice School Association.
M. P., E. C. . .	Miscellaneous Papers, Enlightened Clergyman.
M. P., E. S. . .	Miscellaneous Papers, Narrative of Extraordinary Suffering
M. P., E. T. . .	Miscellaneous Papers, Some Account of an Extraordinary Traveller.
M. P., F. and S. .	Miscellaneous Papers, Fire and Snow.
M. P., F. C. . .	Miscellaneous Papers, Few Conventionalities.
M. P., F. F. . .	Miscellaneous Papers, Frauds on the Fairies.
M. P., F. L. . .	Miscellaneous Papers, Fast and Loose.
M. P., F. O. E. G.	Miscellaneous Papers, Fine Old English Gentleman.
M. P., F. of the L.	Miscellaneous Papers, The Friend of the Lions.
M. P., F. N. P. .	Miscellaneous Papers, Five New Points of Criminal Law.
M. P., F. S. . .	Miscellaneous Papers, Finishing Schoolmaster.
M. P., G. A. . .	Miscellaneous Papers, Gone Astray.
M. P., G. B. . .	Miscellaneous Papers, Great Baby.
M. P., G. D. . .	Miscellaneous Papers, Gone to the Dogs.
M. P., G. F. . .	Miscellaneous Papers, Gaslight Fairies.
M. P, G. H. . .	Miscellaneous Papers " Good" Hippopotamus.
M. P., G. L. A. .	Miscellaneous Papers, Guild of Literature and Art.
M. P., H. H. . .	Miscellaneous Papers, Haunted House.
M. P., H. H. W. .	Miscellaneous Papers, Home for Homeless Women.
M. P., I. . . .	Miscellaneous Papers, Insularities.
M. P., I. and C. .	Miscellaneous Papers, Ignorance and Crime.
M. P., I. C. . .	Miscellaneous Papers, International Copyright.
M. P., I. M . .	Miscellaneous Papers, Idea of Mine.
M. P., I. M. T. .	Miscellaneous Papers, In Memoriam : W. M. Thackeray.
M. P., I. S. H. W.	Miscellaneous Papers, Is She His Wife?
M. P., I. W. M. .	Miscellaneous Papers, Great International Walking Match.
M. P., J. G. . .	Miscellaneous Papers, Joseph Grimaldi.
M. P., J. O. . .	Miscellaneous Papers, John Overs.
M. P., J. S. P. .	Miscellaneous Papers, Judicial Special Pleading.
M. P., J. T. . .	Miscellaneous Papers, Late Mr. Justice Talfourd.
M. P., L. . . .	Miscellaneous Papers, Lamplighter.
M. P., L. A. V.	Miscellaneous Papers, Lost Arctic Voyagers.
M. P., L. E. J. .	Miscellaneous Papers, Legal and Equitable Jokes.
M. P., L. H. . .	Miscellaneous Papers, Leigh Hunt, A Remonstrance.
M. P., L. L. . .	Miscellaneous Papers, Landor's Life.
M. P., L. S. . .	Miscellaneous Papers, Late Mr. Stanfield.

ABBREVIATION.	TITLE.
M. P., L. T. . .	*Miscellaneous Papers, Lively Turtle.*
M. P., L. W. O. Y.	*Miscellaneous Papers, Last Words of the Old Year.*
M. P., M. B. . .	*Miscellaneous Papers, Macready as "Benedick."*
M. P., M. B. S.	*Miscellaenous Papers, Mr. Bull, Somnambulist.*
M. P., M. B. V. .	*Miscellaneous Papers, Mr. Booley's View of the Last Lord Mayor's Show.*
M. P., M. E. . .	*Miscellaneous Papers, Murderous Extremes.*
M. P., M. E. R. .	*Miscellaneous Papers, Curious Misprint in the Edinburgh Review.*
M. P., M. M. . .	*Miscellaneous Papers, Martyr Medium.*
M. P., M. N. D. .	*Miscellaneous Papers, M. Nightingale's Diary.*
M. P., M. P . .	*Miscellaneous Papers, Murdered Person.*
M. P., N. E. . .	*Miscellaneous Papers, Niger Expedition.*
M. P., N. G. K. .	*Miscellaneous Papers, It is not generally known.*
M. P., N. S. . .	*Miscellaneous Papers, New Song.*
M. P., N. S. E. .	*Miscellaneous Papers, Nobody, Somebody, Everybody.*
M. P., N. S. L. .	*Miscellaneous Papers, Nightly Scene in London.*
M. P., N. T. . .	*Miscellaneous Papers, No Thoroughfare.*
M. P., N. Y. D. .	*Miscellaneous Papers, New Year's Day.*
M. P., O. C. . .	*Miscellaneous Papers, Our Commission.*
M. P., O. F. A. .	*Miscellaneous Papers, On Mr. Fechter's Acting.*
M. P., O. L. N. O.	*Miscellaneous Papers, Old Lamps for New Ones.*
M. P., O. S. . .	*Miscellaneous Papers, On Strike.*
M. P., Ox. C. . .	*Miscellaneous Papers, Report of the Commissioners (Oxford)*
M. P., P. A. P. .	*Miscellaneous Papers, Proposals for Amusing Posterity.*
M. P., P. F. . .	*Miscellaneous Papers, Perfect Felicity.*
M. P., P. F. D. .	*Miscellaneous Papers, Prologue to "The Frozen Deep."*
M. P., P. L. U. .	*Miscellaneous Papers, Please to Leave your Umbrella.*
M. P., P. M. B. .	*Miscellaneous Papers, Poor man and his Beer.*
M. P., P. N. J. B.	*Miscellaneous Papers, Proposals for a National Jest-Book.*
M. P., P. P. . .	*Miscellaneous Papers, Pet Prisoners.*
M. P., P. P. D. .	*Miscellaneous Papers, Prologue to "The Patrician's Daughter.*
M. P., P. S. . .	*Miscellaneous Papers, Poetry of Science.*
M. P., P. T. . .	*Miscellaneous Papers, Paradise at Tooting.*
M. P, Q. D. P. .	*Miscellaneous Papers, Quack Doctor's Proclamations.*
M. P., R. D. . .	*Miscellaneous Papers, Railway Dreaming.*
M. P., R. G. . .	*Miscellaneous Papers, Leech's "The Rising Generation."*
M. P., R. H. F. .	*Miscellaneous Papers, From the Raven in the Happy Family."*
M. P., R. L. M. .	*Miscellaneous Papers, Reflections of a Lord Mayor.*
M. P., R. S. . .	*Miscellaneous Papers, Railway Strikes.*
M. P., R. S. D. .	*Miscellaneous Papers, Rather a Strong Dose.*
M. P., R. S. L. .	*Miscellaneous Papers, Restoration of Shakespeare's "Lear.*
M. P., R. T. . .	*Miscellaneous Papers, Red Tape.*
M. P., S. . . .	*Miscellaneous Papers, Supposing !*
M. P., S. B. . .	*Miscellaneous Papers, Spirit Business.*
M. P., S. C. . .	*Miscellaneous Papers, Spirit of Chivalry.*
M. P., S. D. C. .	*Miscellaneous Papers, Slight Depreciation of the Currency.*
M. P., S. F. A. .	*Miscellaneous Papers, Stories for the First of April.*
M. P., S. G. . .	*Miscellaneous Papers, Strange Gentleman.*
M. P., S. O. W. .	*Miscellaneous Papers, "Song of the Wreck."*
M. P., S. for P. .	*Miscellaneous Papers, Subjects for Painters.*
M. P., S. P. . .	*Miscellaneous Papers, Scott and his Publishers.*
M. P., S. Pigs.	*Miscellaneous Papers, Sucking Pigs.*

ABBREVIATION.	TITLE.
M. P., S. Q. F. . .	*Miscellaneous Papers, Slight Question of Fact.*
M. P., S. R. . . .	*Miscellaneous Papers, Smuggled Relations.*
M. P., S. S. . . .	*Miscellaneous Papers, Sunday Screw.*
M. P., S. S. U. . .	*Miscellaneous Papers, Sleep to Startle us.*
M. P., T. B. . . .	*Miscellaneous Papers, Tattlesnivell Bleater.*
M. P., T. D. . . .	*Miscellaneous Papers, Trading in Death.*
M. P., T. F. . . .	*Miscellaneous Papers, Tooting Farm.*
M. P., T. L. . . .	*Miscellaneous Papers, The Lighthouse.*
M. P., T. O. H. . .	*Miscellaneous Papers, Thousand and One Humbugs.*
M. P., T. O. P. . .	*Miscellaneous Papers, That other Public.*
M. P., T. T. . . .	*Miscellaneous Papers, Toady Tree.*
M. P., T. T. D.	*Miscellaneous Papers, Things that cannot be done.*
M. P., T. W. C. . .	*Miscellaneous Papers, To Working Men.*
M. P., Th. L. T. H.	*Miscellaneous Papers, Threatening Letter to Thomas Hood.*
M. P., U. N. . .	*Miscellaneous Papers, Unsettled Neighbourhood.*
M. P., V. and B. S.	*Miscellaneous Papers, Virginie and Black-eyed Susan.*
M. P., V. C. . . .	*Miscellaneous Papers, Village Coquettes.*
M. P., V. D. . . .	*Miscellaneous Papers, Verdict for Drouet.*
M. P., W. . . .	*Miscellaneous Papers, Why ?*
M. P., W. A. R. . .	*Miscellaneous Papers, Well-authenticated Rappings.*
M. P., W. H. . .	*Miscellaneous Papers, Whole Hogs.*
M. P., W. L. . .	*Miscellaneous Pieces, Hymn of the Wiltshire Labourers.*
M. P., W. M. . .	*Miscellaneous Papers, Worthy Magistrate.*
M. P., W. S. .	*Miscellaneous Papers, Word in Season.*
M. P., W. S. . .	*Miscellaneous Papers, Where we Stopped Growing.*
M. P., Y. M. C. .	*Miscellaneous Papers, Young Man from the Country.*
Mud. Pap. . . .	*Mudfog Papers.*
N. N.	*Life and Adventures of Nicholas Nickleby.*
O. C. S. . . .	*Old Curiosity Shop.*
O. M. F. . . .	*Our Mutual Friend.*
O. T.	*Adventures of Oliver Twist.*
P. P.	*Posthumous Papers of the Pickwick Club.*
P. F. I.	*Pictures from Italy.*
P. N. P. . . .	*Pic-nic Papers.*
R. P., B. L. W. .	*Reprinted Pieces, Begging Letter Writer.*
R. P., B. M. S. .	*Reprinted Pieces, Births, Mrs. Meek, of a Son.*
R. P., B. S. . .	*Reprinted Pieces, Bill Sticking.*
R. P., C. D. S. .	*Reprinted Pieces, Child's Dream of a Star.*
R. P., C. S. . .	*Reprinted Pieces, Child's Story.*
R. P., C. T. . .	*Reprinted Pieces, Christmas Tree.*
R. P., D. P. . .	*Reprinted Pieces, Detective Police.*
R. P., D. W. T. T.	*Reprinted Pieces, Down with the Tide.*
R. P., F. . . .	*Reprinted Pieces, Flight.*
R. P., G. A. . .	*Reprinted Pieces, Ghost of Art.*
R. P., L. A. . .	*Reprinted Pieces, Lying Awake.*
R. P., L. V. . .	*Reprinted Pieces, Long Voyages.*
R. P., M. F. F. .	*Reprinted Pieces, Monument of French Folly.*
R. P., N. Sa. . .	*Reprinted Pieces, Noble Savage.*
R. P., N. S. . .	*Reprinted Pieces, Nobody's Story.*
R. P., O. B. . .	*Reprinted Pieces, Our Bore.*
R. P., O. D. . . .	*Reprinted Pieces, On Duty with Inspector Field.*
R. P., O. E. W. P. .	*Reprinted Pieces, Our English Watering Place.*
R. P., O. F. W. P.	*Reprinted Pieces, Our French Watering Place.*
R. P., O. H. F. .	*Reprinted Pieces, Our Honourable Friend.*
R. P., O. o. T. .	*Reprinted Pieces, Out of Town.*

ABBREVIATION.	TITLE.
R. P., O. of the S.	Reprinted Pieces, Out of the Season.
R. P., O. S.	Reprinted Pieces, Our School.
R. P., O. V.	Reprinted Pieces, Our Vestry.
R. P., P. A.	Reprinted Pieces, Plated Article.
R. P., P. B.	Reprinted Pieces, Prince Bull.
R. P., P. M. T. P.	Reprinted Pieces, Poor Man's Tale of a Patent.
R. P., P. R. S.	Reprinted Pieces, Poor Relation's Story.
R. P., S. S.	Reprinted Pieces, Schoolboy's Story.
R. P., T. D. A.	Reprinted Pieces, Three Detective Anecdotes.
R. P., W. W.	Reprinted Pieces, Walk in the Workhouse.
S. B. B., Char.	Sketches by Boz, Characters.
S. B. B., O. P.	Sketches by Boz, Our Parish.
S. B. B., Scenes.	Sketches by Boz, Scenes.
S. B. B., Tales.	Sketches by Boz, Tales.
S. U. T. H.	Sunday under Three Heads.
S. Y. C.	Sketches of Young People.
S. Y. G.	Sketches of Young Gentlemen.
T. T. C.	Tale of Two Cities.
U. T.	Uncommercial Traveller.

Introduction

Two extremes have been the fashion at different times and with different people : on the one hand it has been asserted that all *Dickens*'s characters and places had originals on which they were founded, and prototypes have been found or imagined ; on the other hand it has been stated, on what should be good authority, that with a few notable exceptions the novelist had no real people or scenes in his mind's eye when he drew the exquisite pictures which are caricature and human nature at the same time. To me it appears that neither of these rather wholesale statements is correct. It is quite obvious to any one who " feels " as he reads that *Dickens* was not an imaginative writer. It is impossible to imagine his having written a story from his own fancy : even his fairy stories, the tales of the spirits, the goblins, and sprites are not fanciful ; each one is a moral, a sentiment, or a thought masquerading very heavily in a flimsy disguise. The characters are evidently founded on the men and women and children of all classes, of various nations, and of innumerable dispositions which jostled him in the street, and the field-path, in the village inn, and in the hotel, and at every point of his varied life. An almost infallible memory made possible what might otherwise appear improbable. From this it follows that each character was portrayed from a vivid and permanent picture in the author's mind ; but it is equally certain that each of these mind pictures was a very composite photograph, the characteristics of many men entering into the making of one portrait. Even those characters which are admittedly based upon actualities, such as Harold Skimpole, cannot be attributed to one original—in this case alone at least two men entered into the making of one minor character. It is therefore useless to hope to identify in the world of names and addresses all those people who have sat consciously or unconsciously to the facile pen of the great writer.

The case is somewhat different with regard to the localities and the houses which enter so largely into the novels. It is impossible to point to any novelist in the English language in which locality and local colour play so important a part. And the thin disguise covering the identity of some of the scenes leaves no doubt that the place, and the one place only, is being described, although the one place may be typical of a whole class. But even places and houses are sometimes composite, as were the characters, instancing Jasper's Gatehouse, which is neither of the gatehouses in Rochester, but is all three of them. That real places entered into even the apparently minor scenes of the novels is evident from *Dickens* telling his daughter, many years after the publication of *Pickwick*, that a certain spot was where the redoubtable Nimrod lost his whip. The scene was a picture drawn with a fine sweep on large canvas and touched in with the inimitable individuality of the author.

In estimating the probability, or otherwise, of originals having existed for this character or that place, it is necessary to probe the psychology of

the writer as expressed in his works—in short, as Mr. Micawber would say
to feel with him and think with him, to allow ourselves to be carried along
on the stream of the story. An array of facts, with a counter array of facts
on the negative side, are of little value in the analysis of the thoughts of a
man whose brain probably teemed with plots and plans and characters and
incidents. And there is probably no better example of the development
the expansion, and the growth of Dickens's thought than that expressed
in *Pickwick*. One can see there the young author feeling his feet, and as he
gains assurance, allowing his satire freer play, pointing his wit more broadly
and indicating more clearly the places and people who were held
up to his kindly ridicule or roundly abused for their betrayal of their
trust or the public good. To indicate the way in which this development
made itself felt it is necessary only to lightly sketch the salient features of
the topography of the work.

Rochester is avowedly Rochester, but there is nothing against Rochester
in *Pickwick*—when it is treated disparagingly it becomes "Dulborough."
Muggleton, however, and the people and places in connection with it are
disguised most thoroughly, and yet it is probable that the picture is nothing
more than a humorous caricature of Gravesend. Farther on in the book the
placenames are more obvious. Ipswich, *Bath*, and *Bury* are named, although
the mention of the Mayor of Ipswich must have given rise to a great deal
of chaff to that individual in the flesh. But the name of "Boz" was by that
time a household word, and the famous young writer could do many things
he would not have ventured on a few months previously. In the same way
the disguise of Justice Stareleigh was so thin that Gazlee was immediately
recognized. But Mr. Wardle has not yet been identified with the certainty
that could be desired.

The allusion to the identity of Mr. Wardle reminds me that I have been
informed that a farm "*Dingle Dell*," corresponding in every respect
to the Manor Farm, *Dingley Dell*, and owned by an English Yeoman, the
prototype of Wardle, existed in the early part of the nineteenth century
somewhere between Gravesend and Rochester. This is an old family tradition which may or may not be founded on fact—there is an illimitable fund
of anecdote and story to be gleaned from Kentish family tradition—but as I
have been unable to verify it by a search through early directories and
local papers, I have been obliged to omit it from my "originals."

One peculiar feature of *D*ickens and his work seldom sufficiently allowed
for is the fact that he was a novelist by intention. Some writers write
to please themselves, or because they have a mission, or it may be for the
sake of the pounds, shillings and pence which so many thousands of words
represent, while the motives of others are a conglomeration of all three.
*D*ickens, however, was, or appears to have been, actuated by the singular
idea of amusing and interesting his readers, the people. This solicitude for
the people was revealed in his politics and his political writings, and was due
possibly to the histrionic strain that manifested itself in his amateur theatricals and in his lectures. I can think of no closer simile than that of an actor
acting—acting and conscious meanwhile that he is acting. The knowledge
lends itself to the highest art, while it inflicts an enormous strain on the actor
or writer, and, above all, it produces a mind which cannot be measured by
the ordinary rules of thought nor gauged by the limitations of ordinary ideas.
The conscious artist has an eye for his public and posterity, for the super

...al and for the heart of things. His art is not to produce the perfect work to satisfy the arbitrary canons of his own taste, but to draw forth the acclamations of his readers. It is this that has led to the otherwise incomprehensible state of affairs when Dickens is condemned as a mountebank, and lauded as a wit, praised as a humorist and sneered at as a caricaturist of the small beer of humanity : read and re-read as a transcendental limner of the everlasting traits of human nature ; and thrown aside as the originator of the gutter press. And he is not only a great artist but a bold man who will like to throw down the gauntlet to posterity in the firm faith that no matter how much the dogs may snarl and snap in the arena the work of true genius will endure.

The reason just mentioned gives the clue to the cause of hiding Rochester under the guise of Cloisterham so late in the day that he could have written but Heaven without offending his readers ; and for depicting Uptown so truely that it may have been Rochester, Chatham, Stroud, or Gravesend. Possibly Dickens desired to arouse curiosity regarding Pip's village in the marshes, and the identification may have been intentionally simplified, while sufficient alteration was made to cause a momentary doubt. Joe Gargery's forge, too, has been the subject of a good deal of controversy ; and even quite recently the church in the marshes has been subjected to a search-ing review of the "higher criticism " kind with interesting results.

Possibly none of Dicken's works give so much evidence of conscious art this unfinished romance, the *Mystery of Edwin Drood*. I do not want to appear to labour this idea of intentional genius, but few people are aware of its existence. The " small " man limited by his capacity, and striving with art-sickness to cross the narrow border line between clever facility and genius, apes genius, and because he has it not he falls away even from that position of brilliance he might have occupied had he limited the cravings of his ambition to the ability of his mental gifts. From this cause come most failures in life. Most successes in life are due to unconscious genius, but they are the mediocrity of genius. The world-genius who demands with a feeling of defiance a universal admiration of his gifts and succeeds in fixing the eyes of the world in the dimension of time is a genius of the transcendental order. Bacon as Bacon does not possess it, but Shakespeare whether as himself or as Bacon is the age-long embodiment of the conscious possession of genius with the power of grasping by personal force a commensurate cognition. Dickens is of this plane and of this class. Many of his admir-ers will say that I have belittled the genius of the writer when I endeavour to show that he was aware of his lustrous possession, and wrote with an eye to its proper setting and perpetuation. This is not true. I have added lustre to his genius.

One sometimes wonders where the vivid compelling charm of Dickens lies in his works. Obviously it is not in the beauty of the language ; some-times his construction is ungrammatical, and in other cases it is harsh and forced. There is none of that limpid poetry in prose that gives a fascination to the writings of some authors who have nothing more to put into them. There are, in fact, very few elaborately drawn scene pictures, and few of the characters are dressed in a point-to-point fashion with the finicky taste and detail of a court tailor or dressmaker. Human nature on the whole, how-ever, is the same to-day as it was yesterday ; woad and a girdle of grass are only names for coats and dresses. Hate, greed, and the lust of body and mind, with their body servants of cant, hypocrisy and duplicity are the same now as they were a hundred or a thousand years ago with, perhaps, a freer leaven of love and good feeling. One at least of the irresistible attractions of the master's works is to be found in his portrayal of people as they were. The character may be a composite one, in fact each character usually is, but because it is true it is complete. Imagination sees only the broad outlines of human nature, with the result that a man is a devil or an "angel" according to the immediate requirements of the creator of the character. The student of human nature, however, sees that the human character is a piece of machinery much more complex than the mechanism of the body. It may be said with truth, therefore, that although Dickens drew his characters from the flesh, he portrayed life as it was, with the inevitable advantage that life always appeals to life.

There are characters in the novels which at first sight appear all black. But on a closer acquaintance the tar-brush is found to be streaked with lighter shades. Sikes is capable of affection, and of remorse, and of fear. The wickedness of Jonas Chuzzlewit is the result of his cupidity and his cowardice. Pecksniff cherished his two daughters. Magwitch had a lasting gratitude for Pip. Uriah Heep and his mother loved one another. Steerforth was not all rogue. On the other hand, David made many errors. Agnes was too indulgent to her father ; and a weaker writer would have made her the unconscious instrument or unintentional reward of her father's deliverance instead of leaving that release from the bondage of Heep to the accident of Micawber's impecuniosity. There is just that difference between melodrama and tragedy. The delineator of life as it stands is a realist, but the realist can only describe with the faithfulness of a journalist the minutiae of filth and indecency, separating the garbage from the profitable refuse with the care of a rag-picker. There are other rooms in the house than the scullery ? There are other things in the garden than the manure ? But for some inexplicable reason the writer who includes in his word-picture the rose and the thorn, the dead leaves and the new shoots is a caricaturist. On these lines Dickens was a caricaturist.

There are certain recognized methods of discovering the history of localities, and in the same way there are methods of conducting the search for Dickens' originals. All the work our author can put forth is based on the knowledge he has assimilated and moulded by the fingers of his genius ; therefore we may look for prototypes with some hope of discovering the individuals, and with the certainty of learning the nature of the world in the early Victorian era and feeling that change which overtook England, and the outward appearance and the superficial nature of the men and women who inhabited it, with those great changes of the forty years of the growth of steam.

Places have changed and the difficulties of identification are immeasurably increased, which, together with the disguise, more or less thin, which Dickens often spread over both scenes and characters sometimes make it impossible to identify a place with certainty. There will be found amongst other identifications in the following pages suggestions as to the originals of Muggleton, Dingley Dell, the Manor House, and the Ship. Some are doubtful, others are more probable. The Ship can be only the Ship and Lobster ; Joe's forge can be only the forge at Chalk : but probably it will be impossible to demonstrate beyond doubt that Gravesend is the Muggleton of Pickwick.

It does not find a legitimate place in this book to describe the finding of the most likely house in which *Dickens'* honeymoon was spent, but it is most interesting as an example of the way in which such things " come about."

At least two routes have been mapped out as that taken by " Little Nell " and her grandfather. And while I do not doubt for a moment that Dickens travelled with the people of his brain along a well remembered road and met with well defined curiosities of humanity which he had fallen in with on other roads, I do not think that either route can be pointed to with certainty. And I think it extremely likely that many roads of real life were pressed into the service of the one. No doubt it is a sign of the truth that so many places live on the memories of the great novelist, and although the fifty-five inns and hotels of *Pickwick* have dwindled to a paltry dozen, the only result so far has been to increase the interest of those remaining.

With the exception of Bath it is rather curious that *Dickens'* books deal in a great measure with East and South East England, a part of England which still appears to enjoy the greatest popularity with the Londoner.

There are endless phases of the novelist's [works, but even if I were able it would not be desirable to deal here with more than those two which are responsible for the existence of the book. Of these, the first is the belief that it will assist the study of *Dickens* to be the re-creation of the material aspect of the country and town as it was in his day. Quite apart from the possible value of the work as a book of reference, I would fain hope that it will show that *Dickens'* novels may be relied upon for this purpose. The second reason for the compilation of the book is a similar one regarding the people of the period. It would be easy to write a vivid description, a life-like picture, of the Victorian era from *Dickens'* works. Our doubt of the works ; and the accusation of exaggeration, which has been so often levelled against them ; are due to our own ignorance of life at that time. The incident of the coachman cutting at Jonas with his whip when that ill-fated man was engaged on his second great crime seems unreal and impossible, until it is remembered that the coachman was king of the road, and so literally did he realize this position that he demanded *pourboire* with the effrontery of a footpad, and met a refusal with the same methods of foul language and fisticuffs. Even the children's games, some of them still seen in the poorer London districts, were real, and were played by the many girls and boys who then made walking in the London byways somewhat hazardous. The rhyme of the *Deputy Winks*—

> "Widdy Widdy wen !
> I—ket—ches—I'm—out—ar—ter—ten.
> Widdy Widdy wy !
> Then—E—don't—go—then—I—shy—
> Widdy Widdy wake—cock warning ! "

was in part a warning note in a rough and tumble boys' game, although I must confess myself quite unable to give any explanation of its meaning or the origin of its use.

Here are two minute details, but the thousands of pages of *Dickens'* novels teem with many more thousands of incidents or unconsidered trifles which either are or will become priceless gems of folklore and its study.

THE DICKENS DICTIONARY

A

"A." *M. P., F. N. P.*

"A." Colonel. "Nobody."
R. P., N. S.

A. Miss=Miss Havisham. (*Which see.*) *G. E.* xxvii.

A. Mr.=Mr. Arndt. *A. N.* xvii.

AARON. Mr. Mr. Riah. (*Which see.*)

ABADEEN=The Addled. Lord Aberdeen. *M. P., T. O. H.*

ABBAYE. Prison of the. Paris. *T. T. C.* b. ii., ch. xxiv.

Note.—The prison in which Gabelle was incarcerated.

ABBAYE. The. *R. P., O. o. S.*

ABBEVILLE. *R. P., A. F.*

ABBEY. "Short for Abigail." *See* Potterson (Miss). *O. M. F.* vi.

ABBEY TOWN. Scene of Gabriel Grub's adventures. *P. P.* xxix.
Original: Rochester or Canterbury, with the possibility of Town Malling or Maidstone.

ABEL. One of Kit's children. *O. C. S.* Chap. The last.

ABEL COTTAGE. Finchley. *O. C. S.* xxi.
It was a beautiful little cottage with a thatched roof and little spires at the gable ends, and pieces of stained-glass in some of the windows.

ABERDEEN. Lord. *See also* Abadeen. *M. P., I.*

ABERDEEN. *U. T.* xxii.

ABÔH. *M. P., N. E.*

ABOU SIMBEL. Temple of. *M. P., E. T.*

ABRAHAM. Deceased brother of Philip Pirrip. *G. E.* i.

ABSENT. City of the. *U. T.* xxi.

ABSOLON. Mr. *M. P., C. f. B.*

ABSTINENCE SOCIETY. Grand Amalgamated Total. *U. T.* xxxi.

ABYSSINIA *R. P., M. O. F. F.,* and *T. L. V.*; *U. T.*, xv.

ACADEMY. The Royal. *B. H.* xiv.; and *R. P., O. B.*

ACADEMY. Mr. Cripples' Evening. *L. D.* ix.
Combining day and Evening Tuition. . . . She (Little *Dorrit*) had herself received her education, such as it was, in Mr. Cripples' Evening Academy.

ACADEMY. Mr. Turvedrop's. *B. H.* xiv.
Original: Was situated at No. 26, Newman Street.

ACADEMY. Signor Billsmithi's Dancing. *S. B. B., Char.* ix.
Not a dear dancing academy —four-and-sixpence a quarter is decidedly cheap on the whole.

ACCOUNTANT-GENERAL. The. *B. H.* ix.

ACHILLES. The, Iron armoured plated ship. *U. T.* xxiv.

1

B

ACQUAPENDENTE.
P. F. I., R. P. S.

ACTON. *U. T.* xx.

ACTOR. An. *M. P., G. F.*

ADA'S MOTHER. *Deceased.*
B. H. vi.

ADAM. *M. P., L. A. V.* i.

ADAM AND EVE COURT.
S. B. B., Scenes xx.

ADAMS. Head boy at School.
D. C. xvi.

ADAMS. Captain. Friend of Sir
Mulberry Hawk. *N. N. L.*

ADAMS. Jane. *S. Y. C.*

ADAMS. Mr., Confidential Clerk
of Mr. Sampson. *H. D.* ii.

ADAMS. W. P. Jack Adams.
D. and S. xxxvi.
A man with a cast in his eye,
and slight impediment in his
speech—sat for somebody's borough. We used to call him W. P.
Adams, in consequence of his
being Warming Pan for a young
fellow who was in his minority.

ADELAIDE. Queen *Dowager.*
M. P., C. C.

ADELINA. *Only daughter of Lady*
Fareway. *G. S. E.* vii.

ADELPHI. The. *D. C.* xi. and
L. D. xlv.; *M. C.* xiii.; *M. P., O. S.*;
P. C. lvii.; *S. B. B.,* Tales iii.;
U. T. xiv.

ADELPHI HOTEL.
A. N. I.; and *C. S., M. L. L.* i.

ADELPHI THEATRE. *P. P.* xxxi.

ADMIRAL BENBOW. The. An
Inn. *R. P., O. O. S.*

ADMIRAL NAPIER. An *Omnibus.*
S. B. B., Tales xi.

ADMIRAL NELSON. A *Dining*
House. *C. S., S. L.* i.

ADMIRAL. Aboard the Argonaut.
U. T. xv.

ADMIRAL. Presiding.
M. P., N. Y. D.

ADMIRALTY. *L. D.* xxi.; *M. P.,*
T. O. H.; and *M. P., L. A. V.*

ADMIRALTY PIER. *Dover.*
U. T. xvii.

ADRIATIC. *C. S., N. T., Act* i.

ADVERTISER. *N. N.* iv.

ADVOCATE. In High Court of
Chancery. *B. H.* i.
Large, with great whiskers, a
little voice, and an interminable
brief, and outwardly directing his
contemplation to the lantern in the
roof, where he can see nothing but
fog.

ADVOCATE. Italian.
U. T. xxviii.

AFFERY. *See* Flintwinch, Affery.

AFRICA. *L. D.* xxi.; and *M. C.* vi.;
M. P., A. P.; *M. P., B. A.*;
M. P., N. E.; *R. P., A. P. A.*;
U. T. xix.

AFRICAN KNIFE SWALLOWER.
N. N. xlviii.

AFRICAN STATION. *B. H.* xiii.

AGED. The. Wemmick's Father.
G. E. xxv.
A very old man in a flannel
coat : clean, cheerful, comfortable
and well cared for, but intensely
deaf.

AGENT. Parliamentary.
M. P., H. H.

AGENTS. Maid and Courier.
L. D. li.
Sent to Paris for purchase of an
outfit for a bride.

AGGS. Mr. . *O. M. F.* viii.

AGNES. *See* Wickfield, Agnes.

AGNES. Mrs. *Bloss'* servant.
S. B. B., Tales i.
In a cherry-coloured merino dress, openwork stockings and shoes with sandals like a disguised Columbine.

AGNES. Little. David Copper-field eldest child. *D. C.* xxxiv.

AIREY ! Sir Richard. *M. P., S. F.A.*

AIX ROADS. *M. P., L. A. V.* ii.

AKERMAN. Mr. Head jailer at Newgate. *B. R.* lxiv.

AKERSHEM. Horatio. The late. *O. M. F.* x.

AKERSHEM. Sophronia. The mature young lady, who marries Mr. Lammle. *O. M. F.* x.

ALABAMA. *M. C.* xvi.

ALBANO. *L. D.* 1. ; and *P. F. I., R.*

ALBANY. A large and busy town. *A. N.* xv.

ALBANY. The. *U. T.* x. ; and *O. M. F.* xxii.

ALBARO. *P. F. I., A. G.*

ALBEMARLE. St., *M. P., N. J. B.*

ALBERT. H. R. Prince. *M. P., E. S., M. P., N.E.*

" ALBERT." Ship. *M. P., N. E.*

ALBINA. Lady, One of Magsman's troupe. *C. S., G. i. S.*
Showing her white air to the army and navy in correct uniform.

" ALCOHOL." Steamboat. *A. N.* xi.

ALDBOROUGH. Lord. *M. P., I.*

ALDERMAN. *B. R.*, lxi. ; and *M. H. C.* i.

ALDERMAN. An ex-M.P.
S. B. B., Scenes xviii.
Small gentleman with a sharp nose—a sort of amateur fireman.

ALDERMANBURY. *M. C.* xxxvii.

ALDERMEN. Of the City of London. *M. P., M. B. V.*

ALDERSGATE STREET. *E. D.* xxiii., and *L. D.* xiii. ; *M. P., L. T., U. T.*

ALDERSHOT. *M. P., S. F. A.*

ALDGATE. *P. P.* i. and *S. B. B.* xlii.

ALDGATE PUMP. *D. and S.* lvi. ; and *N. N.* xli. ; *U. T.* iii.

ALDRICH. Mr. *M. P., I. W. M.*

ALDRICH. Mrs. *M. P., I. W. M.*

ALDRIDGE. Mr., as a monk. *M. P., N. Y.*

ALE HOUSE. Blunderstone. *D. C.* *Original : The Plough, Blundeston.*

ALESSANDRIA. *P. F. I., P. M. B.*

ALEXANDER. Deceased brother of Philip Pirrip. *G. E.* i.

ALEXANDER. Mr. Grazinglands. *U. T.* vi.

ALFRED. Alfred Heathfield. *C. B., B. O. L.* i.

ALFRED. Alfred Lammle. (*Which see.*)

ALFRED. Alfred Raybrock. *C. S., M. f. T. S.* ii.

ALFRED. Alfred Starling. *C. S., H. H.*

ALFRED. Fifth and youngest son of Mrs. Pardiggle. *B. H.* viii.

ALGERIA. *U. T.* xxv.

ALICE. *R. P., A. C. T.*

ALICE. Alice Rainbird. *H. R.* i.

ALICE. *Daughter of* " Good Mrs. Brown." *See Brown Alice.*

ALICE. The youngest of the Five Sisters of York. *N. N.* vi.
The blushing tints in the soft bloom on the fruit, or the delicate painting on the flower, are not more exquisite than was the blending of the rose and lily in her gentle face, or the deep blue of her eye.

ALICE. Mistress, Only daughter of Bowyer. *M. H. C.* i.

ALICIA. Princess, Eldest child of King Watkins the First. *H. R.* ii.

ALICK. Son of Mr. and Mrs. *Octa-vius* Budden. *S. B. B.*, Tales ii.

ALICK. Child on board Gravesend Packet. *S. B. B.*, Scenes x.
A damp earthy child in red worsted socks.

ALICUMPAINE. Mrs. *H. R.* iv.

"ALL IN A MIND." *M. P., O. S.*

ALLAH. *M. P., W. S.*

ALLEGHANY MOUNTAINS.
A. N. x.

ALLEN. Arabella, Sister of Benja-min Allen. *P. P.* xxviii.
Black-eyed young lady, in a very nice little pair of boots with fur round the top.
Note.—Designed by her brother to marry Bob Sawyer, she ran away and married Winkle, largely with the assistance of Sam Weller and Mr. Pickwick.

ALLEN. *Benjamin, Brother* of Arabella Allen. *P. P.* xxx.
A coarse, stout, thick-set young man, with black hair cut rather short, and a white face cut rather long—embellished with spectacles.
Note.—A friend of Bob Sawyer, both rollicking medical students rather disreputable in appearance, and intro-duced in an atmosphere of beer and oysters. Reconciled to his sister after her marriage, and went to Bengal with Bob Sawyer.

ALLEN. Benjamin, Mr., Aunt of. *P. P.* xlviii.

ALLEN. Capt. William. *M. P., N. E.*

ALLEN. Mr. *M. P., E. T.*

ALLEY. Mr. *O. M. F.* viii.

ALLIGWY. *U. T.* ii.

ALLISON. Major. *A. N.* xvii.

ALLISON. Miss, as Mrs. Lovetown. *M. P., I. S., H. W.*

ALLISON AND CO. T. G., Mer-cantile Merchants. *A. N.* xvii.

ALL MUGGLETONIAN CLUB. The Muggleton Cricket Club which played the Dingley Dellers. *P. P.* vii.

ALMACK'S. Assembly-room of the Five Point fashionables. *A. N.* vi.

ALMACK'S. Landlady of, A buxom fat mulatto woman. *A. N.* vi.

ALMSHOUSE. Workhouse of New York. *A. N.* vi.

ALMSHOUSES. Of the Cork Cutter's Company. *C. S., S. L.* i.

ALMSHOUSES. Titbull's. *See* Tit-bull's Almshouses.

ALPHONSE. Mrs. Wititterley's page. *N. N.* xxi.

ALPS. The. *L. D.* xxxvii. ; *P. F. I., L. R. G. A.* ; and *R. P., O. o. T.*

ALREDAH. Character in Nursery Story. *U. T.* xv.

ALTHORP. Lord. *M. P., R. T.*

AMATEUR GALLERY. 121, Pall Mall. *M. P., C.*

AMAZON. The. An Emigrant Ship. *U. T.* xx.

AMAZON. Captain of the. *U. T.* xx.

AMBASSADOR. *M. P., I.*

AMBIGU. Paris. *M. P., W.*

AMBIGUOUSLY COMIC THEATRE· *M. P., N. Y. D.*

AMBLER. *M. P., S. B.*

AMBOISES. Bay of. *M. P., N. E.*

AMELIA. Another daughter of stout lady visitor at Ramsgate. library. *S. B. B.*, Tales iv.

AMELIA. *M. P., S. R.*

AMELIA COTTAGE. Stamford Hill. *S. B. B.*, Tales ii.

AMERICA. *See* United States.

AMERICA JUNIOR. *M. C.* xxii.

AMERICA. South. *C. B., C. H.* i. ; *C. S., H. H.* ; *C. S. M.ƒ.T. S.* ii.

AMERICA. South, Waters. *C. S., P. o. C. E. P.*

AMERICA SQUARE. *C. S., M. ƒ. T. S.* v.

AMERICAN. *M. P., N. J. B.*

AMERICAN COURT OF LAW. *A. N.* iii.

AMERICAN FALL. The. *A. N.* xiv.

AMERICAN MINISTER. (1834). *M. P., N. G.K.*

AMETER. Mr. X. *M. P., T. B.*

AMETER. Mr., X., butcher of *M. P., T. B.*

AMETER. Mr. X., great uncle of. *M. P., T. B.*

AMETER. Mr. X., second son of. *M. P., T. B.*

AMIENS. *C. S., M. J.* v ; *R. P., A. F., M. T.* xvii.

AMPHITHEATRE. Old, of Rome. *L. D.* li.

AMPHITHEATRE. Roman. *P. F. I., V. M. M. S. S.*

AMSTERDAM. *B. R.* lxxxii. ; and *L. D.* lxvii.

AMY. " Little *Dorrit* " (*which see*.)

AMY. Old woman in Workhouse nursing dying inmate. *O. T.* xxiv.

ANALYTICAL. The, Veneering's. Butler. *O. M. F.* xx.

ANCESTOR. Veneering's Crusading, *O. M. F.* ii.

ANCIENT BRITONS. *M. P., H. H.*

ANDERSON. John. A Tramp. *U. T.* xi.

ANDERSON. Mr., Actor. *M. P., M. B.* ; *M. P., R. S. L.*

ANDERSON. Mrs., Wife of John Anderson. *U. T.* xi.

ANDREWS. Jack. *M. P., N. E.*

ANDREWS. Little. *M. P., V. D.*

ANGEL. *P. P.* xxix. Looking down upon, and blessing.

" ANGEL. The," in Bury St. Edmunds. *P. P.*, xvi. In a wide open street, nearly facing the old abbey.

" ANGEL. The," Islington. *O. T.* xlii. Where—London began in earnest.

" ANGEL. The," Public House. *C. S., H. T.*

ANGEL COURT. *L. D.* Pref.

ANGELA. Emmeline's cousin and sweetheart of Charley. *C. S., H. T.*

ANGELICA. A sometime sweetheart of the Uncommercial Traveller. *U. T.* ix.

ANGLAIS, L'. Monsieur—the Englishman Mr. Langley. *C. S., S. L.* ii.

ANGLER'S INN.
Original: Red Lion Inn, Henley.
O. M. F. li.

ANGLESEY. *U. T.* ii.

ANGLO-BENGALEE DISINTERESTED LOAN AND LIFE ASSURANCE COMPANY. Offices of the.
M. C. xxvii.
ᶜ In a new street in the City, comprising the upper part of a spacious house, resplendent in stucco, and plate glass, with wire blinds in all the windows, and "Anglo Bengalee" worked into the pattern of every one of them.

ANIMALS. Society for the Prevention of Cruelty to. *U. T.* xxxv.

ANIO. The river. *P. F. I., R.*

ANNE. *S. Y. C.*

ANNE. Queen, Late Queen Dowager. *M. P., T. D.*

ANNE. Dombey's housemaid.
D. and S. xviii.
Note.—Towlinson and Anne "make it up" and agree to set up together in the general greengrocery line.

ANNE. Mrs. Chickenstalker.
C. B., C. G. iv.

ANNIE. Dr. Strong's Wife's cousin.
D. C. xvi.

ANNUNCIATA. The Church of the.
P. F. I., G. A. N.

ANNY. *O. T.* xxiv.

"ANOTHER." Husband of *Dust* Contractor's daughter.
O. M. F. ii.
Was so cut up by the loss of his young wife that if he outlived her a year it was as much as he did.

ANTHONY. Doctor Jeddler.
C. B., B. o. L. iii.

ANTHONY. Runaway Slave.
A. N. xvii.

ANTHONY. William S.,
M. P., I. W. M.

ANTIPODES. The. *U. T.* v.

ANTOINE. A son of Madame. Doche. *R. P., M. O. F. F.*

ANTONIO. *P. F. I., G. A. N.*

ANTONIO. A lodger at Meggisson's.
U. T. v.
A swarthy youth with a guitar. A young foreign sailor—a Spaniard.

ANTWERP.
H. T., R. vii. ; and *L. D.* lxvi.

ANYSHIRE. *D. and. S.* xxxvi.

APARTMENT. French.
D. and S. liv.
Comprising some half dozen rooms—a dull cold hall or corridor, a dining-room, a drawing-room, a bed chamber, and an inner drawing-room or boudoir, smaller and more retired than the rest.

APENNINES. The. *P. F. I., R.*

APOTHECARY. *O. T.* xxiv.

APOTHECARY. A certain calm.
D. and S. xiv.
Who attended at the establishment when any of the young gentlemen were ill.

APOTHECARY. Attending deathbed of Nicholas Nickleby, senior.
N. N. i.
Cheer up said the Apothecary.

APPARITOR. The, The officer of the Court. *S. B. B.,* Scenes viii.

APPIAN WAY. *P. F. I., R.*

APPIUS CLAUDIUS.
M. P., V. and *B. S.*

APPLICANT. Next, for lodgings.
S. B. B., O. P. vii.
A tall thin gentleman with a

profusion of brown hair, reddish whiskers and very slightly developed moustaches and had altogether a military appearance.

APPRENTICE. *S. B. B., O. P.*, viii.
Pauses every other minute from his task.

APPRENTICE. Apothecary's, the parish. *O. T.* xxiv.

APPRENTICE. Engravers', who painted Miss Bravassa's likeness.
N. N. xxiii.

APPRENTICE. Lobbs'.
P. P. xvii.
Bony apprentice with the thin legs.

APPRENTICES. At Greenwich fair.
S. B. B., Scenes xii.

APPRENTICES. Four London.
S. B. B., Characters i.
They are only bound, now, by indentures. Four all arm in arm, with white kid gloves like so many bridegrooms, light trousers of unprecedented patterns ; and coats for which the English language has yet no name—a kind of cross between a great-coat and a surtout, with the collar of the one, the skirts of the other, and pockets peculiar to themselves. Each of the gentlemen carried a thick stick with a large tassel at the top, the whole four walking with a paralytic swagger. . . . They are a peculiar class and not the less pleasant for being inoffensive.

APPRENTICES. Milliners'.
S. B. B., Scenes i.
The hardest worked—the worst paid—poor girls.

APPRENTICES. Staymakers'.
S. B. B., Scenes i.
Poor girls !—the hardest worked —the worst paid.

APPRENTICES. Two, of Peffer and Snagsby. *B. H.* x.

ARA COELI. Church of.
P. F. I., R.

ARABELLA. Mrs. Grazinglands.
U. T. vi.

ARABELLA. *See* Allen, Arabella.

ARABS. *L. D.* lxx.

ARAGO. M. *M. P., M. M.*

ARAMINTA. *M. P., G. D.*

ARCADE. The. *U. T.* x.

ARCADE. *Beadles* of the.
U. T. xvi.

ARCHBISHOP. *M. P., C. C.*

ARCHBISHOP OF GREENWICH.
O. M. F. liv.
Head waiter in Hotel.

ARCHES. Adelphi. *See* Adelphi.

ARCHES. Commemorative of Rome. *L. D.* li.

ARCHES COURT. The, In Doctors' Commons.
S. B. B., Scenes viii.

AREZZO. *P. F. I., R. D.*

ARGONAUT. The, A ship.
U. T. xv.

ARIEL. *M. P., R. T.*

ARIOSTO'S HOUSE.
P. F. I., T. B. F.

ARISTOTLE. *M. P., P. L. U.*

ARKANSAS.
A. N. xvii. ; and *M. C.* xvi.

ARMES. Place d'—of High Town
R. P., O F. W.
A little decayed market is held.

ARMY. The, Characters in Play.
S. B. B., Scenes xiii.
Two dirty men with corked countenances in very old green tunics, and dirty drab boots.

ARMY. British. *M. P., T. I. P.*

ARMY. Nephews in the, Character in play given by Mr. V. Crummles' Company. *N. N.* xxiii.

ARNDT. The Hon. Charles C. P. *A. N.* xvii.
Member for the Council of Brown County.

ARNO. River. *P. F. I., R. D.*; and *R. P., D. W. T. T.*

ARNO. Valley of the. *P. F. I., R. D.*

ARNOTT. Dr. *M. P., A. J. B.*; and *M. P., S. S. U.*

ARPIN. Mr. P. *A. N.* xvii.

ARRAS. *C. S., M. J.* v.; and *U. T.* xvii.

ARROW. An Indian Chief. *A. N.* ix.

ARSENAL. The, at Woolwich. *B. R.* lxvii.

ARTFUL DODGER. *See also* Dawkins, Jack. *M. P., T. T. C. D.*

ARTHUR Half-brother to Miss Havisham. *G. E.* xlii.

ARTHUR. Negro slave. *A. N.* xvii.

ARTHUR'S SEAT. Edinburgh. *P. P.* xlix.

ARTICLE. Plated. *R. P., P. A.*

ARTIST. A Street. *C. S., S. L.* iii.
A shabby person of modest appearance who shivered dreadfully (though it wasn't at all cold) was engaged in blowing the chalk-dust off the moon.

ARTISTS. *M. P., T.B.*

Individual artists will be found under their names both in real life and the artistic characters of the books.

ARUNDEL. *C. S., M. L. Lo.* i.

ASCENSION. Island of. *M. P., L. T.*; and *M. P., N. E.*

ASHBURTON. Lord. *A. N.* xiv.

ASHES. Name of a Bird. *B. H.* xiv.

ASHFORD. *D. C.* xviii.; and *R. P., A. F.*

ASHFORD. Nettie, A schoolgirl. *H. R.* i.
Aged half-past six.

ASHLEY. Lord. *M. P., S. S.*

ASHLEY. Hon. William. *M. P., C. C.*

ASIA. *M. P., B. A.*; and *M. P., N. S. E.*

ASSEMBLY ROOMS. The. *P. P.* xxxv.

ASSEMBLY ROOMS. At English Watering Place. *R. P., O. E. W.*
A bleak chamber—understood to be available on hire for balls or concerts.
Original: In Nuckall's Place, Broadstairs. Later turned into a club.

ASSEMBLY ROOMS. Library attached to. *R. P., O. E. W.*
This is the library for the Minerva Press.

ASSEMBLY. Two Houses of. Washington. *A. N.* viii.

ASSOCIATED BORES. My Club. *M. P., I. M.*

ASSOCIATION. A certain *Brandy-wine.* *M. C.,* Preface.

ASSURANCE COMPANY. The Anglo-Bengalee *Disinterested* Loan and Life. *M. C.* xxvii.

ASTERISK. *M. P.W.*

ASTLEY'S. A circus. *O. C. S.,* xxxix; and *S. B. B.,* Scenes xi.
It was not a Royal Amphitheatre in those days . . . with all the paint, gilding, and looking-glass; the vague smell of horses suggestive of coming wonders."

ASTLEY'S THEATRE.
B. H. xxi. ; *M. P., M. B. V.* ; and
    M. P., R. H. F.

ASTLEY'S VISITORS. (Audience in
Circus).   *S. B. B.*, Scenes xi.
    Three little boys and a little
girl occupied the front row (of
box), then two more little girls,
ushered in by a young lady, evidently the governess. Then came
three more little boys, dressed
like the first, in blue jackets and
lay down shirt collars : then a
child in a braided frock—Then
came ma and pa, and then the
eldest, a boy of fourteen years old.

ASYLUMS.   *A. N.* iii.
    *The various asylums mentioned
in the works will be found under
their names.*

ATHENAEUM. The. *M. P., B. A.* ;
    M. P., I. M. T. ; and *N. N.* i.

ATHERFIELD. Mrs. Passenger on
board the *Golden Mary.*
    C. S., W. o. G. M.
    A blooming young wife, who
was going out to join her husband
in California.

ATKINS. Will. Personage in Nursery Tale.   *U. T.* xv.

ATKINSONS. Mr., The perfumers.
    U. T. xvi.

ATLANTIC. The. *A. N.*, ii ; *H. T.
R.* i. ; *M. C.*, xiii. ; *R. P., T. D. P.*,
and *U. T.* xx.

ATTÀH OF IDDAH. *M. P., N. E.*

ATTENDANT. At *Bachelors'* Inns
at *Temple Bar.   M. C.* xlv.
    A Fiery-faced matron attired in
a crunched bonnet with particularly long strings to it hanging
down her back.

ATTENDANT. Female, at Ralph
Nickleby's.   *N. N.* xxix.

ATTENDANT. Of Lady Client of
General Agency Office. *N. N.* xvi.
    A red-faced, round-eyed, sloven-
ly girl.

ATTENDANT. Upon the stranger.
    M. H. C. i.

ATTORNEY. A Small.
    S. B. B., O. P. vii.

ATTORNEY. An. *M. P., H. H.*

ATTORNEY. London. *P. C.* xxi.
    A man of no great nicety in
his professional dealings.

ATTORNEY'S CLERK. Making a
search in Vestry.   *D. and S.* v.
    Over-aged, and over-worked, and
underpaid.

ATTORNEY-GENERAL. The.
    M. P., S. F. A. ; *R. P., P. M. T. P.
T. T. C.*, bk. ii., ch. ii., and
U. T. xi.

**ATTORNEY-GENERAL'S CHAM-
BERS.**   *R. P., P. M. T. P.* ;

ATTORNEY-GENERAL. For Ireland.   *M. P.*, Ag. Int.

ATTORNEYS.   *P. P.* xl.

AUBER. M.   *M. P., M. M.*

AUBURN. Mount, Suburb of Cincinnati.   *A. N.* xi.

AUBURN. Prison.   *A. N.* vi.

AUGUSTA.   *B. H.* x.
    A lean young woman from a
workhouse has fits which the
parish can't account for ; aged
three or four and twenty, but
looking a round ten years older.

AUGUSTUS. Son of Mr. and Mrs.
Borum.   N. N. xxiv.
    A young gentleman who was
pinching the phenomenon apparently with a view of ascertaining
if she were real.

AUNT. Allen's.   *P. C.* xlviii.

AUNT. Grey-haired, of Kate.
    D. and S. xxiv.

AUNT. Miss Pankey's at Rottingdean.   *D. and S.* viii.

AUNT. Mr. F's, Flora's Legacy. *L. D.* xiii.

An amazing little old woman, with a face like a staring wooden doll too cheap for expression, and a stiff yellow wig, perched unevenly on the top of her head ... seemed to have damaged her face in two or three places with some blunt instrument in the nature of a spoon ; particularly the tip of her nose—several dints—answering to the bowl of that article. The major characteristics were extreme severity and grim taciturnity ; sometimes interrupted by a propensity to offer remarks in a deep warning voice traceable to no association of ideas.

Note.—Flora had inherited the aunt from her late husband. The "staring wooden doll" took a great dislike to Arthur Clenman and let off her remarks, of which "There's milestones on the Dover Road" is perhaps the best known, at him with the deadliest marksmanship.

AUNT. Mr. Home's. *M. P., M. M.*

AUNT. My. *See* Trotwood, Betsy.

AUSTERLITZ. *R. P., O. F. W.*

AUSTIN. John. *M. P., P. F.*

AUSTIN. Mrs. *M. P., R. H. F.*

AUSTIN FRIARS. *M. C.* xxxviii ; *M. P., G. A.*

AUSTRALIA. *C. S., S. L.* i. ; *D. C.* xxii ; *D. and S.* xxv. ; *M. P., C.* ; *M. P., E. T.* ; *M. P., P. P.* ; *M. P., S. R.* ; *M. P., W.* ; *U. T.* ii.

AUSTRIA. *C. S.,* ii ; *M. P., W. H.* ; *R. P., O. B.* ; *U. T.* xxviii.

AVALLON. *P. F. I., G. T. F.*

AVENGER. The. *See* Pepper.

AVIGNON. *B. H.* xii ; *C. S.* ii ; *L. D.* xi ; *P. F. I., L. R. G. A.* ; *P. F. I., P. M. B.*

AVVOCATE. *P. F. I.*

AWKWARD SQUAD. Full Private Number One in The. *See* Sloppy.

AYLESBURY. *M. P., C. P.*

AYNHO. *M. P., E. S.*

AYRESLEIGH. Mr., under arrest. *P. P.,* xl.

A middle-aged man in a very old suit of black, who looked pale and haggard.

AZORES. *M. P., L. A. V.* ii.

B

"B." C. of. The Countess. *N. N.* xxviii.

B. Count de. *M. P., M. M.*

"B." D. of. The Duchess. *N. N.* xxviii.

B. M. *M. P., F. S.*

B. Madame. *M. P., A. A. P.*

B. Major. "Nobody." *R. P., N. S.*

B. Master, Ghost of. *C. S., H. H.* Dressed in an obsolete fashion, or rather was not so much dressed as put into a case of inferior pepper-and-salt cloth, made horrible by means of shining buttons.

B. Miss L., of Bungay, Suffolk *M. P., W. R.*

B. Mr. *M. P. W. R.*

B. Mr. Mr. Bridgman. *A. N.* xvii

B. Mr. John. *M. P., R. T.*

B. Mrs. Mrs. Benjamin Britain *C. B., B. o. L.* iii

B. Mrs. *M. P., S. F. A.*

B. Mrs. *M. P., W. R.*

B. Young. *M. P., W. R.*

BABBY. The Young Peerybingle. *C. B., C. o. H.* iii.

BABER. *M. P., C. Pat.*

BABIES. (In arms) at Tea Gardens. *S. B. B.* Scenes ix.

BABLEY. Mr. Richard. *See Dick,* Mr.

BABY. Great, The Public. *M. P., G. B.*

BABY. Kitterbell's baby. *See* Kitterbell, Master Frederick Charles William.

BABY. *See* Meagles, Minnie.

BABY. *D*ying, of *B*rickmaker's wife. *B. H.* viii.

BABY. New, of the Kenwigs. *N. N.* xxvi.

BABY. The Old, Lillyvick Kenwigs. *N. N.* xxxvi.

BACHELOR. The. *O. C. S.* lii.
The little old gentleman was the active spirit of the place, the adjuster of all the differences, the promoter of all the merry-makings, the dispenser of his friend's bounty, and of no small charity of his own besides.

Note.—The extract admirably illustrates the Bachelor's character. Nell and her father made acquaintance with him at the village where the schoolmaster procured them the appointment of caretakers of the old church. The little old gentleman had lived at the Parsonage House for fifteen years.

BACHELOR'S HALL. The name given to Quilp's riverside place, first named in chapter l. of Old Curiosity Shop. This was the Counting House which the dwarf converted into a temporary dwelling place during his "displeasure" with his wife. *See also* Quilp.

"BACHELORS. The Three Jolly." *D. and S.* xxvii.

BACK. *M. P., L. A. V.* i.

BACK YARD. Of Mrs. Chivery's Establishment. *L. D.* xxii.
In this yard a wash of sheets and table cloths tried (in vain for want of air) to get dried on a line or two.

BACON. Friar. *M. P., P. M. B.*
Note.—The originator and supporter of the men's village club.
Original: Sir John Bennet Lawes, of Rothamsted.

BACON. Lawyer. *M. P., C. P.*

BADAJOS. *C. S., S. P. T.* ii.

BADEN-BADEN.
D. C. xxxi.; and *M. P., P. M. B.*

BADGER. Black. *D. and S.* xxii.

BADGER. Mr. Bayham, Physician. Mr. Kenge's Cousin. *B. H.* xiii.
A pink, fresh faced, crisp-looking gentleman, with a weak voice, white teeth, light hair and surprised eyes.
Note.—This Chelsea practitioner was the one to whom Richard Carstone was articled in his first choice of a profession. Besides his Chelsea practice he attended a large public institution. His most prominent trait was a habit of praising the two former husbands of his wife.

BADGER. Mrs. Laura, wife of Mr. Bayham *Badger.* *B. H.* xiii.
A lady of about fifty, youthfully dressed, and of a very fine complexion.
Note.—Her "first" was Captain Swosser of the Royal Navy, her "second" Professor Dingo: Mr. Badger was her "third."

BAGDAD. *U. T.* xv.

BAGDAD. The Bazaar at. *M. P., G. A.*

BAGGS. Mr. *O. M. F.* viii.

BAGGS. Lilburn W., late Governor of State, at Independence. *A. N.* xvii.

BAGMAN. The, Traveller at the "Peacock." *P. P.* xiv.

A stout hale personage of about forty, with only one eye—a very bright black eye, which twinkled with a roguish expression of fun and good humour.

Note.—The Bagman was the narrator of the now famous "Bagman's Story" and the "Story of the Bagmans Uncle." The latter contains incidentally a lively account of the old coaching days. Pickwick meets the Bagman on two occasions, first at Eatanswill and afterwards at Bristol.

BAGMAN'S UNCLE. Employee of Tiggin and Welps, and friend of Tom Smart. *P. P.* xlix.

One of the merriest, pleasantest, cleverest fellows that ever lived. In appearance, my uncle was a trifle shorter than the middle size—a trifle stouter, too— his face might be a trifle redder.

BAGNERELLO. Signor.
P. F. I., G. A. N.

BAGNERELLO. Villa.
P. F. I., G. A. N.

BAGNET. Matthew, an ex-artillery-man and proprietor of musician's shop. *B. H.* xxvii.

Tall and upright, with shaggy eyebrows, and whiskers like the fibres of a cocoanut, not a hair upon his head, and a torrid complexion. Voice, short, deep and resonant, not at all unlike the tones of the instrument (bassoon) to which he is devoted.

Note.—Friend of George Rouncewell. Formerly an artilleryman, but when he enters the story he is in " the musical business." His wife has the head of the family but to maintain " discipline " he never admits it to her. The story leaves him and his family as occasional visitors at " Chesney Wold."

very rigid pair of jawbones, and long-flapped elephantine ears.

Note.—The major lives near Miss Tox, whom he watches from his window. He exchanges little courtesies with her. Makes the acquaintance of Mr. Dombey, and introduces him to Edith Grainger his second wife. The friendship between the Major and Miss Tox comes to nothing.

BAIAE. *P. F. I., R. D.*

" BAIL." A. Trader in bailing prisoners out. *P. P.* xl.
" What, am I to understand that these men earn a livelihood by walking about here to perjure themselves before the judges of the land at the rate of half a crown a crime ? "

BAILEY. *Benjamin. Belonging to Commercial Boarding House.*
M. C. viii.
With a large red head, and no nose to speak of, and a very dirty Wellington boot on his left arm —" I thought you was the Paper," replied the boy, " and wondered why you didn't shove yourself through the grating as usual."

Note.—The boy at Mrs. Todger's boarding - house. He has a variety of names bestowed upon him by the boarders. He is a friend of Mr. Sweedlepipe, with whom he afterwards enters the hairdressing business. In the meantime he has been " tiger " to Tigg Montague.

BAILEY. Captain. *D. C.* xviii.

BAILEY. Old, Courts at. *C. S.,* *T. C. S.* i ; *N. N.* xx ; and *S. B. B.,* Scenes xxiv.
Nothing so strikes the person who enters them for the first time, as the calm indifference with which the proceedings are conducted.

BALIM. Mr. *S. Y. G.*

BAILLIE. A. *P. P.* xlix.
Mac something and four syllables after it, who lived in the old town of Edinburgh.

BAILLIE'S GROWN-UP SON.
P. P. xlix.

BAILLIE'S THREE DAUGHTERS.
P. P. xlix.
Very pretty and agreeable.

BAILLIE'S WIFE. *P. P.* xlix.
" One of the best creatures that ever lived."

BAINES. Mr, An Actor.
R. P., O. O. S.

BAKER. Mr. *S., Y. G., Y. L.*

BAKER. Mr., A Coroner. *U. T.* iii.

BAKER. Mr. E. S., Nominated Member of Grant County.
A. N. xvii.

BAKER. A. *M. P., G. A.*

BAKER. A (in Somerstown).
B. H. xliii.
A sort of human hedgehog rolled up said Mr. Skimpole— from whom we borrowed a couple of armchairs when they were worn out, he wanted them back. He objected to their being worn.

BAKER. The. *G. E.* viii.

BAKERS' TRAP. A Thames *Dock,* famous for Suicide Scenes.
U. T. iii.

Original : Old Gravel Lane Bridge, St. George's-in-the-East. Locally known as the " Bridge of Sighs."

BAKERS. *S. B. B.,* Scenes i.

BALAKLAVA. *M. P., G. D. ; M. P. N. S. E. ; and M. P., S. F. A.*

BALDERDASH. Great Parochial Joint Stock *Bank* of. *R. P., O. V.*

BALDERSTONE. Thomas, Mrs. Gauleton's brother.
S. B. B.; Tales ix.

BÂLE. P. F. I., V. M. M. S.S.

BALFE. Mr. M. P., M. M.

BALLANTYNE FAMILY. Scott's Publishers. M. P., S. P.

BALLANTYNE. Alexander.
M. P., S. P.

BALLANTYNE. James.
M. P., S. P.

BALLANTYNE. John. M. P., S. P.

BALLAST-HEAVERS. At Ratcliff.
U. T. xxx.
Occupants of one room.

BALLEY. Mr. O. M. F. viii.

BALLON. Rev. Adin.
M. P., S. B.; M. P., R. S. D.

BALLS. Golden, in connection with uncle. M. C. i.
Certain entertainments, so splendid and costly in their nature, that he calls them "Golden Balls."

BALL'S POND. D. S. xviii; and S. B. B., Tales iii.

BALSAMO. Mr. M. P., M. M.

BALTIC SEA. D. and S. iv.

BALTIMORE, U.S.A.
A. N. viii.; and M. P., I. W. M.

BAMBER. M. H. C. iv.
He is a strange secluded visionary.

BAMBER. Residence of. M. H. C. iv.
One of these dull lonely old places—often shut up close for several weeks together.

BAMBER. Jack, An attorney's clerk. P. P. xx.
Never heard to talk of anything else but the inns, and he has lived alone in them till he's half crazy. . . .

A little yellow high - shouldered man . . . a fixed grim smile perpetually on his countenance . . . a long skinny hand with nails of extraordinary length.
Note.—The old man knew more about the "Inns" (of Court), than any one. Mr. Pickwick succeeded in "drawing" him when he joined Mr. Lowten's convivial company at the "Magpie and Stump" on the occasion of his search after Mr. Perker's clerk regarding the Bardell case.

BAMBINO. P. F. I.

BAND. A brass. D. and S. xxxi.
In the person of an artful trombone, lurks and dodges round the corner, waiting for some traitor tradesman to reveal the place and hour of the wedding - breakfast, for a bribe.

BAND. The, taking part in election.
P. P. xvi.

BAND OF MUSIC. In pasteboard caps. P. P. xv.

BAND OF PENSIONERS. Captain and Lieutenant of. M. P., M. B.V.

BANDOLINING ROOM. At Mugby Junction. C. S., M. J. v.
It's led to by the door behind the counter, which you'll notice usually stands ajar, and it's the room where our missis and our young ladies *Bandolines* their hair.

BANDS OF HOPE. Juvenile.
M. P., F. F.

BANGER. CAPTAIN, A vestryman.
R. P., O. V.

BANGHAM. Mrs., Charwoman and messenger. L. D. vi.
Who was not a prisoner (though she had been once) but was the popular medium of communication with the outer world.

BANGOR.
M. P., E. S.; and U. T. ii.

BANJO BONES. Mr., A professional at the Snug. *U. T.* v.
Comic favourite — looking very hideous with his blackened face and limp loaf-sugar hat.

BANJO BONES. Mrs., Wife of Mr. Banjo Bones. *U. T.* v.
In her natural colours—a little heightened.

BANK. The. Coketown. *H. T., R.* i.
Red brick house, with black outside shutters, green blinds inside, a black street door up two white steps, a brazen door plate, and a brazen door handle full stop.

BANK IN SALISBURY. *M. C.,* v.
Original : Probably Wilts and Dorset Bank.

BANK. In Venice. *L. D.* xlii.

BANK. Mill Pond. *G. E.* xlvi.

BANK OF ENGLAND. *B. R.* lxvii. ; *C. S., G. S.* ; *D. S.* xiii. ; *L. D.* xxvi. ; *M. C.* xxxvii. ; *M. P., E. T.* ; *M. P., I. M.* ; *N. N.* xxxv. *P. C.* lv. ; *U. T.* ix.

BANK. The, and National Credit Office. *M. C.* xxiii.

BANK CLERK. Tim Linkinwater's friend. The Superannuated. *N. N.* xxxvii.

BANKER. *Banker* at *Rouge-et-noir* table. *N. N.* l.
A plump, paunchy, sturdy-looking fellow, with his under-lip a little pursed from a habit of counting money inwardly as he paid it.

BANKS. Major. An old East India Director. *H. D.* iv.

BANKS. *U. T.* xxi.

BANQUO. Character in play. *S. B. B.,* Scenes xiii.
Snuff-shop looking figure.

BANTAM. Angelo Cyrus. *P. P.* xxxv.
Dressed in a very bright blue coat with resplendent buttons, black trousers, and the thinnest possible pair of highly polished boots. A gold eye-glass was suspended from his neck by a short broad black ribbon ; a gold snuff-box was lightly clasped in his left hand ; gold rings innumerable glittered on his fingers ; and a large diamond pin, set in gold, glistened in his shirt frill. He had a gold watch, and a gold curb chain with large gold seals ; and he carried a pliant ebony cane with a heavy gold top. His linen was of the very whitest, finest, and stiffest ; his wig of the glossiest, blackest, and curliest. His snuff was prince's mixture ; his scent *bouquet du roi.* His features were contracted into a perpetual smile ; and his teeth were in such perfect order that it was difficult at a small distance to tell the real from the false.

Note.—The Grand Master at Ba-ath is of secondary importance, but is an example of Dickens' faculty of introducing a character "full grown." Bantam is Bantam and could be nobody else, and no other could be Bantam. The above description is of interest, as it contains one of Dickens' errors, which occurs in stating Bantam's cane to have been pliant ebony.

Original : The original of Cyrus Angelo Bantam's house has been identified as No. 12, *Queen Square, Bath.*

BANVARD. Mr. *M. P., A. P.* ; and *M. P., E. T.*

BAPS. Mr., Dancing master at Dr. Blimbers. *D. and S.* xiv.

BAPS. Mrs., Wife of dancing master. *D. and S.* xiv.

BAPTISTE. Billeted on the poor water-carrier. *C. S., S. L.* ii.

Sitting on the pavement, in the sunlight—his martial legs asunder, one of the water-carrier's spare pails between them, which he was painting bright-green outside and bright red within.

BAPTISTERY. Parma.
P. F. I., P. M. B.

BAPTISTERY. The, Pisa.
P. F. I., R. P. S.

"BAR." Guest of Mr. Merdle.
L. D. xxi.
With the jury droop, and persuasive eyeglass.

BARBADOES.
D. S. xiii. ; and M. P., L. A. V. v.

BARBARA. One of Kit's children.
O. C. S. Chap. The last.

BARBARA. The Garland's maid.
O. C. S. xxii.
A little servant girl, very tidy, modest and demure, but very pretty too.

Note.—The servant at Mr. Garland's where she first enters the story. She makes friends with Kit and his mother and the other members of the family and eventually marries Kit.

BARBARA'S MOTHER.
O. C. S. xxxix.

BARBARY. Miss, Godmother and aunt of Esther Summerson.
B. H. iii.
She was a good, good woman. She went to Church three times every Sunday, and to morning prayers on Wednesdays and Fridays. She was handsome ; and if she had ever smiled would have been like an angel—but she never smiled.

Note.—Miss Barbary resided at Windsor where Esther stayed with her until her death. Presumably she was the sister of Lady Dedlock, to which entry reference may be made.

BARBARY. Mrs. Captain. L. D. xii.

BARBARY CORSAIRS.
P. F. I., G. A. N.

BARBER. C. S., H. H.

BARBER. C. S., M. H. C.

BARBER. C. S., S. L.

BARBER. The talkative = Praymiah. M. P., T. O. H.

BARBICAN. B. R. viii.; L. D. xiii. ; M. C. xxxvii. ; and O. T. xxi.
One of the narrow streets which diverged from that centre, from the main street, itself little better than an alley, a low-browed doorway led into a blind court or yard, profoundly dark, unpaved, and reeking with stagnant odours.

BARBOX BROTHERS. The firm of.
C. S., M. J. ii.
Had been some off-shoot or irregular branch of the Public Notary, and bill-broking tree.

BARBOX BROTHERS. Mr. Jackson. C. S., M. J. i.
A man within five years of fifty either way, who had turned grey too soon, like a neglected fire ; a man of pondering habit, brooding carriage of the head, and suppressed internal voice.

Note.—Mr. Jackson is the last member of the firm. He has been disappointed and resolves to travel. He alights on the impulse of the moment at Mugby Junction. The experiences and adventures he goes through from that time have a beneficial effect on his character, and so compensate him for his earlier disappointment.

BARCLAY AND PERKINS. Brewers.
D. C. xxviii.

BARDELL. Master Tommy, The son of Mr. Pickwick's landlady.
P. P. xii.

Note.—Master Tommy appears on several occasions, but does not occupy a very important place in the story. His most noticeable appearance is probably that in the " trial " scene.

BARDELL. Mrs. Martha, Mr. Pickwick's landlady ; and the plaintiff in *Bardell* v. *Pickwick. P. P.* xii.
The relict and sole executrix of a deceased custom-house officer.

Note.—Mrs. Bardell was Mr. Pickwick's landlady. Possibly because the wish was father to the thought, she jumped to the conclusion that, when Mr. P. was gently breaking the news to her that he proposed engaging a manservant (Sam Weller), he was proposing to her. This led to the famous trial Bardell v. Pickwick in chap. xxxiv. Mrs. Bardell is imprisoned by Dodson and Fogg for costs, but is released on Mr. Pickwick's paying them.

Original : Said to have been founded on Mrs. Ann Ellis, " who kept an eating house near Doctors' Commons."

BARGE. A lime.   *N. T.* xxiv.
A white horse on a barge's sail, that barge is a lime barge.

BARGEMAN. A, *Bradley Headstone. O. M. F.* li.

BARING. Mr.   *M. P., T. B.*

BARING BROTHERS.
        M. P., G. A. ; and *M. P., F. L.*

BARK. Lodging - house keeper and receiver of stolen goods.
        R. P., D. W. I.F.

BARK'S. Deputy.
        R. P., D. W. I. F.

BARKER. Owner of an assumed name.   *S. B. B.,* Scenes xiii.

BARKER. Phil.   *O. T.* xxvi.

BARKER. R. B.   *M. P., S. B.*

BARKER. William.
        S. B. B., Scenes xvii.
Assistant waterman to the Hackney Coach Stand, and later 'Bus Conductor. A distant relative of a waterman of our acquaintance —weakness in his early years—a love of ladies, liquids, and pocket-handkerchiefs.

BARKING CREEK.
        R. P., D. W. T. T.

BARKIS. Clara Peggotty.   *See* Peggotty.

BARKIS. Mr., Carrier.   *D. C.* ii.
Of a phlegmatic temperament, and not at all conversational.

Note.—The carrier who sent his message, " Barkis is willin'," to Peggotty by little David. He married Peggotty, and when he died left his money to her.

Original : A Mr. Barker, a carrier of the time at Blundeston.

BARKLEMYS.   *M. C.* xlix.

BARKS. Light screw, At Chatham.
        U. T. xxiv.

BARKSHIRE.   *D. and S.* xxxvi.

BARLEY. Miss Clara.   Clara.
        G. E. xlvi.
Pretty, gentle, dark-eyed girl.

BARLEY. Old, Mr., Clara's father.
        G. E. xlvi.

BARLOW. Mr., A tutor.
        U. T. xxxiii.
Irrepressible, instructive monomaniac.

" BARLOW." Mr. Gifts on Christmas tree.   *R. P., A. C. T.*

BARMAID. Of the " George and Vulture."   *P. P.* xxxi.

BARMAID. At " Town Arms."
        P. P. xiii.
" Bribed to hocus the brandy and water of fourteen unpolled electors as was a stoppin' in the house."

BARMAIDS. In gin palace.
S. B. B. xxii.
Two showily - dressed damsels with large necklaces.

BARMECIDE. *M. P., T. O. H.*

BARNACLE. Clarence, Tite Barnacle's son. *L. D.* xvii.
The born idiot of the family —most agreeable and most endearing blockhead !—with a kind of cleverness in him too.
Original : So far as the name is concerned this has been traced to Bath, but it appears probable that the name was used as being descriptive of the character.

BARNACLE. Ferdinand, Private Secretary to Lord Decimus.
L. D. xlviii.
The sprightly young Barnacle.

BARNACLE. John. *L. D.* xxvi.

BARNACLE. Junior, Son of Mr. Tite - Barnacle. In Circumlocution Office. *L. D.* x.
Had a youthful aspect, and the fluffiest little whisker, perhaps that ever was seen.

BARNACLE. Lord Decimus Tite, Pilot of the ship-circumlocution office. *L. D.* xiii.
In the odour of circumlocution —with the very smell of despatch-boxes upon him.

BARNACLE. Mr. Tite, High in the Circumlocution Office. *L. D.* x.
He wound and wound folds of white cravat round his neck, as he wound and wound folds of tape and paper round the neck of the country. His wristbands and collar were oppressive, his voice and manner were oppressive.

BARNACLE. Tom, Dick, or Harry.
L. D. xxvi.

BARNACLE. William. *L. D.* xxvi.

BARNACLE FAMILY. The Tite,
L. D. ix.
The Barnacle family had for some time helped to administer the Circumlocution Office. The Tite-Barnacle Branch, indeed, considered themselves in a general way as having vested rights in that direction, and took it ill if any other family had much to say to it.

BARNACLES. Less distinguished Parliamentary. *L. D.* xxxiv.

BARNACLES. Three other young.
L. D. xxxiv.
Insipid to all the senses, and terribly in want of seasoning.

BARNARD. Sir Andrew.
M. P., C. C.

BARNARD CASTLE. *N. N.* vii.

BARNARD'S INN. Young Mr. Pocket's rooms. *G. E.* xx.
The dingiest collection of shabby buildings ever squeezed together in a rank corner as a club for tomcats.

BARNET.
B. H. vi. ; *O. T.* vii. ; *U. T.* xiv.

BARNEY. One of Fagin's confederates. *O. T.* xv.
Waiter in a low public house in Saffron Hill.

Note.—Barney is one of those casual elusive characters for which Dickens was so famous. He appears to have neither beginning nor end in the story. As his name implies, he was a Jew. He was engaged at the Three Cripples and always spoke through his nose.

BARNSTAPLE. *C. S., M. f. T. S.* v

BARNUM. Mr. *M. P., Th. Let.*

BARNUM'S HOTEL. Baltimore.
A. N. ix

BARNWELL. George.
R. P., A. C. T.

BARNWELL. *Benjamin Bailey.*
M. C. ix.

BARON. A. *M. P., S. D. C.*

BARON. A lusty young, Son of Baron von Koëldwethout.
N. N. vi.
In whose honour a great many fireworks were let off, and a great many dozens of wine drunk.

BARONESS. Young, *Daughter* of Baron von Koëldwethout.
N. N. vi.

BARRACK CABARET.
P. F. I., L. R. G. A.

BARRACKS. The, Room in.
B. R. lviii.
A stone-floored room, where there was a very powerful smell of tobacco, a strong thorough draught of air, and a great wooden bedstead.

BARRIERS. *M. P., N. Y. D.*

BARRISTERS. *S. B. B.,* Scenes xxiv.

BARRONNEAU. Monsieur Henri (Publican of the Cross of Gold)
L. D. i.
Sixty-five at least, and in a failing state of health, had the misfortune to die.

BARRONNEAU. Madame, widow of M. Henri Barronneau. *L. D.* i.
She was two-and-twenty, had gained a reputation for beauty, and was beautiful. Unfortunately the property of Madame Barronneau was settled on herself.

BARROW. Sir John.
M. P., L. A. V. ii.

BARRY. *M. P., R. S. L.*

BARRY'S PALACE. Sir Charles.
M. P., M. P.

BARSAD. John. The assumed name of Solomon Pross, *which see.*

BART. *See* Smalleed, Bartholomew.

BARTHÉLÉMY. *M. P., M. E.*

BARTHOLOMEW. Deceased brother of Philip Pirrip. *G. E.* i.

BARTHOLOMEW CLOSE. *G. E.* xx.

BARTHOLOMEW FAIR.
M. P., J.G.

BARTHOLOMEW'S. Nursing Institution. *M. C.* xxv.

BARTLEY. Mr. *M. P., R. S. L.*

BARTON. Mr. Jacob, brother of Mrs. Malderton. *S. B. B.,* Tales v.
A large grocer—never scrupled to avow that he wasn't above his business.

BARTON. Mr. *S. B. B.,* Tales v.

BASLE. *C. S., N. T.,* Act iii.

BASS. Thin faced man in black.
S. B. B., Scenes ii.
He can go down lower than any man. So low sometimes that you can't hear him.

BASTILLE. *M. P., C. S., M. P., W. H., M. P., W. S. G.; T. T. C.,*
bk. ii., ch. xxi.
So resistless was the force of the [human] ocean bearing him on . . . he was landed in the outer courtyard of the *Bastille.* (*T. T. C.*)

BATES. *Belinda.* *C. S., H. H.*
A most intellectual, amiable and delightful girl, has a fine genius for poetry, goes in for woman's mission, woman's rights, woman's wrongs.

BATES. Charles. *O. T.,* ix.
Note.—Bates was one of Fagin's "pupils." In spite of his trade and surroundings he was a jolly boy always laughing. After Sikes' crime and Fagin's execution he relinquished his former life, and, "from being a farmer's drudge, and a carrier's lad, he is now the merriest young grazier in all Northamptonshire."

BATH.   *B. H.* xxviii. ;   *M. P.,*
L. L. ; and *P. C.* xxxv.

BATTENS. Mr., a Titbull Pensioner.   *U. T.* xxvii.
This old man wore a long coat,
such as we see Hogarth's chairmen
represented with—of that peculiar
green-pea hue without the green,
which seems to come of poverty.
*Original : A one time mayor of
Rochester bore the same name.*

BATTERSEA.   *C. B., H. M.* i. ;
and *R. P., D. W. T. T.*

BATTERY GARDENS. New York.
                      A. N. vi.

BATTERY. Old, on the Marshes.
                      G. E. i.

BATTLE BRIDGE. *D. and S.* xxxi.,
M. P., R. H. F. ; *O. M. F.* iv. ;
O. T. xxxi. ; and *S. B. B.,* Scenes
                               xx.

BATTLE MONUMENT. *Baltimore.*
                      A. N. ix.

BATTY.   *M. P., M. B. V.*

BAUDI. Countess Cornelia de.
B. H., Pref. and xxxiii.

BAVARIAN COUNTESS. A Pilgrim
to Rome.   *P. F. I., R.*

BAY OF BISCAY. *D. and S.* xxxix.

BAY OF FUNDY.   *A. N.* ii.

BAY o' NAPLES. *R. P., G. o. A.*

BAYSWATER.   *U. T.* x.

BAYTON. Mrs.   To be buried
parochially.   *O. T.* v.

BAZAAR. In Soho Square, London.
                 M. P., N. Y. D.

BAZANCOURT. M. de.
                 M. P., S. F. A.

BAZZARD. Mr.   Mr. Grewgious's
Clerk.   *E. D.* xi.

BEADLE.   *L. D.* ii.
If there is anything that is not
to be tolerated on any terms—a
type of Jack-in-office insolence
and absurdity—that represents
in coats, waistcoats, and big
sticks, our English holding-on by
nonsense, after every one has
found it out, it is a beadle.

BEADLE.
        B. H. xi. ; and *P. C.* xvii.

BEADLE. A.   *B. H.* iv.

BEADLE. A portentous in the
Church where Paul Dombey was
christened.   *D. and S.* v.

BEADLE. Of Church where
Walter and Florence are married.
                  D. and S. lvii.

BEADLE. Of some deceased old
Company.   *U. T.* ix.

BEADLE. Of the Tallow Chandlers'
Company.   *M. P., M. B. V.*

BEADLE. Coroner's. *U. T.* xviii.

BEADLE. Under of the Worshipful
Company of Tallow Chandlers.
                 M. P., M. B. V.

BEADLE. Harriet. *See* Tattycoram.

BEADLE'S SON-IN-LAW. *M. C.* xxv.

BEAK. A Magistrate. *O. T.* viii.

BEAN. Mrs.   *M. P., S. R.*

**" BEAR YE ONE ANOTHER'S
BURTHENS."**   *M. P., O. S*

BEAR. Prince, At war with Prince
Bull.   *R. P., P. B*

BEARER. A.   *M. C.* xix.

BEARER. Nat., Captain of a Merchantman.   *C. S., H. H*
A thick-set wooden face, and
figure—an intelligent man, with a
world of watery experiences in
him.

BEARERS. Of sedan chair, Two. B. R. xxiii.; also P.P. xxxvi.

BEAST MARKET. A.
R. P. M. O. F. F.

BEATRICE. Polly's mother.
C. S., M. J. iv.
A careworn woman, with her hair turned grey.

BEAUFORD PRINTING House.
C. S., S. L. iv.

BEAUTY. Famous. M. P., C. P.

BEAUVAIS.
T. T. C., Book iii., Chap. i.
But when they came to the town of Beauvais he could not conceal from himself that the aspect of affairs was very alarming.

BEAVERTON, BOONE CO. Ill., U.S.   M. P., S. F. A.

BEBELLE. Playful name for Gabrielle. Which see.

BECKWITH. Alfred. H. D. iii.

BEDFORD.   D. and S. lx.

BEDFORD. The.   D. and S. xli.

BEDFORD ROW.
S. B. B., Scenes xvi.; and U. T. xiv.

BEDFORD SQUARE.
M. P., A. P.; S. B. B., Tales v.

BEDFORD STATION. M. P., R. S.

BEDFORD STREET.
M. P., W. S. G.

BEDLAM.   B. H. xlvii.; B. R, lxvii.; C. B., C. C., S. i.; C. B., C. H. ii.; L. D. lxvii.; M. P., K. C.; and M. P., W. H.

BEDLAMITE.   D. and S. xxvii.

BEDWIN. Mrs., Mr. Brownlow's housekeeper.   O. T. xii.
A motherly old lady, very neatly and precisely dressed.

Note.—Mrs. Bedwin was a kindly old soul, who had great difficulty in believing any evil of Oliver, and welcomed him back on his restoration.

BEECHER. Rev. Charles.
M. P., R. S. D.

BEECHER. Rev. Henry Ward.
M. P., R. S. D.

BEECROFT. Mr., Pilot.
M. P., N. E.

BEEF HOUSE. À LA MODE,
D. C. xi.
Original: Johnson's in Clare Court, the New Thirteen Canons.

"BEER." The nine o'clock.
S. B. B., Scenes ii.
Comes round with a lantern in front of his tray.

BEETHOVEN. M. P., O. L. N. O.

BEFILLAIRE. Colonel, Character in a novel read by Kate Nickleby to Miss Wititterly. N. N. xxviii.

BEGGING-LETTER WRITER.
R. P., T. B. W.

BEGGING - LETTER WRITER. Brother of.   R. P., T. B. W.

BEGGING - LETTER WRITER. Wife of.   R. P., T. B. W.

BEGS. Mrs. Ridger, late |Miss Micawber.   D. C. xxxiv.

BEINGS. Such. S. B. B., Scenes iii.
Who can walk from Covent Garden to St. Paul's Churchyard and back into the bargain without deriving some amusement—instruction—from his perambulation—and yet there are such. Large stocks and light waistcoats, jet canes and discontented countenances, are the characteristics of the race.

BELGIAN VILLAGES. *R. P., N. S.*

BELGIUM.
   M. P., C. P.; and *U. T.* xxv.

BELGRAVE SQUARE. *N. N.* xxi.;
P. F. I., G. T. F.; and *R. P., O. T.*

BELGRAVIA.
   M. P., F. C.; and *M. P., S. D. C.*

BELGRAVIAN BORDERS.
           O. M. F. xx.

BELINDA. A correspondent of
Master Humphrey's. *M. H. C.* ii.

BELINDA. Mrs. Matthew Pocket
—*which see.*

BELINDA. Mrs. Walter Waters.
        S. B. B., Tales iv.

BELIZE. *C. S., P. o. C. E. P.*

BELL & CO. *O*xford Street.
         M. P., W. R.

BELL YARD. A narrow alley.
         B. H. xiv.

BELLA. Refer to Wilfer, *B*ella.

BELLA. Housemaid of Miss Pupford.   *C. S., T. T. G.* vi.

BELLA. The younger prisoner
about to enter prison van.
       S. B. B., Char. xii.

BELLA. *B*aby, *D*aughter of John
and *B*ella Rokesmith.
       O. M. F. lxii.

BELLA. Isola.
    P. F. I., V. M. M. S. S.

BELLAMY'S. *S. B. B.*, Scenes xviii.

BELLE. Spirit of. *C. B., C. C.* s. ii.

BELLE. Spirit of husband of.
      C. B., C. C. s. ii.

BELLE SAVAGE.   *P. P.* x.
  "Parish?" says the lawyer.
"*B*elle Savage," says my father;

for he stopped there wen he drov
up, and he know'd nothing abou
parishes, *he* didn't."

BELLER. Henry, Convert t
temperance.   *P. P.* xxxii
  For many years toast-maste
at various Corporation dinners
during which time he drank a grea
deal of foreign wine; is out c
employ now; and never touche
a drop of foreign wine by an
chance.

BELLEVILLE.   *A. N.* xii
  A small collection of woode
houses, huddled together in th
very heart of the bush an
swamp.

BELLING. Master, A Taunto
boy, pupil of Mr. Squeers.
         N. N. iv
  On the trunk was perched—hi
lace-up half-boots and corduro
trousers dangling in the air—
diminutive boy, with his shoulder
drawn up to his ears, and hi
hands planted on his knees.

   Note.—Belling was a natural chil
confided to the tender mercies of th
Yorkshire schoolmaster.

BELLOWS. Fictitious name c
correspondent leaving gift for th
father of the Marshalsea. *L. D.* v

"BELLOWS." *B*rother. Guest c
Mr. Merdle.   *L. D.* xx

BELLOWS. Mrs. *M. P., S. Pig*

BELLS. The. *Chimes*, 3rd quarter

BELLS. The men who play.
       D. and S. xxx
  Have got scent of the marriage
—are practising in a back settle
ment near Battle *B*ridge.

BELL TOTT. Miss Bell Tott.
     C. S.; P. o. C. E. P

BELL TOTT. Mrs. *Bell Tott.*
         C. S., P. o. C. E. P.

BELMORE. Mr. G., as Mr. Bintry.
         M. P., N. Y.

BELVAWNEY. Miss, Member of Mr. Crummles' Company.
         N. N. xxiii.
    Seldom aspired to speaking parts, and usually went on as a page, in white silk hose, to stand with one leg bent, and contemplate the audience, or twisting up the ringlets of the beautiful Miss Bravassa.
    Note.—A member of Crummles' company. Looked with some favour on Nicholas, and when he hinted at his departure, "actually shed tears."

BELVILLE. Assumed name.
         S. B. B., Scenes xiii.

BEN.   *Laz. Tour.*

BEN. Guard of mail from London.
         O. T. xlviii.

BEN. Negro-slave.   *A. N.* xvii.

BEN. Waiter at inn in Rochester.
         C. S., S. P. G. i.

BENBOW. Admiral.
         R. P., O. of the S.

" BENCH." Guest of Mr. Merdle.
         L. D. xxi.

BENCHERS. Old.   *B. H.* i.
Blue-nosed, bulbous-shoed.

BENEDICT. Mr.   *M. P., M. M.*

BENGAL.   *D. S.* viii. ; *P. P.* lvii. ; and *R. P., T. B. W.*

BENJAMIN.   *B. R.* viii.

BENJAMIN. Thomas, Suitor in a divorce suit.   *D. C.* iv.
    Under an ingenious little statute (repealed now, I believe, but in virtue of which I have seen several

marriages annulled) The husband had taken out his marriage licence as Thomas only. *Not* finding himself as comfortable as he expected, he now came forward, by a friend, after being married a year or two, and declared that his name was Thomas Benjamin, and therefore he was not married at all. Which the court confirmed.

BENNETT. Mr. George.
         S. Y. G., Theat.

BENNETT. Dr. Sterndale.
         M. P., M. M.

BENNETT. Mr. W. Actor.
         M. P., M. B.

BENNETT. As George Edmunds.
         M. P., V. C.

BENSON. Lucy.   *M. P., V. C.*

BENSON. Old.   *M. P., V. C.*

BENSON. Young.   *M. P., V. C.*

BENTING.   *M. P., S. R.*

BENTON. Miss, Housekeeper to Master Humphrey.   *M. H. C.* i.

BERBERNI.   *P. F. I., R.*

BERINTHIA. Mrs. Pipchin's middle - aged niece. *D. and S.* viii.
    Possessing a gaunt and ironbound aspect, and much afflicted with boils on her nose.

BERKELEY. Assumed name.
         S. B. B., Scenes xiii.

BERKELEY. Mr. = Bob Tample.
         M. P., G. D.

BERKELEY HEATH.   *P. C.* l.

BERKELEY PLACE. London.
         M. P., N. Y. D.

BERMONDSEY.
    L. D., Pref. ; and *R. P., a. F.*

BERNERS STREET. *M. P.*, *W. S. P.* ; and *S. B. B.*, Char. ix.

BERRY. *See* Berinthia.

BERTHA. *Dolls' dressmakers.* *C. B.*, *C. o. H.* ii. *Blind daughter of Caleb Plum-mer.*

BERWICK. Miss Mary. *M. P.*, *A. A. P.* *Original : Miss Adelaide Anne Procter.*

BERWICK. *R. P.*, *O. H. F.* ; and *S. B. B.*, Tales viii.

BEST AUTHORITY. *M. P.*, *B. A.*

BETHEL CHAPEL. *S. B. B.*, Char. ix.

BETHEL. Little. *O. C. S.* lxi. *Original : Said to have been founded on Zoar (Strict Baptist) Chapel, Great Ailie Street.*

BETHLEHEM HOSPITAL. *U. T.* xiii.

BETHNAL GREEN. *O. M. F.* xliii. ; and *U. T.* x.

BETHNAL GREEN ROAD. *O. T.* xxi.

BET. BETSY. Fagin's accomplice. *O. T.* ix. Wore a good deal of hair, not very neatly turned up behind.

Note.—One of Fagin's female thieves and on rather friendly terms with Tom Chitling.

BETLEY. Mr. *C. S.*, *Mrs. L. Lo.*
BETSEY. *M. P.*, *N. G. K.*

BETSEY. Maid of Britain (Mr. and Mrs.). *C. B.*, *B. o. L.* iii.

BETSEY JANE. Mrs. Wickam's uncle's child. *D. and S.* viii. As sweet a child as I could wish to see. Everything that a child could have in the way of illness,

Betsey Jane had come through The cramps was as common to her, said Mrs. Wickam, " as bile is to yourself, Miss *Berry.*"

BETSEY. Miss. *See* Trotwood Miss Betsey.

BETSY. *Betsy White.* *U. T.* v

BETSY. A black woman (slave) *A. N.* xvii

BETSY. Mrs. Cluppins. *P. P.* xlvi

BETSY. Bob Sawyer's maid. *P. P.* xxxii A dirty slipshod girl in black cotton stockings, who might have passed for the neglected daughter of a superannuated dustman in very reduced circumstances.

BETSY. *See* Quilp, Mrs.

BETTERTON. *M. P.*, *R. S. L.*

BEVAN. Boarder at Pawkins'. *M. C.* xvi A middle-aged man, with a dark eye, and a sunburnt face . . . something very engaging and honest in the expression of his features.

Note.—A contrast to most of those Martin meets in America : a good friend who provides the necessary money for the return of Martin and Mark Tapley to England.

BEVERLEY. Mr. *M. P.*, *G. F*

BEVERLEY. Mr., Otherwise Log gins. *S. B. B.*, Scenes xiii

BEVIS MARKS. In the city o London. *O. C. S.* xi

Note.—The locality of the offic of Sampson Brass and his sister Sally

BIANCHINI. Prebendary of Verona *B. H.* Pref. ; and *B. H.* xxxiii

BIB. Mr. Julius Washingto Merryweather. *M. C.* xxiv A gentleman in the lumber line

" BIBLES. The Three." A Publisher's place on London Bridge.
M. H. C. iii.

BIBO. *B. H.* xxxii. ; and *M. P.*
L. E. J.

BICKLE, BUSH AND BODGER.
U. T. xiv.

BIDDY. Mr. Wopsle's Great-Aunt's Grand-daughter. *G. E.* vii.
Her hair always wanted brushing, her hands always wanted washing, and her shoes always wanted mending and pulling up at heel. On Sundays she went to Church elaborated.

Note.—She is introduced in her grandmother's little general shop and school. When the old lady conquered a " confirmed habit of living " Biddy came to the forge to nurse Pip's sister, Mrs. Gargery. Pip is much taken with Biddy, but when his fortunes improve he overlooks her. In the meantime she has become a schoolmistress. When later he would make amends he finds she has become Joe's second wife on the death of the first.

BIFFINS. Miss
N. N. xxxvii. ; and *M. C.* xxviii.

BIG BIRD. Indian brave.
M. P., E. T.

BIG CANOE. An Indian Chief.
A. N. ix.

BIG GRAVE CREEK. *A. N.* xi.

BIGBY. Mrs., Mrs. Meek's mother.
R. P., B. M. S.

BIGWIG FAMILY. *R. P., N. S.*
Composed of the stateliest people thereabout.

BILBERRY. Lady Jemima.
L. D. xvii.

BILER. Toodles, Robin —*which see.*

BILKINS. *M. P., W.*

BILKINS. An Authority on Taste.
R. P., O. F. W.

BILL. Driver of Omnibus.
S. B. B., Scenes xvi.

BILL. A Turnkey. *P. P.* xli.
Very old, of No. 20, Coffee Room Flight.

BILL. Aggerawatin, Bill Borker.
S. B. B., Scenes xvii.

BILL. Black, Prisoner in Newgate.
G. E. xxxii.

BILL. My. Melia's husband.
G. E. xx.

BILL. Plain, Alphonse. *N. N.* xxi.

BILL. Uncle, At Tea Gardens.
S. B. B., Scenes ix.

BILL. Uncle, Niece of in Tea Gardens. *S. B. B.,* Scenes ix.

BILLICKIN. Mrs., Lodging-house keeper. *E. D.* xxii.
Personal faintness and overpowering personal candour were the distinguishing features of Mrs. Billickin's organisation.

Note.—A casual character. Rosa Bud's landlady and widowed cousin of Mr. Bazzard, clerk to Mr. Grewgious.

BILLINGS. Ann, A spirit.
M. P., S. B.

BILLINGSGATE. *G. E.* liv. ; *L. D.* vii. ; and *M. P., N. J. B.*

BILLINGTON. Mr., as Mrs. Walter Wilding. *M. P., N. T.*

BILLINGTON. Mrs., as the Veiled Lady. *M. P., N. T.*

BILLSMETHI. Signor, Of the King's Theatre, Teacher of dancing.
S. B. B., Char. ix.

BILLSMETHI. Master.
S. B. B., Char. ix.

BILLSMETHI. Miss, Daughter of Billsmethi. *S. B. B.,* Char. ix.

BILLSMETHI. Fourteen pupils of.
S. B. B., Char. ix.
Who danced a grand Sicilian shawl-dance. The most exciting thing that ever was beheld —such a whisking, rustling and fanning, and getting ladies into a tangle with artificial flowers and then disentangling them again.

BILLSMETHI. Pupil of Signor.
S. B. B., Char. ix.
In brown gauze over white calico.

BILLSTICKERS. King of the.
R. P., B. S.
A good-looking little man of about fifty, with a shining face, a tight head, a bright eye, a moist wink, a quick speech, and a ready air. The oldest and most respected member of the " old school of bill sticking."

BILLSTICKERS. Father of the King of the. *R. P. B. S.*
Was Engineer, Beadle, and Billsticker to the Parish of St. Andrew's, Holborn. Employed women to post bills for him.

BILSON AND SLUM. Commercial House. *P. P.* xiv.

BILSTON. *M. P., I. S.*

BINKLE. Lady Fitz.
S. B. B., Scenes xiv.

BINTRY. Mr., Solicitor.
C. S., N. T., Act i.
A cautious man with twinkling beads of eyes in a large overhanging bald head.

BINTRY. Mr. *M. P., N. T.*

BIRD FANCIERS. *S. B. B.*, Scenes v.

BIRDS. The Prisoners in Marseilles prison. *L. D.* i.

BIRMINGHAM. A Drysalter. George Silverman's Guardian. *G. S. E.* iii.

BIRMINGHAM. Mr. and Mrs.
U. T. xxii.
Host and Hostess of the Lord Warden Hotel.

BIRMINGHAM. *B. R.* lxxxii.; *D. and S.* xx.; *M. H. C.* iii.; *M. P.*, Ag. Int.; *M. P., E. S.*; *M. P., F. S.*; *M. P., M. E. R.*; *N. N.* xxvii.; *O. T.* xlviii.; *P.P.* l.; *R.P., P. M. T. P.*; *R. P., T. D. P.*

BIRMINGHAM. Intelligent workmen of. *M. P., E. T.*

BIRMINGHAM. Member for.
M. P., S. S.

BIRMINGHAM. Town Hall.
M. P., Ag. Int.

BIRMINGHAM TUNNEL. *M.P., F.S.*

BIRTHDAY CELEBRATION. Heroine of. *U. T.* xix.
Peach-faced creature in a blue sash, and shoes to correspond.

BISCUIT BAKER'S DAUGHTERS. Fourteen, from Oxford Street.
N. N. xlix.

" BISHOP." Guest of Mr. Merdle.
L. D. xxi.

BISHOP. A. *P. P.* xvii.
Once, and only once in his life Nathaniel Pipkin had seen a bishop—a real bishop with his arms in lawn sleeves, and his head in a wig.

" BISHOP MAGNATE." Guest of Mr. Merdle. *L. D.* xxi.

BISHOP OF LONDON. *M. P., G. B.*

BISHOPS. An Extra Waiter.
C. S., S. L. i.
By calling a plate-washer.

BISHOP'S STORTFORD. *M.P., E.S.*

BISHOPSGATE STREET.
B. R. lxxvii. ; and *M. P., W.*

BISHOPSGATE STREET WITHIN.
N. N. ii.

BISHOPSGATE STREET WITHOUT.
D. and S. ix.

BITHERSTONE. Pupil at Dr.
Blimber's. *D. and S.* viii.
No longer Master Bitherstone
of Mrs. Pipchin's—in collars and
a neckcloth, and wears a watch.

BITHERSTONE. *Bill,* Father of
Master Bitherstone. *D. and S.* x.
His friend (Major Bagstock's)
who had written to ask him, if he
ever went that way (*Brighton*)
to bestow a call upon his only son.

BITZER. A Pupil at Coketown.
H. T. ii.
Light-eyed, and light-haired,
afterwards Light Porter, and then
clerk at Bounderby's *Bank* in
Coketown.

Note.—Introduced early in the book
as a special example of the pupils in
Gradgrind's school, from which all
fancy is eliminated, and in which fact,
fact, fact is taught. After leaving
school he is employed in Bounderby's
Bank where Tom Gradgrind occupies
a higher position. Tom robs the
bank, and Bitzer discovers it. In the
hope of being given Tom's post he
captures the culprit and almost succeeds in securing him. It is only due
to Sleary that he fails. Nevertheless
Bitzer becomes the "show young
man" of Josiah Bounderby.

BISCAY. Bay of. *S. B. B.,* Scenes x.

BIZAGNO. The river.
P. F. I., G. A. N.

BLACK. A Constable.
R. P., D. W. I. F.

"BLACK BADGER." The.
D. and S. xxii.

"BLACK BOY." At Chelmsford.
P. C. xx.

BLACK COUNTRY. Round about
Birmingham. *U. T.* xxiii.

BLACK HOLE. Regimental Prison.
C. S., S. P. I. ii.

"BLACK LION." Inn. *B. R.* xiii.
Instructed the artist who painted
his sign to convey into the features
of the lordly brute, whose effigy
it bore, as near a counterpart
of his own face (the landlord's),
as his skill could compass, and
devise—supposed to be the veri-
table portrait of the host as he
appeared on the occasion of some
great funeral ceremony or public
mourning.
*Original : Black Lion, White-
friars.*

"BLACK LION." Landlord of the.
B. R. xxxi.

Note.—Landlord of the inn of the
same name. He could only see things
from one point of view, that of his
pocket, and had no regard for glory
as represented by the army.

BLACK. Mrs., One of Mrs. Lemon's
pupils. *H. R.* iv.

"BLACK" or "*Blue Boar*" or
"*Bull.*" *U. T.* iii.

BLACK SEA. *M. P., S. F. A.*

BLACKBIRD. Joseph.
M. P., P. M. B.

BLACKBOY AND STOMACHACHE.
Mudfog papers 2nd meet.

BLACKBOY. Mr., A Fictitious name.
D. C. ii.
Elaborately written on lid of a
box carried by Mr. Barkis, con-
taining his hoards and labelled,
"Mr. *Blackboy,* to be left with
Barkis till called for.

BLACKBURN. *G. S. E.* v. ; *M.P.O. S.*

BLACKDASH. *M. P., W*

BLACKEY. A *Beggar.*
                    R. P., D. W. I. F.
Who stood near London *B*ridge
these five and twenty years, with
a painted skin to represent disease.

BLACK-EYED SUSAN.
                    M. P., N. Y. D.

BLACKFRIARS. *B. R.* xlix. ; *D. C.*
    xi. ; *R. P., D. W. T. T.*

BLACKFRIARS BRIDGE. *B. H.*
xix. ; *D. C.* xvii. ; *G. E.* xlvi. ;
L. D. xii. ; *S. B. B.*, Scenes xv.

BLACKFRIARS BRIDGE. Toll
Houses on.   *B. R.* lxvii.

BLACKHEATH. Home of Mr. and
Mrs. Rokesmith.   *O. M. F.* liv.
A modest little cottage, but a
bright and fresh, and on the
snowy tablecloth the prettiest of
little breakfasts.
Also *C. S., S. P. T.* ; *D. C.* xiii. ;
U. T. vii. *See also* Salem House.

BLACK-MAN. A Greyhaired.
                    M. C. xvii.

BLACKMORE. Mr., Entertainer in
Vauxhall Gardens.
            S. B. B., Scenes xiv.

BLACKPOOL. Stephen. A Mill
Hand.   *H. T.* x.
A rather stooping man, with a
knitted brow, a pondering expression of face, and a hard-
looking head, sufficiently capacious, on which his iron-grey hair
lay long and thin. Forty years of
age—looked older.

Note.—He is married to a woman
who proves a drunkard and ruins his
home. He turns to Rachael for com-
fort, but cannot marry her. He is a
hand in Mr. Bounderby's factory, but
when the others unite he will not join
them, but because he does not agree

with Mr. Bounderby in running them
down he is discharged. Every man's
hand is against him in Coketown and
he leaves to look for work elsewhere.
He is accused of robbing the bank, and
on his way back to refute the charge
he falls down a disused shaft. After
some days he is rescued, but he has
suffered such injuries that he dies.
His name is cleared by the discovery
that the theft was committed by young
Gradgrind.

BLACKPOOL. Wife of Stephen.
                    H. T. x.
Such a woman ! a disabled
drunken woman—a creature so
foul to look at, in her tatters,
stains and splashes . . . dangling in
one hand, by the string, a dung-
hill fragment of a bonnet.

BLACKPOT. =*B*lackpool.
                H. T., R. viii.

BLACKSMITH.   *M. P., B.*

BLACKSTONE. Lawyer.
                    M. P., C. P.

BLACKWALL. *M. P., C. J.* ; *R. P.,*
    T. D. P. ; *S. B. B.*, Scenes x.

BLACKWALL RAILWAY.
        R. P., T. D. P. ; *U. T.* ix.

BLACKWOOD. Messrs., Mercers.
                    M. P., S. P.

BLADUD. Prince, Founder of the
public baths in *B*ath.
                    P. P. xxxvi.
The illustrious Prince being
afflicted with leprosy — shunned
the Court of his royal father, and
consorted moodily with husband-
men and pigs—Among the herd
was a pig of solemn countenance.
This sagacious pig was fond of
bathing in rich moist mud. The
prince resolved to try the purifying
qualities. He washed and was
cured. Hastening to his father's
court, he paid his best respects,
and returning founded the city
and its famous baths.

BLAIZE. Madame. *M. P., C. P.*

BLAKE. Jim, Runaway Negro Slave. *A. N.* xvii.

BLAKE. Mr. Warmint. *S. Y. G.*

BLANDOIS. M. *See* Rigaud, Monsieur.

BLANK. Mr. *Mudfog Papers.*

BLANK BLANK. The Reverend. *O. M. F.* x.

BLANK. Mount. Mont Blanc. *C. S., H. T.*
So-called by Americans.

BLANKSHIRE. *M. P., W.*

BLANQUO. Pierre, A Guide. *R. P., O. B.*

BLATHERS. Bow Street Officer. *O. T.* xxxi.

A portly man in a great-coat—a stout personage of middle height, aged about fifty : with shiny black hair, cropped pretty close ; half whiskers, a round face, and sharp eyes.

Note.—Bow Street officers engaged on the attempted burglary at Mrs. Maylie's house. Blathers and Duff have wonderful thories, but they do not meet with much success.

BLAZE AND SPARKLE. Jewellers. *B. H.* ii.

BLAZES. M. Tuckle. *P. P.* xxxvii.

BLAZO. Sir Thomas, Jingle's opponent in a cricket match in the West Indies. *P. P.* vii.

BLEAK HOUSE. Near to St. Alban's. *B. H.* i.

What seemed to be an old-fashioned house, with three peaks in the roof in front, and a circular sweep leading to the porch.

One of those delightfully irregular houses where you go up and down steps out of one room into another, and where you come upon more rooms when you think you have seen all there are—a bountiful provision of little halls and passages—where you find still older cottage-rooms in unexpected places, with lattice windows and green growth pressing through them.

Original : The original of Bleak House has never been identified with certainty. General credence, however, is given to a house at the top of Gombard's Road, St. Albans. "Fort House," Broadstairs ; and Cobley's (Fallow) Farm, Finchley, have been suggested, but the former has nothing to do with the venue of the story and the latter is simple conjecture.

BLEEDING HEART YARD. *L. D.* ix.

No inappropriate destination for a man who had been in official correspondence with my lords and the Barnacles—and perhaps had a misgiving also that Britannia herself might come to look for lodgings in Bleeding Heart Yard.

Note.—The yard in which Casby's property lay, and where Doyce and Clenman had their office in the neighbourhood of Hatton Gardens.

BLESSINGTON. LADY, *M.P., L. L.*

BLIGH. *M. P., L. A. V.* ii.

BLIGH. Captain, Of the " Bounty." *R. P., T. L. V.*

BLIGHT. Mortimer Lightwood's Clerk. *O. M. F.* viii.
Dismal boy.

BLIMBER. Doctor. *D. and S.* xi.

A portly gentleman in a suit of black, with strings at his knees, and stockings below them. He had a bald head, highly polished ; a deep voice ; and a chin so very double, that it was a wonder how he ever managed to shave into the creases. He had likewise a pair of little eyes that were always half shut up, and a mouth that was always half expanded into a grin

Note.—The proprietor of the school to which Paul Dombey was sent was an educational gardener of the forcing variety. He produced mental fruit at all seasons of the year. This he did from a sense of duty, as he was always sufficiently kind to the ten pupils he took. Curiously enough there are seventeen boys shown in the illustration of the pupils enjoying themselves. The Dr. is last seen at Mrs. Feeder's wedding.

Original : Dr. Everard who kept a school such as that described at Brighton.

BLIMBER'S HOUSE. Doctor.
D. and S. xi.
A mighty fine house, fronting the sea. Not a joyful style of house within, but quite the contrary. Sad-coloured curtains, whose proportions were spare and lean, hid themselves despondently behind the windows. The tables and chairs were put away in rows, like figures in a sum : fires were so rarely lighted in the rooms of ceremony, that they felt like wells, and a visitor represented the bucket.

BLIMBER'S SCHOOL. Dr.
D. and S. xi.
Was a great hot house, in which there was a forcing apparatus incessantly at work. Mental green peas were produced at Christmas, and intellectual asparagus all the year round. Mathematical gooseberries (very sour ones too) were common at untimely seasons, and from mere sprouts of bushes, under *Doctor* Blimber's cultivation. Every description of Greek and Latin vegetable was got off the driest twigs of boys under the frostiest circumstances. No matter what a young gentleman was intended to bear, *Doctor* Blimber made him bear to pattern somehow or other.
Original of the School : A school kept by Dr. Everard, and termed the " Young House of Lords."

BLIMBER. Mrs., Doctor Blimber's wife. *D. and S.* xi.
Was not learned herself, but she pretended to be, and that did quite as well. She said at evening parties, that if she could have known Cicero, she thought she could have died contented.

BLIMBER. Miss Cornelia, Doctor Blimber's daughter. *D. and S.* xi.
A slim and graceful maid. She kept her hair short and crisp, and wore spectacles. She was dry and sandy with working in the graves of deceased languages. None of your live languages for Miss Blimber. They must be dead —stone dead—and then Miss Blimber dug them up like a ghoul.

BLINDER. Chandler's shop, name of. *B. H.* xiv.

BLINDER. *Bill* (deceased), An Hostler. *M. H. C.* iv.
Had charge of them two well-known piebald leaders.

BLINDER. Mrs. *B. H.* xv.
A good-natured-looking old woman, with a dropsy or an asthma, or perhaps both.

BLINKINS. Mr., Latin Master at Our School. *R. P., O. S.*

BLOCKADE MAN. At Ramsgate. *S. B. B.,* Tales iv.

BLOCKITT. Mrs., Mrs. *Dombey's* nurse. *D. and S.* i.
A simpering piece of faded gentility, who did not presume to state her name as a fact, but merely offered it as a mild suggestion.

BLOCKSON. Mrs., Charwoman employed by Knags. *N. N.* xviii.
Employed in the absence of the sick servant and remunerated with certain eighteenpences to be deducted from her wages due.

BLOGG. Mr., The *Beadle* of Poorhouse. *O. M. F.* xvi.

BLOODY ISLAND. *O. N.* xiii.
The dwelling-ground of St. Louis.

BLOOMER. Mrs. Colonel.
M. P., F. F. ; *M. P., S. Pigs.*

BLOOMSBURY SQUARE. *E. D.*
xxii. ; *M. H. C.* i.

BLOOMSBURY SQUARE. Lord
Mansfield's House in. *B. R.* lxvi.

BLORES. Mrs., Wooden Leg Walk,
Tobacco Stopper Row, Wapping.
M. P., G. A.

BLOSS. Mr., Deceased husband of
Mrs. *Bloss.* *S. B. B.,* Tales i.

BLOSS. Mrs., Relict of the departed
Bloss. *S. B. B.,* Tales i.
A boarder at Mrs. Tibbs.

In a pelisse the colour of the
interior of a damson-pie ; a bonnet
of the same, with a regular con-
servatory of artificial flowers ; a
white veil, and a green parasol
with a cobweb border. Mrs.
Bloss was very fat and red-
faced, an odd mixture of shrewd-
ness and simplicity, liberality and
meanness.

BLOSSOM. Little, *Dora.*
D. C., xii.

BLOTTON. Mr., Member of the
Pickwick Club. *P. P.,* i.
With a mean desire to tarnish
the lustre of the immortal name
of Pickwick, actually undertook a
journey to Cobham, in person, to
disprove the antiquity of the
inscription on the famous stone
found at Cobham.

Note.—Mr. Blotton of Aldgate is
one of the earliest characters in the
Pickwick Papers, but he drops out of
the narrative in the earlier chapters.
Possibly this is due to the change
that takes place in the character of
the papers themselves.

BLOWERS. Mr., " Eminent Silk
gown." *B. H.* i.
Said " Such a thing might
happen when the sky rained
potatoes."

BLUBB. Mr.
Mudfog Papers, 2nd meet.

BLUE ANCHOR ROAD.
C. S., S. L. i.

" **BLUE BOAR.** The," An Inn.
G. E. xiii.
*Original : The " Blue Boar " in
High Street, Rochester, does not
agree with the house of the story,
and it is suggested that the " Bull
Inn," Rochester, is the original.
From internal evidence it is sup-
posed that Pip's dinner took place
in Room No.* 3.

" **BLUE BOAR.**" Leadenhall Market.
P. P. xxxiii.
*Original : Suggested that the
" Green Dragon," Bull's Head Pas-
sage, Gracechurch Street, was the
original of the " Blue Boar " in
Leadenhall Market, which did not
exist.*

BLUE CANDIDATE. The Hon. Mr.
Slumkey. *P. P.,* li.

BLUE DRAGON. Sign before Village
Ale-house door. *M. C.* ii. and iii.
A faded, and an ancient dragon
he was ; and many a wintry
storm of rain, snow, sleet, and
hail, had changed his colour from
a gaudy blue to a faint lack-
lustre shade of grey. But there
he hung ; rearing, in a state of
monstrous imbecility, on his hind
legs.

*Original : Generally thought to
be the " George " at Amesbury,
but also claimed on behalf of the
" Green Dragon " at Alderbury,
" three miles on the Southampton
Road from Salisbury. The " Blue
Dragon " is also said to be a composite picture of both. Another
prototype of the " Blue Dragon " has
been found at Winterslow, a few
miles east of Salisbury—" a locality
which exactly corresponds with the indications of the tale " in the " Lion's
Head." The " Half Moon and
Seven Stars " is pointed to as the*

alehouse where the family conference took place.

The "*Green Dragon*" at Market Lavington has also been advanced to claim the honour of being the original of the "*Blue Dragon.*"

BLUE FISH. Indian brave.
M. P., E. T.

BLUE LION AND STOMACH WARMER. *S. B. B.,* Tales viii.
"The Lion" Inn at Great Winglebury.

BLUE LION AND STOMACH WARMER. Upper *Boots* of the.
S. B. B., Tales viii.
A man thrust in a red head with one eye in it, and being asked "to come in" brought in the body and the legs to which the head belonged, and a fur cap which belonged to the head.

BLUE LION INN. Muggleton.
P. P. vii.
Original: Suggested as "Swan Hotel," Town Malling, but refer to Muggleton.

BLUE LION STREET. *M. P., G. H.*

BLUEBOTTLE. Mrs.   *S. Y. C.*

BLUES. Parliamentary Candidates.
P. P. xiii.

BLUFFY. Mr. George. *B. H.* xxvii.

BLUMB. Of the Royal Academy.
R. P., O. B.

BLUNDER-BRITON. A Vestry, man.   *R. P., O. V.*

BLUNDER-SNOZZLE. A Vestry-man.   *R. P., O. V.*

BLUNDERBORE. A legendary being.   *P. P.* xxii.
The ferocious giant *Blunderbore* was in the habit of expressing his opinion that it was time to lay the cloth, Ha Hum!

BLUNDERBORE. Capt.
Mudf. Papers 2nd meet.

BLUNDEREM. Mr. *Muf. Papers.*
1st meet.

BLUNDERSTONE. In Suffolk.
D. C. i.
Note.—The village in Suffolk where David Copperfield was born.
Original: Blundeston (pronounced Blunston) near Yarmouth.

BLUNDERSTONE CHURCH.
D. C. ii.
What a high-backed pew! With a window near it.
Original: Has been suggested that the old Parish Church of Chatham was the original of this, although Blundeston Church itself is held to satisfy the details of the description.

BOAR. The Squires of The,
G. E. lviii.
Landlord of the *Blue Boar.*

"BOAR'S HEAD." *M. C.* xxxviii.

BOARD. The, Administrators of Parish relief.   *S. B. B., O. P.* i.
All sit behind great books, with their hats on.

BOARD. Of the Workhouse.
O. T. ii.
Eight or ten fat gentlemen . . . very sage, deep, philosophical men.

BOARD. The Treasury.
D. and S. lxi.

BOARD OF HEALTH. *M. P., P. T.*

"BOARD OF HONOUR. The."
A. N. xvii.

BOARDING-HOUSE. The.
S. B. B., Tales i.
There were meat-safe looking blinds in the parlour windows, blue and gold curtains in the drawing-room, and spring roller blinds all the way up.

BOAT. Releasing passengers from Quarantine.   *L. D.* ii.
Was filled with the cocked hats

to which Mr. Meagles entertained a natural objection.

BOATMAN. At *Broadstairs.*
R. P.; O. W. P.
Original : The particular Broad-stairs boatman who claimed to be the original of the sketch was Harry Ford. This is established in an interview Mr. Hughes had with him.

BOATMEN. *O. C. S.* iii.

BOB. *S. B. B.,* Tales ix.

BOB. Bob Redforth. *H. R.* i.

BOB. Guard of Early Coach.
S. B. B., Scenes xv.

BOB. The Marshalsea Turnkey.
L. D. vii.

Note.—Turnkey at the Marshalsea. A favourite of Mr. Dorrit's and god-father to Little Dorrit. It is for Bob Mr. Dorrit calls when in his last illness he thinks himself back in the Marshal-sea.

BOB. Runaway Slave of J. Surgette.
A. N. xvii.

BOB. Tom, Servant of English Prime Minister. *M. P., W.*

BOBADIL. Captain.
M. P., R. S. D.

Note.—Dickens' acting part.

BOBBO. In love with Seraphina's Sister. *C. S., M. L. Lo.* ii.

BOBBS AND CHOLBERRY.
M. C. xliv.

BOBSTER. Mr., Father of Miss Cecilia. *N. N.* xl.

Note.—The father of the young lady whom Newman Noggs mistook for Madeline Bray. Nicholas was desi-rous of discovering the identity of the beautiful visitor of the Cheeryble Brothers, and Newman watched for the servant, but he followed the wrong person.

BOBSTER. Miss Cecilia.
N. N. xl.
An only child, her mother was dead ; she resided with her father.

Note.—Miss Cecilia was persuaded by Newman to see his friend and let him plead his cause. Newman had made the unfortunate mistake of following the wrong person and thought that Miss Bobster was Madeline Bray. Nicholas and Newman were admitted into a back kitchen or cellar, and just as the mistake had been discovered Bobster knocked thunderously at the front door.

BOCCACCIO'S HOUSE.
P. F. I., R. D.

BOCKER. Tom. *O. M. F.* ix.

BODDLEBOY. *M. P., T. B.*

BODGER. *M. P., I.*

BODLEIAN LIBRARY.
M. P., T. O. H.

BOFFER. Expelled the Exchange.
P. C. lv.

BOFFIN. Henrietty, Wife of N. Boffin. *O. M. F.* v.
A stout lady of a rubicund and cheerful aspect, dressed in a low evening dress of sable satin, and a large velvet hat and feathers. A Highflyer at Fashion.

Note.—The wife of the Golden Dust-man. A motherly old soul, who, when they inherit the Harmon money, flies high at fashion. She befriends Bella Wilfer, and when she recognises John Harmon in Rokesmith enters heartily into the scheme to bring him and Bella into closer touch. After the marriage and the settling down of the young couple Mr. and Mrs. Boffin are left staying with them indefinitely.

BOFFIN. Father of Mrs., named Henery. In the Cannie Provision Trade. *O. M. F.* v.

BOFFIN. Mother of Mrs., named. Hetty. *O. M. F.* v.

BOFFIN. Nicodemus. *O. M. F.* v.
A broad, round-shouldered, one-
D

sided old fellow in mourning, dressed in a pea overcoat and carrying a large stick. He wore thick shoes, and thick leather gaiters, and thick gloves like a hedger's—with folds in his cheeks, and his forehead, and his eyelids, and his lips, and his ears ; but with bright, eager, childishly-enquiring grey eyes, under his ragged eyebrows, and broad-brimmed hat.

Note.—The illiterate but good-hearted servant of John Harmon. Harmon leaves his property to his son on condition that he marries Miss Bella Wilfer : in the event of his not doing so the property falls to Noddy Boffin. Young John Harmon returns from Africa, to fulfil the conditions of the will, but disappears immediately on his arrival, and a drowned body in the Thames is identified as his. As a result of this Boffin inherits the great wealth of his old master. One of his first acts is to offer a large reward, through Mortimer Lightwood, for the identification of the murderer of John Harmon. The supposed murdered man is not dead, however, and enters Boffin's employment as private secretary. Bella Wilfer is adopted by the Boffins and they are thrown together. Rokesmith (the name assumed by John Harmon) falls in love with her.

Original : The prototype of Boffin is said to have been a Mr. Henry Dodd, a contractor, of City Wharf, New North Road, Hoxton.

BOFFIN'S BOWER. *O. M. F.* v.

A charming spot, is the *Bower*. It is a spot to find out the merits of, little by little, and a new 'un every day. There's a serpentining walk up each of the mounds, that gives you the yard and neighbourhood changing every moment. When you get to the top, there's a view of the neighbouring premises, not to be surpassed. And the top of the High Mound is crowned with a lattice-work arbour.

Original : Was situated on ground now occupied by the Great Northern and Midland Railways.

BOFFIN'S EQUIPAGE. The driver of. *O. M. F.* ix.

A long hammer-headed young man—had been formerly used in the business, but was now entombed by an honest jobbing tailor of the district in a perfect sepulchre of coat and gaiters sealed with ponderous buttons.

BOGSBY. Mr. James George. *B. H.* xxxiii.

Landlord of the " Sol's Arms."

BOGUEY. Old. Mr. Krooks. *B. H.* xxxii.

BOGUS. Mr. and Mrs. *U. T.* vi.

BOHEME. *M. P., R. S. L.*

BOILED BEEF OF NEW ENGLAND. *U. T.* xxiii.

Original : House at the corner of Commercial Street and Flower Street.

BOILER. " *Boanerges.*" *U. T.* ix.

BOILER MAKER. *U. T.* xxx.

Wife of out-of-work. She did slop-work ; made pea-jackets—she got for making a pea-jacket, ten-pence-halfpenny, and she could make one in something less than two days.

BOKUM. Widow of Mr., dearest friend of Mrs. Macstinger. *D. and S.* lx.

BOLBY. A Policeman. *U. T.* iii.

BOLDER. Little. Pupil at Dotheboy's Hall. *N. N.* vii.

An unhealthy-looking boy, with warts all over his hands.

BOLDERS' FATHER. Father of one of Squeers' pupils. *N. N.* viii.

" Two pound ten short."

BOLDHEART. Capt. *H. R.* iii.

BOLDWIG. Captain, Sir Geoffrey Manning's neighbour. *P. P.* xix.

A little fierce man, in a stiff black neckerchief, and blue surtout, who when he did condescend to walk about his property, did it in company with a thick rattan stick with a brass ferule, and a gardener, and sub-gardener, with meek faces, to whom (the gardeners, not the stick) Captain Boldwig gave his orders with all due grandeur and ferocity.

Note.—Captain Boldwig is an imperious gentleman with high ideals regarding the sacred nature of land and game. Mr. Pickwick, who was temporarily lame, had been left in a barrow by his friends, while they continued their sport. It appeared they were trespassing, however, and Mr. Pickwick was discovered by the captain and his keepers asleep after too much cold punch. As the keeper was unable to wheel the somnolent Pickwick to the " devil "—the first destination proposed by Boldwig—he took him to the pound, where the redoubtable founder of the Pickwick Club was found by his friends. (*See* Muggleton, etc.)

BOLES. Miss. *M. P., N. Y. D.*

BOLES. Mr. *M. P., N. Y. D.*

BOLES. Mrs., Wife of Mr. *Boles.*
U. T. xii.

BOLES'S. A School of *Boles.*
U. T. xii.

BOLO. Miss., One of Whist Party at Assembly Rooms, *Bath.*
P. P. xxxv.

Of an ancient and whist-like appearance.

BOLOGNA. *P. F. I., P. M. B.*

BOLOGNA CEMETERY. *P. F. I.*

BOLSENA. Lake of.
P. F. I., R. P. S.

BOLTER. Morris, Mr. and Mrs. The names assumed by Noah Claypole and Charlotte in their dealings with Fagin. *See* Claypole, Noah and Charlotte.

BOLTON. Mr. *R. B.*

BOMBAY. *M. P., O. P.; P. F. I., V. M. M. S. S. ; R. P., A. C. T.*

BONAPARTE. Napoleon. *C. S., M. J.; C. S., S. P. T., U. T.* xii.

BOND STREET. *D. and S.,* xxxi. ; *M. P., I. M.; N. N.* xxxii. ; *O. M. F.* lviii. ; *S. B. B.,* Tales v.
U. T. xvi.

BONDSMAN. An Hereditary.
S. B. B., Scenes xviii.
An Irish Correspondent of an Irish Newspaper.

BONDY. Forest of. *M. P., A. P.*

BONES. Mr., *Banjo. See Banjo Bones* Mr.

" BONNET." A friend of the *D*warf at a gaming-booth.
C. S., G. i. S.

BONNET. Father of. *C. S., G. i. S.* In the livery-stable line.

BONNEY. Mr. Promoter of United Metropolitan Improved Hot Muffin and Crumpet and Punctual Delivery Company. *N. N.* ii.
A pale gentleman with his hair standing up in great disorder all over his head, and a very narrow cravat tied loosely round his throat. Taking off a white hat which was so full of papers that it would scarcely stick upon his head.

BONNY. African town.
M. P., N. E.

BONOMI. Mr. *M. P., E. T.*

BOOBY. The. The last of the Patriarchs. *L. D.* xiii.
Drifting *Booby,* much as an

unwieldy ship on the Thames river may sometimes be seen heavily driving with the tide—making a great show of navigation.

BOODLE. *M. P., W.*

BOODLE. Lord. *B. H.* xii.

BOOKING OFFICE CLERK. At "White-horse Cellar." *P. P.* xxxv.

BOOKSTALL KEEPER. *O. T.* xi.
An elderly man of decent but poor appearance, clad in an old suit of black.
Original: The original of this bookseller has been identified as a bookseller in Hampstead Road to whom Dickens used to be sent by his father.

BOOLEY. Mr., Extraordinary traveller. *M. P., C. M. B.; M. P., E. I.; M. P., M. B. V.*

BOON ISLAND. *M. P., L. A. V.* ii.

BOONE CO. III., U.S. *M. P., S. F. A.*

BOORKER. *Bill*, William *Barker*. *S. B. B.*, Scenes xvii.

"BOOT. The." A tavern. *B. R.* xxxvii.
A lone house of public entertainment, situated in a field at the back of the Foundling Hospital— a very solitary spot and quite deserted after dark.
Original: The site of the old "Boot" is now occupied by a new "Boot" behind the Foundling Hospital." Identified as 116, Cromer St.

BOOTH. *M. P., R. S. L.*

BOOTH. An immense, At Greenwich Fair. *S. B. B.*, Scenes xii. With the large stage in front,

so brightly illuminated with variegated lamps.

BOOTH. The, Circus. *H. Ts., S.* vi.

BOOTJACK. The, and Countenance. *Mud. Pap.* ii.

BOOTLE. *M. P., E. S.*

BOOTS. *S. B. B.*, Tales viii.

BOOTS. At Inn. *M. C.* xlii.

BOOTS. Guest of Veneerings. *O. M. F.* ii.

"BOOTS." The, of "Holly Tree Inn." *C. S., H. T.*

BOOZEY BILL. A mutinous sailor. *H. R.* iii.

BOOZLE. *S. Y. G.*

BOOZLE. Earl of. *M. P., N. G. K.*

BOOZLE. Castle. *M. P., N. G. K.*

BO-PEEP POLICE OFFICE. *M. P., G. B.*

BORDEAUX. *M. P., H. J. B. U. T.* xxiii.

BORE. Our. *R. P., O. B.*
He may put fifty people out of temper, but he keeps his own.

BOROUGH. *B. R.* lxxxii.; *L. D.* lxx.; *M. S., E. S.; R. P., D. W. I. F.; U. T.* xiii.

BOROUGH. Sequestered pot-shop in. *P. P.* lii.

"BOROUGH." King's Bench Prison. *D. C.* xi.

BOROUGH CLINK. *B. R.* lxvii.

BOROUGH HIGH STREET. *L. D.* xxxvi., *P.P.* xxi.

BOROUGH MARKET. *P. P.* xxxiii.

BOROUGHBRIDGE. *N. N.* xiii.

BORRIOBOOLA-GHA. *B. H.* iv.

BORRIOBOOLA. King of.
B. H. lxvii.
Wanting to sell everybody.

BORUM. Mr., Patron of Mr. V. Crummles' Company. *N. N.* xxiv.

BORUM. Mrs., Wife of Mr. *Borum.*
N. N. xxiv.

BOSTON U.S.A. *A. N.* i. ; *M.P., I. C.* ; *M. P., R. S. D.* ; *M. P., S. B.* ; *R. P., T. D. P.* ; *U. T.* iii. ; *U. T.* xxiii.

BOSTON. South. *A. N.* iii.

BOSTON BANTAM=James Ripley Osgood. *M. P., I. W. M.*

BOSTON MELODEON. *M. P., S. B.*

BOSWELL COURT.
S. B. B., Tales vii.

BOTANY BAY. *N. N.* xli.

BOTELER. *M. P., R. S. L.*

BOTTLE-OF-BEER. *M. P., N. E.*

BOTTLES. Stable-man. *C. S., H. H.*
Deaf tenant of haunted house. A phenomenon of moroseness not to be matched in England.

BOUCLET. Madame, Concierge.
C. S., S. L. ii.
A compact little woman of thirty-five or so.

BOUCLET. Monsieur, Husband of Madame. *C. S., S. L.* ii.
Great at billiards.

BOUCLET. Husband, and two children of married sister of madame. *C. S., S. L.* ii.

BOUCLET. Nephew and book-keeper of. *C. S., S. L.* ii.
Who held the pen of an angel.

BOULEVARD. The.
M. P , N. Y. D. ; and *R. P., A. F.*

BOULEVARDE THEATRES.
M. P., W.

BOULOGNE. *S. B. B.,* Tales i.

BOUNDERBY. Mr., a *B*anker.
H. T. iv.
A big loud man, with a stare, and a metallic laugh. A man made out of coarse material—with great puffed head and forehead, swelled veins in his temples, and such a strained skin to his face, that it seemed to hold his eyes open. Seven or eight and forty.

Note.—Close *friend* of Gradgrind. Successful man in Coketown. He is interested in many concerns of magnitude and appeared to have all the faults without any of the redeeming features of the rich man. After he attains to riches he pays his mother to keep away, but she comes on occasion just to "take a proud peep" at him. He marries Louisa Gradgrind, but the union is an unhappy one. His wife is assailed by an accomplished man and flies to her father. Her husband insists on her return, but she does not comply, and he casts her off. He dies and leaves a will providing for "five and twenty humbugs."

BOUNDERBY. Father of. *H. T.* v.
Died when he (Bounderby) was eight years old.

BOUNDERBY. Mother of=Pegler, Mrs. *H. T.* s. iv.

BOUNDERBY. Grandmother of, kept a chandler's shop. *H. T.* s. iv.

BOUNDERBY. Loo, Née Louisa Gradgrind, *which see.*

BOURNE. Old. *E. D.* xi.

BOURSE. The.
M. P., R. D. ; and *O. M. F.* xxi.

BOUSEFIELD. William.
M. P., D. M.

BOW. Little house at. *N. N.* xxxv.
Original : Grove Hall Estate at Bow : formerly the site of Byas's Private Lunatic Asylum.

BOW BELLS. *D. and S.* iv.

BOW STREET. Police Court.
O. T. xliii.
The room smelt close and unwholesome, the walls were dirt-discoloured; and a dusty clock above the dock. The only thing present which seemed to go on as it ought; for depravity, or poverty, or an habitual acquaintance with both, had left a taint, on all the animate matter.
Also *B. R.* lviii.; *M. P.*, *W. M.*; *S. B. B.*, Scenes xiv.; *S. B. B.*, Char. xi.; *U. T.* iv.

BOW STREET MEN. *G. E.* xvi.

BOWER. The. *O. M. F.* xv.
A gloomy house, with sordid signs on it of having been, through its long existence—in miserly holding—bare of paint, bare of paper on the walls, bare of furniture, bare of experience of human life.

BOWERY. The, Street in New York. *A. N.* vi.

BOWERY THEATRE. The, New York. *A. N.* vi.

BOWES. *See* Dotheboy's Hall.

BOWLEY. Sir Joseph.
C. B., C. G. ii.
I am the poor man's friend and father.

BOWLEY. My Lady, Wife of Sir Joseph *Bowley.* *C. B., C. G.* ii.
A stately lady in a bonnet.

BOWLEY. Master, The heir of *Bowley.* *C. B., C. G.* iii.
Son of Sir Joseph *Bowley.*

BOWLEY. Porter of Sir Joseph.
C. B., C. G. ii.
Underwent some hard panting before he could speak, his voice—a long way off, and hidden under a load of meat.

"BOWLEY HALL." Residence of Sir Joseph *Bowley. C. B., C. G.* iii.

BOWYER. Honest, a money lender. *M. H. C.* i.
Was in the habit of lending money on interest to the gallants of the Court.

BOWYER. Sam'l, Workhouse inmate. *R. P., W. I. A. N.*

BOXALL. *M. P., L. L.*

BOY. King,
O. M. F. ; *M. P., N. E.*

BOY. *Haunted Man,* i.

BOY. *L. D.,* Pref.
The smallest I ever conversed with, carrying the largest baby I ever saw, offered a supernaturally intelligent explanation of the locality in its old uses, and very nearly correct.

BOY. A rioter. *B. R.* lxxvii.
Hanged in Bow Street.

BOY. At George and Vulture.
P. P. xxxiii.
A young boy of about three feet high, or thereabouts; in a hairy cap, and fustian overalls, whose garb bespoke a laudable ambition to attain, in time, the elevation of an hostler.

BOY. Carrying Tim Linkinwater's sister's cap. *N. N.* xxxvii.

BOY. Emerging from Fort at Chatham. *U. T.* xxiv.
A young boy, with an intelligent face burnt to dust colou by the summer sun, and with crisp hair of the same hue.

BOY. Errand, of Mr. Pickles.
H. R. ii.

BOY. Ginger-beer, of the audience in theatre.   *N. N.* xxiv.

BOY. In common lodging-house in Liverpool.   *U. T.* v.
Carefully writing a copy in a copying-book in the middle of the night.

BOY. In grey livery—of Sawyer's late Nockemorf.   *P. P.* l.
Busily employed in putting up the shutters.

BOY. Inattentive, from inn in Rochester.   *C. S.* ; *S. P. T.* i.
With hot plates.

BOY. Little, In tea gardens.
                    S. B. B., Scenes ix.
Diminutive specimen of mortality in the three-cornered pink satin hat with black feathers.

BOY. Little, Son of lady in distress.
                    S. B. B., *O. P.* v.

BOY. Little, Walter and Florence Gay's.   *D. and S.* lxii.

BOY. Living in back attic of No. 6, The Court.   *N. N.* xl.
Hyacinths, blossoming in old blacking-bottles belong to a sickly bed-ridden hump-backed boy. There he lies, looking now at the sky, and now at his flowers, which he still makes shift to trim and water, with his own thin hands.

BOY. Monotonous, Theatre employé.   *L. D.* xx.

BOY. Negro, Slave.   *A. N.* xvii.
Had round his neck a chain dog-collar with De Lampert on it.

BOY. Patient in hospital.
                    P. P. xxxii.
Said he wouldn't lie there to be made game of.

BOY. Of young medical practitioner.   *S. B. B.*, Tales vi.
A corpulent round-headed boy, who in consideration of the sum of one shilling per week and his food, was let out by the parish to carry medicine and messages.

BOY. The prowling.   *See* Pirip, Philip.   *G. E.* xxi.

BOY. Queer small.   *U. T.* vii.

BOY. Saved from the wreck.
                    M. P., S. W.

BOY. Sharp.   *M. P., S. S. U.*

BOY. Sharpest small.   *M. P., B. S.*

BOY. Sir Jeoffrey Manning's.
                    P. P. xix.
There's the boy with the basket as punctual as clockwork . . . taking from his shoulder a couple of large stone bottles fastened together by a leathern strap. Cold punch in t'other !

BOY. Small, In the fleet. *P. P.* xlv.

BOY. Small, Passenger in stage coach.   *S. B. B.*, Scenes xvi.
Of a pale aspect, with light hair, and no perceptible neck, coming up to town under the protection of the guard.

BOY. Son of brother of Lieutenant.
                    M. H. C. ii.
Confided to care of lieutenant's wife.

BOY. Son of George and Mary.
                    P. P. xxi.
The hard realities of the world, with many of its worst privations —hunger and thirst, and cold and want—had come home to him from the first dawnings of reason. "The child's young heart was breaking." The child was dead.

BOYLSTON SCHOOL. South *Boston*
                    A. N. iii.
Asylum for neglected and indi-

gent boys who have committed no crime.

BOYS. At tea gardens.
S. B. B. xvi.
With great silk hats just balanced on the top of their heads, smoking cigars, and trying to look as if they liked them.

BOYS. Foundlings. *M. P., N. Y.*

BOYS. Gay old.
S. B. B., Char. vii.
Paunchy old men in the disguise of young ones—who assume all the foppishness and levity of boys, without the excuse of youth or inexperience.

BOYS. Interviewing Martin.
M. C. xxii.

BOYS. New York paper. *M. C.* xvi.

BOYS. Seeing Mark Tapley off.
M. C. vii.

BOYS. Steady old.
S. B. B., Char. vii.
Certain stout old gentlemen of clean appearance, who are always to be seen in the same taverns, at the same hours every evening, smoking and drinking in the same company.

BOYS. Two, *D*emanded money for the rioters. *B. R.* lxvii.
Armed with bars taken from the railings of Lord Mansfield's House.

BOYS. Two other, Pupils of Mr. Squeers. *N. N.* v.

BOYTHORN. Lawrence, School-fellow of Mr. Jarndyce's. *B. H.* ix.
His head thrown back like an old soldier, his stalwart chest squared, his hands like a clean blacksmith's, and his lungs!—talking, laughing or snoring, they make the beams of the house shake . . . a very handsome old gentleman—with a massive grey head.

Note.—Friend of Mr. Jarndyce, residing in Lincolnshire. His land adjoined the estate of Sir Leicester Dedlock, with whom he had a standing feud as to a right of way. After Sir Leicester's misfortunes, Mr. Boythorn would have sunk his differences, but the baronet took this as pity, and so the feud had to be revived and continued.

Original : Walter Savage Landor.

" BOZ." Pseudonym of Charles Dickens, Esquire. *A. N.* xiv.; *M. P., E. C.* ; *S. B. B. O. P.* i.

BOZZOLO. *P. F. I., V. M. M. S. S.*

BRA. Piazza di,
P. F. I., V. M. M. S. S.

BRACCO. Pass of,
P. F. I., R. P. S.

BRADBURY AND EVANS. Printing house of. *M. P., M. E. R.*

BRAHAM. Mr., as Squire Norton.
M. P., V. C.

BRANDLEY. Mrs., A widow.
G. E. xxxviii.
Complexion was pink . . . set up for frivolity.

BRANDLEY. Miss, *D*aughter of Mrs. *B*randley. *G. E.* xxxviii.
Complexion was yellow . . . set up for theology.

BRANSCOMBE. Mr., as Jean Paul.
M. P., N. Y.

BRASS. Foxey, The father of Sampson and Sally. *Dead.*
O. C. S. xxxvi.

BRASS. Sally, Sister to Sampson *B*rass. *O. C. S.* xxxiii.
A kind of amazon at common law . . . a lady of about thirty-five or thereabouts, of a gaunt and bony figure . . . Miss *B*rass wore

no collar or kerchief except upon her head, which was invariably ornamented with a brown gauze scarf.

Note.—The sister of Sampson Brass and, if that were possible, more villanous than he. She was his able partner in their business of attorney, and when he was ruined she too was seen " in the obscene hiding-places in London, in archways, dark vaults and cellars."

BRASS.   Sampson, Mr. Quilp's
lawyer.   *O. C. S.* xi.
An attorney of no very good repute. . . he was a tall, meagre man, with a nose like a wen, a protruding forehead, retreating eyes, and hair of a deep red.

Note.—Brass, although himself a rogue, was the catspaw of Quilp, the dwarf. He was a disreputable attorney living in Bevis Marks, with his sister. At Quilp's command he engages Dick Swiveller as clerk. Ultimately his villanies and illegalities lead to his imprisonment with hard labour, after that he became a bird of evil omen haunting the byways of the city.
Original : Brass's House may have been No. 10, Bevis Marks.

BRASS AND COPPER FOUNDER.
                        M. C. ix.
Middle-aged gentleman with a pompous voice and manner.

BRASS PEOPLE.   African tribe.
                        M. P., N. E.

BRATS.   Two, " Farmed " out to branch workhouse.   *O. T.* ii.

BRAVASSA. The beautiful Miss, Member of Mr. V. Crummles' Company.   *N. N.* xxiii.
Had once had her likeness taken in character—whereof impressions were hung up for sale in the pastry cook's window, and the greengrocer's, and the circulating library, and the box office, whenever the announce bills came out for her annual night.

Note.—Usually went " on " in white silk hose as a page boy. Actually shed tears when Nicholas expressed the fear that he must leave the company.

BRAVE.   The, The Courier.
                P. F. I., P. M. B.

BRAY.   Miss Madeline.   *N. N.* xvi.
The beautiful girl who had so engrossed his (Nicholas Nickleby's) thoughts—seemed now a thousand times more beautiful. Not nineteen—dark eyes, long eyelashes, ripe and ruddy lips.

Note.—Nicholas first meets Madeline in the registry office, where he was immediately struck with her appearance. Later he recognises her at the Cheeryble brothers. Although not related to them, she was the daughter of a friend of theirs. Her mother had died early. Her father was one of those selfish, debased characters which Dickens could draw so well. He endeavoured to force her into a repulsive marriage with Gride. While Nicholas is preventing this as far as he is able, Bray dies in the floor above. Nicholas removes Madeline, in spite of all opposition, to his mother's and Kate's care. He afterwards marries her.

Original : So far as the name is concerned at least, this was founded on one of Dickens's schoolfellows at Wellington House.

BRAY.   Mr.   Walter,   Madeline Bray's father.   *N. N.* xlvi.
He was scarce fifty, perhaps, but so emaciated as to appear much older. His features presented the remains of a handsome countenance.

Note.—The miserable and selfish debauchee, father of Madeline. He had so far forgotten his duty as a father that he endeavoured to force his daughter into a marriage with Gride. He dies suddenly just as his plan appears to be on the point of completion.

BRAY'S WIFE. Walter, Madeline's deceased mother.   *N. N.* xlvii.

BRAZEN HEAD. The, of the Circumlocution Office.   *L. D.* x.

BRAZIL. *M. P., L. A. V.* ii.

BREAK NECK STAIRS. Main approach to business of Wilding and Co. *C. S., N. T.*, Act i.

" BREAK OF DAY." The, *L. D.* xi.
Curtained windows clouded the " *Break* of Day," but it seemed light and warm. There one could find meat, drink, and lodgings, whether one came on horseback, or came on foot.

" BREAK OF DAY." Landlord of the. *L. D.* xi.
Who acted as cook.

" BREAK OF DAY." Landlady of the. *L. D.* xi.
A smart, neat, bright little woman, with a good deal of cap, and a good deal of stocking.

BREES. Mr. *M. P., E. T.*

BRENTFORD. *G. E.* xlii. ; *M. P., M. M.* ; *O. M. F.* xvi. ; *O. T.* xxi.; *U. T.* x.

BRENTFORD. King of. *M. P., I.*

BREWER. Guest of Veneerings. *O. M. F.* ii.

BREWSTER. *M. P., R. S. D.*

BRICK. Mr. Jefferson, War Correspondent of Rowdy Journal. *M. C.* xvi.
A small young gentleman of very juvenile appearance, and unwholesomely pale in the face. He wore his shirt collar turned down over a black ribbon ; and his lank hair, a fragile crop, was not only smoothed and parted back from his brow—but had, here and there, been grubbed up by the roots. He had that order of nose, on which the envy of mankind has bestowed the appellation " snub."

BRICK. Mrs. Jefferson. *M. C.* xvi.
The matron in blue.

BRICK. Two young children of Mrs. Jefferson *Brick*. *M. C.* xvi.

BRICK. The, fictitious name of correspondent leaving gift for Father of Marshalsea. *L. D.* vi.

BRICK LANE BRANCH. Of the united Grand Junction Ebenezer Temperance Association.
P. P. xxxiii.
Original : The Brick Lane Branch had its origin in a meeting room at the back of one of the shops in Brick Lane, situated at the bottom instead of the top of a ladder.

BRICKLAYER AND HIS FAMILY. *M. P., G. D.*

BRICKLAYER'S LABOURER.
S. B. B., Scenes v.
There they are in their fustian dresses, spotted with brick-dust and whitewash leaning against posts. We never saw a regular bricklayer's labourer' take any other recreation, fighting excepted.

BRICKMAKER. *B. H.* viii.
All stained with clay and mud, lying at full length on the ground, smoking a pipe.

BRICKMAKER. Wife of. *B. H.* viii.
A woman with a black eye, nursing a poor little gasping baby by the fire.

BRIDE. Lucretia. *D. and S.* v.

BRIDE. The, in a thin white dress.
S. B. B., Scenes vii.

BRIDE'S AUNT. Aunt of Sophronia Akershem. *O. M. F.* x.
A widowed female of a medusa sort, in a stony cap, glaring petrefaction at her fellow-creatures.

BRIDE'S TRUSTEE. *O. M. F.* x.
An oilcake-fed style of business-gentleman with mooney spectacles.

BRIDEGROOM. At wedding.
D. and S. v.

BRIDEGROOM. In hackney coach.
S. B. B., Scenes vii.
In blue coat, yellow waistcoat, white trousers, and *B*erlin gloves to match.

BRIDEGROOM. Chosen friend of, in hackney coach.
S. B. B., Scenes iii.

BRIDESMAID.
D. and S. xxxi.
*D*istantly connected with the family . . . who so narrowly escaped being given away by mistake.

BRIDESMAID. In hackney coach.
S. B. B., Scenes vii.

BRIDESMAIDS. Of Cornelia *B*limber. *D. and S.* lx.
*G*auzy little bridesmaids.

BRIDESMAIDS. *O. M. F.* x.

BRIDEWELL.
B. R. lxvii.; *R. P.*, *L.A.*

BRIDGE. *G. E.* xlvi.
Original: It is considered by some that the bridge referred to may have been that at Aylesford.

BRIDGE. Canal, *U. T.* xviii.
See also Baker's Trap.

BRIDGE. The Iron. *L. D.* ix.
Original: Southwark Bridge.

BRIDGE OF SIGHS.
P. F. I., *A. I. D.*

BRIDGE OF THE GANTHER.
C. S., *N. T.*, Act iii.

BRIDGE ROAD. *B. R.* xlviii.

BRIDGEMAN Laura, Inmate of *B*lind Asylum. *A. N.* iii.
*B*lind, deaf and dumb girl.

BRIDGMAN. Mr. *A. N.* xvii.

BRIEG. Town. *C. S.*, *N. T.*, Act iii.

BRIG PLACE. *D. and S.* ix.

BRIGAND. Mr. Tupman in costume of. *P. P.*, x.
A very tight jacket; sitting like a pincushion over his back and shoulders: the upper portion of his legs encased in the velvet shorts, and the lower part thereof swathed in the complicated bandages to which all brigands are peculiarly attached.

BRIGGS. Pupil of Dr. Blimber.
D. and S. xii.
The stony pupil—sat looking at his task in stony stupefaction and despair . . . he should wish himself dead, if it weren't for his mother and a blackbird he had at home.

BRIGGS. Mr. Alexander, *B*rother of Samuel *B*riggs.
S. B. B., Tales vii.
Under articles to Mr. Samuel *B*riggs.

BRIGGS. Mr. Samuel, An attorney.
S. B. B., Tales vii.

BRIGGS. Mrs., A widow.
S. B. B., Tales vii.

BRIGGS. Mr. and Mrs.
S. Y. C. Egotistical.

BRIGGS SENIOR. Father of pupil. at Dr. Blimber's. *D. and S.* xii.

BRIGGSES. The, family of
S. B. B., Tales vii.

BRIGHT. Mr. John. *M. P.*, *T. B.*

BRIGHT CHANTICLEER = Boston Bantam. *M. P.*, *I. W. M.*

BRIGHTON. *B. H.* xiv.; *D. and S.* viii.; *M. P.*, *G. D.*; *M. P.*, *N. S.*; *N. N.*, 1.; *S. B. B.*, Tales iv.; *U. T.* xi.
All the coaches had been upset. in turn, within the last three weeks; each coach had averaged two passengers killed, and. six wounded; and in every case—no blame whatever was attributable to the coachman.

BRIMER. Mr., Fifth mate of the Halsewell. *R. P., T. L. V.*

BRINKLE. Lord Fitz, Chairman of Indigent *Orphans' Friend's Bene-* volent Institution.
S. B. B., Scenes xix.
A little man, with a long and rather inflamed face, and grey hair brushed bolt upright in front. He wears a wisp of black silk round his neck, without any stiffener, as an apology for a neckerchief.

BRISTOL. *B. R.* lxxxi. ; *M. P., L. W. O. Y.* ; *P. P.* xxxviii. ; *U. T.* xx.

BRISTOL. *Dean of* in 1850.
M. P., L. W. O. Y.

BRITAIN. Mrs., Née Clemency Newcome. *C. B., B. O. L.* iii.

BRITAIN. Manservant of Doctor Jeddler. *C. B., B. O. L.* i.
A small man, with an uncommonly sour and discontented face.

Note.—The landlord of the " Nutmeg Grater," as Britain became, was known as " Little Britain."

BRITAIN. Great. *C. S., H. T.*

BRITAIN. Little, *Benjamin Britain. C. B., B. O L.* i.

BRITAINS. Two Masters, Sons of *Britain.* *C. B., B. O. L.* iii.

BRITANNIA. The Captain of the. *A. N.* i.
A well-made, tight-built dapper little fellow, with a ruddy face.

BRITANNIA AT HOXTON. *U. T.* iv.
A gallery at threepence, another gallery at fourpence, a pit at sixpence, boxes and pit-stalls at a shilling, and a few private boxes at half-a-crown.

BRITISH LION. *M. P., B. L.*

BRITISH MUSEUM. *A. N.* xii. ; *L. D.* iii. ; *M. P., N. J. B.* ; *M. P., O. C.* ; *M. P., S. F. A.* ; *R. P., D. W . I. F.* ; *S. B. B.,* Scenes xxiii. *U. T.* xxiii.

BRITON. Old. A Juryman.
G. E. xxv.

BRITTANY. *M. P., L. A. V.,* ii.

BRITTEEN.=*Britain.*
M. P., T. O. H.

BRITTLES. Lad of all work to Mrs. Maylie. *O. T.* xxviii.

Note.—One of Mrs. Maylie's servants. A rather weak-minded boy, who had been a " slow boy " for upwards of thirty years. Brittles " assisted " in the capture of Oliver after the burglary.

BRIXTON. *M. C.* xxvii. ; *P. P.* i. ; *S. B. B.,* Tales v. ; *U. T.* vi.

BROAD COURT. Bow Street.
N. N. xxx.

BROAD STREET. Cross in.
N. N. xxxi.

BROADWAY. The. *M. C.* xvi.

BROADWAY. The, New York.
A. N. vi.

BROBINGNAY. *U. T.* xv.

BROBITY. Miss, Proprietress of a School. *E. D.* iv.

BROGLEY. *Broker and appraiser. D. and S.* ix.
Who kept a shop where every description of second-hand furniture was exhibited in the most uncomfortable aspect, and under circumstances and in combinations the most completely foreign to its purpose.
Mr. *Brogley* was a moist-eyed, pink-complexioned, crisp-haired man, of a bulky figure and an easy temper.

BROGSON. Guest of *Budden.*
S. B. B., Tales iii.
An elderly gentleman in a

black coat; drab knee-breeches, and long gaiters.

BROKER. A bill.
S. B. B., O. P. vii.

BROKER. Neighbouring, of the Kenwigs. *N. N.* xvi.

BROKER. Stout, Visitor in Bar parlour. *S. B. B.,* Char. iii.
In a large waistcoat.

BROKER'S MAN. Mr. *Bung.*
S. B. B., O. P. v.

BROKER'S MEN. In Fancy Stationer's. *S. B. B.,* Scenes iii.
Removing the little furniture there was in the house.

BROKERS' SHOPS.
S. B. B., Scenes xxi.
Strange places—would furnish many a page of amusement, and many a melancholy tale. The goods here are adapted to the taste, or rather the means, of cheap purchasers—a turn-up bedstead is a blunt, honest piece of furniture—ornament it as you will—seems to defy disguise—how different—a sofa-bedstead —it has neither the respectability of a sofa—nor the virtues of a bed. A small dirty shop exposing for sale the most extraordinary and confused jumble of old, worn out, wretched articles. Our wonder at their ever having been bought, is only to be equalled by our astonishment at the idea of their ever being sold again. Some half dozen high-backed chairs, with spinal complaints and wasted legs—pickle-jars, and surgeon's ditto—miscellanies of every description.

BROKERS' SHOPS. In Seven Dials.
S. B. B., Scenes v.
Which would seem to have been established by humane indi-

viduals, as refuges for destitute bugs.

BROMPTON. New, *Refer* to New *Brompton.*

BROMPTON. *N. N.* xxi.

BROOK STREET. Grosvenor Square. *D. and S.* xxx.; *U. T.* xvi.

BROOKE. Rajah. *M. P., P. F.*

BROOKER. Mr. *N. N.* xliv.
A spare dark withered man, with a stooping body and a very sinister face rendered more ill-favoured by hollow and hungry cheeks deeply sunburnt; and thick black eyebrows, blacker in contrast with the perfect whiteness of his hair. Roughly clothed in shabby garments, of a strange and uncouth make, and having about him an indefinable manner of depression and degradation.

Note.—The hand of Brooker is observable throughout the book, but it is only in the later chapters that he appears. He had been in Ralph Nickleby's employ, with, possibly a natural result, that he hated his master. Taking the opportunity when offered, he persuaded Ralph that his boy was dead. In reality it is poor Smike, left at Squeer's school, that we find Ralph's boy; only to see his father hunt him and persecute him.

BROOKS. Pupil at Dotheboys' Hall. *N. N.* vii.

BROOKS. Hon. Preston S., Kansas. *M. P., M. E.*

BROOKS. Mr., A Pieman; fellow-lodger of Weller's. *P. C.* xix.

BROOKS. Of Sheffield. The name by which Murdstone referred to David Copperfield before he married Mrs. Copperfield, when in the company of his friends. *D. C.* ii.

BROOKS'S. *D. and S.* xli.

BROOKS DINGWALLS. The.
S. B. B., Tales iii.

BROTHARTOON. Chamber candle-
stick. M. P., T. O. H.

BROTHER. A Lonely, of Josephine's. H. T., G. ix.
Died in hospital of fever—died
in penitence and love of you.

BROTHER. (Deceased) of Joey B.
(Major Bagstock). D. and S. x.

BROTHER. Plymouth,
C. S., M. L. Leg. i.

BROTHER of Passenger on Coach.
N. N. v.

BROTHER SOLDIER. Who had
served with Lieutenant.
M. H. C. ii.

BROTHERS TWIN. The, Charles
and Edwin Cheeryble—which see.

BROUGHAM. Lord. M. P., F. C.;
M. P., M. M., and M. P., S. S.

BROWDIE. John, Son of corn-
factor. Miss Price's fiancé.
N. N. ix.
His hair very damp from recent
washing, and a clean shirt, whereof the collar might have belonged
to some giant ancestor . . . together
with a waistcoat of similar dimensions—something over six feet
high.

Note.—A Yorkshire farmer, big and
strong, but kindly and jolly. 'Tilda
Price is a friend of Fanny Squeers, and
John Browdie is betrothed to, and
ultimately marries Miss Price; on his
first meeting with Nicholas—at a tea-
party with Miss Squeers—he is jealous,
but Nicholas afterwards owes much to
honest John, who becomes his good
friend. Browdie assists at the break
up of Dotheboy's Hall, and aids the
boys with food and sundry sixpences
and shillings.

Original : John S——, of Broodis-
wood in Yorkshire, to whom Dickens
had a letter of introduction when

getting " local colour." The character also recalls Scott's Dandie
Dinmont.

BROWDIE. Mrs., née Price—which
see.

BROWN. P. P. xxxix.

BROWN. Alice. D. and S. xxxiii.
A solitary woman of some thirty
years of age; tall; well formed;
handsome; miserably dressed; the
soil of many country roads in
varied weather—dust, chalk, clay,
gravel, clotted on her grey cloak
by the streaming wet; no bonnet
on her head, nothing to defend
her rich black hair from the rain,
but a torn handkerchief.

Note.—Known as Alice Marwood,
Alice Brown was first cousin to Mrs.
Edith Dombey, and daughter of
"Good" Mrs. Brown. She enters the
story on her return from transportation,
and is befriended by Harriet Carker.
She leaves the tale on her death, still
befriended by the same good woman.

BROWN. Conversation, at the
Treasury Board. D. and S. lxi.
Four-bottle man—with whom
the father of my friend Gay was
probably acquainted.

BROWN. Of Muggleton. Maker of
Miss Rachael Wardle's book.
P. P. x.

BROWN. One of Mrs. Lemon's
pupils. H. R. iv.

BROWN. Passenger on Gravesend
Packet. S. B. B., Scenes x.

BROWN. Captain John, of the
Polyphemus. D. and S. iv.

BROWN. Emily. S. B. B., Tales viii.
Married at Gretna Green to
Horace Hunter.

BROWN. Fanny. M. P., L.

BROWN. Miss. M. P., S. P.

BROWN. Mr. M. P., F. S.

BROWN. Mr. *O. C. S.*, xxi.
Who was supposed to be then a corporal in the East Indies.

BROWN. Mr.
Mud. Pap. ii.

BROWN. Mr. *S. B. B.*, Tales ix.
Plays the Violoncello.

BROWN. Mr. Henry.
S. B. B., O. P. vi.

BROWN. Mrs., Rag and bone vendor. *D. and S.* vi.
A very ugly old woman, with red rims round her eyes, and a mouth which mumbled and chattered of itself when she was not speaking. She was miserably dressed, and carried some skins over her arm.

Note.—The mother of Alice Marwood. She kidnaps Florence Dombey and steals her clothes. She leaves the story on the death of her daughter.

BROWN. Room—dark and ugly—of good Mrs.
D. and S. xxxiv.
There was no light in the room save that which the fire afforded—a heap of rags, a heap of bones, a wretched bed, two or three mutilated chairs or stools, the black walls and blacker ceiling, were all its winking brightness shone upon.

BROWN. Tom. *M. P., N. Y. B.*

BROWN AND CO. Misses.
S. B. B., O. P. vi.

BROWNDOCK. Miss, Kate Nickleby's father's cousin's sister-in-law
N. N. xvii.
Was taken into partnership by a lady that kept a school at Hammersmith—and made her fortune in no time at all. Was the same lady that got the ten thousand pounds prize in the lottery.

BROWNLOW. Mr. *O. T.* x.
A very respectable-looking personage, with powdered head and gold spectacles. He was dressed in a bottle-green coat, with a black velvet collar; wore white trousers; and carried a smart bamboo cane under his arm.

Note.—Mr. Brownlow was a benevolent old gentleman, who ultimately adopted Oliver Twist as his son. The introduction was effected by the Artful Dodger stealing Mr. Brownlow's pocket-handkerchief: Oliver is captured as the thief and taken to the magistrate's office, and doubtless would have been conveyed to prison but for the opportune arrival of a witness in the person of the bookseller. Mr. Brownlow takes Oliver home with him and tends him during his weakness, but he is recaptured by Nancy's aid. Mr. B. is greatly distressed by Oliver's non-return, and is forced to the conclusion that he must have decamped. Future events, however, reinstate Oliver in Mr. Brownlow's opinion, with the result already mentioned.

Original of Mr. Brownlow's residence: Situated in Craven Street.

BROWNS. The three Miss.
S. B. B., O. P. vi.

BROWNS. Three Miss.
S. B. B., O. P. ii.

BRUCE. Traveller.
M. P., E. T.; M. P., L. A. V. ii.

"BRUIN." Hugh of the Maypole.
B. R. xl.

BRUNEL. *M. P., S.*

BRUSSELS. *C. S.; S. P. T.* ii.;
M. P., S. F. A.; N. N. l., *O. M. F.*
ii.; *U. T.* xvii.

BRUSSELS. School at.
O. M. F. xxx.

BRYANSTONE SQUARE.
D. and S. iii.

BUCKET. Mr., a detective officer.
B. H. xxii.
A stoutly-built, steady-looking, sharp-eyed man in black, of about the middle age, with a face as unchanging as the great mourning

ring on his little finger, or the brooch, composed of not much diamond and a good deal of setting, which he wears in his shirt.

Note.—Detective officer whose industry and penetration make him appear more than mortal to the poor wretches he hunts down. He is good-hearted, however, and does what he can. He is closely connected with the main threads of the story, and it is he who in company with Esther Summerson tracks Lady Dedlock, although he is too late to be of any service. He is the means of obtaining possession of the later will from Smallweed, but that, too, is of no value, as the case has eaten up the estate. He leaves the story unceremoniously and unostentatiously seeing to the chairing-home of Grandfather Smallweed.

BUCKET. Mr., Aunt of. *B. H.* liii.

BUCKET. Mr., *B*rother-in-law of. *B. H.* liii.

BUCKET. Mr., Brother of. *B. H.* liii.

BUCKET. Mr., Father of. *B. H.* liii.

BUCKET. Mrs., Wife of Mr. *Bucket.* *B. H.* xlix.
A lady of natural detective genius—dependent on her lodger for companionship and conversation."
Note.—Leads on Mademoiselle Hortense to incriminate herself.

BUCKINGHAM. Duke of. *S. B. B.*, Scenes xiii.

BUCKINGHAM. Duke of, and tenants. *M. P., Ag. Int.*

BUCKINGHAM PALACE. *M. P.; Th. Let., M. P., N. G. K.*

BUCKLERSBURY. *S. B. B.*, Char. i.

BUD. Miss Rosa, A pupil at Mrs. Twinkleton's. *E. D.* iii.
Wonderfully pretty, wonder-

fully childish, wonderfully whimsical. A husband has been chosen for her by will and bequest.

Note.—One of the principal characters of the story. She is introduced as the pet pupil of the Nuns' House. She and Edwin Drood are betrothed while children by their parents, and they have grown up accepting that condition of affairs. They discover, however, that they cannot be made to love by order, and agree to become "brother and sister." Rosa is loved by John Jasper, but does not reciprocate, and to some extent fears him.

BUDDEN. Mr. *O*ctavius, Cousin of Minns. *S. B. B.*, Tales ii.

BUDDEN. Master Alexander Augustus. *S. B. B.*, Tales ii.
Habited in a sky-blue suit with silver buttons—possessing hair of nearly same colour as metal.

BUDDEN. Son of *O*ctavius. *S. B. B.*, Tales ii.
Mr. Augustus Minns—consented to become godfather by proxy.

BUDDEN. Mrs., Amelia, Wife of *O*ctavius Budden. *S. B. B.*, Tales ii.

BUDDEN. "Boy" of Mr. *S. B. B.*, Tales ii.
"In drab livery, cotton stockings and high lows."

BUDDEN. House of Mr. *S. B. B.*, Tales ii.
"Yellow brick house with a green door, brass knocker and door-plate, green window frames—a garden—a small bit of gravelled ground with one or two triangular beds—a Cupid on each side of the door, perched upon a heap of chalk flints, variegated with pink conch shells.

BUDGER. Mrs. *P. P.* ii.
A little old widow, whose rich dress and profusion of ornament

BULDER. Colonel. Head of the garrison.   *P. P.* ii.
Present at the charity ball, Rochester.

BULDER. Mrs., Colonel.   *P. P.* ii.
Present at the charity ball, Rochester.

BULDER. Miss.   *P. P.* ii.
Present at the charity ball, Rochester.

BULE. Miss, Pupil of Miss Griffin.
C. S., H. H.

BULL. Mr. John Bull.   *M. P., A. J. B.*; *M. P., B. S.*; *M. P., H. H.*; *M. P., M. E.*; *M. P., N. J. B.*; *M. P., O. C.*

BULL. Mrs.   *M. P., A. J. B.*; *M. P., N. J. B.*

BULL. Prince, A Powerful Prince.
R. P., P. B.

BULL'S FAMILY. Mr., members of.
M. P., H. H.

"BULL." The *B*lack, At Holborn.
M. C. xxv.
Original.—May have been the "Bull and Anchor."

"BULL." Chambermaid of the.
M. C. xxv.

"BULL." Head-chambermaid of the.   *M. C.* xxv.

"BULL." Landlady of the.
M. C. xxv.

"BULL." Landlord of the.
M. C. xxv.

"BULL INN." High Street, Rochester.   *P. P.* ii.
Good house—nice beds—half-a-crown in the bill if you look at the waiter—charge you more if you dine at a friend's than they would if you dined in the coffee-room.

Note.—The real name of the "Bull" since Queen Victoria passed a night there has been "The Royal Victoria and Bull Hotel." Mr. Pickwick's room has been identified as No. 17, Mr. Tupman's as No. 13, and Mr. Winkle's as No. 19.

"BULL" INN. Whitechapel.
P. P. xxii.

"BULL'S HEAD." The Old Hotel.
U. T. vi.

With its old-established knife boxes on its old-established sideboards, its old-established flue under its old-established four-post bedsteads, in its old-established airless rooms, its old-established frowziness upstairs and downstairs, its old-established cookery and its old-established principles of plunder.

BULLAMY. Porter in the service of the Anglo-Bengalee *Disinter*ested *L*oan and *L*ife Assurance Company.
M. C. xxvii.

A wonderful creature, in a vast red waistcoat, and a short-tailed pepper-and-salt coat.

Note.—His evident respectability was one of the company's assets.

BULLDOG. *M. P., F. L.*

BULLDOGS. The United.
B. R. viii.

BULLFINCH. *U. T.* xxxii.

BULLMAN. At law against Ramsey.
P. P. xx.

BULLOCK. Churchwarden.
D. C. xxix.

Excommunication case in court. Tipkins against *B*ullock, of a scuffle between two churchwardens.

BULLS OF ROME. *M. P., A. J. B.*

"BULLUM." *Boulogne.*
R. P., A. F.

BULPH. A pilot. *N. N.* xxiii.

Who sported a boat green door, with window-frames of the same colour, and had the little finger of a drowned man on his parlour mantelshelf, with other maritime and natural curiosities.

BUMBLE. Mr., Workhouse beadle.
O. T. ii.

A fat man, and a choleric.

Note.—The Beadle, who ever since the publication of "Oliver Twist" has stood for the symbol of the office. It was he who "invented" Oliver's name. When the poor orphan was nine years old he is removed by the Beadle from the "farm" to the workhouse. Later on he "sells" himself as a husband to Mrs. Corney, matron of the workhouse "for six tea-spoons, a pair of sugar-tongs, and a milk-pot, with a small quantity of second-hand furniture, and twenty pound in money." Mrs. Corney, when she becomes Mrs.Bumble, subjugates the Beadle, who is now master of the workhouse. Together they sell the locket and ring left by Oliver's mother, when she died in the workhouse, to Monks. Misfortune overtakes them: they are deprived of their situation, and eventually become inmates of the same workhouse.

BUMBLE. Mrs., *See* Corney, Mrs.

BUMPLE. Defendant in brawling case. *S. B. B.*, Scenes viii.

BUN HOUSE. The old original.
B. H. liii.

"BUNCH." Mother." Gift on Xmas tree. *R. P., A. C. T.*

BUNG. Spruggins' opponent.
S. B. B., O. P. iv.

In a cast-off coat of the captain's a blue coat with bright buttons, white trousers, and a description of shoes familiarly known by the appellation of "high lows."

BUNGAY. Suffolk. *M. P., W. R.*

BUNKER HILL STREET.
M. C. xxii.

BUNKIN. Mrs. *P. C.* xxxiv.
Which clear-starched.

BUNSBY. Captain, *D. and S.* xv.
With one stationary eye in the mahogany face, and one revolving one, on the principle of some lighthouses. This head was decorated with shaggy hair like oakum, which had no governing inclination towards the north, east, west, or south, but inclined to all four quarters of the compass, and to every point upon it. The head was followed by a dreadnought pilot-coat and by a pair of dreadnought pilot-trousers, whereof the waistband was so very broad and high, that it became a succedaneum for a waistcoat : being ornamented nearer the wearer's breast-bone with some massive wooden buttons, like backgammon men. Would deliver such an opinion on this subject, or any other that could be named, as would give Parliament six and beat 'em. . . . Been knocked overboard twice, and none the worse for it. Was beat in his apprenticeship, for three weeks (off and on) about the head with a ringbolt. And yet a clearer-minded man don't walk.

Note.—The eccentric captain of the "Cautious Clara." He is regarded by Captain Cuttle as infallible. He is vastly afraid of his landlady, Mrs. MacStinger, and is eventually captured by her and married.

BUNSBY. Mrs., late Mrs. MacStinger. *D. and S.* lx.

BURFORD. Mr. *M. P., E. T.*

BURGESS AND CO. Toots' tailor.
D. and S. xii.

BURIAL GROUND. *N. N.* lxii.
A dismal place, raised a few feet above the level of the street, and parted from it by a low parapet-wall, and an iron railing; a rank, unwholesome, rotten spot, where the very grass and weeds seemed, in their frowsy growth, to tell that they had sprung from paupers' bodies, and had struck their roots in the graves of men, sodden while alive, in steaming courts and drunken hungry dens.

BURLINGTON. Iowa. *A. N.* xvii.

BURLINGTON ARCADE. London.
M. P., I.; U. T. xvi.

BURLINGTON GARDENS.
U. T. xvi.

BURLINGTON HOUSE GARDENS.
U. T. x.

BURNETT. Henry. *M. P., I. G.*

BURNINGSHAME. Borough of.
M. P., H. H.

BURNLEY. Workman from.
M. P., O. S.

BURNS. Spirit of Robert.
M. P., S. F. A.

BURTON. Mr., of the General Furnishing Ironmongery Warehouse.
M. P., S. S.

BURTON. Thomas, Convert to Temperance. *P. C.* xxxiii.
Purveyor of cat's meat to the Lord Mayor and sheriffs and several members of the Common Council—has a wooden leg; finds a wooden leg expensive, going over the stones; used to wear second-hand wooden legs,—wears new wooden legs now, and drinks

nothing but water and weak tea. The new legs last twice as long as the others.

BURY. A man named,
A. N. xvii.

BURY. George, *Brother* of John's wife. *R. P., P. M. T. P.*

BURY. *M. P., O. S.*

BURY St. Edmunds.
D. C. xxx.; P. P. xv.
S. B. B. liv.; U. T. xxiii.
A handsome little town, of thriving and cleanly appearance.

"BUSH." The, Inn. *P. P.* xxxviii.
Original: Stood where the Wilt-shire Bank was erected in Corn Street, near the Guildhall, Bristol.

BUSHMEN. The. *R. P., T. N. S.*

BUSINESS. A Man of, Trustee for Miss Wade. *L. D.* lvii.

BUSTS. Waxen, In hairdressers.
N. N. lii.
Of a light lady, and a dark gentleman.

BUTCHER. William, A moderate Chartist. *R. P., P. M. T. P.*

BUTCHERS. A syndicate or guild of. *R. P., M. O. F. F.*

BUTLER. Mrs. Lavinia.
S. B. B., Tales iii.

BUTLER. Dr. BLIMBER'S.
D. and S. xii.
In a blue coat and light buttons, who gave quite a winey flavour to the table beer; he poured it out so superbly.

BUTLER. Mr. Merdle's chief.
L. D. xxi.
Stateliest man in the company. He did nothing, but he looked on as few other men could have done.

BUTLER. Cheeryble *Brothers'*.
N. N. lxiii.

BUTLER. Of Great Sibthorp.
M. P., S. P.

BUTLER. Silver-headed, hired by Mrs. Skewton. *D. and S.* xxx.

BUTLER. Theodosius, Miss Crumpton's Cousin. *S. B. B.,* Tales iii.
One of those geniuses to be met with in almost every circle. They usually have very deep monotonous voices.

BUTTON. Mr. William, Signor Jupe.
H. T., S. iii.

BUXTON. Sir Thomas Fowell.
M. P., N. E.

BUZFUZ. Serjeant, *Barrister for* Bardell. *P. P.* xxxiv.
With a fat body and a red face.
Note.—Buzfuz was counsel for the plaintiff in the trial. Although drawn from nature, the introduction of the character is supposed to have had as its object the lessening of the bullying of witnesses.
Original: Serjeant Bompas of the time.

BWISTOL. *Bristol.* *P. P.* xxxv.

BYRON. Honourable Lord. *M. C.* xxii.; *M. P., L. A. V.* ii.; *S. B. B.,* Scenes xiii.

C

C.D. Captains, "Nobodies."
R. P., N. S.

CAB. Fare of red.
S. B. B., Scenes xvii
A tall weazen-faced man, with an impediment in his speech.

CAB. Another fare of red.
S. B. B., Scenes xvii
A loquacious little gentleman in a green coat—had paid more than he ought and avowed his deter-

mination to 'pull up' the cabman in the morning.

"CABBAGE AND SHEARS." Inn.
C. S., D. M.

CABBERY. Another suitor of Mrs. Nickleby. *N. N.* xli.

CABBURN. *R. P., B. S.*

CAB-DRIVER. The last.
S. B. B., Scenes xvii.
A brown-whiskered white-hatted, no-coated cabman, his nose was generally red, and his bright blue eye not unfrequently stood out in bold relief against a black border of artificial workmanship. His boots were of the Wellington form, pulled up to meet his corduroy knee smalls—his neck was usually garnished with a bright yellow handkerchief. In summer he carried in his mouth a flower; in winter a straw.

CAB-DRIVERS. *S. B. B.,* Scenes i.
Wondering how people can prefer them wild beast cariwans of homnibuses, to a regular cab with a fast trotter.

CABINET. A. *B. H.* xii.

CAB'NET MAKER. *P. C.* xlv.

CACHOTS. The.
P. F. I., L. R. G. A.

CACKLES. My Cousin.
M. P., B. A.

CAD. Conductor of Omnibus.
S. B. B., Scenes xvi.

CADDO GAZETTE. A newspaper.
A. N. xvii.

CADELL. *M. P., S. P.*

CADI. Chief. *M. P., T. O. H.*

CADOGAN PLACE. Sloane Street.
N. N. xxi.

CAEN WOOD. Lord Mansfield's Country Seat. *B. R.* lxvi.
O. T. xlviii.

CAESARS. The Palace of the.
P. F. I., R.

CAFÉ DE LA LUNE. *M. P., R. D.*

CAFFRARIA. *R. P., T. L. V.*

CAGGS. Mr. *O. M. F.* viii.

CAGLIOSTRO. Spirit of.
M. P., M. M.

" CAIN, A MYSTERY." *M. C.* xxii.

CAIRAWAN. The Caravan.
C. S., G. i. S.

CAIRO. *M. P., E. T.*

CAIRO. On the Mississippi.
A. N. xii.
Detestable morass.

CAIUS CESTIUS. Burial place of.
P. F. I., R.

CALAIS. *L. D.* xxiv. ; *M. P., W.* ;
O. M. F. lxvii. ; *R. P., B. S.* ;
and *U. T.* xvii.

CALAIS. A native of. *L. D.* lvi.
In a suit of grease, and a cap of the same material.

CALAIS. Hôtel de, Calais.
U. T. xvii.

CALAIS HARBOUR. *U. T.* xvii.

CALCRAFT. Mr. *M. P., F. S.* ;
M. P., I. M. ; *M. P., M. P.* ;
M. P., T. B.

CALCUTTA.
M. P., E. T. ; and *U. T.* viii.

CALEB. Caleb Plummer.
C. B., C. O. H. i.

CALIFORNIA. *C. S., H. N.*; *C. S., W. O. G. M.*; *M. P.*, *R. H. F.*; and *R. P., O. S.*

CALLEY. Mr. *O. M. F.* viii.

CALLOW. An eminent physician. *R. P., O. B.*

CALOMEL. *C. S., H. H.*, ii.

CALTON. Mr., A boarder at Mrs. Tibbs'. *S. B. B.*, Tales i.
He used to say of himself that although his features were not regularly handsome, they were striking. . . . It was impossible to look at his face without being reminded of a chubby street-door knocker, half-lion, half-monkey. He was exceeding vain, and inordinately selfish.

CALTON HILL. *P. C.* xlix.

CAMBERLING TOWN. *D. and S.* vi.

CAMBERWELL. *L. D.* viii.; *M. C.* ix.; *N. N.* xxxvii.; *P. C.* xx.; *S. B. B.*, Tales v.

CAMBERWELL GREEN. *G. E.* lv.

CAMBERWELL GROVE. *S. B. B.*, Tales v.

CAMBRIDGE. *C. S., M. L. Leg.* i.; *G. E.* xxiii.; *G. S. E.* vi.; *M.P.*, *C. H. T.*; *R. P., T. B. W.*; *T. T. C.*, bk. ii, ch. x.

CAMBRIDGE. University of. *A. N.* iii.

CAMBRIDGE. Young Duke of. *M. P., G. H.*

CAMDEN TOWN. *C. B., C. C.*, *S.* i.; *C. S., H. H., D. C.* xxvii.; *D. and S.* vi.; *M. P., R. S.*; *O. T.* xlii.; *P. C.* xxi.; *S. B. B.*, Scenes i.; *S. B. B.*, Scenes xx.

CAMDEN TOWN. Post office. *D. C.* xxviii.

CAMEL. In Zoological Gardens. *M. P., R. H. F.*

CAMEL - CUM - NEEDLE'S-EYE. Extensive parish. *M. P., G. B.*

CAMILLA. Mr., Husband of Mrs. Camilla. *G. E.* xi.

CAMILLA. Mrs., Mr. Pocket's sister. *G. E.* xi.
Note.—One of the most prominent of Miss Havisham's fawning relatives.

CAMOGLIA. *P. F. I., R. P. S.*

CAMPAGNA. The solitary. *L. D.* lv.

CAMPANILE. Parma. *P. F. I., P. M. B.*

CAMPBELL. Dr. John, *M. P., R. S. D.*

CAMPBELL. Lord. *M. P., M. E.*

CAMPBELL. Mr., Mr. Provis (alias Abel. Magwich.) *G. E.* xlvi

CAMPBELL. Sir John. *M. P., S. F. A.*

CAMPO SANTO. *P. F. I., R. D*

CAMPO SANTO. The Church of Pisa. *P. F. I., R. P. S*

CANADA. *A. N.* ix.; *L. D.* vii

CANAL BRIDGE. *U. T.* xviii
See also Baker's Trap.

CANE. Grotto del. *P. F. I., R. D.*

CANNANA. Mr. Hamet Safi, Secretary to H[is] R[olling] H[ulk] the Hippopotamus. *M. P., R. G. H*

CANNING. Mr. *M. P., W*

CANNON STREET. *M. C.* ix

CANONGATE. Edinburgh. *M. P.* *S. P.*; and *P. P.* xlix.; and *H. T.* xxxiv.
There shot up against a dark sky, tall, gaunt straggling houses

with time-stained fronts, and windows that seemed to have shared the lot of eyes in mortals, and to have grown dim and sunken with age. Six, seven, eight. stories high were the houses; story piled above story, as children build with cards.

CANTERBURY. A. N. xviii.; B. R. li.; D. C. xvi.; L. D. liv.; U. T. vii.

CANTERBURY. Archbishop of. B. R. lxxxii.; M. H. C iii.

CANTERBURY POST OFFICE. D. C. xx.

CANTERBURY PRECINCT. M. P., N. Y. D.

CANTON DE VAUD. L. D. i.; M. P., C. H. T.

CAPE COAST CASTLE. M. P., N. E.

CAPE. Mr. S. B. B., Tales ix. Practised the violin.

CAPITOL. The. L. D. li.

CAPITOL. The, Washington. A. N. viii. A fine building of the Corinthian order.

CAPPER. Mr. S. Y. G.

CAPPER. Mrs. S. Y. G.

CAPPUCCHINO. P. F. I.

CAPRI. P. F. I., R. D.

CAPTAIN. Of the Screw. M. C. xvi.

CAPTAIN. The, a very old frequenter of Bellamy's. S. B. B., Scenes xviii. Spare, squeaking old man—a cracked bantam sort of voice—much addicted to stopping " after the House is up;"—a complete

walking reservoir of spirits and water.

CAPTING. Of " The Esau Slodge." M. C., xxxiii.

CAPUANA. Porta. P. F. I., R. D.

CAPULETS. The House of the, P. F. I., V. M. M. S. S.

CARAVAN. Sombre, A hearse. S. B. B. Scenes xvi. In which we must one day make our last earthly journey.

CARBOY. Of Kenge and Carboy. B. H. iii.

CARDINALS. P. F. I., R.

CAREW. Bamfylde Moore, the reigning successor of. M. P., G. A.

CARKER. Harriet, Sister of John and James Carker. D. and S. xxxiii. This slight, small, patient figure, neatly dressed in homely stuffs—leaning on the man still young, but worn and grey—his sister, who of all the world, went over to him in his shame, and put her hand in his, and with a sweet composure and determination, led him hopefully upon his barren way.

Note.—She befriends Alice Brown She lives quietly with her brother John, who is under a cloud, and eventually marries Mr. Morfin.

CARKER. Mr. James, Manager in Dombey and Son's office. D. and S. iv. A gentleman thirty-eight or forty years old, of a florid complexion, and with two unbroken rows of glistening teeth, whose regularity and whiteness were quite distressing—bore so wide a smile upon his countenance—that there was something in it like the snarl of a cat.

Note.—Brother of John and Harriet Carker. Manager of the house of Dombey and Son. He is entirely in Mr. Dombey's confidence, and possesses a great amount of influence over him. He is employed by his master to carry messages to his wife with the object of humiliating her. In return she elopes with Carker, and then leaves Carker when he thinks he has obtained his desire. Dombey's manager uses his position in the firm to further his own ends, and by doing so amasses a fortune. Although he does not lay hands on any of the firm's money, he has so involved it in rash and extensive speculation that it fails. In an endeavour to escape Mr. Dombey, Carker is killed on the railway. Paddock Wood Station in Kent, has been suggested as the scene of his death.

CARKER JUNIOR. Mr. John, in Dombey and Sons.
D. and S. vi.

He was not old, but his hair was white; his body was bent, or bowed as if by the weight of some great trouble: and there were deep lines in his worn and melancholy face. The fire of his eyes, the expression of his features, the very voice in which he spoke were all subdued and quenched, as if the spirit within him lay in ashes. He was respectably, though very plainly, dressed in black, but his clothes, moulded to the general character of his figure, seemed to shrink—and seemed to join in the sorrowful solicitation which the whole man from head to foot expressed, to be left unnoticed, and alone in his humility. *Brother of Carker the manager.* Two or three years older than he, but widely removed in station.

Note.—Brother of James and Harriet Carker. When he is introduced in the story he occupies a very junior position which he discharges with patient industry. It transpires that in his youth he robbed the firm, but that, instead of being dismissed, he was put into the post in which he is found, while his brother occupies the

position of manager. After his brother elopes with Mrs. Dombey, he is discharged. But when his brother meets with his accidental death he inherits the wealth accumulated by his brother. As, however, he looks upon his brother's fortune as in some measure due to his abuse of his position in the firm, John secretly makes over the interest year by year to old Mr. Dombey, after his bankruptcy.

CARLAVERO. Giovanni, Wine shopkeeper. *U. T.* xxviii.
His striking face is pale, and his action is evidently that of an enfeebled man—was a galley-slave in the north of Italy—a political offender.

CARLAVERO. Wife of Giovanni.
U. T. xxiii.

CARLISLE. *C. S., D. M.*

CARLISLE HOUSE. *B. R.* iv.

CARLO FELICE. The.
P. F. I., G. A. N.

CARLTON CLUB HOUSE.
M. P., B. A.

CARLTON HOUSE HOTEL. New York. *A. N.* vi.

CARLTON NEPHEWS.
M. P., S. for P.

CARLTON TERRACE.
S. B. B., Scenes xx.

CARLYLE. Mr. Thomas, Author. *A. N.* iii.; *M. P., P. F.*; *M. P., W. H.*; *M. P., W. S. G.*

CARNAK. Temple of. *M. P., E. T.*

CAROLINA. North. *A. N.* xvii.

CAROLINA. South. *A. N.* xvii.

CAROLINE. *C. B., C. C.*, s. iv.
A mild and patient creature.

CAROLINE. A Negress slave.
A. N. xvii.

CAROLINE. Queen.
M. P., L. A. V. i.

CARONDELET. Nicknamed Vide Poche. *A. N.* xiv.

CARPET-BEATER. A.
S. B. B., Scenes v.

CARR. Mr. Alfred, A West Indian gentleman of colour. *M. P., N. E.*

CARRARA. *P. F. I., R. P. S.*

CARIBBEAN SEAS.
C. S., P. O. C. E. P.

CARROT. Matthew.
M. P., P. M. B.

CARSTONE. Ada, née Clare.
B. H. li.

CARSTONE. Richard, ward in chancery and distant cousin of Ada Clare. *B. H.* iii.
A handsome youth, with an ingenious face, and a most engaging laugh—he was very young ; not more than nineteen then.

Note.—Ward of Mr. Jarndyce, and a party to the great case Jarndyce *v.* Jarndyce. His want of fixity of purpose and his slackness in his expenditure, based on the prospect of the termination of the chancery suit, spoil a character otherwise charming. He first tries law, from that he studies medicine under Mr. Bayham Badger, and then turns his attention to the Army. But he is unable to concentrate his attention on either, and returns to the chancery suit, which he resolves to watch in person. The anxiety undermines his health and breeds distrust of his guardian. He marries Ada Clare the other ward of John Jarndyce. The chancery suit terminates with the absorption of the estate in costs, and this accelerates Richard's death.

CARSTONE. Richard, Son of Ada and Richard. *B. H.* lxvii.

CARTER. Mr. *Mud. Pap.* 1.

CARTER. A. *B. R.* xxxi.
In a smock frock.

CARTHAGE. *A. N.* xvii.

CARTON. Captain (Admiral Sir George). *C. S., P. O. C. E. P.*
With bright eyes, brown face, and easy figure.

CARTON. Lady, Née Marion Maryon. *C. S., P. O. C. E. P.*

CARTON. Sydney, Stryver's Jackal.
T. T. C., Book ii., Chap. iii.
" I am a disappointed drudge, sir. I care for no man on earth, and no man on earth cares for me."

Note.—One of the most dramatic figures in the story. A debauched lawyer, and jackal to Mr. Stryver. He is instrumental in obtaining the discharge of Darnay on the count of treason by the close resemblance existing between them. He falls in love with Lucy Manette although, to others, he affects indifference to her. But he declares his love for her and leaves her. After she is married to Darnay her husband is obliged to go to Paris. He is arrested by the Revolutionists and sentenced to death. Carton follows, takes his place in prison and suffers execution by the guillotine.

CASBY. Mr. Christopher, Landlord of *B*leeding Heart Yard, formerly town agent to Lord *D*ecimus Tite-Barnacle. *L. D.* xii.
A man advanced in life, whose smooth grey eyebrows seemed to move—as the firelight flickered on them, sat in an armchair, with his list-shoes on the rug, and his thumbs slowly revolving over one another. His shining bald head, which looked so large, because it shone so much ; long grey hair at its sides and back, like floss silk, or spun glass, which looked so benevolent because it was never cut.—Various old ladies in the neighbourhood spoke of him as the " Last of the Patriarchs." His smooth face had a bloom upon it like ripe wall-fruit.—He had a

long wide-skirted bottle-green coat on, and a bottle-green pair of trousers, and a bottle - green waistcoat.

Note.—The Patriarch was the landlord of Bleeding Heart Yard, which he bled by means of Mr. Pancks. He was the father of Mrs. Flora Finching. He is shown up eventually by Pancks, to the whole yard.

CASGAR. Great plain at the feet of the mountains of.
M. P., T. O. H.

CASHIM TAPA. *M. P., T. O. H.*
Rich elder brother of Scarli Tapa.

CASHIM TAPA. Wife of.
M. P., T. O. H.

CASSIM. *Barrister's* clerk.
O. M. F. iii.

CASSINO. Monte, *P. F. I., R. D.*

CASTEL-A-MARE. *P. F. I., R. D.*

CASTIGLIONE. *P. F. I., R. D.*

CASTLE. Abode of Mrs. Pipchin.
D. and S. viii.
The castle was in a steep by-street at *Brighton*—where the front-gardens had the unaccountable property of producing nothing but marigold, whatever was sown in them. In winter time the air couldn't be got out of the castle, and in the summer-time it couldn't be got in.

CASTLE. Coavinse's, In Cursitor Street. *B. H.* xiv.
A house with barred windows.

CASTLE. The, Mr. Wemmick's house. *G. E.* xxv.

CASTLE DUNGEON. Room in Mrs. Pipchin's. *D. and S.* viii.
An empty apartment at the back, devoted to correctional purposes . . . looking out upon a chalk wall and a water-butt, and made ghastly by a ragged fireplace without any stove in it.

CASTLES. German. *R. P., A. C. T.*
Where we sit up alone to wait for the spectre.

CASTRO. *M. P., L. L.*

CASUALTY WARD. In hospital.
S. B. B., Char. vi.

CASWELL. Oliver, Inmate of Asylum for the Blind at *Boston.* Blind, deaf and dumb. *A. N.* iii.

CAT. In " Happy Family."
M. P., R. H. F.

CAT. Le. Historian. *B. H.*, Pref.
One of the most renowned surgeons produced by France.

CATACOMBS. *P. F. I.*

CATESBY. *S. B. B.*, Scenes xiii.

CATHEDRAL. In Florence.
P. F. I., R. D.

CATHEDRAL. Old. *E. D.* i.
The massive gray square tower of an old cathedral rises before the sight of a jaded traveller. The Virginia creeper on the cathedral wall has showered half its deep red leaves on the pavement.
*O*ther Cathedrals will be found under their various names.

CATHERINE STREET. Strand.
S. B. B., Scenes xiii. ; *U. T.* iv.

CATLIN. Mr. *R. P., T. N. S.*

" CATTIVO SOGGETTO MIO."
L. D. xlii.

CAUKABY. Lady, Mrs. Dombey.
D. and S. i.

CAULON. Brother of Walker.
U. T. v.

CAVALIER. A masked.
M. H. C. iii.

A man pretty far advanced in life, but of a firm and stately carriage. His dress was of a rich and costly kind—but soiled and disordered.

CAVALLETTO. Signor John Baptist. *L. D.* i.

A sunburnt, quick, lithe, little man, though rather thick-set. Ear-rings in his brown ears, white teeth lighting up his grotesque brown face, intensely black hair clustering about his brown throat, a ragged red shirt open at his brown breast. Loose, seamanlike trousers, decent shoes, a long red cap, a red sash round his waist, and a knife in it. The little man was an Italian.

Note.—Introduced as a prisoner in the same cell with Rigaud, who dominates him and abuses him, and of whom he is always somewhat afraid. He finds his way to England, and is eventually employed by Arthur Clennam in the works. He is instrumental in finding Rigaud and, having lost his fear, he accompanies his former prison companion, as servant.

CAVENDISH SQUARE.
L. D. xx.; *N. N.* x.; *O. M. F.* v.

CAVETON. *S. Y. G.*

CAWBERRY. *M. P., F. C.*

CAY. Mr. Sheriff. *M. P., S. P.*

CECIL STREET. Strand.
S. B. B., Tales x.

CECILIA METELLA. Tomb of.
P. F. I., R.

CELIA. Charity child. *U. T.* xxi.

Shaking mats in City churchyard.

CELLAR. In house near *Barbican*.
B. R. viii.

Where there was a small copper fixed in one corner, a chair or two, a form and a table, a glimmering fire, and a truckle bed, covered with a ragged patchwork rug.— The floors were of sodden earth, the walls and roof of damp, bare brick, tapestried with the tracks of snails and slugs.

CEMETERY. The. *C. S., S. L.* ii.

In all Britain you would have found nothing like it.—There were so many little gardens and grottos made upon graves in so many tastes, with plants and shells and plaster figures and porcelain pitchers, and so many odds and ends . . . nothing of the solemnity of death here.

CENCI. Palace of the. *P. F. I., R.*

CENTRAL CRIMINAL COURT.
C. S., T. G. S. i.; and *M. P., I.*

CENTRAL DISTRICT. London.
M. P., F. F.

CERTAINPERSONIO. Prince.
H. R. ii.

CEYLON. *M. P., E. T.*

CHADBAND. Mr., In the ministry.
B. H. xix.

A large yellow man, with a fat smile, and a general appearance of having a good deal of train-oil in his system.

Note.—Friend of Mrs. Snagsby. A canting hypocrite of no defined denomination. He is engaged in an attempt by Smallweed to blackmail Sir Leicester Dedlock.

CHADBAND. Mrs., Formerly Mrs. Rachael. *B. H.* xix.

A stern, severe-looking, silent woman.

Note.—Introduced as the austere and self-seeking servant of Esther Summerson's aunt. Becomes the wife of Chadband and is concerned with him in the blackmail of Sir Leicester Dedlock.

CHADWICK. Mr. *M. P., S. S. U.*

CHADWICK. Mr. *U. T.* xxix.

CHADWICK'S ORCHARD. Preston.
M. P., O. S.

CHAFFWAX. Deputy.
R. P., P.M. T. P.

CHAIRMAKER. Cornish.
C. S., H. T.
The chairs assigned were mere frames, altogether without bottoms of any sort, so that we passed the evening on perches.

CHAIRMAN. A Preston weaver.
M. P., O. S.

CHAIRMAN. At a harmonic meeting. *S. B. B.,* Scenes ii.
Little pompous man, with the bald head, just emerging from the collar of his green coat.

CHAIRMAN. The. *O. M. F.* lxvii.

CHAIRMEN. Guests at *Dombey's* housewarming. *D. and S.* xxxvi.

CHAIRMEN. One short and fat and one long and thin. *P. P.* xxxvi.
Original : Said to have been real and well-known characters in Bath a hundred years ago.

CHALK FARM. *U. T.* xviii.

CHALONS. *L. D.* xi.; *P.F.I., G.T.F.*
The flat expanse of country about Chalons lay a long, heavy streak, occasionally made a little ragged by a row of poplar trees, against the wrathful sunset.

CHALONS. The Café. *L. D.* xi.
With its bright windows and its rattling of dominoes.

CHALONS. *D*yers in. *L. D.* xi.
With its strips of red cloth on the doorposts.

CHALONS. Hotel in. *L. D.* xi.
With its gateway, and its savoury smell of cooking.

CHALONS. Its silversmiths.
L. D. xi.
With its earrings, and its offerings for altars.

CHALONS. Tobacco dealers.
L. D. xi.
With its lively group of soldier customers coming out pipe in mouth.

CHAMBERMAID. Head, at Furnival's Inn. *E. D.* xx.

CHAMBERMAID. Head.
C. S., S. L. i.

CHAMBERS. *P. P.* xxi.
What is there in Chambers in particular ?

CHAMOUNI. *R. P., O. B.*

CHAMPEAUX. Café, near the Bourse. *M. P., N. Y. D.*

CHAMPLAIN. Lake. *A. N.* xv.

CHAMPS ELYSÉES. *M. P., R. D.*

CHANCELLOR. Lord.
R. P., P. M. T. P.

CHANCELLOR. Lord, in 1813.
M. P., C. P.

CHANCELLOR. The Lord High.
B. H. i.
With a foggy glory round his head, softly fenced in with crimson cloth and curtains.

CHANCELLOR OF THE EXCHEQUER. The. *S. B. B.,* Scenes xviii. ; *U. T.* xxii.

CHANCELLOR OF THE EXCHEQUER. *O*ffice of.
M. P., R. T.

CHANCERY.
P. P. xliv. ; *S. B. B.,* Scenes iii.

CHANCERY. Court of. *B. H.* i. ; *M. P., L. W. O. Y.* ; *P. P.* xliv. ; *S. B. B.,* Scenes iii.
Which has its decaying houses and its blighted lands in every shire, its worn-out lunatics in every mad-house.

CHANCERY. Master in.
R. P., P. M. T. P.

CHANCERY. Masters in.
U. T. xxvi.
Holding up their black petti-coats.

CHANCERY BAR. M. P., L. E. J.

CHANCERY LANE. B. H. i.;
O. M. F. viii.; P. C. xl.; R. P.,
B. S.; S. B. B. viii.

CHANCERY PRISONER. In the
Fleet. P. C. xlii.
A tall, gaunt, cadaverous man,
in an old great-coat and slippers;
with sunken cheeks, and a restless,
eager eye. His lips were bloodless
and his bones sharp and thin.
God help him! The iron teeth of
confinement and privation had
been grinding him down for twenty
years.

CHANDLER. The little, Shop of.
S. B. B., Scenes ii.
The crowds which have been
passing to and fro during the whole
day are rapidly dwindling away.

CHANEY. (China.) D. and S. iii.

'CHANGE. See Exchange, Royal.

CHANNEL. The.
C. S., M. f. T. S. v.; L.D. lvi.;
O. M. F. xxi.; R. P., O. F. M.

CHANNEL ISLANDS. M. P., G. D.

CHANNING. Dr., A preacher.
A. N. iii.

CHAPEL. Newgate prison.
S. B. B., Scenes xxv.
The meanness of its appoint-
ments—the bare and scanty pulpit
—the women's gallery with its
heavy curtain—the tottering little
table at the altar—so unlike the
velvet and gilding, marble and
wood of a modern church, are
strange and striking.

CHAPEL. Newgate prison, Condemned pew in.
S. B. B., Scenes xxv.
Immediately below the reading-
desk, on the floor of the chapel,
and forming the most conspicuous
object in its little area—black pen,
in which the wretched people,
who are singled out for death, are
placed on the Sunday preceding
their execution—to hear prayers
for their own souls, and join in
responses of their own burial
service.—At one time—the coffins
of the men about to be executed
were placed—upon the seat by
their side.

CHAPEL. Of the Holy Office.
P. F. I., L. R. G. A.

CHAPEL WALKS. Preston.
M. P., O. S.

CHAPLIN. Miss Ellen, as, Rosina.
M. P., M. N. D.

CHARACTER. A well-known. An
M.P.   S. B. B., Scenes xviii.
The quiet gentlemanly - looking
man in the blue surtout, grey
trousers, white neckerchief and
gloves, whose closely - buttoned
coat displays his manly figure and
broad chest He has fought a
good many battles in his time.

CHARACTERS. S. B. B., Char. i.

CHARING CROSS. C. S., M. L. Lo.
i.; M. P., T. D.; N. N. ii.;
O. M. F. xliii.; S. B. B., Scenes
vii.

CHARING CROSS. The golden cross.
D. C. xix.

CHARING CROSS. The statue at.
N. N. xli.

CHARIOTEER. At Ramsgate pier
S. B. B., Tales iv.
Offering services to the Tuggs.

CHARITABLE GRINDERS.   A Worshipful Company. *D. and S.* v.

An ancient establishment; where not only is a wholesome education bestowed upon the scholars, but where a dress and badge is likewise provided for them. The dress—is a nice warm, blue baize tailed coat and cap, turned up with orange - coloured binding; red worsted stockings; and very strong leather small clothes.

CHARKER. Harry, Corporal of marines in chase of pirates.
C. S., P. O. C. E. P.

CHARLES.   *S. Y. C.*

CHARLES. Old, Waiter at west country hotel.   *C. S., S. L.* i.
Considered Father of the waitering.

CHARLES. Old, Widow of.
C. S., S. L. i.
An inmate of the Almshouses of the Cork Cutters' Company.

CHARLES STREET.   *Drury Lane. U. T.* xxxvi.

CHARLESTON.   *A. N.* viii.

CHARLEY. *See* Hexam, Charley.

CHARLEY. *See* Neckett, Charlotte.
B. H. xv.

CHARLEY. The bashful man. A barrister.   *C. S., H. T.*

CHARLEY. Little, Son of Mrs. Blockson.   *N. N.* xviii.
Fell down an airy and put his elber out.

"CHARLEY." Marine store shop-keeper.   *D. C.* xiii.
An ugly old man, with the lower part of his face all covered with a stubbly grey beard.

Note.—The marine store's man to whom David sells his jacket.

CHARLEY. Potboy of " Magpie and Stump."   *P. P.* xx:
A shambling potboy, with a red head.

CHARLEY AND ANGELA.   Eight children of.   *C. S., H. T.*

CHARLOTTA.   Charlotte Tuggs.
S. B. B., Tales iv

CHARLOTTE.   *O. T.* iv

CHARLOTTE.   *S. Y. C*

CHARLOTTE. An old lady of ninety-nine.   *R. P., A. C. T*

CHARLOTTE. Daughter of John
R. P., P. M. T. P

CHARLOTTE. Daughter of Mr. and Mrs. Borum.   *N. N.* xxiv

CHARLOTTE. Deceased daughter of Mr. Pocket.   *G. E.* xxx

CHARLOTTE. One of the children brought up with Miss Wade.
L. D. lvii
Stupid mite—my chosen friend —one time I went home with her for the holidays—my false young friend.

CHARLOTTE. Mrs. Sowerberry's maid.   *O. T.* iv.
A slatternly girl in shoes down at heel, and blue worsted stockings very much out of repair.

Note.—Servant of Mrs. Sowerby wife of the undertaker to whom Oliver was apprenticed. She robs the till and travels to London with Noah Claypole There they fall in with Fagin and become thieves. Afterwards with Noah she becomes an informer.

CHARLOTTE. *See* Neckett, Charlotte.

CHARLOTTE STREET.
S. B. B., Char. ix

CHARLOTTE'S AUNT.   *L. D.* lvii

CHARLOTTE'S CROWD. Of cousins and acquaintances. *L. D.* lvii.

CHARTERHOUSE. The. *B. R.* iv.

CHARTRES STREET. *A. N.* xvii.

CHARWOMAN. Phantom.
C. B., C. C. S. iv.
I wish it was a little heavier judgment, and it should have been—if I could have laid my hands on anything else.

CHÂTEAU. Of the Old Guard.
R. P., O. F. W.

CHATHAM. *B. R.* xxxi.; *C. S., P. O. C. E. P.*; *C. S., S. P. T.*; *D. C.* xiii.; *P. P.* ii.; *R. P., T. B. W.*; *R. P., T. D. P.*; *U. T.* v.

CHATHAM. Dockyard. *U. T.* xxiv.
Made no display, but kept itself snug under hillsides of cornfields, hopping gardens, and orchards; its great chimneys smoking with a quiet—almost a lazy air, like giants smoking tobacco. It resounded with the noise of hammers beating upon iron.

CHATHAM DOCKYARD. Workshop in. *U. T.* xxiv.
Where they make all the oars used in the British Navy.

"CHAUNTER." A. *L. D.* xii.
Not a singer of anthems, but a seller of horses.

CHAYMAID. Chambermaid at coffee-house. *L. D.* iii.

CHEAP. The ward of. *M. C.* xxxv.

CHEAP JACK. *U. T.* xi.

CHEAPSIDE. *B. R.*, xxxvii.; *D. and S.* xiii.; *G. E.* xx.; *L. D.* iii.;

M. C. xxv.; *M. P., M. B. V.*; *N. N.* xxvi.; *O. M. F.* iv.; *P. P.* xx.; *R. P., T. D. A.*; *U. T.* xii.

CHEERFUL. Mr. *M. P., B. S.*

CHEERYBLE. Mr. Charles, Younger twin-brother of Mr. Ned.
N. N. xxxv.
A sturdy old fellow in a broad skirted blue coat, made pretty large to fit easily, with no particular waist; his bulky legs clothed in drab breeches, and high gaiters, and his head protected by a low-crowned, broad-brimmed white hat, such as a wealthy grazier might wear. He wore his coat buttoned, his dimpled double-chin rested in the folds of a white neckerchief—not one of your stiff starched, apoplectic cravats, but a good easy, old-fashioned white neck-cloth.—What principally attracted the attention—was the old gentleman's eye—never was such a clear, twinkling, honest, merry happy eye as that.

Note.—The Cheeryble Brothers were merchants in a prosperous business. They were exceedingly charitable and good, so much so that it has been urged that their character is an impossible one. They befriended Nicholas and employed him in their office. And Nicholas' whole fortunes are due in a large measure to them; as was also the happiness and prosperity of other characters of the book. The brothers retire from the business, which is carried on by Frank Cheeryble and Nicholas.

Originals : Brothers William and Daniel Grant. Young Scotsmen who settled in Manchester and became wealthy calico printers with warehouse in 15, Cannon Street, Manchester, and another house in Moseley Street. Dickens first met them in 1838. William died in 1842 and Daniel in 1855. William was Ned, and Daniel, brother Charles of the story.

CHEERYBLE. Frank, Nephew of Cheeryble brothers. *N. N.* xliii.
A sprightly, good - humoured, pleasant fellow, with much both in his countenance and disposition that reminded Nicholas very strongly of the kind - hearted brothers. His manner was as unaffected as theirs.

Note.—Nephew of the brothers Cheeryble. He eventually succeeds to the business with Nicholas and marries Kate Nickleby.

CHEERYBLE. Kate, Mrs. Frank. Kate Nickleby. *N. N.* lxv.

CHEERYBLE. Ned (Edwin), Twin brother of Mr. Charles Cheeryble. *N. N.* xxxv.
Another old gentleman, the very type and model of himself (Mr. Charles Cheeryble). The same face, the same figure, the same coat, waistcoat, and neckcloth, the same breeches and gaiters, nay there was the very same white hat hanging against the wall.

CHEESEMAN. Mrs., Née Jane Pitt. *R. P., T. S. S.*

CHEESEMAN. Old, The school-boy. *R. P., T. S. S.*
Wasn't Latin master then ; he was a fellow—very small—never went home for his holidays. At last made second Latin master.

CHEESEMONGER'S. A. *S. B. B.*, Scenes ii.

CHEGGS. Mr. Alick, *Dick* Swiveller's successful rival for the fair Sophia Wackles. *O. C. S.* viii.
Mr. Cheggs was a market-gardener and shy in the presence of ladies.

CHEGGS. Miss. *O. C. S.* viii.
Mr. Cheggs came not alone or unsupported, for he prudently brought along with him his sister, Miss Cheggs.

CHELSEA. *B. H.* xiii. ; *B. R.* xvi. *N. N.* xxi. ; *O. C. S.* viii. ; *R. P. T. D. P.* ; *R. P., P. M. T. P.*

CHELSEA. Bun-house. *B. R.* xlii

CHELSEA FERRY. *O. M. F.* xv

CHELSEA PENSIONER. *U. T.* xxvii

CHELSEA WATERWORKS. *P. P.* xxiii

CHELTENHAM. *L. D.* xii. ; *M. P. E. S.* ; *R. P., T. D. P.*

CHEMIST. Gloomy analytical Fifth retainer of Veneering's. *O. M. F.* ii

CHERRY. "Fond " for Charity Pecksniff—*which see.*

CHERTSEY. *O. M. F.* xli. ; *O. T.* xix

CHERUB. Amiable. *See* Wilfer, Mr.

CHESAPEAKE BAY. *A. N.* ix

CHESELBOURNE. *O. C. S.* lxvi.
Rebecca Swiveller . . . of Cheselbourne in *Dorsetshire.*

CHESHIRE COAST. *U. T.* xxxi.

CHESHIREMAN FAMILY. Mr. Cheeseman's. *R. P., T. S. S.*

CHESNEY WOLD. Sir Leicester and Lady *Dedlock's* home in Lincolnshire. *B. H.* vii.
Original : Rockingham Castle.

CHESNEY WOLD. Little church in the park in. *B. H.* ii.
Is mouldy—and there is a general smell and taste as of the ancient *Dedlocks* in their graves.

CHESNEY WOLD. Ghosts' Walk in Lady *Dedlock's* place in. *B. H.* ii.
Broad-flagged pavement, called from old time the Ghosts' Walk.

CHESNEY WOLD VILLAGE.
B. H. vii.
Original: Rockingham.

CHESTER. Mr. *M. H. C.* vi.

CHESTER. Edward. *B. R.* i.

A young man of about eight-and-twenty, rather above the middle height—gracefully and strongly made. He wore his own dark hair, and was accoutred in a riding-dress—together with his large boots (resembling those of our lifeguardsmen of the present day).—Lying upon the table beside him—were a heavy riding-whip and a slouched hat—a pair of pistols in a holster-case, and a short riding-cloak.

Note.—Edward is in love with Emma Haredale. Both her father and his endeavour to prevent the marriage, but eventually the former relents. The wedding takes place and Edward and his wife go abroad, although they return to England when " the riots are many years old."

CHESTER. Edward, Great-grand-father of. *B. R.* xv.

CHESTER. Edward, Maternal grandfather of. *B. R.* xv.

CHESTER. Edward, Mother of. *B. R.* xv.

CHESTER. Edward and Emma, Children of. *B. R.* lxxxii.

CHESTER Edward, Wife of, née Emma Haredale—*which see.*

CHESTER. Old Mr. (Sir John). *B. R.* v.

A staid, grave, placid gentleman, something past the prime of life, yet upright in his carriage for all that. He wore a riding-coat of a somewhat brighter green than might have been expected of a gentleman of his years, with a short black velvet cape, and laced pocket-holes and cuffs,—his linen,

too, was of the finest kind, worked in a rich pattern at the wrists and throat, and scrupulously white.

Note.—Father of Edward Chester; becomes Sir John in chap. 21. He endeavours, by all the means in his power, to prevent the marriage of his son and Miss Emma Haredale. He obtains control of Hugh and uses him for his own ends. Utterly without honour in the real sense he discards his tools when they are of no further use to him. He is eventually killed by Mr. Haredale in a duel.

Original : Supposed to have been based on Lord Chesterfield.

CHESTER. Son of Mr. *M. H. C.* vi.

CHESTERTON. Mr., Prison Governor. *M. P., C. and E.*

CHESTLE. Mr. *D. C.* xviii.

Note.—The hop-grower who supplants David and marries the eldest Miss Larkins.

CHEVALIER. The. *P. F. I., L. R. G. A.*

CHEYPE. The ward of. *M. H. C.* i.

CHIAJA. The, Or public gardens. *P. F. I., R. D.*

CHIB. Mr., A vestry-man. *R. P., O. V.*
Father of the vestry.

CHICK. Young Smallweed—*which see.*

CHICK. Frederick. *D. and S.* i.

CHICK. John, Husband of Dombey's sister. *D. and S.* i.

A stout old gentleman, with a very large face, and his hands continually in his pockets, and who had a tendency to whistle and hum tunes. In their matrimonial bickerings they were, upon the whole, a well-matched, fairly balanced, give-and-take couple.

CHICK. Louisa, Sister of Dombey. *D. and S.* i.

A lady rather past the middle

F

age than otherwise, but dressed in a very juvenile manner, particularly as to the tightness of her bodice.

Note.—Mr. Dombey's sister and friend of Miss Tox. She entreats everybody, from the first Mrs. Dombey, at the birth of little Paul, to her brother, on the ruin of the house, to "make an effort." The latter is the last occasion on which she emerges from her obscurity.

CHICKABIDDY LICK. Plains of. *M. C.* xxi.

CHICKENSTALKER. Mrs., Shopkeeper. *C. B., C. G.* ii. In the general line.

CHICKENSTALKER. Shop of Mrs. *C. B., C. G.* iv. Crammed and choked with the abundance of its stock—everything was fish that came to the net of this greedy little shop, and all articles were in its net.

CHICKETT. The girl from the workhouse. *D. C.* xi.

CHICKSEY AND STOBBLES. *O. M. F.* iv. Former masters of Veneering.

CHICKSEY, VENEERING, AND STOBBLES. *O. M. F.* iv. Drug house.

CHICKWEED. Conkey, A burglar. *O. T.* xxxi. Kept a public-house, and he had a cellar, where a good many young lords went to see cockfighting, and badger-drawing, and that.

CHICK-WEED. Young Smallweed—*which see.*

CHIEF. Of the gravediggers. *M. P., L. W. O. Y.*

CHIEF. The, Mr. *Dorrit*—*which see.*

CHIGGLE. Sculptor. *M. C.* xxxiv.

CHIGWELL. Essex. *B. R.* i.

CHIGWELL CHURCH. *B. R.* xxxi.

CHIGWELL ROW. *B. R.* i.

CHILD. *R. P., C. D. S.* Original : Dickens himself.

CHILD. *M. P., C. H.*

CHILD. A washerwoman's. *S. B. B., O. P.* ii.

CHILD. In common lodging-house in Liverpool. *U. T.* v. She drags out a skinny little arm from a brown dust-heap on the ground.

CHILD. Of *Betsy* Martin's. Convert to temperance. *P. P.* xxxiii.

CHILD. Of prisoner in the Fleet. *P. P.* xli.

CHILD-BED-LINEN SOCIETY. *S. B. B., O. P.* vi.

CHILDERS. E. W. B., One of Sleary's Troupe. *H. T., S.* vi. His face close-shaven, thin and sallow, was shaded by a quantity of dark hair, brushed into a roll all round his head, and parted in the centre. He was dressed in a Newmarket coat, and tight-fitting trousers, wore a shawl round his neck.

CHILDERS. Mrs. E. W. B., Josephine. *H. T., G.* vii.

CHILDREN. *S. B. B.,* Scenes i.

CHILDREN. Four or five. in house in George's Yard. *S. B. B., O. P.* v. Grovelling about among the sand on the floor, naked.

CHILDREN. Groups of (singing carols). *P. P.* xxix. Curly-headed little rascals.

CHILDREN. In chaises, at tea-gardens.   *S. B. B.*, Scenes i.

CHILDREN. Of fancy stationer.
    S. B. B., Scenes iii.
In mourning — in the little parlour behind the shop—clean, but their clothes were thread-bare.

CHILDREN. Of Mr. and Mrs. Britain.   *C. B., B. o. L.* iii.

CHILDREN. Our.   *M. P., W. L.*

CHILDREN. Rosy, living opposite to Mr. Dombey's house.
    D. and S. xviii.

CHILDREN. Seeing Mark Tapley off.   *M. C.* vii.

CHILDREN. Six, of brother of passenger on coach.   *N. N.* v.

CHILDREN. Six small, of widow.
    S. B. B., O. P. i.

CHILDREN. Some ragged, of corpse.   *O. T.* v.

CHILDREN. Three or four, of lady in distress.   *S. B. B., O. P.* v.
Fine-looking little children.

CHILDREN. Two little.
    M. P., L. W. O. Y.

CHILDREN-IN-ARMS. Taking part in election.   *P. P.* xiii.
"To pat on the head and inquire the age of " ... "if you *could* manage to kiss one of 'em."

CHILDREN'S HOSPITAL. The.
    O. M. F. xxvi.

Original : Said to have been the Children's Hospital, Gt. Ormond St.

CHILL. Uncle, Relation of Mr. Michael.   *R. P., P. R. S.*

CHILLIP. Dr.   *D. C.* i.
He walked as softly as the ghost in Hamlet, and more slowly. He carried his head on one side, partly in modest depreciation of himself, partly in modest propitiation of everybody else.

Note.—He ushers little David into the world. Some years later he left Blunderstone and vanishes until David meets him in a coffee-house. He has bought a little practice within a few miles of Bury St. Edmunds where he is doing well.

Original : Sketched from the Dickens' " old family medical attendant in the Devonshire Terrace days."

CHILLIP'S BABY.   *D. C.* xxii.
A weazen little baby, with a heavy head that it couldn't hold up, and two weak staring eyes, with which it seemed to be always wondering why it had ever been born.

CHILLIP'S. Mr., Second wife.
    D. C. xxii.
Tall, raw-boned, high-nosed.

CHIMES. The, Church bells.
    C. B., C. i.
Centuries ago, these bells had been baptized by bishops.
Original : St. Dunstan's, Fleet Street.

CHIMNEY-SWEEPER. Master.
    D. and S. xv.
A man who had once resided in that vanished land (Stagg's Gardens), who now lived in a stuccoed house three stories high, and gave himself out, with golden flourishes upon a varnished board, as contractor for the cleaning of railway chimneys by machinery.

CHIN TEE. Chinese idol.
    M. P., C. J.

CHINA. (Country.) *B. H.* xi. ; *C. S., D. M.* ; *H. T., S.* xv. ; *L. D.* v. ; *M. P., S. R.* ; *M. P., T. O. H.* ; *R. P., B. S.* ; *R. P., T. B. W.*

CHINA. In London.   *M. P., C. J.*

CHINAMAN.   *E. D.* i.

CHINAMAN. Sailor.   *U. T.* xx.

CHINAMAN. Jack.   *E. D.* i.
   Original: " George Ah Sing, who had an opium den in Cornwall Road, St. George's-in-the-West. He died in 1889."

CHINCK'S BASIN.   *G. E.* xlvi.

CHIPPING NORTON.   *R. P., O. S.*

CHIPS. Character in one of Nurse's
   Stories.   *U. T.* xv.
   Had sold himself to the devil for an iron pot, and a bushel of tenpenny nails, and half a ton of copper and a rat that could speak.

CHIRRUP. Mr.   *S. Y. C.*

CHIRRUP. Mrs.   *S. Y. C.*

CHISWICK. *O. M. F.* vi. ; *O. T.* xxi.

CHISWELL STREET.   *O. T.* xxi.

CHITLING. Tom, Recently released
   prisoner.   *O. T.* xviii.
   He had small twinkling eyes, and a pock-marked face ; wore a fur cap, a dark corduroy jacket, greasy fustian trousers, and an apron.
   Note.—Another of Fagin's pupils. Rather more than friendly with Bet. Is first met with when he comes out of prison and last seen in the house by the Folly Ditch.

CHIVERY AND CO. Tobacconists.
                   L. D. xxii.
   Importers of pure Havannah cigars, Bengal cheroots, and fine-flavoured Cubas, dealers in fancy snuffs, etc., etc.
   It was a very small establishment, wherein a decent woman sat behind the counter working at her needle. Little jars of tobacco, little boxes of cigars, a little assortment of pipes, a little jar or two of snuff, and a little instrument like a shoeing horn for serving it out, composed the retail stock in trade.

CHIVERY. Mrs., Mother of young
   John.   *L. D.* xviii.
   Kept " a snug tobacco business round the corner of Horsemonger Lane."

CHIVERY. Senior, A non-resident turnkey at the Marshalsea.
                  L. D. xviii.

CHIVERY. Young John, Sentimental son of the turnkey.
                  L. D. xviii.
   Was small of stature, with rather weak legs and very weak light hair. One of his eyes was also weak, and looked larger than the other, as if it couldn't collect itself. Young John was gentle likewise ; but he was of great soul. Poetical, expansive, faithful. Was neatly attired in a plum-coloured coat, with as large a collar of black velvet as his figure could carry ; a silken waistcoat bedecked with golden sprigs ; a chaste neckerchief much in vogue in that day—pantaloons so highly decorated with side stripes—and a hat of state very high and hard— a pair of white kid gloves, and a cane like a little finger-post.

   Note.—Son of John Chivery. Lover of Little Dorrit at first in secret Eventually he tells her of his love, but she refuses him. The blow upsets him very much but he continues to love her. He is last seen at Little Dorrit's wedding.

CHIZZLE. Mr.   *B. H.* i

CHOBBS AND BOLBERRY.
                  M. C. xliv

CHOCTAW TRIBE. Of Indians.
       A. N. xii. ; *M. P., E. T*

CHOKE. General. *M. C.* xxi.
Very lank gentleman, in a loose limp white cravat, a long white waistcoat and a black great-coat.

CHOKESMITH. *See* Rokesmith.

CHOLLOP. Hannibal. *M. C.* xxxiii.
A lean person in a blue frock and a straw hat, with a short black pipe in his mouth ; and a great hickory stick, studded all over with knots, in his hand, smoking and chewing as he came along.

CHOPPER. Great-uncle of William Tinkling. *H. R.* i.

CHOPPER. Mrs. *S. Y. C.*

CHOPS. The dwarf. *C. S., G. i. S.*

CHOPSKI. The dwarf. *C. S., G. i. S.*

CHORLEY. Mr. *M. P., A. P.*

CHOWLEY. *See* Mac Stinger, Charles.

CHOWSER. Colonel, Guest of Ralph Nickleby. *N. N.* xix.

CHRIST. *M. P., M. M.*

CHRISTCHURCH, Oxford. Library of. *M. P., T. O. H.*

CHRISTIAN. Fletcher.
R. P., L. P. V.
One of the officers of the "*Bounty.*"

CHRISTIAN. Thursday October.
R. P., T. L. V.
Son of Fletcher Christian by a savage mother.

CHRISTIANA. One-time sweetheart of Mr. Michael.
R. P., P. R. S.

CHRISTIANA. Widowed mother of.
R. P., P. R. S.

CHRISTINA. *Donna, Only* daughter of Don Bolaro Fizzgig. *P. P.* ii.
Note.—One of Jingle's imaginary conquests.

CHRISTMAS FAMILY-PARTY.
Grandmama at. *S. B. B.*, Char. vii.

CHRISTMAS. Rev. Henry.
M. P., I. M.

"CHRISTMAS PAST." First spirit.
C. B., C. C., S. ii.

CHRISTOPHER. A waiter.
C. S., S. L. i.

"CHRISTOPHER HARDMAN'S MEN." *M. P., O. S.*

CHRISTOPHER-WREN CHURCH.
C. S., N. T., Act i.

"CHRONICLE." *N. N.* iv.

CHRONICLE. The gentlemanly, writer of a letter to Master Humphrey. *M. H. C.* i.

CHRONOLOGY. Precincts of.
M. P., L. W. O. Y.

CHUCKSTER. Mr., Clerk to Mr. Witherden. *O. C. S.* xiv.
Note.—Mr. Chuckster was Mr. Witherden's clerk, a friend of Dick Swiveller, and, in his own way, Kit's enemy. When Kit's name was cleared, Mr. Chuckster thought him rather worse than before because his guilt would have shown his spirit. Chuckster leaves the story as the occasional visitor of Dick and the Marchioness.

CHUFFEY. Anthony Chuzzlewit & Son's clerk. *M. C.* xi.
A little blear-eyed, weazen-faced, ancient man. He was of a remote fashion, and dusty like the rest of the furniture ; he was dressed in a decayed suit of black ; with breeches garnished at the knees with rusty wisps of ribbon, the very paupers of shoe-strings ; on the lower portion of his spindle legs were dingy worsted stockings of the same colour.—He looked as if he had been put away and forgotten half a century before, and somebody had just found him in a lumber-closet.
Note.—The old clerk of Anthony Chuzzlewit is so wrapped up in his

master that he seems dead to the rest of the world. He is rather badly treated by Jonas, and, as a result, always distrusts his master's son.

CHUMBLEDON SQUARE.
R. P., O. V.

CHURCH. *R. P., C. D. of S.*
Original: Supposed to be the Parish Church of Chatham.

CHURCH. The. *B. R.* i.

CHURCH. An old city. *U. T.* ix.
Christening would seem to have faded out of this church long ago, for the font has the dust of desuetude thick upon it, and its wooden cover (shaped like an old-fashioned tureen cover) looks as if it wouldn't come off, upon requirement. The altar—rickety and the Commandments damp.

CHURCH. In which Wemmick and Miss Staffins were married. *G.E.* lv.
Original: Possibly Emanuel Church, Camberwell.

CHURCH. Anglo-Norman style.
D. and S. xli.
They've spoilt it with whitewash.

CHURCH. Belonging to Foundling Hospital. *L. D.* ii.
I saw all those children ranged tier above tier, and appealing from the Father none of them had known on earth, to the Father of us all in heaven.

CHURCH. Down in Devonshire.
D. C. xxvii.

CHURCH. In which Paul Dombey was christened. *M. C.* v.
Original: Suggested by one writer as Marylebone Church.

CHURCH. Little, In the park.
B. H. xviii.

CHURCH. Near Rood Lane.
U. T. ix.
There was often a subtle flavour of wine.

CHURCH. New, In Coketown.
H. T., s. v.
A stuccoed edifice with a square steeple over the door, terminating in four short pinnacles like florid wooden legs.

CHURCH. New, Saint Pancras.
S. B. B., Tales i.

CHURCH. One obscure, In the heart of City. *U. T.* ix.
Which had broken out in the melodramatic style, and was got up with various tawdry decorations, much after the manner of the extinct London maypoles.

CHURCH. Where Bella Wilfer and Rokesmith were married.
O. M. F. liv.
Original: Said to have been the Church of St. Alphege, Greenwich.

CHURCH. Where Little Nell was buried. *O. C. S.* lxxii.
Original: Tong Church, dedicated to St. Mary the Virgin and St. Bartholomew.

CHURCH. Where Walter and Florence were married. *D. and S.* lvi.
A mouldy old church in a yard, hemmed in by a labyrinth of back streets and courts, with a little burying-ground round it, and itself buried in a kind of vault, formed by the neighbouring houses, and paved with echoing stones. It was a great, dim, shabby pile, with high old oaken pews, among which about a score of people lost themselves every Sunday.

CHURCH IN THE MARSHES. Pip's village. *G. E.* i.
Original: The church is a composite picture of several churches in the neighbourhood of Cooling, Kent, including that of Higham.

CHURCH OF ENGLAND MISSIONARY SOCIETY. *M. P., N. E.*

CHURCH STREET. *O. M. F.* xviii.

CHURCHES. City of London.
U. T. x.

CHURCHWARDEN. The Senior.
S. B. B., O. P. i.

CHURCHWARDENS. The.
S. B. B., O. P. i.

CHURCHYARD. P. P. xxi.
Beneath a plain gravestone, in one of the most peaceful and secluded churchyards in Kent, where wild-flowers mingle with the grass, and the soft landscape around forms the fairest spot in the garden of England.
Original: There is little doubt that the churchyard here referred to is that of Shorne, about two miles from Gravesend, where Dickens himself wished to be buried.

CHURCHYARD. G. E. i.
Bleak place, overgrown with nettles.
Original : Cooling Churchyard, Kent, where the curious stone lozenges are to be found, although not in the same numbers.

CHURCHYARD. A., O. M. F. xxxii.
A paved square court, with a raised bank of earth about breast-high in the middle, enclosed by iron rails.

CHURCHYARD. A hemmed-in.
B. H. xi.
Whence malignant diseases are communicated to the bodies of our dear brothers and sisters who have not departed.
Original : " On the left-hand side as you go down Russell Court from Catherine Street to Drury Lane."

CHURCHYARD. Approach to a City. U. T. xxi.
A dairy exhibiting in its modest window one very little milk-can and three eggs, would suggest to me the certainty of finding the poultry, hard by, pecking at my forefathers.

CHURCHYARD. In Bedfordshire.
L. D. xxv.

CHURCHYARD. Of a City church.
U. T. ix.
Like the great, shabby, old mignonette box, with two trees in it and one tomb.

CHURCHYARD. Phantom.
C. B., C. C., s. iv.

CHURCHYARDS. City, U. T. xxi.
Sometimes so entirely detached from churches, always so pressed upon by houses ; so small, so rank, so silent, so forgotten, except by the few people who ever look down on them from their smoky windows.

CHURCHYARDS. City, Visitors to.
U. T. xxi.
Blinking old men, let out of workhouses—have a tendency to sit on bits of coping stone—with both hands on their sticks, and asthmatically gasping. The more depressed class of beggars, too, bring hither broken meats, and munch.

CHUZZLEWIT. M. P., T. O. P.

CHUZZLEWIT. A certain male Chuzzlewit. M. C. i.
Whose birth must be admitted to be involved in some obscurity, was of very mean and low descent.

CHUZZLEWIT. A, In the Gunpowder Plot. M. C. i.

CHUZZLEWIT. Anthony, M. C. iv.
The face of the old man was so sharpened by the wariness and cunning of his life, that it seemed to cut him a passage through the crowded room, as he edged away behind the remotest chairs.
Note.—Old Anthony was brother to the elder Martin, and father of Jonas Chuzzlewit. He was cunning, and to some extent unscrupulous. This is reflected in his son, who makes an unsuccessful attempt to poison his father. Old Anthony, however, soon dies.

CHUZZLEWIT. Diggory, *M. C.* i.

Making constant reference to an uncle, in respect of whom he would seem to have entertained great expectations, as he was in the habit of seeking to propitiate his favour by presents of plate, jewels, books, watches, and other valuable articles.

CHUZZLEWIT FAMILY. *M. C.* i.

Undoubtedly descended in a direct line from Adam and Eve.

CHUZZLEWIT. George, A gay bachelor cousin of Mr. Martin Chuzzlewit. *M. C.* iv.

Who claimed to be young, but had been younger, and was inclined to corpulency, and rather overfed himself : to that extent, indeed, that his eyes were strained in their sockets, as if with constant surprise ; and he had such an obvious disposition to pimples, that the bright spots on his cravat, the rich pattern on his waistcoat, and even his glittering trinkets, seemed to have broken out upon him.

CHUZZLEWIT. Jonas, Son of Anthony Chuzzlewit. *M. C.* iv.

Had so profited by the precept and example of his father, that he looked a year or two the elder of the twain, as they stood winking their red eyes, side by side.

Note.—Young Jonas has inherited his father's cunning without his knowledge. He is cruel and miserly. He makes an attempt to poison his father, old Anthony, and as his intended victim soon dies, he believes he has succeeded. With the object of removing traces of the crime he takes precautions. But the secret is known to old Chuffey. He marries " Merry " Pecksniff, and carrying out his intention, he breaks her spirit with harshness and cruelty. Still under the impression that his plot to murder his father succeeded, he believes himself in the power of Montague of the Anglo-Bengalee. Acting under this influence, he pays a good amount of his

Owing to the influence of his grandfather, however, Pecksniff turns him out. He then emigrates to America with Mark Tapley. Their ideas regarding the new continent are scarcely realized. Their money is invested in land in the City of Eden, which is described in glowing terms by the agent. They discover it to be a dismal swamp, fever infected; without drainage, clearings, or houses. Martin is attacked by the prevalent fever, and is only saved by the attentions of Mark Tapley, who, in turn, is stricken down. They leave Eden, and with the assistance of Mr. Beavan return to England. Martin goes back to Peckmiff's to acknowledge his error to his grandfather, but is turned from the door. He returns to London, and eventually finds that his grandfather has been proving Pecksniff's intentions. After the denunciation of the hypocritical architect, Martin finds himself reinstated in his uncle's affections, and marries Mary Graham.

CHUZZLEWIT. Mrs. Ned, Widow of a deceased brother of Mr. Martin Chuzzlewit. *M. C.* iv.
Having a dreary face, and a bony figure and a masculine voice, was, in right of these qualities, what is commonly called a strongminded woman.

CHUZZLEWIT. One. *M. C.* i.
Came over with William the Conqueror.

CHUZZLEWIT. Toby, Son of a certain Male Chuzzlewit. *M. C.* i.
Upon his deathbed this question was put to him, in a distinct, solemn, and formal way: "Toby Chuzzlewit, who was your grandfather?" to which he replied— and his words were taken down— the Lord No. Zoo.

CHUZZLEWIT AND CO. Martin Chuzzlewit and Mark Tapley. *M. C.* xxiii.

CHUZZLEWIT AND SON. The firm of Anthony, *M. C.* xi. Manchester Warehousemen.

CHUZZLEWIT AND SON. Place of business of Anthony, *M. C.* xi.
In a very narrow street behind the Post Office. A dim, dirty, smoky, tumbledown, rotten old house it was, as any one would desire to see, but there the firm —transacted all their business and their pleasure too, such as it was; for neither the young man nor the old had any other residence, or any care or thought beyond its narrow limits.

CHUZZLEWITS. Many. *M. C.* i.
Being unsuccessful in other pursuits,have, without the smallest rational hope of enriching themselves, or any conceivable reason, set up as coal merchants.

CICERO. Negro Emancipated Slave. *M. C.* xvii.
Bought his freedom, which he got pretty cheap at last, on account of his strength being nearly gone, and he being ill.

CICERONE. *P. F. I., P. M. B.*

CIGAR SHOP. A West End. *S. B. B.*, Scenes iii.

CINCINNATI. *A. N.* x.; *M. P., E. T.; M. P., S. B.*

CINDERELLA. *M. P., F. F.*

CIRCUMLOCUTION OFFICE. *L. D.* ix.; *M. P., M. in E. R.*

The Most Important Department under Government . . . no public business of any kind could possibly be done at any time without the acquiescence of the Circumlocution Office.—Whatever was required to be done, the Circumlocution Office was beforehand with all the public departments in the art of perceiving—*How Not to Do It.*

CIRCUMLOCUTION OFFICE. Pagoda Department of. *U. T.* viii.

CIRCUMLOCUTION SAGES.
L. D. x.

CIRCUS OF ROMULUS. *P. F. I., R.*

CIRENCESTER. *M. P., E. S.*

CITIZEN. A substantial.
M. H. C., i.

CITY. (London). *C. S., M. L. L.*
i.; *C. S., S. L.* iv.; *G. E.* xxiv.;
M. C. viii.; *M. H. C.* i.; *N. N.*
xi.; *O. M. F.* xxxiv.; *P. P.*
xxxii.; *R. P., A. F.*; *R. P.,*
B. S.; *S. B. B.,* Scenes i.;
S. B. B., Scenes xvii.

CITY CHURCHYARD. Another.
U. T. xxi.
In another City Churchyard of
—cramped dimensions, I saw—
two comfortable Charity children.

CITY CLERK. Occupant of house
next door, without the knocker.
S. B. B., O. P. vii.

CITY COUNTING HOUSES. Youths
from, *S. B. B.,* Scenes xiii.

CITY OF THE ABSENT. *U. T.* xxi.

CITY SQUARE. *N. N.* xxxvii.

CIVITA VECCHIA.
L. D. liv.; *R. P., P. M. T. P.*

CLAPHAM. *M. P., N. Y. D., M. P. I.*

CLAPHAM GREEN. *P. P.* xxxv.

CLAPHAM ROAD. *R. P., P. R. S.*

CLAPPERTON. *M. P., N. E.*

CLAPTON. *S. B. B.,* Scenes ix.

CLARA. Secretly engaged to Herbert Pocket. *G. E.* xxx.

CLARE. *R. P., T. D. P.*

CLARE. Miss Ada, Ward in Chancery. *B. H.* iii.
A beautiful girl, with such rich
golden hair, such soft blue eyes,
and such a bright, innocent, trusting face—about seventeen.

Note.—A ward of Mr. Jarndyce.
She is troubled about her cousin
Richard Carstone on account of his
shiftlessness and his absorption in the
chancery suit. But in spite of her
entreaties he is unable to alter what is
really his nature, and in spite of her
knowledge of his temperament, Ada
marries him, but is early left a widow.
Unlike Richard, she continues her trust
in their guardian, and is a close friend
of Esther Summerson.

CLARE MARKET. *B. R.* lvi.
P. P. xx.; *R. P., L. A.*; *R. P.,*
M. F. F.; *S. B. B.,* Scenes xxii.

CLARENCE DOCK. *R. P., B.*

CLARENDON. *M. P., L. T.*

CLARIONET. The, One of the
Waits. *C. S.*; *S. P. T.* iii.

CLARISSA. The other Miss Spenlow. *D. C.* xli.

CLARK. *Betsy.* Servant next
door. *S. B. B.* Scenes i.

CLARK. Mr., Employed by Dombey and Son. *D. and S.* vi.
Looking at the neighbouring
masts and boats, a stout man
stood whistling, with his pen behind his ear, and his hands in his
pockets, as if his day's work were
nearly done.

CLARK. Mrs. *N. N.* xvi.

CLARK'S CIRCUS. *M. P., J. G.*
The illegitimate drama.

CLARKE. Maria. *M. P., F. S.*

CLARKE. Mr., Mrs. Weller's first
husband. *P. P.* xxvii.
Relict and sole executrix of
the dead and gone Mr. Clarke. *See*
Weller, Mrs.

CLARKE. Mr. Samuel, of *Beaver*-
ton, *Boone* Co., U.S.
M. P., S. F. A.

CLARKE COUNTY. (Mo).
A. N. xviii.

CLARKINS. Mr., " Old."
M. P., W. R.

CLARKINS. Mrs.   *M. P., W. R.*

CLARKINS. Mrs. " Young."
                  M. P., W. R.

CLARKSON. Mr.   *M. P., V. D.*

CLARKSON. Mr., A Solicitor.
                  R. P., T. D. P.

CLARRIKER AND CO. House of.
                  G. E. xxxvii.

I must not leave it to be supposed that we were ever a great house. We were not in a grand way of business, but we had a good name.

CLATTER. A physician.
                  R. P., O. B.

CLAXTON. Mr. Marshall. *M. P., C.*

CLAY. Mr.   *M. P., I. C.*

CLAYPOLE. Noah, A Charity boy.
                  O. T. v.

A large-headed, small-eyed youth, of lumbering make, and heavy countenance—a red nose, and yellow smalls.—Mother a washerwoman and father a drunken soldier.

Note.—Noah Claypole is the elder apprentice at Sowerby's the undertaker, who relieves the workhouse of Oliver Twist. He robs his master and makes for London. Here he becomes one of Fagin's dupes. He is set to watch Nancy, and it is through him that her friendship for Oliver is discovered, and she suffers death at the hands of Sikes. On the break-up of the thieves' school he turns Queen's evidence, and from that he becomes an informer.

CLEAR. Cape.   *A. N.* xvi.

CLEAVER. Fanny, *Dolls' Dress-maker.*   *O. M. F.* xviii.

A child—a dwarf—a girl—a something—sitting on a little low old-fashioned armchair, which had a kind of little working bench before it. . . .

" I can't get up " " because my back's bad, and my legs are queer." A queer, but not ugly face,—bright grey eyes.

Note.—" Jenny Wren " was Lizzie Hexam's "landlady" after the death of the latter's father. The deformed dolls' dressmaker was greatly exercised by her " bad child,"—her drunken, dissolute father. She is a friend to Lizzie Hexam. Her bad child dies in the street. She is called to Eugene Wrayburn's bedside, where she guesses the magic word. The last seen of her is where she is receiving a visit from Sloppy, and the inference is that Sloppy *is* " he " who was expected.

CLEAVER. Mr.   *O. M. F.* xviii.

Note.—Mr. Dolls was Jenny Wren's " bad child," but her father. He was in a chronic state of drunkenness through multitudinous threepennyworth's o' rum. He betrays his trust for the same fiery liquor and meets his death through his debauchery. Jenny finds him on a police stretcher in the street, but when he is conveyed to the nearest " doctor's shop " it is found that he is dead.

CLEEFEWAY. Ratcliffe Highway.
                  R. P., O. F. W.

CLEM. Little, *Daughter* of Mr. and Mrs. Britain.
                  C. B., B. O. L. iii.

CLEM.   *G. E.* xii.

Note.—Pip's song is from the song of the blacksmiths of Chatham which was sung on St. Clement's Day.

CLEM. Poor. *See* Clemency.

CLEMENCY. Maidservant of Dr. Jeddler.   *C. B., B. o. L.* i.

About thirty years old, had a plump and cheerful face—twisted up into an odd expression of tightness that made it comical. Her dress was a prodigious pair of self-willed shoes—blue stockings; a printed gown of many colours, and the most hideous pattern procurable for money, and a white apron—She always wore short sleeves.—In general a little cap placed somewhere on her head.

CLEMENT'S DANES.
                  C. S., M. L., Leg. i.

CLEMMY. *See* Clemency.

CLENNAM. Arthur. *L. D.* ii.

A grave, dark man of forty. The brown, grave gentleman who smiled so pleasantly, who was so frank and considerate in his manner.

Note.—One of the chief characters of the story. He is first seen on his return from China, where he has been assisting his father in business. His supposed mother, however, shows no great love for him. At his mother's house, he meets Little Dorrit, whom he befriends and assists. He enters into partnership with Doyce, but he is unfortunate and is thrown into the Marshalsea for debt. While there Little Dorrit tends him, and she having lost her money, they are married. Doyce sets the business on its legs again, and Clennam takes up his old position. It transpires that Arthur was the son of Mr. Clennam, but by another woman before he married : thus explaining Mrs. Clennam's coldness to him and want of interest.

CLENNAM. Arthur's father's Uncle Gilbert. *L. D.* xv.

CLENNAM. Mr., Arthur's father. *L. D.* iii.

Your ascendency over him was the cause of his going to China to take care of the business there.

CLENNAM. Mrs., Widowed stepmother of Arthur. *L. D.* iii.

On a black bier-like sofa—propped up behind with one great angular black bolster, like the block at a state execution in the good old times, sat his mother in a widow's dress—cold grey eyes, and her cold grey hair, and her immovable face, as stiff as the folds of her stony head-dress.—On her little table lay two or three books, her handkerchief, a pair of steel spectacles—and an old-fashioned watch in a heavy double case.

Note.—When she is introduced to the reader she is a crippled invalid, although her business capacity is unimpaired and she continues to manage the English affairs of the firm. She is supposed to be the mother of Arthur Clennam, but it transpires that she is only the wife of his father. She has suppressed a will by which Little Dorrit would have benefited. Rigaud or Blandois discovers it and endeavours to blackmail her. But she appeals to Little Dorrit, who not only forgives her, but accedes to her request to keep the information from Arthur until she shall be dead.

CLENNAM'S HOUSE. Mrs. *L. D.* iii.

An old brick house, so dingy as to be all but black, standing by itself within a gateway. Before it, a square courtyard where a shrub or two or a patch of grass were as rank (which is saying much) as the iron railings enclosing them were rusty ; behind it, a jumble of roots. It was a double house, with long, narrow, heavily-framed windows.—It had been propped up, and was leaning on some half-dozen gigantic crutches.

CLENNAM. Parents of Mr. *L. D.* ii.

I am the only son of a hard father and mother—parents who weighed, measured, and priced everything ; for whom what could not be weighed, measured, and priced, had no existence.

CLENNAMS. Of Cornwall. *L. D.* xiii.

CLEOPATRA. Mrs. Skewton. *D. and S.* xxi.

CLERGYMAN. *C. B., C. C.*, s. i.

CLERGYMAN. Attending deathbed of Nicholas Nickleby, Sr. *N. N.* i.

" It is very sinful to rebel."

CLERGYMAN. *Benevolent old. P. P.* xxviii

Guest at wedding of *Bella* and Trundle.

Note.—As the " Ivy Green " was not originally written for " Pickwick," it is possible that the Clergyman was not intended as a character; this would no doubt account for the very small place he occupies in the story •

CLERGYMAN. Officiating.
S. B. B., O. P. i.

CLERGYMAN. Who christened Paul *Dombey.* *D. and S.* v.
An amiable and mild-looking young curate, but obviously afraid of the baby—like the principal character in a ghost story " a tall figure all in white "—at sight of whom Paul rent the air with his cries.

CLERICAL GENTLEMAN. Chaplain. Prisoner in the Fleet. *P. P.* xlii.
Who fastened his coat all the way up to his chin by means of a pin and a button alternately had a very coarse red face, and looked like a drunken chaplain : which, indeed, he was.

CLERK. *C. B., C. C.,* s. i.

CLERK. A. *P. P.* xl.
In spectacles, standing on a box behind a wooden bar at another end of the room, who was "taking the affidavits," large batches of which were, from time to time, carried into the private room, for the judge's signature.

CLERK. Angular, Mr. Grewgious. *E. D.* ix.

CLERK. Attorney's, In *Doctors'* Commons. *S. B. B.,* Scenes viii.

CLERK. Common law. *P. P.* xl.
With a bass voice.

CLERK. Copying, in " Six Clerks' Office." *B. H.* i.

CLERK. Early. *S. B. B.,* Scenes i.

CLERK. In a Government Office. *P. P.* xliv.
A very pleasant gen'l'm'n too—

one o' the precise and tidy sort, as puts their feet in little india-rubber fire-buckets wen it's wet weather—he saved up his money on principle, wore a clean shirt every day on principle; never spoke to none of his relations on principle, " fear they shou'd want to borrow money of him "—dined every day at the same place.

CLERK. In church where Paul was christened. *D. and S.* v.
The only cheerful-looking object there, and *he* was an undertaker.

CLERK. Of church where Walter and Florence are married. *D. and S.* lvii.
A dusty old clerk, who keeps a sort of evaporated news-shop underneath an archway opposite.

CLERK. Of Mr. Jaggers'. *G. E.* xxiv.
A high-shouldered man with a face-ache tied up in dirty flannel, who was dressed in old black clothes that bore the appearance of having been waxed.

CLERK. Of Mr. Jaggers'. *G. E.* xxiv.
A little flabby terrier of a clerk with dangling hair.

CLERK. Of Mr. Jaggers'. *G. E.* xxiv.
Looked something between a publican and a rat-catcher.

CLERK. Of hotel in *Brook* Street. *L. D.* lii.

CLERK. Of the Patents. *R. P., P. M. T. P.*

CLERK. Office of the Judges. *P. P.* xl.
A room of specially dirty appearance, with a very low ceiling and old panelled walls.

CLERK. Parish. *M. H. C.* i.

CLERK. Postal, On Railway Train.
U. T. xiii.

CLERK. Superannuated Bank, friend of Tim Linkinwater.
N. N. xxxvii.

CLERKENWELL. *B. H.* xxvi. ;
B. R. iv. ; *M. P., M. P.* ; *O. M. F.*
vii. ; *O. T.* x. ; *T. T. C.* bk. ii.,
ch. vi.
Although there were busy trades
—and working jewellers by scores,
it was a purer place, with farm-
houses nearer to it than many
modern Londoners would readily
believe, and lovers' walks at no
great distance, which turned into
squalid courts.

CLERKENWELL. House in a street
in. *B. R.* iv.
A modest building, not over-
newly fashioned, not very straight,
not large, not tall ; not bold-
faced, with great staring windows,
but a shy, blinking house, with a
conical roof going up into a peak
over its garret window of four
small panes of glass.

CLERKENWELL. New jail at.
B. R. lxvi.

CLERKENWELL GREEN. *U. T.* x.

CLERKENWELL SESSIONS.
O. T. xvii.

CLERKS. Articled. *B. H.* i.

CLERKS. At Gray's Inn Square.
P. P. liii.

CLERKS. In Mr. *Dombey's Office.*
D. and S. xiii.
Not a whit behindhand in their
demonstrations of respect. The
wit of the counting-house became
in a moment as mute as the row
of leather fire-buckets hanging up
behind.

CLERKS. Managing. *P. P.* xl.

CLERKS. Two spare, in a Bank in
Venice. *L. D.* xlii.
Like dried dragoons, in green
velvet caps adorned with golden
tassels.

CLEVELAND. *A. N.* xiv.

CLEVERLY. Susannah, Emigrant.
U. T. xx.

CLEVERLY. William, Emigrant.
U. T. xx.

CLICK. Mr., A Lodger.
C. S., S. L. iii.
The rest of the house generally
give him his name, as being first,
front, carpeted all over, his own
furniture, and if not mahogany, an
out-and-out imitation.

CLICK. Mister, A Pickpocket.
R. P., D. W. I. F.

CLICKITS. *S. Y. C.*

CLICKITT. The youngest Miss, but
one. *M. P., N. Y. D.*

CLIFFORD'S INN. *B. H.* xxxiv. ;
L. D. vii. ; *O. M. F.* viii. ; *P. P.*
xxi.

CLIFFORD'S INN. Plantation in.
O. M. F. viii.
Mouldy little plantation, or cat
preserve—sparrows were there,
cats were there, dry rot and wet
rot were there.

CLIFFORD STREET. *U. T.* xvi.

CLIFTON. *P. P.* xxxviii.

CLIP. Mr. *Mr. R. B.*

CLISSOLD. Lawrence, A Clerk.
C. S., M ʃ. T. S. v.

CLIVE. Mr., Clerk in another Department of Circumlocution Office.
L. D. x.

CLOCK ROOM. In haunted house.
C. S., H. H.

CLOCK TOWER. Of Royal Exchange. *C. S., W. O. G. M.*

CLOCKER. Mr., A Grocer.
R. P., O. O. S.

CLOISTERHAM. *E. D.* iii.
An ancient city,—and no meet dwelling-place for any one with hankerings after the noisy world, deriving an earthy flavour throughout from its cathedral crypt. The streets are little more than one narrow street.
Original: Rochester.

CLOISTERHAM. Mayor of. *See* Sapsea, Mr. *E. D.* xii.

CLOISTERHAM JAIL. *E. D.* v.

CLOISTERHAM WEIR. *E. D.* vi.
Original : There is no great certainty about this, but it is generally agreed that of the weirs which Dickens might have had in view, Snodland is the most likely. The others are Allington and Farleigh.

CLOSE. The. *E. D.* ii.

CLOWN. At Astley's.
S. B. B., Scenes xi.

CLOWN. On stage in *Britannia.*
U. T. iv.

CLOWNS. Four, in Booth at Greenwich Fair. *S. B. B.*, Scenes xii.
In Roman dresses, with their yellow legs and arms, long black curly heads, bushy eyebrows, and scowl expressive of assassination, and vengeance, and everything else that is grand and solemn.

CLOWNS. Two, May Day dancers.
S. B. B., Scenes xx.
Walked on their hands in the mud.

CLUB. Allotment. *M. P., P. M. B.*

CLUB HOUSE. The Strangers'.
N. N. l.

CLUBBER. Sir Thomas, Head of the *Dockyard.* *P. P.* ii.
Tall gentleman in blue coat and bright buttons.
Note.—Present at Charity Ball, Rochester.

CLUBBER. Lady, Wife of Sir Thomas Clubber. *P. P.* ii.
Large lady in blue satin.
Note.—Present at Charity Ball, Rochester.

CLUBBERS. The Miss, Daughters of Sir Thomas Clubber.
P. P. ii.
Two large young ladies in fashionably made dresses of blue satin.
Note.—Present at Charity Ball, Rochester.

CLUBMEN. *M. P., P. M. B.*

CLUBMEN. Of St. James's Street.
M. P., P. M. B.

CLUPPINS. Mrs., Particular acquaintance of Mrs. Bardell.
P. P. xxvi.
A little brisk, busy-looking woman.

CLY. Roger, Servant to Charles Darnay.
T. T. C., Book ii. ; Chap. iii.
Police spy and witness against Darnay at the Old Bailey.
Note.—Spy. Partner with "Barsad" in the accusation against Darnay and other evil plots. Occupies the position of servant to Darnay. According to the "prophetic vision" he suffered death by the guillotine.

CLYDE. The Banks of the.
L. D. xvi.

COACH AND HORSES. The.
O. T. xxi.
Original : Of the same name close to the entrance to Sion Park, "where Brentford ends and Isleworth begins."

COACH OFFICE. *D. C.* xvii.

COACH-OFFICE. All alive.
S. B. B., Scenes i.
Surrounded by the usual crowd of Jews and Nondescripts.

COACH OFFICE. Booking clerks of. *S. B. B.*, Scenes xv.
One with a pen behind his ears, and his hands behind him, is standing in front of the fire, like a full-length portrait of Napoleon.

COACH OFFICE. *Booking* office of. *S. B. B.*, Scenes xv.

COACH OFFICE. Porters of.
S. B. B., Scenes xv.
Stowing the luggage away, and running up the steps of the booking-office, and down the steps of the booking-office, with breathless rapidity.

COACH STANDS. *S. B. B.*, Scenes i.

COACHING HOUSE. *U. T.* xxii.

COACHMAKER. A. *U. T.* xxii.
A dry man, grizzled, and far advanced in years, but tall and upright, who,—pushed up his spectacles against his brown paper cap.

COACHMAKER. Gallant.
B. R. xxxi.
Vowed that Mrs. Varden held him bound in adamantine chains.

COACHMAKER. Mother of gallant.
B. R. xxxi.

COACHMAKER. The. *G. E.* viii.

COACHMAN. *D. C.* xix.

COACHMAN. *P. P.* xxxvii.
In an embroidered coat reaching down to his heels, and a waistcoat of the same.

COACHMAN. First. *P. P.* lv.
Mottle-faced man.

COACHMAN. Of coach. *N. N.* v.

COACHMAN. Of coach to Yorkshire.
C. S., *H. T.*

COACHMAN. Of doctor attending on Jinkinson. *M. H. C.* v.

COACHMAN. Of hackney-coach.
M. C. xxviii.

COACHMAN. Of hackney-coach.
S. B. B., Scenes vii.
In his wooden-soled shoes.

COACHMAN. Of stage-coach.
S. B. B., Scenes xvi.

COACHMAN. On box of coach.
M. C. xi.

COACHMAN. Requested to find Staggs's Gardens. *D. and S.* xv.

COACHMAN. Second. *P. P.* lv.

COACHMAN. Third. *P. P.* lv.
A hoarse gentleman.

COALHEAVER. Visiting hairdresser's. *N. N.* lii.
Big, burly, good-humoured, with a pipe in his mouth,—requested to know when a shaver would be disengaged.

COAL PORTER. Out of work.
U. T. xxx.

COAL-PORTERS. At Ratcliff.
U. T. xxx.
Occupants of one room.

COAN. Mrs., Medium.
M. P., *S. F. A.*

COASTGUARD. *U. T.* ii.

COAVINSES' A 'ouse. *B. H.* vi.

COAVINSES' OFFICE. Boy in.
B. H. xiv.
A very hideous boy.

COAVINSES. *See* Neckett, Mr.

COBB TOM. General Chandler and Post Office Keeper. *B. R.* i.
Beyond all question—the dullest dog of the party.

COBBEY. Pupil at Dotheboys' Hall. *N. N.* viii.
Cobbey's grandmother is dead, and his Uncle John has took to drinking, which is all the news his sister sends, except eighteen-pence, which will just pay for that broken square of glass.

COBBLER. *M. P., T. O. H.*

COBBLER. Prisoner in the Fleet. *P. P.* xliv.
Who rented a small slip-room in one of the upper galleries—bald-headed. He was a sallow man—all cobblers are—and had a strong bristly beard—all cobblers have. His face was a queer, good-tempered piece of workmanship.

"COBBLER DICK." *M. P., O. S·*

COBBLER'S WIFE. *Deceased.* *P. P.* xliv.

COBBS. *M. P. T. T.*

COBBS. The *Boots* at the "Holly Tree Inn." *C. S., H. T.* v.
Formerly under-gardener to Mr. Walmer. A mowing and sweeping, and weeding and pruning and this and that.

COBBY. The Giant. *U. T.* xi.

COBDEN. Richard. *M. P., Ag. Int.*

COBHAM CHURCHYARD. *P. P.* xi.

COBHAM HALL.
P. P. xi., *C. S., S. P. T.* iii.
An ancient hall, displaying the quaint and picturesque architecture of Elizabeth's time.

COBHAM VILLAGE. *P. P.* xi.
Really, for a misanthrope's choice, this is one of the prettiest and most desirable places of residence I ever met with.

COBHAM WOODS.
C. S.; S. P. T. iii.

COBURG. *A. N.* xv.

"COBURG, THE." *N. N.* xxx.

COBURG DOCK. At Liverpool. *A. N.* i.

COBWEB. Esther Summerson. *B. H.* viii.

COCKER. Mr. Indignation, guest at Temeraire. *U. T.* xxxii.

COCKSPUR STREET. Charing Cross. *M. P., T. D.*

COCKSWAIN. The, of boating party. *S. B. B.,* Scenes x.

COE. Mrs., As Susan. *M. P., M. N. D.*

CODGER. Miss, Literary lady. *M. C.* xxxiv.
Sticking on the forehead—by invisible means, was a massive cameo, in size and shape like the raspberry tart which is ordinarily sold for a penny, representing on its front the Capitol at Washington.

CODGERS. *M. P., N. G. K.*

CODGERS. Mr. *L. T.*

CODLIN. Thomas, "Punch" showman. *O. C. S.* xvi.
Had a surly, grumbling manner, and an air of always counting up what money they hadn't made.

Note.—One of the two men with the Punch, Little Nell and her grandfather meet with early in their travels. The showmen had the idea that there was something to be made out of the two wanderers, and the one endeavoured to influence Nell at the other's expense. Hence arose the saying "Codlin's the friend, not Short."

Original : Tom Willis, a showman.

COFFEE-HOUSE. In Covent Garden. *B. R.* xxviii.
Original : Probably Tom's, 17, Russell Street. Although Cutriss's is generally accepted as the prototype of the "noted coffee-house."

COFFEE-HOUSE. Serjeant's Inn.
P. P. xliii.

COFFEE-ROOM FLIGHT. Stairs
in the Fleet.   P. P. xli.
These staircases received light
from sundry windows placed at
some little distance above the
floor, and looking into a gravelled
area bounded by a high brick wall,
with iron *chevaux-de-fris* at the
top.

COFFEE-SHOP. Theatrical.
S. B. B., Scenes xiii.

COFFIN. The, The Argonaut.
U. T. xv.

COFFIN LANE. Which led to the
churchyard.   P. P. xxix.
Into which the townspeople did
not much care to go, except in
broad daylight.

COGSFORD. Of Cogsford *Brothers*
and Cogsford.   M. P., S. R.

COGSHALL.   M. P., S. B.

COILER. Mrs., A widow.
G. E. xxiii.
Of that highly sympathetic
nature that she agreed with everybody, blessed everybody, and shed
tears on everybody, according to
circumstances.

COINER. A, Prisoner in Newgate.
G. E. xxxii.
In a well-worn olive-coloured
frock-coat, with a peculiar pallor
overspreading the red in his complexion—his hat, which had a
greasy and fatty surface like cold
broth.

COKE. Caleb, of Wolverhampton.
M. P., R. S.

COKETOWN.   H. T., s. iv.
A town of red brick, or of brick
that would have been red if the
smoke and ashes had allowed it.
A town of machinery and tall
chimneys. It had a black canal
in it, and a river that ran purple
with ill-smelling dye. It contained several large streets, all very
like one another.
*Original : A composite picture,
but generally agreed to represent
Manchester.*

COLDVEAL. Lady. M. P., T. T.

COLE. King, " The venerable "
illustrious potentate. P. P. xxxvi.

COLEMAN STREET. P. P. xl. ; and
S. B. B., Char. v.

COLERIDGE. Mr. Justice.
M. P., C. P.

COLES. Mrs., Wife of Mr. Coles.
U. T. xii.

COLES. Rev. T. S.   M. P., E. C.

COLES'S. Coles's School. U. T. xii.

COLESHAW.   Miss, Passenger on
board " Golden Mary."
C. S., W. o. G. M.
A sedate young woman in black,
about thirty I should say, who
was going out to join a brother.

COLISEUM. At Rome.
P. F. I., R. ; R. P., L. A.

COLLAN. *See Bailey, Benjamin.*
M. C. ix.

COLLEGE. The.   M. C. xxvii.

COLLEGE. The.   P. P. xliv.

COLLEGE. Lilliputian (Miss Pupford's).   C. S., T. T. G. vi.

COLLEGE. Of Upper Canada,
Toronto.   A. N. xv.

COLLEGE GREEN.
S. B. B., Tales i.

COLLEGE HILL. Mark Lane.
U. T. xxi.

COLLEGE YARD. The aristocratic,
or pump side.   L. D. xix.

COLLEGE YARD. The poor side. *L. D.* xix.

COLLEGIAN. The. *L. D.* xix.
In the seaside slippers, who had no shoes.

COLLEGIAN. The. *L. D.* xix.
In the dressing-gown, who had no coat.

COLLEGIAN. The poor lean clerk. *L. D.* xix.
In buttonless black, who had no hopes.

COLLEGIAN. The stout greengrocer. *L. D.* xix.
In the corduroy knee-breeches, who had no cares.

COLLIERS. Heavy old, at Chatham. *U. T.* xxiv.

COLLINGSWORTH. John, a spirit. *M. P., S. B.*

COLLINS. *M. P., O. L. N. O.*

COLLINS. Police-officer. *S. B. B.,* Scenes xviii.

COLLINS. Mr. Wilkie. *M. P., E. C.; M. P., N. T.*

COLLINS. Mr. Wilkie, as Lithers. *M. P., M. N. D.*

COLMAN. Mr. *M. P., A. in E.*

COLONIAL OFFICE. *M. P., R. T.*

COLOSSEUM. *U. T.* xxi.

COLUMBIA. *A. N.* xvii.

COLUMBINE. A stage, in Britannia. *U. T.* iv.

COLUMBINE. In Booth at Greenwich Fair. *S. B. B.* xix.

COLUMBUS. *A. N.* xiv.

COMEDIAN. The low, Of the establishment. *S. B. B.,* Scenes xii.
Whose face is so deeply seared with the small-pox, and whose dirty shirt-front is inlaid with openwork and embossed with coral studs like ladybirds.

COMEDIAN. Principal, At Astley's. *S. B. B.,* Scenes xi.

COMIC ACTOR. *M. P., G. A.*

COMIC SINGER. The, At Vauxhall Gardens. *S. B. B.,* Scenes xiv.
A marvellously facetious gentleman.

COMMERCIAL ROAD. London. *D. S.* ix.; *R. P., T. D. P.*; and *U. T.* iii.

COMMERCIAL STREET. Whitechapel. *U. T.* xxiii.

COMMISSIONER. *M. P., S. R.*

COMMISSIONER. A, School Inspector. *H. T.,* s. ii.
A Government officer—in his way a professed pugilist—always in training with a system to force down the general throat like a bolus.

COMMISSIONER. Chief, of police. *U. T.* xxxiv.

COMMISSIONER. Mrs., Mrs. Pordage. *C. S., P. o. C. E. P.*

COMMISSIONER. Mrs. *M. P., S. R.*

COMMISSIONER. Of bankrupts. *P. P.* xlvii.

COMMISSIONERS. *M. P., N. E.*

COMMISSIONERS. Lottery. *R. P., B. S.*

COMMITTEE. Ladies' sick visitation. *S. B. B., O. P.* vi.

COMMITTEE. Of the Methodistical Order. *P. P.* xxii.
Fourteen women a passin "resolutions, and wotin" supplies, and all sort o' games.

COMMITTEE. Slumkey's, One of.
P. P. xiii.
Addressing six small boys . . . as men of Eatanswill.

COMMON. A. *M. P., U. N.*

COMMON. The. *D. C.* xiv.

COMMON COUNCIL. *M. P., P. F.*

COMMON COUNCIL. Court of.
N. N. xli.

COMMON COUNCILMAN.
M. H. C. i.

COMMON HARD. Portsmouth.
N. N. xxiii.

COMMON PLEAS. Court of.
U. T. xxvi.

COMMON SENSE. An ill-conditioned friend of mine.
M. P., T. T. C. D.

COMMONS. House of. *D. and S.* xxxi.; *M. C.* xxix.; *M. H. C.* i.; *M. P., H. H.* xli.; *N. N.*; *S. B. B.*, Scenes xiv.

COMMONS. A member of the House of. *S. B. B.*, Scenes xviii.
Singularly awkward and ungainly.

COMMONS. Messenger of the House of. *S. B. B.*, Scenes xviii.
With the gilt order round his neck.

COMMONS. An officer of the House of. *B. R.* xlix.

COMO. Lake of. *P. F. I., R. D.*

COMPAGNIA DELLA MISERICORDIA. Member of.
P. F. I., R. D.

COMPANION. A. *M. P., N. S. L.*

COMPANION. My old, Master Humphrey's clock. *M. H. C.* i.

COMPANY. St. Katherine's *Dock,*
S. B. B., Scenes x.

COMPEYSON. Miss Havisham's false lover. *G. E.* xlii.
Note.—The second convict Pip sees on the marshes. He is recaptured with Magwitch. After his return from penal servitude he sees Magwitch, and gives information. He is killed at the recapture of Magwitch. He proves to have been the villanous lover of Miss Havisham.

COMPEYSON. Wife of. *G. E.* xlii.

COMPORT. Jane, Sweetheart of young Dowgate. *U. T.* ix.

COMPTON. Mr., Actor.
M. P., M. B.

CONCIERGERIE.
T. T. C., bk. iii., ch. xiii.
In the black prison of the Conciergerie, the doomed of the day awaited their fate.

CONCORD. A room in the Royal George Hotel, *Dover. T. T. C.* iv.

CONCORDE. Place de la.
R. P., O. o. S.; *U. T.* xxiii.

CONDEMNED CELLS. In Newgate prison. *S. B. B.*, Scenes xxv.
The entrance is by a narrow and obscure passage leading to a dark passage, in which a charcoal stove casts a lurid tint over the objects in its vicinity. There are three of these passages, and three of these ranges of cells. Prior to the recorder's report being made, all the prisoners under sentence of death are removed from the day-room at five o'clock in the afternoon, and locked up in these cells, where they are allowed a candle until ten o'clock ; and here they remain till seven next morning. When the warrant for a prisoner's execution arrives, he is removed to the cells, and confined in one of them until he leaves it for the scaffold.

CONGRESS. *M. P., Y. M. C.*

CONDUCTOR. Gold-laced, The beadle. *S. B. B., O. P.* i.

CONDUCTOR. Of omnibus, Cad. *S. B. B.*, Scenes xvi.
His great boast is that he can chuck an old gen'lm'n into the buss, shut him in, and rattle off, before he knows where it's a going to.

CONDUCTOR. Of this Journal (*Household Words*).
M. P., B. A.

CONDUCTOR. To one of the omnibuses. *N. N.* xlv.
Wears a glazed hat.—He has a wart on his nose.

CONFRATÉRNITA.
P. F. I., G. A. N.

CONFRATÉRNITA. Blue.
P. F. I., G. A. N.

CONNECTICUT. *A. N.* iii.

CONNECTICUT RIVER. *A. N.* v.

CONOLLY. Dr. *M. P., S. B.*

CONSCRIPTS. French-Flemish. *U. T.* xxv.
Who had drawn unlucky numbers in the last conscription and were on their way to a famous French garrison town.

CONSORT. Prince. *M. P., N. E.*

CONSTABLE. *O. T.* xxx.
Had a large staff, a large head, large features, and large half-boots.

CONSTABLE. A. *G. E.* iv.

CONSTABLE. The. *B. H.* xix.

CONSTABLES. *S. B. B.*, Scenes xvii.

CONSTABLES. The. *G. E.* xvi.
The extinct red waistcoated police.

CONSTABLES. With blue staves. *P. P.* xiii.

CONSTANT COMPANION.
R. P., C. D. O. S.
Original : Dickens' sister Fanny or Harriet Ellen.

CONSUL. The British. *L. D.* li.

CONSUL'S. A gentleman from the. *C. S., M. L. Leg.* ii.
Dark, with his hair cropped what I should consider too close.

CONTADINI. *P. F. I., R.*

CONTRACTOR. Railway.
M. P., T. B.

CONTRACTOR. The.
O. M. F. lxvii.

CONVENT. In St. Louis. *A. N.* xii.
For the ladies of the Sacred Heart.

CONVICT HULKS. *G. E.* i.
Original : A convict ship lay just outside the Navy yard at Chatham, and probably supplied the convict hulks of the story.

CONWAY. General, A soldier.
B. R. xlix.
I am a soldier—and I will protect the freedom of this place with my sword.

COODLE. Lord. *B. H.* xii.

COOK. At number 25.
S. B. B., O. P. iii.

COOK. Captain. *M. P., E. T.*

COOK. Capt., Captain of steam ship " Russia." *U. T.* xxxi.

COOK. In the house with the green gate. *P. P.* xxiii.

COOK. In Weller's service.
P. P. lii.
A very buxom-looking cook, dressed in mourning, who had been bustling about in the bar, glided into the room—and be stowed many smirks of recognition on Sam, silently stationed herself at the back of his father's chair, and announced her presence by a slight cough.

COOK. Mrs. Jellyby's. *B. H.* iv.
In pattens — frequently came and skirmished with the house-maid at the door. There appeared to be ill-will between them.

COOK. Of Cheeryble Brothers·
N. N. xxxv.

COOK. Of Mrs. Maylie.
O. T. xxviii.

COOK'S COURT. *B. H.* x.
Original : Took's Court, Cursitor Street.

COOK'S STRAITS. *M. P., E. T.*

COOKING DEPÔT. For the working classes. *U. T.* xxiii.
Where accommodation is provided for dining comfortably 300 persons at a time.

Note.—This was one of the earliest experiments of "Cheap food." The building has been converted to other uses.

COOPER. Augustus. In the oil and colour line. *S. B. B.*, Char. ix.
Just of age, with a little money, a little business, and a little mother.

COOPER. Apprentice of Augustus.
S. B. B., Char. ix.

COOPER. Mr. Artist. *A. N.* xii.

COOPER. Mr. *M. P., F. C.*

COOPER. Mother of Mr. Augustus.
S. B. B., Char. ix.
Managed her husband and his business in his lifetime, took to managing her son and his business after his decease.

COPE. *M. P., O. L. N. O.*

COPELAND. *R. P., A. P. A.*

COPENHAGEN HOUSE.
S. B. B., Scenes xx.

COPPERFIELD. Agnes, David's eldest child. *D. C.* xxxiv.

COPPERFIELD. Clara, David's mother. *D. C.* i.
My mother was, no doubt, unusually youthful in appearance, even for her years.

Note.—David's mother. Some years after the death of her husband she marries Mr. Murdstone. Her life after this is an unhappy one ; so unhappy, in fact, that she dies under the treatment of her husband and his sister, her baby being buried with her.

COPPERFIELD. David, The elder.
D. C. i.
My father's eyes had closed upon the light of this world six months, when mine opened on it.

COPPERFIELD. David. *D. C.* i.
Born at Blunderstone, in Suffolk, or " thereby " as they say in Scotland, I was a posthumous child. My father's eyes had closed upon the light of this world six months, when mine opened on it.

Note.—The title-character of the book is usually considered to have many of the characteristics of and similar experiences to those of Dickens himself. Little David was born at Blunderstone in Suffolk, with a caul, some six months after his father's death. The child lived with his mother, attended by old Peggotty, for some years until the appearance of Mr. Murdstone. During David's visit to Peggotty's brother at Yarmouth, his mother and Mr. Murdstone are married. Then commences a period of misery for him : a misery accentuated by the loss of a great deal of his mother's kindness. Murdstone and his sister inaugurate a system to train up the mother and to break down the child, which culminates in a dramatic outburst. David is sent to Creakle's school, where he meets Steerforth and Traddles, two characters who occupy important places in the narrative. David's mother and her child die and are buried together : David is first neglected and then put to the lowest kind of work at the counting-house of Murdstone and Grinby, in the wine trade. Lodgings are taken for him by his stepfather with Mr. Micawber. The life is more than the sensitive boy can bear and he leaves it, tramping on foot to Dover, where he succeeds in finding his aunt. His aunt, Betsey Trotwood, puts him to a good school in Canterbury. Later on he is articled to Messrs. Spenlow and Jorkins, proctors. His aunt loses her money and he takes to reporting and literary work, in which he succeeds. He marries Dora, Spenlow's daughter. Spenlow himself having died, leaving her only a comparatively small sum. Dora dies and he marries Agnes, the daughter of Mr. Wickfield, his aunt's solicitor in Canterbury. The story leaves him and his wife in happiness.

Original : Charles Dickens himself.

COPPERFIELD. Mrs. David. *See* Spenlow, Dora.

COPPERFIELD. Mrs. David. *See* Copperfield, Mrs. Clara.

COPPERFULL. Mr., Name given to David by Mrs. Crupp.

COPPERNOZE. Mr. *Mud. Pap.* ii.

COPPICE ROW. *O. T.* viii.

COPYING - CLERKS. Low.
S. B. B., Scenes xiii.

CORAM. " Originator of the Institute for these poor Foundlings."
L. D. ii.

CORINTHIAN PILLARS.
P. P. xxxvi.

CORNEY. Mr., Deceased husband of matron of workhouse.
O. T. xxiii.
Who had not been dead more than five-and-twenty years.

CORNEY. Mrs., The matron of the workhouse. *O. T.* xxiii.
A poor desolate creature . . . a discreet matron.

Note.—Mrs. Corney was matron of the workhouse at which Oliver was born. In that capacity she obtains possession of a locket and ring stolen from the dead body of Oliver's mother, and disposes of them to Monks. She marries Bumble the beadle. They lose their situations and both become inmates of the workhouse over which they had formerly reigned as master and matron.

CORNHILL. *B. R.* i. ; *C. B.*, *C. C.*, *S.* i. ; *C. S.*, *S. L.* iv. ; *C. S.*, *W. o. G. M.* ; *M. C.* xxxviii. ; *M. P.*, *L. H.* ; *P. P.* xx. ; *R. P.*, *B. S.* ; *U. T.* ix.

CORNICE ROAD. *P. F. I.*, *G. A. N.*

CORNISH GENTLEMAN. A, An Athlete. *D. and S.* xxii.

CORNWALL. *D. and S.* iv. ; *L. D.* xiii. ; *N. N.* x. ; *S. B. B.*, Char. iii. ; *U. T.* xxvii.

CORNWALL. Mining districts of.
M. C. xxi.

CORONER. *B. H.* xi.

CORONER'S JURY. *U. T.* xviii.

CORPORALS. Certain, Of Royal East London Volunteers.
B. R. xliii.

CORPORATION. Eden Land-
M. C. xxi.

CORRECTION. House of.
O. T. xiii. ; *S. B. B.*, Scenes xvi.

CORRECTION. Middlesex house of.
R. P., *W. I. A. W.*

CORRESPONDING SOCIETY. Of the Pickwick Club. A branch of the United Pickwickians, or the Pickwick Club. *P. P.* i.

Note.—The members of the branch were Pickwick, Tupman, Snodgrass, and Winkle. They were requested to forward, from time to time, authenticated accounts of their journeys, and investigations . . . to the Pickwick Club stationed in London.

" CORRESPONDING SOCIETY. Of Begging-Letter Writers."
R. P., *T. B. W.*

CORSO. The. *L. D.* xliii. ; *P. F. I.*, *V. M. M. S. S.*

COSTA. Signor. *M. P.*, *M. M.*

COSTELLO. Mr. Dudley, As Mr. Nightingale. *M. P.*, *M. N. D.*

COSTERMONGERS.
S. B. B., Scenes v.

COSY. Room in Six Jolly Fellow-ship Porters. *O. M. F.* vi.

COTTAGE. Miss Trotwood's.
D. C. xiii.
A very neat little cottage with cheerful bow-windows; in front of it, a small square gravelled court, or garden full of flowers, carefully tended, and smelling deliciously.
Original: In Nuckalls Place, Broadstairs, since named after the novelist, Dickens House.

COTTAGE. Next door to that of Mrs. Nickleby. *N. N.* xli.
Which, like their own, was a detached building.

COTTAGERS. *O. C. S.* xv.

COTTINGHAM. James. *A. N.* xvii.

COULSON. Mr., as Will, a waiter at the St. James's Arms.
M. P., S. G.

COUNCIL CHAMBER. The.
A. N. xvii.

COUNSEL. *M. P., P. L. U.*

COUNSEL. *M. P., L. E. J.*

COUNSEL. *B. H.* i.
A very little Counsel, with a terrific bass voice.

COUNSEL. In the cause. *B. H.* i.

COUNSEL. The, in the Arches Court. *S. B. B.,* Scenes viii.
Wore red gowns.

COUNSEL. Two or three, never in any cause. *B. H.* i.

COUNSEL'S OFFICE. *P. P.* lv.

COUNT. The usual French.
L. D. lv.
Guest of Mrs. Merdle.

COUNTESS. Eliza Grimwood.
R. P., T. D. A. i.

COUNTESS. Guest of Mr. Merdle
L. D. xxi
Secluded somewhere in the core of an immense dress, to which she was in the proportion of the heart to the overgrown cabbage.

COUNTING HOUSE. At the works of Doyce and Clennam. *L. D.* lxiii

COUNTING HOUSE. *See* Cheeryble Brothers.

COUNTRY. French-Flemish.
U. T. xxv
Three-quarters Flemish, and a quarter French.

COUNTRYMAN. *M. P., S. D. C.*

COUNTRYMAN. Comic, Member of Mr. V. Crummles' Company.
N. N. xxiii
" With a turned-up nose, a large mouth, broad face, and staring eyes."

COUNTRYMAN. Prisoner in " the poor side " of the Fleet. *P. P.* xlii.
Flicking with a worn-out hunting-whip, the top boot that adorned his right foot; his left being (for he had dressed by easy stages) thurst into an old slipper. Horses, dogs, and drink had brought him there.—There was a rusty spur on the solitary boot.

COUNTY. English. *M. P., P. M. B.*
Original: Stevenage, in Hert-fordshire.

COUNTY GAOL. Reading.
M. P., P. P.

COUNTY INN. Canterbury.
D. C. xvii.
Original: Fountain Hotel, in St. Margaret's Street, is generally recognised as the County Inn, where Mr. Dick slept.

COUNTY INSTITUTIONS. For idiots. *B. R.* xlvii.

COUNTY JUSTICE. The.
B. R. xlvii.

COUNTY MEMBER. Of Parliament.
S. B. B., Scenes xviii.

The old, hard-featured man—a good specimen of a class of men, now nearly extinct.—Look at his loose, wide, brown coat, with capacious pockets on each side ; the knee-breeches and boots, the immensely long waistcoat, and silver watch-chain dangling below it, the wide-brimmed brown hat, and the white handkerchief tied in a great bow, with straggling ends sticking out beyond his shirt frill.

COUPLE. Some three or four. At Greenwich Fair.
S. B. B., Scenes xii.

COURIER. A, of Dorrit's party.
L. D. xxxvii.

COURIER. French.
P. F. I., *G. T. F.*

COURT. The, No. 6 in. *N. N.* xl.

COURT-HOUSE. *C. S., T. G. S.* li.

COURT-KEEPER. The, in Doctor's Commons. *S. B. B.,* Scenes viii.
A respectable-looking man in black, of about twenty stone weight or thereabout.

COURTIER. A spruce young.
M. H. C. i.

COURTIER. A better—still.
M. H. C. i.

COURTIERS. Of the goblins.
P. P. xxix.
Who kick whom royalty kicks, and hug whom royalty hugs.

COURTS OF LAW. *B. R.* lxvii. ; and *U. T.* xiii.

COURVOISIER. *M. P., C. P.*

COUSIN. A, of Sir Leicester Dedlock. *B. H.* xl.
A languid cousin with a moustache.

COUSIN. Debilitated, Of Sir Leicester Dedlock. *B. H.* liii.

COUSIN. Solitary female, Of Mr. Martin Chuzzlewit. *M. C.* iv.
Who was remarkable for nothing but being very deaf, and living by herself, and always having the toothache.

COUSIN. Young scapegrace of a. *S. B. B.,* Char. ii.
Guest at Christmas family party.

COUSIN JOHN. Mr. Jarndyce.
B. H. vi.

COUSIN TOM. Captain Boldheart's cousin. *H. R.* iii.

COUSINS. Rest of the, Of Sir Leicester Dedlock. *B. H.* xxviii.
Ladies and gentlemen of various ages and capacities.

" COVE." A, A thief.
R. P., D. W. T. T.

COVENT GARDEN. *G. E.* xlv. ; *L. D.* xiii. ; *M. P.. W. M.* ; *M. P., W. S. G.* ; *S. B. B.,* Scenes i. ; *S. B. B.,* Scenes vi. ; *U. T.* i.

COVENT GARDEN MARKET. *D. C.* xxiv. ; *G. E.* xxi. ; *M. C.* xl. ; *O. C. S.* i. ; *O. M. F.* lix. ; *P. P.* xlvii. ; *U. T.* xiii.
Of dozing women—drunkards especially, you—come upon such specimens there, in the morning sunlight—such stale, vapid rejected cabbage-leaf, and cabbage-stalk dress, such damaged-orange countenance, such squashed pulp of humanity.

COVENT GARDEN THEATRE. *C. S., M. L. Leg.* i. ; *D. C.* xix. ; *M. P., A. G. L.* ; *M. P., S. Q. F.* ; *M. P., T. Let.*

COVENTRY. *P. P.* li.
Note.—Said also to be the town where Mrs. Jarley gave the performance on the night after meeting Nell and her grandfather.

COWER'S. Clerk from, The solicitors. *S. B. B.*, Tales iv.
Habited in black cloth, and bore with him a green umbrella, and a blue bag.

COWER'S. Solicitors. *S. B. B.*, Tales iv.

CRACKIT. Mr. Toby, Confederate of Fagin. *O. T.* xxii.
He was dressed in a smartly-cut snuff-coloured coat, with large brass buttons; an orange neckerchief; a coarse staring shawl-pattern waistcoat; and drab breeches.—Had no very great quantity of hair, either upon his head, or face; but what he had, was of a reddish dye, and tortured into long corkscrew curls.—He was a trifle above the middle size, and apparently rather weak in the legs.
Note.—A housebreaker belonging to Fagin's gang. He and Sikes were the principal operators in the attempt on Mrs. Maylie's house. After the failure, he repairs to the house on Jacob's Island, where he is last seen.

CRADDOCK. Mrs., Landlady of a house in Royal Crescent, Bath, where Pickwick took lodgings for self and friends. *P. P.* xxxvi.
Original : According to the most recent discoveries, the original of this character was Mrs. Craddock, the wife or mother of a well-known Gravesend cabdriver. See Pickwick Mr.

CRAGGS. Mr., A lawyer. *C. B., B. O. L.* i.
A cold, hard, dry man, dressed in grey, and white, like a flint; with small twinkles in his eyes, as if something struck sparks out of them.

CRAGGS. Mrs., Wife of Mr. Craggs. *C. B., B. O. L.* ii.

CRATCHIT. Bob, Scrooge's clerk. *C. B., C. C., S.* i.

CRATCHIT. Master Peter, Son of Bob Cratchit. *C. B., C. C., S.* iii.

CRATCHIT. Mrs., Wife of Bob Cratchit. *C. B., C. C., S.* iii.
Dressed out but poorly, in a twice-turned gown, but brave in ribbons, which are cheap, and make a goodly show for sixpence.

CRATCHIT. Mrs. *M. P., I. W. M.*

CRATCHIT BELINDA. Second daughter of Bob Cratchit. *C. B., C. C., S.* iii.

CRATCHITS. Two smaller. *C. B., C. C., S.* iii.
Boy and girl.

CRAVEN STREET, STRAND. *O. T.* xli.

CRAWLEY. Mr. (the youngest), Visitor at the Assembly Rooms, Bath. *P. P.* xxxv.
His father has eight hundred a year, which dies with him.

CREAKLE. Mr., Schoolmaster of Salem House. *D. C.* v.
Mr. Creakle's face was fiery, and his eyes were small, and deep in his head; he had thick veins in his forehead, a little nose, and a large chin. . . . I'll tell you what I am. . . . I'm a Tartar.
Note.—The master and proprietor of Salem House. His son left home and he terrorises over his wife and daughter. After David leaves the school Creakle drops out of the story until he is disposed of finally by being exhibited as a Middlesex magistrate tenderly considerate of the prisoners.
Original : The character of Creakle is generally supposed to have been founded on that of Mr. Jones, the head master of Wellington House Academy at the corner of

Hampstead Road and Granby Street. Dickens was sent to this school after his father's discharge from the debtors' prison.

CREAKLE. Mrs. *D. C.* v.

CREAKLE. Miss. *D. C.* v.
I heard that Miss Creakle was regarded by the school in general as being in love with Steerforth.

CREDITORS. Unlucky.
M. P., L. E. J.

CREEBLE. Miss, Of the Misses Creeble's Boarding and Day Establishment for Young Ladies.
M. P., E. T.

CREEVY. Miss La. *See* La Creevy, Miss. *N. N.* lxiii.

CREMONA. *P. F. I., V. M. M. S. S.*

CREMORNE GARDENS.
M. P., R. H. F.

CREWLER. Mrs., Sophy's mama.
D. C. xli.

CREWLER. Reverend Horace, Sophy's papa. *D. C.* xli.
An excellent man, most exemplary in every way.

CREWLER. Sophy, *Dearest girl in the world. D. C.* xxxiv.
*Note.—*Daughter of the Rev. Horace Crewler. She is the moral mainstay of the family. After waiting some years she and Traddles are married— on the Britannia metal footing, though the silver plate arrives in time.

CRIEL. *R. P., A. F.*

CRIMEA. *M. P., S. F. A.*

CRIMINAL COURTS.
S. B. B., Scenes xxiv.

CRIMP. David, Tapster at "Lombards' Arms." *M. C.* xxvii.

CRIMPLE. David, Esquire (Secretary and resident *Director* of the Anglo-Bengalee *Disinterested*

Loan and Life Assurance Company. This gentleman's name, by the way, was originally Crimp, but as the word was susceptible of an awkward construction and might be misrepresented, he had altered it to Crimple. *M. C.* xxvii.

CRINKLES. *Mud. Pap.* ii.

CRIPP. Mrs., Bob Sawyer's boy's mother. *P. P.* l.

CRIPPLE CORNER. *Belonged to* Wilding and Co.
C. S., N. T., Act i.
There was a pump in Cripple Corner. There was a tree in Cripple Corner. All Cripple Corner belonged to Wilding and Co. Their cellars burrowed under it, their mansion towered over it.

CRIPPLES. Master. *L. D.* ix.
Behind the blind was a little white-faced boy, with a slice of bread and butter, and a battledore.

CRIPPLES. Mr., Of Mr. Cripples' Academy. *L. D.* ix.

CRIPPLES. Pupils of Mr. *L. D.* ix.

" CRIPPLES. The Three ", Inn in Saffron Hill frequented by Fagin.
O. T. xxvi.

CRIPPLES. Two, *Both* mere boys.
B. R. lxxvii.
One with a leg of wood, one who dragged his twisted limbs along by the help of a crutch, were hanged in the same *Bloomsbury* Square.

CRISPARKLE. Mrs., Mother of the Rev. Septimus. *E. D.* vi.
Pretty old lady. " What is prettier than an old lady—when her eyes are bright, when her figure is trim and compact, when her face is cheerful and calm, when her dress is as the dress of a china shepherdess, so dainty in its colours."

CRISPARKLE.   Sister of Mrs., A childless widow.   *E. D.* vi.
Another piece of *D*resden china.

CRISPARKLE.   The Reverend Septimus, Minor Canon. *E. D.* ii.
Fair and rosy—early riser, musical, cheerful, classical, kind, good-natured, social, contented, and boy-like; feinting and dodging with the utmost artfulness, while his radiant features teemed with innocence, and soft-hearted benevolence beamed from his boxing-gloves.

> *Note.*—A minor canon of Cloisterham, living with his mother in Minor Canon Corner. He takes Neville Landless as pupil, and it is while with him that Neville is suspected of the murder of Edwin Drood.

CRISPARKLES. Six little, *D*eceased brothers of the Reverend Septimus Crisparkle.   *E. D.* vi.
Went out, one by one, as they were born, like six weak little rushlights, as they were lighted.

CROCUS.   *D*octor, A phrenologist.
A. N. xiii.
A tall, fine-looking Scotchman, but rather fierce and warlike in appearance.

CROFTS.   *S. Y. C.*

CROOKED BILLET.   *B. R.* xxxi.

CROOKEY. Attendant.   *P. P.* xl.
Who might have passed for a neglected twin brother of Mr. Smouch . . . looked something between a bankrupt grazier, and a drover in a state of insolvency.

CROPLEY. Miss, A friend of Mrs. Nickleby's.   *N. N.* xxxiii.

"CROSS KEYS." The, Wood Street.
G. E. xx.; *L. D.* i.; *N. N.* xxxiii.; *S. B. B.*, Scenes xvi.; *U. T.* xii.

CROWL.   Mr., Fellow-lodger of Newman Noggs.   *N. N.* xiv.

CRUMLINWALLINER. A bard whose name sounded like.
B. H. xvii.

CRUMMLES. Master, Elder son of Mr. Vincent Crummles.
N. N. xxii.

CRUMMLES. Master Percy, Younger son of Mr. Vincent Crummles.
N. N. xxiii. ; *N. N.* xxii.

CRUMMLES. Mr. Vincent, Manager of travelling theatre.
N. N. xxii.

He had a very full under-lip, a hoarse voice, as though he were in the habit of shouting very much, and very short black hair, shaved off nearly to the crown of his head —to admit of his more easily wearing character wigs of any shape or pattern.

Note.—Crummles is manager-proprietor of a travelling theatre and company. He met Nicholas and Smike, and persuades them to enter the company. After Nicholas leaves the company he lost sight of the Crummleses until he accidentally saw a bill advertising positively the last appearance of Mr. Crummles outside a Minor Theatre. It turned out that the family was on the point of their departure for America. Crummles was nicknamed old " bricks and mortar " by subordinate members of his company.

Original : The Pilot's house where Crummles stayed is supposed to have been No. 78, St. Thomas' Street.

CRUMMLES. Miss Ninetta, daughter of Mrs. Vincent Crummles.
N. N. xxiii.

A little girl in a dirty white frock, with tucks up to the knees, short trousers, sandalled shoes, white spencer, pink gauze bonnet, green veil and curl-papers.

Note.—" The Infant Phenomenon," who had been ten years old for the past five years. Daughter of Mr. and Mrs. Crummles. She was always given good parts in the plays at the theatre, much to the disgust of some of the other members of the company.

CRUMMLES. Mrs., Wife of Mr. Vincent Crummles. *N. N.* xxiii.

A stout, portly female, apparently between forty and fifty, in a tarnished silk cloak, with her bonnet dangling by the strings in her hand, and her hair (of which she had a great quantity) braided in a large festoon over each temple.

Note.—A wonderful woman : mother of the Phenomenon.

CRUMPTON. Miss Amelia.
S. B. B., Tales iii.
Owned to thirty-eight.

CRUMPTON. Miss Maria.
S. B. B., Tales iii.
Admitted she was forty.

CRUMPTON. The Misses, Proprietresses of boarding-school.
S. B. B., Tales iii.
They dressed in the most interesting manner—like twins ! and looked as happy as a couple of marigolds run to seed. They were very precise—wore false hair —always smelt strongly of lavender.

CRUNCHER. Jeremiah, General messenger, and in particular for Tellson and Co's Bank during the day, and Resurrectionist at night.
T. T. C. ii.
He had eyes . . . of a surface black, with no depth in the colour or form, and much too near together.

Note.—He is present at the trial of Darnay, and crops up repeatedly in the story. The scenes of the French Revolution so affect him, however, that he renounces his nightly trade and resolves not to ill-treat his wife for " flopping."

CRUNCHER. Mrs., Wife of Jerry Cruncher. *T. T. C.*, bk. ii., ch. i.
You're a nice woman ! What do you mean by flopping yourself down and praying agin me ?

CRUNCHER. Young Jerry.
T. T. C., bk. ii., ch. i.
He (Jerry's father) was never absent during business hours, unless upon an errand, and then he was represented by his son, a grisly urchin of twelve.

Note.—Son of Jerry Cruncher, and general assistant to his father when he is away from his post outside Tellson's. Young Jerry is very curious to discover the trade his father practises by night. He is supposed to succeed his father as outside messenger.

CRUPP. Mrs., *David's* landlady in chambers in the Adelphi.
D. C. xxiii.

Note.—After Miss Trotwood's loss of fortune she comes up to David, and there is war between her and Mrs. Crupp, in which the latter is worsted.

Original : York House, 15, Buckingham Street, since demolished.

CRUSHTON. The Honourable Mr., Lord Mutanhed's bosom friend.
P. P. xxxv.
The other gentleman, in the red under-waistcoat, and dark moustache.

CRUSOE. Robinson. *M. C.* v.

CRUSOE'S ISLAND. *M. C.* xxi.

CRYPT. The. *E. D.* xii.

CRYSTAL PALACE. *U. T.* xxxi.

CUFFY. *B. H.* xii.

CUMMINS. Tom. *P. P.* xx.

CUNARD LINE. Shipowners.
U. T. xxxi.

CUNARD. The, Steam packet.
A. N. xvi.

CUNNING. Name of bird.
B. H. xiv.

" CUPID." Clipper, schooner.
M. C. xliv.

CUPID. Kidderminster.
H. T., *S.* vi.

CURATE. Our. *S. B. B., O. P.* ii.
A young gentleman of prepossessing appearance, and fascinating manners. He parted his hair on the centre of his forehead in the form of a Norman arch, wore a brilliant of the first water on the fourth finger of his left hand, which he always applied to his left cheek when he read prayers.

CURDLE. Mr., Literary man.
N. N. xxiv.
Had written a pamphlet of sixty-four pages, post octavo, on the character of the nurse's deceased husband in Romeo and Juliet.
He wore a loose robe on his back, and his right forefinger on his forehead, after the portraits of Sterne . . . to whom somebody or other had once said he bore a striking resemblance.

CURDLE. Mrs., Patroness of Mr. V. Crummles' Company.
N. N. xxiv.
Dressed in a morning wrapper, with a little cap stuck upon the top of her head.

CURÉ. Monsieur, The. *U. T.* vii.

CURIOSITY DEALER'S WAREHOUSE. *See* Old Curiosity Shop.

CURSITOR STREET. *B. H.* x. ; *R. P., B. S.* ; *S. B. B.*, Tales x.

CURSITOR STREET. Little dairy in. *B. H.* xxv.

CURZON. Daughter of Thomas.
B. R. viii.

CURZON. Thomas, Hosier.
B. R. viii.
Mark Gilbert's master.

CUSTOM-HOUSE. *D. and S.* lx. ; *G. E* xlvii. ; *L. D.* xxix. ; *O. M. F.* iv. ; *P. F. I., G. A. N.* ; *U. T.* vii.

CUSTOM-HOUSE   OFFICERS.
Calais.   *U. T.* xvii.
  In green and grey.

CUSTOMER.   Of Kidney Pie Merchant.   *S. B. B.*, Scenes ii.

CUT.   New, London.
                  S. B. B., Scenes xi.

"CUTAWAY."   Fictitious name.
                          L. D. vi.

CUTE.   Alderman, A justice.
                      C. B., C. G. i.
  Coming—at that light heavy
pace—that peculiar compromise
between a walk and a jog-trot—
which a gentleman upon the
smooth down-hill of life, wearing
creaking boots, a watch-chain, and
clean linen, *may* come out of his
house.

CUTE.   Alderman, Mrs.
                      C. B., C. G. i.

CUTLER.   Mr. and Mrs. *N. N.* xiv.
  Newly married couple, who had
visited Mr. and Mrs. Kenwigs in
their courtship.

CUTTLE.   Captain Ned, Late pilot,
privateer's man or skipper.
                      D. and S. iv.
  A gentleman in a wide suit of
blue, with a hook instead of a hand
attached to his right wrist; very
bushy black eyebrows; and a
thick stick in his left hand, covered
all over (like his nose) with knobs.
He wore a loose silk handkerchief
round his neck, and such a very
large coarse shirt-collar, that it
looked like a " small sail." When
you see Ned Cuttle bite his nails,
Wal'r, then you may know that
Ned Cuttle's aground.
  Note.—Captain Cuttle, who is best
known for his now famous saying,
" when found, make a note of," was the
friend of Sol Gills. He is a fairly
constant figure throughout the story,
and befriends Florence Dombey. He
leaves the story the partner of Sol
Gills, proud of the fact that he is now a
man of science.

CYMON.   Simon Tuggs.
                      S. B. B., Tales iv.

D

D. A. J.,   *M. P., S. B.*

DABBER.   Sir, Dingleby.
                          N. N. xxvii.

DADSON.   Mr., Writing-master at
Minerva House.
                      S. B. B., Tales iii.
  In a white waistcoat, black knee-
shorts, and ditto silk stockings,
displaying a leg large enough for
two writing-masters.

DADSON.   Wife of Mr.
                      S. B. B., Tales iii.
  In green silk, with shoes and
cap-trimmings to correspond.

DAGGS.   Mr.   *O. M. F.* viii.

DAIRY.   Late ladies' school.
                      S. B. B., Scenes iii.

DAISY.   Solomon, Parish clerk and
bell-ringer.   *B. R.* i.
  A little man—had round black
shiny eyes like beads—wore at the
knees of his rusty black breeches,
and on his rusty black coat, and
all down his long-flapped waistcoat, queer little buttons like
nothing except his eyes.   He
seemed all eyes from head to foot.

DALLEY.   Mr.   *O. M. F.* viii.

DAMASCUS.   *U. T.* xv.

DAME DURDEN.   *See* Summerson,
Esther.

DAMIENS.   *T. T. C.*, bk. ii., ch. xv.

DAMON AND PYTHIAS.
                      S. B. B., char. xi.

DAMSEL.   A   wiry-faced   old,
Guest at Pawkins.   *M. C.* xvi.
  Who held strong sentiments
touching the rights of women, and
had diffused the same in lectures.

DANBY. *M. P., O. L. N. O.*

DANCER. A May day,
S. B. B., Scenes xx.
The " green " animated by no less a personage than our friend in the tarpauling suit.

DANCING-MASTER. A, Inmate of the Marshalsea. *L. D.* vii.

" DANDO." Head man at Searle's boating establishment.
S. B. B., Scenes x.
Magnificent, though reddish whiskers.

DANTE. *L. D.* xlii.

DANTE. The spirit of.
M. P., S. F. A.

DANTON. Mr., Guest at Christening party of the Kitterbells.
S. B. B., Tales xi.

DAPH. Pointer belonging to Sir Jeoffrey Manning. *P. C.* xix.

DARBEE. *Derby. M. P., T. O. H.*

DARBY. A constable. *B. H.* xxii.

DARBY'S. A lodging-house.
U. T. v.

DARBY'S. A weekly lodger at.
U. T. v.
A deserter.

DARDANELLES. *M. P., L. A. V.*

DARK JACK. Landlord of little public house in *Liverpool. U. T.* v.
A negro—in a Greek cap, and a dress half-Greek and half-English.

DARLING. Grace. *M. P., S. Pigs.*

DARNAY. Charles.
T. T. C., bk. ii., ch. ii.
A young man of about five-and-twenty, well-grown and well-looking, with a sunburnt cheek and a dark eye.

Note.—Son of Marquis St. Evrèmond. A French Emigré, who renounces his fortune in France in favour of his poor

tenants. He becomes a teacher, etc. in London. Tried for treason in England and discharged. He marries Lucy Manette. In Paris he is arrested and sentenced. By the sacrifice of Sydney Carton, who dies in his stead, he is saved.

DARNAY. Mrs. *See* Manette, Miss Lucie.

DARTFORD. *L. D.* liv.

DARTLE. Miss Rosa, Mrs. Steerforth's companion. *D. C.* xx.
She had black hair and eager black eyes, and was thin and had a scar upon her lip. She was a little dilapidated—like a house—with having been so long to let.

Note.—Companion to Mrs. Steerforth. She loves Steerforth in her own fierce way, and despises the Peggottys—particularly Little Emily. She is left alternately caressing and quarrelling with Mrs. Steerforth.

Original : The name is said to be an old Rochester one.

DARWEN. River. *G. S. E.* v.

DASH. *Dash*, The Reverend.
O. M. F. x.

DASH BLANK. Lord. *M. P., T. T.*

DATCHERY. *Dick*, A mysterious personage. *E. D.* xviii.
Buttoned up in a tightish blue surtout, with a buff waistcoat and grey trousers. He had something of a military air. This gentleman's white head was unusually large, and his shock of white hair was unusually thick and ample. A single buffer.

Note.—The identity of Datchery is one of the secondary mysteries of the book upon which probably the principal mystery depends. He enters the story rather late, after Edwin Drood's disappearance, with the object of watching John Jasper. In this work he keeps a tally of the points he makes by a score of uncouth chalk marks on his cupboard wall. He has been identified with Edwin Drood, Helena Landless, Bazzard, and Tartar by different writers.

DAUGHTER. Eldest, Of the widow.
                    M. C. iv.
   Expressed a general hope that
some people *would* appear in
their own characters.

DAUGHTER. Of Baron von Swillenhausen.   *N. N.* vi.

DAUGHTER. Of elderly lady—
poultry-dealer in Leadenhall Market.   *D. and S.* xlix.
   Engaged by Captain Cuttle to
come and put Florence *D*ombey's
room in order and render her any
little services she required.

DAUGHTER. Of Mrs. Wugsley.
                  P. P. xxxv.
   Much older than her sister.
   Lord Mutanhed has been introduced to me. I said I thought I was
not engaged.

DAUGHTER. Of old lady, married.
             S. B. B., Scenes vii.

DAUGHTER. Of Prison-keeper.
                  L. D. i.
   Three or four years old—fair
little face, touched with divine
compassion—was like an angel's
in the prison.

DAUGHTER. Of the deaf old
gentleman.   *M. H. C.* vi.
   Who fled from her father's
house.

DAUGHTERS. Growing up, of
Majestic English Mama and Papa.
                  L. D. ii.
   Who were keeping a journal
for the confusion of their fellow-
creatures.

DAUGHTERS. Of Matchmaking
Mamas — visitors in Assembly
Rooms, *B*ath.   *P. P.* xxxv.
   Remembering the maternal in-
junction to make the best use of
their youth, had already commenced incipient flirtations in the
mislaying of scarfs, putting on
gloves, setting down cups, and so
forth.

DAUGHTERS. Three, Of widow of
deceased brother of Mr. Martin,
Chuzzlewit.   *M. C.* iv.
   Three in number, and of gentlemanly deportment, who had so
mortified themselves with tight
stays that their tempers were
reduced to something less than
their waists, and sharp lacing was
expressed in their very noses.

D'AULNAIS. The name of Charles
Darnay's mother, from which he
forms the name he adopts in
England. *See Darnay.*

DAVENPORT. Mr., Actor.
          M. P., V. and B. S.

DAVENTRY.   *P. P.* li.

DAVID. Ancient Butler of
Cheeryble Brothers. *N. N.* xxxvii.
   Of apoplectic appearance, with
very short legs.
   *Original: Alfred Boot, engaged
by the Brothers Grant in the capacity
of the character of the book.*

DAVID. Gravedigger. *O. C. S.* liv.
   You're getting very deaf, *D*avy,
very deaf to be sure.

DAVID. Shopman in pawnbroker's.
                  M. C. xiii.

DAVIES. Mr., English tourist.
                 P. F. I., R.

DAVIES. Mrs., English tourist.
                 P. F. I., R.

DAVIES. Sir *D*.   *M. P., C. C.*

DAVIS. Andrew Jackson.
   M. P., R. S. D.; M. P., S. B.

DAVIS. Father of Gill.
            C. S., P. o. C. E. P.
   A shepherd.

DAVIS. Gill, Private in the Royal
Marines.   *C. S., P. o. C. E. P.*

"DAVY." Or safety-lamp.
                 N. N. vi.

DAWES. Nurse in the poor nobleman's family.   *L. D.* lvii.

H

DAWKINS. Jack, A thief.
O. T. viii.

He was a snub-nosed, flat-browed, common-faced boy enough; and as dirty a juvenile as one would wish to see; but he had about him all the airs of a man. He was short of his age; with rather bow legs, and little sharp ugly eyes. His hat was stuck on the top of his head so lightly that it threatened to fall off every moment. He wore a man's coat, which reached nearly to his heels. He had turned the cuffs back, half way up his arm, to get his hands out of his sleeves : apparently with the ultimate view of thrusting them into the pockets of his corduroy trousers ; for there he kept them !

Note.—The most interesting and successful of Fagin's young thieves. The Dodger finds Oliver weak and tired and hungry on his way to London. He shares his "only one bob and a magpie" with Oliver and carries him off to London. In spite of his adroitness in thieving he is captured while attempting to pick a pocket. In court he maintains a game sang-froid, and carries it off with a commendable boldness, from his own point of view. While in the "jug" before his transportation he is maintained by Fagin "like a gentleman," to compensate for the possibility of his not finding a place in the Newgate Calendar.

DAWS. Mary, Young kitchenmaid.
D. and S. lix.

Of inferior rank—in black stockings who, having sat with her mouth open for a long time, unexpectedly discharges from it words to this effect : "Suppose the wages shouldn't be paid"—"If *that* is your religious feelings,"—says cook warmly, "I don't know where you mean to go."

DAWSON. Mr., Surgeon.
S. B. B., O. P. iii.

DAYVLE. The devil. *B. H.* xl.

DEAD SEA. *M. P., T. O. H.*

DEAF AND DUMB ESTABLISH-MENT. *C. S., D. M.*

DEAL. *B. H.,* xlv. ; *M. P., F. S.*

DEALER. In Marine Stores.
S. B. B., Scenes xxi.

DEALER. Marine Store.
S. B. B., Scenes iii.
At corner of the street.

DEALER. Principal slipper and dog's-collar man.
D. and S. xiii.

Who considered himself a public character—threw up his forefinger to the brim of his hat as Mr. Dombey went by.

DEAN. Miss. *E. D.* ii.

DEAN. Mr. *E. D.* ii.

DEAN. Mrs. Abigail. The Earl of Aberdeen. *M. P., B. S.*

DEAN. The. *E. D.* ii

DEATH. *M. P., D. V.*

DEATH. Name of bird.
B. H. xiv

DEBT. A payer off of the National
O. M. F. ii
Guest of Veneerings.

DEBTOR. A, A Plasterer.
L. D. vi

Who had been taken in execution for a small sum the week before, had "settled" in the course of that afternoon, and was going out.

DEDLOCK. Favourite brother of wife of Sir Morbury. *B. H.* vii
Killed in the civil wars.

DEDLOCK. Lady, Wife of Sir Morbury. *B. H.* vii
She was a lady of haughty temper, lamed—never spoke of

being crippled—or in pain—said "I will die here where I have walked, and I will walk here, though I am in my grave.

EDLOCK. My Lady, Wife of Sir Leicester Dedlock. *B. H.* ii.

For years now, my Lady Dedlock had been at the centre of the fashionable intelligence, and at the top of the fashionable tree.— An exhausted composure, a worn-out placidity, an equanimity of fatigue not to be ruffled by interest or satisfaction, are the trophies of her victory.—She has a fine face. Her figure is elegant, and has the effect of being tall.

Note.—Wife of Sir Leicester Dedlock. Before she is married she has a child, the Esther Summerson of the story, by Captain Hawdon. She is a true wife to Sir Leicester, and although she has no "family" to match his own, successfully supports the dignity of the position. She always retains the knowledge of her early secret, which is hidden from her husband. The family lawyer, Tulkinghorn, becomes acquainted with it, however, and threatens to disclose. She leaves home, and with the assistance of some brickmakers succeeds in putting off pursuit. She is found dead at the gate of the cemetery in which Captain Hawdon lies buried, by her illegitimate daughter Esther and Inspector Bucket, who carries her husband's full forgiveness.

Original: Said to have been Hon. Mrs. Watson, of Rockingham Castle: Friend of Dickens.

EDLOCK. Sir Leicester, Bart.
B. H. ii.

There is no mightier baronet than he. His family is as old as the hills, and infinitely more respectable.—The world might get on without hills, but would be done up without Dedlocks. He is honourable, obstinate, truthful, high-spirited, intensely prejudiced, a perfectly unreasonable man. He will never see sixty-five again, nor perhaps sixty-six, or sixty-seven

—has a twist of the gout now and then.—He is of a worthy presence, with light grey hair and whiskers, his fine shirt-frill, his pure white waistcoat, and his blue coat with bright buttons always buttoned.

Note.—Owner of Chesney Wold, and the head of a great county family, Conservative and reserved, not to say haughty, he becomes the husband of a woman beautiful and witty, but without "family." She has had a child by Captain Hawdon, before her marriage. Sir Leicester Dedlock is ignorant of the secret. But Tulkinghorn becomes acquainted with it and threatens to expose her. She leaves home on the eve of the threatened disclosure and dies. Sir Leicester forgives his wife and instructs Mr. Bucket to find her and bring her home. He only succeeds in finding her dead at the gate of the cemetery in which Captain Hawdon was buried. Sir Leicester never recovers from his illness and the shock, but lives a broken man in the quiet of his place in Lincolnshire.

DEDLOCK. Sir Leicester.
M. P., L. L.

DEDLOCK. Sir Morbury. Ancestor of Sir Leicester. *B. H.* vii.

DEDLOCK. Volumnia, cousin of Sir Leicester Dedlock.
B. H. xxviii.

A young lady (of sixty) who is doubly highly related; having the honour to be a poor relation, by the mother's side, to another great family—lives slenderly on an annual present from Sir Leicester—and makes occasional resurrections in the country houses of her cousins.

Note.—Cousin of Sir Leicester Dedlock. She is one of his annuitants, and after Lady Dedlock's death she takes up her residence at Chesney Wold, where she reads to the invalided Sir Leicester; cheered in the dull surroundings by a glimpse she has obtained of a paper providing for the contingency of "something happening" to her kinsman.

DEDLOCK'S. Lady, woman.
B. H. xii.

DEDLOCK'S. Sir Leicester, man.
B. H. xii.

" DEDLOCK ARMS." The, Clean little tavern. *B. H.* xxxvi.
A long sanded passage to his best parlour ; a neat carpeted room with more plants in it than were quite convenient, a coloured print of Queen Caroline, several shells, a good many tea-trays, two stuffed and dried fish in glass cases, and either a curious egg, or pumpkin—hanging from his ceiling.
Original : Sondes Arms, Rock-ingham.

DEEDLES. The banker.
C. B., C. G. ii.

DEEDLES BROTHERS. *Bankers.*
C. B., C. G. iii.

DEFARGE. Ernest, Keeper of a wineshop. *T. T. C.* v.
A bull-necked, martial-looking man of thirty.

Note.—Husband of Madame Defarge. He is a leader of men of the Revolution as she is of the women. Together they keep a wineshop in St. Antoine. He is concerned with the release of Dr. Manette, whose servant he had been in his youth, and discovers a document which the old man had hidden. This is produced against Darnay when he is imprisoned in Paris.

DEFARGE. Madame Thérèse, wife of the wine-shop keeper.
T. T. C. v.
A stout woman, with a watchful eye, a large hand heavily ringed, a steady face, strong features, and great composure of manner.

Note.—One of the knitting women. Wife of M. Defarge. A notable character and leader of the women of the Revolution. She shows herself dispassionate, and, to modern ideas, utterly unwomanly. She is killed in a struggle with Miss Pross in Paris.

DEFRESINER. Of Defresiner et Cie. *C. S. N. T.* Act iii.

DEFRESINIER ET CIE. Cham-pagne Merchants.
C. S., N. T. Act i.

DELAFONTAINE. Mr.
S. B. B., Tales v.

DELAWARE. *A. N.* xiii.

DELEGATES. *M. P., O. S.*

DEMERARA.
D. and S. lvi. ; *P. P.* liii.

DEMON OF UNREST. Sloppy. *Which see.* *O. M. F.* lxiii.

DEMPLE. George, Boy at Salem House. *D. C.* v.
Father was a doctor.

DENBIGH. Lord. *M. P., C. C.*

DENHAM. Mr., A student.
C. B., H. M. ii

DENNIS. Joe, Negro slave.
A. N. xvii

DENNIS. Mr. *B. R.* Pref

DENNIS. Ned, The hangman.
B. R. xxxvi
A squat, thick-set personage with a low, retreating forehead, coarse shock of red hair, and eye so small and near together tha his broken nose alone seemed t prevent their meeting and fusin into one of the usual size. dingy handkerchief, twisted lik a cord about his neck—his dres was of threadbare velveteen— faded, rusty, whitened black, lik the ashes of a pipe—in lieu buckles at his knees, he wor unequal lengths of pack-threa

Note.—The common hangman wh with a certain amount of secrecy is ringleader in the Gordon Riots. F virtue of his trade he wants to "work off" all the opponents, but when he is arrested and condemned to the death he has seen so many suffer, he becomes a coward and cries continuously for a reprieve.

Original : John Dennis, hangman at the time of the riots ; ringleader of the rioters, but obtained a reprieve.

DENTIST'S SERVANT. *U. T.* xvi.
He knows what goes on in the little room where something is always being washed or filed.

DEPTFORD. *B. H.* xx. ; *C. S., G. i. S.* ; *D. and S.* iv. ; *R. P., P. M. T. P.* ; *U. T.* vi.

DEPUTY. The carriers.
C. B., C. O. H. iii.

DEPUTY. In charge of lodging-house. *R. P., D. W. I. F.*

DEPUTY. *E. D.* v.
I'm man-servant up at the Travellers' Twopenny in Gasworks Garding.

Note.—" Deputy " or " Winks " or both combined was employed at " The Traveller's Twopenny " in Cloisterham. He is first seen as the guardian angel, or devil, of Durdles, whom he is pelting with stones to make him go home. The doggerel rhyme he chants was at one time and in one form well known as entering into a boys' street game :

Widdy, widdy wen !
I-ket-ches-Im-out-ar-ter-ten,
Widdy Widdy wy !
Then-E-don't-go-then-I-shy—
Widdy Widdy Wake-cock warning.

So far as the book goes he is seen as the enemy of Jasper, obtaining information for Datchery.

DERBY. Late Lord. *M. P., O. S.*

DERBY. Lord.
M. P., T. B., M. P., T. O. H.

DERRICK. John. *C. S., T. G. S.* i.

DESDEMONA. *P. F. I., A. I. D.*

DESERT. The, The plains.
U. T. xx.

DESOLATION. Great desert of.
M. P., T. O. H.

DESPAIR. Name of bird.
B. H. xiv.

DESPARD. *M. P., S. for P.*

DESSIN. Hôtel, Calais.
U. T. xvii.

D'ESTE. Mrs., As the second wife.
M. P., N. T.

D'ESTE. Villa. *P. F. I., R.*

DESTRUCTIVES. M.P's.
S. B. B., Scenes xviii.

DETAINERS. *S. B. B.,* Tales x.

DETECTIVE SERGEANT. Of Police. *R. P., D. W. I. F.*

DETECTIVES. *R. P., T. D. P.*

DEVASSEUR. Loyal.
R. P., O. F. W.
In that part of France a husband always adds to his own name the family name of his wife.

Note.—Landlord of house in French watering-place, and town councillor.

DEVIL'S PUNCH BOWL.
N. N. xxv.

DEVON. *D. and S.* xxi. ; *M. P., P. F. D.* ; *N. N.* i. ; *R. P., A. P. A.* ; *S. B. B.,* Tales x. ; *T. T. C.,* bk. ii., ch. xiii.

DEVONSHIRE FLOWER. Kitty.
C. S., M. f. T. S. ii.

DEVONSHIRE. North.
C. S., M. f. T. S. i. ; *G. S. E.* vii.

DEVONSHIRE HOUSE.
M. P., G. L. A., M. P., M. N. D.

DEVONSHIRE TERRACE.
M. P., I. C.

DIALS. The. Seven *D*ials.
S. B. B., Scenes v.

DIAVOLO. Piazza del, (Mantua).
P. F. I., V. M. M. S. S.

DIBABS. Jane. *N. N.* lv.
Married a man who was a great deal older than herself, and she *would* marry him.

DIBABSES. The. *N. N.* lv.
Lived in a beautiful little thatched white house one story high, covered all over with ivy and creeping plants—where the earwigs fell into one's tea on a summer evening.
Original : Said to have been Mile End Cottage " about a mile south of the city (Exeter) boundary on the high road to Plymouth," which Dickens took and furnished for his parents, but this is doubtful.

DIBBLE. Dorothy, Emigrant.
Wife of Sampson. *U. T.* xx.

DIBBLE. Sampson, Emigrant.
U. T. xx.

DIBBS. *M. P., F. S.*

DIBDIN. Mr., The late, Poet.
P. P. xxxiii.
Seeing the error of his ways, had written " Who hasn't heard of the Jolly Young Waterman," a temperance song.

DICK. *See* Wilkins, *D*ick.

DICK. *L. T.*

DICK. An orphan playmate of *O*liver's. *O. T.* vii.
Good-bye, dear, God bless you— The blessing was the first *O*liver had ever heard invoked upon his head.

Note.—The little friend of Oliver a the branch workhouse where Olive was farmed for sevenpence-halfpenny a week. Oliver says good-bye to him when running away from Sowerby He is a delicate child not rendere any stronger by " farming " and, a the doctor said, dying.

DICK. Guard of coach. *N. N.* v
A stout old Yorkshireman.

DICK. Hostler at tavern in Salis bury. *M. C.* v

DICK. Joram's younger apprentice
D. C. xxii

DICK. Mr., Miss Trotwood's gues or lodger. *D. C.* xiii
A florid, pleasant-looking gen tleman with a grey head.

DICK. One of Kit's children.
O. C. S. Chap. The last

DICK. Sally's sweetheart.
C. S., N. T. O

DICKENS. Charles. *A. N.* i.; *M P., A. in H. H.*; *M. P., A. T. V.*; *M. P., C. H. T.*; *M. P., I. W. M.*; *M. P., L. S.*; *M. P., M. E. R.*; *M. P., M. N. D.*; *M. P., N. S. L.*; *M. P., S. F. A.*; *M. P., V. C*

DICKENSON'S LANDING. St Lawrence. *A. N.* xv

DIDCOT. *M. P., E. S*

DIGBY. Mr., Smike acting as a tailor. *N. N.* xxx
With one tail to his coat, and a little pocket-handkerchief with a hole in it, and a woollen nightcap and a red nose, and other distinctive marks peculiar to tailors on the stage.

DIJON. *D. and S.* lii

DILBER. Mrs., Phantom laundress
C. B., C. C. S. iv
Produced sheets and towels, a little wearing apparel, old fashioned silver teaspoons, sugar tongs and a few boots.

DINGLEY DELL. *P. P.* v.
Dingley Dell, gentlemen—fifteen miles, gentlemen—cross road [from Rochester]. *See also* Muggleton.

Original : If one could say with absolute certainty which town sat for its portrait in Muggleton, it might be easy to light on Dingley Dell. In the meantime it appears probable that if Gravesend were Muggleton, Northfleet was Dingley Dell. Singlewell, the name of a hamlet some two miles distant, may have suggested the jingle of the name. There was just that amount of friendly rivalry or quarrelsome friendship between the two places as there is shown to be between Muggleton and Dingley Dell. It is also said to have been founded on Burnham and Frindsbury and Sandling near Maidstone.

DINGLEY DELL CLUB. The cricket club which played the All-Muggleton. *P. P.* vii.

DINGO. Professor, Of European reputation. *B. H.* xiii.
Second husband of Mrs. *Badger.*

DINGWALL. Esq., M.P., Cornelius Brook. *S. B. B.*, Tales iii.
He had, naturally, a somewhat spasmodic expression of countenance, which was not rendered the less remarkable by his wearing an extremely stiff cravat.

DINGWALL. Master Brook, Son of M.P. *S. B. B.*, Tales iii.
One of those public nuisances, a spoilt child—in a blue tunic, with a black belt, a quarter of a yard wide, fastened with an immense buckle, looking like a robber in melodrama seen through a diminishing glass.

DINGWALL. Miss Brook (Lavinia). *S. B. B.*, Tales iii.
Daughter of M.P.

DINGWALL. Mrs. Brook, Wife of M.P. *S. B. B.*, Tales iii.

DIOGENES. Dr. Blimber's dog. *D. and S.* xiv.
Had never in his life received a friend into his confidence, before Paul . . . a blundering, ill-favoured, clumsy, bullet-headed dog.

Note.—Florence Dombey's dog, given her by Mr. Toots.

DIRECTOR. A bank, Guest at Dombey's housewarming. *D. and S.* xxxvi.
Reputed to be able to buy up anything, but who was a wonderfully modest-spoken man.

DIRECTOR. East India, Guest at Dombey's housewarming. *D. and S.* xxxvi.
Of immense wealth, in a waistcoat apparently constructed in serviceable deal by some plain carpenter, but really engendered in the tailor's art, and comprised of the material called nankeen.

DIRECTORS. *M. P., R. S.*

DIRECTORS. More, Guests at Dombey's housewarming.
: *D. and S.* xxxvi.

DIRTY DICK. See Dorrit, Mr. Frederick. *L. D.* ix.

DISMAL JEMMY. The teller of "The Stroller's tale." *P. P.* iii.
His eyes were almost unnaturally bright and piercing ; his cheekbones were high and prominent ; and his jaws were long and lank.

Note.—A member of the theatrical profession and a friend of Jingle.

DISPENSARY. Ladies'. *S. B. B., O. P.* vi.

DISRAELI. Mr. Benjamin. *M. P., T. B.*

D'ISRAELI. Isaac. *See also* Dizzee. *M. P., L. L. M. P., T. O. II.*

DISSENTERS' MISSIONARY SOCIETY. *S. B. B., O. P.* vi.

DIVER. Colonel, Editor of New York Rowdy Journal.
M. C. xvi.
A sallow gentleman, with sunken cheeks, black hair, small twinkling eyes, and a singular expression.

DIURNO. The Teatro.
P. F. I., G. A. N.

DIXON. Mr., Mr. *Dick.*
D. C. xxiii.

DIXON. Mr. Hepworth,
M. P., P. P.

DIXONS. The. *S. B. B.,* Tales ix.

DIZZEE=Disraeli. *M. P., T. O. H.*

" DOADY." Corruption of *David.*
See Copperfield, *David.*

DOBBLE. *Daughters* of Mr.
S. B. B., Char. iii.

DOBBLE. Mr., Junior, Son of Mr. Dobble. *S. B. B.,* Char. iii.

DOBBLE. Mrs., Wife of Mr. Dobble.
S. B. B., Char. iii.

DOBBS. *M. P., T. T.*

DOBBS. Julia. *M. P., S. G.*

DOCHE. Madame, Selling calves.
R. P., M. O. F. F.

DOCK-LABOURERS. At Ratcliff.
U. T. xxx.

DOCK SLIP. In Government yard.
U. T. xv.

DOCKHEAD. *U. T.* x.

DOCKHEAD. *O. T.* l.

DOCKS. *C. S., M. L. L.* i. ; *D. C.* xxii. ; *E. D.* i. ; *O. M. F.* iii. ; *S. B. B.,* Scenes ii. ; *S. B. B.,* Tales vii.

DOCKS. East India. *U. T.* xxxiv.

DOCTOR. *P. P.* xliv.
In a green fly, with a kind o' Robinson Crusoe set o' steps, as he could let down when he got out, and pull up arter him wen he got in, to perwent the necessity o' the coachman's gettin' down, and thereby undeceivin' the public by lettin' em see that it wos only a livery coat as he'd got on, and not the trousers to match.

DOCTOR. Astonishing.
M. P., Q. D. P.

DOCTOR. Attending Anthony Chuzzlewit. *M. C.* xix.
Looked as distant and unconscious as if he had heard, and read of undertakers, and had passed their shops, but had never before been brought into communication with one.

DOCTOR. Attending birth of Marigold accepting no fee but a tea-tray. *C. S., D. M.*

DOCTOR. Attending Jinkinson.
M. H. C. v.

DOCTOR. Attending patient at the " *Bull.*" *M. C.* xxv.

DOCTOR. Attending Sam Weller's mother-in-law at time of her demise. *P. P.* lii.

DOCTOR. Examining emigrants on board the Amazon. *U. T.* xx.

DOCTOR. Of Civil Law.
S. B. B., Scenes viii.
His wig was put on all awry, with the tail straggling about his neck, his scanty grey trousers and short black gaiters, made in the worst possible style, imparted an inelegant appearance to his uncouth person, and his limp, badly-starched shirt-collar almost obscured his eyes.

DOCTORS. Some. *B. H.* xi.

DOCTOR'S SERVANT. *U. T.* xvi.

A confidential man—he lets us into the waiting-room, like a man who knows minutely what is the matter with us, but from whom the rack would not wring the secret.

DOCTORS' COMMONS. *D. C.* xxiii. ; *M. H. C.* iv. ; *O. M. F.* viii. ; *P. P.* x. ; *S. B. B.,* Scenes viii.

A quiet and shady court-yard, paved with stone, and frowned upon by old red-brick houses. . . . A lazy old nook near St. Paul's Churchyard. . . A little out-of-the-way place, where they administered what is called ecclesiastical law, and play all kind of tricks with obsolete old monster Acts of Parliament, which three-fourths of the world know nothing about. . . . The place where they grant marriage-licences to love-sick couples, and divorces to unfaithful ones ; register the wills of people who have any property to leave.

DODD. Dr. *M. P., P. P.*

DODDLES. Blinkiter. *L. D.* xlviii.

DODGER. The artful. *See* Dawkins, Jack. *O. T.* viii.

"DODO." The, An inn. *R. P., A. P. A.*

DODSON. Mr., Of *Dodson* and Fogg. *P. P.* xx.

A plump, portly, stern-looking man.

DODSON AND FOGG. His Majesty's attorneys. *P. P.* xx.

At the Court of King's Bench, and Common Pleas at Westminster.

Note.—The plaintiff's attorney (Mrs. Bardell's) in the "Case." Typical specimens of shady lawyers. They take up the case as a speculation, trusting to get costs from Mr. Pickwick.

Failing to do so, however, they incarcerate Mrs. Bardell in the Debtors' Prison, where she is discovered by Sam Weller. In this way she is the indirect means of enabling Messrs. Dodson and Fogg to obtain their costs, as Pickwick's obstinacy is not proof against Perker's pleading for Mrs. Bardell.

DOE. John. *B. H.* xx. ; *M. P., L. E. J.*

DOFFIN. *O. M. F.* xxv.

DOG. In "Happy Family." *M. P., R. H. F.*

DOGE. The. *C. S., N. T.,* Act i.

DOGGINSON. A vestryman. *R. P. O. V.*

DOGS. The. *M. P., G. D.*

DOGS. The, Seeing Mark Tapley off. *M. C.* vii.

DOGS' MEAT MAN. Fictitious name. *L. D.* vi.

DOKE. Mr. *M. P., R. S. D.*

DOLBY. George, "The man of Ross." *M. P., I. W. M.*

DOLLOBY. Mr. *D. C.* xiii.

Who kept a shop, where it was written up that ladies' and gentlemen's wardrobes were bought.

DOLLS. Mr., *See* Cleaver, Mr.

DOLLY. *Dear faithful. B. H.* iii.

DOLLY'S CHOP HOUSE. *R. P., L. A.*

DOLLYS. Small children of Joe and *Dolly* Willet. *B. R.* lxxxii.

DOLPH. Adolphus Tetterby *C. B., H*t maid. *¡. H.* iii.

DOLPHIN. The. *D* n sisters.

DOLPHIN'S HEAD. Ex-sta *U*' *B. H.* iii. house.

DOLPHIN'S HEAD. W ¡, *N. G. K.*

A mournful young w *B. H.* vii. one eye susceptible of and one uncontrollab)ora.

'DOLPHUS. *See* Tetterby, Adolphus.

DOMBEY. Mr. Paul. *D. and S.* i.

About eight-and-forty years of age—was rather bald, rather red, and though a handsome, well-made man, too stern and pompous in appearance to be prepossessing. On the brow of *D*ombey, Time and his brother Care had set some marks, as on a tree that was to come down in good time—remorseless twins they are for striding through their human forests, notching as they go.

Note.—The existing head of the firm. The "house" of Dombey and Son fills his horizon. His daughter Florence is obnoxious to him because she was not born a boy, and his son Paul is weak and dies a child. After this he marries again, but the marriage is rendered an unhappy one because there is no love, and an infinity of pride, in both husband and wife. This culminates in the elopement of the second Mrs. Dombey with Carker, the manager for the firm. But having punished her husband in this way, she immediately leaves Carker as revenge on him. Carker leaves the firm in an embarrassed position, and Dombey now proves himself incapable of nursing it over the crisis, and the crash comes. His bankruptcy has the effect of breaking his pride, and when his despised daughter comes to him, he is persuaded to go with her to her home with Walter Gay, where he ends his days in the receipt of a mysterious income.

DOMBEY. Florence. *D. and S.* i.

*D*eep dark eyes, the child in her grief and neglect was so gentle, so quiet and uncomplaining; was possessed of so much affection that no one seemed to care to have; and so much sorrowful intelligence that no one seemed to mind, or think about the wounding of.

Note.—Florence was the neglected sister of little Paul. Paul loves her, and she tends and nurses him. Ultimately she marries Walter Gay, and her father eventually relies upon his despised daughter in his adversity.

DOMBEY. Mrs. Fanny, Wife of *D*ombey and mother of Florence and Paul. *D. and S.* i.

Clinging fast to that slight spar (her little daughter) within her arms, the mother drifted out upon the dark and unknown sea that rolls round all the world. . . . Had always sat at the head of his table, and done the honours of his table, in a remarkably ladylike and becoming manner.

Note.—Dombey's first wife and mother of Florence and Paul. Apparently a gentle, patient woman, she dies at Paul's birth for want of " an effort."

DOMBEY. Paul, Son of Mr.

D. and S. i.

He was a pretty little fellow; though there was something wan and wistful in his small face. His temper gave abundant promise of being imperious in after life. He had a strange, old-fashioned, thoughtful way—of sitting brooding in his miniature armchair; when he looked (and talked) like one of those terrible little beings in the fairy tales, who at a hundred and fifty, or two hundred years of age, fantastically represent the children for whom they have been substituted.

Note.—The long-hoped-for heir of the house of Dombey and Son. His mother dies at his birth, leaving him a frail child, to the care of strangers. As he grows his health does not improve. His father sends him to Brighton to the care of Mrs. Pipchin. From there he goes to Dr. Blimber's school. But this educational hothouse does not improve his strength and he returns home. Here he takes to bed, and gradually sinks, until he leaves the " house " without a successor, tended to the last by his sister.

Original : Little Paul Dombey is founded upon Harry, the crippled son of the Burnetts (who lived in

*Upper Brook Street, Manchester).
Mrs. Burnett was Dickens's eldest
sister Fanny.*

DOMBEY. Second Mrs.
                              D. and S. xxi.
Very handsome, very haughty,
very wilful, who tossed her head
and drooped her eyelids, as though,
if there were anything in all the
world worth looking into, save a
mirror, it certainly was not the
earth or sky. Married at eighteen.

Note.—The second Mrs. Dombey
was the widow of Colonel Granger
and the daughter of Mrs. Skewton.
She makes an unhappy marriage with
Dombey. She marries him as a
business proposition : her beauty in
return for his wealth and position.
The two proud spirits clash, and the
aversion which takes the place of mere
indifference is fostered by Carker,
Dombey's manager, with an object in
view. He believes he has attained
this object when Edith elopes with
him. She deliberately takes this course
to punish her husband, and having
done so she immediately leaves Carker,
in this way revenging herself on him
for his unwelcome attentions. The
story leaves her seeking oblivion—
a changed woman to some extent.

" DOMBEY AND SON." The house
of. (The Firm.)   *D. and S.* i.
The earth was made for *Dombey
and Son* to trade in, and the sun
and moon were made to give them
light. Rivers and seas were
formed to float their ships ; rain-
bows gave them promise of fair
weather. Stars and planets cir-
cled in their orbits—to preserve
inviolate a system of which they
were the centre.

DOMBEY'S HOUSE. Mr.
                              D. and S. iii.
It was a corner house, with
great wide areas containing cellars
frowned upon by barred windows,
and leered at by crooked-eyed
doors leading to dustbins. It was
a house of dismal state, with a
circular back to it, containing a

whole suit of drawing-rooms looking upon a gravelled yard, where
two gaunt trees, with blackened
trunks and branches, rattled,
rather than rustled, their leaves
were so smoke-dried.

*Original : Pointed out as a house
at the corner of Mansfield Street
and Queen Anne Street, between
Portland Place and Bryanston
Square, although this is doubtful.*

DOMESTIC. Female, At Dr. Blimber's.   *D. and S.* xli.

DOMESTICS. Two female, Of six
Jolly Fellowship Porters.
                              O. M. F. vi.
Two robust sisters with staring
black eyes, shining flat red faces,
blunt noses, and strong black
curls, like dolls.

DON DIEGO. Inventor of flying
machines.   *R. P., A. F.*

DON QUIXOTE. Character in
Nursery Story.   *U. T.* xv.

DONCASTER.   *U. T.* xvi.

DONKEY.   *M. P., R. H. F.*

" DONKEY DRIVER." *M. P., O. S.*

DONNY. Miss, Proprietress of
boarding-school.   *B. H.* iii.

Note.—Meets Esther Summerson and
takes her to " Greenleaf," her own
boarding-school, where Esther spends
six years at Mr. Jarndyce's expense.
She occupies no other position in the
narrative beyond that short notice.

DONNY'S. Miss, A very neat maid.
                              B. H. iii.

DONNYS. Miss, Two — twin sisters.
                              B. H. iii.

DOODLE. Cocker, Esq.
                        M. P., N. G. K.

DOODLE. Sir Thomas. *B. H.* vii.

DORA. *See* Spenlow, Dora.

DORR. Madame, Marguerite's companion. *C. S., N. T.*, Act i.

A true Swiss impersonation—from the breadth of her cushion-like back, and the ponderosity of her respectable legs, to the black velvet band tied tightly round her throat for the repressing of a rising tendency to goître; or higher still, to her great copper-coloured gold earrings, or higher still, to her head-dress of black gauze stretched on wire.

DORKER. A former pupil of Mr. Squeers. *N. N.* iv.

Who unfortunately died at Dotheboys' Hall. . . . Dry toast and warm tea offered him every night and morning when he could not swallow anything—a candle in his room on the very night he died.

DORKING. *U. T.* x.; *P. P.* xxvii.

DORKING CHURCHYARD. *P. P.* lii.

DORNTON. Sergeant, A detective. *R. P., T. D. P.*

About fifty years of age, with a ruddy face, and a high sunburnt forehead.

DORRIT. Amy. *L. D.* iii.

Her diminutive figure, small features, and slight spare dress, gave her the appearance of being much younger than she was.—A woman, probably of not less than two-and-twenty, she might have been passed in the street for little more than half that age. At so much—or at so little—from eight to eight, Little Dorrit was to be hired. It was not easy to make out Little Dorrit's face; she was so retiring.—Born in the Marshalsea. She was christened one Sunday afternoon, when the turnkey, being relieved, was off the lock—went up to the font of Saint George's Church, and promised, and vowed, and renounced on her behalf.

Note.—Amy Dorrit is the title-character of the book. She is the daughter of William Dorrit, born in the Marshalsea. She is the mainstay of her father. Being at liberty to leave the prison, she goes to Mrs. Clennam's to do needlework, where she meets Arthur, through whose assistance her father is released from the Marshalsea. She accompanies her father on his travels. And when he dies and their money is lost she nurses Arthur Clennam in the same old Marshalsea, and after his recovery marries him.

DORRIT. Edward. Tip. *L. D.* vi.

Tip tired of everything . . . his small second mother got him into a warehouse, into the hop trade, into the law again, into an auctioneer's, into a brewery, into a stockbroker's, into the law again, into a coach-office, etc., etc. . . . but whatever Tip went into, he came out of tired, announcing that he had cut it.

Note.—Tip was the brother of Little Dorrit. His sister obtained numerous situations for him, but he is too deeply imbued with the spirit of the Marshalsea to remain long in any employment. He is in his majesty when the family inherit their wealth, but is returned to his natural element by their loss of it.

DORRIT. Fanny. *L. D.* vii.

Became a dancer. A pretty girl of far better figure and much more developed than Little Dorrit, though looking younger in the face when the two were observed together.

Note. Fanny is the spoilt elder sister of Little Dorrit. When the story opens she is a dancer where her uncle is in the orchestra. Mr. Sparkler is infatuated with her, but Fanny is bought off by Mrs. Merdle. Later on when the Dorrits acquire wealth, Fanny again meets the Sparkler and they are married.

Original : Fanny Dorrit is said to have been founded in some measure on Dickens' sister Fanny. The name has been traced to the burying-ground in Rochester, where " Fanny Dorrett " was found on a stone.

DORRIT. Frederick, *Brother of William Dorrit.* *L. D.* vii.

He was dirtily and meanly dressed, in a threadbare coat, once blue, reaching to his ankles and buttoned to his chin, where it vanished in the pale ghost of a velvet collar—a confusion of grey hair and rusty stock and buckle which altogether nearly poked his hat off. A greasy hat it was, and a napless. His trousers were so long and loose, and his shoes so clumsy and large, that he shuffled like an elephant.

Note.—Brother of Mr. William Dorrit, He is a clarionet player in a small theatre orchestra. When his brother enters on his inheritance Frederick accompanies the family on its travels, when he is the principal companion of Little Dorrit.

DORRIT. Mrs., Wife of debtor. *L. D.* vi.

Came—with a little boy of three years old, and a little girl of two . . . . When his youngest child (Little *Dorrit*) was eight years old, his wife, who had long been languishing away of her own inherent weakness—not that she retained any greater sensitiveness as to her place of abode than he did—went upon a visit to a poor friend and old nurse in the country, and died there.

DORRIT. William, A debtor in the Marshalsea. *L. D.* vi.

A very amiable and very helpless middle-aged gentleman—shy retiring man ; well-looking, though in an effeminate style ; with a mild voice, curling hair, and irresolute hands—rings upon the fingers in those days—which nervously wandered to his trembling lips a hundred times in the first half-hour of his acquaintance with the jail. The Father of the Marshalsea. . . . Brought up as a gentleman . . .

with the soft manner and white hair.

Note.—First introduced as the Father of the Marshalsea, a prisoner for debt for some twenty-five years. He was dependent upon his daughter, Little Dorrit, to a very large extent, but he was looked up to by all the other prisoners, largely on account of "his family." Later on he inherits a very large estate which has lain unclaimed and has accumulated. He immediately travels in a style fitting his new rank, engaging Mrs. General as a companion for his daughters. He makes himself rather ridiculous. His long imprisonment has had its effect on him. Not only are his ideas somewhat old, but his mind has become a little impaired. Through it all Little Dorrit comforts him. He is taken ill at a dinner-party given by the Merdles, calling on Bob the Marshalsea turnkey to assist him. A few days later he dies under the impression that he is still in the prison, giving instructions to pawn his jewellery to purchase delicacies. His vast wealth has been handed over to Mr. Merdle, and when the great financier breaks, the Dorrits' money is gone.

Original : A foundation for the name has been found in the name of a prisoner Dorrett, confined in the King's Bench at the time Dickens' father was in one of the debtor's prisons.

DORRIT'S ROOM. In Marshalsea, Mr. *L. D.* viii.

The bare walls had been coloured green, evidently by an unskilled hand, and were poorly decorated with a few prints. The window was curtained, and the floor carpeted ; and there were shelves and pegs, and other such conveniences, that had accumulated in the course of years, It was a close, confined room, poorly furnished ; and the chimney smoked to boot, but constant care had made it neat, and—comfortable.

D'ORSAY. Count. *M. P., L. L.*

DORSETSHIRE.
    O. C. S. vii.; *R. P., A. P. A.*
See also Cheselbourne.

D'OSSOLA. Domo.
                    P. F. I., V. M. M. S. S.

DOT. *See* Peerybingle, Mrs.
                    C. B., C. O. H. i.

DOTHEBOYS' HALL.   *N. N.* iii.
    A long, cold-looking house, one
story high, with a few straggling
outbuildings behind, and a barn
and stable adjoining.
    *Original : A long dwelling-house
of one story at Bowes, Yorkshire.*

DOT'S FATHER. *C. B., C. O. H.* iii.

DOT'S MOTHER.
                    C. B., C. O. H. iii.

DOUAI.   *U. T.* xvii.

DOUBLEDICK. Richard, Enlisting
as a soldier.   *C. S., S. P. T.* ii.
    Age, twenty-two, height five
foot ten, had gone wrong, and run
wild. His heart was in the right
place, but it was sealed up. . . .
This made him Private Richard
Doubledick, with a determination
to be shot.
        Note.—Private Richard turns over a
    new leaf—with the aid of his officer, and
    becomes Corporal, Sergeant, Lieutenant,
    Captain, and Major.

DOUBLEDICK. Son of Major
Richard.   *C. S., S. P. T.* ii.

DOUGLAS. Rev. Dr., Bishop of
Salisbury.   *M. P., R. S. D.*

DOUGLAS.   *M. P., E. S.*

DOUNCE. Mr. John, A widower.
                    S. B. B., Char. vii.
    He was a short, round, large-
faced, tubbish sort of man, with a
broad-brimmed hat, and a square
coat, and had that grave, but confident kind of roll, peculiar to old
boys in general—a retired glove-
and-braces maker—a widower

with three daughters—all u.
married. Married his cook, a
lives, a henpecked husband.

DOUNCES. Miss, Three.
            S. B. B., Char. v
Went off on small pensions.

DOVE DELEGATE. [From Americ
                    M. P., W.

DOVE. In " Happy Family."
                    M. P., R. H.

DOVE. Mr.   *M. P., M.*

DOVE. Mrs.   *M. P., M.*

DOVER. *D. C.* xiii.; *G. E.* xlv.
    L. D. iii.; *M. P., W.*; *P. F.*
    V. M. M. S. S.; *R. P., B. S*
    R. P., O. F. W.; *T. T. C.* iv
                    U. T.

DOVER. *See also* Royal Georg
Hotel.

DOVER CASTLE.   *B. H.* l

DOVER HARBOUR.   *U. T.* xvi

DOVER ROAD. *D. C.* xii.; *L. I*
    liv.; *P. P.* xliii.; *T. T. C.*
    The *Dover* road lay beyon
the *Dovermail* as it lumbered u
Shooters' Hill.

DOW. Lorenzo, A spirit.
                    M. P., S. l

DOWGATE. Young, Courting Jar;
Comport.   *U. T.* i:

DOWGATE FAMILY.   *U. T.* i:

DOWLER. Mr., An officer in H.
Majesty's Service, traveller o
coach to *Bath.*   *P. P.* xxxv
    A stern-eyed man of about five
and-forty, who had a bald an
glossy forehead, with a good dea
of black hair at the sides and bac
of his head, and large blac
whiskers. He was buttoned up t
the chin in a brown coat; an
had a large seal-skin travellin;
cap, and a great coat and cloak.

Note.—A would-be redoubtable ex-army officer. First makes the acquaintance of Mr. Pickwick and his friends at the White Horse Cellar, where they are all waiting for the Bath coach. Captain and Mrs. Dowler relieve the Pickwickians of a bedroom and sitting-room at the house in the Royal Crescent, Bath. Captain Dowler fell asleep while waiting up for his wife ; this led to Mr. Winkle's amusing adventure of the sedan chair. Captain Dowler threatens to cut Winkle's throat from ear to ear ; but in the morning both endeavour to avoid each other from a feeling of cowardice.

Original : May have been founded, at all events so far as the name is concerned, on Vincent Dowling, one of Dickens' associates on the reporting expedition to Bath.

DOWLER. Mrs., Mr. Dowler's wife. *P. P.*, xxxv.
A rather pretty face in a bright blue bonnet.

DOWN EASTERS. *A. N.* x.

DOWNING STREET. *M. P., O. C. ; M. P., R. T. ; M. P., T. T. ; M. P., T. W. M.*

DOWNS. The. *B. H.* xlv. ; *M. P., L. A. V.* ii. ; *P. P.* xxxix.

DOYCE. *Daniel,* A smith and engineer. *L. D.* x.
A short, square, practical-looking man, whose hair had turned grey, and in whose face and forehead there were deep lines of cogitation, which looked as though they were carved in hard wood. He was dressed in decent black, a little rusty, and had the appearance of a sagacious master in some handicraft—a certain free use of the thumb that is never seen, but in a hand accustomed to tools.

Note.—An inventor who is driven from pillar to post in his endeavour to get an invention adopted by Government. In the end he takes it abroad, where it is at once adopted and Doyce made much of. Arthur Clennam becomes his partner in the home firm, but meets with financial reverses. Doyce, however, clears him and reinstates him.

DOYCE. Daniel, Partner of. *L. D.* xvi.
A good man he was. But he has been dead some years.

DOZE. Prof. *Mud. Pap.* i.

DRAGON. The. *See* Blue Dragon. *M. C.* ii.

DRAGOONS. Piedmontese. *P. F. I., R.*

DRAGOONS. Pope's. *P. F. I., R.*

DRAWER. In cotton works. *M. P., O. S.*

DRAWLEY. Mr. *Mud. Pap.* ii.

DRAYTON. *M. P., T. D.*

DREARY ONE. I, the. *M. P., P. M. B.*

DREDGERMEN. Water thieves. *R. P., D. W. T. T.*
Who under pretence of dredging up coals—from the bottom of the river, hung about barges and other undecked craft, and when they saw an opportunity, threw any property they could lay their hands on overboard.

DRESSMAKER. Lodger in two-pair back. *N. N.* xiv.
Young lady who made Mrs. Kenwigs' dress.

DRINGWORTH BROTHERS. *C. S., M. f. T. S.* v.

DRIVER. New, of fresh coach. *N. N.* vi.

DRIVER. Of coach. *L. D.* liii.

DRIVER. Of coach. *M. C.* xx.

DRIVER. Omnibus, Of rival. *S. B. B., Scenes* xvi.
Taunts our people with his having "regularly done " 'em out of that old swell "—an old gentleman.

DRIZZLE. *B. H.* i.

DROOCE. Sergeant of Marines.
C. S., P. o. C. E. P.
Most tyrannical non-commissioned officer in His Majesty's service.

DROOD. Father of Edwin. *E. D.* ix.
Left a widower in his youth.

DROOD. Young, Edwin *Drood*.
E. D. ii.

Note.—The title-character of the story. He is an orphan and betrothed by his father to Rosa Bud. He studies in London, but in the opening of the story he is visiting his uncle, John Jasper, at Cloisterham, at the same time he is to see Rosa who is at the Nun's House in the same town. Possibly as a result of this early arrangement of their destinies they rebel against it and agree to abandon it. The appearance of Helen and Neville Landless completely alter the relations. Rosa takes a great interest in Neville, while Edwin is drawn to Helen. The two young men, on the other hand, dislike one another. This dislike is fostered by Jasper for his own ends, and after a bitter quarrel at Jasper's house, they are induced to make it up. For this purpose they again repair to Jasper's room, but after that Edwin is missed, and his watch found in the river. Neville has set off on a walking tour and is suspected.

Originals : The origin of the Drood mystery has been traced to a Rochester mystery. A bachelor living in High Street was trustee for his nephew. The nephew went to the West Indies but returned unexpectedly. He disappeared as suddenly, and some time later a skeleton of a young man was discovered close by ; this naturally led to the conclusion that the uncle had murdered his nephew and buried the body.

The landlord of the Falstaff Inn, opposite Gad's Hill, was named Edwin Trood.

DROUET. *M. P., H. H. W.* ; *M. P. P. P.* ; *M. P., P. T.*

DROUET'S. Mr., *Brother*.
M. P., P. ?

DROUET'S. Mr., Farming establish ment. *M. P., P.* ?

DROWSYSHIRE. Member for.
M. P., F. (

DROWVEY AND GRIMMER.
School mistresses. *H. R.*

DROWVY. Miss, A teacher. *H. R.*

DRUID. A. *U. T.*

DRUM. The, A private friend (
Trotty's. *C. B., C. G.* i

DRUMMLE. Bentley. *G. E.* xxii
An old-looking young man, of heavy order of architecture . . '
next heir but one to a Baronetc
. . . A sulky kind of fellow—idl(
proud, niggardly, reserved, an
suspicious.

Note.—Boards at Mr. Pocket's, whe
Pip stays. Although not a friend (
Pip's he is what Wemmick calls one (
the gang." He marries Estella ; il
treats her in all possible ways, and
himself killed " consequent on his il
treatment of a horse." He is known a
" The Spider."

DRUMMLE. Mrs. Bentley. *S(*
Estella.

DRUMMOND STREET.
S. B. B., Char. vii

DRUNKARD. The.
S. B. B., Tales xi
His dress was slovenly and di
ordered, his face inflamed, his eye
bloodshot and heavy . . . poore
shabbier, but the same irreclaim
able drunkard.

DRUNKARD. Mother-in-law of th
S. B. B., Tales xii
With her face bathed in tear
supporting the head of the dyin,
woman—her daughter.

DRUNKARD. Wife of the, *Dyin*
S. B. B., Tales xi
Grief, want, and anxious car

had been busy at the heart for many a weary year.

DRURY LANE. *M. P., C. P.; M. P., G. F.; M. P., W. M.; O. C. S.* vii.; *S. B. B.,* Scenes xi.; *M. P.,* Scenes xxi.; *U. T.* x.

DRURY LANE THEATRE. *M. P., B. S.; M. P., M. B.; M. P., S. Q. F.; N. N.* xxv.; *P. P.* xliv.; *R. P., D. W. T. T.; R. P., L. A.; U. T.* iv.

DUBBLEY. Officer of justice.
P. P. xxiv.
A dirty-faced man, something over six feet high, and stout in proportion.

DUBLIN. *M. P., E. S.; S. B. B.,* Tales i.; *R. P., D. W. T. T.*

DUCROW. A rider at Astley's.
S. B. B., Scenes xi.

DUCROW. Mr. *M. P., C. C.*

DUFF. Bow Street officer.
O. T. xxxi.
A red-headed, bony man, in top boots; with a rather ill-favoured countenance, and a turned up sinister-looking nose.

Note.—Bow Street officer engaged, in company with Blathers, on the attempted burglary at Mrs. Maylie's house.

DUFFY. *B. H.* xii.

DUKE. *M. C.* xxviii.

DUKE OF YORK. *M. P., N. E.*

DUKE STREET.
B. R. 1.; *O. M. F.* ii.

DULL. Mr. *Mud. Pap.* ii.

DULL LITTLE TOWN. Rochester.
M. P., J. G.

DULLBOROUGH. *U. T.* xii.
Original : Rochester.

DULLBOROUGH. Fishmongers in.
U. T. xii.
A compact show of stock in his

window, consisting of a sole and a quart of shrimps.

DULLBOROUGH. High Street.
U. T. xii.

DULLBOROUGH. Mechanics' Institution. *U. T.* xii.
"It led a modest and retired existence up a stable-yard—no mechanics belonged to it, and it was steeped in debt to the chimney-pots."
Original : This was undoubtedly represented by the Mechanics' Institute at Chatham which Dickens assisted.

DULLBOROUGH. Serious Booksellers in. *U. T.* xii.

DULLBOROUGH. Theatre.
U. T. xii.

DULLBOROUGH. Town Hall of.
U. T. xii.
Original : Corn Exchange, Rochester.

DULLBOROUGH TOWN. Playing-field. *U. T.* xii.
The station had swallowed up the playing-field.

DULWICH CHURCH. *P. P.* lvii.

DULWICH GALLERY. *P. P.* lvii.

DULWICH. House of Pickwick.
P. P. lvii.
The house I have taken—is at Dulwich. It has a large garden, and is situated in one of the most pleasant spots near London.
Original : Charles Dickens the Younger avers that his father had no house in his mind when he made Mr. Pickwick settle at Dulwich. A house at Dulwich has since been named " Pickwick Villa".

DUMBLEDON. A parlour-boarder at our school. *R. P., O. S.*

DUMBLEDON. Mrs., Mother of Dumbledon. *R. P., O. S.*

DUMKINS. Mr., A most renowned member of the All-Muggletonian. *P. P.* vii.

DUMMINS. Mr. *S. Y. G.*

DUMMY. Mr. *Mud. Pap.* ii.

DUMPS. Mr., Nicodemus, *Bank* clerk. *P. P.* vii. ; *S. B. B.,* Tales xi.
A bachelor, six feet high, and fifty years old : cross, cadaverous, odd, and ill-natured. He was afflicted with a situation in the *Bank* worth five hundred a year.

DUNCAN. *P. F. I., R.*

DUNCAN. King of Scotland, Character in play. *S. B. B.,* Scenes xiii.
Boy of fourteen, who is having his eyebrows smeared with soap and whitening.

DUNCHURCH. *P. P.* li.

DUNDAY. Dr. *R. P., D. P.*

DUNDEE. *M. P., E. S., P. P.* xlix.

DUNDEY. Doctor, A Robber. *R. P., T. D. P.*

DUNKLE. Doctor Ginery, a shrill boy. *M. C.* xxxiv.
A gentleman of great poetical elements.

DUNN. Judge. *A. N.* xvii.

DUNSTABLE. *Butcher. G. E.* iv.

DURDLES. A stonemason. *E. D.* iv.
Chiefly in the gravestone, tomb, and monumental way, and wholly of that colour from head to foot. In a suit of coarse flannel with horn buttons, a yellow neckerchief with draggled ends, an old hat more russet-coloured than black, and laced boots of his stony calling.

Note.—Stonemason in Cloisterham. He appears to spend most of his time in and about the cathedral finding, by tapping with his ever ready hammer, where long-buried celebrities have been built in. He is the foil for Jasper's evil intentions. Jasper obtains possession of Durdles' keys and thoroughly examines the locked portion of the cathedral. There is little doubt that Durdles would have entered the story, again, but for some chapters he is lost sight of.

Original : A drunken old German stonemason who was always prowling about the cathedral trying to pick up little bits of broken stone ornaments, carved heads, crockets, finials, and such like, which he carried about in a cotton handkerchief. Also said to have been founded on a verger of the cathedral.

DURHAM. A clerk at. *L. D.* xxv.

DUST. Name of bird. *B. H.* xiv.

DUST-BIN. The, Royal old *Dust*-bin. *C. S., S. L.* i.

DUSTMAN. The Golden. *See* Boffin, Mr.

DUSTMEN. The National, Members of Parliament. *H. T., R.* xii.

DUSTWOMAN. My lady. *See* Boffin, Mrs.

DUTCHMAN. Cheeseman. *R. P., T. S. S.*

DWARF. *M. P., T. O. P.*

DWARF. A, One of Magsman's Showmen. *C. S., G. i. S*
A most uncommon small man with a most uncommon large Ed ; and what he had inside that Ed, nobody ever knowed but himself. It was always his opinion that he was entitled to property.

DWARF CHILD. An unlucky, A nursemaid. *D. and S.* xxxi
With a giant baby, who peeps in at the porch.

EASTERN PENITENTIARY. Prison in Philadelphia.   *A. N.* vii.
    The system here is rigid, strict, and hopeless solitary confinement —cruel and wrong.

EASTERN POLICE MAGISTRATE.
                        U. T. iii.
    Said, through the morning papers, that there was no classification at the Wapping Workhouse for women.

EASTLAKE.   *M. P., O. L. N. O.*

EASTLAKE. Mr., *Sec.* to Fine Arts Commission.   *M. P., S. of C.*

EATANSWILL. Pocket borough returning member.   *P. P.* xi.
    We have traced every name in Schedules A and B without meeting with that of Eatanswill . . . we are therefore led to believe that Mr. Pickwick, with that anxious desire to abstain from giving offence to any, and with those delicate feelings for which all who knew him well know he was so eminently remarkable, purposely substituted a fictitious designation.

Original : It is suggested that the name was taken from Eaton Socon, a small town on the Norwich Road. The place has been variously identified as Ipswich, Bury St. Edmunds, Norwich, and Sudbury. The first held the field for many years. Bury St. Edmunds' claims are not convincing, and the evidence is generally in favour of Sudbury. Dickens reported elections at both Ipswich and Sudbury in 1835, for the Morning Chronicle. *The Sudbury election was a bye-election for the return of one member only. The evidence is fully set out in the* Daily News *and other papers, of April 1907. And the coach distances fit in with the latter place.*

EATON SQUARE.
                    S. B. B., O. P. vii.

EBENEZER JUNCTION.
                    P. P. xxxiii.

ECCLES. Late, of Blackburn.
                    M. P., O. S.

ECCLESIASTICAL COURT. The.
                    B. R. lxxxii.

" EDDARD." Coster's donkey.
                    O. M. F. v.

EDDY. *See* Drood, Edwin.

EDDYSTONE LIGHTHOUSE.
                    M. P., L.

EDEN.   *M. C.* xxi.
    A flourishing city ! an archi-
tectural city. There were banks,
churches, cathedrals, market-
places, factories, hotels, stores,
mansions, wharves ; an exchange,
a theatre ; public buildings of all
kinds. ... So choked with slime and
matted growth was the hideous
swamp which bore that name.
    *Original : A place known as
Cairo in U.S.A.*

EDEN. The valley of. *M. C.* xxi.

EDEN SETTLEMENT. The office
of the.   *M. C.* xxi.
    It was a small place ; something
like a turnpike. But a great deal
of land may be got into a dice-
box, and why not a whole territory
be bargained for in a shed.

EDEN STINGER. The office of.
                    M. C. xxi.

EDGE-ER. (Edgware) Road.
                    S. B. B., lv.

EDGWARE ROAD.   *N. N.* xl.

EDINBURGH. *M. P., E. S.* ; *M. P.,
S. S.* ; *P. P.* xlix. ; *R. P., O. H. T.* ;
                    U. T. xxiii.

EDINBURGH AND LONDON MAIL.
                    P. P. xlix.

EDINBURGH APPRENTICE
SCHOOL ASSOCIATION.
                    M. P., E. A. S.

EDITH. Mrs. Granger.
                    D. and S. xxi.

EDKINS. Mr., A member of the
Honourable Society of the Inner
Temple.   *S. B. B.,* Tales vii.
    A pale young gentleman in a
green stock, and spectacles of the
same colour. Member of a debating society.

EDMONDS. George.   *V. C.*

EDMONTON.   *O. T.* xxxi.

EDMUND. Mr., Mr. Longford,
alias Denham.   *C. B., H. M.* iii.

EDMUNDS. George. *M. P., V. C.*
    John, the subject of " The
Convict's return" told at the
Manor Farm.   *P. P.* vi.

    Note.—The hero or villain of the
clergyman's story of " The Convict's
Return." If Gravesend is Muggleton,
the churchyard of the story is probably
that of Shorne—a favourite place with
Dickens.

EDMUNDS. The father of John
Edmunds, the returned convict.
                    P. P. vi.

EDMUNDS. Mrs., The mother of
John Edmunds the returned convict.   *P. P.* vi.

EDSON. Mr., A lodger of Mrs.
Lirriper's.   *C. S., M. L. Lo.* i.

EDSON. Mrs., supposed wife of
Mr. Edson.   *C. S., M. L. Lo.* i.
    A pretty young thing and
delicate.

EDWARD. Bertha's brother.
                    C. B., C. O. H. iii.

EDWARD. The Deaf man in the
cart.   *C. B., C. O. H.* iii.

EDWARD. Lord.   *M. P., T. T.*

ELFIN. The, Smallweed.
>   *B. H.* xxi.

ELIZABETH. Miss.   *O. M. F.* v.
Inhabitant of Corner House.

ELLENBOROUGH. Lord.
>   *M. P., C. P.*

ELLIE. " Negro boy " slave.
>   *A. N.* xvii.

ELLIS. Mr., Visitor to Bar Parlour.
>   *S. B. B.*, Char. iii.
Sharp-nosed, light-haired man
in a brown surtout reaching nearly
to his heels.

" ELMESES." The.   *C. S., H. T.*

ELMS. The city of, New Haven.
>   *A. N.* v.

ELTON. Mr.   *M. P., R. S. L.*

ELTON DISTRICT.   *M. P., O. S.*

ELY PLACE.   *D. C.* xxiv.

ELYSIAN FIELDS.
>   *B. H.* xii. ; *M. P., N. Y. D.*

EMANUEL. Stiggins' chapel.
>   *P. P.* lii.

EMERSON. Mr. Ralph Waldo,
author.   *A. N.* iii.

EMIGRANTS. On board the
" Amazon."   *U. T.* xx.
Some with cabbages, some with
loaves of bread, some with cheese
and butter, some with milk and
beer, some with boxes, beds, and
bundles, some with babies—nearly
all with children—nearly all with
bran new tins for their daily
allowance of water.

EMILE. Billeted at the clockmaker's.
>   *C. S., S. L.* ii.

EMILIA. Mrs. *Orange's* baby.
>   *H. R.* iv.

EMILY.   *M. P., A. A. P.*

EMILY. Little. *D. C.* iii.

Note.—Mr. Peggotty's niece. David meets her, while they are both children, on his visit to her uncle at Yarmouth, and falls in love with her. She is afterwards affianced to Ham Peggotty. David takes Steerforth on a visit with him to Yarmouth and eventually Emily elopes with Steerforth. After some time he tires of her and proposes to hand her over to Littimer. Thereupon she leaves him, but is ultimately discovered by her uncle, and they emigrate together. They do well in Australia.

EMILY. A suicide. *U. T* iii.

EMILY. The elder prisoner.
S. B. B., Tales i.
About to enter prison van.

EM'LY. *See* Emily, Little.

EMMA. Little. *D. C.* xii.
The girl twin.

EMMA. Maid at Manor Farm.
P. P. xxviii.

EMMA. Servant at the Manor Farm, Dingley Dell. *P. P.* v.

EMMA. Waitress at an Anglers' Inn. *C. S., H. T.*

EMMELINE. Angela's cousin, and Edwin's sweetheart. *C. S., H. T.*

EMMY. *M. P., S. R.*

EMPEROR. *M. P., S. F. A.*

ENCHANTRESS. Compact, Passenger in train. *R. P., A. F.*

" ENDEAVOUR." Steward of the.
S. B. B., Tales vii.

" ENDEAVOUR." Steward's wife of the. *S. B. B.*, Tales vii.

ENDEAVOUR STRAITS.
M. P., L. A. V. ii.

ENDELL. Martha, Schoolfellow of Em'ly's and used to work for Mr. Omer. *D. C.* xxii.

Note.—The " unfortunate " who discovers Little Em'ly for her uncle. She was at one time at Omer's working side by side with Little Em'ly.

ENGINE DRIVER. American Railway train. *M. C.* xxi.
He leaned with folded arms and crossed legs against the side of the carriage smoking.

ENGINE DRIVER. On G.W.R.
M. P., R. S.

ENGINEER. An. Guest of Veneerings. *O. M. F.* ii.

ENGINEERS. *Officer of, At Chatham.*
U. T. xxiv.

ENGINEMEN AND FIREMEN. On the Bedford Station. *M. P., R. S.*

ENGLAND. Sir Richard.
M. P., S. F. A.

ENGLAND. *A. N.* ii. ; *C. B., B. o. L.* i. ; *C. S., N. T.* iv. ; *C. S., S. P. T.* i. ; *C. S., T. G. S.* ; *H. R.* iii. ; *H. T., S.* ii. ; *L. D.* xi. ; *M. P., A in E.* ; *M. P., A. P.* ; *M. P., B.* ; *M. P. E. S.,* *M. P., I. C.* ; *M. P., I. M.* ; *M. P., J. T., M. P., L. A. V.* ; *M. P., L. L.* ; *M. P., L. W. I. Y.* ; *M. P., N. E.* ; *M. P., N. G. K.* ; *M. P., N. J. B.* ; *M. P., O. F. A.* ; *M. P., P. A. P.* ; *M. P., P. M. B.* ; *M. P., P. P.* ; *M. P., R. D.* ; *M. P., R. S.* ; *M. P., R. T.* ; *M. P. S.* ; *M. P., S. D. C.* ; *M. P., S. S.* ; *M. P., T. T.* ; *N. N.* vi. ; *R. P., T. H. S.* ; *U. T.* iii.

ENGLAND. West of.
M. P., L. W. O. Y. ; *O. M. F.* xvii.

ENGLISH COURT. *M. P., C. C.*

ENGLISH PUBLIC. *M. P., R. S.*

ENGLISH WATERING-PLACE.
R. P., O. E. W.
Original : Broadstairs.

ENGLISH WATERING-PLACE.
Boatmen of our. *R. P., O. E. W.*
Looking at them, you would say that surely these must be the

laziest boatmen in the world— let them hear—the signal guns of a ship in distress, and these men spring into activity, so dauntless, so valiant, and heroic, that the world cannot surpass it.

ENGLISH WATERING-PLACE.
Church in our.　　*R. P., O. E. W.*
A hideous temple of flint, like a great petrified haystack.

ENGLISH WATERING-PLACE. Main street of our.　　*R. P., O. E. W.*
Always stopped up with donkey chaises.''

ENGLISH WATERING-PLACE. Pier at.　　*R. P., O. E. W.*
A queer old wooden pier, fortunately without the slightest pretensions to architecture, and very picturesque in consequence.

ENGLISH WATERING-PLACE. Preventive station at our.
R. P., O. E. W.

ENGLISH WATERING-PLACE. The sands at our.　*R. P., O. E. W.*
The children's great resort. They cluster there, like ants.

ENGLISHMAN. *Daughter of Mr. The.*　　*C. S., S. L.* ii.
His erring and disobedient and disowned daughter.

ENGLISHMAN. Monsieur The. *See* Langley, Mr.

ENGLISHMEN.　　*M. P., N. J. B.*

ENGLISHMEN. A few shadowy.
U. T. xvii.
Passengers on Dover-Calais Packet.

ENGROSSING CLERK. Of Patent Office.　　*R. P., P. M. T. P.*

" ENOUGH," HOUSE. " Satis."
G. E. viii.

ENTERPRISE. Fort,
M. P., L. A. V. i.

ENTRIES. Blind Alleys in Liverpool.　　*U. T.* v.
Kept in wonderful order by the police.

EPPING FOREST.
B. R. i. ; *U. T.* xxvii.

EPPS. Dr.　　*M. P., C.*

EPSOM.　　*R. P., T. D. A.* ii.

EQUITY. Court of.
B. H. xv. ; *M. P., L. E. J.*

ERIE. Lake.　　*A. N.* xiv.

ERIE. The town of.　*A. N.* xiv.

ERINGOBRAGH. Miss=Ireland.
M. P., A. J. B.

ESQUIMAUX.　　*M. P., L. A. V.* i.

ESSEX. *G. E.* liv.; *M. P., N. S. L.* ;
D. and S., i. ; *O. M. F.* xii.

ESSEX MARSHES.　　*B. H.* i.

ESSEX STREET.　　*G. E.* xl.

ESTABLISHMENT. Normal,
R. P., T. D. P.

ESTELLA. *Daughter of Magwich. Adopted by Miss Havisham.*
G. E. viii.
Who was very pretty and seemed very proud—pretty brown hair.
Note.—She is first seen by Pip at Miss Havisham's, who has adopted her. She is being trained by her deranged foster-mother to break men's hearts, as the only possible revenge on the sex for the injury done to her by Compoyson. She marries Bentley Drummle, the Spider, a man with much money, a family pedigree, but no intelligence. Pip loves her, and even after the marriage cannot quite forget her. Drummle illtreats her, and she separates from him. Later on he is killed by an accident " consequent on his ill-treatment of a horse." Estella and Pip accidentally meet on the site of the old Satis House some two years after Drummle's death, and when Pip leaves with her, it is with " no shadow

of another parting from her." She proves to be the daughter of Magwich and Molly, Mr. Jaggers' housekeeper.

ESTELLA. Mother of.
G. E. xlviii.

ETERNAL CITY. The.
P. F. I., R. P. S.

ETERNAL HEAVENS. *M. P., D. V.*

ETHELINDA. Reverential wife of Thomas Sapsea.   *E. D.* iv.

ETON.   *M. P., I. M. T.*

ETON SLOCOMB.   *N. N.* v.
Original: Eaton Socon.

ETTY.   *M. P., O. L. N. O.*

EUGÈNE. Billeted at the Tinman's.
C. S., S. L. ii.
Cultivating, pipe in mouth, a garden four foot square, for the Tinman, behind the shop.

EUGENE. A solicitor, Friend of Mortimer, guest of Veneerings.
O. M. F. ii.
Buried alive in the back of his chair, behind a shoulder—and gloomily resorting to the champagne chalice whenever proffered.

EUPHEMIA. Miss Pupford's assistant.   *C. S., T. T. G.* vi.

EUROPE. *A. N.* xviii.; *M. P., B. A.*; *M. P., C. C.*; *M. P., E. C.*; *M. P., G. H.*; *M. P., I.*; *M. P., I. C.*; *M. P., N. S. E.*; *M. P., S. B.*; *M. P., S. F. A.*; *R. P., O. H. T.*

EUROPE. The capital of.
M. H. C. i.

EUSTACE. The celebrated Mr.
L. D. xli.
The classical tourist.

EUSTON HOTEL. *M. P., E. S.*

EUSTON SQUARE. *A. N.* i.; *M. P., E. S.*; *N. N.* xxxvii.; *S. B. B.,* Char. viii.

EVANS. Miss Jemima, a shoe binder and straw-bonnet maker.
S. B. B., Char. iv
In a white muslin gown—a little red shawl—a white straw bonnet trimmed with red ribbons, a small necklace, a large pair of bracelets, Denmark satin shoes, and open work stockings, white cotton gloves —and a cambric pocket handkerchief.

EVANS. Mr., Friend of the Gattletons.   *S. B. B.,* Tales ix
A tall, thin, pale young gentleman, with extensive whiskers, talent for writing verses in albums and playing the flute.

EVANS. Richard, schoolboy.
O. C. S. li
An amazing boy to learn, blessed with a good memory and a ready understanding.

EVANS. Superintendent, Thames Police Officer. *R. P., D. W. T. T*

EVANS AND RUFFY. Messrs., Bill Printers.   *R. P., B. S*

EVENSON. Mr. John, Boarder at Mrs. Tibbs.   *S. B. B.,* Tales i
Very morose and discontented; a thorough Radical, and used to attend a great variety of public meetings, for the express purpose of finding fault with everything that was proposed; was in receipt of an independent income— from various houses he owned in the different suburbs.

EXCAVATORS' HOUSE OF CALL The.   *D. and S.* vi

" EXCHANGE OR BARTER." Boy at Salem House.   *D. C.* vi
One boy, who was a coal-merchant's son, came as a set-off against the coal bill, and was called, on that account, " Exchange or Barter."

EXM

EXM

EXT

EYE

EZE

FA

FA

EXCHANGE. Royal. *M. P.*, *G. A.
N. N.* xli. ; *U. T.* iv.

EXCHEQUER. *M. P., R. T.*

EXCHEQUER COFFEE - HOUSE.
O. M. F. iii.

EX-CHURCHWARDEN. The.
S. B. B., O. P. iv.
Supporter of Spruggins.

EXCISE OFFICE. The.
O. M. F. iv.

EXETER. *C. S., D. M.* ; *N. N.*
xxi. ; *U. T.* xxiii.

EXETER. Bishop of. *M. P.,
Ag. Int.* ; *M. P., L. W. O. Y.* ;
M. P., P. F.

EXETER 'CHANGE.
S. B. B., Char. i.

EXETER HALL. *M. P., G. B.* ;
M. P., N. E. ; *M. P., S. S.* ;
N. N. v. ; *S. B. B., O. P.* vi.

EXETER STREET.
R. P., T. D. A. i.

EXHIBITION. Miss Linwood's.
D. C. iv.
Mausoleum of needlework.

EXMOUTH. *C. S., S. P. T.* ii.

EXMOUTH STREET. *O. T.* viii.

EXTERNAL PAPER - HANGING
STATION. The. *R. P., B. S.*

EYE. A little town in Suffolk.
M. P., E. C.

EZEKIEL. The boy at Mugby Junction. *C. S., M. J.* v.

F

FACCIO. Monte. *P. F. I., G. A. N.*

FACE-MAKER. The. *U. T.* xxv.
A corpulent little man in a
large white waistcoat, with a
comic countenance, and with a
wig in his hand.

FACTORY. The. *H. T., S.* xii.

FAGGS. Mr. *O. M. F.* viii.

FAGIN. A thief. *O. T.* viii.
A very old, shrivelled Jew,
whose villainous and repulsive face
was obscured by a quantity of
matted red hair. He was dressed
in a greasy flannel gown, with his
throat bare.

Note.—The crafty old Jew who kept
a thieves' school near Field Lane in
Saffron Hill, and acted as receiver to
the older members of his gang of
burglars. Oliver falls into his hands
and he is paid by Monks to make the
boy into as bad a thief as the companions he is forced to associate with.
His dupes are detected, but the Jew
himself escapes until the murder of
Nancy breaks up the whole gang. Fagin
is charged with complicity in the
murder, and after being sentenced to
death becomes mad in his cell and
beseeches Oliver to assist him to
escape. He suffers the extreme penalty of the law.

*Original : So far as the name is
concerned Fagin appears to have
been founded on one of Dickens'
fellow boy-workers in the blacking
factory, who befriended him.*

FAHEY. Mr. *M. P., E. T.*

FAIDO. A Swiss village.
P. F. I., R. D.

FAIR. The, In the Fleet.
P. P. xli.
" You don't really mean that any
human beings live down in those
wretched dungeons ? " " *Don't I,*"
said Mr. Roker.

FAIR GUVAWNMENT. Fair Government. *M. P., T. O. H.*

FAIRFAX. Mr. *S. Y. G.*

FAIRIES. *M. P., F. F.* ; *M. P., G. F.*

FAIRY. John Kemble.
M. P., G. F.

FAIRY. Master Edmund.
M. P., G. F.

FAIRY. Miss. *M. P., G. F.*

FAIRY. Miss Angelica.
M. P., G. F.

FAIRY. Miss Rosina. *M. P., G. F.*

FAIRY. Mr. *M. P., G. F.*

FAIRY. Mrs. *M. P., G. F.*

FALKLAND ISLANDS. *B. R.* Pref.

FALKNER AND CO. *M. P., S. P.*

FALL. Mr., Editor of the *Vicksburg Sentinel.* *A. N.* xvii.

FALLEY. Mr. *O. M. F.* viii.

FALMOUTH. *C. S., M. f. T. S.* v.

FALSTAF INN. The *P. P.* v.
A little roadside public-house, with two elm-trees, a horse-trough, and a sign-post in front.

Note.—The Falstaf stands opposite Gad's Hill Place, and this is probably what Dickens had in his mind's eye when he wrote.

FAMILY. An Irish. *P. P.* l.
Keeping up with the chaise and begging all the time.

FAMILY MANSION. Of Uncommercial traveller. *U. T.* xviii.
In a certain distinguished metropolitan parish.

FAMILY PARTY. Christmas.
S. B. B., Char. ii.
Not a mere assemblage of relations. It is an annual gathering of all the accessible members of the family, young or old, rich or poor ; and all the children look forward to it, for two months beforehand, in a fever of anticipation.

FAMILY PARTY. Grandpapa at Christmas. *S. B. B.,* Char. ii.
Produces sprig of mistletoe from his pocket, and tempts the little boys to kiss their little cousins under it—says, that when

he was just thirteen and three months old, he kissed grandmama under a mistletoe too.

FAMILY SPY. New York.
M. C. xvi.

FAN. Scrooge's sister.
C. B., C. C. s. ii.

FANCHETTE. *R. P., O. B.*

FANE. General. *M. P., S. F. A.*

FANG. Mr., Police Magistrate.
O. T. xi.
A lean, long-backed, stiff-necked middle-sized man, with no great quantity of hair, and what he had, growing on the back and sides of his head. His face was stern, and much flushed.

Note.—The police-magistrate before whom Oliver was taken when charged with stealing Mr. Brownlow's handkerchief. He is overbearing in manner, violent in language, and without any regard for justice. He had summarily sentenced Oliver to three months' hard labour on the flimsiest evidence, when the keeper of the bookshop breathlessly arrived with testimony which could not be ignored.

Original : Mr. Laing, a magistrate of the period. Several houses have been pointed out as the original of Mr. Fang's office ; the weight of evidence appears to be in favour of No. 54, Hatton Garden.

FANG'S. Mr., Office. *O. T.* xi.

FANNY. Father and mother of.
S. B. B., Tales x.

FANNY. Guest at Christmas party.
R. P., T. C. S.

FANNY. Mrs. Parsons.
S. B. B., Tales x.

FARADAY.
M. P., M. M. ; M. P., R. S. D.

FAREWAY. Lady, Widow of Sir Gaston Fareway. *G. S. E.* vii.

FAREWAY. Mr., Second son of Lady Fareway. *G. S. E.* vii.

FAREWAY PARK. Home of Lady
Fareway.   *G. S. E.* ix.

FARM HOUSE. Deputy of landlady
of.   *R. P., D. W. I. F.*

FARM HOUSE. Landlady of.
R. P., D. W. I. F.

FARM HOUSE. The old, Common
lodging-house. *R. P., D. W. I. F.*

FARMER.   *M. P., A. A. P.*

FARMER'S SON.   *M. P., A. A. P.*

FARMERS. Young and old, In
Salisbury Market Place. *M. C.* v.
With smock-frocks, brown
great-coats, drab great-coats,
red worsted comforters, leather
leggings, wonderful-shaped hats,
hunting whips, and rough sticks.

FARMERS' WIVES. In Salisbury
Market Place.   *M. C.* v.
In beaver bonnets and red
cloaks.

FARRIER. A tall.   *M. H. C.* iii.
Who having been engaged all
his life in the manufacture of horse-
shoes must be invulnerable to the
power of witches.

FARRINGDON STREET. *B. R.* lx. ;
C. S., S. L. iv. ; *M. P., S. S. U.* ;
P. P. xli. ; *S. B. B.,* Scenes xvi.

FAT BOY. Joe.   *P. P.* xxviii.

FAT BOY.   *P. P.*
Original : Was Mr. James Bud-
den, at one time landlord of the
" Red Lion Inn " in Military
Road, Chatham ; also claimed by
Richard Cockerill (alias of Charles
Peace ?) as founded on himself.

FATHER. Aged, Of Mr. Vholes.
B. H. xxxvii.

FATHER. A stout, Of a stout
family.   *S. B. B.,* Scenes x.
On board the " Gravesend
Packet."

FATHER. Briggs'. *D. and S.* xiv.
Never would leave him alone.

FATHER. Husband of mother illus-
trated by Goblin.   *P. P.* xxix.
Wet and weary. . . . the children crowded round him, and seiz-
ing his cloak, stick, and gloves—
with busy zeal, ran with them from
the room.

FATHER. Monsieur Rigaud's.
L. D. i.
My father was Swiss.

FATHER. Of George, Prisoner
at Marshalsea.   *P. P.* xxi.
Who *would* have let him die in
gaol, and who *had* let those who
were far dearer to him than his
own existence, die of want, and
sickness of heart that medicine
cannot cure—had been found dead
on his bed of down.

FATHERS. One of the young, At
Great St. Bernard. *L.D.* xxxvii.
The host, a slender, bright-eyed,
young man of polite manners,
whose garment was a black gown
with strips of white crossed over
it like braces, who no more resembled the conventional breed
of the Saint Bernard Monks,
than he resembled the conventional breed of the Saint Bernard
dogs.

FATHERS. Two young, On the
Great St. Bernard. *L. D.* xxxvii.

FAUNTLEROY. Criminal.
M. P., C. P.

FECHTER. Mr. Actor.   *M. P.,*
O. F. A. ; *M. P., M. M.*

FECHTER. Mr., As Jules Obenreizer.   *M. P., N. T.*

FEE. Dr.   *Mud. Pap.* i.

FEEDER, B. A. Mr., Dr. Blimber's
Assistant.   *D. and S.* xi.
He was a kind of human barrel-

organ, with a little list of tunes at which he was continually working, over and over again, without any variation.

Note.—Assistant in Dr. Blimber's school. He afterwards marries Miss Blimber and succeeds the doctor in the school.

FEEDER, M. A. The Reverend Alfred, *B*rother of Mr. Feeder.
D. and S. lx.

FEEDER. Mrs., née Cornelia Blimber. *D. and S.* lx.

FEENIX. Mrs. Granger's cousin.
D. and S. xxi.
A man about town forty years ago.

Note.—Cousin of the second Mrs. Dombey, and therefore nephew to Mrs. Skewton. Although he is a rather ancient nobleman, he endeavours to appear youthful. Albeit he is good at heart, and he is last seen on an errand of mercy, taking Florence to bid farewell to her stepmother.

FEENIX. Old cousin.
M. P., P. M. B.

FEENIX. The late Lord, Brother of the Honourable Mrs. Skewton.
D. and S. xxi.
The family are not wealthy—they're poor, indeed—but if you come to blood, sir.

FELIX. Fourth son of Mrs. Pardiggle. *B. H.* viii.

FELLOW. A tall, Fresh from a slaughter-house, a rioter.
B. R. lxiv.
Whose dress and great thigh-boots smoked hot with grease and blood.

FELLOW. Passenger by coach.
P. P. xlix.
An uncommonly ill-looking fellow in a close brown wig and a plum-coloured suit, wearing a very large sword, and boots up to his hips.

FELLOW. That young, Hanging outside stage-door at Astley's.
S. B. B., Scenes xi.
In the faded brown coat, and very full light green trousers, pulls down the wrist-bands of his check shirt, as ostentatiously as if it were of the finest linen, and cocks the white hat of the summer before last as knowingly over his right eye, as if it were a purchase of yesterday.

FELLOWS IN THE WEST INDIES. Some of our. *L. D.* lx.

FEMALE. A, Guest at *D*ombey's housewarming. *D. and S.* xxvi.
A bony and speechless female with a fan.

FEMALE. From Inn in Rochester.
C. S.; *S. P. T.* i.

FENCHURCH STREET.
O. M. F. xxv.

FENDALL. Sergeant, A detective.
R. P., T. D. P.
A light-haired, well-spoken, polite person.

FENNING. Eliza. *M. P., C. P.*

FERDINAND. Miss, Pupil at the Nun's house. *E. D.* ix.

FERGUSON. *M. P., F. C.*

FERGUSON. *N. N.* ii.

FERN. William, Will Fern.
C. B., C. G. ii.
A sun-browned, sinewy, country-looking man, with grizzled hair, and a rough chin—in worn shoes—rough leather leggings, common frock, and broad slouched hat.

FERNANDO PO. *M. P., N. E.*

FEROC. M., Bathing machine proprietor. *R. P., O. F. W.*
Gentle and polite, immensely stout—of a beaming aspect, deco-

rated with so many medals (for saving people from drowning) that his stoutness seems a special dispensation of Providence to enable him to wear them.

FERRARA.   *P. F. I., T. B. F.*

FETTER LANE. *S. B. B.*, Char. ix.

FEZZIWIG. Mrs. *C. B., C. C.* s. ii.

FEZZIWIG. Old. *C. B., C. C.* s. ii.
    An old gentleman in a Welsh wig.

FEZZIWIG. Two 'prentices of old.
            C. B., C. C. s. ii.
    Their beds—under a counter in the back shop.

FEZZIWIGS. Three Miss.
            C. B., C. C. s. ii.
    Daughters of old Fezziwig.

FIBBITSON. Mrs., An inmate of the almshouses.   *D. C.* v.
    Another old woman in a large chair by the fire.

FIDDLER. At Uncle Tom's Cabin blowing room.   *M. P., O. S.*

FIELD. Rev. Mr.   *M. P., P. P.*

FIELD. Sacred.   *P. F. I., R.*

FIELD AND CO. Inspector, policemen.   *R. P., D. W. I. F.*

FIELD LANE. *M. P., C. and E.* ;
    M. P., S. S. U. ; *O. T.* viii.

FIELDING. Emma.   *S. Y. C.*

FIELDING. May, Tackleton's fiancée.   *C. B., C. o. H.* ii.
    Her hair is dark . . . her shape —there's not a doll's in all the room to equal it . . . and her eyes.

FIELDING. Mrs., Mother of May.
            C. B., C. o. H. ii.
    A little querulous chip of an old lady with a peevish face, who in right of having preserved a

waist like a bedpost, was supposed to be a most transcendent figure.

FIELDING. Sir John, A magistrate.
            B. R. lviii.

FIELDS. James T. *M. P., I. W. M.*

FIELDS. Mistress Annie.
            M. P., I. W. M.

FIERY FACE. Ruth. *M. C.* xliii.

FIESOLE.   *M. P., L. L.*

FIESOLE. The Convent at.
            P. F. I., R. D.

FIGURE. Ghost in wooden press.
            P. P. xxi.
    A pale and emaciated figure in soiled and worn apparel. The figure was tall and thin, and the countenance expressive of care and anxiety.

FIKEY. A forger. *R. P., T. D. P.*

FILER. Mr.   *C. B., C. G.* i.
    A low-spirited gentleman of middle age, of a meagre habit, and a disconsolate face ; who kept his hands continuously in the pockets of his scanty pepper-and-salt trousers, very large and dog-eared from that custom ; and was not particularly well brushed or washed.

FILEY.   *H. D.* iv.

FILLETOVILLE. Marquess of, Only son of.   *P. P.* xlix.
    The young gentleman in sky blue.

FINCHBURY. Lady Jane.
            D. and S. xli.

FINCHES. A club. *G. E.* xxxiv
    The members should dine expensively once a fortnight.

FINCHING. Flora. *L. D.* xiii.
    Always tall, had grown to be

very broad, too, and short of breath—a lily, had become a peony—Flora, who had seemed enchanting in all · she said and thought, was diffuse and silly.

Note.—The relict of Mr. Finching and daughter of Casby. Formerly a sweetheart of Arthur Clennam, she is introduced desiring to practise all those endearing, artless wiles of twenty years before. She is last seen at Little Dorrit's wedding with Arthur Clennam.

Original : Said to be founded on Miss Beadwell in later life.

FINCHING'S. Aunt, *See* Aunt, Mr. F's.

FINCHLEY. *See* Abel Cottage.

FINCHLEY. *D. and S.* xxxii. ; *B. R.* lxviii.

FINE ARTS COMMISSIONERS. *M. P., S. of C.*

FINLAYSON. Mr., The Government actuary. *M. P., Th. Let.*

FINSBURY SQUARE. *O. T.* xxi. ; *S. B. B.,* Char. *V.*

FIPS. Mr. *M. C.* xxxviii.
Grave, business-like, sedate-looking . . . small and spare, and looked peaceable, and wore black shorts, and powder.

Note.—The mysterious lawyer who is in old Martin's confidence to some extent, and who acts as his agent in doing good while old Martin himself is acting the part he has chosen.

Original of Mr. Fips' Chambers : Probably situated in Pump Court.

FIRE ENGINE. The parish. *S. B. B., O. P.* i.

FIREMAN. The, Of American railway train. *M. C.* xxi.
Who beguiled his leisure by throwing logs of wood from the tender, at the numerous stray cattle on the line.

FIREMAN. Waterman, An old. *S. B. B.,* Tales vii.

Dressed in a faded red suit, just the colour of the cover of a very old Court-Guide.

FIREWORKS. Rev. Jabez. *M. P., W. H.*

" FIRST AND LAST. The," A beer shop. *U. T.* xxii.

FISH. An Indian chief. *A. N.* ix.

FISH. Mr., Confidential Secretary to Sir Joseph Bowley. *C. B., C. G.* ii.
A not very stately gentleman in black, who wrote from dictation.

FISH. Mrs. *M. P., S. B.*

FISH STREET HILL. *D. C.* xxx. ; *O. M. F.* xx.

FISHER. Fanny, Married daughter of Mrs. Venning. *C. S., P. o. C. E. P.*
Quite a child she looked, with a little copy of herself holding to her dress.

FISHMONGERS' HALL. *M. P., N. G. K.*

FITZ. Lord Fitz-Brinkle. *S. B. B.,* Scenes xix.

FITZBALL. *S. Y. G.*

FITZ-JARNDYCE. Miss Flite's name for Esther Summerson. *Which see.*

FITZ-LEGIONITE. Percival. *M. P., C. Pat.*

FITZ-MARSHALL. Mr. Charles. *See* Jingle, Mr. Alfred.

FITZROY SQUARE. *S. B. B.,* Scenes vii.

FITZ-SORDUST. Col. *S. Y. G.*

FITZ-WARREN. Mr. *M. P., G. A.*

FIVE POINTS. New York. *A. N.* vi.

FIXEM. Old, A bailiff, The broker's man's master. *S. B. B., O. P.* v.

FIZKIN. Horatio, Esq. of Fizkin Hall. *P. P.* xiii.
A tall, thin gentleman, in a stiff white neckerchief . . . desired by the crowd . . . to send a boy home, to ask whether he hadn't left his voice under the pillow.

Note.—The defeated candidate for Parliamentary honours at the Eatanswill election.

FIZKIN'S COMMITTEE. *P. P.* xiii.

FIZMAILE. Mr. *M. P., T. T.*

FIZZGIG. Don Bolaro, Jingle's Spanish grandee. *P. P.* ii.

FIZZGIG. *Donna* Christina, Jingle's imaginary conquest. *P. P.* ii.
Splendid creature—high-souled daughter . . . never recovered the [effects of] the stomach pump.

FLABELLA. Lady, Character in a novel read by Kate to Mrs. Wititterly. *N. N.* xxviii.

FLADDOCK. General, A passenger in the "Screw." *M. C.* xvii.

FLAIR. The Honourable Augustus. *S. B. B.,* Tales viii.

FLAM. Hon. Sparkins. *M. P., V. C.*

FLAM. Mr., Of the Minories. *M. P., N. G. K.*

FLAM. The real doctor. *M. P., Q. D. P.*

FLAMWELL. Mr. *S. B. B.,* Tales v.
A little spoffish man, with green spectacles—one of those gentlemen—who pretend to know everybody, but in reality know nobody.

FLANDERS. *U. T.* xxvi.

FLANDERS' NEPHEW. *U. T.* xxvi.
To whom, Flanders, it was rumoured, had left nineteen guineas.

FLANDERS. Sally, A married servant. *Once* nurse of Uncommercial Traveller. *U. T.* xxvi.
After a year or two of matrimony, became the relict of Flanders . . . an excellent creature, and had been a good wife.

FLANDERS' UNCLE. *U. T.* xxvi.
A weak little old retail grocer, had only one idea, which was that we all wanted tea.

FLANDERS' WIFE'S BROTHER. *U. T.* xxvi.
Guest at funeral of Flanders.

FLASHER. Wilkins, Esq., Stockbroker. *P. P.* lv.

FLASHER. Wilkins, Clerk of. *P. P.* lv.

FLASHER. Wilkins, Esq., Groom of. *P. P.* lv.
On his way to the West End to deliver some game.

FLASHER. Wilkins, Esq., House of. *P. P.* lv.
The house of Wilkins Flasher Esq., was in Surrey. The horse and "Stanhope" of—were at an adjacent stable.

FLAY. George. *M. P., E. S.*

FLEANCE. Character in Play. *S. B. B.,* Scenes xiii.
Young lady with the liberal display of legs.

FLEDGEBY. Mr., Father of (deceased). *O. M. F.* xxii.
Had been a money-lender.

FLEDGEBY. Mr., Mother of (deceased). *O. M. F.* xxii.

FLEDGEBY. Young. *O. M. F.* xxi.
Had a peachy cheek, or a cheek compounded of the peach, and the red red wall on which it grows, and

was an awkward, sandy-haired, small-eyed youth, exceeding slim— and prone to self examination in the articles of whiskers and moustache.

Note.—Fledgeby has a dual personality in the story ; one, his own ; the other as Pubsey and Co., money-lenders and bill-brokers. He wishes to be married and agrees to pay Mr. Lammle a thousand pounds when he is united to Miss Georgina Podsnap. The marriage does not take place, however, and Lammle does not receive his money. Pubsey and Co. are hard dealers, and Fledgeby carries out the deceit in detail by pleading for some mercy for the creditors. Retribution overtakes him in the form of Mr. Alfred Lammle and in the shape of a " stout lithe cane."

FLEECE. Golden, Shop of Thomas Curzon. *B. R.* xxxviii.

FLEET. The. *B. H.* xxiv. ; *B. R.* viii. ; *M. P., S. S. U.* ; *N. N.* lv. ; *P. P.* xl.

FLEET MARKET. *B. R.* viii. ; *M. P., S. S. U.*
At that time, a long irregular row of wooden sheds and pent-houses, occupying the centre of what is now called Farringdon Street.

FLEET PRISON. The poor side. *P. P.* xlii.
In which the most miserable and abject class of debtors are confined. A prisoner having declared upon the poor side pays neither rent nor chummage. His fees, upon entering and leaving the gaol, are reduced in amount, and he becomes entitled to a share of some small quantities of food : to provide which, a few charitable persons have, from time to time, left trifling legacies in their wills.

FLEET STREET. *B. R.* xv. ; *C. S. H. T.* i. ; *D. C.* xxiii. ; *G. E.* xlv. ; *M. P., T. D.* ; *O. M. F.* viii. ;

P. P. xl. ; *S. B. B.,* Scenes xviii *S. B. B.,* Tales x

FLEETWOODS. The, Mr. Flee wood. *S. B. B.,* Tales v.
Mrs. Fleetwood, and Mast Fleetwood, of the steam excursio party.

FLEMING. Agnes, *Oliver Twist* mother. *O. T.*
Note.—The mother of Oliver Twi and sister of Rose Maylie. Betraye by the father of Monks she makes h way to the workhouse where she di in giving birth to Oliver.

FLEMING. Rose, Miss Maylie. *O. T.* li

FLESTRIN. Junior, Quinbus, The Young Man Mountain, E mund Sparkler. *L. D.* l

FLETCHER. Christian. *R. P., L.*

FLIMKINS. Mr. *S. Y.*

FLIMKINS. Mrs. *S. Y.*

FLINTWINCH. Ephraim. *L. D.* lxv
Twin brother of Jeremiah' The lunatic keeper.

Note. — Jeremiah's brother. keeper of a lunatic asylum who obliged to leave the country. Wh he does so he is entrusted, by l brother, with a box of papers stol from Mrs. Clennam. This box ge into the hands of Rigaud, who ende vours to make money by the content

FLINTWINCH. Jeremiah. *L. D.* i
An old man, bent and drie but with keen eyes. He was short, bald old man, in a hig shouldered black coat, and wais coat, drab breeches, and long dre gaiters. He might, from his dres have been either clerk, or servan and in fact had long been bot His neck was so twisted, that th knotted ends of his white crav usually dangled under one ear

he b
havin
—and
since
time

partn

Clen

get i
lose
how
sum

T
sine
you
Foo
of d
the
man

N
dent
sees
terro

FLIPF
mer

FLIPF

FLIPF
field

FLIPF
of l
V
of t
nec

FLITI
in
squ
(Ch
pre
in
sui
tai
cat
cu

ments ; principally consisting of
paper, matches, and dry lavender.

Note.—A suitor in chancery, a
regular attendant who had become
rather mad through the never-ending
proceedings. She was a good little soul.
She appointed Richard her executor,
in the event of her death, to watch over
her interests, as he, too, was such a
regular attendant ; but on the result of
the Jarndyce case being known she
liberates the birds she had caged and
named so oddly.

*Original : An actual character
who travelled from court to court,
with a real or fancied grievance.*

FLITE'S. Miss, Brother (deceased).
B. H. **xxxv.**
Had a builder's business.

FLITE'S. Miss, Father (deceased).
B. H. **xxxv.**
Had a builder's business.

FLITE'S. Miss, Sister (deceased).
B. H. **xxxv.**
A tambour worker.

FLOPSON. One of the young
Pocket's nurses. *G. E.* **xxii.**

FLORENCE. *L. D.* li. ; *M. P.*,
L. L. ; *N. N.* i. ; *P. F. I.*, *T. B. F.*

FLORENCE STREET. 30. *U. T.* **xx.**
Latter-Day Saints' Book Depôt.

FLOUNCEBY. *M. P., B. A.*

FLOUNCEBY. Mrs. *M. P., B. A.*

FLOWER. The, Of ours. *See* Bagstock.

"FLOWER - POT. The," Bishopsgate Street. *S. B. B.*, xlvi.
A public house.

FLOWERS. Mrs. Skewton's maid.
D. and S. xl.

FLOWERS. Tom. *M. P., G. D.*

FLUGGERS. Old, Member of Mr. V.
Crummles' Company. *N. N.* xxx.
Does the heavy business.

FLUMMERY. Mr. *Mud. Pap.* ii.

FLY. A, A werry large—reg'lar bluebottle. *S. B. B.*, Tales iv.

FLYNTERYNGE. Mynheer von Jeremiah. *See* Flintwinch.

FOGG. Mr., Of *D*odson and Fogg. *P. P.* xx.
An elderly, pimply-faced, vegetable diet sort of man, in a black coat, dark mixture trousers, and small black gaiters : a kind of being who seemed to be an essential part of the desk at which he was writing, and to have as much thought and sentiment.

FOGLE. Jackson. *U. T.* v.

FOLEY. Acquaintance of Cousin Feenix; on a blood mare. *D. and S.* xli.

FOLIAR. Mr., Pantomimist in Mr. Vincent Crummles' Company. *N. N.* xxiii.
Note.—A somewhat mischievous member of Crummles' company, acting the savage on his first introduction. It was he who carried the cartel of defiance from Mr. Lenville, and in the capacity of mutual friend acted as tale-bearer.

FOLKESTONE. *M. P.*, *S. R.* ; *R. P.*, *A. F.*

FOLLY. Name of one of Miss Flite's birds. *B. H.* xiv.

FOLLY DITCH. *O. T.* l.

FONDI. *P. F. I.*, *R. D.*

FONDLING. The. *N. N.* xxxvi.

FOODLE. *D*uke of. *B. H.* xii.

FOOTBOY. Of Mrs. Gowan. *L. D.* xxvi.
Microscopically small . . . who waited on the malevolent man who hadn't got into the post office.

FOOTMAN. *M. C.* ix.
With such great tags upon his liveried shoulder, that he wa perpetually entangling and hook ing himself among the chairs an tables, and led such a life of to ment, which could scarcely hav been surpassed if he had been bluebottle in a world of cobwebs

FOOTMAN. *P. P.* xxxvi
Gentleman in a yellow waistcoa with coach trimming border.

FOOTMAN. *P. P.* xxxvi
Selection in purple cloth.

FOOTMAN. *P. P.* xxxvi
Gentleman in light blue suit.

FOOTMAN. Dr. Blimber's footman *D. and S.* x
A weak-eyed young man, wit the first faint streaks or early daw of a grin on his countenance.

FOOTMAN. Liveried, of Mada Mantalini. *N. N.*

FOOTMAN. Mr. Bantam's. *P. P.* xxx
Powder-headed, tall footman

FOOTMAN. Mr. Tite-*B*arnacle's. *L. D.*
The footman was to the Gro venor Square footmen, what th house was to the Grosvenor Squa houses. Admirable in his way, h way was a back and a bye wa His gorgeousness was not u mixed with dirt ; and both i complexion and consistency he ha suffered from the closeness of h pantry—had as many large bu tons with the Barnacle crest upo them, on the flaps of his pocket as if he were the family strong-bo and carried the family plate an jewels about with him buttone up.

FOOTMAN. Mr. Wititterley's. *N. N.* xx

FOOTMAN. Of doctor attending o Jinkinson. *M. H. C.*

FOUNDLING CHILDREN. Hospital for. *B. R.* xxxviii. ; *C. S., N. T.* o. ;
L. D. ii.
Time was, when the foundlings were received without question in a cradle at the gate. Time is, when inquiries are made respecting them, and they are taken as by favour from the mothers, who relinquish all natural knowledge of them and claim to them for ever-more.

FOUNDLING HOSPITAL. Governors of the.   *C. S., N. T.* o.

FOUNDLING HOSPITAL. Matron of.   *C. S., N. T. o.*
An elderly female attendant.

FOUNDLING HOSPITAL. Neat attendants of.   *C. S., N. T.* o.
Silently glide about the orderly and silent tables.

FOUNDLING HOSPITAL. Treasurer of.   *C. S., N. T.*, Act i.

FOUNTAIN. Runaway man-slave. *A. N.* xvii.

FOUNTAIN. The, In Vauxhall Gardens.   *S. B. B.*, Scenes xiv.
That had sparkled so showily by lamp-light, presented very much the appearance of a water-pipe that had burst · all the orna-ments were dingy.

FOUNTAIN COURT. Temple.
B. R. xv. ; *M. C.* xlv.

FOUR ASHES.   *M. P., E. S.*

FOX. George.   *M. P., R. S. D.*

FOX. The Misses.   *M. P., S. B.*

FOX. Mr.   *M. P., T. O. H.*

FOX. Mr., of Oldham. *M. P., P. F.*

FOXEY. Dr.   *Mud. Pap.* ii.

FRA DIAVOLO. Fort of.
P. F. I., R. D.

FRANCE. *B. H.* iii. ; *B. R.* lxxxii. ; *C. S., M. L. Lo.* i. ; *D. C.* xxii. ; *D. and S.,* Pref. ; *L. D.* i. ; *M. H. C.* i. ; *M. P., A. in E.* ; *M. P., C. P.* ; *M. P., E. S.* ; *M. P., L. A. V.* ii. ; *M. P., N. G. K.* ; *M. P., N. J. B.* ; *M. P., R. D.* ; *M. P., T. O. H.* ; *N. N.* vi. ; *P. F. I., G. T. F.* ; *R. P., O. B.* ; *T. T. C.* i. ; *U. T.* vii.

FRANCE. The inns of. *C. S., H. T.*
With the great church-tower rising above the courtyard—and clocks of all descriptions in all the rooms, which are never right.

FRANCE. King of.
M. P., L. W. O. Y.

FRANCE. Mouse, delegate from.
M. P., W. H.

FRANCE. Queen of. *B. R.* lxxxii.

FRANCIS. Father. *M. P., N. T.*

FRANCO. Porto.
P. F. I., G. A. N.

FRANÇOIS. From restaurant.
D. and S. liv.
A dark bilious subject in a jacket, close shaved, and with a black head of hair cropped.

FRANÇOISE. Monsieur, A butcher.
R. P., M. O. F. F.

FRANK. Little, Child of first cousin of poor relation. *R. P., P. R. S.*
A diffident boy by nature.

FRANK. Mother of little.
R. P., P. R. S.

FRANKFORT. *U. T.* xxiii.

FRANKLIN. *M. P., P. F. D.* ; *M. P., R. S. D.*

FRANKLIN. Benjamin, the spirit of.
M. P., S. B.

FRANKLIN. Sir John.
M. P., L. A. V. i.

FRASCATI. *P. F. I., R.*

"FRATERNITY'" *M. P., O. ?*

FRED. Mrs. *C. B., C. C.* s. i
A dimpled, surprised-looking capital face ; a ripe little mouth that seemed made to be kissed— as no doubt it was.

FRED. Scrooge's nephew.
C. B., C. C. s. i

FREDERICKSBURG. *A. N.* i

FREE TRADE HALL. Manchester
M. P., Ag. In

FREEDOM. Fair, A lovely princess. *R. P., P. ?*

FREEMAN'S COURT. Cornhill.
P. P. xvi
House of Dodson and Fogg.
Original : Probably drawn from Newman's Court, Cornhill, with name borrowed from a court neighbouring Cheapside.

FREEMASONS'. The.
S. B. B., Scenes xi

FRENCH. Emperor of the.
M. P., R. S.

FRENCH. The. *C. S., S. P. T.*

FRENCH-FLEMISH COTTAGES.
U. T. xx
In the wayside cottages the loom goes wearily—rattle and click, rattle and click—a poor weaving peasant—man or woman, bending at the work, while the child working too, turns a hand-wheel upon the ground to suit its height.

FRENCH - FLEMISH COUNTRY CHAPELS. *U. T.* x?
Little whitewashed black holes —with barred doors and Flemish inscriptions, abound at roadside corners, and often they are garnished with a sheaf of wooden crosses, like children's swords.

FRENCH WATERING-PLACE.
French visitors to.
R. P., O. F. W.
Bathe all day long, and seldom appear to think of remaining less than an hour at a time in the water.

FRENCH WATERING-PLACE. Fish market in.   R. P., O. F. W.

FRENCHMAN.   S. B. B., Scenes v.

FRENCHMAN. A, Passenger in train.   R. P., A. F.
In Algerine wrapper, with peaked hood behind, who might be Abd-el-Kader dyed rifle-green.

FRENCHMAN. Melancholy, Passenger in train.   R. P., A. F.
With black vandyke beard, and hair close-cropped, with expansive chest to waistcoat, saturnine as to his pantaloons, calm as to his feminine boots, precious as to his jewellery, smooth and white as to his linen.

FRENCHMEN.   M. P., N. J. B.

FRENCHMEN. Shadowy.
U. T. xvii.
Passengers on Dover-Calais Packet.

FRIAR. Carthusian.
P. F. I., G. A. N.

FRIAR. Of Saint Benedict.
N. N. vi.

FRIARS.   P. F. I., T. R. P.

FRIARS. Dominican.
P. F. I., V. M. M. S. S.

FRIBOURG. P. F. I., V. M. M. S. S.

FRIDAY. Character in Nursery Tale.   U. T. xv.

FRIDAY STREET. R. P., T. D. P.

FRIEND. Giving bride away at wedding.   D. and S. v.
A superannuated beau, with

one eye, and an eyeglass stuck in its blank companion.

FRIEND. Landor's. *M. P., L. L.*

FRIEND. Our Honourable, M.P. *R. P., O. H. F.*

FRIEND. To Em'ly abroad. *D. C.* xxii.
In a little cottage she found room for Em'ly (her husband was away at sea).

FRIENDS. Two or three of Toots. *D. and S.* xxii.

FRITHERS. Mr. *S. Y. C.*

FROME. *C. S., S. P. T.* ii.

FROST. Miss. *R. P., O. S.*
A pupil in our school.

FROST AND CO. *M. P., S. for P.*

FRRWENCH CONSUL'S. *C. S., M. L. Leg.* i.

FRY. Mrs. *M. P., S. Pigs.*

FRY. Mrs. *S. B. B.*, Scenes xxiv.

FRYING-PAN. The. *A. N.* v.

FUFFY. *B. H.* xii.

FULHAM. *D. and S.* xxiii. ; *L. D.* xvi. ; *R. P., O. F. W.*

FUNAMBULES. *M. P., W.*

FURNIVAL'S INN. *E. D.* xi. ; *S. B. B.*, Tales vii.

G

G. Mr. J. *M. P., S. F. A.*

G. Mrs. *M. P., S. F. A.*

G. P., A widow lady. *L. D.* xlviii.

"G." Supposed ex-lover of M's Pupford. *C. S., T. T. G.* i.
A short chubby old gentlem, with little black sealing-wax bo s up to his knees.

GABELLE. Monsieur Théoph, Postmaster and tax functiona. *T. T. C.*, bk. ii. ch. v.
Note.—Local functionary in the l- lage by the estate of the St. Evrémor. He is imprisoned by the Republics and liberated to appear as a witns against Charles Darnay in Paris.

GABLEWIG. Mr., of the In r Temple. *M. P., M. N.* .

GABRIELLE. Child at the barb's shop. *C. S., S. L* i.

GAD'S HILL. *U. T.* i.

GAD'S HILL GASPER = Cha s Dickens. *M. P., I. W.* .

GAFF. Tom. *M. P., N. G.* .

GAG. Tom. *M. C.* xx i.

GAGARINES QUAY. St. Petersb g. *M. P., M.* .

GAGGS. Mr. *O. M. F.* i.

GAIETY. Theatre of. *M. P., N. Y* .

GAL. The, Jonas Chuzzlewit's m d. *M. C.* x i.

GALLANBILE. Mr. M. P., Far ly of. *N. N.* i.
Applicant of General Age y Office for cook.

GALLAND. Mr. *M. P., T. O* .

GALLERY. Mr. Catlin's. *A. N.* ii.

GALLERY. Reporters'. *S. B. B.*, Scenes x ii.

GALLERY. The Strangers'. *B. R.* x.

GALLEY. Mr. *O. M. F.* iii.

GALLEY-SLAVES' PRISON.
P. F. I., G. A. N.

GALILEO. The Tower of.
R. F. I., R. D.

GALLY. Major C. A. N. xvii.

GALT HOUSE. Hotel in Louisville.
A. N. xii.

GAMBAROON. Lord. M. P., T. T.

GAME CHICKEN. The.
D. and S. xxii.
Was always to be heard of at
the bar of the " Black Badger,"
wore a shaggy white great-coat
in the warmest weather, and
knocked Mr. Toots about the
head three times a week, for the
small consideration of ten and
six per visit.
Note.—The pugilistic attendant of
Mr. Toots.

Original : Was founded on a
real character with the same
sobriquet in the earlier half of
the nineteenth century.

GAMFIELD. Mr., Chimney-sweep.
O. T. iii.
Whose villanous countenance
was a regular stamped receipt
for cruelty.

GAMMON. Name of a bird.
B. H. xiv.

GAMMONRIFE. Member for.
M. P., F. C.

GAMP. Husband deceased of Mrs.
Gamp. M. C. xix.
When Gamp was summoned to
his long home, and I see him
a lying in Guy's Hospital with a
pennypiece on each eye, and his
wooden leg under his left arm, I
thought I should have fainted
away.

GAMP. Mr. M. P., G. B.

GAMP. Mrs. M. P., S. F. A.

GAMP. Mrs., midwife. M. C. xix.
A fat old woman with a husky
voice, and a moist eye, which she
had a remarkable power of turning
up and only showing the white
of it. Having very little neck, it
cost her some trouble to look over
herself, if one may say so, at
those to whom she talked. She
wore a very rusty black gown,
rather the worse for snuff, and a
shawl and bonnet to correspond.
The face—the nose in particular—
somewhat red and swollen.

Note.—The story of Mrs. Gamp
shows a picture of the very unpro-
fessional nurse, now happily seldom
met with. Her care for herself and
her creature comforts is the sole
end she has in view. She appears on
the scene on several occasions in the
capacity of monthly nurse, sick nurse,
and "layer out" of the dead. She is
dismissed, and, if exposure were necessary in such a case, exposed at the
general family meeting when Pecksniff
is awarded his just dues. It is Mrs.
Gamp's friend, Mrs. Harris, who has
become a household word.

GANDER. Mr., Boarder at Todger's
establishment. M. C. ix.
Of a witty turn, who had origin-
ated the sally about "collars."

GANGES. River. M. P., T. O. H. ;
U. T. xv.

GARDEN COURT. Temple. G. E.
xli. ; M. C. xlv.

GARDEN ON THE ROOF. The.
O. M. F. xxii.
A blackened chimney-stack
over which some humble creeper
had been trained—a few boxes
of humble flowers and evergreens
completed the garden.

GARDENER. A market.
S. B. B., Scenes vi.

GARDENER. Miss Donny's.
B. H. iii.
Ugly, lame, old gardener.

GARDENS. Tea.
S. B. B., Scenes ix.

GARDINER. Captain.
M. P., L. A. V. ii.

GARDNER. Dr.   *M. P., R. T.*

GARDNER. Mr., as Mr. Lanbury.
M. P., I. S. H. W.

GARDNER. Mr., as John Maddox.
M. P., V. C.

GARDNER. Mr., as Tom Sparks.
M. P., S. G.

GARGERY. Joe, The blacksmith.
G. E. i.
A fair man with curls of flaxen hair on each side of his smooth face, and with eyes of such a very undecided blue that they seemed to have somehow got mixed with their own whites. Mild, good-natured, sweet-tempered, easy-going, foolish, dear fellow.

Note.—The blacksmith of the story; and one of its chief characters. He is the husband of Pip's sister, and both he and Pip are badly treated by her. Joe makes up to Pip for this by taking him as something of a friend and companion. In the course of the story it transpires that Joe was the son of a drunken father. He went to work and kept his father until that individual went off in a " purple leptic " fit. He then had to keep his mother until she also died. After that he got acquainted with Pip's sister and married her, when his " hammering " was still continued. His wife is savagely attacked by Orlick and subsequently dies. Joe comes up to London when Pip is ill and nurses him and pays his debts. When Pip goes down to see Joe again, he finds he has married Biddy. In later years Joe and Biddy are seen living happily with a little Pip of their own.

Original of Joe's Forge: Generally believed to have been situated in Cliffe-at-Hoo. But later traced to Chalk, close by Dickens's honeymoon house.

GARGERY. Little girl, daughter of Joe and Biddy.   *G. E.* lix.

GARGERY. Mrs. Biddy (second wife).   *G. E.* lix.

GARGERY. Mrs. Joe, Sister of Philip Pirrip.   *G. E.* i.
She was not a good-looking woman, with black hair and eyes, and such a prevailing redness of skin. She was tall and bony, and almost always wore a coarse apron fastened over her figure behind with two loops, and having a square, impregnable bib in front that was stuck full of pins and needles.

Note.—Wife of Joe Gargery, and sister of Pip. She is killed by the results of a murderous attack made on her by Orlick.

GARGERY. Pip., Son of Joe.
G. E. lix.
" We giv' him the name of Pip for your sake, dear old chap."

GARLAND. Mr. Abel. *O. C. S.* xiv.
Mr. Abel had a quaint old fashioned air about him, looked nearly of the same age as his father, and bore a wonderful resemblance to him in face and figure . . . in the neatness of the dress and even in the club-foot he and the old gentleman were precisely alike.

Note.—The son of Mr. Garland articled to Witherden. Mr. Abel enters in due time, into partnership with Witherden and marries a bashful young lady.

GARLAND. Mr.   *O. C. S.* xiv.
A little, fat, placid-faced old gentleman.

Note.—Mr. Garland is introduced driving a fat pony. Kit Nubbles hold the pony while the old gentleman visits Witherden. Mr. Garland has no small change to give Kit and tells him to return on another occasion to work out the remainder. Much to the general surprise Kit does this. When Kit leaves Little Nell's service he is engaged by Mr. Garland, who befriend him.

GASPER=Charles Dickens.
                    M. P., I. W. M.

GASWORKS GARDING.   *E. D.* v.

GATE OF ST. MARTIN. Theatre of
the.   *M. P., N. Y. D.*

GATE OF SAN GIOVANNI LATER-
ANO. (Rome.)   *P. F. I., R. D.*

GATE OF THE STAR. The.
                    B. H. xii.

GATE. The traitor's. *M. H. C.* i.,
                    G. E. liv.

GATEHOUSE. The old stone, (crossing the Close).   *E. D.* ii.
    Pendent masses of ivy and
creeper covering the building's
front.

GATEWAY. Old, In which Little
Nell saw Quilp. *O. C. S.* xxvii.
    *Original: Suggested as the ancient
gate in Much Park Street, Coventry.*

GATTLETON. Lucinia. *S. B. B.,*
                    Tales ix.

GATTLETON. Mr. A stock-broker
in especially comfortable circumstances.   *S. B. B.,* Tales ix.

GATTLETON. Mr.   Sempronius.
                    S. B. B., Tales ix.
    Son of Mr. Gattleton.

GATTLETON. Mrs., Wife of Mr.
Gattleton.   *S. B. B.,* Tales ix.
    A kind, good-tempered, vulgar
soul, exceedingly fond of her
husband and children.

GAY. Walter.   *D.* and *S.* iv.

    Note.—Sol Gills' nephew. He is
    employed in the house of Dombey and
    Son. He is able to render some service
    to Florence Dombey when she is lost.
    Mr. Dombey is displeased with him,
    and to get him out of the way sends
    him to the Barbadoes branch of the
    firm. The ship in which he sails is lost,
    it is believed, with all on board. But
    some time after Walter returns and
    marries Florence. Later on old Mr.
    Dombey comes to live with them.

GAZINGI. Miss, Member of Mr. V. Crummles' Company. *N. N.* xxiii. With an imitation ermine boa tied in a loose knot round her neck, flogging Mr. Crummles Junior for fun.

GENERAL ASSEMBLY. *A. N.* ii.

GENERAL BOARD OF HEALTH. *M. P., F. F.; R. P., O. o. T.*

GENERAL COVE. A gentleman. *U. T.* iii.

GENERAL. The, King of Bill-stickers. *R. P., B. S.*

GENERAL. Mrs., Matron or Cha-peron of Mr. Dorrit's daughters. *L. D.* xxxvii. The daughter of a clerical digni-tary in a cathedral town. A lady, well-bred, accomplished, well connected. . . . In person, Mrs. General, including her skirts, was of a dignified and imposing appear-ance ; ample, rustling, gravely voluminous. Her countenance and hair had rather a floury appearance. If her eyes had no expression, it was probably be-cause they had nothing to express.

Note.—An aristocratic widow en-gaged by Mr. Dorrit after his accession of wealth to be a companion to his daughters and to improve their minds and manners. It is presumed that she has designs of becoming Mrs. Dorrit, and almost gets this length. But after Mr. Dorrit's attack at the Merdles he does not know her and thinks she wishes to take the place of a woman at the Marshalsea.

GENERAL. Old. *B. H.* liii.

GENERAL AGENCY OFFICE. *N. N.* xvi. For places and situations of all kinds enquire within. . . a little floor-clothed room, with a high desk railed off in one corner.

GENERAL AGENCY OFFICE. Pro-prietress of. *N. N.* xvi.

A very fat old lady in a mob c —who was airing herself at 1 fire.

GENERAL POST OFFICE. Lond *O. T.* xxx

GENERIC FRENCH OLD LAI *M. P.,*

GENEVA. *L. D.*, xxiii. ; *C. N. T.* Act

GENEVA. The Lake of. *L. D.* xxx'

GENIE. *M. P., T. O.*

GENII. *M. P,.*

GENII. The Guardian, of the Ci Gog and Magog. *M. H. C*

GENIUS. Aspiring, of Harmo Meeting. *S. B. B.,* Scenes

GENIUS. Of *Despair* and Suici *N. N.* A wrinkled, hideous figure, w deeply sunk and bloodshot ey and an immensely long cadaver face, shadowed by jagged matted locks of coarse black h He wore a kind of tunic, of a bluish colour, which—was clas or ornamented down the fr with coffin-handles. His l too, were encased in coffin-pla as though in armour, and c his left shoulder he wore a sl dusky cloak, which seemed mad a remnant of some pall.

GENOA. *P. F. I., T. R. P.; R. P. M. T. P.; U. T.* xx

GENTLEMAN. Accomplice of tl thimbles' man. *S. B. B.,* Scenes In top boots, standing regrets his inability to bet— his purse at home.

GENTLEMAN. American, passe in the Screw. *M. C.* Wrapped up in fur and skin, . . . [appeared in a ' shiny, tall, black hat, and constantly overhauled a very little valise of pale leather.

GENTLEMAN. (Another clerk) in Secretarial *Department* of Circumlocution Office. *L. D.* x.

GENTLEMAN. Another elderly, Member of Mr. V. Crummles' Company. *N. N.* xxiii.
Paying especial court to Mrs. Crummles, a shade more respectable, who played the irascible old man.

GENTLEMAN. Another masked. *M. H. C.* iii.

GENTLEMAN. At dining-room of house which shall be nameless. *C. S., S. L.* iv.
He had one of the new-fangled uncollapsible bags in his hand. His hair was long and lightish.

GENTLEMAN. Boarder at Pawkin's. *M. C.* xvi.
Started that afternoon for the Far West on a six months' business tour; his equipment—just such another shiny hat—and just such another little pale valise, as had composed the luggage of the gentleman who came from England in the Screw.

GENTLEMAN. Boarder at Todger's. *M. C.* ix.
Of a theatrical turn, recites.

GENTLEMAN. Boarder at Todger's *M. C.* ix.
Of a literary turn, repeated (by desire) some sarcastic stanzas he had recently produced.

GENTLEMAN. Boarder at Todger's. *M. C.* ix.
Of a debating turn, rises and suddenly lets loose a tide of eloquence which bears down everything before it.

GENTLEMAN. Brother of Jewish, *U. T.* ii.
One of the drowned at wreck of the "Royal Charter."

GENTLEMAN. Brother of Smike's mother. *N. N.* lx.
A rough, fox-hunting, hard-drinking gentleman, who had run through his own fortune, and wanted to squander away that of his sister.

GENTLEMAN. Catholic, of small means. *B. R.* lxi.
Having hired a waggon to remove his furniture by midnight, had had it all brought down into the street to save time in the packing. The poor gentleman, with his wife and servant and their little children, were sitting trembling among their goods in the open street.

GENTLEMAN. Children of Catholic. *B. R.* lxi.

GENTLEMAN. Corpulent, with one eye. *M. P., T. B.*

GENTLEMAN. *Deaf* old, Friend of Master Humphrey. *M. H. C.* i.
His hair was nearly white—I never saw so patient and kind a face.

GENTLEMAN. Elderly inebriated. Member of Mr. V. Crummles' Company. *N. N.* xxiii.
In the last depths of shabbiness, who played the calm and virtuous old men.

GENTLEMAN. Fat old, In the pit of theatre. *N. N.* xxiv.

GENTLEMAN. Fine old English. *M. P., F. O. E. G.*

GENTLEMAN. Foreign. *O. M. F.* xi.

GENTLEMAN. French. *C. S., Mrs. L. L.*

GENTLEMAN. Frequenter of the "Magpie and Stump."
P. P. xx.
In a checked shirt and mosaic studs, with a cigar in his mouth.

GENTLEMAN. Friend of Alderman Cute's. *C. B., C. G.* i.
Had a very red face, as if undue proportion of the blood in his body were squeezed up into his head, which perhaps accounted for his having also the appearance of being rather cold about the heart. . . . A full-sized, sleek, well-conditioned gentleman, in a blue coat with bright buttons, and a white cravat.

GENTLEMAN. Guest at Pawkins'.
M. C. xvi.
From neighbouring states; on monetary affairs.

GENTLEMAN. Guest at Pawkins'.
M. C. xvi.
From neighbouring states, on political affairs.

GENTLEMAN. Guest at Pawkins'.
M. C. xvi.
From neighbouring states—on sectarian affairs.

GENTLEMAN. Guest in a great Hotel at Marseilles. *L. D.* ii.
A tall French gentleman, with raven hair and beard, of a swart and terrible, not to say genteely diabolical aspect, but who had shown himself the mildest of men.

GENTLEMAN. In a flannel jacket and a yellow neck-kerchief.
M. P., G. A.

GENTLEMAN. In office of Dombey and Son. *D. and S.* li.
Who has been in the office three years, under continual notice to quit on account of lapses in his arithmetic.

GENTLEMAN. Harpist of Gravesend Packet. *S. B. B.,* Scenes xii "In the forage cap."

GENTLEMAN. Hoarse. *O. M. F.* v
Driving his donkey in a truck with a carrot for a whip.

GENTLEMAN. In next house to Mr. Nickleby. *N. N.* xxxvii
He is a gentleman, and has the manners of a gentleman, although he does wear smalls, and grey worsted stockings.

GENTLEMAN. Legal. *O. M. F.* xx
At Pocket Breaches Branch Station, with an open carriage with a printed bill "Veneering for ever."

GENTLEMAN. Mature young (guest of Veneerings). *O. M. F.* ii
With too much nose on his face, too much ginger in his whiskers, too much torso in his waistcoat, too much sparkle in his studs, his eyes, his buttons, his talk, and his teeth.

GENTLEMAN. Member of Mr. V Crummles' Company.
N. N. xxii
Who played the low-spirited lovers and sang tenor songs.

GENTLEMAN. A neighbour.
S. B. B., O. P. vi
Red-faced in a white hat.

GENTLEMAN. Number four, A Barnacle. *L. D.* x
Clerk in Circumlocution office

GENTLEMAN. Of a Mosaic Arabia cast of countenance.
D. and S. lix
With a massive watch-guard, whistles in the drawing-room, and while he is waiting for the other gentleman, who always has pen and ink in his pocket, asks

Mr. Towlinson (by the easy name of Old Cock) if he happens to know what the figure of them crimson and gold hangings might have been, when new bought.

GENTLEMAN. Of the Palace.
M. P., F. L.

GENTLEMAN. Old. *C. B., C. o. H. i.*

GENTLEMAN. Old, for whom Cobbler in the Fleet used to work.
P. P. xliv.

GENTLEMAN. Old, one of the Board. *O. T.* iii.
In tortoise-shell spectacles.

GENTLEMAN. Old, who lives in our row. *S. B. B., O. P.* iv.
A tall thin, bony man, with an interrogative nose, and little restless perking eyes.

GENTLEMAN. One of the Board. In white waistcoat. *O. T.* iii.
Most positively and decidedly affirmed that not only would Oliver be hung, but that he would be drawn and quartered into the bargain.

GENTLEMAN. One of the visitors to Vauxhall Gardens.
S. B. B., Scenes xiv.
With his dinner in a pocket-handkerchief.

GENTLEMAN. One, boarder at Todger's. *M. C.* ix.
Who travelled in the perfumery line, exhibited an interesting nick-nack in the way of a remarkable cake of shaving-soap which he had lately met with in Germany.

GENTLEMAN. "Ordered six" at Searle's Boating Establishment.
S. B. B., Scenes x.

GENTLEMAN. Pale young. *See* Pocket, Herbert.

GENTLEMAN. Particularly small.
S. B. B., Scenes xiv.
Entertainer at Vauxhall Gardens, in a dress coat.

GENTLEMAN. "Pink-faced."
P. P. xiii.
Who delivered a written speech of half-an-hour's length.

GENTLEMAN. Powder-headed, of No. 3. *S. B. B., O. P.* vii.

GENTLEMAN. Red-faced.
M. H. C. iii.
With a gruff voice.

GENTLEMAN. Retired from business and owner of a garden.
S. B. B., Scenes ix.
Always something to do there—digging—sweeping and cutting and planting with manifest delight.

GENTLEMAN. Since deceased.
M. C. i.
Credible and unimpeachable member of the Chuzzlewit family.

GENTLEMAN. Solitary, Inside passenger in coach. *N. N.* v.
Of very genteel appearance, dressed in mourning, his hair was grey.

GENTLEMAN. Son of, died about five years old. *S. B. B.*, Scenes i.

GENTLEMAN. Straightforward, who trains the birds and mice.
M. P., G. H.

GENTLEMAN. Successor to officer in our Chapel of Ease.
S. B. B., O. P. ii.
A pale, thin, cadaverous man, with large black eyes, and long straggling black hair—dress slovenly in the extreme, manner ungainly, doctrines startling.

GENTLEMAN. Traveller by coach.
                              P. P. xlix.
In a powdered wig, and a sky-blue coat trimmed with silver, made very full and broad in the skirts, which were lined with buckram.

GENTLEMAN. Venerable, 1850.
                    M. P., L. W. O. Y.

GENTLEMAN. Very fine.
                              M. P., F. L.

GENTLEMAN. Very old.
                    S. B. B., Scenes vi.
With a silver-headed stick.

GENTLEMAN. Very quiet, respectable, dozing, old.
                    S. B. B., O. P. ii.
Who had officiated in our Chapel-of-ease for twelve years.

GENTLEMAN. Vocal, *Boarder* at Todger's.   *M. C.* ix.
Regales them with a song.

GENTLEMAN. Walking.
                    S. B. B., Scenes xi.
The dirty swell.

GENTLEMAN. Wife of Catholic.
                              B. R. lxi.

GENTLEMAN. Wife of—retired from business.   *S. B. B.*, Scenes ix.
Takes great pride in the garden too on a summer's evening—you will see them sitting happily together in the little summer-house.

GENTLEMAN. With one eye. The *Bagman.*   *P. P.* xlviii.
Smoking a large *D*utch pipe; with his eye intently fixed on the round face of the Landlord.

GENTLEMAN. Young, Attached to the stable department of "The Angel."   *P. P.* xvi.

GENTLEMAN. Young, Clerk in Kenge and Carboy's.   *B. H.* iii.

GENTLEMAN. Young, May Day dancer.   *S. B. B.*, Scenes xx
In girl's clothes and a widow's cap.

GENTLEMAN. Young, under articles to a civil engineer.
                    M. P., O. L. N. O

GENTLEMAN. Youngest, At Todger's Establishment.   *M. C.* ix

GENTLEMAN'S WHIST CLUB.
                    S. B. B., Tales viii
Winglesbury Buffs at "The Lion Inn."

GENTLEMAN'S WHIST CLUB.
Winglebury Blues at the "Winglebury Arms."
                    S. B. B., Tales viii

GENTLEMANLY INTEREST, The member for.   *M. C.* xxxv

GEN'L'M'N. The next, in restaurant
                              P. P. xliv

GENTLEMEN. A stream of, interviewing Martin.   *M. C.* xxii
Every one with a lady on his arm—came gliding in; every new group fresher than the last.

GENTLEMEN. Country.
                    S. B. B., Scenes i

GENTLEMEN. In Tea Gardens.
                    S. B. B., Scenes ix
In alarming waistcoats, and steel watch-guards, promenading about, three abreast, with surprising dignity.

GENTLEMEN. In Tea Gardens.
                    S. B. B., Scenes ix
In pink shirts and blue waistcoats, occasionally upsetting either themselves or somebody else, with their own canes.

GENTLEMEN. Old decrepid, visitors in Assembly Rooms, Bath
                              P. P. xxxv

GENTLEMEN. Three, In another department of Circumlocution Office. *L. D.* x.
Number one doing nothing particular; number two doing nothing particular; number three doing nothing particular.

GENTLEMEN. Two. *B. H.* xxiii.

GENTLEMEN. Two.
M. P., P. M. B.

GENTLEMEN. Two portly.
C. B., C. C., s. i.
Desiring some slight provision for the poor and destitute from Scrooge.

GENTLEWOMAN. The, Character in play. *S. B. B.,* Scenes xiii.
Black-eyed female.

GEORGE. Mrs. Jarley's servant.
O. C. S. xxvi.
Appeared in a sitting attitude, supporting on his legs a baking-dish and a half-gallon stone-bottle, and bearing in his right hand a knife, and in his left a fork.
Note.—George ultimately marries Mrs. Jarley, whose caravan he has driven for so long.

GEORGE. *N. N.* xii.
A young man, who had known Mr. Kenwigs when he was a bachelor, and was much esteemed by the ladies.
Note.—The bachelor friend of the Kenwigses, who attempted to joke about the rate collector.

GEORGE. Articled clerk of Mr. Buffle. *C. S., M. L. Leg* i.

GEORGE. Aunt, *S. B. B.,* Char. ii.
On Christmas morning at home dusting decanters and filling castors.

GEORGE. Eldest son of visitors to Astley's. *S. B. B.,* Scenes xi.
Who was evidently trying to

look as if he did not belong to the family.

GEORGE. Friend of Mr. Weller Senior, insolvent. *P. P.* xliii.
Had contracted a speculative but imprudent passion for horsing long stages, which led to his present embarrassments . . . soothing the excitement of his feelings with shrimps and porter.

GEORGE. Guard of coach.
C. S., H. T.

GEORGE. King. *M. P., N. E.*

GEORGE. Master. *O. M. F.* v.
Inhabitant of Corner House.

GEORGE. Master, *See* Vendale, George.

GEORGE. Mrs., One of Mrs. Quilp's visitors. *O. C. S.* iv.
Before I'd let a man order me about as Quilp orders her . . . I'd kill myself and write a letter just to say he did it.

GEORGE. One of boating-crew training for race.
S. B. B., Scenes x.

"GEORGE." Porter at Railway Station. *U. T.* xxi.

GEORGE. Queer client—prisoner in Marshalsea. *P. P.* xxi.
Deepest despair and passion scarcely human had made such fierce ravages on his face and form . . . that his companions in misfortune shrunk affrighted from him as he passed by.

GEORGE. Second lieutenant at bar of dining-rooms of house which shall be nameless. *C. S., S. L.* iv.

GEORGE. Son of Mrs. Chick.
D. and S. i.

"GEORGE." The, Inn.
O. T. xxxiii.

GEORGE. Uncle, Host at Christmas family party. *S. B. B.*, Char. ii.
On Christmas Eve—coming down into the kitchen, taking off his coat, and stirring the pudding for half an hour or so—to the vociferous delight of the children and servants. On Christmas day Uncle George tells stories, carves poultry, takes wine, and jokes with the children at the side table.

GEORGE. Visitor at Greenwich Fair. *S. B. B.*, Scenes xii.

GEORGE AND FREDERICK. Sons of Mrs. Chick. *D. and S.* viii.
Both ordered sea air.

"GEORGE AND NEW INN." *N.N.*vi.
Original : The name a compound of the names of two inns some half a mile apart. Also suggested to have been " King's Head," Barnard Castle.

" GEORGE AND THE GRIDIRON." Dining Rooms. *C. S. S. L.* i.

" GEORGE AND VULTURE." Tavern and Hotel, George Yard, Lombard Street. *P. P.* xxvi.

GEORGE'S ST. *U. T.* iii.

GEORGE STREET.
S. B. B., Char. viii.

" GEORGE THE SECOND." The. *D. and S.* iv.

GEORGE THE THIRD. His Majesty King, *O. M. F.* x.

" GEORGE THE THIRD." Kept by a Watkins. *N. N.* xviii.

GEORGE TOWN. Suburb of Washington. *A. N.* viii.

GEORGE TOWN. Jesuit College in, *A. N.* viii.

GEORGE TOWN. President of Jesuits' College (Mansion of the). *A. N.* viii.
More like an English club-house,

both within and without, than any other kind of establishment.

GEORGE YARD. *P. P.* xxxi

GEORGE'S YARD. Lombard Stree *S. B. B., O. P.* '
That little dirty court at the back of the gas-works.

GEORGIANA. A cousin of M Pocket. *G. E.* xx
An indigestive single woma who called her rigidity her religi and her liver love.
Note.—One of Miss Havishan fawning relatives who is left " twer pound down."'

GEORGIANA. Deceased mother Philip Pirrip. *G. E.*

GEORGIANA M'RIA. Pip's sist *G. E.* lvi

GERMAN. *M. P., N. J.*

GERMANS. *M. P., W.*

GERMANS. Shadowy, Passenge on *Dover-Calais* Packet. *U. T.* xv
In immense fur coats and boo

GERMANY. *C. S., S. P. T.* i *L. D.* xvi. ; *M. C.* ix. ; *M. W. H.* ; *R. P., O. B.* ; *U. T.* x

GERRARD STREET. Soho. *G. E.* xx

GHASTLY GRIM. Saint. *U. T.* x

A City churchyard.
It is a small churchyard with a ferocious strong spiked iron ga, like a jail. This gate is or mented with skulls and cro bones, larger than the life wrou t in stone. The skulls grin a t horribly, thrust through d through with iron spears . . . It s in the City, and the Blackv ll railway shrieks at it daily.

GIBBS. Villain, A young hairdresser.   *M. H. C.* v.

GIBRALTAR.   *M. P., E. T.*

GIBRALTAR OF AMERICA. Quebec.   *A. N.* xv.

GIGGLES. Miss, Pupil at the Nun's House.   *E. D.* ix.

GIL BLAS. Character in Nursery Story.   *U. T.* xv.

GILBERT. Gill. *C. S., P. o. C. E. P.*

GILBERT. Mark, Apprentice of a hosier.   *B. R.* viii.
Age nineteen, loves Curzon's daughter, cannot say that Curzon's daughter loves him—an ill-looking, one-sided, shambling lad, with sunken eyes set close together in his head.

GILDED HOUSE. *M. P., N. Y. D.*

GILES. Jeremie, and Messrs., Bankers.   *C. S., N. T.* Act i.

GILES. Mr., Butler and steward to Mrs. Maylie.   *O. T.* xxviii.

Note.—The would - be valiant butler of Mrs. Maylie. A kind - hearted man with the failings of his exalted situation. Accompanied by two other servants he pursues Sikes and Toby Crackit after the attempted burglary—for a short distance. Giles is parted with in the last chapter, when he is quite bald, although he still remains in his old post.

GILL. Mr. and Mrs.   *M. C.* xxix.

GILLESPIE. Mr. James, of Allison and Co.   *A. N.* xvii.

GILLS. Gill.   *C. S., P. o. C. E. P.*

GILLS. Solomon, Instrument maker and proprietor of a ship's chandler's shop.   *D. and S.* iv.
An elderly gentleman, in a Welsh wig, which was as plain and stubborn a Welsh wig as ever was worn, and in which he looked

anything but a Rover. He was a slow, quiet-spoken, thoughtful old fellow, with eyes as red as if they had been small suns looking at you through a fog—and a newly awakened manner. The only change ever known in his outward man, was from a complete suit of coffee-colour, cut very square, and ornamented with glaring buttons, to the same suit of coffee-colour minus the inexpressibles, which were then of a pale nankeen.—He wore a very precise shirt frill, and carried a pair of first-rate spectacles on his forehead, and a tremendous chronometer in his fob.

Note.—Walter Gay's uncle. He keeps a nautical instrument maker's shop without having many customers or doing much business. When Walter's ship is lost, he refuses to believe that the boy has gone down with her, and starts out in search of him. Afterwards his investments prove a success, and he takes Captain Cuttle into partnership, although he no longer troubles about the absence of custom.

Original of Sol. Gill's House: Divided between 99, Minories, and Messrs. Norie and Wilson, afterwards at 156, Minories, and 157, Leadenhall St.

GILTSPUR STREET. *G. E.* li.

GIMBLET. *B*rother, A drysalter.
G. S. E vi.
An elderly man with a crabbed face, a large dog's-eared shirt-collar, and a spotted blue neckerchief reaching up behind to the crown of his head.

GIN SHOP. Customers.
S. B. B., Scenes xxii.
Two old washerwomen—rather overcome by the head dresses and haughty demeanour of the young ladies who officiate.
Young fellow in a brown coat and bright buttons ushering in two companions. . . . Female in faded

feathers. Two old men come in ju to have a drain—finished their thi quartern, have made themselv crying drunk . . . fat comfortab. looking elderly women . . . thron of men, women and children . . knot of Irish labourers.

GIN SHOP. *O*stensible propriet of. *S. B. B.*, Scenes xx
A stout coarse fellow in a f cap, put on very much on o side to give him a knowing a and display his sandy whiskers the best advantage.

GINGERBREAD AND TOYS. V€ dors of, at Greenwich Fair.
S. B. B., Scenes ₃

GIPSY. At Greenwich Fair.
S. B. B., Scenes ₃
A sunburnt woman in a r cloak.

GIPSY. Sentenced to die.
B. R. lx₃
A sunburnt, swarthy fellow, most a wild man.

GIPSY-TRAMP. *U. T.*

GIPSY WOMAN. Good Mrs. Brov
D. and S. xx
A withered and very ugly (woman, dressed not so much li a gipsy as like any of that med race of vagabonds who tra about the country, begging a stealing, and tinkering and we ing rushes, by turns, or all gether—munching with her ja as if the death's head bene her yellow skin were impatient get out.

GIRL. A bold, In brickmake
B. H. v
*D*oing some kind of washing very dirty water.

GIRL. Case No. 13.
M. P., H. H.

GIRL. Case No. 14.
M. P., H. H.

GIRLS. Two.   *M. P., N. T.*

GIRARD COLLEGE. The, Philadelphia.   *A. N.* vii.
A most splendid unfinished
marble structure.

GLAMOUR. Bob.   *O. M. F.* vi.

GLASGOW.   *M. P., C. P.; M. P.,
G. S.; M. P., S. S.; P. P.,*
xlix.; *R. P., T. D. P.; U. T.* xxiii.

GLAVORMELLY. Mr., Actor at the
Coburg.   *N. N.* xxx.

GLIB. Mr.   *M. P., W. H.*

GLIBBERY. Bob, Potboy of Six
Jolly Fellowship Porters.
O. M. F. vi.

GLIBBERY. Late mother of Bob.
O. M. F. vi.
Systematically accelerated his
retirement to bed with a poker.

"GLIMPSE OF GREEN." Common
public house.   *M. P., G. B.*

GLOBSON. Bully.   *U. T.* xix.
Schoolfellow of Uncommercial
Traveller.

GLOGWOOD. Sir Chipkins.
S. Y. C.

GLORIOUS APOLLERS.
O. C. S. xiii.
A convivial circle, of which Mr.
Dick Swiveller had the honour to
be " Perpetual Grand."
*Original : A song book was
issued from Paternoster Row in
the early nineteenth century under
the title of the " Apollo," giving
a toast or sentiment at the top of each
page. Also said to have been
founded on the Royal Antediluvian
Order of Buffaloes.*

"GLORY." Monsieur the Landlord of
the.   *R. P., M. O. F. F.*

"GLORY." The, An Inn.
_R. P., M. O. F. F._

GLOSS. Mr. _M. P., W. H._

GL'OSTER. _Duke of._
_S. B. B._, Scenes xiii.

GLO'STERMAN. _Double, Cheese-man._ _R. P., T. S. S._

GLOUCESTERSHIRE. _A. N._ xv.

GLUBB. _Drawer of Paul's little carriage._ _D. and S._ viii.
Grandfather of ruddy-faced lad —a weazen, old, crab-faced man, in a suit of battered oilskin, who had got tough and stringy from long pickling in salt water, and who smelt like a weedy sea-beach when the tide is out.

GLUMPER. Sir Thomas.
_S. B. B._, Tales ix.
Knighted in the last reign for carrying up an address on some-body's escaping from nothing.

GLYM AND HALIFAX. _M. P., G.A._

GLYN. Mr. _M. P., R. S._

GLYN AND CO. _U. T._ xxi.

"GOAT AND BOOTS." The, An inn.
_S. B. B., O. P._ ii.

GOAVUS. Mr. _M. P., G. D._

GOBLER. Mr., Boarder at Mrs. Tibbs'. _S. B. B._, Tales i.
In a very delicate state of health —a lazy, selfish, hypochondriac—tall, thin, and pale—his face invariably wore a pinched, screwed-up expression . . . he looked as if he had got his feet in a tub of exceed-ingly hot water against his will.

GOBLER. Mrs., Late Mrs. Bloss.
_S. B. B._, Tales i.

GOBLIN. Of the Bells.
_C. B., C. G._ iii.

GOBLIN. Seated on an uprigl tombstone. _P. P._ xxi
A strange unearthly figur His long fantastic legs, whic might have reached the groun were cocked up, and crossed aft a quaint, fantastic fashion : h sinewy arms were bare ; and h hands rested on his knees . . . l was grinning at Gabriel Grub wi such a grin as only a goblin cou call up.

GOBLINS. King of the.
_P. P._ xxi

GOBLINS. Troups of.
_P. P._ xxi

GODALMING. _N. N._ xx

"GODMOTHER." See Riah, M

GOFF. George. _A. N._ xv.

GOG. The elder giant. _M. H .C._
Had a flowing grey bea. The giant warder of this ancie city, [London].

GOG AND MAGOG.
D. and S. iv. ; _M. H. C._ i. ; _N. N._ .

GOLDEN APE. The. _B. H._ .

GOLDEN CROSS. _D. C._ xx ;
_P. P._ ii. ; _S. B. B._, Scenes .
_S. B. B._, Scenes xv ;

GOLDEN DUSTMAN. See Bofi Nicodemus.

GOLDEN HEAD. A French r. taurant. _D. and S._ .

"GOLDEN LION." Hotel of t, Mantua. _P. F. I., V. M. M. S_

GOLDEN LION COURT. _B. R._

"GOLDEN MARY." Armourer, r smith of. _C. S., W. O. G._ .

"GOLDEN MARY." Carper r aboard of. _C. S., W. O. G._ .

"GOLDEN MARY." Second m e of. _C. S., W. O. G._ .

John Barsad, who was thought to be dead.

GOODCHILD. Francis. *L. T.*
Original : This was, of course, the name adopted by Dickens, who was one of the two idle apprentices.

GOODLE. *B. H.* xii.

GOODMAN'S FIELDS. *M. P., G. A.*

GOODWIN. Mrs. Potts' " Body-guard." *P. P.* xviii.
A young lady, whose ostensible employment was to preside over her toilet, but who rendered herself useful in a variety of ways, and none more so than in the particular department of constantly aiding and abetting her mistress in every wish and inclination opposed to the desires of the unhappy Pott.

GOODWINS. The. *D. and S.* xxiii. *R. P., O. E., W. P.*

GOODY. Old Mrs., Grandchild of. *O. M. F.* ix.

GORDON. Colonel, near relation of Lord George Gordon. *B. R.* xlix.

GORDON. Emma, Tight-rope Lady . . . one of Sleary's Troup.
H. T., S. vi.

GORDON. Lord George.
B. R. xxxv.
About the middle height, of a slender make, and sallow complexion, with an aquiline nose, and long hair of a reddish-brown, combed perfectly straight and smooth about his ears, and slightly powdered, but without the faintest vestige of a curl. He was attired, under his great-coat, in a full suit of black, quite free from any ornament, and of the most precise and sober cut.
President of the great Protestant Association.

Note.—The Lord George Gordon of the book is very faithful to the real Lord George Gordon of the historic

"No Popery" riots. Lord George was the third son of the third Duke of Gordon, and was born on September 19, 1750. Although he was the chief actor in the dramatic scenes of the Gordon riots of 1780, he was not convicted on the charge of high treason. Later on, however, he was convicted of writing a libellous pamphlet on the queen of France. He escaped to Holland, but was refused sanctuary and returned to England, where he died on November 1, 1793, a professed member of the Jewish religion.

Original of Gordon House : Said to have been 64, *Welbeck Street, Cavendish Square.*

GORDON. Mr. Sherriff.
M. P., E. A. S.

GORDON PLACE. No 25, Residence of the Miss Willises.
S. B. B., O. P. iii.

It was fresh painted and papered from top to bottom ; the paint inside was all wainscoted, the marble all cleaned, the old grates taken down, and register stoves, you could see to dress by, put up.

GORE HOUSE. *M. P., L. L.*

GORHAM. *M. P., R. H. F.*

GORHAMBURY. *U. T.* xiv.

GORHAMBURY. *Brother-in-law of* the Bishop of. *M. P., T. T.*

GORTON DISTRICT. *M. P., O. S.*

GOSWELL STREET. *P. P.* ii.

Mr. Samuel Pickwick . . .threw open his chamber window. . . Goswell Street was at his feet, Goswell Street was on his right hand—as far as the eye could reach, Goswell Street extended on his left ; and the opposite side of Goswell Street was over the way.

Original : The name was later changed to Goswell Road.

GOTHARD. Great Saint,
P. F. I., R. D.

GOUDO. The Gorge of.
P. F. I., V. M. M. S. S.

GOUNOD. M. *M. P., M. M.*

GOVERNESS. Of visitors to Astley's. *S. B. B.,* Scenes xi.

Peeped out from behind the pillar, and timidly tried to catch ma's eye, with a look expressive of her high admiration of the whole family.

GOVERNOR. Jack, A sailor.
C. S., H. H.

The finest-looking sailor that ever sailed—gray now, but as handsome as he was a quarter of a century ago. A portly, cheery, well-built figure of a broad-shouldered man, with a frank smile, a brilliant dark eye, and a rich dark eyebrow. . . A man of wonderful resources.

GOVERNOR. Our, *See* Tackleton, Mr.

GOVERNOR. The Landlord of "Holly Tree" Inn. *C. S., H. T.*

GOWAN. Harry. *L. D.* xviii

This gentleman looked barely thirty. He was well dressed— "An artist, I infer from what he says.?" "A sort of one", said Daniel Doyce—"What sort of one?" asked Clennam. "Why he has sauntered into the arts at a leisurely Pall-Mall pace."

Note.—A young artist, marrie Minnie Meagles. He lives to a larg extent on his wife's father's generosity Eventually he discovers that it woul be better for him not to know th Meagles, but the money still continue to come to Minnie.

GOWAN. Mrs., Family servant of
L. D. xxv.

Who had his own crow to pluc with the public, concerning situation in the Post Office whic he had for some time been ex pecting, and to which he was not yet appointed.

GOWAN. Mrs. *See* Meagles, Minnie.

GOWAN. Mrs., Mother of Henry Gowan. *L. D.* xvi.

A courtly old lady, formerly a beauty, and still sufficiently well favoured to have dispensed with the powder on her nose, and a certain impossible bloom under each eye.

Note.—Henry Gowan's mother. Living on a pension in apartments at Hampton Court Palace.

GOWAN FAMILY. *L. D.* xvii.

A very distant ramification of the Barnacles; . . . the paternal Gowan, originally attached to a legation abroad, had been pensioned off as a commissioner of nothing particular somewhere or other, and had died at his post with his drawn salary in his hand, nobly defending it to the last extremity.

GOWER. Tomb of old—in St. Saviour's, Southwark. *U. T.* ix.

He lies in effigy with his head upon his book.

GOWER STREET.
P. P. xxxi.; *S. B. B.,* Char. ix.

GRACECHURCH STREET.
R. P., B. S.; U. T. xxi.

GRADGRIND. Jane. *H. T.,* s. iv.

GRADGRIND. Louisa. *H. T.,* s. iii.

A child . . . of fifteen or sixteen; but at no distant date would seem to become a woman all at once. . . . She was pretty.

Note. — Louisa eventually marries Bounderby without having any love for him. She is persecuted by another man and takes refuge with her father. Her husband insists on her immediate return; failing this he casts her off and she remains with her father.

GRADGRIND. Mr. Thomas, A mill-owner. *H. T.,* s. iii.

The speaker's square forefinger

emphasized his observations by underscoring every sentence with a line on the schoolmaster's sleeve. The speaker's voice—inflexible, dry and dictatorial—hair, which bristled on the skirts of his bald head—all covered with knobs, like the crust of a plum pie.

Note.—A wealthy man retired from business living at Stone Lodge near Coketown. He is obsessed with figures and facts, and their importance; and rules his life by them, as well as a school he controls. On the same principles he arranges the marriage of his daughter with Mr. Bounderby. The marriage turns out an unhappy one. His son Tom is placed in Bounderby's bank, but he becomes wild as a result of the earlier repression, and robs the bank. These two failures result in changing Gradgrind's point of view, particularly as the only friendship and assistance he meets with is from Sleary and the members of his circus troupe, and he realizes that his facts and figures must be leavened by love and forbearance.

GRADGRIND. Mrs., Wife of Thomas Gradgrind. *H. T.,* s. iv.

A little, thin, white, pink-eyed bundle of shawls, of surpassing feebleness, mental and bodily, who was always taking physic.

GRADGRIND. Thomas. Clerk in Bounderby's Bank. *H. T.,* s. iii.

Note.—A sullen, selfish cub. He enters Bounderby's Bank. Before long he robs the safe. The blame falls on Blackpool. But he is cleared. Tom eventually manages to escape from the country by the aid of Sleary and his troup.

GRADGRINDS. Five young, Children of Mr. Gradgrind. *H. T.,* s. iii.

GRAHAM. Hugh, Apprentice of Bowyer. *M. H. C.* i.

GRAHAM. Mary. *M. C.* iii.

She is very young; apparently no more than seventeen. She was short in stature; and her figure was slight. Her face was very pale. Her dark brown hair —had fallen negligently from its bonds, and hung upon her neck.— Her attire was that of a lady, but extremely plain.

Note.—Mary Graham is first introduced tending to old Martin Chuzzlewit. It was because of his love for her that young Martin displeased his grandfather. The young people remain true to one another, however, and after Martin's return from America they are finally married.

GRAINGER.   Dr.   *M. P., P. T.*

GRAINGER.   Steerforth's friend.
           D. C. xxiv.

GRAND CAIRO.   *M. P., E. T.*

GRAND CANAL. The, Venice.
           L. D. xli.

CRAND DUKE. At Baden-Baden.
           D. and S. xxxi.

GRAND VIZIER.   *C. S., H. H.*

GRANDFATHER. Doctor Marigold.
           C. S., D. M.

GRANDFATHER. Little Nell's. *See* Trent, Little Nell's Grandfather.

GRANDMAMA. Kate Nickleby's.
           N. N. xxxv.

When she was a young lady, before she was married—ran against her own hairdresser, as she was turning the corner of Oxford Street,—the encounter made her faint away.

GRANDMARINA. Fairy.   *H. R.* ii.
Dressed in shot-silk of the richest quality, smelling of dried lavender.

GRANDMOTHER. Cinderella's.
           M. P., F. F.

GRANDMOTHER. Of Tom Pinch.
           M. C. ii.

A gentleman's housekeeper— died happy to think she had put me with such an excellent man.

GRANDMOTHER. Of unimpeachable member of the Chuzzlewit family.   *M. C.* i.

Contemplating venerable relic —a dark lantern of undoubted antiquity; rendered still more, interesting by being, in shape and pattern, extremely like such as are in use at the present day. "Aye, Aye! This was carried by my fourth son on the fifth of November, when he was a Guy Fawkes."

GRANDMOTHER. Of (Mr.) Vholes.
           B. H. xxxvii.
Who died in her hundred-and-second year.

GRANDMOTHER. Of (Miss) Wade.
           L D. lvii.
A lady who represented that relative to me, and who took that title on herself. She had some children of her own family in her house, and some children of other people.

GRANDMOTHER. Old, In tea gardens.   *S. B. B.* Scenes ix.

GRAND-NEPHEW. Of Mr. Martin Chuzzlewit.   *M. C.* iv.
Very dark, and very hairy, and apparently born for no particular purpose but to save looking-glasses the trouble of reflecting more than just the first idea and sketchy notion of a face, which had never been carried out.

GRANDPAPA. With a beautifully plaited shirt-frill and white neckerchief.   *S. B. B.*, Char. ii.

GRANGER. Edith. *See* Dombey, Mrs.

GRANGER. Colonel, of Ours (deceased).   *D. and S.* xxi.
A de-vilish handsome fellow, sir, of forty-one.

GRANNETT. Mr., Overseer at workhouse.   *O. T.* xxiii.
Who relieved an outdoor dying pauper with offer of a pound of potatoes, and half a pint of oatmeal.

RANT COUNTY. Sheriff of.
A. N. xvii.

RANTHAM. *N. N.* v.

RANVILLE. Mr. *See* Wharton,
Mr. Granville. *G. S. E.* ix.

RAVE-DIGGER. The. *B. R.* i.
Ill in bed from long working in
a damp soil and sitting down to
take his dinner on cold tombstones.

RAVE. Family, Of the Chuzzlewits. *M. C.* i.

RAVES. Phantom.
C. B., C. C., S. iv.

RAVESEND. *B. R.* xxxi.; *D. C.*
xiii.; *D. and S.* xviii.; *G. E.*
lii.; *L. D.* liv.; *S. B. B.*, Scenes x.
S. B. B., Tales iv.; *U. T.* vii.

RAY. Dr., the residence of.
M. P., S. B.

RAYMARSH. Pupil at Dotheboys'
Hall. *N. N.* vii.
Graymarsh's maternal aunt—is
very glad to hear he's so well and
happy and sends her respectful
compliments to Mrs. Squeers, and
thinks she must be an angel.

RAYPER. Mrs., Neighbour of the
Copperfields. *D. C.* ii.
She's going to stay with Mrs.
Grayper.

RAYPER. Mr. and Mrs.
D. C. xxii.

RAY'S INN. *P. P.* xx.
Curious little nooks in a great
place like London, these old inns
are.

RAY'S INN. Chambers in.
U. T. xiv.
An upper set on a rotten staircase with a mysterious bunk or
bulkhead on the landing outside
them, of a rather nautical and
screw collier-like appearance, than
otherwise, and painted an intense
black.

GRAY'S INN. The Honourable
Society of. *U. T.* xiv., *D. C.* xxx.

GRAY'S INN. Traddles' Chambers.
D. C.
Original: Supposed to have
been described from Dickens' own
chambers at 15, Furnival's Inn.

GRAY'S INN GARDENS. *L. D.* xiii.

GRAY'S INN LANE. *O. T.* xlii.;
P. P. xlvii.; *R. P.*; *D. W. I. F.*;
S. B. B., Scenes xiii.
Intricate and dirty ways—
lying between Gray's Inn Lane
and Smithfield—render that part
of the town one of the lowest and
worst that improvement has left
in the midst of London.

GRAY'S INN ROAD. *M. P., V. D.*

GRAY'S INN ROAD. Lodgings
which Mr. Micawber occupied
as Mr. Mortimer prior to coach
journey to Canterbury.
D. C. vii.

GRAY'S INN ROAD. A street in.
L. D. xiii.
Which had set off from that
thoroughfare with the intention
of running at one heat down into
the valley, and up again to the
top of Pentonville Hill; but which
had run itself out of breath in
twenty yards, and had stood still
ever since.—It remained there for
many years, looking with a baulked
countenance at the wilderness
patched with unfruitful gardens,
and pimpled with eruptive summer-
houses, that it meant to run over
in no time.

GRAY'S INN SQUARE. Set of
chambers in, of Mr. Percy Noakes.
S. B. B., Tales vii.
His sitting-room presented a
strange chaos of dress-gloves,
boxing-gloves, caricatures, albums,
invitation cards, foils, cricket-bats
—in the strangest confusion.

GRAZINGLANDS. Mr., Of the Mid-land Counties. *U. T.* vi.
A gentleman of a comfortable property.

GRAZINGLANDS. Mrs., Wife of Mr. Grazinglands. *U. T.* vi.
Amiable and fascinating.

GREAT BRITAIN. *A. N.* xiv.; *H. T., R.* ii.; *L. D.* xi.; *M. P., E. T.; M. P., L. A. V.* ii.; *M. P., N. E.; M. P., R. S.; M. P., R. T.; U. T.* x.

GREAT CORAM STREET.
S. B. B., Tales i.

GREAT DESERT. The.
R. P., D. W. T. T.

GREAT FATHERS. Of the Revolution. *M. P., Y. M. C.*

GREAT HORSESHOE FALL. The.
A. N. xiv.

GREAT MARLBOROUGH STREET.
C. S., S. L. iv.; *S. B. B.,* Tales vii.

GREAT NATIONAL SMITHERS' TESTIMONIAL. *B. H.* viii.

GREAT NORTH ROAD.
C. S., H. T.; O. T. xlii.

GREAT ORMOND STREET. Lord Chancellor's in. *B. R.* lxvii.

GREAT PAVILIONSTONE HOTEL.
R. P., O. O. T.
Original : Pavilion at Folke-stone.

GREAT PORTLAND STREET.
R. P., O. B.

GREAT PYRAMID. *M. P., T. B.*

GREAT QUEEN STREET.
O. C. S. viii.; *S. B. B.,* Scenes xix.

GREAT RUSSELL STREET.
U. T. iv.

GREAT SAINT BERNARD. The pass of the.
L. D. xxxvii.; *R. P., L. A.*

GREAT SALT LAKE. The.
U. T. x

GREAT SPHINX. *M. P., E. !*

GREAT SQUARE. *P. F. I., :*

GREAT TWIG STREET.
M. P., U. ;

"GREAT WHITE HOUSE." Chambermaid of the. *P. P.* xx

"GREAT WHITE HORSE." Chambermaids at the. *P. P.* xxi

"GREAT WHITE HORSE." Ipswich. *P. P.* xi
Famous in the same degree as prize ox, or unwieldy pig, for enormous size.

"GREAT WHITE HORSE." Landlord of the. *P. P.* xi.
A corpulent man, with a fortnight's napkin under his arm, and coeval stockings on his legs.

GREAT YARMOUTH. *M. P., E.!*
See also Yarmouth.

GREEK WARRIOR. *P. F. I.,*

GREEN. A constable.
R. P., D. W. I.

GREEN. Miss. Child sweetheart Uncommercial Traveller.
U. T. i.
Original : Generally believed to be Lucy Stroughill, at No. 1, Ordnance Terrace, the sister of Dickens' friend and playmate.

GREEN. Miss. *N. N.* :.
Elderly lady from back parlour.

GREEN. Mr. *M. P., R. H.*

GREEN. Mr. An Aeronaut.
S. B. B., Scenes :.

GREEN. Mr., Jun.
S. B. B., Scenes :.

GRETA

REEN. Mrs. *O. C. S.* xxi.
Lodger at the cheesemonger's
round the corner.

REEN. Mrs., Son of, a law writer.
B. H. xi.
Aboard a vessel bound for
China.

REEN. The. *O. T.* x.

REEN. The, Richmond.
G. E. xxxiii.

REEN. Tom. A gonoph.
R. P., D. W. I. F.

REEN. Tom, A soldier.
B. R. lviii.
A gallant, manly, handsome
fellow, but he had lost his left
arm—his empty coat-sleeve hung
across his breast—he wore a jaunty
cap and jacket.

REEN GATE. The very, Belonging to Mr. Nupkin's residence.
P. P. xxv.

*Original : Believed locally to be
that adjoining the churchyard a few
yards from Church Street, Ipswich.*

GREEN LANES. *B. R.* xliv.

GREEN PARK *C. S., S. L.* iii.

GREEN YARD. Of *Dockhead* district. *U. T.* x.

GREENACRE. Mr. *M. P., T. F.*

GREENGROCER. *U. T.* xii.

GREENGROCER. Hired to wait by
the Kitterbells at christening
party. *S. B. B.,* Tales xi.
Hired to wait for seven-and
sixpence, and whose calves alone
were worth double the money.

GREENGROCER'S SHOP, BATH.
P. P. xxxvii.
*Original : The Beaufort Arms
public house.*

GREENHORNS. Some, At Greenwich Fair. *S. B. B.,* Scenes xii.

GREEN

" GREE
house

GREEN

GREEN\

GREENV
A p
sort of
fever.

GREENW

GREENW
iii. ; *M.*

GREENWI

GREENWO

GREENWO

GREGOIRE
Doche.

GREGORY.
Murdston

GREGSBUR'
The gre
ment, war
keep his pa
in order.
headed ge
voice, a
tolerable c
with no me

*Note.—*Th
Parliament w
and to whom

GRENELLE.

BRIDGE. In Yorkshire.
N. N. iii.
·inal : Barnard Castle.

◄ GREEN.
C. S., H. T. ; M. P., S. G.

·IOUS. Mr., Rosa's guar-
·an official receiver of rents).
E. D. ix.
arid, sandy man. He had a
·y flat crop of hair, in colour
consistency like some very
·y yellow fur tippet. Cer-
notches in his forehead, as
·;h nature had been about to
·◄ them into sensibility or
·ment, when she had thrown
· the chisel.

·te.—Rosa Bud's guardian with
·bers in Staple Inn. He pays
·; visits to his ward in Cloisterham,
·when, after Edwin Drood's dis-
··arance, she leaves Cloisterham, it
·her guardian she travels. He is
·much upset by her recital of John
··er's persecutions, and takes apart-
·◄ts for her with Billickin. He then
·des to investigate Edwin's dis-
··arance, with his suspicions very
··h pronounced against John Jasper.

·JGIOUS. Angular Clerk of Mr.
E. D. ix.

·VGIOUS. Clerk of Mr.
E. D. xi.
·◄ pale, puffy-faced, dark-haired
··n of thirty, with big dark eyes
·t wholly wanted lustre, and a
··satisfied doughy complexion
·t seemed to ask to be sent to
·· baker's. A gloomy person, with
·◄gled locks.

·Y. Lord.   M. P., P. P.

·Y. Misses.   S. Y. G.

·Y. Sir George.   M. P., S.

·DE. Arthur, A money-lender.
N. N. xlvii.
A little old man of about seventy
seventy-five years of age, of a

very lean figure, much bent, and
slightly twisted. He wore a grey
coat with a very narrow collar
an old-fashioned waistcoat o
ribbed black silk, and such scanty
trousers as displayed his shrunker
spindle-shanks.

Note.—A miserly old money - lender
He arranges with Ralph Nickleby'
assistance to compel Mr. Bray to per
suade Madeline to marry him. Mr
Bray is heavily in debt to both Grid
and Ralph, and the scheme prospers
The interposition of Nicholas and th
timely death of her father save Made
line from her threatened fate. Som
years later his house was broken int
and he himself murdered.

GRIDLEY. Mr., The man from
Shropshire.   B. H. xv
" A tall, sallow man, with a care
worn head, on which but littl
hair remained, a deeply-lined fac
and prominent eyes. He had ;
pen in his hand, and in the glimps
I caught of his room in passing,
saw that it was covered with ;
litter of papers."

Note.—A suitor in chancery. On
of two brothers. By his father's deatl
he inherited the farm with a legacy o
£300 to pay to his brother. The ques
tion was whether his brother had no
received part of this in board, lodging
etc. The brother took this questio
to chancery, and there it became ·
problem of infinite ramification. H
and his brother were ruined. H
attends the court, unable to understan
that he can do nothing, and alway
hoping for something. He is com
mitted for contempt, but offends again
He ends his days, utterly worn out, i
George Rouncewell's shooting-gallery
hiding from the officers of the law.

GRIDLEY. Mr., Brother of.
B. H. xv
Claimed his legacy of three hun
dred pounds—I, and some of m
relations, said he had had a par
of it already in board and lodgings
and some other things. That wa
the question and nothing else—

GRI
I wa·
accur·
GRIDL·
ner.
Lei
forth
GRIEV
ings,
GRIE·
GRIFF
GRIG.
GRIG·
GRIG·
GRIG·
GRIMI
Hall
A
gro·
park
GRIM
GRIM
the
GRIM
GRIM
GRIN
of
·
lan
in
nai
a l
the
A
a
wi·
da·

Note.—A friend of Mr. Brownlow. Somewhat short-tempered, but good-hearted. He is quite sure Oliver will not return when he is trusted with books and money by Mr. Brownlow, and as Oliver does not return he maintained he was correct. His characteristic phrase is "Or, I'll eat my head." At the end of the book he is left a frequent visitor of Mr. Losberne, on which occasions he "plants, fishes, and carpenters with great ardour."

GRIMWOOD. Eliza, A young woman.   *R. P., T. D. A.* i.

GRINDER. A, A coach, or tutor.
                                     G. E. xxiii.

GRINDER. Mr., Travelling showman.   *O. C. S.* xvii.

GRINDER. Toodles junior.
                                     D. and S. xxii.

GRINDER'S LOT. A travelling show.
                                     O. C. S. xvii.

Consisted of a young gentleman and a young lady on stilts. . . the public costume of the young people was of the Highland kind.

GRINDOFF. The miller.
                               R. P., A. P. A.

" GRIP." Barnaby's raven.
                                       B. R. vi.

Balancing himself on tiptoe, as it were, and moving his body up and down in a sort of grave dance, rejoined, " I'm a devil, I'm a devil, I'm a devil."

Note. Barnaby's raven, Grip, was his constant companion, even in Newgate when his master was imprisoned for complicity in the riots. He recovered his good looks " and became as glossy as ever." He had lost his gift of speech, however, in prison. At the end of a year he again speaks " and from that period . . . he constantly practised and improved himself in vulgar tongue."

Originals : Dickens' own ravens. One of which died in 1841 and another in 1845.

GRISE. Wife of Hown, Negro slave.
                                       A. N. xvii.

GRISSELL AND PETO. Messrs.
             R. P., B. S.

GRITTS. Right Hon. Mr.
             M. P., C. Pat.

GROBUS. Right Hon. Sir Gilpin
Grobus.   *M. P., C. Pat.*

GROCER. The.   *G. E.* viii.

GROFFIN. Thomas,   Juryman-
Chemist.   *P. P.* xxxiv.
    A tall, thin, yellow-visaged man.
I am to be sworn, my lord, am I.
Very well, my lord, then there'll
be murder before this trial's over.
. . . I've left nothing but an errand
boy in my shop. . . . The prevail-
ing impression on his mind is, that
Epsom salts means oxalic acid;
and syrup of senna, laudanum.

    Note.—The chemist on the jury at
the " trial."

GROGGLES. Mr., Member of the
Common Council.   *M. P., L. T.*

GROGGLES. Mrs.   *M. P., L. T.*

GROGINHOLE. Hon.   member
for.   *M. P., F. C.*

GROGUS. The great ironmonger.
         S. B. B., Tales ii.

GROGZWIG. In Germany.
             N. N. vi.

GROMPUS. Mr., Guest of Mr. Podsnap.   *O. M. F.* xi.

GROOM. A, At Astley's.
         S. B. B., Scenes xi.

GROOMBRIDGE WELLS.
         C. S., N. T. Act i.

GROPER. Colonel.   *M. C.* xxxiv.

"GROSVENOR." Carpenter of the.
         R. P., T. L. V.

"GROSVENOR." Cooper of the.
         R. P., T. L. V.

"GROSVENOR." Little child
seven on board the.   A passenge
         R. P., T. L.

"GROSVENOR." Steward of the
         R. P., T. L.

GROSVENOR PLACE.
     C. S., S. L. iii. ; *N. N.* x

GROSVENOR SQUARE.
     L. D. ix ; *S. B. B.*, Scenes x

GROSVENOR SQUARE.   Lo:
Rockingham's in.   *B. R.* lxv

GROSVENOR REGION. By-stree
in.   *L. D.* xxv
    Parasite little tenements, wi
the cramp in their whole fram
from the dwarf hall-door on t
giant model of His Grace's in t
square to the squeezed window
the boudoir. Rickety dwellin
of undoubted fashion, but of
capacity to hold nothing co
fortably except a dismal sme
looked like the last result of t
great mansions' breeding in-and-
and where their little suppleme
tary bows and balconies we
supported on thin iron colum
seemed to be scrofulously resti
upon crutches.

GROUND. Tom Tiddler's.
         C. S., T. T. G.
    A nook in a rustic by-road.

GROVE. The.
     G. E. xxxiv. ; *U. T.*

GROVE HOUSE ACADEMY.
         M. C.

GROVES. James.   Public hou
keeper and gambler.
         O. C. S. xx
    Jem Groves — honest Je
Groves, as is a man of unblemish
moral character, and has a go
dry skittle-ground.
    Note.—The unimpeachable landl
of the " Valiant Soldier," who assist

GROWL
Hous
A
librar
Whe
and

GRUB.

Ar

man
but
bott
and
who
pass
scow
it w

No
"Sto
sexto

treat
on h

GRUB.

GRUB
"De
A
mide
seen
dres
out
whe
at

GRUI
V.

I
bea
Cru
anc

and dressed the ladies, and swept
the house, and held the prompt
book when everybody else was on
for the last scene.

GRUEBY. John, Servant of Lord
George Gordon.   *B. R.* **xxxv.**
A square-built, strong-made,
bull-necked fellow of the true
English breed—was to all appearance five-and-forty—Had a great
blue cockade in his hat, which he
appeared to despise mightily.

> *Note.*—Grueby, as personal servant
> to Lord George Gordon, did all in his
> power to preserve his master, and
> attended him with a touching devotion.
> When Lord George was eventually
> imprisoned, John Grueby continued to
> serve him to the last.

GRUFF AND GLUM. An old pensioner.   *O. M. F.* liv.
Two wooden legs had this
gruff and glum old pensioner.

GRUFF AND GRIM. Mr. Barley.
G. E. xlvi.

GRUFF AND TACKLETON. Toymaker.   *C. B., C. o. H.*

GRUFFSHAW.   Professional
speaker.   *M. P., O. S.*

GRUMMER.   *P. P.* xxiv.
Elderly gentleman in top-boots,
who was chiefly remarkable for a
bottle nose ; a hoarse voice, a
snuff coloured surtout and a
wandering eye. A somewhat forbidding countenance.

GRUMMIDGE. Dr.   *Mud. Pap.* ii.

GRUNDY. Madam.   *M. P., I.*

GRUNDY. Mr., At number twenty.
M. P., R. H. F.

GRUNDY Mr., Frequenter of
" Magpie and Stump."   *P. P.* xx

Note.—An example of a type of London clerk. Met with at the "Magpie and Stump," where each of Mr. Lowten's friends is an illustration of a class, less than a study of an individual.

GRUNDY. Mrs.　　*M. P., R. H. F.*

GUARD. At Mugby Junction.
　　　　　　C. S., M. J. i.

GUARD. Collected, of train.
　　　　　　R. P., a. F.

GUARD. Of coach.　*P. P.* xxviii.

GUARD. Of coach.　*P. P.* xlix.
　With a wig on his head, and most enormous cuffs to his coat, had a lantern in one hand, and a huge blunderbuss in the other.

GUARD. Of coach to Yorkshire.
　　　　　　C. S., H. T.

GUARD. Of stage-coach.
　　　　　S. B. B., Scenes xvi.

GUARD. On railway train.
　In a red coat.　*U. T.* xiii.

GUARDIAN.　　*M. P., P. T.*

"GUARDIAN." Mr. Jarndyce.
　　　　　　B. H. viii.

GUARDIANS. Stepney Board of.
　　　　　　U. T. xxix.

GUBBINS. Mr.　*S. B. B., O. P.* ii.

GUBBINSES. The, Guests of the Gattletons.　*S. B. B.*, Tales ix.

GUBBLETON. Lord
　　　　　S. B. B., Tales v.

GUDGEON. Mr. J.　*M. P., E. C.*

GUEST. At Mr. Podsnap's.
　　　　　　O. M. F. xi.
　With one eye screwed up into extinction and the other framed and glazed.

GUESTS. At Pawkins' boarding house.　　*M. C.* xvi.
　All the knives and forks were working away at a rate which was quite alarming,—everybody seemed to eat his utmost in self-defence, as if a famine were expected to set in before breakfast-time to-morrow morning.

GUEST. At Wedding of Caroline Jellyby.　　*B. H.* xxx.
　An extremely dirty lady, with her bonnet all awry, and the ticketed price of her dress still sticking on it, whose neglected home—was like a filthy wilderness; but whose church was like a fancy fair.

GUEST. Gentleman at Caroline Jellyby s wedding.　*B. H.* xxx.
　Who said it was his mission to be everybody's brother, but who appeared to be on terms of coolness with the whole of his large family.

GUFFY.　　　　*B. H.* xii.

GUILD. Of literature and art.
　　　　　　M. P., G. L. A.

GUILDFORD.
　N. N. xxv. ; *R. P., T. D. A.* ii

GUILDFORD. Picnic held near.
　　　　　　D. C. iv

GUILDHALL.　*B. R.* lxvii. ; *M. H.* *C.* i. ; *M. P., R. L. M.* ; *P. P.* xxxv. ; *S. B. B.*, Scenes xix

GUILDHALL. The.　Canterbury.
　　　　　　D. C. xxii.

GUINEA-PIG. In happy family
　　　　　　M. P., P. F.

GULD PUBLEEK=Gulled Public.
　　　　　　M. P., T. O. H.

GULPIDGE. Mr., Something to do at secondhand with the law business of the Bank.　*D. C.* xxv

GULPIDGE. Mrs., Wife of Mr. Gulpidge.　　*D. C.* xxv

clothes on, a shining hat, lilac kid gloves, a neckerchief of a variety of colours, a large hot-house flower in his buttonhole, and a thick gold ring on his little finger.

Note.—A burlesque character employed as a clerk by Kenge and Carboy. Sometimes engaged on private matters for the firm, he obtains a good deal of information. On these occasions he is sometimes brought in contact with Esther Summerson, with whom he falls in love. She is only amused at his subsequent offer and refuses him. After her illness when her face is disfigured, she again meets Mr. Guppy, who is afraid she has come to claim fulfilment of his promise, and is only reassured with much difficulty and quasi-legal formality that she has no desire to marry him. Guppy, with the meanness of an unauthorised amateur detective, also obtains information of the secret of Lady Dedlock. He again offers marriage to Esther, having reconsidered it.

GUSHER. Mr., A missionary.
                    B. H. viii.

A flabby gentleman with a moist surface, and eyes much too small for his moon of a face.

Note.—Friend of Mrs. Pardiggle.

GUSTER. Augusta.   *B. H.* x.

Note.—Servant to the Snagsbys. She has fits and falls into anything handy, convenient, or inconvenient. She is useful in clearing up the mystery of Lady Dedlock's flight.

GWYNN. Miss, Writing and ciphering governess at " Westgate House."   *P. P.* xvi.

GYE AND BALNE. Messrs., Bill Printers.   *R. P., B. S.*

GYMNASE. Paris.   *M. P., W.*

H

HACKNEY.   *S. B. B.,* Scenes ix.

HACKNEY COACH STANDS.
              S. B. B., Scenes vii.

HACKNEY-COACHMEN.
S. B. B., Scenes i.
Admiring how people can trust their necks into one of them crazy cabs, when they can have a 'spectable 'ackney cotche with a pair of 'orses as von't run away with no vun.

HACKNEY ROAD. *U. T.* x.

HAGGAGE. *Doctor.* In Marshalsea.
L. D. vi.
Amazingly shabby, in a torn and darned rough-weather sea jacket, out at elbows, and eminently short of buttons (he had been in his time the experienced surgeon carried by a passenger ship) the dirtiest white trousers conceivable by mortal man, carpet slippers, and no visible linen.

HAGUE. The. *L. D.* lxvii.

HAIRDRESSER. Journeyman.
N. N. lii.
Who was not very popular among the ladies, by reason of his obesity and middle age.

"HALF MOON AND SEVEN STARS." The, An obscure alehouse.
M. C. iv.

HALFPAY CAPTAIN. *S. B. B.*, *O. P.* ii.
Near neighbour, a retired officer. Ordnance Terrace.

HALFWAY HOUSE. *G. E.* xxviii.

HALFWAY HOUSE. *N. N.* xlix.

HALFWAY HOUSE. *B. R.* ii.
Original: "The Green Man," *Leytonstone.*

HALIFAX. *A. N.* i.

HALIFAX HARBOUR. *A. N.* ii.

HALL. Mr. *M. P., W. M.*

HALL. The. *M. C.* xxvii.

HALL. The, In Budden's house
S. B. B., Tales
Passage, denominated by courtesy "The Hall."

HALL FLIGHT. In the Fleet.
P. P. x
A dark and filthy staircase which appeared to lead to a range of damp and gloomy stone vault beneath the ground and those suppose are the little cellars where the prisoners keep their small quantities of coals.

HALL OF EXAMINATION. In the Hôtel de Ville.
T. T. C. bk. ii. ; ch. x.

HALLEY. Mr. *O. M. F.* v.

HALLIDAY. *Brother,* A Mormon agent. *U. T.*

HALLIFORD. *O. T.* ii.

HALLIFORD. Lower. *O. T.* ii.

HALLOCK. Dr., the residence of
M. P., S ?.

"HALSEWELL." Crew of the
R. P., T. L. ?.

"HALSEWELL." Petty officer of the. *R. P., T. L.* ?.

"HALSEWELL." Soldiers on e.
R. P., T. L. ?.

HAMMERSMITH. *G. E.* x. ;
M. P., G. D. ; *N. N.* xvii. ; *C. T.* xxi. ; *S. B. B.*, Tales iii. ; *U.* ?. x.

HAMMERSMITH SUSPENSION BRIDGE. *S. B. B.*, Scene vi.

HAMMOND. Rev. Charles.
M. P., ? B.

HAMPSTEAD. *B. R.* xvi.; *D. C* vi.
M. P., G. B.; *R. P.,* ? A.

HAMPSTEAD. Village of.
O. T. x iii.

HAMPSTEAD HEATH.
M. P., N. S. E., O. T. xlviii.

HAMPSTEAD PONDS. *P. P.* i. ;
U. T. x.
This Association has heard read
. . . the paper communicated by
Samuel Pickwick, Esq., . . . entitled, Speculations on the Source
of the Hampstead Ponds.

Note.—There is no doubt that the
ponds here referred to are those close
to Hampstead Heath Station. Although the reference to them is facetious, their source was at one time a
matter of some small interest. They
are fed by a small stream having its
rise in Caen Wood.

HAMPSTEAD PONDS. Miss Griffin's establishment in.
C. S., H. H.

HAMPSTEAD ROAD.
S. B. B., Scenes ix.

HAMPTON. *N. N.* l. ; *O. T.* xxi. ;
O. M. F. xii.

HAMPTON CLUB HOUSE. *N. N.* l.

HAMPTON COURT. *L. D.* xii. ;
S. B. B. Scenes v., *M. P., G. B.*

HAMPTON COURT PALACE.
M. P., P. L. U.

HANAPER. The clerk of the.
R. P., P. M. T. P.

HANAPER. *Deputy* clerk of the.
R. P., P. M. T. P.

HANCOCK. Mr. *M. P., F. M.*

HANCOCK AND FLOBBY.
M. C. xxii.

HANDEL. Herbert Pocket's name
for Pip. *G. E.* xxii.

HANDEL. *M. P., O. L. N. O.*

HANDFORD. Mr. Julius, *See* Harmon, John.

HANDS. The, Mill-workers.
H. T. s.

HANGING-SWORD ALLEY. Whitefriars. *B. H.* xxvii. ; *T. T. C.* bk.
ii. ch. i.
Jerry Cruncher's lodgings were
in Hanging-sword-alley, and they
" were not in a savoury neighbourhood."

HANNAH. Servant girl to Miss La
Creevy. *N. N.* iii.
With an uncommonly dirty
face.

HANOVER. *A. N.* iii.

HANOVER SQUARE.
N. N. xxxvii. ; *U. T.* iii.

HANSARDADE. *Daughter of the*
Grand Vizier Parmarstoon.
M. P., T. O. H.

Note.—Hansard's Parliamentary De-
bates, etc.

HANSARD'S. Luke, pages.
M. P., Q. D. P.

HANWELL. Middlesex.
M. P., S. B.

HAPPY CHARLES. Street of.
M. P., N. Y. D.

HAPPY COTTAGE. *L. D.* xlix.

HAPPY FAMILY. Austin's Animals
in one cage. *M. P., P. F.*

HARDINGE. Miss Emma.
M. P., R. S. D.

HARDY. Mr., " The funny gentleman." *S. B. B.,* Tales vii.
A stout gentleman of about
forty, a practical joker—always
engaged in some pleasure excursion or other—could sing comic
songs, imitate hackney-coachmen
and fowls, play airs on his chin.

and execute concertos on the Jew's harp.

HAREDALE. Miss Emma, Niece of Mr. Geoffrey Haredale.

B. R. i.

An orphan, foster sister of *Dolly Varden*—a lovely girl.

Note.—Emma was the niece of Mr. Geoffrey Haredale, and daughter of Reuben. After many vicissitudes she is married to Edward Chester.

HAREDALE. Mr. Geoffrey.

B. R. i.

A burly, square-built man, negligently dressed, rough and abrupt in manner, stern, and, in his present mood, forbidding both in look and speech.

Note.—Roman Catholic. Somewhat disliked, but, on account of his religion, specially obnoxious to the Gordon Rioters. The Warren, his residence, is burned, and beside the ruins he fights a duel with Sir John Chester, and kills him. He leaves the country and spends the rest of his days under the severe discipline of a monastery.

HAREDALE. Reuben, Father of Miss Haredale and elder brother of Mr. Geoffrey Haredale.

B. R. i.

He is not alive, and he is not dead—not dead in a common sort of way . . . found murdered in his bed-chamber ; and in his hand was a piece of the cord attached to an alarm-bell outside the roof.

HAREDALE. Reuben, Gardener of.

B. R. i.

HAREDALE. Reuben, Steward of.

B. R. i.

HAREDALE. Reuben, Two women servants of. *B. R.* i.

HAR'FORDSHIRE. *M. C.* xxix.

HARKER. Mr., Police officer.

C. S., T. G. S. i.

Sworn to hold us (The Jury) in safekeeping. He had an agree-

able presence, good eyes, enviable black whiskers, and a fine sonorous voice.

HARLEIGH. Mr.

S. B. B., Tales ix.

HARLEQUIN. In booth in Greenwich fair. *S. B. B.*, Tales xii.

HARLEQUIN. On stage in *Britannia.* *U. T.* iv.

HARLEQUIN, A, On stage in *Britannia.* *U. T.* iv

HARLEY. J. P. *M. P., V. C*

HARLEY. Mr., As Felix Tapkins Esq. *M. P., T. S. H. W*

HARLEY. Mr., As Mr. Martin Stokes. *M. P., V. C*

HARLEY. Mr., As the strange gentleman. *M. P., S. G*

HARLEY STREET.

L. D. xx. ; *U. T.* xv.

HARMON. Daughter of dust contractor. *O. M. F.* i

He (the dust contractor) chose a husband for her, entirely to his own satisfaction, and not in the least to hers.—The poor girl respectfully intimated that she was secretly engaged to the popular character whom the novelists and versifiers call "another."—Immediately the venerable parent anathematised, and turned her out.

HARMON. John, Son of dust contractor. (Alias Julius Handford, alias John Rokesmith.) *O. M. F.*

Only son of a tremendous old rascal who made his money by dust. A boy of spirit and resource pleads his sister's cause—venerable parent turns him out—gets aboard ship. A boy of fourteen, cheaply educating at *Brussels*, when his sister's expulsion befell,

Note.—The son of the Harmon of the Harmon estate. He returns from the Cape on the death of his father to take over his inheritance and to fulfil the condition of his father's will by marrying Bella Wilfer. On his return he is attacked, robbed and seriously injured. He is thrown into the Thames as dead, but he revives and swims ashore. In the meantime the man Radfoot, who robs him, quarrels over the spoil and is killed and thrown into the river. When his body is found it is identified as that of John Harmon on account of the property and clothes found on him. Harmon then changes his name to Julius Handford, so that he may make personal investigations without being recognised. He does not retain this alias long, however, but engages himself as private secretary to Mr. Boffin as John Rokesmith. Here he meets Bella Wilfer, and with the assistance of the Boffins, who have recognised him, he succeeds in winning the girl's love. He marries her, and when he is about to reveal his identity to her, he is arrested for his own murder. His identity is discovered by Mrs. Boffin, and she and her husband enter into a scheme to assist him. Noddy Boffin pretends to be miserly, and subjects his secretary to continual insults ; this excites Bella's sympathy, and then her love follows and they are married. Boffin discovers a later will giving everything to him unconditionally. This he ignores, and makes over the greater portion of the property to Rokesmith. His connections with Silas Wegg and Mr. Venus are scarcely essential, but serve to illustrate and illuminate the story.

HARMON. Mrs., Wife of dust contractor—dead. *O. M. F.* ii.

HARMON. Mrs., *See* Wilfer Bella.

HARMON. Old Mr., Deceased dust contractor. *O. M. F.* iii.

HARMON'S. Old. Boffin's Bower. *O. M. F.* v.

HARMONIC MEETING. Waiter at. *S. B. B.,* Scenes ii.
Pale-faced man with the red head.

HARMONIC MEETING. Guests of. *S. B. B.,* Scenes ii.
Some eighty or a hundred.

HARMONIC MEETINGS. Chairman of. *B. H.* xi.

HARMONY JAIL. Boffin's Bower. *O. M. F.* v.
" Not a proper jail, wot you and me would get committed to — they give it the name, on account of old Harmon living solitary there."

HARRIET. *See* Carker, Harriet.

HARRIS. Greengrocer. *P. P.* xxxvii.
Waiting on members and guests of Select Company of Footmen's friendly swarry.

HARRIS. Mary, Nurse at Holborn Union. *M. P., V. D.*

HARRIS. Mr., " Punch showman." *O. C. S.* xvi.
A little merry-faced man, with a twinkling eye and a red nose.
Note.—Harris was Short, Trotters, or Short Trotters indiscriminately to his friends.
Original : Said to have been a showman named Tubby, but as this is all that is known of him the statement is of little value.

HARRIS. Mr. *M. C.* xlix. *M. P., S. F. A.*

HARRIS. Mr. Law stationer. *S. B. B.,* Char. vii.

HARRIS. Mrs. *M. P., L. E. J.*

HARRIS. Mrs., Friend of Mrs. Gamp. *M. C.* xix.
Whom no one in the circle of Mrs. Gamp's acquaintance had ever seen : neither did any human being know her place of residence. The prevalent opinion was that

she was a phantom of Mrs. Gamp's brain.

HARRIS. Thomas L.
M. P., R. S. D.

HARRIS. Tommy, Little.
M. C. xlix.

HARRISBURG. *A. N.* ix.

HARRISON. General. *A. N.* iv.

HARRISON. Little. *O. M. F.* ix.

HARROW. *G. E.* xxiii. ; *U. T.* x.

HARROWGATE. *D. and S.* xxi.

HARRY. Coachman of early coach.
S. B. B., Scenes xv.
In a rough blue coat, of which the buttons behind are so far apart that you can't see them both at the same time.

HARRY. Cousin. *R. P., A. C. T.*

HARRY. Master, Son of Mr. Walmer. *C. S., H. T.*

HARRY. Our eighth royal.
M. P., T. B.

HARRY. A pedlar. *O. T.* xlviii.
This was an antic fellow, half pedlar, half mountebank, who travelled about the country on foot, to vend hones, strops, razors, washballs, harness-paste, medicine for dogs and horses, cheap perfumery, cosmetics, and such-like wares, which he carried in a case slung to his back.

HARRY. The grandson of *Dame* West, and the schoolmaster's favourite scholar. *O. C. S.* xxv.
He was a very young boy ; quite a little child. His hair still clung in curls about his face, and his eyes were very bright ; but their light was of heaven, not earth.

HART. Mr., Assistant master of Asylum for the *B*lind at Bolton.
A. N. iii.

HARTFORD. *A. N.* v.

HARTHOUSE. Mr. James, Political agent. *H. T., R.* ii.
Five-and-thirty, good-looking, good figure, good teeth, good voice, good breeding, well dressed, dark hair, bold eyes.

Note —Friend of Gradgrind. It is largely due to his vile insinuations that Louisa's marriage is such an impossible one.

HARVEYS. *S. Y. C.*

HARWICH. *B. R.* lxxxii.

HASTINGS. *M. P., T. B.*

HATCH. Mrs., Cora.
M. P., R. S. D.

HATCHWAY. *M. P., G. F.*

HATFIELD. *C. S., M. L. Lo.* i.

HATFIELD. Small public house at.
O. T. xlviii.
There was a fire in the taproom, and some country labourers were drinking before it.

Original: Believed to be the " *Eight Bells.*"

HATFIELD CHURCHYARD.
C. S., M. L. Leg. i.

HATTER. The. *U. T.* xvi.

HATTER. Of New York.
M. P., T. O. P.

HATTON GARDEN. *B. H.* xxvi. ; *R. P., B. S.* ; *S. B. B.,* Tales xi.

HAUNTED HOUSE=House of Parliament. *M. P., H. H.*

HAUNTED HOUSE. Cook at the.
C. S., H. H.

old lady who lived in a large and
dismal house barricaded against
robbers, and who led a life of
seclusion. She was dressed in
rich materials, satins and lace
and silks—all of white. Her
shoes were white—a long white
veil depended from her hair, and
she had bridal flowers in her hair,
but her hair was white. Some
bright jewels sparkled on her neck
and on her hands.

Note.—First seen in the story, a
mentally deranged woman living in
Satis House with all daylight excluded.
Pip goes there to play, and meets
Estella, Miss Havisham's adopted
daughter, and sees many strange
things. Miss Havisham is training
Estella to break men's hearts. When
Pip goes no more to Satis House, Miss
Havisham pays Joe a premium of
twenty-five guineas for his indentures.
When she dies she has left most of her
wealth to Estella, " a cool " four thousand to Matthew Pocket, and insigni-
ficant sums to other relatives. It
transpires through the story that Miss
Havisham had been a beautiful heiress
basely deserted on the wedding-day by
Compeyson, the intended husband.
The shock had unhinged her mind.
She then adopted Estella to wreak her
vengeance on the whole of mankind
she came in contact with.

*Original : The original was a
young lady disappointed in the way
Miss Havisham was and, following
the same seclusion, lived " in a
house on the Kettle estate at Newtown,
Sydney, Australia." The story is
said to have been related to Dickens.*

HAVISHAM. Mother of Miss, deceased.   *G. E* xxii.
Died when she was a baby.

HAWDON. A law-writer. *B. H.* x.
His hair is ragged, mingling
with his whiskers and his beard—
dressed in shirt and trousers, with
bare feet.

Note.—Captain Hawdon's identity
is hidden for a long time. He is introduced as an unknown law-writer, living

over Krook's rag-and-bone shop, and going under the name of Nemo. It transpires that he was a military officer, formerly a lover of Lady Dedlock to be, and father of Esther Summerson. He befriends Jo, and dies in his garret. Jo is called up at the "Inkwhich" with unfortunate results to himself. Nemo is buried in the strangers' ground in the neighbouring churchyard, and it is there that Lady Dedlock is found dead clinging to the railings of the closed gate.

HAWDON. Esther. *See* Summerson, Esther.

HAWK. Sir, Mulberry, Guest and client of Ralph Nickleby.
N. N. xix.
Another superlative gentleman, something older, something stouter, something redder in the face.

Note.—A man about town : maintains himself largely by fleecing young men of wealth less versed in the way of the world than himself. One of these, a character in the book, is Lord Verisopht. Hawk fought a duel with him and killed him. This obliged Sir Mulberry to leave the country. He resided abroad for some years, but on returning to this country he was thrown into prison, where he died. Hawk was a connection of Ralph Nickleby's from whom he learns about Kate. Nicholas heard him insult his sister by name in a public place, and in spite of his refusal to disclose his identity, Nicholas managed to inflict punishment upon him.

HAWKINS. A middle-aged baker.
L. D. xxv.
Defendant in Miss Rigg's action for breach of promise.

HAWKINSES. The Landed gentry.
N. N. xxxv.
They are much richer than the Grimbles, and connected with them by marriage.

HAWKINSON. Aunt. *O. M. F.* lii.

HAWKYARD. Mr. Verity.
G. S. E. iv.
A yellow-faced, peak-nosed gentleman, clad all in iron grey to his gaiters.

HAYDEN. Mrs., M. B. *M. P., C.*

HAYMARKET. The. *B. H.* xxi.; *U. T.* x.; *S. B. B.*, Scenes xvii.

HAYNES. Inspector, Of Police Force.
R. P., D. W. I. F.

HAYWARD. Mr. *M. P., S. F. A.*

HAZEBRONCKE. *U. T.* xvii.

HAZEBRONCKE. *C. S., M. J.* v.

HEAD REGISTRAR. Of births.
M. P., L. W. O. Y.

HEADSTONE. Mr. *Bradley*, Schoolmaster. *O. M. F.* xviii.
In his decent black coat and waistcoat, and decent white shirt, and decent formal black tie, and decent pantaloons of pepper and salt, with his decent silver watch in his pocket, and its decent hair-guard round his neck, looked a thoroughly decent young man of six-and-twenty.

Note.—Pauper lad trained as a teacher, and at the opening of the story is master of the boys' department of a school on the borders of Kent and Surrey. Charley Hexam becomes a pupil of his and Bradley falls passionately and unreasoningly in love with Lizzie Hexam. She, however, desires to have nothing to do with him ; in fact, goes rather in fear of him. Bradley broods so much on his unrequited love and is so intensely jealous of Eugene Wrayburn, that his mind becomes distorted. He attempts to murder Wrayburn, and believes he has succeeded. He is dogged by Rogue Riderhood, who has discovered the attempted murder and has traced him to school. Rogue blackmails him heavily and renders his life unbearable by his persecution and insistence. Bradley, while at the Lock, which the Rogue attends, suddenly forces his enemy into the water locked in his own embrace, and both are drowned.

HEALTH. *Officer of.* and **HUMBUGS.** Variety of, in cocked hats. *L. D.* ii.

Original of Heep's house : Supposed to have been situated in North Lane, Canterbury.

HEIDELBERG. Student beerhouses at. *C. S., H. T.*

HEIRESSES. Characters in play. *N. N.* xxiii.
Given by Mr. V. Crummles' Company.

HELENA. Miss Mell, fourth daughter of *Doctor* Mell. *D. C.* xxxiv.

HELL GATE. *A. N.* v.

HELMSMAN. Spirit. *C. B., C. C.* s. iii.

HELVES. Captain, One of Steam Excursion party. *S. B. B.,* Tales vii.

HENDERSON. *M. P., R. S. L.*

HENDERSON. Mrs. *M. P., R. S. D.*

HENDON. *O. T.* xlviii.

HENLEY. *L. D.* xiii.

HENRI. A young man who had belonged to the Inn in Switzerland . . . who had disappeared. *C. S., H. T.*

HENRIETTA. Mr. Click's sweetheart. *C. S., S. L.* iii.
In the bonnet-trimming.

HENRIETTA. Miss Nupkins. *P. P.* xxv.
Possessed all her mamma's haughtiness without the turban, and all her ill-nature without the wig.

HENRY. A Negro man-slave. *A. N.* xvii.

HENRY. Brother of Kate. *P. P.* xvii.
Cousin of Maria Lobbs.

HENRY. Mr., Gentleman behind counter in pawnbroker's shop. *S. B. B.*, Scenes xxiii.
With curly black hair, diamond ring, and double silver watch-guard.

HENRY. Son of the drunkard. *S. B. B.*, Tales xii.
Dead. Shot like a dog by a gamekeeper.

HENRY V. *M. P., W. H.*

HEPBURN. English seaman. *M. P., L. A. V.* i.

HER MAJESTY'S THEATRE. *U. T.* iv.

HERALD. *N. N.* iv.

HERALDS' COLLEGE. *O. M. F.* ii.

HERBERT. *See* Pocket, Herbert.

HERBERT. Mr., *M. P., O. L. N. O.*

HERBERT. Mr., M.P. *B. R.* lxxiii.
Rose, and called upon the House to observe that Lord George Gordon was then sitting under the gallery with the blue cockade, the signal of rebellion in his hat.

HERCULANEUM. *P. F. I., R. D.*

HERMIT. A. *C. S., T. T. G.* i.
A slothful, unsavoury, nasty reversal of the laws of human nature.

HERMITAGE. *P. F. I.*

"HERO OF WATERLOO." A public house. *R. P., D. W. T. T.*

HEROD. *M. P., R. D.*

HEROES. Roman, clowns in *Booth* in Greenwich Fair. *S. B. B.*, Scenes xii.

HERRING. Mr. *M. P., T. C. ʃ. B.*

HERSCHEL. John, John's first cousin. *C. S., H. H.*

HERSCHEL. Mrs., Wife of John Herschel. *C. S., H. H.*

HERTFORDSHIRE. *B. H.* iii.; *C. S., M. L. Lo.* i.; *M. P., C. P.*; *M. P., S. R.*; *O. M. F.* xliii.; *U. T.* xi.; *R. P. T. D. P.*

HERTFORDSHIRE FRIEND. *M. P., P. M. B.*

HE SING. Mandarin passenger. *M. P., C. J.*

HEWITT. Bro. *M. P., S. B.*

HEXAM. Charlie. *O. M. F.* i.
Note.—Son of Gaffer Hexam and brother of Lizzie. His great aim is to become "respectable." His sister assists him to study while he is a boy. He becomes a pupil of Bradley Head-stone, and endeavours to persuade Lizzie to accept the schoolmaster's offer of marriage. When she rejects Bradley he renounces her. And later, he connects Bradley with the attack on Eugene Wrayburn and casts him off—because any acquaintance with a suspected murderer would interfere with his respectability. The story leaves him an under-master at another school, looking forward to filling the shoes of the headmaster and planning, if he desires it, to marry the school-mistress.

HEXAM. *D*welling of. *O. M. F.* iii.
The low building had the look of having once been a mill. There was a rotten wart of wood upon its forehead that seemed to in-dicate where the sails had been. The boy lifted the latch of the door. They passed at once into a low, circular room. The fire was in a rusty brazier, not fitted to the hearth, and a common lamp, shaped like a hyacinth root, smoked and flared in the neck of a stone bottle on the table. There was a wooden bunk or berth in a corner, and in another corner a wooden stair leading above.
Original : Situated in Limehouse.

HEXAM. Gaffer, Jesse Hexam.
O. M. F. i.

HEXAM. Jesse, A waterman.
O. M. F. i.

A strong man with ragged, grizzled hair, and a sun-browned face—no covering on his matted head—brown arms bare to between elbow and shoulder—loose knot of a loose kerchief lying low on his bare breast, in a wilderness of beard and whisker—a hook-nosed man, and with that and his bright eyes and his ruffled head bore a certain likeness to a roused bird of prey.

Note.—Gaffer Hexam was one of the " night birds " of the river robbing dead bodies floating on the tide. He finds the body believed to be that of John Harmon and, chiefly owing to the insinuations of Rogue Riderhood, is accused of his murder. When preparations are made to arrest him on the charge, he is found drowned, trailing in the wake of his own boat.

HEXAM. Lizzie, Daughter of Hexam. *O. M. F.* i.

A dark girl of nineteen or twenty, pulling a pair of sculls very easily.

Note.—Daughter of Gaffer Hexam, and sister of Charley. She is very much opposed to her father's method of making a living, although she assists him, to the extent of rowing his boat. When her father is drowned, she leaves home. Eugene Wrayburn becomes greatly interested in her and assists her. Bradley Headstone falls in love with her, but she refuses his offer of marriage. Headstone becomes intensely, even madly, jealous of Eugene, and annoying his distasteful attentions and to lessen the risk of meeting Eugene, Lizzie leaves London secretly, and with the assistance of Riah obtains employment in a mill up the river. Wrayburn succeeds in tracing her by bribing " Mr. Dolls." He follows her, and is in turn followed by Bradley Headstone. After Eugene has seen Lizzie, Bradley makes a murderous attack upon him. He is rescued by Lizzie, although his life is despaired of. He (Wrayburn) marries her, and recovers.

HEXAM. Lizzie, Temporary lodging of. *O. M. F.* xviii.

Some little quiet houses in a row—one of these. The boy knocked at a door, and the door promptly opened with a spring and a click—a parlour door within a small entry stood open.

HEYLING. George's surname.
P. P. xxi.

Although evidently not past the prime of life, his face was pale and haggard. Disease or suffering had done more to work a change in his appearance than the mere hand of time could have accomplished in twice the period of his whole life.

Note.—Heyling's wife's father casts him into prison for debt. Heyling's father dies leaving him a wealthy man. He at once obtains his release from the Marshalsea. During his imprisonment his wife and child die from poverty and its privation. He devotes himself to revenge. First he sees his wife's brother drown without making an effort to save him, despite the entreaties of the father. He then reduces the father to the state he himself had occupied. The churchyard in which the young mother and child lie buried is that of Shorne.

HICKS. Septimus, A boarder at Mrs. Tibbs. *S. B. B.*, Tales i.

A tallish, white-faced man, with spectacles, and a black ribbon round his neck instead of a neckerchief—a most interesting person : a poetical walker of the hospitals, and a very talented man . . . fond of lugging into conversations all sorts of quotations from Don Juan.

HICKS. Septimus, Father of.
S. B. B., Tales i.

HICKSON. Mr., *S. B. B.*, Scenes xix.

HICKSONS. The, Guests of the Gattletons. *S. B. B.*, Tales ix.

HIGDEN. Betty, Home of.
O. M. F. xvi.

A small home with a very

large mangle in it, at the handle of which machine stood a very long boy.—In a corner below the mangle, on a couple of stools, sat two very little children. The room was clean and neat. It had a brick floor and a window of diamond panes, and a flounce hanging below the chimney-piece and strings nailed from bottom to top outside the window, on which scarlet beans were to grow.

HIGDEN. Mrs. Betty.
O. M. F. xvi.

An active old woman, with a bright dark eye, and a resolute face, yet quite a tender creature too ; nigher fourscore year than threescore and ten.

Note.—Poor old Betty kept a " minding school " and a mangle, at Brentford. By the aid of both she had kept out of the poor house, and hoped to do so throughout. She refuses much assistance from the Boffins, and starts out on a tramp with little goods for sale ; but the " deadness " steals over her more frequently and more completely, until at last she dies in Lizzie Hexam's arms.

HIGHBURY BARN. *M. P., E. T.*

HIGH 'CHANGE. *L. D.* lxi.

HIGHGATE. *B. H.* lvii. ; *B. R.* iv. ; *D. C.* xx. ; *P. P.* i.

HIGHGATE. Dr. Strong's house in.
D. C. vii.

Not in that part of Highgate where Mrs. Steerforth lived, but quite on the opposite side of the little town.

HIGHGATE. Village of.
O. T. xlviii.

HIGHGATE ARCHWAY. *O. T.* xlii. ; *C. S. H. T.*

HIGHGATE HILL. *O. T.* xlviii.

HIGH HOLBORN. *L. D.* xii. *M. C.* xlix.

HIGHLANDS. Of the North River.
A. N. xv.

HIGHLANDS. Scottish.
C. S., H. T. ; *R. P., A. C. T.*

HIGH SCHOOL. Edinburgh.
M. P., S. P.

HIGH SHERIFF. Of Suffolk.
M. P., F. S.

HIGH STREET.
M. P., G. H. ; *N. N.* xxiii. ; *O. M. F.* xli. ; *O. T.* iii.

HIGH STREET. Borough.
P. P. xxx.
See also " White Hart Inn."

HIGH STREET. Cloisterham.
E. D. xii.

The natural channel in which the Cloisterham Channel flows.

HIGH STREET. Mr. Sapsea's premises in. *E. D.* iv.

(*O*ver and against the Nuns' House) irregularly modernised here and there—more and more, that they preferred air and light to Fever and Plague.

HIGH STREET. Of market town.
G. E. viii.

HIGH STREET. Rochester.
E. D. iii. ; *P. P.* ii.
See also " Bull Inn."

HIGH STREET. The, Where the prison stood. *L. D.* ix.

HIGHWAYS. Old trodden, Of Rome. *L. D.* li.

H. I. J. Ensigns. Nobodies.
R. P., N. S.

HILL. Mr. Rowland. *M. P.,* *M. E. R.* ; *M. P., S. S. M. P.,* *R. H. F.*

HILTON. Mr., Guest at Minerva House.   *S. B. B.*, Tales iii.
Undertaken the office of Master of the Ceremonies on occasion of half-yearly ball, given by the Misses Crumpton.

HILTON. Young.
            S. B. B., Tales iii.

HIMALAYA MOUNTAINS.
        M. P., R. T. ; *M. P., S. R.*

HIMSELF. Somebody.
            C. S., S. L. iv.

HINE. William, A young duellist, aged thirteen.   *A. N.* xvii.

HIPPOPOTAMUS. The Good,
                M. P., G. H.

HIS WIFE. And two sisters-in-law."   *U. T.* ii.
Came in among the bodies of ten of the shipwrecked.

HOBBS.   *M. P., T. T.*

HOBLER. Mr., *Driver of the red cab.*   *S. B. B.*, xxiv.

HOCKER. Thomas, Murderer.
                M. P., C. P.

HOCKLEY-IN-THE-HOLE.
                O. T. viii.

HOGARTH.   *M. P., C. P.* ; *M. P. O. L. N. O.* ; *M. P., S.* ; *M. P., S. F. A.*

HOGARTH. James, Mrs. J. Ballantyne's brother.   *M. P., S. P.*

HOGG. Sir James.   *M. P., G. A.*

HOGHTON TOWERS. A farmhouse.
                G. S. E. iv.
A house, centuries old, deserted and falling to pieces.

HOG'S BACK. The.   *A. N.* v.

HOLBEIN.   *M. P., R. D.*

HOLBORN.   *B. H.* iv. ; *E. D.* xi. ; *L. D.* xiii ; *M. C.* xiii. ; *P. P.* xlvii. ; *O. T.* xxi. ; *S. B. B.*, Scenes vii.

HOLBORN COURT. Now South Square.
        D. C. xxx. ; *P. P.* xxxii.

HOLBORN HILL.   *B. H.* i.; *O. T.* xxvi. ; *G. E.* xxi. ; *B. R.* lxi.

HOLBORN UNION.
        M. P., P. T. ; *U. T.* xiv.

HOLLAND.   *B. R.* lxxxii.

HOLLAND. King of.   *M. P., R. S. D.*

HOLLAND STREET.
            R. P., D. W. T. T.

HOLLIDAY. Arthur.   *L. T.*

HOLLIN'S SOVEREIGN MILL. Mr.
                M. P., O. S.

HOLLINSWORTH. Mr., As Mr. Owen Overton.   *M. P., S. G.*

HOLLOWAY.
    O. M. F. iv. ; *S. B. B.*, Scenes xvii.

HOLLOWAY. Professor, Of Holloway's ointment.
        M. P., F. F. ; *M. P. M. P. R. P., B. S.*

HOLLOWAY ROAD.   *N. N.* xxxvi.

"HOLLY TREE." The, An Inn.
                C. S., H. T.
Place of good entertainment for man and beast.

"HOLLY TREE INN." Bedrooms in.   *C. S., H. T.*

"HOLLY TREE INN." Landlady of.   *C. S., H. T.*

"HOLLY TREE INN." Landlord of.   *C. S., H. T.*

"HOLLY TREE INN." The ostler, potboy, and stable authorities of.
                C. S. H. T.

HOLMES. Dr. Oliver Wendell.
                M. P., I. W. M.

HOLMES. Mrs.   *M. P., I. W. M.*

HOLYHEAD. *A. N.* xvi.; *B. H.* xxiv.; *M. P., E. S.*; *S. B. B.* Scenes xv.

HOLYROOD. Palace, and chapel. *P. P.* xlix.; *U. T.* xxxiv.

HOLYWELL STREET. *S. B. B.*, Scenes vi.

HOME. Daniel Dunglas. *M. P., M. M.*; *M. P., R. S. D.*

HOME. Mrs. *M. P., M. M.*

HOME. For homeless women. *M. P., H. H. W.*

HOME. Of James Carker, Manager of *Dombey's. D and S.* xxxiii. Situated in the green and wooded country near Norwood. It is not a mansion; it is of no pretensions as to size; but it is beautifully arranged, and tastefully kept.

HOME. Of John Carker, "the junior" in *Dombey's.*

D. and S. xxxiii. It is a poor, small house, barely and sparely furnished, but very clean; and there is even an attempt to decorate it, shown in the homely flowers trained about the porch and in the narrow garden. The neighbourhood in which it stands has as little of the country to recommend it, as it has of the town.

HOME DEPARTMENT. Secretary of State for. *M. P., F. C.*; *O. T.* xi.

HOME OFFICE. *R. P., P. M. T. P,*

HOME SECRETARY. *R. P., P. M. T. P.*; *M. P., M. P.*; *M. P., S. D. C.*; to *R. P., O. o. T.*

HOMINY. Major. *M. C.* xxii. One of our choicest spirits; and belongs *to* one of our most aristocratic families.

HOMINY. Miss. *M. C.* xxii.

HOMINY. Mrs. Wife of Mr. Hominy. *M. C.* xxii. Very straight, very tall, and not at all flexible in face or figure. On her head she wore a great straw bonnet, with trimmings of the same colour—in her hand she held a most enormous fan.

HONDURAS. *C. S., P. o. C. E. P.*

HONDURAS SWAMPS. *U. T.* xxiv.

HONEST TOM. Colleague of—M.P. *S. B. B.*, Scenes xviii. The large man in the cloak with the white lining, with the light hair hanging over his coat collar.

HONEYTHUNDER. Old Mr. (Luke). Chairman of Committee of Philanthropists. *E. D.* vi. A model philanthropist, who never sees a joke.

Note.—One of those canting hypocrites without which a novel by Dickens would be scarcely complete. He is guardian to Helen and Neville Landless, and is first·seen when he brings his wards to Cloisterham. After Neville is suspected of the murder of Edwin Drood, Mr. Honeythunder gladly washes his hands of his guardianship in favour of the Rev. Crisparkle, who tells him a few truths about himself.

HONG KONG. *B. H.* lv.

HONORIA. Lady *Dedlock.* *B. H.* liv.

HOOD. Mr. Tom. *M. P., Ag. Int.*; *M. P., L. A. V.* i.; *M. P., L. S.*; *M. P., Th. Let.*

HOODLE. *B. H.* xii.

HOOKEM. Sir Snivey. *Mud. Pap.* ii.

HOPE. Miss Flite's bird. *B. H.* xiv.

HOPKINS.   *O. M. F.* xlviii.

HOPKINS. Candidate for beadle's post, with seven small children.
    S. B. B., O. P. iv.

HOPKINS. Captain, *Debtor* in King's Bench prison.   *D. C.* xi.
Shared the room with Mr. Micawber.

HOPKIN'S. Captain, daughters.
    D. C. xi.
Two were girls with shock heads of hair.

HOPKINS. Jack, Hospital Student.
    P. P. xxxii.
He wore a black velvet waistcoat, with thunder-and-lightning buttons ; and a blue-striped shirt, with a white false collar.

  Note.—A medical student at Bartholomews, the friend of Bob Sawyer, and somewhat of the same kidney.

HOPKINS. Mr.   *S. Y. G.*

HOPKINS. Mrs., Captain Hopkins' wife.   *D. C.* xi.
A very dirty lady.

HOPKINS. The Heaven-born.
    M. H. C. iii.
The great witch-finder of the age.

HOPWOOD.   *M. P., O. S.*

HORN. Cape. *C. S., M. f. T. S.* ii.

"HORN COFFEE-HOUSE." In Doctors' Commons. *P. P.* xliv.

HORNBY. Henry, Of Blackburn.
    M. P., O. S.

HORNER. L.   *M. P., O. C.*

HORNER. Mr. *S. B. B.,* Scenes xii.
The man of Colosseum notoriety.

HORNSEY. Churchyard at.
    D. C. xxv.

HORSE GUARDS. The.
  B. R. lxxxii.; *D. C.,* vi.; *M. C.* xiv.; *M. P., Th. Let.*; *M. P., T. O. H.*; *N. N.* xli.

"HORSE GUARDS." Guest of Mr. Merdle.   *L. D.* xxi.

HORSEMAN. A.
  B. R. lvi. ; *M. H. C.* iii.

HORSEMONGER LANE.
    L. D. xviii.; *M. P., F. S.*

HORSEMONGER LANE JAIL.
    R. P., L. A.

HORTENSE. Mlle, Lady *Dedlock's* maid.   *B. H.* xii.
A Frenchwoman of two-and-thirty—a large-eyed brown woman with black hair ; who would be handsome, but for a certain feline mouth, and general uncomfortable tightness of face, rendering the jaws too eager, and the skull too prominent. Like a very neat she-wolf imperfectly tamed.

  Note.—Maid to Lady Dedlock. When she is introduced to the story she has been in the service five years, and becomes jealous of Rosa. She learns something of Lady Dedlock's secret, and shoots Mr. Tulkinghorn. The crime is carefully traced to her by Mr. Bucket, and she leaves the story in custody, still defiant.

HORTON. Miss, P., Actress.
    M. P, R. S. L.

HOSIER LANE.   *O. T.* xxi.

HOSPICE. The.
    C. S., N. T. Act iii.

HOSPICE. The, founded by Napoleon. *P. F. I., V. M. M. S. S.*

HOSPITAL. A patient in casualty ward.   *S. B. B.,* Char. vi.
Her recovery was extremely doubtful. . . . A fine young woman of about two and three and twenty. Her face bore marks of the ill-usage

she had received. She was evidently dying. . . . It was an accident. "He didn't hurt me he
wouldn't for the world." Jack,
they shall not persuade me to
swear your life away. He never
hurt me. Some kind gentleman,
take my love to my poor old
father. He said he wished I had
died a child—oh, I wish I had.

HOSPITAL. *Dressers at.*
         S. B. B., Char. vi.
A couple of young men who
smelt strongly of tobacco.

HOSPITAL. East London Children's.
         U. T. xxx.
Established in an old-sail-loft
or storehouse, of the roughest
nature, and on the simplest means.
I found it airy, sweet and clean.

HOSPITAL. House Surgeon of.
         S. B. B., Char. vi.

HOSPITAL. Medical officers and
directors of East London Children's.   *U. T.* xxx.
A young husband and wife,
both have had considerable practical experience of medicine and
surgery.

HOSPITAL. Some public.
         S. B. B., Char. vi.
A refuge and resting place for
hundreds, who but for such institutions must die in the streets
and doorways.

HOSPITAL. The Royal.
         P. F. I., *R. D.*

HOSPITALS. One of the large, In
London.   *D. C.* xxv.
You understand it now, "Trot,"
said my aunt. "He is gone." "Did
he die in Hospital?" "Yes."

HOSTLER.   *P. P.* li.
Expected the first gold medal
from the Humane Society—for
taking the postboy's hat off;

the water descending from the
brim of which—must inevitably
have drowned him (the postboy)
but for his great presence of mind.

HOSTLER. From Inn in Rochester.
         C. S., *S. P. T.* i.

HOSTLERS. At the Great White
Horse.   *P. P.* xxiv.

HOTEL. At Leamington, where
Dombey stayed.
         Original : Copps's Royal Hotel.

HOTEL. Coketown.   *H. T.*, *R.* ii.

HOTEL. Handsome, Where Nicho-
las overheard Sir Mulberry Hawk.
         N. N. xxxii.
Original : Believed to have been
Mivart's (or Claridge's) then in
Brook Street.

HOTEL. In Brook Street. *L. D.* lii.

HOTEL. In Brook Street. Landlord of.   *L. D.* lii.

HOTEL. At which Mr. *Dick* stopped
in Canterbury.   *D. C.* xvii.
Original : Said to have been the
" *Fleur de Lys Hotel,*" *in High St.*

HOTEL. In Canterbury. *D. C.* lii.
Thro' various close passages;
which smelt as if they had been
steeped, for ages, in a solution of
soap and stables.

HOTEL. In Yarmouth.   *D. C.* v.
Original : Suggested as "Crown
and Anchor," Yarmouth.

HOTEL. National.   *M. C.* xxi.
An immense white edifice, like
an ugly hospital.

HOTEL. Near Charing Cross.
         B. R. lxvi.

HOTEL. Pegwell Bay.
         S. B. B., Tales iv.

HOTEL. Two waiters of Pegwell
Bay.   *S. B. B.*, Tales iv.

HOTEL CAPULET. Padrona of the.
         P. F. I., *V. M. M. S. S.*

HÔTEL DE FRANCE.   Calais.
                          U. T. xvii.

HÔTEL DE VILLE.
                  T. T. C., bk. ii. ch. xxii.

HÔTEL DE VILLE.   Premises of
Monsieur Salcy.   *U. T.* xxv.
    Had established his theatre in
the whitewashed Hotel de Ville.

HOTEL, GREENWICH.   Lovely
women.   *O. M. F.* xxv.
    Original : Was identified as the
" Ship Tavern " at Greenwich.
(By Quartermaine.)

HOUNDSDITCH. *B. R.* lxiii. ; *P. P.*
        xliii. ; *R. P., B. S.*

HOUNDSDITCH CHURCH.
                       U. T. xxxiv.
    Original : Said to be St. Botolph,
Aldgate.

HOUNSLOW.   *M. C.* xiii. ; *O. T.*
        xxi. ; *U. T.* xiv.

HOUNSLOW HEATH.
        G. E. xlviii. ; *M. P., R. T.*

HOUSE.   A large wooden, in Putney.
                         M. H. C. iii.

HOUSE.   In Thames Street.
                          N. N. xi.
    Old and gloomy and black,
in truth it was, and sullen and
dark were the rooms, once so
bustling with life and enterprise.

HOUSE.   In George's Yard.
                    S. B. B., O. P. v.
    There was a little piece of
enclosed dust in front of the
house, with a cinder path leading
up to the door, and an open rain-
water butt on one side.   A dirty
striped curtain, on a very slack
string, hung in the window, and a
little triangular bit of broken
looking-glass rested on the sill
inside.

HOUSE.   In St Mary Axe.
                        O. M. F. xxii.
    A yellow-overhanging plaster-
fronted house.

HOUSE.   In the Common Hard,
Portsmouth, where Nicholas and
Smike lodged.   *N. N.* xxiii.
    Original : Situated in a narrow
lane leading to the wharf.   After-
wards a jeweller's shop.

HOUSE.   Lodging, In Ramsgate.
                     S. B. B., Tales iv.
    With a bay window from which
you could obtain a beautiful
glimpse of the sea—if you thrust
half your body out of it, at the
imminent peril of falling into the
area.

HOUSE.   Near Barbican.
                          B. R. viii.
    From whose defaced and rotten
front the rude effigy of a bottle
swung to and fro like some
gibbeted malefactor.

HOUSE.   Occupied by city clerk.
                   S. B. B., O. P. vii.
    A neat, dull little house, on the
shady side of the way, with new
narrow floorcloth in the passage,
and new narrow stair-carpets up
to the first floor.   The paper was
new, the paint was new, and the
furniture was new, and all three
bespoke the limited means of the
tenant.

HOUSE.   Our, Corner House—not
far from Cavendish Square.
                          O. M. F. v.
    It was a great dingy house, with
a quantity of dim side window and
blank back premises.

HOUSE.   Our.   Joe Gargery's.
                          G. E. ii.
    A wooden house, as many of the
dwellings in our country were.

HOUSE.   Private, Tenant of.
                     S. B. B., Scenes iii.

HOUSE.   Senate.
                     P. F. I., G. A. N.

HOUSE.   Silver, The Fort, the Mine.
                   C. S., P. o. C. E. P.

HOUSE. The. *B. H.* xii.

HOUSE. The, Workhouse.
O. M. F. xvi. ; *S. B. B., O. P.*

"HOUSE. The Early Purl," Inscription on the doorpost of The Six Jolly Fellowship Porters.
O. M. F. vi.

HOUSE. The Haunted. *C. S., H. H.*

HOUSE. The Nuns'. *E. D.* ii.
In the midst of Cloisterham— a venerable brick edifice. The house front is old and worn, and the brass plate is so shining and staring, that the general result has reminded imaginative strangers of a battered old beau with a large modern eyeglass in his blind eye.

HOUSE. Which shall be nameless, where somebody's luggage was left. *C. S., S. L.* i.

HOUSE. With the green blinds.
S. B. B., Char. iii.

HOUSE AT BATH. *P. P.* xxxvi.
Original : Was situated in Royal Crescent, not the Circus.

HOUSE GOVERNMENT.
P. F. I., G. A. N.

HOUSE OF ASSEMBLY. Members of the. *A. N.* ii.

HOUSE OF COMMONS. *M. P., B. S ; M. P., C. P. ; M. P., F. C. ; M. P., G. B. ; M. P., I. M. ; M. P., O. C. ; M. P., P. L. U. ; M. P., R. T. ; M. P., S. S. ; M. P., Th. Let. ; U. T.* xxvi.

HOUSE OF CORRECTION.
M. P., L. W. O. Y. ; M. P., S.

HOUSE OF CORRECTION. Middlesex. *M. P., C. and. E.*

HOUSE OF CORRECTION FOR THE STATE. S. Boston. *A. N.* iii.

HOUSE OF DETENTION. Clerkenwell. *M. P., M. P.*

HOUSE OF INDUSTRY. South Boston. *A. N.* iii.
Worthy of notice. Self Government, quietude and peace.

HOUSE OF LORDS. *M. P., C. P. ; M. P., P. P. ; P. P.* lv. ; *S. B. B.* Scenes xviii.

HOUSE OF REFORMATION. For Juvenile Offenders. South Boston. *A. N.* iii.

HOUSE OF REPRESENTATIVES. Washington. *M. P., Y. M. C.*

HOUSEBREAKER. Keeper of a country Inn. *C. S., H. T.*
Had had his right ear chopped off.

HOUSEBREAKER. Wife of.
C. S., H. T.
Who heated the poker and terminated his career, for which— she received the compliments of royalty on her great discretion and valour.

"HOUSEHOLD WORDS" OFFICE.
R. P., T. D. P.

HOUSEKEEPER. John Podger's.
M. H. C. iii.
Afflicted with rheumatism— burnt as an undoubted witch.

HOUSEKEEPER. Of Cheeryble. Brothers. *N. N.* xxxvii.

HOUSEMAID. At Number 23.
S. B. B., O. P. iii.

HOUSEMAID. Dombey's.
D. and S. xviii.

HOUSEMAID. Mrs. Tibbs'.
S. B. B., Tales i.

HOUSEMAID. Of Cheeryble Brothers. *N. N.* xxxvii.

HOUSEMAID. Of Mrs. Maylie.
O. T. xxviii.

HOUSES. The night.
S. B. B., Scenes i.

HOVELLERS. *R. P., O. o. S.*
Kentish name for longshore boatmen.

HOWARD. Mr. *M. P., S. Pigs.*

HOWE. Dr. Head of Asylum for the Blind at Boston. *A. N.* iii.

HOWE. Lord. *M. P., C. C.*

HOWE. Lord Chamberlain.
M. P., S. for P.

HOWITT. Mr. William.
M. P., M. M. ; M. P., R. S. D.

HOWLER. Reverend Melchisedech Minister of the Ranting Persuasion.
D. and S. xv.
Having been one day discharged from the West India *Docks* on a false suspicion (got up expressly against him by the general enemy) of screwing gimlets into puncheons and applying his lips to the orifice, had announced the destruction of the world for that day two years, at ten in the morning, and opened a front parlour for the reception of ladies and gentlemen of the Ranting persuasion.

HOWN. A runaway negro slave.
A. N. xvii.

HOWSA KUMMAUNS. Peerless Chatterer. *Official* name of wife of Taxedtaurus. *M. P., T. O. H.*
Note.—House of Commons.

HUBBLE. Mr. The Wheelwright.
G. E. iv.
A tough, high-shouldered, stooping old man, of a saw-dusty fragrance, with his legs extraordinarily wide apart.
Note.—Friend of Joe Gargery's wife. Last seen in the funeral procession of Mrs. Gargery.

HUBBLE. Mrs., Wife of wheelwright. *G. E.* iv.
A little curly, sharp-eyed person in sky blue.

HUDDART. Miss. *M. P., R. S. L.*

HUDIBRAS. Lud, King of Great Britain. *P. P.* xxxvi.
He was a mighty monarch. The earth shook when he walked : he was so very stout. His people basked in the light of his countenance : it was so red and glowing. He was indeed every inch a king. And there were a good many inches of him too, for although he was not very tall—the inches he wanted in height he made up for in circumference.

HUDSON. *A. N.* xv.

HUDSON. Mr. *M. P., G. A.*

HUDSON'S BAY COMPANY.
M. P., L. A. V. i.

HUFFY. *B. H.* xii.

HUGGIN LANE. A City church in.
U. T. ix.

HUGH. Father of, Sir John Chester.
B. R. lxxv.

HUGH. Mother of. *B. R.* xi.
Hung when he was a little boy, with six others, for passing bad notes.

HUGH. *O*stler at the " Maypole."
B. R. x.
He sleeps so desperate hard— that if you were to fire off cannonballs into his ears, it would not wake him, said the distracted host. " Brisk enough when he is awake," said the guest. . . . Loosely attired in the coarsest and roughest garb, with scraps of straw and hay—his usual bed—clinging here and there, and mingling with his uncombed locks.
Note.—Hugh enters the story as hostler and general man at the " Maypole Inn." He is *au fait* with everything connected with horses, but he is entangled with the rioters and becomes a prominent figure amongst them.

His extreme strength and wild devil-may-care athleticism render him particularly suitable for the part he plays. He gets into the power, the seductive power, of the superior gentleman, of Sir John Chester, and becomes a tool in his hand. It transpires that he is the illegitimate son of Sir John, but when he is threatened with the gallows, his father refuses to intervene on his behalf. And Hugh, the friend of Barnaby, suffers the extreme penalty with the utmost composure, or, rather, indifference.

HUGHES. Ladies of the family of the Reverend Stephen Roose.
U. T. ii.

HUGHES. R., Grimaldi's executor.
M. P., J. G.

HUGHES. Reverend Hugh Robert, of Penrhos. Brother of Stephen Roose Hughes. *U. T.* ii.

HUGHES. Reverend Stephen Roose. Clergyman of Llanallgo.
U. T. ii.
I read more of the New Testament in the fresh, frank face (going up the village beside me) in five minutes, than I have read in anathematising discourses in all my life.

HUGO. M. Victor. *M. P., L. L.*

HULL. *M. H. C.* i.

HULLAH. John. *M. P., F. C.* ; *M. P., S. F. A.* ; *M. P., V. C.*

HUMAN INTEREST. Brothers.
U. T. i.

HUMBUG. Wan. *M. P. B. L.*

HUME. Joseph. *M. P., S. for P. M. P., T. D.*

HUMM. Mr. Anthony, President of the Ebenezer Temperance Association. *P. P.* xxxiii.
Straight-walking, a converted. fireman, now a schoolmaster, and occasionally an itinerant preacher.

A sleek, white-faced man in a perpetual perspiration.

HUMMUMS. An Inn. In Covent Garden.
G. E. xlv. ; *S. B. B.*, Scenes i.

HUMPHREY. *Duke,* His Grace.
M. C. i.

HUMPHREY. Master. *M. H. C.* i.
A misshapen, deformed old man.
Original : So far as the book-title was concerned, if no farther, this was founded on a clockmaker named Humphreys whose shop could be seen from the "King's Head," Barnard Castle, where Dickens made a brief stay.

HUMPHREY. Master. Such a very old man. *O. C. S.* i.
Note.—The ' I'" of the earlier chapters is supposed to be Master Humphrey, who is narrating the story. The "Old Curiosity Shop," first commenced in the fourth number of "Master Humphrey's Clock," a serial publication edited by Dickens, but which "became one of the lost books of the earth."

HUMPHREY. Master, House of.
M. H. C. i.
A silent, shady place, with a paved courtyard. Its wormeaten doors, and low ceilings crossed by clumsy beams ; its walls of wainscot, dark stairs, and gaping closets ; its small chambers, communicating with each other by winding passages or narrow steps ; its many nooks scarce larger than its corner cupboards ; its very dust and dullness are all dear to me.
For original *see* Humphrey. Master.

"HUNGERFORD STAIRS." Public-house. *D. C.* lvii.
The Micawber family were lodged in a little, dirty, tumble-

down public-house, which in those days was close to the stairs, and whose protruding wooden rooms overhung the river.

Original: "The Swan."

HUNT. Captain Boldwig's head gardener.   *P. P.* xix.

HUNT. Leigh.   *M. P., L. H.*

HUNT. Leigh, Eldest son of.
                M. P., L. H.

HUNT. Robert.   *M. P., P. S.*

HUNT AND ROSKELL. Messrs., Jewellers in New Bond Street.
                M. P., I. M.; U. T. xvi.

HUNTER. Horace.
                S. B. B., Tales viii.
Note.—Party to a duel which never came off—who married Miss Emily Brown at Gretna Green.

HUNTER. Mr., Husband of Mrs. Leo Hunter.   *P. P.* xv.
"Is it a gentleman?" said Mr. Pickwick. "A wery good imitation o' one, if it ain't," replied Mr. Weller. A grave man, with an air of profound respect.
Note.—Mr. Hunter lived in the reflected light of his wife.

HUNTER. Mrs. Fogle.
                Mud. Pap. ii.

HUNTER. Mrs. Leo, Poetess of "The Den," Eatanswill.
                P. P. xv.
"To-morrow morning, sir, we give a public breakfast . . . feasts of reason, sir, and flow of souls." . . . Mrs. Leo Hunter, writer of some delightful pieces. . . . Ode to an Expiring Frog. It commenced:

Can I view thee panting, lying
On thy stomach, without sighing?
Can I unmoved see thee dying
                On a log,
                Expiring frog?

Original: Credited to Mrs. Somerville Wood.

HUSBAND. First.   *M. P., N. T.*

HUSBAND. Of friend to Little Em'ly.   *D. C.* xxii.
The husband was come home then; and the two together put her aboard a small trader.

HUSBAND. Of other lady at wedding of Bunsby.   *D. and S.* lx.
The short gentleman with the tall hat.

HUSBAND. Of the daughter of the deaf gentleman.   *M. H. C.* vi.

HUSBAND. Of the married Miss Hominy.   *M. C.* xxiii.

HUSBAND. Second.   *M. P., N. T.*

HUSBANDS IN PERSPECTIVE. At tea gardens.
                S. B B., Scenes ix.
*O*rdering bottles of ginger-beer for the objects of their affections with a lavish disregard of expense.

HUTCHING. Mr. Thomas.
                M. P., S. B.

HUTLEY. James.   *See* Dismal Jemmy.

HYDE PARK.   *D. C.* xxviii.; *O. T.* xxxix.; *M. P., R. H. F.*

HYDE PARK CORNER.   *G. E.* xxx.; *M. P., T. T.; O. M. F.* xliv.; *O. T.* xxi.; *R. P., T. N. S.*

HYGEIAN COUNCIL of the British College of Health. Members of the.   *M. P., M. P.*

HYGEIAN   ESTABLISHMENT. King's Cross.   *M. P., Ag. Int.*

HYPOLITE. Private, Billeted at the Perfumer's.   *C. S., S. L.* ii.
Volunteered to keep shop, while the fair perfumeress stepped out to speak to a neighbour or so.

HYTHE.   *D. C.* xii.

I

ICELAND.   *O. M. F.* xxviii.

IDDÂH. On the Niger.
      M. P., N. E.

IDLE. Thomas.   *L. T.*
 Original: Thomas Idle was Wilkie Collins, who accompanied Dickens on this idle tour.

IDLERS. Seeing Mark Tapley off.
      M. C. vii.

IDOL. The presiding, Of the Circumlocution *Office.* *L. D.* x.

IKEY. Sheriff officer's mercury.
      S. B. B., Tales x.
 A man in a coarse Petersham great-coat, whity-brown neckerchief, faded black suit. Gamboge-coloured top-boots, and one of those large crowned hats—now very generally patronised by gentlemen and costermongers.

IKEY. Stable man of Inn.
      C. S., H. H.
 A high-shouldered young fellow, with a round face, a short crop of sandy hair, a very broad, humorous mouth, a turned-up nose, and a great sleeved waistcoat of purple bars, with mother-of-pearl buttons.

IMPERIAL.   *M. P., W.*

IMPUDENCE. Little Miss. *E. D.* ii.

IMYANGER. An, A Witch doctor.
      R. P., T. N. S.
 Sent for to Nooker the Umtargartie, or smell out the witch.

INCHBALD. Mrs. *M. P., L. S.*

INDEPENDENCE. *A. N.* xvii.

INDIA. *C. S., S. P. T.*; *C. S., T. T. G.* vi.; *D. and S.* viii.; *H. T., S.* xv.; *L. D.* lvii.; *M. C.,* xxvii.; *M. P., E. T.*; *M. P., L. L.*; *M. P., M. E. R.*; *M. P.,*
N. G. K.; *M. P., S. F. A.*; *R. P., A. C. T.*; *R. P., O. E. W.*; *R. P., P. M. T. P.*; *R. P., T. B. W.*; *R. P., T. C. S.*; *U. T.* iv.

INDIA DOCKS. *D. and S.* ix.

INDIA HOUSE. *M. P., E. T.*; *M. P. G. A.*; *M. P., I. S. H. W.*; *M. P. L. T.*; *U. T.* iii.

INDIAN. *C. S., G. into Soc.*

INDIAN. A wild, Exhibited at Greenwich Fair.
      S. B. B., Scenes xii.
 A young lady of singular beauty, with perfectly white hair and pink eyes.

INDIAN OCEAN. *H. R.* iii.

INDIAN PROPERTY. Mr. Bull's fine.   *M. P., H. H.*

INDIANS. Chiefs of. *A. N.* ix.

INDIANS. North American.
      U. T. xxvi.

INDIANS. Ojibbeway,
      R. P., T. N. S.

INDIANS. Wyandot, *A. N.* xiv.

INDIES. East.   *E. D.* iv.

INDIES. The.   *U. T.* xv.

INDIES. West. *S. B. B., O. P.* i.

INDIGENT ORPHANS' FRIENDS' BENEVOLENT INSTITUTION. A member of. *S. B. B.,* Scenes xix.
 A large-headed man, with black hair and bushy whiskers.

INDIGENT ORPHANS' FRIENDS' BENEVOLENT INSTITUTION.
 A member of.
      S. B. B., Scenes xix.
 A stout man in a white neckerchief and buff waistcoat, with shining dark hair, cut very short in front, and a great, round, healthy face.

INDIGENT ORPHANS' FRIENDS' BENEVOLENT INSTITUTION. A member of. *S. B. B.*, Scenes xix.
A round-faced person, in a dress-stock, and blue under-waistcoat.

INDIGENT ORPHANS' FRIENDS' BENEVOLENT INSTITUTION. Secretary of. *S. B. B.*, Scenes xix.

INDIGENT ORPHANS' FRIENDS' BENEVOLENT INSTITUTION. Titled visitors at dinner of.
S. B. B., Scenes xix.

INESTIMABLE. The, Life Assurance Office. *H. D.* ii.

INFANT BONDS OF JOY.
B. H. viii.

INFANTS. *M. P., L. E. J.*

INGLIS. Sir Robert, Member for the University of Oxford.
M. P., C. J.

INGOLDSBY. Thomas. *M. P., A. P.*

INN. *G. E.* lii.
Once been a part of an ancient ecclesiastical house.

INN. About half a quarter of a mile from the end of the Downs.
P. P. xiv.
A strange old place, built of a kind of shingle, inlaid, as it were, with cross-beams, with gable-topped windows projecting completely over the pathway, and a low door with a dark porch.

Originals : Numerous originals have been claimed for the inn in which Tom Smart experienced the strange events : " Marquis of Ailesbury Arms " at Clatford ; " Catherine Wheel " at Beckhampton ; a former inn at Shepherd's Shord ; " Kennet Inn " at Beckhampton. That at Shepherd's Shore appears to receive the most support.

INN. A famous, in Salisbury.
M. C. xii.
The hall a very grove of dead game, and dangling joints of mutton ; and in one corner an illustrious larder, with glass doors, developing cold fowls and noble joints, and tarts wherein the raspberry jam coyly withdrew itself—behind a lattice-work of pastry.
Original : Supposed to have been the " White Hart," St. John Street, Salisbury ; or by another authority " The Angel."

INN. A spacious. *B. H.* lvii.
Solitary, but a comfortable, substantial building."

INN. At Mugby. *O. S., M. J.* i.

INN. At which Wrayburn was nursed. *O. M. F.* lvi.
Original : Said to have been the " Red Lion " near Henley.

INN. Cornish. *C. S., H. T.*

INN. In Rochester.
C. S., S. P. T. i.

INN. In the North of England.
C. S., H. T.
Haunted by the ghost of a tremendous pie—a Yorkshire pie, like a fort, an abandoned fort, with nothing in it. The waiter had a fixed idea that it was a point of ceremony at every meal to put the pie on the table.

INN. In the remotest part of Cornwall. *C. S., H. T.*

INN. Landlord of an. *C. S., H. T.*
By the roadside, whose visitors unaccountably disappeared for many years, until it was discovered that the pursuit of his life had been to convert them into pies.

INN. Little, At which Micawber stopped in Canterbury. *D. C.* xvii.
Originals : Suggested as the " Sun Inn " in Sun Street, Canterbury, also as the " Queen's Head Inn " at the corner of Watling Street and St. Margaret Street.

INN. On the Welsh border.

C. S., H. T.

In a picturesque old town

INN. Roadside, Where Nicholas met Crummles. *N. N.* xxii.
Original: Coach and Horses, near Petersfield, locally known as the " Bottom Inn."

INN. Swiss. *M. P., N. T.*

INNER TEMPLE. *M. P., M. N. D.*

INNKEEPER. *L. T.*

INNS. English posting. *C. S., H. T.*
Which we are all so sorry to have lost.

INNS. German. *C. S., H. T.*
Where all the eatables are soddened down to the same flavour.

INNS. Highland. *C. S., H. T.*
With the oatmeal bannocks, the honey—the trout from the loch, the whisky and—perhaps the Athol Brose.

INNS. The Anglers. *C. S., H. T.*

INNS. Welsh. *C. S., H. T.*
With the women in their round hats, and the harpers with their white beards (venerable, but humbugs, I am afraid) playing outside the door.

INNS OF COURT. *B. R.* lxvii.
M. H. C. iv.; *S. B. B.*, Scenes i.

INSOLVENT COURT. *P. P.* xlii.

INSOLVENT COURT. Commissioners of the. *P. P.* xliii.
One, two, three, or four gentlemen in wigs, as the case may be, with little writing-desks before them, constructed after the fashion of those used by the judges of the land, barring the French polish. There is a box of barristers on their right hand; there

is an enclosure of insolvent debtors on their left; and there is an inclined plane of most especially dirty faces in their front.

INSOLVENT DEBTORS COURT.
S. B. B. xlii.

INSPECTOR. Connected with Circumlocution Office. *U. T.* viii.

INSPECTOR. Night. *O. M. F.* iii.
With a pen and ink and ruler posting up his books in a whitewashed office.

INSTITUTION. Indigent Orphans' Friends' Benevolent.
S. B. B., Scenes xix.

INSTITUTIONS. Ladies' charitable.
S. B. B., O. P. vi.

INSTITUTION FOR THE FOUND CHILDREN. In Paris. *L. D.* ii.

INTEREST. Monied, Passenger in train. *R. P., A. F.*

IOWA. *A. N.* xvii.; *D. C.* xxvi.; *M. P., F. S.*; *P. P.* xx.

IPSWICH. Market Place.
C. S., D. M.

IPSWICH GAOL. Governor of.
M. P., F. S.

IRELAND. *A. N.* xv.; *B. H.* xxiv.
H. T., R. ii.; *M. P., E. S.*;
M. P., E. T.; *M. P., F. O. E. G.*;
M. P., H. H.; *M. P., L. W. O. Y.*;
M. P., Q. D. P.; *M. P., R. S.*;
S. B. B., Tales i.; *U. T.* xxxi.

IRISH PEDLAR. *S. B. B., O. P.* vi.

IRISHWOMAN. An, at Mr. Skimpole's. *B. H.* lxi.
Breaking up the lid of a waterbutt with a poker, to light the fire with.

IRON BRIDGE. *L. D.* xxii.
Original: Probably Southwark Bridge, on which Dickens himself used to wander when his father was in prison.

IRONWORKER.   *O. C. S.* xliv.

IRVING. Washington.
M. P., I. C.

IRVING. Washington. Appointed Minister at the Court of Spain.
A. N. viii.

ISAAC. Coach driver. *P. P.* xlvi.
A shabby man in black leggings . . . with a thick ash stick in his hand . . . seated on the box (of the coach) smoking a cigar. The bashful gentleman.

ISAAC. Man slave.   *A. N.* xvii.

ISLE OF MAN.   *M. P., E. S., C. S., M. L. Lo.* i.; *U. T.* xvii.

ISLE OF THANET. *R. P., A. P. A.*

ISLE OF WIGHT.   *O. M. F.* x.

ISLEWORTH.   *O. T.* xxi.

ISLINGTON. *B. H.* lix.; *B. R.* xxxi.; *C. S., H. T.* iv.; *C. S., M. L. Lo.* i.; *D. and S.* xiii.; *M. C.* xxxvi.; *M. H. C.* vi.; *M. P., E. T.*. *M. P., P. P.*; *N. N.* xxxix.; *O. T.* viii.; *S. B. B.,* Scenes i.; *S. B. B.,* Char. i.

ISLINGTON ROAD.
S. B. B., Char. i.

ITALIAN BOULEVARD. *U. T.* xii.

ITALIAN BOYS.   *M. P., G. H.*

ITALIAN CAVALIERE.
M. P., N. Y. D.

ITALIAN CITY. Protestant Cemetery near.   *U. T.* xxvi.

ITALIAN PALACE.   *C. S., H. H.*

ITALIAN PRISONER. *U. T.* xxviii.

ITALIANS. *P. P.* xxxiii.; *P. F. I., T. R. P.*

ITALY.   *C. S., H. T.*; *C. S., S. P. T.*; *D. C.* xi.; *M. P., C. P.*; *M. P., M. M.*; *P. F. I.*; *R. P., D. W. T. T.*; *R. P., L. A.*; *R. P., O. B.*; *U. T.* vii.

ITALY. Inns in old monastery.
C. S., H. T.
With their massive quadrangular staircases, whence you may look from among clustering pillars into the blue vault of heaven.

ITALY. Roadside Inns of.
C. S., H. T.
Where the mosquitoes make a raisin pudding of your face in summer, and the cold bites it blue in winter. Where you get what you can, and forget what you can't.

ITALY. The old palace inns.
C. S., H. T.

ITRI.   *P. F. I., R. D.*

IVINS. Friend of Miss Jemima.
S. B. B., Char. iv.

IVINS. Miss, Miss Jemima Evans.
S. B. B., Char. iv.
The pronunciation most in vogue with the circle of her acquaintance.

IVINS. Mrs. Mother of Jemima.
S. B. B., Char. iv.

IVINS. One of the younger Miss.
S. B. B., Char. iv.

IVINS. The youngest Miss.
S. B. B., Char. iv.

IVINS. The youngest Miss—but one.
S. B. B., Char. iv.

IVINS. Young man of friend of. Jemima.   *S. B. B.,* Char. iv.

IVORY. A runaway negro manslave.   *A. N.* xvii.

IZZARD. Mr.   *M. C.* xxxix.

J

JACK. A British, in the "Snug."
U. T. v.
A little maudlin and sleepy, lolling over his empty glass as if he were trying to read his fortune at the bottom.

JACK. Cheap. *U. T.* xxii.

JACK. Engaged at Searle's boating establishment. *S. B. B.*, Scenes x.

JACK. Frying pan. *M. P., N. E.*

JACK. The Lord Mayor. *M. H. C.* i.

JACK. Mrs. Lupin's man.
M. C. xxxvi.

JACK. Of the Little Causeway.
G. E. liv.
Had a bloated pair of boots on, which he exhibited—as interesting relics—taken a few days ago from the feet of a drowned seaman washed ashore. . . . Probably it took about a dozen drowned men to fit him out completely.

Note.—The odd-job man at the Ship. (The "Ship and Lobster" near Gravesend.)

JACK. Prisoner under arrest.
S. B. B., Char. vi.
A powerful, ill-looking young fellow at the bar, undergoing an examination, on the very common charge of having, on the previous night, ill-treated a woman, with whom he lived in some court hard by.

JACK. Runaway "negro boy" slave. *A. N.* xvii.

JACK. Sailor. *U. T.* xx.

JACK. Secretary of Master Humphrey's Club. *M. H. C.* iv.

JACK. Suicide. *R. P., D. W. T. T.*

JACK OF SWEDEN. Visitor at the "Snug." *U. T.* v.

JACK SMOKE. *M. P., N. E.*

JACK SPRAT. *M. P., N. E.*

JACK THE FINN. Visitor at the Snug. *U. T.* v.

JACKMAN. Major, Mrs. Lirriper's lodger. *C. S., M. L. L.* o.

Though he is far from tall, he seems almost so when he has his shirt-frill out, and his frock-coat on and his hat with the curly brim. His mustachios as black and shining as his boots, his head of hair being a lovely white.

JACKS. Cheap, *C. S., D. M.*
We tell 'em the truth about themselves to their faces, and scorn to court 'em.

JACKS. Dear, *C. S., D. M.*
Members of Parliament, platforms, pulpits, counsel learned in the law. These *Dear* Jacks soap the people shameful.

JACKSON. A certain, A turnkey.
L. D. xix.

JACKSON. A crimp. *U. T.* v.

JACKSON. Andrew *Davis.*
M. P., R. S. D.

JACKSON. General. *A. N.* iv.

JACKSON. Joe, A sailor. *U. T.* xx.

JACKSON. Michael. *B. H.* lvii.
With a blue velveteen waistcoat, with a double row of mother-of-pearl buttons.

JACKSON. Mr. *M. P., F. C.*

JACKSON. Mr. *S. Y. C.*

JACKSON. Mr., Clerk of *Dobson* and Fogg. *P. P.* xx.

JACKSON. Mrs. *S. Y. C.*

JACKSON. Trainer for the ring.
D. and S. lxi.
Kept the boxing-rooms in Bond Street—man of very superior qualifications—used to mention that in training for the ring they substituted rum for sherry.

JACKSON. Young, Of the firm of Barbox Brothers. *C. S., M. J.* ii.

JACOB'S ISLAND. *O. T.* l.; *U. T.* x.

JACOBS. Establishment of Mr. Solomon, Lock-up House.
S. B. B., Tales x.

JACOBS. Mr. Solomon.
S. B. B., Tales x.

JACQUES. One to Four.
T. T. C. v.

Note.—Principals in the Revolution, with Defarge.

JACQUES. Five.   *T. T. C.* v.

Note.—The road-mender of the earlier part of the story. He becomes a wood-sawyer, and ignorant but faithful watcher. A member of Defarge's revolutionary party.

JAGGERS. A lawyer. *G. E.* xviii.
A burly man of exceedingly dark complexion, with an exceedingly large head, and a correspondingly large hand—prematurely bald on the top of his head—had bushy black eyebrows that would not lie down, but stood up bristling. His eyes were set very deep in his head, and were disagreeably sharp and suspicious.

Note.—Miss Havisham's legal adviser. He is first met with at Satis House, but he is frequently seen throughout the story in his characteristic attitude of biting his forefinger. He is the only person Pip knows in connection with his great good fortune for a long time, as everything done for him is through Jaggers. He has a large criminal clientèle, and conducted the case for Magwitch when he was recaptured. This is the last time he appears.

JAIL.   *B. H.* vi.

JAIL. Kingston.   *G. E.* xlii.

JAIL. The County.   *G. E.* xii.

JAIL. The Pink. *P. F. I., G. A. N.*

JAILER. Of Marseilles prison.
L. D. i.
Carrying his little daughter.—
"My little one you see, going round with me to have a peep at her father's birds."

JAILS. Her Majesty's.
S. B. B., Char. xii.

JAIRING'S. First waiter at,
U. T. vi.
Denuded of his white tie, making up his cruets.

JAIRING'S. Hotel for families and gentlemen.   *U. T.* vi.

JAIRING'S. Second waiter at.
U. T. vi.
In a flabby undress, cleaning the windows of the empty coffee-room.

JAMAICA.   *C. S., P. o. C. E. P.*;
D. and S. xxxii.; *O. M. F.* ii.

JAMAICA HARBOUR.
D. and S. iv.

JAMANNE. Miss.   *M. P., U. N.*

JAMES.   *S. Y. C.*

JAMES. Henry, Commander of barque "*Defiance.*"
D. and S. xxxi.

JAMES. Mr. Bayham Badger's butler.   *B. H.* xiii.

JAMES. Mr. William Robert, Solicitor and clerk to the Holborn Union.   *M. P., P. T.*

JAMES. Mrs. Tibbs' boy.
S. B. B., Tales i.
In a revived black coat of his master's.

JAMES. Negro boy-slave.
A. N. xvii.

JAMES. Son of John.
R. P., P. M. T. P.

JAMES RIVER.   *A. N.* ix.

JAMES STREET.
N. N. vii.; *U. T.* xiv.

JAMES THE FIRST. King.
M. H. C. iii.

JANE. Aunt, Baby of.
S. B. B., Char. ii.
Guest at Christmas family party.

JANE. Aunt, Inhabitant of corner house.   *O. M. F.* v.

JANE. Daughter of a stout lady visitor at Ramsgate library.
     S. B. B., Tales iv.

JANE. Hebe of Bellamy's.
     S. B. B., Scenes xviii.
Female in black—a character in her way. Her leading features are a thorough contempt for the great majority of her visitors; her predominant quality, love of admiration—no bad hand at re-partees.

JANE. Mr. *O*range's maid.
     H. R. iv.

JANE. Mr. Pecksniff's "Serving-maid."   *M. C.* xxxi.

JANE. Servant at the Manor Farm, *D*ingley *D*ell.   *P. P.* v.

JANE. Servant girl in obscure public-house.   *M. C.* xiii.

JANE. Servant of Mr. and Mrs. Kitterbell.   *S. B. B.*, Tales xi.

JANE. Servant to Mr. and Mrs. Pott.   *P. P.* xiii.

JANE. Sister of young lady, fiancée of great lord.   *N. N.* xviii.

JANE. Suicide.   *U. T.* iii.

JANE. Wardrobe woman at school.
     R. P., T. S. S.

JANE. Wife of Uncle Robert.
     S. B. B., Char. ii.
Guest at Christmas family party.

JANET. Miss Trotwood's maid.
     D. C. xiii.
A pretty, blooming girl of about nineteen or twenty, and a perfect picture of neatness.

JANUS. Sir Jasper.
     M. P., C. Pat.

JAPAN.   *E. D.* iv.

JARBER.   *C. S., G. i. S.*

JARGON. Name of a bird.
     B. H. xiv.

JARLEY. Mrs., Of Jarley's wax-works.   *O. C. S.* xxvi.
At the open door of the caravan sat a Christian lady, stout and comfortable to look upon, who wore a large bonnet trembling with bows.
Note.—The proprietor of the travelling wax-works. She falls in with Little Nell and engages her to display the wax-works to visitors. Eventually she married her driver George. *See also* Coventry.

JARNDYCE. John.   *B. H.* ii.
A handsome, lively, quick face, full of change and motion; and his hair was silvered iron-grey—nearer sixty than fifty, but he was upright, hearty, and robust.
Note.—One of the parties in Jarndyce and Jarndyce, the interminable Chancery case that has become a household word. He was the guardian of Richard Carstone and Ada Clare. He engages Esther Summerson as companion and friend to Ada, but is so pleased with her kindly ways and modest thoughtfulness that he asks her to marry him. She consents. After preparing everything for the wedding he releases her in favour of Allan Woodcourt, as he has seen that there is a greater affection between them. He is a visitor at their house, however, and they erect a "growlery" for him. He detests the great case, and endeavours to keep Richard out of it, but without success. Ultimately it is found that all the estate has been eaten up in costs, without any decision having been arrived at. He is a kindly, generous man, who when he is displeased explains that the "wind is in the East" to account for his ill-humour.

JARNDYCE. Old Tom, of Jarndyce and Jarndyce.   *B. H.* i.
Blew his brains out in a coffee-house in Chancery Lane.

JARNDYCE AND JARNDYCE. The famous chancery suit on which the story hangs.   *B. H.*

Originals : It is not difficult to find prototypes of the case in chancery ; but two, Jennens v. Jennens and Martin v. Earl Beauchamp, have been specially singled out.

JARVIS. A clerk in Wilding and Co.   *C. S., N. T.* Act i.

JASPER. Mr. Jack.   *E. D.* ii.
A dark man of some six-and-twenty, with thick, lustrous, well-arranged black hair and whiskers. His voice is deep and good, his face and figure are good, his manner is a little sombre.

Note.—Uncle of Edwin Drood and secret suitor for the hand of Rosa Bud. He is introduced in an East End opium den. He is addicted to the habit, and it would appear from the story that some discovery of importance hinges upon his infirmity. He foments the ill-feeling between his nephew and Neville Landless, although he appears to be desirous of making them friendly. So far as the book is completed he is suspected of the murder of Edwin by several people, and is being constantly watched by Datchery.

Original : So far as the name is concerned, it was not unknown in Chatham, and has been traced to the Church registers.

JASPER'S GATEHOUSE.
                    E. D. ii.
Original : Probably the College Yard Gate at Rochester, also known as Cemetery Gate, and Chertsey's Gate, but the description also appears to include points from the Prior's Gate and the Deanery Gatehouse.

JAVELIN-MAN.   *B. R.* lxi.

JEAN. A son of Madame Doche.
                    R. P., M. O. F. F.

JEDDLER. Doctor, A great philosopher.   *C. B., B. o. L.* i.
The heart and mystery of his philosophy was to look upon the

world as a gigantic practical joke. Had a streaked face like a winter pippin, with here and there a dimple, and a very little bit of pigtail behind that stood for the stalk.

JEDDLER. Doctor, Wife of.
                    C. B., B. o. L. i.

JEDDLER. Grace.
                    C. B., B. o. L. i.
So gentle and retiring.

JEDDLER. House of Doctor.
                    C. B., B. o. L. i.

JEDDLER. Martha, Spinster sister of *Doctor* Jeddler.
                    C. B., B. o. L. i.

JEFFERSON. Judge.   *A. N.* xiv.

JEFFERY.   *M. P., M. E. R.*

JEFFREYS. [Judge].
                    M. P., A. in E.

JELLYBY. Caddy, Eldest daughter of Mrs. Jellyby.   *B. H.* iv.
From her tumbled hair to her pretty feet, which were disfigured with frayed and broken satin slippers, trodden down at heel, she really seemed to have no article of dress upon her, from a pin upwards, that was in its proper condition, or in its right place.

Note.—Eldest daughter of Mrs. Jellyby. She is introduced working as unpaid secretary to her mother. She has been neglected in many ways, but in spite of this she is a pleasing character. She marries Prince Turveydrop and escapes the uncongenial surroundings of her home. She has to work hard in her new sphere, however, and prospers so much that she keeps her own little carriage. She has a deaf and dumb little girl to whom she devotes her spare time and energies.

JELLYBY. Mr., Husband of Mrs. Jellyby.   *B. H.* iv.
He may be a very superior

man; but he is, so to speak, merged in the more shining qualities of his wife. A mild, bald gentleman in spectacles.

Note.—Mrs. Jellyby's husband. A quiet, unobtrusive man. He is neglected by his wife and becomes bankrupt. In the end Mr. Jellyby is seen spending his evenings at Caddy's new house, still with his head against the wall.

JELLYBY. Mrs.   B. H. iv.
A lady of very remarkable strength of character, who devotes herself entirely to the public— has devoted herself to an extensive variety of public subjects— is at present devoted to the subject of Africa—cultivation of the coffee-berry—and the natives. Pretty, very diminutive, plump woman, of from forty to fifty, with handsome eyes.

Note.—Mrs. Jellyby is a caricature of the woman with a mission; she is first seen promoting a scheme for the natives of Borrioboola-Gha on the Niger. She is so absorbed in this work that she neglects her home, her husband, and her children. Eventually her husband becomes a bankrupt. After the failure of the Niger scheme she takes up the rights of women to sit in Parliament, " a mission involving more correspondence than the old one."

JELLYBY'S.   House in Thavies Inn.
                            B. H. iv.
A narrow street of high houses, like an oblong cistern to hold the fog. The house at which we stopped had a tarnished brass plate on the door, with the inscription Jellyby.

JELLYBYS. One of the young.
Peepy.   B. H. iv.
One of the dirtiest little unfortunates I ever saw—fixed by the neck between two iron railings.

Note.—Son of the Jellybys and rather more neglected than the others. He is befriended by Esther Summerson, and is last seen in the Custom House, " and doing extremely well."

" JEM."   A carol singer.
                        P. P. xxviii.

JEM.   Boy of Mr. Solomon Jacobs.
                    S. B. B., Tales x.
A sallow-faced, red-haired, sulky boy.

JEMIMA.   Sister of Mrs. Toodle.
                        D. and S. ii.

JEMMY.   Dismal, Job's brother.
See Dismal Jemmy.

JEMMY.   Son of Mrs. Edson.
                    C. S., M. L. Lo. i.

JENKINS.   Miss.   S. B. B., Tales ix.
Whose talent for the piano was too well known to be doubted for an instant.

JENKINS.   Mr.   S. Y. C.

JENKINS.   Owner of an assumed name.   S. B. B., Scenes xiii.

JENKINS.   Sir   Mulberry   Hawk's man.   N. N. i.

JENKINSON.   Messenger in Circumlocution Office.   L. D. x.
Who was eating mashed potatoes and gravy behind a partition by the hall fire.

JENNER.   Dr.
    M. P., N. J. B.;   M. P., S. C.

JENNINGS.   Miss, Pupil at the Nuns' House.   E. D. ix.

JENNINGS.   Mr.   Mud. Pap.

JENNINGS.   Mr., Robe-maker.
                    S. B. B., Char. vii.

JENNINGS.   Pupil   at   Dotheboys' Hall.   N. N. vii.

JENNY.   Brickmaker's   wife.
                        B. H. viii.

Note.—Wife of one of the brickmakers. She is not a bad woman, but is dominated by her drunken husband. She changes her outer garment with Lady Dedlock to enable the latter to elude those in search of her.

JERROLD. Mr. *Douglas.*
M. P., I. M. T. ; M. P., V. and B. S.

JERRY. A travelling showman with performing dogs.
O. C. S. xviii.
A tall, black-whiskered man in a velveteen coat.

JERUSALEM BUILDINGS. Row of shops. *C. B., H. M.* i.
Tetterby's was the corner shop in Jerusalem Buildings.
Original : Possibly Jerusalem Buildings was a thin disguise for Jerusalem Passage, St. John's Square, Clerkenwell.

JERUSALEM COFFEE-HOUSE.
L. D. xxix.

JESUITS. The. *P. F. I., G. A. N.*

JEW AND CHRISTIAN VAMPIRES.
Attending sale of *Dombey's* furniture. *D. and S.* lix.
Herds of shabby vampires, Jew and Christian, overrun the house, sounding the plate-glass mirrors with their knuckles, striking discordant octaves on the grand piano, drawing wet forefingers over the pictures, breathing on the blades of the best dinner-knives, punching the squabs of chairs and sofas with their dirty fists, touzling the feather beds, opening and shutting all the drawers, balancing all the silver spoons and forks, looking into the very threads of the drapery and linen, and disparaging everything.

JEWBY. Clients of Snagsby.
B. H. x.

JEWELLER'S SHOP. In Paris. Attendant in. *L. D.* liv.
A sprightly little woman, dressed in perfect taste.

JEWESS. *P. P.* xli.
A magnificent Jewess of surpassing beauty.

JEWESS. The stout.
S. B. B., Scenes xiii.
Mother of the pale, bony little girl, with the necklace of blue glass beads sitting by her. She is being brought up to the profession.

JEWISH GIRL. A beautiful.
B. R. lxxxii.
Who attached herself to him (Lord George Gordon while in Newgate) from feelings half-religious, half-romantic, but whose virtuous and disinterested character appears to have been beyond the censure even of the most censorious.

JEWISH PASSENGERS. On board "Royal Charter." *U. T.* ii.

JEWS. Hawkers. *P. P.* xxxv.
With the fifty-bladed knives.

JEWS. In Holywell Street.
S. B. B., Scenes vi.
Red-headed, and red-whiskered, who forcibly haul you into their squalid houses, and thrust you into a suit of clothes, whether you will or not.

JEWS. Lenders of fancy dresses.
S. B. B., Scenes xiii.
A sure passport to the amateur stage.

JIBBS. *M. P., F. S.*

JIDDA. In the *Dead* Sea.
M. P., L. A. V. ii.

J. J. Mr., of Peckham.
M. P., S. F. A.

JILKINS. A physician.
R. P., O. B.

JIM. Negro man-slave. Ran away. *A. N.* xvii.

JINGLE. Alfred, Strolling player.
P. P. ii.
He was about the middle height, but the thinness of his body, and

the length of his legs, gave him the appearance of being much taller. The green coat had been a smart dress garment . . . the soiled and faded sleeves scarcely reached to his wrists. . . . His scanty black trousers displayed here and there those shiny patches which bespeak long service. . . . His long black hair escaped in negligent waves beneath each side of his old, pinched-up hat. . . . His face was thin and haggard ; but an indescribable air of jaunty impudence and perfect self-possession pervaded the whole man.

Note.—Jingle enters the story at an early chapter as a rollicking, entertaining eccentric ; and leaves it the recipient of Mr. Pickwick's generosity for the West Indies, having passed through real adventures surely as wonderful as those fables he narrated with such profusion. He masquerades as Charles Fitz-Marshall and occasions the Pickwickians a vast amount of trouble, but is discovered by Mr. Pickwick in a most deplorable condition in the debtors' prison.

Original : Is said to have existed in a fellow clerk of Dickens' named Potter.

JINIWIN. Miss Betsy. *See* Quilp, Mrs.

JINIWIN. Mrs., Mrs. Quilp's mother. *O. C. S.* iv.

Mrs. Quilp's parent was known to be laudably shrewish in her disposition and inclined to resist male authority.

Note.—Quilp's mother-in-law, Mrs. Jiniwin, is in mortal dread of the dwarf, but she endeavours to make some show of opposing and defying him. On Mrs. Quilp's second marriage it was made a condition that her mother should be an out-pensioner.

JINKINS. Customer come to redeem some tools. *S. B. B.*, Scenes xxx.

Was enjoying a little relaxation from his sedentary pursuits, a quarter of an hour ago, in kicking his wife.

JINKINS. Mr., Gentleman boarding at Todger's. *M. C.* viii.

Was of a fashionable turn ; being a regular frequenter of the Park on Sundays, and knowing a great many carriages by sight— was much the oldest of the party, being a fish salesman's bookkeeper, aged forty—was the oldest boarder also ; and in right of his double seniority, took the lead in the house.

" **JINKINS.**" Resident at inn in Marlborough *Downs.* *P. P.* xiv.

A very tall man in a brown coat and bright basket buttons, and black whiskers, and wavy black hair, who was seated at tea with the widow, and who it required no great penetration to discover was in a fair way of persuading her to be a widow no longer.

Note.—Introduced in the Bagman's story. Attempts to marry the widowed landlady, but is frustrated by Tom.

JINKINS. Wife of, Takes in mangling. *S. B. B.*, Scenes xxiii.

A wretched, worn-out woman, apparently in the last stage of consumption, whose face bears evident marks of ill-usage, and whose strength seems hardly equal to the burden—light enough, God knows ! of the thin, sickly child she carries in her arms.

JINKINSON. A barber. *M. H. C.* v.

JINKINSON'S. Children of, *M. H. C.* v.

JINKINSON'S. A barber's shop. *M. H. C.* v.

JINKS. Mr., Magistrate's clerk. *P. C.* xxiv.

A pale, sharp-nosed, half-fed, shabbily-clad clerk, of middle age, . . . had a legal education of three years in a country attorney's office.

JO. Crossing-sweeper. *B. H.* xi.
Very muddy, very hoarse, very ragged, knows a broom's a broom, and knows it's wicked to tell a lie.

Note.—The boy is befriended by Captain Hawdon, then an unknown law-writer. He knew nothing—who he was or his name. Questioned before the coroner's jury, he is a pathetic figure. Accidentally he is involved in Lady Dedlock's secret without knowing the meaning of his knowledge. But Mr. Tulkinghorn has him hounded on from one place to another. He falls ill, and communicates the smallpox to " Charley," and " Charley " gives it to Esther. He is found in London by Allan Woodcourt, and taken to George's Shooting Gallery, where he is cared for, but dies and, it is presumable, buried in the strangers' ground beside Captain Hawdon.

JOBBA. Mr.   *Mud. Pap.* i.

JOBBER. A grimly satirical,
                        U. T. xxii.
Who announced himself as having to let " A neat one-horse fly, and a one-horse cart."

JOBBIANA. A discreet slave.
                        M. P., *T. O. H.*
Note.—Jobbery.

JOBBING MAN. A.
                S. B. B., Scenes v.

JOBLING. John, Esquire, M.R.C.S., Medical *O*fficer to the Anglo-Bengalee *D*isinterested Loan and Life Assurance Company.
                        M. C. xxvii.
The same medical officer who had followed poor old Anthony Chuzzlewit to the grave, and who had attended Mrs. Gamp's patient at the " *B*ull." His neckerchief and shirt-frill were ever of the whitest, his clothes of the blackest and sleekest, his gold watchchain of the heaviest, and his seals of the largest. His boots, which were always of the brightest, creaked as he walked.

JOBLING. Tony.   *B. H.* xx.
His hat presents at the rims a peculiar appearance of a glistening nature, as if it had been a favourite snail-promenade. He has the faded appearance of a gentleman in embarrassed circumstances.

Note.—Law-writer to Snagsby. He passes under the name of " Weevle." He is a friend of Mr. Guppy and accompanies that gentleman on his visit to Esther Summerson, when he renews his offer of marriage. It appears then that Jobling will occupy the position of clerk to Mr. Guppy when he sets up his own legal establishment.

JOB-MASTER. A, Who taught riding.   *D. and S.* xxii.

JOBSON FAMILY. Emigrants.
                        U. T. xx.

JOBY.   *C. S., H. H.*
" A hold chap, a sort of one-eyed tramp."

JOCK.   *L. T.*

JOCK. Rev. Jared. *M. P., F. F.*

JOCKEY CLUB. A member of.
                        M. C. xxvi.

JODD. Mr.   *M. C.* xxxiv.

JODDLEBY. A.   *L. D.* xvii.

JOE. Driver of 'bus plying to Cloisterham.   *E. D.* vi.

JOE. Fat boy.   *P. P.* iv.
" Damn that boy, he's gone to sleep again."

Note.—Joe was the celebrated fat boy who was servant to Mr. Wardle. Although he wakened up to do a duty, immediately the task was accomplished he went to sleep. Curiously enough he is one of the few characters in Pickwick which do not undergo some development. He is the same fat boy in chapter lvi. as in chapter iv. The only exception might be his fondness for Mary.

JOE. Guard of the *Dover* mail.
T. T. C. ii.

JOE. Jack Adams' brother.
D. and S. xxxvi.

JOE. Labourer. *D. and S.* vi.

JOE. Man-cook in a family hotel.
O. T. xxxix.
In a quiet but handsome street near Hyde Park.

JOE. Mrs., Mrs. Joe Gargery.
G. E. ix.

JOE. Old, *Dealer in rags and bones.*
C. B., C. C. iv.
A grey-haired rascal, nearly seventy years of age.

JOES. Small, Children of Joe and Dolly Willet. *B. R.* lxxxii.

JOEY. Captain. *O. M. F.* vi.
The bottle-nosed regular customer (at the "Six Jolly Porters") in the glazed hat.

JOEY. Mr., Joey Ladle.
C. S., N. T. Act iii.

JOHN. *C. S., H. H.*

JOHN. *M. P., S. B.*

JOHN. *M. P., S. G.*

JOHN. *M. P., S. R.*

JOHN. *R. P., A. O. T.*

JOHN [*Bull*]. *M. P., T. O. P.*

JOHN. *Boiler maker out of work in Ratcliff.* *U. T.* xxx.

JOHN. Boy of the Parsons.
S. B. B., Tales x.

JOHN. Host at Christmas party.
R. P., P. R. S.

JOHN. Miss La Creevy's brother.
N. N. xxxi.

JOHN. Mr. *S. Y. C.*

JOHN. Mr. Malderton's man.
S. B. B., Tales v.
A man who, on ordinary occa-

sions, acted as half-groom, half-gardener—touched up to look like a second footman.

JOHN. Negro slave. *A. N.* xvii.
Committed to jail.

JOHN. Of Sunderlands.
G. E. liv.
Master of Ship "Betsy" of Yarmouth.

JOHN. Old Charles. *C. S., S.* li.

JOHN. Servant in livery.
S. B. B., O. P. v.

JOHN. Servant to Lovetown.
M. P., I. S. H. W.

JOHN. Son of the drunkard.
S. B. B., Tales xii.

JOHN. Subject of "The Stroller's Tale." *P. P.* iii.
A low pantomime actor. . . an habitual drunkard.

JOHN. Tenant of Haunted House.
C. S., H. H.

JOHN. Very poor man, out of work.
D. and S. xxiv.
Went roaming about the banks of the river when the tide was low, looking out for bits and scraps in the mud.

JOHN. Waiter in "Saracen's Head."
P. P. li.

JOHN EDWARD. Youngest grandson of Nandy. *L. D.* xxxi.
Son of Mr. and Mrs. Plornish.

"JOHN, OLD." John.
R. P., P. M. T. P.
" I have been called ' Old John ' ever since I was nineteen years of age, on account of not having much hair."

JOHNNEE. *M. P., T. O. H.*

JOHNNY. *O. M. F.* xvi.
A pretty boy—blue eyes—fat dimpled hand.

Note.—In their hunt for a child to adopt, the Boffins light on Betty Higden's grandson, but before the project can be carried out Johnny dies.

JOHNNY=Lord John Russell.
M. P., B. S.

JOHNNY CAKES.   *A. N.* x.

JOHNSON. Dr.   *M. P., R. S. D.*

JOHNSON. John.   *M. P., S. G.*

JOHNSON. Mr.
The name which Newman Noggs had bestowed upon Nicholas Nickleby in his conversation with Mrs. Kenwigs. *See* Nickleby, Nicholas.

JOHNSON. Parkers.
S. B. B., O. P. vi.

JOHNSON. Pupil of Dr. Blimber.
D. and S. xii.
"Said *Doctor* Blimber, 'Johnson will repeat to me to-morrow morning before breakfast, without book, and from the Greek Testament, the first chapter of the Epistle of Saint Paul to the Ephesians'."

JOHNSON. Tom, Acquaintance of cousin Feenix.   *D. and S.* xli.
Man with cork leg, from White's.

JOHNSON. Traveller to Paris.
R. P., O. F. W.

JOHNSON'S.   *S. B. B., O. P.* v.

JOHNSON'S. Nursery ground.
S. B. B., Scenes ix.

JOLLIE. Miss.   *M. P., S. P.*

JOLLSON. Mrs., Former occupant of 9, Brig Place.   *D. and S.* xxxix.

JOLLY BARGEMEN. *See* Three Jolly *Bargemen.*

JOLLY BOATMEN.   *Mud. Pap.*

JOLLY SANDBOYS.   *O. C. S.* xvii.
A small roadside inn of pretty ancient date.

JOLLY TAPLEY. The "*Blue* Dragon."   *M. C.* xlii.

JOLTERHEAD. Sir W.
Mud Pap. ii.

JOMILLAH.   *M. P., T. O. H.*

JONATHAN.   *M. P., T. O. P.*

JONATHAN.   *O. M. F.* vi.

JONATHAN. Young.
M. P., A. J. B.

JONES. Barrister's clerk.
S. B. B., Char. vii.
Capital company—full of anecdote.

JONES. Blackberry.
O. M F. xlviii.

JONES. Boy.   *M. P., B. A.*
M. P., Th. Let.
Reference to "General" Tom Thumb.

JONES. George.   *O. M. F.* vi.
In a faded scarlet jacket.

JONES. George, Wife of.
O. M. F. vi.

JONES. Husband of Mary.
B. R. Pref.
It was a time when press warrants were issued. The woman's husband was pressed, their goods seized for some debts of his, and she, with two small children, turned into the streets a-begging.

JONES. Mary, hanged at Tyburn.
B. R. xxxvii.
"Who came up to Tyburn with an infant at her breast, and was worked off for taking a piece of cloth off the counter of a shop—and putting it down again when the shopman see her; and who had never done any harm before, and only tried to do that in consequence of her husband being

pressed three weeks previous, and she being left with two young children."

JONES. Mary, Two small children of. *B. R.* Pref.
The younger suckling at her breast when she (Mary Jones) set out for Tyburn.

JONES. Master. *D. C.* xviii.
A boy of no merit whatever.

JONES. Mr. *B. H.* lviii.
The rawest hand behind the counter.

JONES. Mr., Friend of the *Budden* family. *S. B. B.*, Tales ii.
A little smirking man with red whiskers.

JONES, SPRUGGINS AND SMITH. Messrs. *S. B. B.*, Tales v.

JONES. Tom. *M. P., P. P.*

JOODLE. *B. H.* xii.

JOPER. Billy. *D. and S.* xli.
" A man at *Brook's*—you know him no doubt—man with a glass in his eye."

JORAM. Mrs. *See Omer*, Minnie.

JORAM. Undertaker's assistant to Mr. *Omer*. *D. C.* ix.
Note.—Marries Omer's daughter.

JORGAN. Captain, A new Englander. *C. S., M. f. F. S.* i.
An American-born—a citizen of the world, and a combination of most of the best qualities of most of its best countries. In long-skirted blue coat, and blue trousers.

JORKINS. Mr., Mr. Spenlow's partner. *D. C.* xxiii.
A mild man of a heavy temperament, whose place in the business was to keep himself in the background, and be constantly ex-

hibited by name as the most obdurate, and ruthless of men.

JOSEPH. Charity child. *U. T.* xxi.
Shaking mats in City churchyard.

JOSEPH. Head waiter at Slamjam Coffee-House, London, E.C. *C. S., S. L.* i.

JOSEPHINE. Again a wife. *H. T., G.* ix.

JOSEPHINE. Children of. *H. T., G.* ix.

JOSEPHINE. Son of. *H. T., G.* vii.
" The Little Wonder of Scholastic Equitation. Tho' only three years old, he sticks on to any pony you can bring against him."

JOSIAH. A negro man. *A. N.* xvii.
Branded I.M. on hip.

JOVE. *M. P., G. F.*

JOWL. Mat. Fellow gambler with Isaac List. *O. C. S.* xxix.
A bulky fellow of middle age, with large black whiskers, broad cheeks, a coarse wide mouth, and bull-neck.
Note.—One of the two gamblers who, with the assistance of Groves, tempt Little Nell's grandfather. The gang is broken up by the unintentional intervention of Frederick Trent.

JOY. Name of bird. *B. H.* xiv.

JOY. Thomas, A carpenter. *R. P., P. M. T. P.*

J. U. *M. P., S. B.*

JUDGE. *M. P., P. L. U.*

JUDGE. *T. T. C.* bk. ii, ch. ii.

JUDGE. A certain constitutional. *M. C.* xxi.
Who laid down from the

Bench, the noble principle, that it was lawful for any white mob to murder any black man.

JUDGE. In *Doctors' Commons.*
S. B. B., Scenes viii.
A very fat and red-faced gentleman, in tortoiseshell spectacles.

JUDGE. The, In Court of Chancery.
B. H. i.

JUDGE'S CHAMBERS. *B. H.* x.

JUDGES. The. *C. S., T. G. S.* i.

JUDGES. The. *U. T.* xi.

JUDGES. The wery best-two o' them. *P. P.* lv.
The wery best judges of a horse you ever knowed, added Mr. Weller.

JUDY. Mulatto woman. Runaway slave. *A. N.* xvii.

JUFFY. *B. H.* xii.

JUGGLER. The. *D. and S.* xviii.
A sky-blue fillet round his head, and salmon-coloured worsted drawers.

JUGGLER'S BABY. *D. and S.* xviii.

JUGGLER'S WIFE.
D. and S. xviii.
A child's burial has set her thinking that perhaps the baby underneath her shawl may not grow up to be a man.

JULIA. *R. P., G. o. A.*

JULIUS CAESAR. *B. H.* liv.

JULIUS CAESAR. Mr. Slinkton.
H. D. V.

JULLIEN. M. *R. P., B. S.*

JUMBLE. The. *O. M. F.* xviii.
The school at which young Charley Hexam had first learned from a book—a miserable loft in an unsavoury yard. Its atmo-

sphere was oppressive and disagreeable—half the pupils dropped asleep, or fell into a state of waking stupefaction.

JUPE. Cecilia, A stroller's daughter. *H. T., S.* ii.
So dark-eyed, and dark-haired, that she seemed to receive a deeper and more lustrous colour from the sun.

Note.—Cissy is introduced as a shy girl in Gradgrind's school frightened and browbeaten by Bounderby. She is the daughter of a member of Sleary's troupe, and Bounderby thinks the influence an evil one in the school : so it is decided that Cissy must go. It is found, however, the Signor Jupe has vanished, and Mr. Gradgrind takes her home with him. Although Cissy has not too happy a life with the Gradgrinds, it is due to her that Mr. Gradgrind does not suffer much more than he does. Cissy clears Mr. Harthouse out of the way, and by doing so saves Louisa's reputation, and it is also through her and her influence with Sleary that Tom is enabled to escape.

JUPE. Cissy. Her children.
H. T. bk. iii., ch. ix.

JUPE. Signor, A Clown in Sleary's Circus. *H. T., S.* iii.

JURA MOUNTAINS.
P. F. I., V. M. M. S. S.

JURY. *P. P.* xxxiv.

JURY. *M. P., L. E. J.*

JURY. A member of the. (A vestryman). *C. S., T. G. S.* i.
"The greatest idiot I have ever seen at large."

JURY. At Inquest. *B. H.* xi.

JURY Coroner's. *U. T.* viii.

JURY. Foreman of the.
C. S., T. G. S. i.

JUSTICE. Blind,
M. P., T. T. C. D.

JUSTICE. Courts of.
R. P., T. D. P.

" JUSTICE." Russian officer of, Mr. Potts as. *P. P.* xv.

With a tremendous knout in his hand. Tastefully typical of the stern and mighty powers of the " Eatanswill Gazette."

JUSTICE OF PEACE. *B. R.* xlvii.

A stout gentleman with a long whip in his hand, and a flushed face—called by some a genuine John Bull.

JUSTICES. The. *G. E.* xiii.

JUVENILE DELINQUENT SOCIETY. *O. T.* xix.

K

KATSKILL MOUNTAINS. *A. N.* xv.

KAFFIRLAND. *R. P., T. N. S.*

KAFFIRS. Zulu. *R. P., T. N. S.*

KAGS. A returned transport. *O. T.* l.

A robber of fifty years, whose nose had been almost beaten in, in some old scuffle, and whose face bore a frightful scar, which might probably be traced to the same occasion.

Note.—A member of Fagin's gang who has returned from transportation. He is present in the house on Folly Ditch when Sikes takes refuge in it.

KARS. *M. P., N. S. E.*

KATE. An orphan child. *D. and S.* xxiv.

Note.—She visits at Lady Skettles' while Florence Dombey is there.

KATE. Maria Lobbs' cousin. *P. P.* xvii.

An arch, impudent-looking, be-witching little person.

KEAN. *M. P., D. M.* ; and *M. P., R. S. L.*

KEATS. Grave of the bones of. *P. F. I., R.*

KEDGICK. Captain, Landlord of National Hotel. *M. C.* xxii.

Note.—Captain Kedgick, in his capacity of landlord, arranged a levee for Martin Chuzzlewit, and his mysterious behaviour led Mark Tapley to hope they had discovered the most remarkable man in the United States and so used up the " breed."

KEELEY. *M. P., M. B.*

KEEPER. Of Mrs. Nickleby's neighbour. *N. N.* xli.

A coarse, squat man.

KELEY. Patrick, of Kildare, Ireland. *M. P., F. S.*

KELSO. *M. P., S. P.*

KEMBLE. *M. P., R. S. L.*

KENGE. Mr., Of Kenge and Carboy. Solicitors. *B. H.* iii.

A portly, important-looking gentleman, dressed all in black, with a white cravat, large gold watchseals, a pair of gold eyeglasses, and a large seal-ring upon his little finger.

Note.—Kenge is ushered into the story unostentatiously, and although he is present in some of the most dramatic scenes, it is rather as stage property than as a principal actor, and he disappears with the termination of the famous chancery suit, Jarndyce and Jarndyce, in the same way that he enters the book.

KENILWORTH. *D. and S.* xxvi.

KENNINGTON. *B. H.* xxxix. ; and *R. P.* ; *T. D. A.* i.

KENNINGTON OVAL. *M. P., E. T.*

KENNINGTON STATION HOUSE. *C. S., M. L. Lo.* i.

KENSAL GREEN CEMETERY. *M. P., I. M. T.* and *M. P., T. D.*

KENSINGTON. *B. R.* xvi. ; *M. P., P. T.* ; *M. P., T. B.* ; *O. T.* xxi. ; *P. P.* xliv.

KENSINGTON GARDENS.
S. B. B., Tales x.

KENSINGTON GRAVEL.
N. N. xxviii.

KENSINGTON TURNPIKE.
P. P. xxxv.

KENSINGTON UNION. *M. P., P. T.*

KENT. *B. H.* xxvii. ; *C. S., S. P.
T.* ; *D. S.* lvi. ; *G. E.* liv. ; *O. M.
F.* xii. ; *P. P.* ii. ; *R. P., A. C. T.,
O. o. T.* ; *T. B. W.* ; *U. T.* xii.
Everybody knows Kent—apples,
cherries, hops, and women.

Note. Kent enters largely into the
"Pickwick Papers," and in fact into
many of Dickens' works. It was his
favourite county. Reference should be
made to the various places mentioned,

KENT. The hop grounds of.
M. P., G. A.

KENT ROAD.   *D. C.* xiii.

KENT STREET.   *U. T.* xiii.

KENTISH HEIGHTS.   *B. H.* i.

KENTISH TOWN.   *B. R.* xvi.

KENTUCKY.   *M. P., A. P.*

KENTUCKY GIANT.   *A. N.* xii.

KENWIGS. Lillyvick, Son of Mr.
and Mrs. Kenwigs.   *N. N.* xv.
Christened after the collector.

KENWIGS. Mr., Turner in ivory.
N. N. xiv.
Who was looked upon as a
person of some consideration on
the premises, inasmuch as he
occupied the whole of the first
floor, comprising a suit of two
rooms.

Note.—Kenwigs occupied a floor in
[the house in which Newman Noggs
had a room. Their outlook on life
was limited by their expectations
from Mr. Lillyvick, the water-rate
collector. As is natural, the collector
married and disappointed them, until
his wife ran away. There is a subtle

resemblance in the "atmosphere" of
the Kenwigs' home to that of Micawber's.
Original of Kenwigs' house:
Suggested as having been 48, Car-
naby Street.

KENWIGS. Mrs., Wife of Mr. Kenwigs.   *N. N.* xiv.
Quite a lady in her manners,
and of a very genteel family . . .
was considered a very desirable
person to know.

Note.—Wife of Mr. Kenwigs ; and
mother of the wonderful children. She
was very much upset by the marriage
of the collector ; and when the collector's wife ran away with a half-pay
captain and Lillyvick returned to them
—to the room in which he had met
Miss Petowker—to cast her off for ever,
Mrs. Kenwigs was again upset, but
speedily recovered.

KENWIGS. Morleena.   *N. N.* xiv.
Had flaxen hair, tied with blue
ribands, hanging in luxuriant pigtails . . . and wore little white
trousers with frills round the ankles.

Note.—The eldest daughter of the
Kenwigses. She had acquired, or inherited, her parent's artless hypocrisy
in dealing with Mr. Lillyvick.

KENWIGSES. Little.   *N. N.* xiv.

KENWIGSES. The two eldest.
N. N. xiv.
Went twice a week to a dancing
school in the neighbourhood, and
had flaxen hair, tied with blue
ribands, hanging in luxuriant pigtails down their backs ; and wore
little white trousers with frills
round the ankles.

KESWICK VALE.   *M. P., A. P.*

KETCH. Mr. John, The great state
schoolmaster.
M. P., F. S. ; *Mud. Pap.* 2nd
meeting, and *O. T.* xxvi.

KETTLE. Mr.   *M. P., N. G. K.*

KETTLE. Mr. La Fayette. *M. C.* xxi.
Languid and listless in his looks,
his cheeks were so hollow that he
seemed to be always sucking them

in ; and the sun had burnt him not a wholesome red or brown, but dirty yellow. He had bright dark eyes, which he kept half closed—in the palm of his left hand, as English rustics have their slice of cheese, he had a cake of tobacco : in his right a penknife.

Note.—Kettle is one of the most typical of Dickens' caricatures of American personalities. He was secretary of the Watertoast Association of United Sympathisers, and Martin Chuzzlewit met him on his travels.

KEW.   *G. E.* xxx.

KEW BRIDGE.   *O. T.* xxi.

KEYHOLE   REPORTER. New York.   *M. C.* xvi.

KIBBLE. Mr. Jacob, Fellow-passenger of Mr. John Harmon.
                          O. M. F. iii.

KIDDERMINSTER. One of Sleary's troup.   *H. T., S.* vi.
    A diminutive boy with an old face—made up with curls, wreaths, wings, white bismuth, and carmine. This hopeful young person soared into so pleasing a cupid.

KIDGERBURY. Mrs., A charwoman.
                          D. C. xliv.
    The oldest inhabitant of Kentish Town, I believe, who went out charing, but was too feeble to execute her conceptions of that art.

KILBURN ROAD.
                  S. B. B., Scenes ix.

KILDARE. Ireland. *M. P., F. S.*

KILNS. In Pottery. *R. P., A. P. A.*

KINDHEART. Mr., Friend of Uncommercial Traveller. *U. T.* xxvi.
    An Englishman of amiable nature, great enthusiasm, and no discretion.

KING. The.   *B. R.* lxxviii.

KING. In Cinderella. *M. P., F. F.*

KING. Of Little Dorrit's tale to Maggy.   *L. D.* xxiv.

KING. Christian George. A Sambo.   *C. S., P. o. C. E. P.*
    No more a Christian than he was a King or a George.

" KING ARTHUR'S ARMS." Inn.
                  C. S., M. f. T. S. v.

KING GEORGE THE FOURTH.
                          B. H. xii.

KING OF BILL-STICKERS.
                          R. P., B. S.

KING STREET. Covent Garden.
                  M. P., W. S. G.

KING. Tom,   *S. B. B.,* Scenes v.

" KING'S ARMS." The.
                  D. and S. liii.

KING'S ARMS AND ROYAL HOTEL.
Lancaster.   *C. S., D. M.*

KING'S BATH.   *P. P.* xxxv.

KING'S BENCH.   *B. R.* lxvii.

KING'S BENCH OFFICE. *B. H.* x.

KING'S BENCH PRISON.
                          U. T. xiii.

KING'S BENCH PRISON. Debtor's prison in the *Borough.*
    D. C. xi. ; *N. N.* xlvi. ; *S. B. B.,*
                          Scenes xxi.

KING'S BENCH WALK. *See* Temple.

" KING'S HEAD." Barnard Castle.
                          N. N. vii.

KING'S SON. In Cinderella.
                          M. P., F. F.

KINGSGATE STREET. Holborn.
                          M. C. xix.

KINGSMILL. Rev. Mr.
                          M. P., P. P.

KINGSTON. *A. N.* xv.; *D. S.* xxxvi.; *M. H. C.* iii.; *M. P.*, *E. S.*; *O. M. F.* xli.; *N. N.* xxii.

KIMMEENS. Miss, A pupil of Miss Pupford. *C. S., T. T. G.* vi.
A little girl with beautiful bright hair. She wore a plain straw hat, and had a doorkey in her hand.

KIMMEENS. Papa of Kitty. A widower in India.
C. S., T. T. G. vi.

KITCHEN. *Bellamy's*, A refreshment room. *S. B. B.*, Scenes xviii.
Common to both Houses of Parliament . . . large fire and roasting-jack at one end of the room—the little table for washing glasses and draining jugs at the other—the deal tables and wax candles. The damask tablecloths, and bare floor—the plate and china on the tables, and the gridiron on the fire.

KITCHEN SERVANTS. A select staff of, Hired by Mrs. Skewton.
D. and S. xxx.

KITT. Miss, One of picnic party near Guildford. *D. C.* xxxiii.
Daughter of Mrs. Kitt, dressed in pink . . . with the little eyes.

Note.—David Copperfield went and sat with the "creature in pink and inwardly raged at Red Whisker who was monopolising Dora.

KITT. Mrs., Mother of Miss Kitt.
D. C. xxxiii.
Lady dressed in green.

KITTEN. Mr., Vice-Commissioner and *Deputy* Consul of Silver Store Island. *C. S., P. o. C. E. P.*

KITTERBELL. Charles, Nephew of Dumps. *S. B. B.*, Tales xi.
A small, sharp, spare man, with a very large head, and a broad, good-humoured countenance. He looked like a faded giant, with the head and face partially restored, and he had a cast in his eye which rendered it quite impossible for any one to know where he was looking.

KITTERBELL. Family of Mr.
S. B. B., Tales xi.
Two sons and a daughter.

KITTERBELL. Frederick Charles William. *S. B. B.*, Tales xi.
Infant son of Mr. and Mrs. Charles Kitterbell.

KITTERBELL. Mama of Mrs.
S. B. B., Tales xi.

KITTERBELL. Mrs., Wife of Mr. Charles Kitterbell.
S. B. B., Tales xi.
A tall, thin young lady, with very light hair, and a particularly white face . . . one of those women who almost invariably . . . recall to one's mind the idea of a cold fillet of veal.

KITTERBELL. Papa of Mrs.
S. B. B., Tales xi.

KITTERBELL. Sisters of Mrs.
S. B. B., Tales xi.

KITTERBELL. Son of Mr. and Mrs. Charles. *S. B. B.*, Tales xi.

KITTERBELLS. Guest at Christening party of *S. B. B.*, Tales xi.
An old lady in a large toque, and an old gentleman in a blue coat, and three female copies of the old lady in pink dresses, and shoes to match.

KITTY. Alfred Raybrock's sweetheart. *C. S., M. f. T. S.* i.
A very pretty girl . . . very simply dressed, with no other ornament than an autumnal flower in her bosom. She wore neither hat nor bonnet, but merely a scarf or kerchief, folded squarely back over the head, to keep the sun off.

KLEM. Miss, *Daughter of Mr. and Mrs. Klem.* *U. T.* xvi.
Apparently ten years older than either of them.

KLEM. Mr., *Husband of Mrs. Klem.* *U. T.* xvi.
A meagre and mouldy old man.

KLEM. Mrs., A caretaker.
U. T. xvi.
An elderly woman labouring under a chronic sniff.

KNAG. Miss, *Madame Mantalini's forewoman.* *N. N.* x.
A short, bustling, over-dressed female . . . who still aimed at youth, althouth she had shot beyond it years ago.

Note.—Miss Knag was a typical timeserver. From professing a liking for Kate Nickleby she conceived an intense jealousy. Although manageress, she ultimately acquired Madame Mantalini's business.

KNAG. Mr. Mortimer, *Miss Knag's brother.* *N. N.* xviii.
An ornamental stationer and small circulating library keeper—who let out, by the day, week, month, or year, the newest old novels . . . a tall, lank gentleman of solemn features, wearing spectacles, and garnished with much less hair than a gentleman bordering on forty or thereabouts usually boasts.

KNAG. Uncle of Miss Knag.
N. N. xviii.
Had a most excellent business as a tobacconist. . . had such small feet that they were no bigger than those which are usually joined to wooden legs.

KNIFE-SWALLOWER. African, *Actor. Member of Mr. V. Crummles' company.* *N. N.* xlviii.
Spoke remarkably like an Irishman.

KNIGHT BELL. Dr.
Mud. Papers, 1*st meeting.*

KNIGHTSBRIDGE.
S. B. B., Scenes i.

KNOWLES. Mr.
M. P., V. and B. S.

KNOWSWHOM. Lord. *M. P., I.*

KOËLDWETHOUT. The Baron von. *N. N.* vi.
A fine swarthy fellow, with dark hair and large moustachios, who rode a-hunting in clothes of Lincoln green, with russet boots on his feet, and a bugle slung over his shoulder, like the guard of a long stage.

KOËLDWETHOUT. Baroness, *Daughter of Baron von Swillenhaussen.* *N. N.* vi.

Note.—Characters in a story introduced into the book as being told in an inn on the breakdown of the stage-coach.

KONG. Ty. *M. P., C. J.*

KOODLE. *B. H.* xii.

KROOK. Mr., *Dealer in rags and bones, etc.* *B. H.* v.
An old man in spectacles and a hairy cap . . . short, cadaverous and withered; with his head sideways between his shoulders, and the breath issuing in visible smoke from his mouth, as if he were on fire within. His throat, chin and eyebrows were so frosted with white hairs, and so gnarled with veins and puckered skin, that he looked, from his breast upward, like some root in a fall of snow.

Note.—Krook was the only brother of Mrs. Smallweed. He was the landlord of Miss Flite and Captain Hawdon. Old and eccentric, he was usually accompanied by a large and savage gray cat. He appeared to accumulate "stock" without any idea of disposing of it, and seemed to have no idea of what his place really contained. He was so saturated with spirits that his ultimate end was spontaneous combustion, leaving what seemed to be the " cinder of a small charred and broken log of wood sprinkled with white ashes."

Original of Krook's shop : Is supposed to have been at the end of Bishop's Court, Chancery Lane.

KUFFY. *B. H.* xii.

KUTANKUMAGEN. Dr.
Mud. Papers, 1*st meeting.*

KWAKLEY. Mr.
Mud. Papers, 1*st meeting.*

L

LA COUR. Monsieur Le Capitaine de. *C. S., S. L.* ii.

LA CREEVY. Miss, Miniature painter. *N. N.* iii.
A mincing young lady of fifty, wearer of yellow head-dress, who had a gown to correspond, and was of much the same colour herself.

Note.—The bright little miniature painter with whom the Nickleby's first lodge on their coming to London. In spite of Ralph Nickleby's attempt to influence her against them, she becomes one of the best of friends to Kate and her mother and brother, and assists them in many ways with her kindness. In spite of their ages, she and Tim Linkinwater eventually marry.

Original : May have been a Miss Drummond. Also suggested to have been founded on Janet Barrow, an aunt of Dickens.
Original of Miss La Creevy's residence : Identified as No 11, *Strand.*

LA CROIX. *R. P., O. B.*

LA FORCE. Prison.
T. T. C. bk. iii. ch. ix.

Note.—It was in La Force that Charles Darnay was imprisoned, and from there that Sydney Carton rescued him.

LA SCALA. Theatre in Milan.
P. F. I., V. M. M. S. S.

LA TRANQUILLITÉ. A wineshop.
U. T. xxv.
Opposite the prison in the prison alley.

LABOURER. A bricklayer's.
S. B. B., Scenes i.
With the day's dinner tied up in a handkerchief, walks briskly to his work.

LABOURER. An Irish.
S. B. B., Scenes v.

LABOURERS. At Ratcliff.
U. T. xxx.

LABOURING MEN. Two.
M. P., S. D. C.

LACHINE. The village of.
A. N. xv.

LAD. Office. *P. P.* xl.
Fourteen, with a tenor voice.

LAD. Proposed as drawer of carriage. *D. and S.* viii.
A ruddy-faced lad, set aside by Paul, who selected, instead, his grandfather.

LAD LANE. *L. D.* xiii.

LADELLE. Monsieur Zhoe. *See* Ladle, Joey.

LADIES. All the, In the Prison —Marshalsea. *L. D.* vi.

LADIES. Artistes of Mr. V. Crummles' company. *N. N.* xxiii.

LADIES. At tea gardens.
S. B. B., Scenes ix.
With great, long, white pocket-handkerchiefs like small table-cloths, in their hands, chasing one another on the grass in the most playful and interesting manner.

LADIES. Elderly, Guests at Dombey's housewarming.
D. and S. xxxvi.
Carrying burdens on their heads for full dress.

LADIES. Of distinction and liveliness, three or four. *L. D.* xviii.
Used to say to one another, " Let us dine at our dear Merdle's next Thursday."

LADIES. Of Friar Bacon's family.
M. P., P. M. B.

LADIES. Of the Bedchamber.
M. P., M. E. R.

LADIES. Of the booth at Greenwich Fair. *S. B. B.*, Scenes xii.
Were there ever such innocent and awful-looking beings ?

LADIES. Of the court martial.
M. P., N. Y. D.

LADIES. Old, Visitors in Assembly Rooms, *B*ath. *P. P.* xxxv.

LADIES. Two, In Seven *D*ials.
S. B. B., Scenes v.
On the eve of settling the quarrel satisfactorily by an appeal to blows.

LADIES. Two old maiden, At Peckham. *D. and S.* xiv.

LADIES. Two smart young, Clients (and friends) of General Agency *O*ffice. *N. N.* xvi.

LADIES. Unmarried (diverse). Visitors at Assembly Rooms, Bath.
P. P. xxxv.
Seated on some of the back benches, where they had already taken up their positions for the evening, were diverse unmarried ladies, past their grand climacteric, who, not dancing—and not playing —were in the favourable position of being able to abuse everybody without reflecting on themselves.

LADIES' BIBLE AND PRAYER-BOOK CIRCULATION SOCIETY.
S. B. B., O. P. vi.

LADIES' BLANKET DISTRIBUTION SOCIETY. *S. B. B., O. P.* vi.

LADIES' CHILD'S EXAMINATION SOCIETY. *S. B. B., O. P.* vi.

LADIES' COAL DISTRIBUTION SOCIETY. *S. B. B., O. P.* vi.

LADIES' SCHOOL. *M. P., U. N.*

LADIES' SCHOOL. Mrs. Wilfer's.
O. M. F. iv.

LADIES' SOUP DISTRIBUTION SOCIETY. *S. B. B., O. P.* vi.

LADLE. Joey. *M. P., N. T.*

LADLE. Joey, Head cellarman of Wilding and Co.
C. S., N. T. Act i.
A slow and ponderous man, of the drayman order of human architecture, dressed in a corrugated suit and bibbed apron, apparently a composite of doormat and rhinoceros hide.

LADS. Small office, In large hats.
S. B. B., Scenes i.
Who are men before they are boys.

LADY. Bulky, in charge of shop.
S. B. B., Scenes vi.
Of elderly appearance, who was seated in a chair at the head of the cellar steps.

LADY. Elderly, Selling poultry in Leadenhall Market.
D. and S. xlix.
Who usually sat under a blue umbrella.

LADY. Fastidious, Inside passenger on coach to Yorkshire.
N. N. v.
With an infinite variety of cloaks and small parcels.

LADY. Fat.   *C. S., H. W. L.*

LADY. Foreign, beloved by Prince Bladud.   *P. P.* xxxvi.
   Married to a foreign noble of her own country.

LADY. Husband of old.
          S. B. B., O. P. ii.
   Original : Mrs. Newman, living at No. 5, Ordnance Terrace, Chatham.

LADY. In amber. A Barmaid.
          S. B. B., Scenes iii.
   With large earrings, who, as she sits behind the counter in a blaze of adoration and gaslight, is the admiration of all the servants in the neighbourhood.

LADY. In cloth boots.
          S. B. B., Scenes vi.

LADY. Mature young, Guest of Veneerings.   *O. M. F.* ii.
   Raven locks, and complexion that lights up well when powdered.

LADY. Middle-aged, In yellow curl-papers—in " The Great White Horse " inn.   *P. P.* xxii.

LADY. Munificent.   *M. P., C.*

" LADY. My," *S. B. B.,* Scenes xxi.
   Taking part in May Day dances. To preside over the exchequer.

LADY. Of the counter.
          M. P., R. D.

LADY. Of the establishment where Miss Pinch was governess.
          M. C. ix.
   Curious in the natural history and habits of the animal called Governess, and encouraged her daughters to report thereon whenever occasion served. . . . With what may be termed an exciseable face, or one in which starch and vinegar were decidedly employed.

LADY. Of the house.
          M. P, M. M.

LADY OF THE HOUSE. Landlady in a house in the Rules.
          N. N. xlvi.
   Busily engaged in turpentining the disjointed fragments of a tent bedstead at the door of the back parlour.

LADY. Old, Grandchildren of.
          S. B. B., Scenes vii.

LADY. Old, Guest at *Dombey's* housewarming. *D. and S.* xxxvi.
   Like a crimson velvet pincushion stuffed with banknotes, who might have been the identical Old Lady of Threadneedle Street, she was so rich, and looked so unaccommodating.

LADY. Old, Next door but one to shop.   *S. B. B.,* Scenes iii.

LADY. Old, Of a censorious countenance.   *B. H.* xiv.
   Whose two nieces were in the class.

LADY. Old, Of our parish.
          S. B. B., O. P. ii.
   Her name always heads the list of any benevolent subscriptions subscribed towards the erection of an organ in our church. Her entrance into church on Sunday is always the signal for a little bustle in the side aisle.

LADY. Old, Of ten years.
          M. P., G. F.

LADY. Old, Passenger for Hackney coach.   *S. B. B.,* Scenes vii.

LADY. Old, Pensioners of.
          S. B. B., O. P. ii.
   A regular levee of old men and women in the passage, waiting for their weekly gratuity.

LADY. Old, Residence of.
          S. B. B., O. P. ii.
   The little front parlour is a perfect picture of quiet neatness,

the carpet is covered with brown holland, the glass and picture frames are carefully enveloped in yellow muslin ; the table-covers are never taken off except when the leaves are beeswaxed.

LADY. Particularly tall. Entertainer at Vauxhall Gardens.
S. B. B., Scenes xiv.
In a blue sarcenet pelisse, and bonnet of the same, ornamented with large white feathers.

LADY. Reverend old.
S. B. B., Scenes xi.
Who instilled into our mind the first principles of education for ninepence per week.

LADY. Son of old, In India.
S. B. B., *O. P.* ii.
A fine, handsome fellow.

LADY. The other, At wedding of Bunsby.   *D. and S.* lx.

LADY. Traveller by coach.
P. P. xlix.
Attired in an old-fashioned, green velvet dress, with a long waist and stomacher.

LADY. Under distraint.
S. B. B., *O. P.* v.
"As white as ever I see anyone in my days, except about the eyes, which were red with crying."

LADY. Veiled.   *M. P.*, *N. T.*

LADY. Veiled.   *C. S.*, *N. T.*, *O.*
Who flutters up and down near the postern-gate of the Hospital for Foundling Children.

LADY. Young. *M. P.*, *T. T. C. D.*

LADY. Young, At No. 17.
S. B. B., *O. P.* iii.

LADY. Young, At No. 18.
S. B. B., *O. P.* iii.

LADY. Young, At No. 19.
S. B. B., *O. P.* iii.

LADY. Young, *B*ehind the counter.
M. P., *W. R.*

LADY. Young, Client of General Agency *O*ffice.   *N. N.* xvi.
Who could be scarcely eighteen, of very slight and delicate figure, exquisitely shaped . . . a countenance of most uncommon beauty, though shaded by a cloud of sadness. . . . She was neatly, but very quietly, attired. *See* Bray: Madeline.

LADY. Young, *D*aughter of lady in whose house the brokers were.
S. B. B., *O. P.* v.

LADY. Young, Fiancée of great lord.   *N. N.* xviii.
Of no family in particular.

LADY. Young, Guest at *D*ombey's housewarming. *D. and S.* xxxvi.
Of sixty-five, remarkably coolly dressed, as to her back and shoulders, who spoke with an engaging lisp, and whose eyelids wouldn't keep up well, without a great deal of trouble on her part, and whose manners had that indefinable charm which so frequently attaches to the giddiness of youth.

LADY. Young, In blue.
S. B. B., Char. vii.

LADY. Young, In the Fleet.
P. P. xlv.

LADY. Young, Of five times that age (10 years).   *M. P.*, *G. F.*

LADY JANE. Krook's large grey cat.   *B. H.* v.

LADY VISITOR. Of medical practitioner.   *S. B. B.*, Tales vi.
A singularly tall woman, dressed in deep mourning—the upper part of her figure was carefully muffled in a black shawl, as if for the purpose of concealment, and her face was shrouded by a thick black veil.

LADYBIRD. *See* Manette, Miss Lucie.

LADYSHIP. Her, Partner of " My Lord." *S. B. B.*, Scenes xx.
Attired in pink crape over bed-furniture, with low body and short sleeves. The symmetry of her ankles was partially concealed by a very perceptible pair of frilled trousers—her white satin shoes—a few sizes too large—firmly attached to her legs with strong tape sandals. . . . Her head was ornamented with a profusion of artificial flowers ; and in her hand she bore a large brass ladle, to receive, what she figuratively denominated, " The Tin."

LAGNIER. *See* Rigaud, Monsieur.

LAKE OF GENEVA.
D. and S., Pref. ; *U. T.* vii.

LALLEY. Mr.   *O. M. F.* viii.

LAMBERT. Daniel. *N. N.* xxxvii.

LAMBERT. Mr.   *S. Y. G.*

LAMBETH. *M. P., A. P.* ; *M. P., M. B. V.* ; *N. N.* lvii. *R. P., O. B.*

LAMBETH LODGING. *N. N.* lix.

LAMBKIN FAMILY. *M. P., F. F.*

LAMMLE. Alfred.   *O. M. F.* x.
The mature young gentleman.

Note.—An unscrupulous adventurer. Friend of the Veneerings. He marries Sophronia Akershem. Each believes the other to have money—being led on in that belief by Veneering—and when, after their marriage, they discover their error, they decide to prey upon society in every way they are able. They endeavour to entangle Miss Podsnap in an alliance with young Fledgeby, but fail. They also attempt to obtain a footing in the household of Nicodemus Boffin, but fail also in this. They then leave the country.

LAMMLE. Mrs.   *O. M. F.* x.
Note.—Miss Akershem married Mr. Lammle in the belief that he had a large income, while Mr. Lammle had entertained the same belief with regard to her. When they discover one another, they agree to join forces and prey generally upon their friends. This does not prove very successful, and they are last seen dismissed from the Boffin's with a hundred pounds on their way to France.

LAMPERT, DE. *Owner of slaves.*
A. N. xvii.

LAMPLIGHTER.   *L. D.* iii.

LAMPLIGHTER. In Coketown.
H. T., R. vi.

LAMPS. A porter at Mugby Junction.   *C. S., M. J.* i.
A spare man—with his features whimsically drawn upwards as if they were attracted by the roots of his hair. He had a peculiarly shining, transparent complexion, probably occasioned by constant oleaginous application ; and his attractive hair, being cut short, and being grizzled—was not very unlike a lamp-wick.

LANCASHIRE.   *M. P., O. S.*

LANCASTER.   *C. S., D. M.*

LANDING-PLACE. At New Thermopylae.   *M. C.* xxiii.
A steep bank with an hotel, like a barn, on the top of it ; a wooden store or two, and a few scattered sheds.

LANDLADY.   Mr. Nicodemus Dumps'.   *S. B. B.*, Tales xi.

LANDLADY. Of " Magpie and Stump."   *P. P.* xx.
An elderly female.

LANDLADY. Of spacious inn.
B. H. lvii.

LANDLADY.   Of spacious inn, Daughters of.   *B. H.* lvii.
Three fair girls. The youngest a blooming girl of nineteen.

LANDLESS. Miss Helena. *E. D.* vi.
An unusually handsome little girl, very dark, and very rich in colour—of almost the gipsy type. (Twin sister to Neville.)

Note.—Ward of Mr. Honeythunder and sister of Neville Landless. She was born of English parents in Ceylon. Mr. Honeythunder sends her to Cloisterham to school, where she meets Rosa Bud and Edwin Drood. Afterwards, when Neville is suspected of the murder of Edwin and is obliged to leave Cloisterham, she goes to his rooms in Staple Inn to take him "into the sunlight."

LANDLESS. Neville. *E. D.* vi.
An unusually handsome, little, young fellow—very dark, slender, supple, quick of eye and limb; half-shy, half-defiant; fierce of look.
"I have been always tyranically held down by the strong hand. This has made me secret and revengeful—false and mean."

Note.—Brother of Helen Landless, and ward of Mr. Honeythunder. He goes to study with the Rev. Septimus Crisparkle. He meets Rosa Bud and Edwin Drood. He has the beginnings of a warm attachment for Rosa, but dislikes Edwin: a dislike fostered by John Jasper. After Edwin's disappearance Neville is suspected of his murder, and although there is not sufficient evidence to warrant his detention in custody, public opinion is so strong against him that he is obliged to leave Cloisterham. He then resides in Staple Inn, where the Rev. Septimus visits him occasionally, and where his sister goes to keep him company. His guardian disowns him, but he lives in the hope of being cleared.

Original : It has been suggested that Neville and Helena Landless were founded upon Mulattoes boarding at Wellington House Academy when Dickens himself attended there. See also Drood, Edwin.

LANDLORD.   *M. P., N. T.*

LANDLORD. Mrs. Raddles'.
P. P. xxxii.

LANDLORD. Of house in George's Yard.   *S. B. B., O. P.* v.

LANDLORD. Of inn.   *C. S., H. H.*

LANDLORD. Of lonely inn.
N. N. vi.

LANDLORD. Of private house.
S. B. B., Scenes iii.
Got into difficulties.

LANDLORD. Of "The George."
O. T. xxxiii.
A tall gentleman in a blue neck-cloth, a white hat, drab breeches, and boots with tops to match.

LANDLORD. Of "The Bush."
P. P. xlviii.
A jolly-looking old party.

LANDOR. Robert.   *M. P., L. L.*

LANDOR. Walter Savage.
M. P., L. L.

LANDORA. La Signora.
M. P., L. L.

LANDSEER. E., Sir E. Landseer.
M. P., O. L. N. O. ; *M. P., S. for P.*

LANE. Miss, Governess to young Borums.   *N. N.* xxiv.

LANE. Mr.   *M. P., S.*

LANGDALE. Vintner and distiller.
B. R. lxi.
A portly old man, with a very red, or rather purple face.

Note.—The vintner of Holborn. A rubicund, choleric, but good-hearted gentleman. He takes the part of the *deus ex machina*, and his premises suffer in the riots.

LANGHAM PLACE. London.
P. P. xxxiii.

LANGLEY. Monsieur the Englishman.   *C. S., S. L.* ii.

LANSDOWNE. Marquis of.
M. P., T. B.

LANT STREET. In the *Borough.*
P. P. xxx.

There is a sort of repose in Lant Street, which sheds a gentle melancholy upon the soul. There are always a good many houses to let in Lant Street; it is a by-street, too, and its dulness is soothing. . . . If a man wished to abstract himself from the world—he should by all means go to Lant Street.

LAPUTA.   *U. T.* xv.

LARKINS. Father of Jim.
S. B. B., Scenes xiii.
His line is coal and potatoes.

LARKINS. Jim, Horatio St. Julien.   *S. B. B.,* Scenes xiii.

LARKINS. Miss, the eldest.
D. C. xviii.
Is not a little girl . . . not a chicken . . . perhaps the eldest Miss Larkins may be about thirty. *Original: Obelisk to Charles Larkin of Rochester—is the original of the name only of the elder Miss Larkins.*

LARKINS. Mr.   *D. C.* xviii.
A gruff old gentleman with a double chin, and one of his eyes immovable in his head.

LARNER.   *M. P., S. R.*

LASCAR.   *E. D.* i.

LATHARUTH. Habraham, A Jew.
G. E. xx.
A client of Jaggers'.

LATTER - DAY SAINTS. *U. T.* xx.

LAUNDRESS. Daughter of.
P. P. xlvii.

LAUNDRESS. Mr. Perkers'.
P. P. xx.
A miserable-looking old woman . . . whose appearance, as well as the condition of the office (which she had by this time opened) indi-

cated a rooted antipathy to the application of soap and water.

LAUNDRESSES. Slipshod, At Gray's Inn Square.   *P. P.* liii.

LAUREAU. Village of.
C. S., M. f. T. S. ii.

LAURIE. Sir P.
M. P., I. and C.; M. P., P.F.

"LAW." Mr. Grummer's name.
P. P. xxiv.
Law, civil power, and exekative: them's my titles.

LAW. Name of the awful genie.
M. P., T. O. H.

LAW IN ITS WIG. *M. P., T. T. C. D.*

LAWRENCE. Sir Thomas, Artist.
L. D. x.

LAWYER.   *N. N.* lix.

LAWYER. Attending deathbed of Nicholas Nickleby, Sen. *N. N.* i.
Such things happen every day.

LAWYER. Jinkinson's. *M. H. C.* v.

LAWYERS.   *M. P., D. V.*

LAWYER'S CLERKS. In Court of Chancery.   *B. H.* i.

LAYARD. Mr.   *M. P., S. F. A.*

LAYARDEEN. The troublesome.
M. P., T. O. H.

LAYMEN.   *M. P., D. V.*

LAZZARONE. Capo.
P. F. I., R. D.

LAZZARONI. Ragged.
P. F. I., R. D.

LEAD MILLS.   *O. T.* 1.

LEADENHALL MARKET. *D. and S.* xxxix.; *M. P., I. S. H. W.; M. P., L. T.; N. N.* xl.; *P. P.* xxxiii.; *R. P., B. S.; R. P., M. O. F. F.*

LEADENHALL STREET.   *B. R.* xxxvii. ; *C. S.* ; *W. o. G. M.*

LEAKE COUNTY.   *A. N.* xvii.

LEAMINGTON.   *D. and S.* xx.

LEAMINGTON.   Lodgings in.
                     D. and S. xxi.
The Honourable Mrs. Skewton and her daughter resided, while at Leamington, in lodgings that were fashionable enough, and dear enough, but rather limited in point of space and conveniences—Mrs. Skewton, being in bed, had her feet in the window, and her head in the fireplace ; while the Honourable Mrs. Skewton's maid was quartered in a closet within the drawing-room. Withers, the wan page, slept out of the house immediately under the tiles at a neighbouring milk-shop.

LEATH.   Angela, *Betrothed to the bashful man.*   *C. S., H. T.*

"LEATHER BOTTLE."   Cobham.
                     P. P. xi.
A clean and commodious village alehouse.
Note.—The "Leather Bottle," an old-fashioned village inn, was a singular favourite with Dickens, both before and after he took up his residence at Gad's Hill Place. In his later years all his visitors had to be taken to Cobham.

"LEATHER BOTTLE."   Cobham, *Dickens' Room.*   *P. P.* xi.
A long, low-roofed room, furnished with a number of high-backed, leather-cushioned chairs, of fantastic shapes, and embellished with a great variety of old portraits and roughly-coloured prints of some antiquity.
Note.—The room was not then called the Dickens' Room, of course ; but, although it was at one time in danger of being destroyed by fire, it still remains as it then was, with, perhaps, the only exception, of the prints, which have

now been replaced with prints, drawings, etc., of Dickens and his characters.

LEATHER LANE.   *B. R.* lxviii.

LEAVER.   Mr.   *S. Y. C.*

LEAVER.   Mrs.   *S. Y. C.*

LEAVER AND SONS.   Messrs.
                     Mud. Pap. ii.

LEAVING SHOP.   A pawnbroker's.
                     O. M. F. xxix.

LEBANON.   Village of, near Belleville.   *A. N.* xiii.

LECLERCQ.   Miss Carlotta, as Marguerite.   *M. P., N. T.*

LE DOUANIER.   Monsieur.
                     U. T. xvii.

L'ECU D'OR.   Hôtel de.
                     P. F. I., G. T. F.

LEDBRAIN.   Mr.   *Mud. Pap.* i.

LEDBROOK.   Miss, Member of Mr. V. Crummles' Company.
                     N. N. xxiii.
Note.—A friend of Miss Snevellicci, and one of Mrs. Crummles' theatrical company.

LEE.   *M. P., O. L. N. O.*

LEECH.   Mr. John.   *M. P., R. G.*

LEEDS.   *R. P., O. O. S.*

LEEFORD.   Mrs., Edward Leeford's. mother.   *O. T.* li.

LEEFORD.   *See* Monks.

LEEFORD.   Mr.   *O. T.* xlix.
Note.—The betrayer of Agnes Fleming. The father of Monks and of Oliver Twist. He does not enter the story actively—only as a memory—as he was dead before Oliver's birth.

LEGACY DUTY OFFICE.   *P. P.* lv.

LEGHORN.
                     D. C. xxii ; *R. P., P. M. T. P.*

LEGISLATIVE COUNCIL. *A. N.* ii.

LEICESTER FIELDS.   *B. R.* lvi.

LEICESTERSHIRE.   *N. N.* lx.

LEICESTER SQUARE. *B. H.* xxi. ; *M. P., E. T.* ; *R. P., A. P. A.*

LEIGHTON.   *M. P., E. S.*

LEIPZIG. Poor of.   *M. P., L. L.*

LEITH WALK.   *P. P.* xlix.

LEMON. Mark. *M. P., M. N. D.* ; *M. P., N. S.*

LEMON. Mrs., Kept a preparatory establishment.   *H. R.* iv.

LENVILLE. Mr., First Tragedy in Mr. Vincent Crummles' Company.   *N. N.* xxiii.
A dark-complexioned man, inclining indeed to sallow, with long, thick, black hair, and very evident indications (although he was close-shaved) of a stiff beard, and whiskers of the same deep shade. His age did not appear to exceed thirty—his face was long, and very pale, from the constant application of stage paint. He wore a checked shirt, an old green coat with new gilt buttons, a neckerchief of broad red and green stripes, and full blue trousers ; he carried, too, a common ash walking-stick.

Note.—Tragedian of Mr. Crummles' theatrical company. It was he who issued the cartel of defiance to Nicholas and was so summarily discomfited.

LENVILLE. Mrs., Member of Mr. V. Crummles' Company, and wife of Mr. Lenville.   *N. N.,* xxiii.
In a very limp bonnet and veil.

LESBIA.   *M. P., N. S.*

LESLIE.   *M. P., O. L. N. O.*

LETHBRIDGE. Mr., Property man at *Drury* Lane Theatre.   *R. P., D. W. T. T.*

L'ETOILE. Barrière de. *R. P., A. F.*

LEVI. Negro man ; runaway slave. *A. N.* xvii.

LEWES. Mr.   *B. H.,* Pref.

LEWIS. Mrs. A., As Madam Dor. *M. P., N. T.*

LEWISTON.   *A. N.* xv.

LEWSOME. Mr.   *M. C.* xxix.
Note.—The assistant of the medical man who supplied Jonas Chuzzlewit with the poison he intended for his grandfather Anthony. The suspicion of the purpose for which Jonas required the drug so preyed upon his mind that he made a voluntary confession of his part of the crime which he believed had been committed.

LIBRARY. The, Ramsgate. *S. B. B.,* Tales iv.
Was crowded. The same ladies, the same gentlemen, who had been on the sands, in the morning, and on the pier the day before.

LIBRARY. Ramsgate, One of the presiding goddesses of the. *S. B. B.,* Tales iv.

LIBRARY CART. Of Cheap Jack. *C. S., D. M.*
Dr. Marigold.

LICENSED VICTUALLERS. The. *S. B. B.,* xxvi.

LIEUTENANT. A, In King Charles II's Army.   *M. H. C.* ii.
Never a brave man. Married sister of his brother's wife, who murdered his nephew.

LIEUTENANT. Brother of, deceased. *M. H. C.* ii.
Married sister of lieutenant's wife.

LIEUTENANT. Deceased wife of brother of.   *M. H. C.* ii.

LIEUTENANT. The, Mrs. Pott's brother.   *P. P.* xviii.

LIFE. Name of bird. *B. H.* xiv.

LIFEBOAT. Peckham. *U. T.* xxxv.

LIFEGUARD. A, who taught fencing. *D. and S.* xxii.

LIFEGUARDS. A detachment of. *B. R.* xliii.

LIGHT JACK. *U. T.* v.

LIGHTERMAN'S ARMS. Mud. Pap.

LIGHTHOUSEMEN. Two spirit. *C. B., C. C., S.* iii.

LIGHTWOOD. Mortimer, A barrister. *O. M. F.* ii.
Another of Veneering's oldest friends, who never was in the house before, and appears not to want to come again (who sits disconsolate on Mrs. Veneering's left) who was inveigled by Lady Tippins (a friend of his boyhood) to come to these people's, and talk, and who won't talk.

Note.—Friend of Eugene Wrayburn. A solicitor employed by Mr. Boffin. A small income prevents his exerting himself in his profession, although he realizes more than his friend the need for some stability in life. He sticks to Eugene through his illness and the fight with society as represented by the Tippins, and decides to turn to and do something.

LIGNUM VITAE. Regimental nickname of *Bagnet*—*which see.*

LILIAN. William Fern's dead brother's child. An orphan. *C. B., C., G.* ii.
Nine years old.

LILLE. *U. T.* xvii.

LILLERTON. Miss, Visiting Mr. and Mrs. Gabriel Parsons. *S. B. B.,* Tales x.
A lady—well educated ; talks French ; plays the piano, knows a good deal about flowers, and shells, and all that sort of thing ; and has five hundred a year. A lady of very prim appearance and remarkably inanimate—her fea-tures might have been remarkably pretty when she was younger— her complexion—that of a well-made wax-doll.

LILLIE. Pet's deceased twin sister's name. *L. D.* xvi.

LILLIPUT. *U. T.* xv.

LILLYVICK. Mr., Uncle of Mrs. Kenwigs, a collector of water rates. *N. N.* xiv.
A short old gentleman in drabs and gaiters, with a face that might have been carved out of *lignum vitae,* for anything that appeared to the contrary.

Note.—The uncle of Mrs. Kenwigs. A water-rate collector from whom the Kenwigses have expectations. On this account he is treated by them with a deference which is ludicrous because it is studied and intentional. The collector marries Miss Petowker and disappoints them temporarily. Mrs. Lillyvick soon tires of her somewhat ponderous husband and elopes with a half-pay captain when Lillyvick re-turns to his relatives and casts off his wife for ever.

LIMBKINS. Mr., One of the Board. In the high chair. *O. T.* ii.

Note.—Chairman of the " Board " at the workhouse where Oliver was born.

LIMBURY. Mr. Peter. *M. P., I. S. H. W.*

LIME TREE LODGE. Groombridge. Wells. *C. S., N. T.,* Act i.

LIMEHOUSE. *G. E.* xlv. ; *M. P., C. J.* ; *U. T.* xxxiv.

LIMEHOUSE CHURCH. *O. M. F.* vi. ; *U. T.* xxxiii.

LIMEHOUSE HOLE. *D. and S.* lx. ; *O. M. F.* xii. ; *U. T.* xxix.

LIMERICK. *C. S., M. L. Leg.* i.

LINCOLNSHIRE. *B. H.* ii. ; *C. S., M. L. Lo.* i. ; *M. P., E. S.* ; *M. P., G. F.*

LINCOLN'S INN. *B. H.* i.
Lord High Chancellor's court situated in Lincoln's Inn.

LINCOLN'S INN. The old square. *B. H.* iii.
We passed into sudden quietude, under an old gateway, and drove on through a silent square until we came to an odd nook in a corner, where there was an entrance up a steep, broad flight of stairs, like an entrance to a church. And there really was a churchyard, outside under some cloisters, for I saw the gravestones from the staircase window.

LINCOLN'S INN FIELDS. *B. H.* x. ; *B. R.* l. ; *D. C.*, xxiv. ; *P. P.* xliii. ; *S. B. B.*, Scenes xvi.

LINCOLN'S INN FIELDS. Private hotel in. *D. C.* xxiii.
Where there was a stone staircase, and a convenient door in the roof.

LINCOLN'S INN GARDENS. *B. H.* x.

LINCOLN'S INN HALL. *B. H.* i.

LIND. Jenny. *M. P., T. D.*

LINDERWOOD. Lieut. *Mud. Pap.*

LINDERWOOD. Lieutenant, Officer of Marines in chase of pirates. *C. S., P. o. C. E. P.*

LINENDRAPER. Shopman of. *B. R.*, Pref.

LINENDRAPER'S SHOP. *B. R.*, Pref.

LINENDRAPER'S SHOP. A dirty looking. *S. B. B.*, Tales v.

LINES. Chatham. *P. P.* iv.
A grand review . . . of half-a-dozen regiments . . . was to take place upon the lines.
Original : The open space in front of what is now Fort Pitt.

LINKINWATER. Tim, Clerk of Cheeryble Brothers. *N. N.* xxxv.
Note.—The old clerk and ultimate partner of Cheeryble Brothers. He was at first doubtful about Nicholas, but quickly arrived at the conclusion that he would do for the office. He was a suitable character to associate with the genial and generous brothers. He married Miss La Creevy, much to Mrs. Nickleby's disgust.

Original : Actually engaged in the office of the Brothers Grant.

LINKINWATER'S. Tim, Sister. *N. N.* xxxvii.
Guest of Cheeryble Brothers.

LINNET. Thomas. *M. P., P M. B.*

LINSEED. Duke of. *O. M. F.* xvii.

LINX. Miss, A pupil of Miss Pupford. *C. S., T. T. G.* vi.

"LION." Or " Lion and something Else." *D. C.* xi.
A miserable old public-house.

"LION." Boots at the. *S. B. B.*, Tales viii.

LION HEART. A certain. *B. R.* iv.
Ready to become captain of certain reckless fellows.

LIONS. Friend of the, *M. P., T. L.*
Original : Possibly Sir E. Landseer.

LIRRIPER. Jemmy, Adopted grandson of Mrs. Lirriper. *C. S., M. L. Lo.* i.

LIRRIPER. Jemmy, Godfather to the Major. *C. S., M. L. Lo.* i.

LIRRIPER. Joshua, Youngest brother of deceased. *C. S., M. L. Leg.* i.
Continually being summoned to the county court.

LIRRIPER. Mr., Deceased. *C. S., M. L. Lo.* i.
Was a handsome figure of a man, with a beaming eye and a

voice as mellow as a musical instrument—in the commercial travelling line—behind-hand with the world and buried at Hatfield Church.

LIRRIPER'S. Mrs., Lodgings.
      C. S., M. L. Lo. i.
Eighty-one Norfolk Street, Strand.

LIRRIPER. Mrs., Widow, and lodging-house keeper.
      C. S., M. L. Lo. i.
I am an old woman now and my good looks are gone, but that's me, my dear, over the plate warmer—and considered like.

LISSON GROVE.
      S. B. B., Scenes xvii.

LIST. Isaac, Fellow-gambler with Mat. Jowl.   *O. C. S.* xxix.
A slender figure — stooping, and high in the shoulders—with a very ill-favoured face, and a most sinister and villainous squint.

Note.—The companion of Jowl, *to which refer.*

LISTENER. New York, *M. C.* xvi.

LISTON. Mr.   *S. Y. G.*

LITERARY AND SCIENTIFIC INSTITUTION. At Pavilionstone.
      R. P., O. o. T.

LITTIMER. Servant to Steerforth.
      D. C. xxi.
He was taciturn, soft-footed, very quiet in his manner, deferential, observant, always at hand when wanted, and never near when not wanted, but his great claim to consideration was his respectability. No one knew his Christian name. Distant and quiet as the North Pole.

Note.—Steerforth's servant was a capable hypocrite. After his master tires of Emily he proposes to marry her to Littimer. Littimer is last seen in the model prison in the next cell to that of Uriah Heep.

LITTLE BETHEL.   *O. C. S.,* xxii.

LITTLE BRITAIN.   *G. E.* xx.

LITTLE COLLEGE STREET.
      P. P. xxi.

LITTLE EYES. Nickname for Pubsey and Co.—*which see.*

LITTLE GOSLING STREET. Number thirty, London Docks. *L. D.* xxiv.

LITTLE HELEPHANT. The bar of.
      D. and S. lvi.

LITTLE RIFLE. The, The Kentucky Giant.   *A. N.* xii.

LITTLE SAFFRON HILL. *O. T.* viii.

LITTLE TWIG STREET. No. 14.
      M. P., U. N.

LITTLE WINKLING STREET.
      R. P., O. V.

LIVELY. Mr., Respectable trader.
      O. T. xxvi.

Note.—A casual character who kept a receiver's shop in Field Lane, at the farther end.

LIVERER. Mr., The Marchioness' name for Mr. Swiveller—*which see.*

LIVERPOOL. *A. N.* i.; *B. H.* xxiv.; *C. S., H. T.*; *C. S., M. f. T. S.* ii.; *C. S., N. T.,* Act ii.; *C. S., W. o. G. M.*; *H. T., G.* vii.; *L. D.* vii.; *M. C.* xiii.; *M. P., E. S.*; *M. P., R. T.*; *M. P., S. Pigs.*; *M. P., S. S.*; *R. P., B. S.*; *R. P., T. B. W.*; *R. P., T. D. P.*; *U. T.* ii.

LIVERPOOL MECHANICS' INSTITUTION.   *M. P., E. A. S.*

LIVERY. Two tall young men in.
      D. and S. xxx.
Hired by Mrs. Skewton.

LIZ. Neighbour of *Brickmaker.*
                              B. H. viii.
A. She had no kind of grace about
her, but the grace of sympathy ;
but when she condoled with the
woman, and her own tears fell, she
wanted no beauty.

Note.—Wife of one of the brickmakers, and friend of Jenny.

LLANALLGO.   *U. T.* ii.

LLANALLGO. Church at. *U. T.* ii.
A little church of great antiquity. The pulpit was gone, and
other things usually belonging to
the church were gone, owing to
its living congregation having
deserted it for the neighbouring
schoolroom, and yielded it up
to the dead. Forty-four shipwrecked men and women lay
here at one time, awaiting burial.

LLANDAFF. The Right Reverend
the *B*ishop of.   *N. N.* xxvii.

LLOYD'S.   *S. B. B.*, Scenes ix.

LOAFING JACK. A, of the " Stars
and Stripes."   *U. T.* v.
With his long nose, lank cheek,
high cheek-bones, and nothing soft
about him but his cabbage-leaf
hat.

LOBBS. Maria, *D*aughter of old
Lobbs.   *P. P.* xvii.
A prettier foot, a gayer heart, a
more dimpled face, or smarter
form, never bounded so lightly
over the earth they graced, as did
those of " Maria Lobbs."

LOBBS. Old, The great saddler.
                              P. P. xvii.
Who could have bought up the
whole village at one stroke of his
pen.

LOBBY. The, Of House of Commons.   *S. B. B.*, Scenes xviii.

LOBLEY. Mr. Tartar's man.
                              E. D. xxii.
He was a jolly-favoured man,
with tawny hair and whiskers, and
a big red face—the dead image of
the sun in old woodcuts.

LOBSKIN. Signor, Singing-master at
Minerva House.
                   S. B. B., Tales iii.

LOCH KATRINE.   *M. P., I.*

LOCH LOMOND.   *M. P., I.*

LOCK. House.   *O. M. F.* xli.

LOCK. Plashwater weir mill.
                          O. M. F. xliv.
Twenty mile and odd—call it
five-and-twenty mile and odd—
if you like—up-stream.
Original : Situated at Henley.

LOCK-UP-HOUSE.   In   vicinity
of Chancery Lane.
                   S. B. B., Tales x.

LOCK-UP-HOUSE.   Prisoner in,
Ex-fruiterer, and then coal-dealer.
                   S. B. B., Tales x.

LOCK-UP-HOUSE.   Prisoners.
                   S. B. B., Tales x.
In one of the boxes two men
were playing at cribbage.—In
another box, a stout, hearty-looking man of about forty, eating
some dinner which his wife, an
equally comfortable-looking person
had brought him.

LOCKHART.   Mr., Scott's biographer.   *M. P., S. P.*

LOCOCK. Dr.   *M. P., B. A.*

L'OCTROI. Monsieur Le.
                              U. T. xvii.
In his buttoned black surtout,
with his note-book in his hand,
and his tall black hat.

LODGE. At Newgate.
S. B. B., Scenes xxiv.
A whitewashed apartment.

LODGE. The. P. P. xlii.

LODGE. The, At Marshalsea.
L. D. xviii.

LODGE. The, Residence of the Swidgers. C. B., H. M. i.
At students' college.

LODGER. Of Mrs. Bucket.
B. H. xlix.

LODGER. Of Mrs. Raddle's.
P. P. xlvi.

LODGER. Parlour, In Kenwigs'.
N. N. xvi.
Empowered to treat, with the letting of a small back room on the second floor, reclaimed from the leads, and overlooking a soot-bespeckled prospect of tiles and chimney-pots. As a means of securing the punctual discharge of which service he was permitted to live rent free.

LODGER. Woman, In house for travellers. C. B., H. M. ii.
A young face, but one whose bloom and promise were all swept away. "My father was a gardener, far away, in the country. He's dead to me."

LODGING-HOUSE. In Ramsgate, Rooms in (hired by the Tuggs).
S. B. B., Tales iv.
One ground floor sitting-room, and three cells with beds in them upstairs. Five guineas a week —with attendance (attendance means the privilege of ringing the bell as often as you like, for your own amusement).

LODGING-HOUSE. Travellers'.
E. D. xiv.

Original: Said to have been the "Falcon Hotel," Aldersgate Street.

LODGINGS FOR TRAVELLERS.
C. B., H. M. ii.
House where there were scattered lights in the windows on a waste piece of ground.

LOGGINS. Mr. Beverley.
S. B. B., Scenes xiii.

LOMBARD'S ARMS. M. C. xxvii.

LOMBARD STREET. C. S., M. J. ii.; C. S., N. T., Act i.; M. C. xxvii.; M. P., F. L.; N. N. xxiv.; U. T. xxi.

LONDON. A. N. i.; B. H. i.; B. R. i.; C. B., C. G. ii.; C. S., H. H.; C. S., M. f. T. S. v.; C. S., M. J. ii.; C. S., No. T. i.; C. S., S. L. i.; C. S., S. P. T.; D. and S. iv.; E. D. xiv.; G. E. xvi.; H. D. iv.; L. D. ii.; M. C. v. M. H. C. i.; M. P., A. in E.; M. P., A. P.; M. P., B. A.; M. P., B. S.; M. P., C.; M. P., C. and E.; M. P., C. H. T.; M. P., C. P.; M. P., E. T.; M. P., G. A.; M. P., G. H.; M. P., H. H. W.; M. P., I. M.; M. P., L. A. V.; M. P., L. E. J.; M. P., N. J. B.; M. P., N. S. L.; M. P., O. F. A.; M. P., P. F.; M. P., P. N. J. B.; M. P., P. M. P.; M. P., P. P.; M. P., R. D.; M. P., R. L. M.; M. P., R. T.; M. P., S. B.; M. P., S. F. A.; M. P., S. S.; M. P., T. D.; M. P., T. O. H.; M. P., W.; M. P., Y. M. C.; N. N. i., O. M. F. iv.; O. T. viii.; P. P. i.; R. P., B. S.; R. P., D. W. T. T.; R. P., L. A.; R. P., M. o. F. F.; R. P., O. F. W.; R. P., T. D. P., R. P., P. M. T. P.; S. B. B., Scenes i.; U. T. i.

See also the names of different places in London.

LONDON. Arcadian. U. T. xvi.

LONDON. Bishop of, in 1848.
M. P., Dr. C.

LONDON. Master C. J.
                    M. P., A. J. B.

LONDON BRIDGE. *B. R.* v.; *G. E.*
xliv.; *L. D.* vii.; *M. C.* xlvi.;
M. P., H. H. W.; *M. P., N. G. K.*;
M. P., W.; *O. M. F.* i.; *O. T.* xl.;
R. P., D. W. I. F.; *S. B. B.,*
Scenes x.; *S. B. B.,* Tales iv.;
                    U. T. x.

LONDON CORRESPONDENT.   Of
the Tattlesnivel Bleater.
                    M. P., T. B.

LONDON DOCKS.   *D. and S.* iii.

LONDON HOSPITAL.
                    M. P., H. H. W.

LONDON POST-OFFICE.
                    O. M. F. iii.

LONDON ROAD.   *P. P.* lv.

LONDON TAVERN. *C. S., T. G. S.*
i.; *N. N.* ii.; *R. P., L. A.*

LONDON WALL.   *L. D.* xxvi.
                    M. C. xxxvii.

LONG ACRE. *M. P., E. T.*; *M. P.,*
R. T.; *O. C. S.* viii.; *S. B. B.,*
                    Scenes xxi.; *U. T.* x.

LONG EARS. Hon. and Rev.
                    Mud. Pap. ii.
LONG ISLAND.   *A. N.* vi.

LONG LANE.   *O. T.* xxi.

LONG LOST.   *U. T.* xix.

LONGFORD.   Mr.   Edmund=Mr.
Denham.
                    C. B., H. M. ii.

LONGFORD. Mr., Father of Mr.
Edmund Longford. *C. B., H. M.* ii.

LONGFELLOW.   *M. P., I. W. M.*

LONGFELLOW. Miss.
                    M. P., I. W. M.

LONGINUS.   *M. P., P. L. A.*

LONGMANS. Messrs., and Company.
M. P., M. M.; *M. P., R. S. D.*

LONG'S HOTEL.   In Bond Street.
                    D. and S. xxxi.

LOODLE.   *B. H.* xii.

LOOSE. Mr.   *A. N.* xvii.

LORD. A, Going up in balloon.
from Vauxhall Gardens.
                    S. B. B., Scenes xiv.

LORD CHAMBERLAIN.   *H. R.* ii.

LORD CHAMBERLAIN [of Queen
Adelaide].   *M. P., C. C.*

LORD HIGH CHANCELLOR.   The
                    C. B., B. o. L. i.

LORD-LIEUTENANT.   The Levee
held by.   *S. B. B.,* Tales i.

LORD MAYOR.   *B. R.* lxi.
    Original : Alderman Brackley.

LORD MAYOR.   *C. B., C. C., S.* i.

LORD MAYOR.   *D. and S.* xxv.

LORD MAYOR.   *N. N.* xli.

LORD MAYOR.   *P. P.* xli.

LORD MAYOR.   *S. B. B., O. P.* i.

LORD MAYOR.
                    S. B. B., Scenes xiii.

LORD MAYOR.
                    S. B. B., Scenes xvii.

LORD MAYOR.   And Court of
Aldermen (1857). *M. P., S. F. A.*

LORD MAYOR.   And Uncommon
Counsellors.   *M. C.* xxix.

LORD MAYOR [of London] 1850.
                    M. P., M. B. V.

LORD MAYOR.   Of London.
                    M. P., R. L. M.

LORD MAYOR. Wholesale fruiterer.
M. H. C. i.

A very substantial citizen indeed. His face was like the full moon in a fog, with two little holes punched out for his eyes, a very ripe pear stuck on for his nose, and a wide gash to serve for his mouth. He had once been a very lean, weazen little boy.

LORD MAYOR'S HEAD - FOOTMAN. The. *S. B. B., O. P.* i.

"LORD. My," A sweep on May Day. *S. B. B.*, Scenes xx.

Habited in a blue coat, and bright buttons, with gilt paper tacked over the seams, yellow knee-breeches, pink cotton stockings, and shoes : a cocked hat, ornamented with shreds of various coloured paper, on his head, a *bouquet* the size of a prize cauliflower in his button-hole, a long Belcher handkerchief in his right hand, and a thin cane in his left.

LORD. Noble, In House of Commons. *S. B. B.*, Scenes xviii.

LORD. Old, Of a great family.
N. N. xviii.

Customer of Madame Mantalini, who was going to marry a young lady.

LORD PRESIDENT. *B. R.* lxvii.

LORD WARDEN HOTEL. The, At Dover. *U. T.* xvii.

LORDS. House of. *M. H. C.* i. ; *M. P., P. F.* ; *S. B. B.*, Scenes xvi.

LORDS OF THE ADMIRALTY. The.
B. H. xi.

LORENZO. Church of St.
P. F. I., G. A. N.

LORN. Mr. *L. T.*

LORRY. Mr. Jarvis, Of Tellson and Co.'s Bank. *T. T. C.* ii.

A gentleman of sixty, formally

dressed in a brown suit of clothes, pretty well worn, but very well kept, with large square cuffs and large flaps to the pockets. He had a good leg and was a little vain of it.

Note.—Confidential clerk in Tellson's Bank. He is sent over to France in connection with the case of Dr. Manette and returns with him to England. He is a friend of the Manettes. He assists Lucy and her husband in the trials in Paris and escapes with them. In the " prophetic vision " he is seen ten years later passing peacefully away and leaving his goods to his friends.

LOSBERNE. Mr., A surgeon.
O. T. xxix.

Known through a circuit of ten miles round, as " The Doctor," had grown fat, more from good humour than from good living ; and was as kind and hearty, and withal as eccentric an old bachelor, as will be found in five times that space, by any explorer alive.

Note.—A friend of the Maylies. The surgeon who was called in when Oliver was found shot after the attempted burglary. He was a bachelor, and like so many of Dickens' unmarried men, eccentric but kind - hearted. After Rose Maylie's marriage he settled his practice on his assistant and took a cottage outside the village of which his young friend [Harry Maylie] was pastor, and devoted himself to gardening, fishing, and carpentry work.

LOST. Mr., Of the Maze, Ware.
M. P., E. S.

LOST AND LOST. Woolstaplers.
M. P., E. S.

LOUIS. A son of Madame Doche.
R. P., M. O. F. F.

LOUIS. Belonging to inn in Switzerland. *C. S., H. T.*

LOUIS. Servant of Uncommercial Traveller. *U. T.* vii.

LOUISA. *S. Y. C.*

LOUISVILLE.
A. N. xii. ; *M. P., A. P.*

LOVE LANE. *C. S., H. T.*

"LOVELY." A dog. *L. D.* x.

LOVETOWN. Mr. Alfred, *M. P.,
I. S. H. W.*

LOVETOWN. Mrs. *M. P., I. S. H. W.*

LOWELL. Miss. *M. P., I. W. M.*

LOWELL. Mrs. *M. P., I. W. M.*

LOWELL. Prof. James Russell.
A. N. iv. ; *M. P., I. W. M.*

LOWESTOFT. *D. C.* ii.
We went to an hotel by the sea
—David and Mr. Murdstone.

LOWFIELD. Miss. *S. Y. G.*

LOWTEN. Mr., Clerk to Mr. Perker.
P. P. xx.
A puffy-faced young man.
Note.—Lowton was one of Mr.
Perker's clerks and occupied a position
somewhat in the nature of a confidential one. He was an example of a
class of legal clerk now much rarer
than in Dickens' time.

LOYAL. M., M. Loyal Devasseur.
R. P., O. F. W.

LOYAL. Madame, Wife of M.
Loyal. *R. P., O. F. W.*
An agreeable wife.

LUCAS. Solomon, Dealer in fancy
dresses. *P. P.* xv.
His wardrobe was extensive—
very extensive—not strictly classical, perhaps, not quite new, nor
did it contain any one garment
made precisely after the fashion
of any age or time, but everything
was more or less spangled ; and
what *can* be prettier than spangles.

LUCIFER. Sir, Sir Leicester Dedlock. *B. H.* ix.

LUCY. Only child of Mrs. Atherfield. *C. S., W. O. G. M.*
A little girl of three years old

. . . had a quantity of shining
fair hair, clustering in curls all
about her face.
*Original : Supposed to have
been founded on Lucy Stroughill, a
friend of Dickens in the early
Chatham days.*

LUD. King (Hudibras).
P. P. xxxvi.

LUD-GATE. *M. H. C.* i.

LUDGATE HILL. *B. R.* lxvii. ;
C. S., S. L. iv.; *D. C.* xxx.
M. P., E. S.; *M. P., T. D.*;
N. N. xxxix.

LUDGATE HILL. A coffee-house
on. *L. D.* iii.

LUFFY. *B. H.* xii.

LUFFEY. Mr., The highest ornament of the Dingley Dell Club.
P. P. vii.

LUKIN. Young, Suitor of Mrs.
Nickleby. *N. N.* xli.

LUMBEY. Doctor, Medical adviser
to the Kenwigs. *N. N.* xxxvi.
A stout, bluff - looking gentleman, with no shirt-collar, to speak
of, and a beard which had been
growing since yesterday morning ;
for Doctor Lumbey was popular,
and the neighbourhood was pro-
lific.

LUMMY. Ned, Of the Light Salisbury. *M. C.* xiii.

LUMPERS. Labourers employed
to unload vessels.
R. P., D. W. T. T.

LUMPS OF DELIGHT SHOP.
E. D. iii.
*Original : Was opposite East-
gate House, Rochester.*

"LUNNON." *C. S., H. T.*

LUPIN. Mrs., Mistress of "Blue Dragon." *M. C.* iii.

In outward appearance just what a landlady should be : broad, buxom, comfortable, and good-looking, with a face of clear red and white, which by its jovial aspect at once bore testimony to her hearty participation in the good things in the larder and cellar, and to their thriving and healthful influences. She was a widow, but years ago had passed through her state of weeds, and burst into flower again—with roses on her ample skirts. and roses on her bodice, roses in her cap, roses in her cheeks—ay, and roses worth the gathering, too, on her lips. . . . She had a bright black eye, and jet black hair.

Note.— Mrs. Lupin was the picture of the typical landlady of an inn, as Dickens idealised them. She looked on Mark Tapley with very favourable eyes and regretted his departure for America. On his return they are married.

LUSANNE. *M. P., C. H.* T.

LUSHINGTON. Dr. *M. P., N. E.*

LUTH. Mr. Leary's learned dog. *H. T., G.* viii.

LYCEUM THEATRE. *M. P., M. M.; M. P., W. S. G.; R. P., B. S.*

LYNDHURST. Lord. *M. P., C. P.*

LYONS. *L. D.* xi. ; *P. F. I., L. R. G. A.*

LYONS CATHEDRAL. *P. F. I., L. R, G. A.*

LYONS INN. *U.* T. xiv.

LYRIQUE. Paris. *M. P., W.*

LYTTON. Sir Edward Bulwer. *M. P., G. L. A.*

M

M. C. In linendraper's establishment. *S. B. B.*, Tales v.

The obsequious master of the ceremonies of the establishment, who, in his large white neckcloth and formal tie, looked like a bad portrait of a gentleman.

M. D. Little. *See* Marigold, Doctor. *C. S., D. M.*

M. J. Josiah. *A. N.* xvii.

M.P. An, In Bellamy's. *S. B. B.*, Scenes xviii.

A perfect picture of a regular *gourmand.*

M'ALLISTER. *A. N.* xvii.

MACAULAY. Mr. *M. P., I. ; M. P., I. M.*

MACBETH. Lady. *P. F. I., R.*

MACBETH. Lady, *C*haracter in play. *S. B. B.*, Scenes xiii.

The large woman, who is consulting the stage directions—always selected to play the part, because she is tall and stout.

MACCONNOCHIE. *C*aptain. *M. P., P. P.*

MACCONNOCHIE'S SYSTEM. *C*aptain. *M. P., H. H. W.*

MACCOORTS. The, Of MacCoort. *B. H.* xxx.

A great Highland family.

MACDOODLE. *C*harles, Of Macdoodle. *R. P., A. C. T.*

MACEY. Mr., Brother-in-law to Miss Maryon. *C. S., P. o. C. E. P.*

MACEY. Mrs., Miss Maryon's married sister. *C. S., P. o. C. E. P.*

MACFARREN. Mr. *M. P., M. M.*

MACINTOSH. Sir James.
M. P., I. M.

M'KANE. *A. N.* xvii.

MACKIN. Mrs., Pawnbroker's customer. *S. B. B.*, Scenes xxiii.
A slipshod woman .with two flat-irons in a basket.

MACLEAN. Governor.
M. P., N. E.

MACLEAN. Mrs. *M. P., N. E.*

MACKLIN. Mrs., Of No. 4.
S. B. B., Scenes ii.

MACLISE. Daniel. *M. P., O. L. N. O.* ; *M. P., S. for P.* ; *M. P., S. of C.*

MACMANUS. Mr., A midshipman aboard the " Halsewell."
R. P., T. L. V.

M'NEVILLE. Walter. *S. B. B.,* Tales iii.

MACREADY. *M. P., M. B.* ; *M. P. P. P. D.* ; *M. P., S. Q. F.*

MACSTINGER. Alexander, Son of Mrs. MacStinger. *D. and S.* xxv.

MACSTINGER. Charles, Son of Mrs. MacStinger. *D. and S.* xxxix.

MACSTINGER. Juliana, Daughter of Mrs. MacStinger.
D. and S. xxv.

MACSTINGER. Mrs., Captain Cuttle's landlady. *D. and S.* ix.
A widow lady with her sleeves rolled up to her shoulders, and her arms frothy with soap-suds and smoking with hot water.

Note.—Captain Cuttle's landlady. He is particularly afraid of her, chiefly, apparently, because she is somewhat masterful, but largely because Captain Cuttle is not simple, but not strong-willed. However, the captain succeeds in making a "moonlight flitting" without her knowledge. His precautions are only because the landlady would have prevented his going, and not because he was in her debt. Later

on Mrs. MacStinger runs the captain to earth, and he is in danger of being taken back to bondage, but is rescued by Captain Bunsby. Captain Bunsby suffers the martyrdom of sacrifice, as Mrs. MacStinger marries him against his will.

MACSTINGERS. The little, Mrs. MacStinger's family.
D. and S. ix.

MCWILLIAM. Dr. *M. P., N. E.*

MADDOX. John. *M. P., V. C.*

MADEIRA. *H. R.* iii.

MADGERS. Winifred, A girl of Mrs. Lirriper. *C. S., M. L. Leg* i.
She was what is termed a Plymouth Sister. . . . A tidièr young woman never came into a house.

MADNESS. Name of bird.
B. H. xiv.

MADONNA DELLA GUARDIA. Chapel of. *P. F. I., G. A. N.*

MADRAS. *M. P., L. A. V.* ii.

MAG. Mary Ann. *M. P., E. S.*

MAGDALEN.
M. P., H. H. W. ; *M. P., I. M.*

MAGG. Mr., A vestryman.
R. P., O. V.

MAGGIGG'S. Miss, Boarding establishment. *M. P., G. D.*

MAGGIORE. Lago.
P. F. I., V. M. M. S. S.

"MAGGY." Grand-daughter of my (Little Dorrit's) old nurse.
L. D. ix.
She was about eight-and-twenty, with large bones, large features, large feet and hands, large eyes and no hair. Her large eyes were limpid and almost colourless ; they seemed to be very little affected by light, and to stand unnaturally still. There was also that attentive listening

expression in her face, which is seen in the faces of the blind, but she was not blind, having one tolerably serviceable eye. A great white cap, with a quantity of opaque frilling, that was always flapping about, apologised for Maggy's baldness.—The rest of her dress—had a strong resemblance to seaweed. Her shawl looked particularly like a tea-leaf, after long infusion.

Note.—Granddaughter of Mrs. Bangham. Attached to Little Dorrit. She goes to assist Mrs. Plornish, and reappears for the last time at Little Dorrit's wedding.

MAGICIAN. The African.
U. T. xxvi.
Takes the cases of death and mourning under his supervision, and will frequently impoverish a whole family by his preposterous enchantments.

MAGISTRATE. A. *B. R.* xlix.

MAGISTRATE. County, *M. P., S.*

MAGISTRATE. Suburban,
U. T. xxxvi.

MAGISTRATE. The, One of the Board. *O. T.* iii.

MAGISTRATES. At hospital.
S. B. B., Char. vi.
To take depositions of patient. One complained bitterly of the cold, and the other of absence of any news in the evening paper.

MAGISTRATES. Of Middlesex.
M. P., P. P.

MAGNA CHARTA. *P. P.* xxiv.

MAGNIFICENT DISTANCES. The City of, Washington. *A. N.* viii.

MAGNUS. Mr., Peter. *P. C.* xxii.
A red-haired man with an inquisitive nose, mysterious - spoken personage, with a bird-like habit

of giving his head a jerk every time he said anything. . . . "Curious circumstance about those initials, sir. You will observe P.M. —post meridian."

Note.—Mr. Peter Magnus travelled with Mr. Pickwick from London to Ipswich. The object of his visit to the ancient town was to propose to a lady who was stopping at the " Great White Horse," the hostel at which Mr. Pickwick and his fellow-traveller put up. After retiring for the night Mr. P. discovered he had left his watch downstairs. He returned for it. But having obtained it, he was unable to find his own room. At length he discovered one he believed to be his own. Then followed the tragic comedy of his adventure in the lady's bedroom. The sequel was that he and Tupman were haled before the Mayor of Ipswich on the charge of meditating a duel.

Original : Founded on Lazarus Magnus, the owner of a house in Chatham, at the time the Dickens family lived there.

MAGOG. *M. P., G. A.*

" MAGOG." The younger giant.
M. H. C. i.

MAGPIE. In happy family.
M. P., R. H. F.

" MAGPIE AND STUMP." Inn.
P. P. xx.
The weather-beaten signboard bore the half-obliterated resemblance of a magpie intently eyeing a streak of brown paint, which all the neighbours had been taught from infancy to consider as the " Stump."

Original : Generally identified as having been the " George the Fourth," or the " Old Black Jack " in Portsmouth Street, although there was a " Magpie and Stump " in Fetter Lane.

MAGPIES. The Three. *O. M. F.* xvi.

MAGRA. The river.
P. F. I., R. P. S.

MAGSMAN. A showman.
C. S., G. i. S.
A grizzled personage in velveteen with a face so cut up by varieties of weather that he looked as if he had been tattooed.

MAGSMAN. House of.
C. S., G. i. S.
A wooden house on wheels. The wooden house was laid up in ordinary for the winter, near the mouth of a muddy creek.

MAGWITCH. Abel, *alias* Provis. Escaped convict.   *G. E.* i.
A fearful man, all in coarse-grey, with a great iron on his leg. A man with no hat, and with broken shoes, and with an old rag tied round his head—who limped and shivered and glared and growled.

Note.—Pip's convict. He escapes from the convict hulks, and when in a starving condition he meets Pip, he forces the boy, under threat of untold penalties, to procure food for him, together with a file. He is recaptured (partly) through the agency of Compeyson, to whom his evil career is largely due. He is transported, but in after years he amasses wealth in New South Wales, and anonymously through Jaggers, he makes a gentleman of Pip, with "great expectations." Later on he secretly returns to England under the name of Provis—Uncle Provis—but is recognised by Compeyson. Pip and his friends assist him in an attempt to escape, but their plan is frustrated. Compeyson is killed, and Magwitch so seriously injured that he dies in prison before his execution can be carried out; and ignorant of the fact that all his wealth has been forfeited.

MAID. Fanny's.   *L. D.* xxxix.

MAID. Last new, Of the Nuns' House.   *E. D.* iii.

MAID. Miss Tox's. *D. and S.* x.

MAID. Of Mr. Jarndyce's household.   *B. H.* vi.

MAID. Of Rokesmith's.
O. M. F. liv.
A fluttering young damsel, all pink and ribbons.

MAID. The Blue-eyed, Dover coach.   *L. D.* iii.

MAIDEN LANE.
O. M. F. v.; *S. B. B.,* Scenes xx.
Inhabited by proprietors of donkey-carts, boilers of horse-flesh, makers of tiles, and sifters of cinders.

MAIDSTONE. *C. S., P. o. C. E. P.*; *C. S., S. P. T.* iii.

MAIDSTONE. (Jail.)   *D. C.* xvi.

MAINE.   *A. N.* iii.

MAIRIE. The. *C. S., M. L. Leg.* i.

MAIRRWIE. The, At Sens.
C. S., M. L. Leg. i.

MAJESTY. His, On stage in Britannia.   *U. T.* iv.

MAKER. Bonnet-shape.
S. B. B., Scenes iii.

MALABAR.   *M. P., L. A. V.* ii.

MALAKHOFF.   *M. P., B. A.*

MALAY. Sailor.   *U. T.* xx.

MALAY PIRATES.   *M. P., P. F.*

MALCOLM. Character in play.
S. B. B., Scenes xiii.
Stupid-looking milksop, with light hair and bow legs—a kind of man you can warrant town-made.

MALDEN. Jack, Needy and idle.
D. C. xvi.
Rather a shallow sort of gentleman, with a handsome face, a rapid utterance, and a bold, confident air.

Note.—Mrs. Strong's cousin. He is largely the cause of the temporary estrangement of Mrs. Strong from her husband. The doctor befriends him in every way, but always without any good effect on his dissolute relative.

MALDERTON. Mr.
S. B. B., Tales v.
A man whose whole scope of ideas was limited to Lloyd's, the Exchange, the India House, and the Bank. A few successful speculations had raised him from a situation of obscurity and comparative poverty to a state of affluence.

MALDERTON. Mr. Frederick.
S. B. B., Tales v.
Eldest son of Mr. and Mrs. Malderton.
In full dress costume, was the *beau ideal* of a smart waiter. Had lodgings of his own in town, always dressed according to the fashions of the months—went up the water twice a week in the season.

MALDERTON. Mr. Thomas.
Younger son of Mr. and Mrs. Malderton. *S. B. B.,* Tales v.
With his white dress-stock, blue coat, bright buttons, and red watch-ribbon strongly resembled the portrait of that interesting, but rash, young gentleman, George Barnwell.

MALDERTON. Mrs.
S. B. B., Tales v.
A little fat woman like her eldest daughter multiplied by two.

MALDERTON. Miss Teresa, Elder daughter of Mr. and Mrs. Malderton. *S. B. B.,* Tales v.
A very little girl, rather fat, with vermillion cheeks, but good-humoured, and still disengaged, although, to do her justice, the misfortune arose from no lack of perseverance on her part.

MALE. Elizabeth. *M. P., P. T.*

MALLARD. Mr., *C*lerk to Serjeant Snubbin. *P. P.* xxxi.
An elderly clerk, whose sleek appearance and heavy gold watch-chain, presented imposing indications of the extensive and lucrative practice of Serjeant Snubbin.

MALLET. Mr. *Mudfog Pap.* ii.

MALLEY. Mr. *O. M. F.* viii.

MALLOWFORD. Lord. *N. N.* li.

MALTA. *M. P., E. T.*

MALTA. Little, Daughter of Mr. and Mrs. Bagnet. *B. H.* xxvii.

MALTESE JACK. Visitor at " The Snug." *U. T.* v.

MALTHUS. A young Gradgrind. *H. T., S.* iv.

MALVERN. *M. P., M. N. D.*

MAMMAS. Matchmaking, Visitors in Assembly Rooms, Bath. *P. P.* xxxv.

MAN. Another, In chambers in *C*lifford's Inn. *P. P.* xxi.
Took the chambers, furnished them and went to live there. . . . Somehow or other he couldn't sleep.

MAN. At the Morgue. *M. P., R. D.*

MAN. At the piano. *O. M. F.* xi.
A youngish, sallowish gentleman in spectacles, with a lumpy forehead.

MAN. Baked potatoe, *S. B. B.,* Scenes ii.

MAN. *C*apricious old, Wealthy relative of Jack Redburn and his younger brother. *M. H. C.* ii.

MAN. *C*ustomer at ship chandler's. *D. and S.* iv.
Who came to ask change for a sovereign.

MAN. Dirty-faced, In blue apron.
S. B. B., Scenes viii.
In search of a will in Doctors'
Commons.

MAN. Dull young. *M. P., S. S. A.*

MAN. Friend of John Podgers.
M. H. C. iii.
A little man with a yellow face
and a taunting nose and chin.

MAN. From Dombey's house.
D. and S. xv.

MAN. From inn in Rochester.
C. S., S. P. T. i.
With tray on his head contain-
ing vegetables and sundries.

MAN. From restaurant.
D. and S. liv.
A bald man with a large beard.

MAN. From Shropshire. *See*
Gridley, Mr.

MAN. Humpbacked. *O.* T. xxxii.

MAN. Husband of corpse. *O.* T. v.
Face was thin and very pale;
his hair and head were grizzly;
his eyes were bloodshot.

MAN. Ignorant. *M. P., T. O. H.*

MAN. In uniform. *B. H.* lvii.

MAN. In charge of three saddled
horses. *M. H. C.* iii.

MAN. In the broker's shop.
S. B. B., Scenes v.
In the baked "jemmy" line,
or the firewood or hearthstone line,
or any other line which requires
a floating capital of eighteen-
pence or thereabouts.

MAN. In the Fleet. *P. P.* lxv.

MAN. In splendid armour, At Astley's. *S. B. B.*, Scenes xi.

MAN. Lame. *P. P.* xl.

MAN. The last drunken.
S. B. B., Scenes i.
Has just staggered heavily along,

roaring out the drinking-song of
the previous night.

MAN. Little, A visitor to Vauxhall
Gardens. *S. B. B.*, Scenes xiv.
In faded black, with a dirty
face and a rusty black neckerchief, with a red border, tied in a
narrow wisp round his neck, who
entered into conversation with
everybody.

MAN. Little, ugly humpbacked.
O. T. xxxii.

MAN. Long-legged young.
D. C. xii.

MAN. Looking into church where
Walter and Florence are married.
D. and S. lvii.
With a wooden leg, chewing a
faint apple and carrying a blue
bag in his hand, looks in to see
what is going on.

MAN. Merry-faced little.
M. P., P. M. B.

MAN. Obnoxious young.
M. P., W. R.

MAN. Old. *M. P., P. M. B.*

MAN. Old, A hard-featured, in
Doctors' Commons, probably a
money-lender.
S. B. B., Scenes viii.
A deeply wrinkled face—every
wrinkle about his toothless mouth,
and sharp, keen eyes, told of
avarice and cunning. His clothes
were nearly threadbare—from
choice, not from necessity. All
his looks and gestures, down to the
very small pinches of snuff, which
he every now and then took from
a little tin canister, told of wealth,
and penury, and avarice.

MAN. Old, In the poor side of the
Fleet. *P. P.* xlii.
Seated on a small wooden box,
with his eyes riveted on the floor,

Q

his face settled into an expression of the deepest and most hopeless despair. A young girl, his little granddaughter, was hanging about him.

MAN. The old, Whose son is drowning. *P. P.* xxi.
(The cause of Heyling's incarceration in the Marshalsea.)

MAN. On swing-bridge over some docks in Thames. *U. T.* iii.
With a puffed, sallow face, and a figure all dirty and shiny and slimy, who may have been the youngest son of his filthy old Father Thames.

MAN. Poor, In distress in our parish. *S. B. B., O. P.* i.
Is summoned by—the parish. His goods are distrained, his wife dies—is buried by the parish—his children, they are taken care of by the parish. He is relieved by the parish—maintained in the parish asylum.

MAN. Prisoner, In the Fleet. *P. P.* xli.
His wife and a whole crowd of children might be seen making up a scanty bed on the ground, or upon a few chairs, for the younger ones to pass the night in.

MAN. Regular city, Owner of a garden. *S. B. B.,* Scenes ix.
He never does anything in it with his own hands; but he takes great pride in it notwithstanding —descants at considerable length upon its beauty and the cost of maintaining it. This is to impress you—with a due sense of the excellence of the garden, and the wealth of the owner.

MAN. Seafaring. *C. S., W. o. G. M.*

MAN. Shabby-genteel.
S. B. B., Char. x.
Reading in the British Museum

—he always had before him a couple of shabby-genteel books— he used to sit all day, as close to the table as possible—to conceal the lack of buttons on his coat: with his old hat carefully deposited at his feet.

MAN. Tall, On horseback.
B. R. lxvii.
Made a collection for the same purpose (the rioters) and refused to take anything but gold.

MAN. Ugly old. *D. C.* xiii.

MAN. Velveteen, A porter.
C. S., M. J. ii.
Carrying his day's dinner in a small bundle that might have been larger, without suspicion of gluttony.

MAN. Very red-faced, Frequenting "The Peacock." *P. P.* xiv.

MAN. Wild. *M. P., F. L.*

MAN. With a wooden leg.
M. P., N. Y. D.

MAN. Young, Frequenter of "Magpie and Stump." *P. P.* xx.
With a whisker, a squint, and an open shirt-collar (dirty).

MAN. Young, Hanged in Bishopsgate Street, father of. *B. R.* lxxvii.
Waited for him at the gallows, kissed him at the foot when he arrived, and sat there, on the ground till they took him down.

MAN. Young, In tea gardens.
S. B. B., Tales ix.
Keeping company with Uncle Bill's niece.

MAN. Young, One of the Gordon rioters. *B. R.* lxxvii.
Hanged in Bishopsgate Street.

MAN. Young, powerful, In brickmaker's. *B. H.* viii.

MAN. Young, Visitor to Bob Sawyer. *P. P.* xxxii.

Large-headed young man in a black wig.

MAN. Young, Wall-eyed.
C. S., S. P. T. i.

Connected with the fly department of inn in Rochester.

MAN. Young, With donkey-cart.
D. C. xii.

MAN OF ROSS=George Dolby.
M. P., I. W. M.

MANCHESTER. *C. S. N. T.*, Act ii. ; *M. P., E. S.* ; *M. P., F. S.* ; *M. P., G. F.* ; *U. T.* xxiii.

MANCHESTER BUILDINGS.

N. N. xvi. ; *S. B. B.*, Scenes xviii.

Within the precincts of the ancient city of Westminster—is a narrow and dirty region, the sanctuary of the smaller members of Parliament in modern days. . . . It is comprised in one street of gloomy lodging-houses — from whose windows in vacation time there frown long, melancholy rows of bills "To Let."

MANCHESTER DELEGATES.
M. P., O. S.

MANDANS. (Indians.) *M. P., E.* T.

MANDELL. D. J. *M. P., S. B.*

MANETTE. Dr. Alexandre, French prisoner. *T. T. C.* iv.

With his back towards the door, and his face towards the window, a white-haired man sat on a low bench, stooping forward and very busy, making shoes.

Note.—Physician unjustly incarcerated in the Bastille for eighteen years. He is found as a shoemaker in Paris, having been released on the eve of the Revolution. He is taken to England by Mr. Lorry and Lucie his daughter. There he regains the faculties which have left him in his long imprisonment, and even practises his profession. Lucie, his daughter, marries Charles Darnay, the son of the Marquis St. Evremonde. Darnay has resigned his estates to the country. He returns to Paris at the commencement of the Revolution to obtain the release of an old family servant, and is himself accused and thrown into prison. Dr. Manette follows and obtains his release in turn. But he is arrested again and convicted on the evidence of a document written by Dr. Manette when he was in prison. Darnay is saved by the self-sacrifice of Carton, and Dr. Manette and his friends return to London, where the doctor forgets as far as possible the earlier happenings, and continues to practise medicine for many years.

MANETTE. Miss Lucie, Daughter of the rescued French prisoner.
T. T. C. ii.

A young lady of not more than seventeen . . . with a slight, pretty figure, a quantity of golden hair, a pair of blue eyes, and a forehead with a singular capacity of lifting and knitting itself into an expression that was not quite one of perplexity, or wonder, or alarm, or merely of a bright, fixed attention, though it included all the four expressions.

Note.—Daughter of Dr. Manette. Her mother dies before the opening of the story. Lucie goes to Paris, with Mr. Lorry to bring her father to London. On the journey she meets Darnay and is called as a witness in his trial for treason. She marries him later on. And when he is called to Paris and arrested there, she follows him with her father. Ultimately they succeed in escaping, and return to London, where they live happily.

Original : Believed to have been Lucy Stroughill, a friend of Dickens in the early Chatham days.

Original of Manette's House : Carlisle House, Carlisle Street, leading from the centre of the west side of Soho Square. Also said to have been a shop in Manette Street, then Rose Street, Soho.

MANGEL. Ralph. *M. P., P. M. B.*

MANN. Mrs., Matron of a branch workhouse. *O. T.* ii.

Where the parish authorities magnanimously and humanely resolved that Oliver should be "farmed." A parochial delegate, and a stipendiary.

Note.—The time-serving matron of the branch workhouse, where the workhouse children are "farmed" for sevenpence-halfpenny a week; of this sum Mrs. Mann appropriated the greater part to her own use.

MANNERS. Miss Julia.
S. B. B., Tales viii.

A buxom, richly-dressed female of about forty who by mistake eloped from Great Winglebury with Alexander Trott, and they were married at Gretna Green.

MANNING. Mr.
M. P., D. M. ; *M. P., P. P.*

MANNING. Mrs., An emigrant.
R. P., T. D. P.

MANNING. Sir Geoffrey, Friend of Pickwick's. *P. P.* xviii.

MANNINGS. The, Husband and wife. (Criminals). *R. P., L. A.*

Hanging on the top of the entrance gateway of Horsemonger Jail.

"MANOR FARM." In Muggleton.
P. P. iv.

Scene of wedding of Bella and Trundle.

Original: Manor Farm, Dingley Dell, is generally believed to have been founded on Cob Tree Hall, Sandling, near Maidstone. But it appears quite probable that Parrock Manor, at Gravesend, was the place Dickens had in view at the time. Not only was he working—at the honeymoon cottage at Chalk—within half a mile of the place, but at that time. Parrock Manor, as it is now called, and

its surroundings fulfilled most of the conditions of the author's picture, with one great exception, viz., the owner. This was a military man, who is said to have been the exact antithesis of old Mr. Wardle, irascible and unreasonable; more like Captain Boldwig. But this may have been a gentle method of administering rebuke. At the time in question a long lane bordered with trees appears to have run from Parrock Manor to Milton Old Church, some little distance from the centre of the town and the coaching-houses. From an old tracing in my possession the house is shown to have been very much larger than it is at present, with wings and adjoining houses, now destroyed; but it is even now sufficiently large to have been easily suited to the story. There is also a Manor Farm at Frindesbury, with ponds.

MANOR HOUSE. Miss Havisham's. *See* Satis House.

MANOR HOUSE. The old, The farmhouse. *R. P., D. W. I. F.*

MANSEL. Miss. *R. P., T. L. V.*

One of the five lady passengers on board the "Halsewell."

MANSFIELD. Lady. *B. R.* lxvi.

MANSFIELD. Lord. *B. R.* lxvi.

MANSION. Property of Michael Warden, Esq.
C. B., B. o. L. iii.

MANSION HOUSE. *B. R.* lxi. ;
M. H. C. i.; *M. P., G. A.* ;
M. P., R. L. M. ; *P. C.* xx. ;
S. B. B., Scenes xvii.

MANTALINI. Husband of Madame Mantalini. *N. N.* x.

Dressed in a gorgeous morning

gown, with a waistcoat, and Turkish trousers of the same pattern, a pink silk neckerchief, and bright green slippers, and had a very copious watch-chain wound round his body.

Note.—The man of fashion who lives on his wife's earnings as long as possible, but when she is made bankrupt separates from her. He is imprisoned, and released by a laundress who after the first blush has worn off her acquisition sets him to the mangle, where he is discovered turning the handle by Kate and Nicholas. Originally his name was Muntle, but obviously such a name was of no use to a fashionable man about town or to a high-class millinery and dressmaking business.

MANTALINI. Madam, Dressmaker.
N. N. x.
A buxom person, handsomely dressed.

Note.—The dressmaker to whom Kate was sent by her uncle, Ralph Nickleby. She was made bankrupt by her husband's extravagance, and the business was acquired by her manageress.

Original of the house : Suggested as having been No. 11, *Wigmore St.*

MANTALINI'S SHOP. Ground floor of Madam. *N. N.* x.
Let off to an importer of otto-of-roses.

MANTUA. *L. D.* xlv. ; *P. F. I., V. M. M. S. S.*

MANUEL. A negro slave.
A. N. xvii.

MAPLESONE. Julia.
S. B. B., Tales i.
Aged twenty-two. Afterwards Mrs. Simpson.

MAPLESONE. Matilda, Elder daughter of Mrs. Maplesone.
S. B. B., Tales i.
Aged twenty-five. Afterwards Mrs. Septimus Hicks.

MAPLESONE. Matilda, Mrs. Maplesone. *S. B. B.,* Tales i.

MARCHESE. Italian, The usual.
L. D. lv.
Guest of Mrs. Merdle.

" MARCHIONESS." Servant to the Brasses. *O. C. S.* xxxiv.
A small, slipshod girl in a dirty coarse apron and bib. . . . " Yes, I do plain cooking," replied the child. " I'm housemaid too ; I do all the work of the house."

Note.—There is a good deal of mystery attached to the overworked and underfed drudge discovered by Dick Swiveller at the Brass' house in Bevis Marks. There is no solution of the mystery in the book, although it is hinted at : and Sally Brass is supposed to know a good deal more than she tells. Dick Swiveller and the Marchioness form a friendship, and when Dick is ill the Marchioness attends him. After his recovery Dick sends her to a school and finally marries her, when they go to live in a " little cottage at Hampstead."

Original : The Marchioness is supposed to have been founded on the workhouse girl the Dickens family took from the workhouse as general maid of all work.

MARGARET. Aunt, Guest at Christmas family party.
S. B. B., Char. ii.
Poor Aunt Margaret married a poor man—has been discarded by her friends—but Christmas coming round—the unkind feelings—have melted—like half-formed ice, beneath the morning sun.

MARGARET. Husband of Aunt.
S. B. B., Char. ii.
Turns out to be such a nice man, and so attentive to grandmama—such beautiful speeches and nice songs.

MARGARET. Meg. *C. B., C., G.* iii.

MARGARET. Mr. Winkle Senior's maid. *P. P.* l.

MARGARET. Young child of.
C. S., M. f. T. S. i.

MARGARET. Young widow.
C. S., M. f. T. S. i.
Hugh's widow.

MARGARETTA. Mrs. Frank Milvey.
O. M. F. lxi.

MARGATE. *C. S.*, T. T. *G.* vi. ;
H. R. iii. ; *S. B. B.*, Scenes x. ;
S. B. B., Tales iv.

MARGATE. Mayor of. *H. R.* iii.

MARGATE ROADS. *H. R.* iii.

MARGUERITE. *M. P., N. T.*

MARGUERITE. Miss, Niece of M.
Obenreizer. *C. S., N. T.*, Act i.
The young lady wore an unusual
quantity of fair bright, hair, very
prettily braided about a rather
rounder white forehead than the
average English type, and so her
face might have been a shade
rounder than the average English
face, and her figure slightly rounder
than the figure of the average
English girl at nineteen.

MARIA. Runaway Negro woman
slave. *A. N.* xvii.

MARIE. Jean. *M. P., N. T.*

MARIGOLD. Doctor, A *C*heap Jack.
C. S., D. M.
Born on the queen's highway,
but it was the king's at that time,
on a common—at present a middle-
aged man of a broadish build,
in cords, leggings, and a sleeved
waistcoat, the string of which is
always gone behind. "If I have a
taste in point of personal jewelry,
it is mother-of-pearl buttons."
*Original : So far as the name is
concerned, this has been traced to
Bath.*

MARIGOLD. Wife of Doctor.
C. S., D. M.
She wasn't a bad wife, but she
had a temper.

MARIGOLD. Willum, Father of
Doctor Marigold, also a *C*heap
Jack. *C. S., D. M.*

MARINA. *C*aro Padre Abate.
M. P., L. L.

MARINE STORE DEALERS. In
Ratcliffe High Way.
S. B. B., Scenes xx.
Here the wearing apparel is all
nautical—large bunches of cotton
pocket handkerchiefs, in colour and
pattern unlike any one ever saw
before—a few compasses, a small
tray containing silver watches, in
clumsy thick cases.

MARK LANE. The churches about.
U. T. ix.
There was a dry whiff of wheat.

MARKER. Mrs. Wanting a cook.
N. N. xvi.
Offers eighteen guineas ; tea
and sugar found. Two in family,
and see very little company. Five
servants kept. No man — no
followers.

MARKET. *C*alf, *R. P., M. O. F. F.*

MARKET. *C*attle,
R. P., M. O. F. F.

MARKET. *C*ovent Garden.
S. B. B., Scenes i.
Strewed with decayed cabbage
leaves, broken hay-bands, and
all the indescribable litter of a
vegetable market.

MARKET. Sheep.
R. P., M. O. F. F.

MARKET PLACE. Philadelphia.
A. N. vii.

MARKET PLACE. Salisbury.
M. C. v.
Being market-day—the thor-
oughfares about the market place
—filled with carts, horses, donkeys,
baskets, waggons, garden stuff,
meat, tripe, pies, poultry, and
hucksters' wares of every opposite
description and possible variety
of character.

MARKET TOWN. *B. H.* xviii.
A dull little town, with a church
spire, and a market place, and a

market cross, and one intensely sunny street, and a pond with an old horse cooling his legs in it, and a very few men sleepily lying and standing about in narrow little bits of shade.

MARKHAM. Steerforth's friend.
D. C. xxiv.
Always spoke of himself indefinitely, as a "man."

MARKLEHAM. Mrs., Mrs. Strong's mamma. *D. C.* vol. i., xvi.

MARKS. Will, John Podger's nephew. *M. H. C.* iii.
A wild, roving young fellow of twenty, who had been brought up in his uncle's house, and lived there still.

MARLBOROUGH. Downs, "In the direction of Bristol." *P. P.* xiv.
There are many pleasanter places, even in this dreary world, than Marlborough Downs, when it blows hard.

MARLBOROUGH HOUSE. *M. P., S. D. C.; M. P., S. for P.; M. P., Th. Let.*

MARLEY. Scrooge and, Bill discounters. *C. B., C. C.* s. i.

MARLEY. Late of Scrooge and Marley. *C. B., C. C.* s. i.
Was as dead as a door-nail.

MARLOW. Alice, *See* Brown, Alice.

MAROON. Captain, Friend of Captain Barbary. *L. D.* xii.
A gentleman with tight drab legs, a rather old hat, a little hooked stick, and a blue neckerchief.

MARQUIS. *M. P., T. T.*

"MARQUIS OF GRANBY. The," roadside public-house. *P. P.* xxvii.
Original : Believed to have been founded on the King's Head, Dork-

ing. Sometimes supposed to have been the corner shop in High Street, Dorking, " opposite the post-office, at the side of Chequers Court, which runs between it and the London and County Bank."

MARROW BONES AND CLEAVERS. The, have got scent of the marriage. *D. and S.* xxxi.
Put themselves in communication, through their chief, with Mr. Towlinson, to whom they offer terms to be bought off.

MARS. Sons of, Two former lovers of Mrs. Tetterby. *C. B., H. M.* ii.

MARSEILLES. *L. D.* i.; *M. P., W.; P. F. I., G. T. F.; R. P., M. O. F. F.*

MARSEILLES. Prison dungeon in. *L. D.* i.
A villanous prison. In one of its chambers, so repulsive a place that even the obtrusive stare (of the blazing sun) blinked at it, and left it to such refuse of reflected light as it could find for itself, were two men. Beside the two men, a notched and disfigured bench, immovable from the wall, with a draught-board rudely hacked upon it with a knife, a set of draughts, made of old buttons and soup-bones, a set of dominoes, two mats, and two or three wine bottles. The imprisoned air, the imprisoned light, the imprisoned damps, the imprisoned men, were all deteriorated by confinement.

MARSH GATE. *S. B. B.,* Scenes ii.

MARSHAL. The. *L. D.* vi.

MARSHALL. Mary, Betrothed to Richard Doubledick. *C. S., S. P. T.* ii.

MARSHALL. Miss. *S. Y. G.*

MARSHALL. Mr. Matthew. *M. P., F. L.*

MARSHALSEA. Errand bearers of the. *L. D.* ix.

MARSHALSEA. Go-betweens of the. *L. D.* ix.

MARSHALSEA. Father of the. *See* Dorrit, Mr. *L. D.* vi.

MARSHALSEA. Nondescript messengers of the. *L. D.* ix.

"MARSHALSEA HOTEL." The. *L. D.* ix.

MARSHALSEA PLACE. *L. D.*, Pref.
The houses which I recognized, not only as the great block of the former prison, but as preserving the rooms that arose in my mind's eye, when I became Little Dorrit's biographer.

MARSHALSEA PRISON.
L. D. vi. ; *P. P.* xxi.
An oblong pile of barrack buildings, partitioned into squalid houses standing back to back, so that there were no back rooms ; environed by a narrow-paved yard, hemmed in by high walls duly spiked at top. Itself a close and confined prison for debtors, it contained within it a much closer and more confined jail for smugglers—a blind alley some yard and a half wide, which formed the mysterious termination of the very limited skittle-ground in which the Marshalsea debtors bowled down their troubles.

MARSHES. The, Marsh Country. *G. E.* i.
Down by the river, within, as the river wound, twenty miles of the sea.
Original : Cooling marshes on the Kent bank of the Thames.

MARSHES. Pontine. *P. F. I., R. D.*

MARSIGLIA. *L. D.* lviii.

MARTHA. Eldest daughter of Bob Cratchit. *C. B., C. C., S.* iii.

MARTHA. Aunt, Sister of Doctor Jeddler. *C. B., B. O. L.* iii.

MARTHA. Inmate of workhouse. *O. T.* xxiii.
A withered old female pauper. Her body was bent by age ; her limbs trembled with palsy ; her face, distorted into a mumbling leer, resembled more the grotesque shaping of some wild pencil, than the work of Nature's hand.

MARTHA. John's daughter. *D. and S.* xxiv.
Her mother has been dead these ten year. . . . Ugly, misshapen, peevish, ill-conditioned, ragged, dirty—but beloved !

MARTHA. Maid to the Parsons. *S. B. B.*, Tales x.

MARTIGNY. *L. D.* xxxvii.

MARTIN. Miss, Client of. *S. B. B., Char.* viii.
Lady in service, whose " missis " wouldn't allow a young girl to wear a short sleeve of an arternoon.

MARTIN. Amelia, The mistaken milliner. *S. B. B., Char.* viii.
In a merino gown, of the newest fashion, black velvet bracelets on the genteelest principle, and other little elegancies.

MARTIN. Betsy, Convert to temperance. *P. P.* xxxiii.
Goes out charing and washing by the day, never had more than one eye, knows her mother drank stout, and shouldn't wonder if that caused it.

MARTIN. Betsy. *M. P., L.*

MARTIN. Captain. *L. D.* xix.
. A rather distinguished collegian.

MARTIN. Jack, Bagman's uncle. *P. P.* xlix.

MARY.   Barmaid.
                    S. B. B., Scenes xxii.

MARY.   Black girl runaway slave.
                    A. N. xvii.

MARY.   Daughter of drunkard.
                    S. B. B., Tales xii.

MARY.   Daughter of John.
                    R. P., P. M. T. P.

MARY.   Handmaiden at " The
  Peacock."   *P. P.* xiv.

MARY.   Housemaid in pot-shop in
  Borough.   *P. P.* lii.

MARY.   Mrs. Perrybingle.
                    C. B., C. o. H. i.

MARY.   Negro girl slave.
                    A. N. xvii.

MARY.   Nupkins' maid servant.
                    P. P. xxv.
  The pretty servant girl.

  Note.—The appearance of the Pickwickians before the Mayor of Ipswich
  had another result than the exposure
  of Captain Fitz-Marshall, as it was
  there Sam Weller first met Mary, the
  housemaid, whom he afterwards married. Mary also aided and abetted
  Arabella Allen in her runaway match
  with Mr. Winkle.

  *Original : Mary Weller, Dickens'
  nurse. She became Mrs. Mary
  Gibson of Mont Row, Ordnance
  Place, Chatham, died 1888, at the
  age of 84.*

MARY.   Servant at the Manor Farm,
  Dingley Dell.   *P. P.* v.

MARY.   Sweetheart of Captain
  Ravender.   *C. S., W. o. G. M.*
  She died six weeks before our
  marriage day—and she was golden,
  if golden stands for good.

MARY.   Visitor at Greenwich Fair.
                    S. B. B., Scenes xii.

MARY. Wife of George, Prisoner in Marshalsea—dying woman.
P. P. xxi.
Let them lay me by my poor boy now.

MARY ANN. One of the presiding goddesses in library, Ramsgate, in maroon-coloured gowns.
S. B. B., Tales iv.

MARY ANNE. David and Dora's servant. *D. C.* xv.
She had a written character, as large as a proclamation, and according to this document, could do everything of a domestic nature that ever I heard of, and a great many things that I never did hear of.

MARY ANNE. Favourite pupil of Miss Peecher. *O. M. F.* xviii.

Note.—Miss Peecher's maid and favourite. She conveyed intelligence of the happenings at Mr. Headstone's.

MARY ANNE. Wemmick's maid.
G. E. xlv.

MARYLAND. *A. N.* viii.

MARYLEBONE. *D. and S.* xxx.;
M. P., S. Pigs.

MARYLEBONE THEATRE.
M. P., V. and B. S.

MARYON. Captain, Captain of the sloop "Christopher Columbus."
C. S., P. o. C. E. P.

MARYON. Miss, Sister to Captain Maryon. *C. S., P. o. C. E. P.*
A beautiful young English lady, sister to the captain of our sloop.

MASH. Master, Pupil of Mr. Barlow. *U. T.* xxxiii.
This young wretch wore buckles and powder.

MASK. The cavalier whose face was concealed under a black mask.
M. H. C. iii.

"MASKERY'S MOST FEELING COACHMEN." *M. P., O. S.*

MASON. Monsieur, the tall and sallow. *U. T.* xviii.

MASON. The. *D. and S.* xviii.
Sings and whistles as he chips out PAUL in the marble slab before him.

MASSACHUSETTS.
M. P., L. A. V. ii.; *U. T.* iii.

MASSACHUSETTS JEMMY = James T. Fields. *M. P., I. W. M.*

MAST-MAKER. Purchaser of the old boat. *D. C.* xxii.

MASTER. Deceased, of house which shall be nameless.
C. S., S. L. i.
Was possessed of one of those unfortunate dispositions in which spirit turns to water, and rises in the ill-starred victim.

MASTER. Of servant of all work.
S. B. B., Scenes i.

MASTER. The, Our friend.
M. P., F. L.

MASTER CARPENTERS' SOCIETY.
M. P., R. T.

MASTIFF. The, Evenson.
S. B. B., Tales i.

MATABOOS. A set of personages in Tonga Island.
U. T. xxvi.

"MATCHMAKER." The, A former Chuzzlewit. *M. C.* i.
A matron of such destructive principles, and so familiarised to the use and composition of inflammatory and combustible engines, that she was called the matchmaker, by which nickname and byword she is recognised in the family legends to this day.

MATE. Lock-keeper's.
O. M. F. lvii.

M.

Note.—Mrs. Maylie's son. Originally destined for a prominent public career with Parliamentary prospects, he becomes pastor of a village church and marries Rose Maylie.

MAYLIE. Mrs., Lady of house attempted to be burgled.

O. T. xxix.

Well advanced in years; but the high-backed oaken chair in which she sat was not more upright than she. Dressed with the utmost nicety and precision, in a quaint mixture of bygone costume, with some slight concessions to the prevailing taste—she sat in a stately manner, with her hands folded.

Note.—Mrs. Maylie adopted Rose, and befriended Oliver Twist: beyond these she has no very important place in the story.

Original of Mrs. Maylie's house : " *Following Guildford Street (Chertsey) to the cross-roads, where turn R. and L. at fork along Pycroft Road, the house burgled by Bill Sikes and Toby Crackit in ' Oliver Twist,' may be seen. The high-buttressed wall on L. is the one this choice pair so adroitly climbed over.*"

MAYLIE. Rose Miss, Niece of Mrs. Maylie. *O. T.* xxix.

In the lovely bloom and springtime of womanhood—she was not past seventeen, cast in so slight and exquisite a mould ; so mild and gentle ; so pure and beautiful that earth seemed not her element.

Note.—Rose Maylie was discovered by Mrs. Maylie in the charge of some poor people, miserable and uncared for. Her condition is largely due to the machinations of Monks' mother. Mrs. Maylie took the child home and adopted her as her daughter. It is ultimately discovered that her real name is Rose Fleming ; that she is sister to Agnes Fleming, and therefore Oliver's aunt. She married Harry Maylie.

MAYOR. The, Of Eatanswill.
P. P. xiii.
"May he never desert the nail and sarspan business."

MAYOR. The, Of Ipswich.
P. P. xxiv.

MAYOR. The, Officers of.
P. P. xiii.

MAYPOLE. HUGH. Ostler at Maypole. *See* Hugh.

MAYPOLE INN. The.   *B. R.* i.
An old building, with more gable-ends than a lazy man would care to count on a sunny day; huge zigzag chimneys, out of which it seemed as though even smoke could not choose but come in more than naturally fantastic shapes—and vast stables gloomy, ruinous and empty. The place was said to have been built in the days of King Henry the Eighth; and there was a legend, not only that Queen Elizabeth had slept there one night—but that next morning, while standing on a mounting-block before the door with one foot in the stirrup, the virgin monarch had . . . boxed and cuffed an unlucky page for some neglect of duty . . . a very old house, perhaps as old as it claimed to be, and perhaps older, which will sometimes happen with houses of an uncertain, as with ladies of a certain, age.
Original : Although there is a " Maypole Inn " at Chigwell Green, it is generally considered that the " King's Head " at Chigwell is the original of the " Maypole Inn " of the story.

MAYSVILLE.   *A. N.* xvii.

MAZE. Ware.   *M. P., E. S.*

M'CHOAKUMCHILD.   Mr., A schoolmaster.   *H. T., S.* ii.

MEAGLES. Mr., Retired banker.
L. D. ii.
Who never by any accident acquired any knowledge whatever of the language of any country into which he travelled.
Note.—Enters the story on numerous occasions; although not a chief actor in it. He is the father of Minnie. A retired banker who travels a good deal. Friend of Doyce, and of Arthur Clennam, and benefactor of Tatty Coram.

MEAGLES. Mrs., Wife of Mr. Meagles.   *L. D.* ii.
Like Mr. Meagles, comely and healthy, with a pleasant English face, which had been looking at homely things for five-and-fifty years or more, and shone with a bright reflection of them.

MEAGLES. "Pet," Only daughter of Mr. and Mrs.   *L. D.* ii.
About twenty. A fair girl with brown hair hanging free in natural ringlets. A lovely girl, with a frank face and wonderful eyes; so large, so soft, so bright, set to such perfection in her kind, good face. She was round, and fresh, and dimpled.
Note.—Daughter of the Meagles, Pet marries the young artist Harry Gowan, but is not very happy with him.

MEAGLE'S HOUSE. Mr.
L. D. xvi.
A charming place—on the road by the river—It stood in a garden—and it was defended by a goodly show of handsome trees and spreading evergreens. It was made of an old brick house, of which a part had been altogether pulled down, and another part had been changed into the present cottage—within view was the peaceful river, and the ferry boat.

MEALMAN. Who supplies the Zoological Gardens.   *M. P., G. H.*

MEALY POTATOES.   *D. C.* xi.

MECCA.   *R. P., O. H. F.*

MECHI. *R. P., B. S.*

MEDICAL CHOICE SPIRIT.
M. P., L. E. J.

MEDICAL COLLEGE. Baltimore.
A. N. ix.

MEDICAL STUDENT. *L. T.*

MEDICINE MAN. Of North American Indians. *U. T.* xxvi.
For his legal medicine, he sticks upon his head the hair of quadrupeds, and plasters the same with fats, and dirty white powder—and talks a gibberish.—For his religious medicine, he puts on puffy white sleeves, little black aprons, large black waistcoats—collarless coats, with medicine button-holes, medicine stockings and gaiters and shoes—and a highly grotesque medicinal hat.

MEDICINE MEN. Of civilisation.
U. T. xxvi.

MEDITERRANEAN. *L. D.* liv.; *M. P., L. A. V.* ii.; *M. P., N. Y. D.; P. F. I., A. G.; U. T.* vii.

MEDIUM. A horrible.
M. P., S. B.

MEDUSA. Bride's Aunt.
O. M. F. x.

MEDWAY. *C. S.; S. P. T.* i.; *D. C.* xvii.; *P. P.* v.; *U. T.* xxiv.
The banks of the Medway, covered with cornfields and pastures, with here, and there, a windmill, or a distant church.

MEDWIN. Mr. *M. P., S. S.*

MEEK. Augustus George, Son of Mr. and Mrs. Meek.
R. P., B. M. S.

MEEK. George, Mr. Meek.
R. P., B. M. S.

MEEK. Mrs., Wife of Mr. Meek.
R. P., B. M. S.

MEEK'S MOTHER. Mrs., *See* Bigby, Mrs.

MEGG. Mr., A vestryman.
R. P., O. V.

MEGGISSON'S. A lodging-house.
U. T. v.

MELBOURNE. Lord. *M. P., I. M.*

MELCHISEDECH'S. *B. H.* xxxiv.

'MELIA. Bill's wife. *G. E.* xx.

'MELIA. Housemaid of Dr. Blimber's. *D. and S.* xii.
A pretty young woman in leather gloves, cleaning a stove . . . tied some strings for Paul, aged six, . . . who couldn't dress himself easily, not being used to it . . . and furthermore, rubbed his hands to warm them ; and gave him a kiss.

MELL. Mr. Charles, One of the masters at Salem House. *D. C.* v.
A gaunt, sallow young man, with hollow cheeks.
Original : Mr. Mell is generally regarded as having been based on Mr. Taylor, the English master at Wellington House Academy.

MELL. Mrs., Mother of Mr. Mell, and inmate of the almshouses.
D. C. v.

MELLON. Mr. Alfred.
M. P., M. M.

MELLON. Mrs. Alfred, As Sarah Goldstraw. *M. P., N. T.*

MELLOWS. J. Landlord of "Dolphin's Head." *U. T.* xxii.

MELLUKA. Miss, Polly's doll.
C. S., M. J. iv.

MELTHAM. Major Banks.
H. D. v.

MELTONBURY. *M. P., C. Pat.*

MELVILLE. Assumed name.
S. B. B., Scenes xiii.

MELVILLESON. Miss M.
B. H. xxxii.
Young lady of professional celebrity who assists at the Harmonic Meetings.

Note.—A casual character in the book. One of the entertainers at the "Sol's Arms." Her public name is Miss Melvinson, although she is married and the baby is carried to the "Sol's Arms" each night "to receive its natural nourishment."

MEMBER: A, Guest of Veneerings.
O. M. F. ii.

MEN. *M. P., H. H.*

MEN. Amphibious-looking young.
S. B. B., Scenes x.

MEN. At sale of Dombey's furniture. *D. and S.* lix.
Stout men with napless hats on, look out of the bedroom windows, and cut jokes with friends in the streets—and sit upon everything within reach, mantelpieces included.

MEN. Blossom-faced, Undertakers' men. *O. M. F.* lix.

MEN. "A DOZEN," Mr. Raddle.
P. P. xxxii.

MEN. Middle-aged.
S. B. B., Scenes i.
Whose salaries have by no means increased in the same proportions as their families, plod steadily along, apparently with no object in view but the counting house.

MEN. Mr. Mould's. *M. C.* xix.
Found it necessary to drown their grief.

MEN. Of the House of Mr. John Jarndyce. *B. H.* xxxi.

MEN. Old, Seeing Mark Tapley off.
M. C. vii.

MEN. One of the seven mild, Guest at Dombey's housewarming.
D. and S. xxxvi.

MEN. Seven mild. Guests at Dombey's housewarming.
D. and S. xxxvi.

MEN. Shabby-genteel, At Astley's.
S. B. B., Scenes xi.
In checked neckerchiefs and sallow linen—perhaps carrying under one arm a pair of stage shoes badly wrapped up in a piece of old newspaper.

MEN. Silly young, Visitors in Assembly Rooms, Bath.
P. P. xxxv.
Lounging near the doors . . . displaying various varieties of puppyism and stupidity ; amusing all sensible people near them with their folly and conceit.

MEN. Three or four, lounging about the stage-door.
S. B. B., Scenes xi.
With an indescribable public-house-parlour swagger.

MEN. Turnpike.
S. B. B., Scenes xii.

MEN. Two. *M. P., N. T.*

MEN. Two, In Tea Gardens.
S. B. B., Scenes ix.
In blue coats and drab trousers smoking their pipes. Husbands of the two motherly-looking women.

MEN. Two or three, Prisoners in the poor side of the Fleet.
P. P. xlii.
Congregated in a little knot and talking noisily among themselves.

MEN. Two stout, in centre box of private theatre.
S. B. B., Scenes xiii.

MEN. Two, Travellers in coach : in sky-blue and plum colour.
P. P. xlix.

MEN. Washed, Twenty taking part in election. *P. P.* xiii.

MEN. Young, A group of three or four members of Mr. V. Crummles' Company. *N. N.* xxiii.

With lantern jaws, and thick eyebrows—they seemed to be of secondary importance.

MEN. Young, One of the—in livery in Brook Street.
D. and S. xxxi.

Already smells of sherry, and his eyes have a tendency to become fixed in his head, and to stare at objects without seeing them.

MENAGERIES. Travelling, At Greenwich Fair.
S. B. B., Scenes xii.

MENAI STRAITS.
M. P., C. C.; *M. P., E. T.*

MENDICANTS. Army of shabby.
L. D. li.

MENDICITY SOCIETY.
R. P., T. B. W.

MERCANTILE JACK. Sailor on a merchantman. *U. T.* v.

MERCHANT. A, In Spitalfields.
U. T. x.

A bow-legged character, with a flat and cushiony nose, like the last new strawberry.

MERCHANT. Kidney pie,
S. B. B., Scenes ii.

MERCURY. Another acquaintance of Sir Dedlock's Mercury.
B. H. xvi.

MERCURY. Sir Leicester Dedlock's footman. *B.* xvi.
" Six foot two, I suppose ? " says Mr. Bucket. "Three," says Mercury.

Note.—Sir Leicester Dedlock's footman. He has no other name and he is no more than a "super" in the story.

MERCY. Nurse of the Uncommercial traveller. *U. T.* xv.

MERDLE. Establishment in Harley Street. *L. D.* xxi.

Like unexceptionable Society, the opposing rows of houses—were very grim with one another. —Expressionless, uniform, twenty houses, all to be knocked at and rung at in the same form, all approachable by the same dull steps, all fended off by the same pattern of railings, all with the same impracticable fire-escapes, the same inconvenient fixtures in their heads, and everything, without exception, to be taken at a high valuation.

Original of Merdle's house: Was situated in Harley Street.

MERDLE. Mr. *L. D.* xxi.

A man of prodigious enterprise ; a Midas without the ears, who turned all he touched to gold. He was in everything good from banking to building. He was in Parliament of course. He was in the City necessarily. He was chairman of this, trustee of that, president of the other—he was a reserved man, with a broad, overhanging watchful head, that particular kind of dull-red colour which is rather stale than fresh, and a somewhat uneasy expression about his coat-cuffs, as if they were in his confidence, and had reasons for being anxious to hide his hands.

The greatest Forger and thief that ever cheated the gallows.

Note.—The wealthy financier. Father-in-law of Fanny Dorrit. He becomes a bankrupt and commits suicide. Amongst those who entrust their money to him and lose it are the Dorrits.

Original : John Sadlier, at one time Junior Lord of the Treasury, Chairman of the London and County Joint Stock Bank, and interested in other gigantic financial schemes. Forger and swindler. When his malpractices could be no longer hidden he committed suicide in February, 1856. His body was found in a field behind Jack Straw's Castle and buried in Highgate cemetery.

MERDLE. Mrs., First husband of.
L. D. xxi.
Had been a colonel.

MERDLE. Mrs.   *L. D.* xx.
She had large, unfeeling, handsome eyes, and dark, unfeeling, handsome hair, and a broad, unfeeling, handsome bosom. It was not a bosom to repose upon, but it was a capital bosom to hang jewels upon.

> *Note.*—Wife of Mr. Merdle and mother of Mr. Sparkler, mother-in-law of Fanny Dorrit. She shines in society. Her son becomes entangled with Fanny in the early days, and she buys off the girl, but eventually, when the Dorrits come into money, Fanny marries the Sparkler. When Mr. Merdle fails, his wife receives the pity of Society and lives with her son.

MEREDITH. Sir William.
B. R. Pref.

MERITON. Mr. Henry.
R. P., T. L. V.
Second mate of the "Halsewell."

MERMAN. The, A gondolier.
L. D. xlii.

MERMEN. Gondoliers. *L. D.* xlii.

"MERRIKER."   *P. P.* xxxi.

MERRIWINKLE. Mr. and Mrs.
S. Y. C.

MERSEY. The.   *U. T.* v.

MERTON. Tommy, Pupil of Mr. Barlow.   *U. T.* xxxiii.

MESHECK. A Jew in the billstealing way.   *R. P., T. D. P.*

MESMEREST. Black.
R. P., O. o. S.

MESROUR.   *C. S., H. H.*

MESSENGER. From Somerset House.   *S. B. B.*, Char. iii.
In a blue coat.

METHODISTICAL ORDER. One of.
P. P. xxii.
A lanky chap with a red nose. . . . The red-nosed man warn't by no means the sort of person you'd grub by contract.

METROPOLITAN IMPROVEMENT SOCIETY.   *M. P., R. T.*

MEURICE HÔTEL. Calais.
P. F. I., G. T. F.
U. T. xvii.

MEWS. Two corner rooms over.
B. H. xxxviii.
Residence of Mr. and Mrs. Prince Turveydrop.

MEWS STREET. Number twenty-four. Residence of Mr. Tite-Barnacle.   *L. D.* x.
A squeezed house, with a ramshackle bowed front, little dingy windows, and a little dark area like a damp waistcoat-pocket. To the sense of smell the house was like a sort of bottle filled with strong distillation of mews ; and when the footman opened the door, he seemed to take the stopper out.

MEXICO.   *M. P., S. R.*

MEZZO. Giorno, Italian steampacket.   *R. P., P. M. T. P.*

MIBBS. "A very civil, worthy trader."   *M. P., F. S.*

MIBBS. Young.   *M. P., F. S.*

MIBBS' AUNT. Young.
M. P., F. S.

MIC

ICAWBER. Micawber

MICAWBER stone and A sto son in a

hair upo large one there is up extensive ?

the landlord he is placed uncongenial and Orati state of imp for "somethi event that tra imprisonment Bench Pris under the Ins proceeds to P indore sa and he is

something in Medway. La

Uriah believes shortness of willing and a soon discover him, but chastes schemes of h proceeds to can. This he dies. And at Mrs. Wick nounced undoubted to emigrate paper wrote from Mr Fre Micawber pror and because a

Original father.

MICAWBER ber.

A thin at all one

MICAWBER. Master, Son of Micawber   *D. C.* xi.

MICAWBER. Miss, Daughter of Micawber.   *D. C.* xi. Aged about three.

MICAWBER. Mr., Agent for Murdstone and Grinby.   *D. C.* xi.

A stoutish, middle-aged person in a brown surtout and black tights and shoes, with no more hair upon his head (which was a large one and very shining) than there is upon an egg, and a very extensive face.

Note.—Micawber is introduced as the landlord of David Copperfield when he is placed by his step-father in the uncongenial warehouse of Murdstone and Grinby. Even then he is in a state of impecuniosity and is waiting for " something to turn up." The only event that transpires is Mr. Micawber's imprisonment for debt in the King's Bench Prison. He obtains his release under the Insolvent Debtor's Act, and proceeds to Plymouth. This does not induce anything to turn up, however, and he is next seen selling corn, or trying to, and then endeavours to get something in the coal trade on the Medway. Later on he enters Mr. Wickfield's office, under Uriah Heep. Uriah believes that Micawber's chronic shortness of money will make him a willing and a useful tool. Micawber soon discovers what is expected of him, but instead of assisting in the evil schemes of his employer he quietly proceeds to collect all the evidence he can. This he communicates to Traddles. And at a general meeting at Mrs. Wickfield's house, Uriah is denounced. As some recompense for this undoubted service, Micawber is enabled to emigrate to Australia. From a paper which David Copperfield receives from Mr. Peggotty we learn that Mr. Micawber prospered at Port Middlebay and became a magistrate.

Original : Founded on Dickens' father.

MICAWBER. Mrs., Wife of Micawber.   *D. C.* xi.

A thin and faded lady, not at all young.

MICAWBER. Mrs., Micawber's mamma.   *D. C.* xii.

Departed this life before Mr. Micawber's difficulties commenced, or at least before they became pressing.

MICAWBER'S. Mrs., Twins.   *D. C.* xi.

One of them was always taking refreshment.

MICAWBER. Wilkins.   *D. C.* xii.

The boy-twin.

MICHAEL. Mr., The poor relation.   *R. P., P. R. S.*

MICHAEL. Mr., A rogue.   *R. P., D. W. I. F.*

MICHEL. An Iroquois hunter.   *M. P., L. A. V.* i.

MIDDLE TEMPLE.   *H. D.* iii.

MIDDLE TEMPLE GATE.   *B. R.* xl.

MIDDLESEX.   *B. R.* xlviii.; *C. S., D. M.* ; *C. S., N. T.* Act i. ; *M. P., C. P.*; *M. P. S. B.*; *M. P., W. M.*; *O. M. F.* xviii. ; *S. B. B.,* Scenes xvii.

MIDDLESEX. Grand Jury.   *M. P., S. Pigs.*

MIDDLESEX. House of Correction of.   *M. P., C. and E.*

MIDDLESEX. DUMPLING. Pugilist.   *P. P.* xxiv.

MIDLAND COUNTIES.   *U.* T. vi.

MIDSHIPMAN. The Wooden. *See* Gills' shop.

MIFF. Mr., Deceased husband of Mrs. Miff.   *D. and S.* xxxi.

He held some bad opinions, it would seem, about free seats ; and though Mrs. Miff hopes he may be gone upwards, she couldn't possibly undertake to say so.

R

MIFF. Mrs., Pew-opener.
D. and S. xxxi.

The wheezy little pew-opener, a mighty dry old lady, sparely dressed with not an inch of fulness anywhere about her. A vinegary face has Mrs. Miff, and a mortified bonnet, and eke a thirsty soul for sixpences and shillings.

MIGGOT. Mrs., Parkle's laundress.
U. T. xiv.

MIGGS. Married sister of Miss.
B. R. ix.

MIGGS. Miss, Domestic servant to the Vardens. *B. R.* vii.

A tall young lady, very much addicted to pattens in private life; slender and shrewish, of a rather uncomfortable figure, and though not absolutely ill-looking, of a sharp and acid visage.

Note.—Mrs. Varden's servant and maid-of-all-work. She ably seconds her mistress in her pretended indispositions, and together they render the old locksmith's life anything but pleasant. Miggs has her eye on Varden's apprentice Tappertit, and when he follows the rioters she leaves her mistress to act the part of guardian angel to Sim, who regards her with disfavour. After the riots she returns to her old situation. In the meantime, however, Mrs. Varden has undergone a change and her eyes have been opened regarding Miggs. The result is that the at one time indispensable companion is no longer required. She is appointed female turnkey at the Bridewell, a position for which her shrewish disposition is supposed to fit her. She retains the post for some thirty years, until she dies.

MIGGS. Nephew of. *B. R.* lxxx.

Born in Golden Lion Court, number twenty-sivin, and bred in the very shadow of the second bell-handle on the right-hand doorpost.

MIKE. Client of Jaggers.
G. E. xx.

A gentleman with one eye, in a velveteen suit, and knee-breeches.

MILAN. *C. S. N. T.* Act ii.; *P. F. I., V. M. M. S. S.; U. T.* iv.

MILE END. *B. H.* xiii.; *B. R.* lxi.; *P. P.* xxii.

MILES. Bob, A pickpocket.
R. P., D. W. I. F.

MILES. Mr. Owen, Fourth member of Master Humphrey's Club.
M. H. C. ii.

Once a very rich merchant—retired from business—an excellent man of sterling character: not of quick apprehension, and not without some amusing prejudices.

MILITARY. A strong body of.
B. R. lxxvii.

MILITARY. Character A.
C. S., M. L. Leg. i.

A military character in a sword and spurs and a cocked hat and a yellow shoulder-belt, and long tags about him that he must have found inconvenient.

MILITIA. Northumberland.
B. R. lxvii.

MILKMAN. A. *B. H.* iv.

MILKMAN. The. *O. M. F.* iv.

MILKMAN. Who supplies the Zoological Gardens. *M. P., G. H.*

MILKWASH. John. *S. Y. G.*

MILL. In Coketown.
H. T., S. xi.

MILL. Paper. *O. M. F.* lvi.
Original: Marsh Mill.

MILL DAM ROAD. Boston.
M. P., I. W. M.

MILL POND. *O. T.* l.

MILLBANK.   *B. R.* lxxxii. ; *D. C.* xviii. ; *O. M. F.* xviii. ; *R. P.*, *O. B.* ; *S. B. B.*, Scenes xvii.

MILLBANK STREET.
      S. B. B., Scenes xviii.

MILLER. Joe.   *C. B., C. C., S.* v.

MILLER. Joe.   *M. P., W. H.*

MILLER. Mrs., Jane Ann, A widow
      C. S., N. T. Act i.

MILLER. Mr., Old acquaintance of Mr. Pickwick.   *P. P.* xxviii.
The hard-headed old gentleman.

MILLER. The Hon. Mr.
      M. C. xxii.

MILLERS. The second nurse of the young Pockets.   *G. E.* xxii.

MILLINER. The mistaken.
      S. B. B., Char. viii.

MILLINER. Inmate of the Marshalsea.   *L. D.* vii.

MILLINGTARY. The.   *O. T.* vi.

MILLS. Miss Julia.
      R. P., O. E. W.

MILLS. Miss (Julia), Bosom friend of Dora Spenlow.   *D. C.* iv.
Comparatively stricken in years . . . almost twenty. . . Having been unhappy in a misplaced affection, and being understood to have retired from the world, on her awful stock of experience, but still able to take a calm interest in the unblighted hopes and loves of youth.

MILLS. Mr., Father of Miss Mills.
      D. C. iv.

MILLS. Mr.   *M. P., P. T.*

MILTON STREET.
      S. B. B., Char. xi.

MILTON'S TOMB. Cripplegate.
      U. T. ix.

MILVEY. Mrs. Margaretta.
      O. M. F. ix.
Quite a young wife—a pretty, bright little woman, something worn by anxiety.

MILVEY. The Reverend Frank.
      O. M. F. ix.
He was quite a young man, expensively educated and wretchedly paid.
Note.—A secondary, but nevertheless an interesting character. He is consulted by the Boffins when they propose to adopt a child, and he reads the service at Betty Higden's burial. He is a hard-working, generous-minded curate.

MILVEY. Six children of the Rev. Frank.   *O. M. F.* ix.

MIM. Proprietor of Travelling Show.
      C. S., D. M.
A very hoarse man—a ferocious swearer.

MIM. Step-daughter of.
      C. S., D. M.
Deaf and dumb. The poor girl had beautiful long dark hair, and was often pulled down by it and beaten.

MINCIN. Mr.   *S. Y. G.*

MINCING LANE.   *O. M. F.* iv.

MINCING LANE. One church near.
      U. T. ix.
Smelt like a druggist's drawer.

MINDERS. Nurse children.
      O. M. F. xvi.
In a corner below the mangle, on a couple of stools, sat two very little children : a boy and a girl.

MINDERSON. Mrs.   *M. P., U. N.*

MINDING-SCHOOL. A.
      O. M. F. xvi.

MINE. The, On Silver Store Island.
      C. S., P. o. C. E. P.
A sunken block like a powder magazine—(a walled square of

building, with a sort of pleasure ground inside) with a little square trench round it, and steps down to the door. The silver from the mine was stored there . . . brought over from the mainland.

MINERS.   *C. B., C. C., S.* iii.

MINERS. *C*ornish.   *C. S., H.* T.
Dancing before the *C*ornish inn by torchlight.

MINERVA. Esther.   *B. H.* li.

MINISTER. Preaching at Britannia Theatre on Sunday evening.   *U.* T. iv.
I could not possibly say to myself that he expressed an understanding of the general mind and character of his audience—is it necessary or advisable to address such an audience continually as " fellow sinners " ?

MINISTER OF STATE.   *M. P. D. V.*

MINISTERIALISTS. In Parliament.   *S. B. B.,* Scenes xviii.

MINISTERS. Three of his.   *O. M. F.* liv.
Under-waiters at Greenwich Hotel.

MINNS. Mr. Augustus, A clerk in Somerset House.   *S. B. B.,* Tales ii.
A bachelor of about forty, as he said—of about eight-and-forty as his friends said. He was always exceedingly clean, precise, and tidy ; perhaps somewhat priggish, and the most retiring man in the world. Usually wore a brown frock-coat, without a wrinkle, light inexplicables without a spot, a neat neckerchief with a remarkably neat tie, and boots without a fault : he always carried a brown silk umbrella with an ivory handle.

MINOR CANON CORNER.   *E. D.* vi.
A quiet place in the shadow of the *C*athedral, which the cawing of the rooks, the echoing footsteps of rare passers, the sound of the *C*athedral bell, or the roll of the *C*athedral organ, seemed to render more quiet than absolute silence. Red-bricked walls harmoniously toned down in colour by time, strong rooted ivy, latticed windows, panelled rooms, big oaken beams and stone-walled gardens, where annual fruit yet ripened upon monkish trees.
Original : Minor Canon Row, Rochester.

MINORIES. The.   *M. P., N. G. K.* ; *R. P., D. W. I. F.*

MINT. The.   *B. R.* lxvii. ; *C. S., G. i. S.* ; *M. C.* xxi.

MISANTHROPISTS.   *S. B. B.,* Char. i.
Generally old fellows with white heads and red faces, addicted to port wine and Hessian boots— taking great delight in thinking themselves unhappy, and making everyone that came near miserable —you may know them—at church by the pomposity with which they enter and the loud tone in which they repeat the responses— at parties, by their getting cross at whist, and hating music.

MISENO.   *P. F. I., R. D.*

MISERERE.   *P. F. I., R.*

MISSIONARY. A.   *S. B. B., O. P.* vi.

MISSIS. My, Wife of Magwich.   *G. E.* xlii.
Molly, at Jaggers'.

MISSIS. Of Servant of all work.   *S. B. B.,* Scenes i.

MISSIS. Our, Head of Refreshment Room at Mugby Junction.
C. S., M. J. v.

MISSISSIPPI.   *A. N.* x.; *M. C.* xvii.; *M. P., A. P.; M. P., E. T.; M. P., Y. M. C.; R. P., D. W. T. T.; U. T.* xvii.

MISSOURI.   *A. N.* xvii.; *M. C.* xvii.; *M. P., A. P.; M. P., E. T.; U. T.* xx.

MISTAFOKS=Fox. *M. P., T. O. H.*

MISTAPIT=Pitt.   *M. P., T. O. H.*

MISTASPEEKA=Chief of the officers of the Royal Seraglio.
M. P., T. O. H.
Speaker of the House of Commons.

MISTRESS. Mary's, Landlady of potshop in Borough.   *P. P.* lii.

MISTRESS. My, Mother of Miss Wade's pupil.   *L. D.* lvii.

MISTRESS. Of house which shall be nameless.   *C. S., S. L.* i.
A widow in her fourth year.

MISTY. Messrs   *Mud. Pap.* ii.

MITCHELL.   *M. P., F. L.*

MITCHELL. Mr., Manager of the Olympic.   *A. N.* vi.

MITH. Sergeant, A detective.
R. P., T. D. P.
A smooth-faced man with a fresh, bright complexion, and a strange air of simplicity, is a dab at housebreakers.

MITHERS. Client of Miss Moucher's.
D. C. xxii.

MITHERS. Lady, Client of Miss Moucher's.   *D. C.* xxii.

MITHERS' SCHOOL. *M. P., G. D.*

"MITRE." The, An inn in cathedral town.   *C. S., H. T.*
Where friends used to put up, and where we used to go to see

parents, and to have salmon and fowls, and to be tipped.
Original: "Mitre Inn," and "Clarence Hotel," in High Street, Rochester.

MITTS. Mrs., A Titbull's Alms House inmate.   *U. T.* xxvii.
A tidy, well-favoured woman.

MITTS. Mrs., Parlour of.
U. T. xxvii.
A gloomy little chamber, but clean, with a mug of wallflower in the window. On the chimney-piece were two peacocks' feathers, a carved ship, a few shells, and a black profile with one eyelash; —her only son—cast away in China.

MIVINS. Mr., A prisoner in the Fleet.   *P. P.* xli.
A man in a broad-skirted green coat, with corduroy knee-smalls, and grey cotton stockings, was performing the most popular steps of a hornpipe, which, combined with the very appropriate character of his costume, was inexpressibly absurd.

MIZZLE.   *B. H.* i.

MOB. Divisions of.   *B. R.* xlix.
The London, Westminster, Southwark, and Scotch.

MOB. The swell, Pickpockets.
R. P., T. D. A. ii.

MOBBS. Pupil at Dotheboys' Hall.
N. N. viii.
"Mobbs' mother-in-law," said Squeers, "took to her bed on hearing that he wouldn't eat fat, and has been ill ever since. She wishes to know, by an early post, where he expects to go to, if he quarrels with his vittles."

MOCHA.   *M. P., L. A. V.* ii.

MODDLE. Augustus, The youngest boarder at Todgers.
M. C. xxxii.

MODEL. A, An artist's model.
R. P., G. o. A.

MODEL PRISON. Pentonville.
M. P., P. P.

MODENA. *P. F. I., P. M. B.;*
U. T. xxviii.

MOFFIN. ¦ *O. M. F.* xxv.

MOGLEY. Suitor of Mrs. Nickleby.
N. N. xli.

MOLA DI GAËTA.
P. F. I., R. D.

MOLLY. Mr. Jaggers' housekeeper.
G. E. xxvi.
About forty—rather tall, of a lithe, nimble figure, extremely pale, with large faded eyes, and a quantity of streaming hair— her lips—parted as if she were panting, and her face to bear a curious expression of suddenness and flutter. One wrist deeply scarred across and across.

Note.—Mr. Jaggers' housekeeper Pip recognises in her Estella's mother.

MOLOCH. Little, Tetterby's baby.
C. B., H. M. ii.

MOMUSES. Mississippi, Negro singers. *U. T.* xxxiii.
Nine dressed alike, in the black coat and trousers, white waistcoat, very large shirt-front, very large shirt-collar, and very large white tie and wristbands.

MONASTERY. Interior of.
M. P., N. T.

MONASTERY RUIN. *E. D.* vi.

MONFLATHERS. Miss, Boarding school mistress. *O. C. S.* xxix.

MONKEY. Mr., Judge's rendering of Phunky. *P. P.* xxxiv.

MONKS. A confederate of Fagin.
O. T. xxvi.

Note.—Monks was the name adopted by Edward Leeford when endeavouring to procure the ruin of Oliver Twist. Leeford's father had betrayed Agnes Fleming, although fully intending to marry her on his wife's death. He was, therefore, Oliver's father ; and Monks was Oliver's half-brother. Leeford, senior, died suddenly at Rome, and his wife and son destroyed his will leaving the bulk of his property to the girl he had wronged and the child Oliver which was to be born. The son Edward, at the age of eighteen, left his mother, after robbing her, and spent his money wildly and shamelessly. His mother, just before her death, disclosed the secret of the will, and bequeathed to him the letter she had withheld, to-gether with her deadly hatred. Edward Leeford, or Monks, as he is more gener-ally termed, entered into the object with wholehearted villany. He finds Oliver in Fagin's hands, and bribes the Jew to force him into crime. This evil design is frustrated largely by Nancy's evidence, and Monks is forced by Mr. Brownlow and the others to relinquish half the remainder of his father's large fortune to Oliver. The other moiety, amounting to little more than three thousand pounds, Monks retains. He emigrates to the New World, but soon returns to his former courses and ends his days in prison.

MONKS. Two. *M. P., N. T.*

MONKS. Cappucini.
P. F. I., A. G.

MONKS' MOUND. The, Ancient Indian burial-place.
A. N. xiii.
In memory of a body of fanatics of the order of La Trappe.

MONK'S VINEYARD. *E. D.* xii.
Original : An open space in front of Restoration House, Roches-ter. At one time a vineyard in the possession of the monks. The vines.

MONMOUTH STREET.
S. B. B., Scenes vi.
The only true and real em-porium for second-hand wearing apparel. Venerable for its anti-quity, and respectable for its use-fulness.

MONMOUTH STREET. The inhabitants of. *S. B. B.*, Scenes vi.

A peaceable and retiring race, who immure themselves for the most part in deep cellars, or small back parlours, and who seldom come forth into the world, except in the dusk and coolness of the evening. Their countenances bear a thoughtful and dirty cast.

MONOMANIACS. *M. P., G. B.*

MONT BLANC. *M. P., L. A. V.* ii.

MONT BLANC. A good inn in the shadow of. *C. S., H. T.*

Where one of the apartments has a zoological papering on the walls not so accurately joined—the elephant rejoices in a tiger's hind legs and tail, while the lion puts on a trunk and tusks.

MONT BLANC. Inn, In shadow of. *C. S., H. T.*

Cheerful landlady, and honest landlord of.

MONTAGUE. Miss Julia, Singer at White Conduit.
S. B. B., Char. viii.

MONTAGUE. Mr. Basil.
M. P., C. P.

MONTAGUE. Mr. Wortley.
M. P., T. *O. H.*

MONTAGUE PLACE. Russell Square. *P. P.* xlvii.

MONTAGUE SQUARE. Mr. Jorkins' house near. *D. C.* vi.

MONTAGUE. Tigg, Esquire.
M. C. xxvii.

MONTEFIAXHONE.
P. F. I., R. P. S.

MONTMARTRE. Abattoir.
R. P., M. O. F. F.

Surrounded by a high wall, and

looking from the outside like a cavalry barrack.

MONTREAL. *A. N.* xv.

MONTROSE. *M. P., E. S.*

MONUMENT. The. *B. R.*, xiii. ; *M. C.* viii. ; *O. M. F.* iii. ; *R. P. P. R. S.*

MONUMENT. A church behind the, had a flavour of damaged oranges.
U. T. ix.

MONUMENT YARD. *M. C.* xliv.
Original : Supposed to have been intended for Monument Square.

MOODLE. *B. H.* xii.

MOON. A physician.
R. P., O. B.

MOON. *M. P., L. W. O. Y.*

MOON. *M. P., W.*

MOON = Paris. *M. P., R. D.*

MOONEY. Mr. *M. P., L.*

MOONEY. The active and intelligent beadle. *B. H.* xi.

MOONONIANS. Parisians.
M. P., R. D.

MOORE. Ralph. *M. P., N. E.*

MOORFIELDS. *L. D.* vii.

MOORFIELDS. House near.
B. R. lii.

They (the rioters) found in one of the rooms some canary birds in cages, and these they cast into the fire alive.—At the same house, one of the fellows—found a child's doll—a poor toy—which he exhibited at the window—as the image of some unholy saint, which the late occupants had worshipped.

MOORSHEAD. Captain.
M. P., L. A. V. ii.

MOPES. Mr., The hermit.
C. S., T. T. G. i.
Dressing himself in a blanket and skewer, and steeping himself in soot and grease, and other nastiness, had acquired great renown. A compound of Newgate, Bedlam, a Debtors' prison in the worst time, a chimney-sweep, a mudlark, and the noble savage. *Original : James Lucas, the " Hertfordshire Hermit," then living near Stevenage.*

MOPS. Fictitious name. L. D. vi.

MORAN AP KERRIG. Ancestor of Mrs. Woodcourt. B. H. xvii.

MORDLIN. Brother, Of the Ebenezer Temperance Association.
P. P. xxxiii.
Had adapted the beautiful words of " Who hasn't heard of a jolly young waterman " to the tune of the Old Hundredth.

MORFIN. Mr., In Dombey and Son's office. D. and S. iv.
A cheerful-looking, hazel-eyed, elderly bachelor : gravely attired, as to his upper man in black ; and as to his legs, in pepper-and salt-colour. His hair was just touched here and there with specks of grey, as though the tread of time had splashed it ; and his whiskers were already white.

Note.—Mr. Morfin is head clerk at Dombey and Son's. He is under James Carker, and sometimes overhears Carker and Mr. Dombey, although he adopts various artifices to inform them of his presence. He hears enough to make him friendly towards John Carker, the brother in disgrace. He is the " unknown friend " of Harriet Carker, whom he afterwards marries.

MORFIN. Mrs., née Harriet Carker.
D. and S. lxii.

MORGAN, ·· S. Y. C.

MORGUE. The, in Paris. M. P. R. D. ; P. F. I., G. T. F. ; R. P., L. A. ; U. T. vii.

MORGUE. Two custodians of the.
U. T. xviii.

MORGUE IN LONDON. Desolate open-air. U. T. xviii.
Right hand of Canal Bridge, near the cross-path to Chalk Farm —lying on the towing-path, with her face turned up towards us, a woman, dead a day or two, and under thirty, as I guessed, poorly dressed in black.

MORISON AND MOAT. Messrs.
M. P., Ag. Int.

MORMON AGENT. The.
U. T. xx.
A compactly-made, handsome man in black, rather short, with rich brown hair and beard, and clear bright eyes.

MORMON· AGENTS. Two or three.
U. T. xx.

MORTIMER. Assumed name of Mr. Micawber. *Which see.*

MORTIMER'S. Man. O. M. F. x.
Looking rather like a spurious Mephistopheles,

MOSELLE. The. R. P., D. W. T. T.

MOSES. M. P., I. M.

MOSES. E, and Son. M. P., F. F.

MOSES. (And Sons.)
M. P., S. D. C.

MOSES AND SON. R. P., B. S.

MOSES AND SON. Messrs.
M. P., E. S.

MOSQUITO SHORE.
C. S., P. o. C. E. P.

MOTHER. Demonstrated by Goblin to Gabriel Grub. P. P. xxix.
Drew aside the window curtain,

as if to look for some expected object.

MOTHER. Mr. Home's.
M. P., M. M.

MOTHER. Of discharged prisoner.
S. B. B., Scenes xxiv.
An elderly woman, of decent appearance, though evidently poor.

MOTHER. Of Monsieur Rigund.
L. D. i.
My mother was French by blood, English by birth.

MOTHER. Of Neckett's children.
B. H. xv.
Died just after Emma was born.

MOTHER. Our, To the memory of.
N. N. xxxvii.
Toast of Cheeryble Brothers.

MOTHER. Our dear, Of the five sisters. *N. N.* vi.

MOULD. Mr., Undertaker.
M. C. xix.
A little elderly gentleman, bald, and in a suit of black ; with a notebook in his hand, a massive gold watch-chain dangling from his fob, and a face in which a queer attempt at melancholy was at odds with a smirk of satisfaction.

MOULD. Mrs., Wife of undertaker.
M. C. xxv.
Was plumper than the two (daughters) together.

MOULD. Premises of Mr.
M. C. xxv.
Nestled in a quiet corner, where the city strife became a drowsy hum, that sometimes rose, and sometimes fell, and sometimes ceased altogether. The light came sparkling in among the scarlet runners, as if the churchyard winked at Mr. Mould.

MOULD. The Misses, Daughters twain of Mr. Mould. *M. C.* xxv.
So round and chubby were their fair proportions, that they might have been the bodies once belonging to the angels' faces in the shop below, grown up, with other heads attached to them to make them mortal.

MOUNT MISERY. *M. P., L. A. V.* ii.

MOUNT PLEASANT. *B. H.* xxi.

MOUNT VERNON. *A. N.* ix.

MOUNT VESUVIUS. *C. S., S. L.* iii.

MOUNTAIN PASS. *M. P., N. T.*

MOURNER. Chief. *C. B., C. C.* s. i.

MOUSE. In " Happy Family."
M. P., R. H. F.

MOWATT. Mrs., Actress.
M. P., V. and B. S.

MOWCHER. Miss, Masseuse, etc.
D. C. xxii.
A pursy dwarf of about forty or forty-five, with a very large head and face, a pair of roguish grey eyes, and such extremely little arms. Her chin, which was what is called a double chin, was so fat that it entirely swallowed up the strings of her bonnet, bow and all. Throat she had none, waist she had none, legs she had none worth mentioning. This lady, dressed in an off-hand, easy style.

MOWCOP. *M. P., E. S.*

MOZART. *M. P., O. L. N. O.*

MUDBERRY. Mrs. *P. P.* xxxiv.
"Which kept a mangle."

MUDDLEBRANES. Mr.
Mud. Pap. ii.

MUDFOG. *Mud. Pap.*

Original : Rochester.

MUDFOG.   *P. L. M. I.*

MUDFOG ASSOCIATION. *Mud. Pap.*
*Original : Association of British
Science.*

MUDGE. Jonas, Secretary of the
Ebenezer Temperance Association.
           P. P. **xxxiii.**
*C*handler's shopkeeper, an enthusiastic and disinterested vessel,
who sold tea to the members.

     Note.—Secretary of the Brick Lane
Branch of the United Grand Junction
Ebenezer Temperance Association, who
was addicted to the immoderate consumption of toast and tea.

MUFF. Prof.   *Mud. Pap.* i.

MUFFIN-BOY. The.
           S. B. B., Scenes ii..

MUFFIN-MAKER. Former pastrycook and.   *E. D.* v.

MUFFY.   *B. H.* xii.

MUGBY. The boy at refreshment
room.   *C. S., M. J.* v.
He'll appear in an absent manner to survey the line through a
transparent medium composed of
your head and body, and he won't
serve you as long as you can
possibly bear it.

MUGBY HIGH STREET.
         C. S., M. J. ii.

MUGBY JUNCTION. *C. S., M. J.* i.
A place replete with shadowy
shapes, this Mugby Junction in the
small black hours of the four-and-
twenty mysterious goods trains,
covered with palls, and gliding on
like vast, weird funerals. Red-hot
embers showering out upon the
ground.

MUGBY JUNCTION. Down refreshment room at.
         C. S., M. J. v.
Up in a corner—behind the
bottles, among the glasses, bounded
on the nor' west by the beer, stood
pretty far to the right of a metallic object, that's at times the tea-
urn and at times the soup-tureen
—fended off from the traveller by a
barrier of stale sponge-cakes erected
atop of the counter—you ask a boy
so situated—for anything to drink
—he'll try to seem not to hear you.

MUGBY JUNCTION. Lamps' cabin
in.   *C. S., M. J.* i.
A greasy little cabin it was,
suggestive, to the sense of smell,
of a cabin in a whaler. But
there was a bright fire burning
in its rusty grate, and on the
floor there stood a wooden stand
of newly trimmed and lighted
lamps ready for carriage service.

MUGGLETON.   *P. P.* vii.
Everybody whose genius has a
topographical bent knows perfectly well that Muggleton is a
corporate town, with a mayor,
burgesses, and freemen.
     *Original : Numerous towns have
been identified with more or less
success as the original of Muggleton.
Faversham, Maidstone, Tenterden,
and Town Malling. The theories
for these places have been elaborated
on numerous occasions. Gravesend,
however, has a substantial claim,
which has received very little attention, and for that reason it has
appeared advisable to deal with it
in rather more detail. The requirements of Muggleton have been
tabulated as follows.*
a. A corporate town.
b. County Jail and Sessions House.
c. Keenly interested in politics.
d. Interested in cricket.
*e. Open Market Square and " Blue
     Lion Inn."*
     *Gravesend is a corporate town
it had a Court House, though not a
County Jail ; the town was intensely
political ; and it was interested in*

cricket. *The market, though not a "square," was a very large open hall. And at the time Pickwick was written, a long low inn stood at the corner of one of the approaches to the market. It is difficult, if not impossible, to describe with any certainty the houses at that time, but it is of additional interest to note that in the chase after Jingle the "stages" coincide very well with those of the book, except that there is one, rather vaguely introduced in the book, which cannot be placed on the road. Additional evidence is found in "Pickwickian manners and customs." There Mr. Fitzgerald draws attention to a passage in Miss Dickens' "My father as I recall him :" "The late Miss Dickens—'Mamie' as she was affectionately called—in her pleasing and very natural little book, has casually dropped a hint which puts us on the right track. When driving with her on the 'beautiful back road to Cobham once, he [her father] pointed out a spot. There it was, he said, where Mr. Pickwick dropped his whip.' The distressed travellers had to walk some twelve or fourteen miles—about the distance of Muggleton—which was important enough to have a mayor and corporation, etc. We ourselves have walked this road and it led us to Gravesend." It is worth noting, too, that Dickens was extremely interested in this portion of Kent at the time the early chapters of Pickwick were appearing, See also Dingley Dell.*

The feature of the cricket match finds its origin in the Gravesend Club, which at that time was amongst the best known in the county. The matches took place between Gravesend and Chalk, where Dickens was stopping, and they invariably terminated with a cold dinner or supper, or were broken by a cold lunch to the visitors. More fre-

quently the former, however, when, judging from early newspapers, the club and the visitors did justice to the viands both solid and liquid : all, it will be remembered, quite in keeping with the story.

MUGGS. Sir A. *S. B. B.*, Tales iii.

MULATTO. A young, Pupil at our school. *R. P., O. S.*

MULBERRY. *See* Trotter, Job.

MULLINS. Jack. *O. M. F.* vi.

MULLIN'S MEADOWS. *P. P.* vi.
No better land in Kent.

MULLION. John. *C. S., W. o. G. M.*
One of crew of "Golden Mary."

MULLIT. Professor of education; schoolmaster. *M. C.* xvi.
"Very short gentleman with red nose . . . he is a man of fine moral elements, Sir—has written some powerful pamphlets, under the name of 'Suturb,' or Brutus reversed."

MULREADY. *M. P., O. L. N. O.*

MUMLER. Medium, a photographer.
M. P., R. S. D.

MUNTLE. Mr. Mantalini. *Which see.*

MURDERER. Captain. Character in one of Nurse's Stories.
U. T. xv.
An offshoot of the Bluebeard family—Captain Murderer's mission was matrimony—of a cannibal appetite with tender brides.

MURDERER. The. *C. S., D. M. P.*

MURDSTONE. Edward, Mrs. Copperfield's second husband. *D. C.* ii.
He had that kind of shallow black eye, which when it is abstracted, seems, from some pecu-

liarity of light, to be disfigured, for a moment at a time, by a cast. His hair and whiskers were blacker and thicker, looked at so near, than even I had given them credit for being. His regular eyebrows, and the rich white, and black, and brown of his complexion— confound his complexion and his memory—made me think him, in spite of my misgivings, a very handsome man.

Note.—Mr. Murdstone marries Mrs. Copperfield and so becomes David's stepfather. With the assistance of his sister he endeavours to train his wife to be "firm." He succeeds so well in this that she dies, together with the baby that is born to them. David he endeavours to break. After his wife's death he marries again and carries out the same programme, accompanied by a fitting gloom and dark religious fanaticism, and reduces her to the condition of an incipient imbecile.

MURDSTONE. Miss Jane, Mr. Murdstone's sister.   *D. C.* iv.
And a gloomy-looking lady she was . . . very heavy eyebrows, nearly meeting over her large nose, as if, being disabled by the wrongs of her sex from wearing whiskers, she had carried them to that account.

Note.—Mr. Murdstone's sister is a fitting assistant in the course of re- pression. She relieves the former Mrs. Copperfield of all housekeeping and dominates her and David. David again meets her as companion to Dora Spenlow.

MURDSTONE AND GRINBY. In the wine trade.   *D. C.* x.
Original : Murdstone and Grin- by is said to be a thin disguise for Warren's Blacking Manufactory, then at 30, Hungerford Stairs, where Dickens was employed for some short time. Another account of the blacking factory, on his experi- ences in which Dickens founded

Murdstone and Grinby, explains that James Lamert and his cousin George Lamert, backed by Jonathan Warren, who claimed the blacking recipe, started in opposition to the older established Warren's blacking and employed Dickens.

MURGATROYD. Mr.   *M. R. B.*

MURPHY.   *N. N.* ii.

MURPHY. Friend of Mrs. Nickleby. *N. N.* xxxvii.

MURPHY FAMILY. Tramps.
   R. P., D. W. I. F.

MURPHY'S TEMPERANCE HOTEL. Chapel Walks, Preston.
   M. P., O. S.

MURRAY. Honest, Publishers.
   M. P., N. J. B.

MUSES. Hall of the. *R. P., O. o. S.*

MUSEUM. The.   *D. C.* xx.

MUSIC. Director of the.
   S. B. B., Scenes xix.
In the blue coat and bright buttons.

MUSIC GALLERY.   *N. N.* ii.

MUTANHED. Lord (young) of the élite of Bath.   *P. P.* xxxv.
Splendidly dressed young man . . . with long hair and particularly small forehead. The richest man in Ba-ath at this moment.

MUTES. Two.   *M. C.* xix.
Looking as mournful as could be reasonably expected of men with such a thriving job in hand.

MUTTON HILL.   *O. T.* xi.

MUTUEL. Monsieur. *C. S., S. L.* ii.
A spectacled, snuffy, stooping old gentleman, in carpet shoes, and a cloth cap, with a peaked shade, a loose blue frock-coat reaching to his heels, a large limp white shirt- frill, and cravat to correspond, that

is to say, white was the natural colour of his linen on Sundays, but it toned down with the week.

MUZZLE. Mr. Nupkins' footman. *P. C.* xxiv.
With a long body and short legs.

MYRA. Negro wench ; a slave. *A. N.* xvii.

MYSELF. A bashful man. *C. S. H.* T.

MYSTERY. Passenger in train. *R. P., A. F.*
Not young, not pretty, though still of an average candle-light passability.

N

NADGETT. Mr., Secret agent of the Anglo-Bengalee Disinterested Loan and Life Assurance Company. *M. C.* xxvii.
He was the man at a pound a week who made the inquiries—he was born to be secret. He was a short, dried-up, withered old man, who seemed to have secreted his very blood. How he lived was a secret, where he lived was a secret. In his musty old pocket-book he carried contradictory cards, in some of which he called himself a coal-merchant, in others a wine-merchant in others a commission-agent, in others a collector, in others an accountant : as if he didn't know the secret himself. He was mildewed, thread-bare, shabby ; always had flue upon his legs and back ; and kept his linen so secret, by buttoning up and wrapping over, that he might have had none—perhaps he hadn't.

NAMBY. Sheriff's deputy. *P. C.* xl.
Dressed in a particularly gorgeous manner, with plenty of articles of jewellery about him—and a rough great-coat to crown the whole.

NAMELESSTON. Place of seaside resort. *U. T.* xxxii.

NAN. A female crimp. *U. T.* v.

NAN. Dark Jack's delight. *U. T.* v.
His white un-lovely Nan.

NANCY. *U. T.* iii.

NANCY. *O. T.* ix.
Rather untidy about the shoes and stockings.

Note.—Nancy was a member of Fagin's gang, possibly the only one with any remaining feelings of humanity. She was devoted to Sikes and was the means of recapturing Oliver Twist after his escape from Fagin. It was she, however, who revealed Oliver's secret, and so made it possible to discover his parentage and restore his fortunes. She was spied upon whilst doing this, by Noah Claypole, who was watching her on Fagin's behalf. Fagin told Sikes, and Sikes brutally murdered the woman who was willing to do so much for him and beseeched him, even while he struck her, to go to foreign parts with her, where they could live a new life.

NANDY. Mr., John Edward, Mrs. Plornish's father. *L. D.* xxxi.
If he were ever a big old man, he has shrunk into a little old man. His coat is of a colour and cut that never was the mode anywhere, at any period. It has always large, dull metal buttons, similar to no other buttons—a thumbed and napless and yet an obdurate hat—his coarse shirt and his coarse neckcloth have no more individuality than his coat and hat ; they have the same character of not being his—of not

being anybody's. . . . A poor little reedy piping old gentleman, like a worn-out bird who had been in the music-binding business—had retired of his own accord to the workhouse.

NAPIER. Admiral Sir Charles.
M. P., N. G. K.

NAPLES. *M. P., N. G. K.; M. P., W. H.; M. P., W. M.; P. F. I., R. D.; R. P., O. F. W.; R. P., P. M. I. P.; U.* T. iv.

NAPLES. King of. *P. F. I., R.*

NAPOLEON. Spirit of.
M. P., R. S. D.

NAPOLEON BONAPARTE.
M. C. iv.; *O. M. F.* lvi.; *R. P., B. S.; R. P., O. F. W.*

NATHAN. Messrs., In Titchbourne Street, Haymarket. *M. P., I. M.*

NATHAN. Mr., The dresser in private theatre. *S. B. B.*, Scenes xiii.
A red-headed, red-whiskered Jew.

NATIONAL CINDER HEAP. Houses of Parliament. *H. T., R.* xi.

NATIONAL GALLERY. *U.* T. xxiii.

NATIONAL HOTEL. *M. C.* xxxiv.

"NATIVE. The," Dark servant of Major Bagstock's.
D. and S. vii.

Note.—Major Bagstock's coloured servant. He was christened "The Native," by Miss Tox, and having no name to the Major, being called by any opprobrious term, he naturally becomes "the native" throughout. His last appearance is watching Dombey's house to satisfy the curiosity of his master.

NATURAL. A, A silly.
O. M. F. xvi.

NAVAL OFFICER. An old—on half-pay. *S. B. B., O. P.* ii.
His bluff and unceremonious behaviour disturbs the old lady's domestic economy—he will smoke

cigars in the front court—and lifts up the old lady's knocke with his walking-stick—He attends every vestry meeting that is held; always opposes the constituted authorities of the parish, denounces the profligacy of the churchwardens, contests legal points against the vestry clerk will make the tax-gatherer call for his money till he won't call any longer—then he sends it Is a charitable, open-hearted fellow at bottom, after all.

NAVY ISLAND. *A. N.* xv

NEAPOLITAN INN. Woman servant at. *U.* T. xxviii
A bright, brown, plump little woman-servant.

NEAPOLITAN NOBILITY.
L. D. li

NECKETT. "A Follower."
B. H. xiv
"Industrious ? He'd set upon a post at a street corner, eight or ten hours at a stretch, if he undertook to do it."

Note.—The Coavinses of Mr. Skimpole. He is sheriff's officer, but his duty, such as it is, he does well. He dies and leaves three children, who are befriended by Mr. Jarndyce.

NECKETT. CHARLOTTE. *B. H.* xv

Note.—Eldest daughter of Coavinses the sheriff's officer. She is introduced after her father's death, working for her brother and baby sister, locking them up during her absence. Mr Jarndyce visits them, with the result that little Emma is "took" care of by Mrs. Blinder, Tom is put to school, and Charley is sent as a "present" to Esther Summerson as her maid Charley catches smallpox from Jo and gives it to Esther, who has nursed her and Charley in turn nurses her mistress She is eventually married to a miller well to do.

NECKETT. EMMA. *B. H.* xv

Note.—Sister of "Charley" Neckett She is a baby of eighteen months when she is first introduced, but the family is befriended by Mr. Jarndyce. And when "Charley" is married to the miller, Emma appears to take her place as maid to Esther.

NECKETT. Tom.   *B. H.* xv.
A mite of a boy, some five or six years old, nursing and hushing a heavy child of eighteen months.

Note.—Son of the sheriff's officer. The family is befriended by Mr. Jarndyce and Tom is put to school. He is afterwards apprenticed to the well-to-do miller whom his sister marries ; and is always falling in love and being ashamed of it.

NED. Chimney-sweep.   *O. T.* xix.

NED. Negro man slave.
    A. N. xvii.

NED. Young boy of.   *O. T.* xix.

NEESHAWTS. Dr.   *Mud. Pap.* i.

NEGRO. At Pawkins.   *M. C.* xvi.
In a soiled white jacket, busily engaged in placing on the tables two long rows of knives and forks, relieved at intervals by jugs of water, and as he travelled down one side of this festive board, he straightened with his dirty hands the dirtier cloth, which was all askew, and had not been removed since breakfast.

NEGRO SINGERS. *M. P., P. L. U.*

NEIGHBOUR. Our next door.
    S. B. B., O. P. vii.

NEIGHBOURS. Of Nicholas Nickleby, Senr.   *N. N.* i.

NEIGHBOURS. Shy.   *U. T.* x.

NEILL HOUSE. Hotel in Columbus.
    A. N. xiv.
Richly fitted with the polished wood of the black walnut.

NELL. Little. *See* Trent. Little Nell.

NELSON.   *M. P., R. T.* ; *M. P., T. O. P., U.* T. xv.

NEMO. *See* Hawdon, Captain.

NEPAULESE PRINCES. [In Vauxhall Gardens.]   *M. P., R. H. F.*

NEPHEW. Pebbleson, Predecessors of Wilding and Co.
    C. S., N. T. Act i.

NEPHEW. Scrooge's, Son of Fan.
    C. B., C. C., S. ii.

NEUCHÂTEL.   *C. S., N. T.* Act i.

NEUF. Pont.   *P. F. I., G. T. F.*

NEVILLE. Mr., H. G. as George Vendale.   *M. P., N. T.*

NEWARK.   *N. N.* v.

NEW BOND STREET. *M. P., I. M.*

NEW BROMPTON.   *P. P.* ii.
The streets present a lively and animated appearance occasioned chiefly by the conviviality of the military.

NEW BRUNSWICK. *R. P., T. D. P.*

NEWBURGH. The town of.
    A. N. xv.

NEW BURLINGTON STREET.
    C. S., S. L. iv.

NEW CHURCH. *S. B. B.,* Char. i.

NEWCOME. Clemency,
    C. B., B. o. L. i.

NEW CROSS STATION.
    R. P., A. F.

NEW CUT.   *M. P., A. P.*

NEW ENGLAND.   *A. N.* iii.

NEWGATE.   *B. H.* xxvi. ; *B. R.* lviii. ; *C. S., T. G. S.* i. ; *G. E.* xx. ; *M. P., C. P.* ; *M. P., G. B.* ; *M. P., N. G. K.* ; *M. P., N. S. E.* ; *M. P., R. G.* ; *M. P., S. F. A.* ; *M. P., W. S. G.* ; *N. N.* iv. ; *O. M. F.* xxii. ; *O. T.* xi. ; *P. P.* xxi. ; *R. P., L. A.* ; *S. B. B.,* Scenes xvii. ; *S. B. B.,* Scenes

xxiv.; *S. B. B.*, Scenes xxv.;
T. T. C., Bk. ii.; *Ch.* ii.; *U. T.*
xiii.

NEWGATE. Discharged prisoner
from.   *S. B. B.*, Scenes xxiv.
Had been long in prison, and
had been ordered to be discharged
that morning. He had formed
dissolute connections: idleness
had led to crime.

NEWGATE. Prisoner.
    S. B. B., Scenes xxiv.
Boy of thirteen is tried, say
for picking the pocket of some
subject of Her Majesty. The
boy is sentenced, perhaps, to
seven years' transportation.

NEWGATE. Turnkey at.
    S. B. B., Scenes xxiv.
An ill-looking fellow, in a broad-
brimmed hat, belcher handkerchief and top-boots, with a brown
coat—something between a great-
coat and a sporting jacket on his
back, and an immense key in his
left hand.

NEWGATE MARKET. *B. H.* v.;
R. P., *M. O. F. F.*; *R. P.*, *T. D. P.*

NEWGATE PRISON. Condemned
cell in.   *S. B. B.*, Scenes xxv.
A stone dungeon, eight feet
long by six wide, with a bench
at the upper end, under which
were a common rug, a bible, and
prayer book. An iron candle-
stick fixed into the wall at side.—
and a small high window . . . admitted air and light. It contained
no other furniture of any description.
At the top of a staircase, and
immediately over the press room.
The room was large, airy and clean.

NEWGATE PRISON. Wardswomen
and wardsmen of.
    S. B. B., Scenes xxv.
Are all prisoners selected for

good conduct. They alone are
allowed the privilege of sleeping
on bedsteads.

NEWGATE SCHOOL.
    S. B. B., Scenes xxv.
A portion of the prison set apart
for boys under fourteen. A toler-
ably-sized room, in which were
writing materials. Fourteen in
all, some with shoes, some without; some in pinafores without
jackets, others in jackets without
pinafores and one in scarcely
anything at all.—And fourteen
such terrible little faces we never
beheld. There was not one redeeming feature among them.

NEWGATE. The gibbet.
    S. B. B., Scenes xxiv.

NEWGATE. Whipping place.
    S. B. B., Scenes xxiv.

NEWGATE. Yard for men.
    S. B. B., Scenes xxv.
In one of which—that towards
Newgate Street—prisoners of the
more respectable class are confined. The different wards necessarily partake of the same character. They are provided, like
the wards on the women's side—
the only very striking difference—
is the utter absence of employment. Huddled together—by the
fireside sit twenty men perhaps—
all idle and listless—with the
exception of a man reading an old
newspaper.

NEWGATE STREET. *B. R.* lxiv.;
N. N. xxvi.; *P. P.* xxxi.;
G. E. xxxiii.

NEW HAMPSHIRE. *A. N.* iii.

NEW HAVEN. Known also as the
City of Elms.   *A. N.* v.

NEW INN. *M. P.*, *B. S.*; *P. P.* xx.

NEW INN. Near R——.
R. P., T. D. P.

NEW JERSEY. *R. P., T. D. P.*

NEWMAN STREET.
B. H. xxiii.; *S. B. B. Char.* ix.

NEWMAN STREET. Mr. Turvey-drop's Academy in. *B. H.* xiv.

NEWMARKET.
D. C. xxv.; *R. P., A. C. T.*

NEW ORLEANS. *A. N.* iii.;
A. N. xiv.; *M. P., A. P.; M. P., E. T.*

NEW OXFORD STREET.
R. P., D. W. I. F.

NEW PAVILIONSTONE.
R. P., O. O. T.

NEWPORT MARKET. *P. P.* xlix.;
R. P., M. O. F. F.; R. P., T. D. P.

NEW RIVER. *B. R.* iv.

NEW RIVER 'ED. *D. C.* xxv.
A sort of private hotel and boarding 'ouse.

NEW RIVER HEAD. *B. R.* lxvii.
Detachment of soldiers were stationed to keep guard.

NEW ROAD. The.
S. B. B., Char. v.

NEW ROYAL ADELPHI THEATRE.
M. P., N. T.

NEWSBOY. Uncommonly dirty.
M. C. xvi.

NEW SOUTH WALES. *R. P., D. W. I. F.; R. P., P. M. T. P.*

NEW THERMOPYLAE. *M. C.* xxii.

NEWTON CENTRE.
M. P., I. W. M.

NEWTON CONN. *M. P., S. B.*

NEW YORK. *A. N.* ii.; *C. S., H. H.; M. C.* xiii.; *M. P., C. P.; M. P., L. A. V.* ii.; *M. P., R. S. D.; M. P., S. B.; M. P., W. R.; R. P., L. A., R. P., T. D. P.; U. T.* xx.

NEW YORK. Bay of. *U. T.* xxxi.

NEW YORK. State.
R. P., T. D. P.

NEW YORK. State House of.
M. C. xvi.

"NEW WHITE HART." An Inn.
U. T. xxii.
Opposition house to the Dolphin.

NEW WORLD. The. *C. S., H. T.*

NEW ZEALAND. *B. H.* xxvii.; *C. S., N. T. Act* i.; *M. P., E. T.; M. P., R. I.*

NEXT DOOR NEIGHBOUR. Our.
S. B. B., O. P. vii.

NIAGARA. *A. N.* xiv.; *R. P., D. W. T. T.; R. P., L. A.*

"NIBBLING JOE." *M. P., O. S.*

NIBLOS. A small summer theatre—New York. *A. N.* vi.

NICE. *P. F. I., A. G.*

NICHOLAS. Butler at Bellamy's.
S. B. B., Scenes xviii.
Steady, honest-looking old fellow in black. An excellent servant is Nicholas, an unrivalled compounder of salad-dressing—an admirable preparer of soda-water and lemon—a special mixer of cold grog and punch—and, above, all an unequalled judge of cheese. His prim white neckerchief, with the wooden tie, into which it has been regularly folded for twenty years past, merging by degrees into a small-plaited shirt-frill—would give you a better idea of

his character than a column of our poor description could convey.

NICK. Emperor of Russia.

M. P., B. S.

NICKETS. Late owner of Bounderby's Retreat. *H. T., R.* vii.

NICKLEBY. Godfrey, Grandfather of Nicholas. *N. N.* i.

A worthy gentleman, who taking it into his head rather late in life that he must get married, and not being young enough, or rich enough to aspire to the hand of a lady of fortune, had wedded an old flame out of mere attachment. Mr. Nickleby's income at the time of his marriage fluctuated between sixty and eighty pounds per annum.

Note.—Father of Ralph and Nicholas Nickleby, senr.

Original of Godfrey Nickleby's home : Probably Mile End Cottage, "about a mile south of the city (Exeter) boundary on the high road to Plymouth," which Dickens took, and furnished for his parents.

NICKLEBY. Kate, Sister of Nicholas. *N. N.* i.

Fourteen, as near as we can guess.

Note.—Sister of Nicholas. She is placed by her uncle, Ralph Nickleby, with Madame Mantalini. She is the object of the undesirable attentions of some of Ralph's evil-minded clients, chiefly those of Sir Mulberry Hawk, who suffers at Nicholas' hand in consequence. Ultimately she marries Frank Cheeryble.

Original : Founded on Dickens' sister, Mrs. Burnett.

NICKLEBY. Mrs., Wife of Godfrey Nickleby. *N. N.* i.

After five years—presented her husband with a couple of sons.

NICKLEBY. Mrs., Mother of Nicholas. *N. N.* i.

Daughter of a neighbouring gentleman, a well-meaning woman enough, but weak withal. . . . She dearly loved her husband, and still doted on her children.

Note.—Mother of Kate and Nicholas; weak-minded and with a strong inclination to dwell on unimportant details. Her remarks were more often than not without point, and far beside the subject of conversation. She is devotedly attached to her son and daughter, although she is of little assistance to them, and accompanies them in their pursuit of fortune. She is firmly convinced that the mad gentleman next door to the house at Bow was reduced to that state of mind by her rejection of his addresses. She is highly indignant at Miss La Creevy's betrothal to Tim Linkinwater. After their marriages she sometimes resided with Nicholas, sometimes with Kate.

Original : Founded on Dickens' mother. Strong hints that Mrs. Nickleby is a portrait of Mrs. Dickens in later life. This is impossible, as N. N. was written soon after marriage.

NICKLEBY. Nicholas, senr., Father of Nicholas. *N. N.* i.

Was of a timid and retiring disposition. Embraced his wife and children — solemnly commended them to the One who never deserted the widow and her fatherless children, and smiling gently on them — observed, that he thought he could fall asleep.

Note.—The father of Nicholas and Kate, brother of Ralph and the son of Godfrey. Left with a very small fortune, he speculated and lost what he had. He died and left his widow and son and daughter to the tender mercies of Ralph and the world.

NICKLEBY. Nicholas, Hero of tale. *N. N.* i.

About nineteen. His figure was somewhat slight, but manly and well-formed ; and apart from all the grace of youth and come-

liness, there was an emanation from the warm young heart in his look and bearing—bright with the light of intelligence and spirit. . . . First assistant master at Dotheboys' Hall.

Note.—The hero of the book. By his father's unfortunate speculations he is reduced to poverty and faced with the problem of supporting himself and his mother and sister. They all come to London and attempt to interest Ralph Nickleby in their case. Nicholas is packed off to Squeers' school as usher. Kate is placed in Madame Mantalini's dressmaking establishment. Nicholas discovers early the state of things at the school, a state of things made worse for him by his rejection of the advances of Miss Squeers. The end of it is that he thrashes Squeers and leaves the school accompanied by Smike. He returns to London, but finds it necessary to leave soon after. He reaches Portsmouth, meets Mr. Vincent Crummles, and joins the theatrical company. He makes a decided success in this until he is recalled to London by an urgent letter from Newman Noggs, relating to Kate. He removes his mother and sister from the charge, such as it was, of his uncle, and is fortunate enough to fall in with the Cheeryble brothers. From this point his success is unbroken. He rises in the estimation of the brothers, marries Madeline Bray, and buys a partnership in the business with her fortune.

Original : Was founded in some considerable degree on Mr. Henry Burnett, the husband of Dickens' sister, Fanny.

NICKLEBY. Ralph, junr., Uncle of Nicholas.   *N. N.* i.

Deduced from the tale (of his father's sufferings in his days of poverty) the two great morals that riches are the true source of happiness and power, and that it is lawful and just to accomplish their acquisition by all means short of felony. . . . He wore a bottle-green spencer over a blue coat : a white waistcoat, grey mixture pantaloons, and Wellington boots drawn over them. The

corner of ɛ frill struggl to show its chin and tl spencer . . . composed of which had i handle of a ɛ termination ir a sprinkling head, as if to benevolent . . cold restless e) tell of cunning t. itself in spite of the old man featured and for old man's eye w twinklings of ava

Note.—Uncle to lender with a goc clientèle. The fathe believes dead. He kind, for Nicholas a come to London. B mer and endeavours sible to thwart him a future. Eventually plans recoil on himse himself in his house i His relatives take nc his ill-gotten wealth, a Crown.

Original : Recalls in " Guy Mannering

NICKLEBY. Ralph, Godfrey Nickleby.

Left him (Mr. Godfr the bulk of his littl amounting in all to fiʼ pounds sterling.

NICKS. Nehemiah.   *M*

NICOLL.   *ʜ*

NIECES AND NEVYS. Of old gentleman.   *ɪ*

NIGER.   *M.*

NIGER. The, Left bank of

-PORTER. In Lincoln's Inn.
B. H. xxxii.
solemn warder, with a mighty
er of sleep, keeps guard in
lodge.

TINGALE. John.
M. P., P. M. B.

TINGALE. Mr.
M. P., M. N. D.

. *H. T.,' G.* ii. ; *M. P., E. T.* ;
U. T. xv.

ER. Miss Margaret.
H. D. iv.
Niece of Mr. Julius Slinkton.

EVEH. *M. P., N. J. B.*

PER. Susan, Florence Dom-
ey's nurse. *D. and S.* iii.
A short, brown, womanly girl of
ourteen, with a little snub nose,
nd black eyes like jet beads.
Note.—Eventually Susan marries
oots.

SBETT. Mrs., Actress.
M. P., M. B.

X. Mr. *R. P., D. W. I. F.*

IXON. Mr. *S. B. B.*, Scenes xix.

IXON. Mr. Charles.
S. B. B., Scenes xix.

IXON. Mr. James.
S. B. B., Scenes xix.

IIXONS. The, Guests of the Gattletons. *S. B. B.*, Tales ix.

OAKES. Mr. Percy, A law student. *S. B. B.*, Tales vii.
Was what is generally termed a
devilish good fellow. If any old
lady whose son was in India gave a
ball, Mr. Percy Noakes was master
of the ceremonies—if any member
of a friend's family died, Mr. Percy
Noakes was invariably to be seen
in the second mourning coach

with a white handkerchief to his
eyes, sobbing—like winkin . . . was
smart, spoffish, and eight-and-
twenty.

NOAKES. Mrs. *M. P., S. G.*

NOAKES AND STYLES. Messrs.
Mud. Pap. ii.

NOBBS. *M. P., T. T.*

NOBLEMAN. A poor, Family of.
L. D. lvii.
Miss Wade became governess
to the family.

NOBLEMAN. Another, House of.
M. P., L. L.

NOBLEMAN. English, Deceased.
U. T. xxiii.
Generous and gentle.

NOBLEMAN. Good-natured.
M. P., L. L.

NOBLEMAN. Mother of two daughters of poor. *L. D.* lvii.
Young and pretty.

NOBLEMAN. Two daughters of
poor. *L. D.* lvii.
They were timid, but on the
whole disposed to attach themselves to me.

NOBLEMAN'S FAMILY. Nurse in
poor *L. D.* lvii.
A rosy-faced woman.

NOBLEY. Lord. *M. C.* xxviii.

NOBODY. *M. P., N. S. E.*

NOBODY. *R. P., U. S*
Lived on the bank of a mighty
river, broad and deep . . . one of
an immense family.

NOBODY'S MASTER. *R. P., U. S*

NOBS. Old. Mr. Weller, senior
Which see.

NOCKEMORF. Sawyer late,
P. P. xxxviii

NODDY. Mr., Visitor, accompanying young man to Bob Sawyer's. *P. P.* xxxii.

A scorbutic youth in a long stock.

NOGGS. Newman, Clerk to Ralph Nickleby. *N. N.* ii.

A tall man of middle age, with two goggle eyes, whereof one was a fixture, a rubicund nose, a cadaverous face, and a suit of clothes (if the term be allowable when they suited him not at all) much the worse for wear, very much too small, and placed upon such a short allowance of buttons that it was marvellous how he contrived to keep them on. Kept his horses and hounds once— squandered his money, invested it anyhow, borrowed at interest, and in short made first a thorough fool of himself and then a beggar.

Note.—At one time a well-to-do gentleman in Yorkshire. But he squandered his money and eventually became clerk and general drudge to Ralph Nickleby. He is filled with the intention of exposing Ralph and his nefarious practices, and when Nicholas appears on the scene he befriends him. While Nicholas is away at Squeers' school and at Portsmouth he watches over Kate. It is largely through him that Nicholas and his friends are able to checkmate Ralph Nickleby. After the happy ending to the story he lives in a cottage close by Nicholas's house and delights in amusing the children.

Original : The character is taken from the life—a man well known in the neighbourhood of Barnard Castle. It is also said that it was founded on Newman Knott, who received an allowance through Ellis and Blackmore, where Dickens was at one time engaged.

NOGO. Prof. *Mud. Pap.* i.

NOLAND. Sir Thomas. *S. B. B.*, Tales v.

NOLLY. *O. T.* xiii.

NON-COMMISSIONED OFFICERS. Seven. *R. P., N. S.* Nobodies.

NONDESCRIPT. The, Connected with the Marshalsea. *L. D.* ix.

NOODLE. *B. H.* xii.

NORAH. Sweetheart of Master Harry. *C. S., H. T.*

Long, bright, curling hair and sparkling eyes in little sky-blue mantle.

NORE. The. *D. and S.* xv. ; *S. B. B.*, Tales vii. ; *U. T.* xxiv.

NORFOLK. *C. S., M. L. Lo.* i. ; *D. C.* xxxiv. ; *H. D.* iii.

NORFOLK. Duchess of. *M. P., C. C.*

NORFOLK ISLAND. *M. P., P. P.; R. P., T. B. W.*

NORFOLK STREET. Strand. *C. S., M. L. Leg.* i.

NORMAN. The, William the Conqueror. *M. P., T. B.*

NORMANDY. Bonnet. *C. S., G. i. S.*

NORMANDY. Robert of. *M. P., F. C.*

NORRIS. Mr., Engaged in mercantile affairs. *M. C.* xvii.

NORRIS. Mr., Junior, Son of Mr. Norris. *M. C.* xvii.

A student at college.

NORRIS. The Misses, Daughters of Mr. Norris. *M. C.* xvii.

One eighteen, the other twenty— both very slender, but very pretty. They sang in all languages except their own.

NORRIS. Mrs. *M. C.* xvii

Looked much older and more faded than she ought to have looked.

NORRIS. Mrs., Senior, Mother of Mr. Norris. *M. C.* xvii.

A little sharp-eyed, quick, old woman.

NORRIS. S, F. *M. P., S. B.*

NORTH BARRIER.
     T. T. C. bk. iii. ch. x.

The carriage left the street behind, passed the North Barrier, and emerged upon the country road. In Dr. Manette's story.

NORTH BRIDGE. *P. C.* xlix.

NORTH END. *O.* T. xlviii.

NORTH FORELAND.
     R.|*P.* ; *C. E. W. P.*

NORTH POINT. *A. N.* ix.

NORTH POLE. *B. H.* xviii. ; *M. P., R. T.* ; *O. M. F.* ii. ; *U.* T. xv.

NORTH SEA. *N. N.* xli.

NORTH TOWER. In the Bastille. *T. T. C.* bk. ii. ; ch. xxi.

Through gloomy vaults where the light of day had never shone, past hideous doors of dark dens and cages, down cavernous flights of steps, and again up steep, rugged ascents.

Note.—The North Tower was where Dr. Manette had been confined, in "One Hundred and Five."

NORTH-WESTERN LINE OF RAIL-WAY. L.N.W.R. *M. P., R. S.*

NORTHAMPTONSHIRE. *M. P., E. S.* ; *M. P., O. L., N. O.* ; *O.* T. liii. ; *R. P., T. D. P.*

NORTHFLEET. Kent. *O. M. F.* xii.

NORTHUMBERLAND HOUSE. In the Strand. *M. P., G. A.*

NORTON. *C*harles Eliot. *M. P., I. W. M.*

NORTON. Mrs. *M. P., I. W. M.*

NORTON. Squire. *M. P., V. C.*

NORWEGIAN FROSTS.
     U. T. xxiv.

NORWICH. *D. C.* iii. ; *E. D.* ix. ; *M. P., W.* ; *P. P.* xiii.

NORWICH CASTLE. *M. P., U. N.*

NORWOOD. *D. C.* xxvi. ; *D. and S.* xxxiii. ; *U.* T. xiv.

NORWOOD ROAD. *D. C.* xxvi.

"NOT TIRED YET." *M. P., O. S.*

NOTRE DAME. *L. D.* liv. ; *R. P., M. O. F. F.* ; *U.* T. vii.

NOTTING HILL. *U.* T. x.

NO-ZOO. The Lord, Toby Chuzzle-wit's grandfather. *M. C.* i.

It *has* been said—for human wickedness has no limits—that there is no lord of that name—and that among the titles which have become extinct, none at all resembling this, even in sound, is to be discovered.

NUBBLES. *C*hristopher, Shop-boy to Trent and then servant to the Garlands. *O. C. S.* i.

Kit was a shock-headed, sham-bling, awkward lad with an un-commonly wide mouth.

Note.—Kit was errand-boy and shop-boy to Nell's grandfather. He is Nell's willing slave, but the grand-father takes it into his head that Kit has injured him and discharges him. Kit enters the employ of Mr. Garland, where he prospers. He is accused of theft, however, through the instru-mentality of the Brasses and im-prisoned. He is soon cleared, and his case arouses some interest, so that he is able to better his position. In the end he marries Barbara.

NUBBLES. Mrs., Kit's mother. *O. C. S.* x.

Wait till he's a widder and works like you do, and gets as little, and does as much, and keeps his spirits up the same.

Note.—Mrs. Nubbles is Kit's mother : a hardworking laundress, who is eventu-ally placed out of the reach of want.

NUGENT. Lord. *M. P., C. P.*

NUMBER ONE. Another refractory in Wapping Workhouse.

U. T. iii.

"NO. 20—COFFEE-ROOM FLIGHT." Prisoner in the Fleet. *P. P.* xli.

" Little dirty-faced man in the brown coat. If he got any wrinkles in his face they was stopped up with the dirt . . . he got into debt . . . and in course o' time he come here in consekens. It warn't much execution for nine pound nothin' multiplied by five for costs. He wos a very peaceful inoffendin' creetur—the turnkeys they got quite fond on him."

NO. 924. Cabdriver. *Refer to* Sam.

NUMSKULL. Sir Arrogant. *See* Dedlock, Sir Leicester.

NUPKINS. George, Principal Magistrate of Ipswich. *P. P.* xxiv.

As grand a personage as the fastest walker would find out, between sunrise and sunset, on the twenty-first of June, which being, according to the almanack, the longest day in the whole year, would naturally afford him the longest period for his search.

Note.—Mr. Nupkins was Mayor of Ipswich and therefore chief magistrate of the town. Wiss Witherfield, the lady into whose bedroom Mr. Pickwick had accidentally strayed, lodged information with Mr. Nupkins that Mr. Pickwick was to fight a duel, with Mr. Tupman as his second. The two Pickwickians were accordingly arrested and carried before His Worship. The following proceedings are very diverting, as a skit on the ignorance of the elective magistracy. Mr. Pickwick and his friend owe their release to their knowledge of Jingle who, masquerading as Captain Fitz-Marshall, was intended for the " rich " husband of Miss Nupkins.

NUPKINS. Miss, Daughter of chief magistrate. *P. P.* xxv.

NUPKINS. Mrs., Wife of chief magistrate. *P. P.* xxv.

A majestic female in a pink gauze turban, and a light brown wig.

Note.—Mrs. Nupkins is one of Dickens' best examples of the lady who always knew a thing after it had happened.

NURSE. Attending deathbed of Nicholas Nickleby, senior.

N. N. i.

NURSE. Moloch's. *C. B., H. M.* ii.

NURSE. The, Mrs. Kitterbell's.

S. B. B., Tales xi.

With a remarkably small parcel in her arms, packed up in a blue mantle trimmed with white fur.

NURSEMAIDS. Twenty, In Mr. Dombey's Street.

D. and S. xxxi.

Have promised twenty families of little women, whose instinctive interest in nuptials dates from their cradles, that they shall go and see the marriage.

"NUTMEG GRATER." Landlord of the. *C. B., B. o. L.* iii.

"NUTMEG GRATER." Roadside inn. *C. B., B. o. L.* iii.

Snugly sheltered behind a great elm-tree with a rare seat for idlers. . . . the horse trough full of clear, fresh water . . . the crimson curtains in the lower rooms, and the pure white hangings in the little bedchambers above, beckoned, *Come in !*

O

O——. Mr. *M. P., R. T.*

OAK LODGE. Camberwell.

S. B. B., Tales v.

Residence of the Maldertons.

OAKUM HEAD. Chief of Refractories.   *U. T.* iii.

OBELISK. The.   *C. S.*, *S. L.* iii. ;
                        D. C. xii. ; *U. T.* x.

OBENREIZER. Friend and compatriot of.   *C. S.*, *N. T.* Act ii.
The friend's face was mouldy. and the friend's figure was fat. His age was suggestive of the autumnal period of human life.

OBENREIZER. M. Jules, Agent of " Defresnier et Cie."
  :*C. S.*, *N.* T. Act i. ; *M. P. A. T.*
Champagne-making friends of Wilding and Co. . . . A black-haired young man of dark complexion. through whose swarthy skin no red glow ever shone. He was robustly made, well proportioned, and had handsome features.—If his lips could have been made a little thicker, and his neck much thinner, they would have found their want supplied.

OBENREIZER. Woman-servant of M.   *C. S.*, *N.* T. Act ii.

OBENREIZER'S HOUSE.
                        M. P., *N.* T.

OBI. King.   *M. P.*, *N. E.*

O'BLEARY. Mr., Boarder at Mrs. Tibbs.   *S. B. B.*, Tales i.
An Irishman, recently imported —had come over to England to be an apothecary, a clerk in a Government office, an actor, a reporter, or anything else that turned up— he was not particular—wore shepherd's plaid inexpressibles, and used to look under all the ladies' bonnets as he walked along the streets.

O'BOODLEOM. Irish member.
                        M. P., *B. A.*

O'BRIEN.' Mr., Passenger on Gravesend packet.   *S. B. B.*, Scenes x.

OBSERVATORY. The.
                        O. M. F. liv.

OBSERVATORY. The.
                S. B. B., Scenes xii.

OBSERVATORY. A room in Grad. grind's house.   *H. T.*, *S.* xv.

OBSTACLE. The, The Obelisk.
                        C. S., *S. L.* iii.

OCEAN CLIFFS.   *M. P.*, *T. O. P.*

O'CONNELL. Mr.   *M. P.*, *C. P.*

O'DONOVAN. Wife and daughter. Tramps.   *R. P.*, *D. W. I. F.*

OFFENDER. (Murdered person.)
                        M. P., *F. N. P.*

O. F. F. I. C. E.=Antediluvian Cave.   *M. P.*, *T. O. H.*

OFFICER. Brother, Of soldier.
                        M. H. C. ii.

OFFICER. Commanding, Of the Horse Guards.   *B. R.* xlix.

OFFICER. From India on leave.
                        L. D. ii.
Guest in Great Hotel in Marseilles.

OFFICER. In Doctors' Commons.
                S. B. B., Scenes viii.
A little thin old man, with long grizzly hair—whose duty—was to ring a large handbell when the Court (Arches) opened in the morning, and who, for aught his appearance betokened to the contrary, might have been similarly employed for the last two centuries at least.

OFFICER. Militia. M.P.
                S. B. B., Scenes xviii.
With a complexion almost as sallow as his linen, and whose large black moustache would give him the appearance of a figure in a hairdresser's window.—The

most amusing person in the house—very punctual in his attendance, generally harmless, and always amusing.

OFFICER. Night. *M. P., S. S. U*

OFFICER. Police. *O. T.* xi.
A bluff old fellow—kind-hearted thief-taker.

OFFICER. Public, Guest of Veneerings. *O. M. F.* ii.

OFFICER. Sturdy old, of the Army.
M. H. C. i.

OFFICER. Young. *M. P., L. L.*

OFFICER. Young, Of the audience in the theatre. *N. N.* xxiv.
Supposed to entertain a passion for Miss Snevelicci.

OFFICER OF THE COURT. In Doctors' Commons.
S. B. B., Scenes viii.
A fat-faced, smirking, civil-looking body, in a black gown, black kid gloves, knee-shorts, and silks, with his shirt-frill in his bosom, curls on his head, and a silver staff in his hand

OFFICERS. *Custom 'Us, Custom House Officers.* *G. E.* liv.

OHIO. *M. P., S. B.; R. P., D. W. T. T.*

OHIO. The. *A. N.* xi. ; *M. P., E. T.*

OJIBBEWAY BRIDE.
M. P., Th. Let.

O'KILLAMOLLYBORE. Young.
M. P., C. Pat.

OLD BAILEY. *A. N.* xiv. ; *B. R.* xxxix. ; *M. C.* ix. ; *M. P., A. in E.; M. P., C. P.; M. P., Dr. C.; M. P., D. M.; M. P., L. E. J.; M. P., N. S. E.; M. P., P. L. U.; M. P., T. D.; P. C.* xxxiii. ; *T. T. C.* bk. ii. ch. ii.
U. T. iii.

A vile place, in which most kinds of debauchery and villany were practised, and where dire diseases were bred. The court was all bestrewn with herbs and sprinkled with vinegar, as a precaution against gaol air and gaol fever.

OLD BOAR. The, Kept by a Watkins. *N. N.* xxiii.

" OLD BRICKS AND MORTAR."
Crummles, Mr. V. *Which see.*

OLD BURLINGTON STREET.
U. T. xvi.

OLD CHARON. *B. H.* xxxii.
Original : The name was taken from a schoolfellow of Dickens at Chatham.

OLD CURIOSITY SHOP. *O. C. S.*
The title-piece of the novel of the name.
One of those receptacles for old and curious things which seem to crouch in odd corners.
Original : Said to have been pointed out by Dickens as then 10, Green Street, Leicester Square. Cannot be connected with the house at the corner of Lincoln's Inn Fields, so often thought to be the original.
Another " original " has been found in No. 24, Fetter Lane, demolished about 1891.

OLD FILE. *L. D.* xlii.

OLD GOOSEBERRY. Fictitious name of donor of gift to the Father of the Marshalsea. *L. D.* vi.

OLD GRANITE STATE.
M. P., T. O. P.

OLD HELL SHAFT. A disused pit.
H. T., G. vi.

OLD HUMMUMS. *M. P., W. S. G.*

OLD KENT ROAD. *U. T.* vii.

OLD MINT. The. *R. P., D. W. I. F.*

OLD PALACE YARD.   *U.* T. xiii.

OLD PANCRAS ROAD.   *P. P.* xxi.

OLD ROYAL HOTEL.   *P. P.* l.

OLD SQUARE. Lincoln's Inn.
B. H. iii.

OLD STREET ROAD.   *B. H.* ix.

OLD 'UN. The, Mr. Gummidge.
D. C. xxii.

OLYMPIC THEATRE. The, New
York.   *A. N.* vi. ; *U.* T. iv.

'OMAN. A young.
S. B. B., Scenes v.
" As takes in tambour work, and
dresses quite genteel."

OMER. Minnie, Afterwards Mrs.
Joram.   *D. C.* ix.

OMER. Mr., Draper, tailor, haber-
hasher, funeral furnisher, etc.
D. C. ix.
A fat, short-winded, merry-look-
ing little old man in black, with
rusty little bunches of ribbons at
the knees of his breeches, black
stockings, and broad-brimmed hat.
*Original of Omer's shop: Has
been identified as " an old-fashioned
shop at the corner of a row, miscalled
Broad Row (Yarmouth), that precisely corresponds with the description ; and, singularly enough it
is used as a clothing establishment,
and in silver letters on a black
board inside the shop is the announce-
ment, "Funerals furnished."*

ONE. The Nobby Shropshire,
D. and S. xxxii.

ONE HUNDRED AND FIVE. North
Tower.   T. T. *C.* bk. ii. ch. xxi.
" Monsieur, it is a cell."

ONOWENEVER. Mrs. *U.* T. xix.

ONTARIO LAKE.   *A. N.* xv.

strength, never in a hurry, and always slouching.

Note.—Joe Gargery's man. Enormously strong and with an unreasoning grudge against Pip and his sister. He kills Pip's sister and later on endeavours to do the same to Pip. The arrival of Herbert and others prevents the execution of the design.

ORPHAN BOY. The. *R. P., A. C. T.*

ORSON. O'Bleary. *S. B. B.*, Tales i.

OSBORNE'S HOTEL.   *P. C.* liv.

OSGOOD. James Ripley=The Boston Bantam.   *M. P., I. W. M.*

OTAHEITE.
     M. P., E. T. ; *M. P., L. A. V.* ii.

OTRANTO. Castle of.
                    P. F. I., R. D.

OUR ENGLISH WATERING PLACE.
                    R. P., O. E. W. P.
Original: Broadstairs.

OUR FRENCH WATERING-PLACE.
                    R. P., O. F. W. P.
Original: Boulogne.

OUR SCHOOL.   *R. P., O. S.*
Original: Probably Wellington House Academy in Hampstead Road.

OUTSIDES. Passengers outside on coach.   *P. P.* xxxv.

OVERS. John.   *M. P., Overs.*
Working-man author.

OVERSEERS. The.
                    S. B. B., O. P. i.
They are usually respectable tradesmen, who wear hats with brims inclined to flatness.

OVERTON. Joseph, Mayor of Great Winglebury. Solicitor.
                    S. B. B., Tales viii.
A sleek man—in drab shorts and continuations, black coat, neckcloth and gloves.

OVERTON. Mr. Owen, Mayor of a small town on the road to Gretna.
                    M. P., S. G.

OWEN. John, Schoolboy.
                    O. C. S. lii.
"A lad of good parts, sir, and frank honest temper."

OWEN. Mr. Robert.
     M. P., S. B. ; *M. P., S. F. A.*

OWEN. Professor.   *U. T.* xxix.

OWL. In "Happy Family."
                    M. P., R. H. F.

OXENFORD.   *M. P., V. and B. S.*

OXFORD.   *M. P., I. M. F.* ; *M. P., L. L.* ; *M. P., T. O. H.* ; *R. P., T. B. W.*

OXFORD. Colleges of.
                    M. P., L. W. O. Y.

OXFORD. Member for the University of.   *M. P., H. H.*

OXFORD MARKET.
                    D. and S. xviii.

OXFORD ROAD. *B. R.* xvi. ; *P. P.* xxxiii.

OXFORD STREET. *B. H.* xiii. ; *D. C.* xxviii. ; *L. D.* xxvii. ; *M. H. C.* i. ; *M. P., N. Y. D.* ; *M. P., P. F.* ; *M. P., W. R.* ; *N. N.* xxxv. ; *R. P., D. W. I. F.* ; *S. B. B.*, Scenes xv. ; *S. B. B.*, Scenes xvi. ; *S. B. B.*, Tales vii. ; *T. T. C.* bk. ii. ch. vi ; *U. T.* x.

OXFORD UNIVERSITY.
                    M. P., O. C.

OXFORDSHIRE.   *O. M. F.* xlii.

P

PA. Husband of lady in distress.
                    S. B. B., O. P. v.

PAAP. Mr., *Celebrated dwarf.*
                    A. N. v.

PACIFIC OCEAN.
                    N. N. xli. ; *U. T.* xx.

PACKER. *C*lient of Snagsby.
                              B. H. x.

PACKER. Tom, In the Marines.
              C. S., P. o. C. E. P.
   A wild, unsteady young fellow,
son of a respectable shipwright—
a good scholar who had been well
brought up.

PACKET. The.   *R. P., O. o. S.*

PADDINGTON.
   S. B. B., Scenes xvii. ; *U. T.* iii.

PADDINGTON ROAD.
              S. B. B., Scenes xvii.

PADUA.   *P. F. I., A. I. D.*

PAESTUM.   *P. F. I., R. D.*

PAGE. A, David Copperfield's.
                              D. C. xix.
   The principal function of this
retainer was to quarrel with the
cook ; in which respect he was
a perfect Whittington, without
his cat, or the remotest chance of
being made a Lord Mayor.

PAGE. A dissipated, Of the Pockets'.
                              G. E. xxiii.
   Who had nearly lost half his
buttons at the gaming-table.

PAILLASSE.   *M. P., R. D.*

PAINE. Thomas, The spirit of.
                              M. P., S. B.

PAINTER   AND   DECORATOR'S
JOURNEYMAN.
              S. B. B., *C*har. viii.
   Husband of Miss Martin's friend.

PAINTED GROUND.   *P. P.* xli.
   From the fact of its walls
having once displayed the sem-
blances of various men-of-war in
full sail, and other artistical effects,
achieved in bygone times by
some imprisoned draughtsman in
his leisure hours.

PALACE.   *M. H. C.* i.

PALACE. Farnese.
              P. F. I., P. M. B.

PALACE COURT.   *L. D.* vii.

PALACE YARD. *B. R.* xliii. ; *M. P.*
   O. C.; *O. M. F.* iii. ; *S. B. B.*,
                        Scenes xviii.

PALACES. Royal.   *B. R.* lxvii.

PALAIS ROYAL. *M. P., N. Y. D.* ;
              R. P., A. F. ; *U. T.* vii.

PALAIS ROYAL. Theatre of the.
              M. P., N. Y. D.

PALEY. Poor.   *M. P., R. S. D.*

PALL MALL. *C. S., G. i. S.* ; *C. S.*,
   W. o. G. M. ; *M. C.* xxvii. ;
   M. P., B. A. ; *M. P., C.* ; *M. P.*,
   T. D. ; *O. M. F.* xliv. ; *R. P.*,
   B. S. ; *S. B. B.*, *C*har. i. ; *U. T.*
                              xvi.

PALL MALL. *C*lubmen of.
              M. P., P. M. B.

PALMAS. *C*ape.   *M. P., N. E.*

PALMER. Mr.   *M. P., B. A.* ;
   M. P., M. P. ; *M. P., S. F. A.*

PALMERSTON. Lord.
   M. P., I. ; *M. P., T. B.* ;
              M. P., T. O. H.

PANCKS. Mr., Mr. Casby's agent.
                              L. D. xiii.
   Short dark man—dressed in
black and rusty iron-grey ; had
jet-black beads of eyes ; a scrubby
little black chin ; wiry black
hair striking out from his head in
prongs, like forks or hairpins—
dirty hands, and dirty broken
nails—snorted and sniffed and
puffed and blew, like a labouring
steam-engine.
   Note.—Mr. Casby's agent. He is
moral whipping-boy to the Patriarch.
He squeezes the tenants of Bleeding
Heart Yard, who are quite sure that if
only Mr. Casby knew he would dis-
approve. But when Pancks returns
from collecting rents, the Patriarch

Left margin notes:

I., P. M. B.

D. vii

M. P.
S. B. B.
...nes xviii

B. R. lxvii.

.. Y. Y. D.
T. vii

:e of the
Y. D

S. D.

.. i.; U. T

of.

P.. S. F. A

P., T. B.;
P., T. O. R.

's agent
L. D. xii.
...ssed i
...y; had
.. scrubbi
..y black
.. head t
hairpins—
..y broke
...d an
labourin

.. He i
Patriard
..f Bleedin:
cure that
would do
..s return
Patriard

---

grumbles because he has not squeezed enough. He assists very much in the discovery of Rigaud, and is a friend of Arthur Clennam. Before leaving Casby's employment he shows the Patriarch in his true colours to the people of the yard.

PANCRAS ROAD.
　　　　　　S. B. B., Char. iv.

PANGLOSS. Officer of Circumlocution Office. 　　*U. T.* viii.

PANIZZI. Signor. 　*M. P., N. J. B.*

PANKEY. Miss, Boarder at Mrs. Pipchin's. 　　*D. and S.* viii.
A mild, little blue-eyed morsel of a child, who was shampooed every morning, and seemed in danger of being rubbed away altogether.

PANKEY'S FOLKS. The little, Boarders at Mrs. Pipchin's.
　　　　　　D. and S. lix.

PANTALOON. On the stage in the Britannia. 　　*U. T.* iv.

PANTHEON. At Rome.
　　P. F. I., R.; R. P., A. P. A.

PAOLINA CAPELLA. A chapel.
　　　　　　P. F. I., R.

PAPA'S. Grave,
　　　　　　S. B. B., O. P. ii.

PAPER-BUILDINGS. 　*B. R.* xv.
A row of goodly tenements shaded in front by ancient trees, and looking at the back upon the Temple Gardens.

PAPER-BUILDINGS. 　*See also* Temple.

PAPERS. Boy at Smith's bookstall.
　　　　　　C. S., M. J. v.

PARADIS. Hôtel du.
　　　　　　P. F. I., A. G.

PARDIGGLE. Francis. 　*B. H.* viii.

PARDIGGLE. Mr. O. A., F.R.S., Husband of Mrs. Pardiggle.
　　　　　　B. H. viii.
Mr. Pardiggle brings up the rear. . . . An obstinate-looking man with a large waistcoat and stubby hair.

Note.—A member of the charitable army who make a lot of noise and do little work. Occupies no important place in the story, and is chiefly of interest as the friend of the Jellybys.

PARDIGGLE. Mrs. Distinguished for rapacious benevolence.
　　　　　　B. H. viii.
A formidable style of lady, with spectacles, a prominent nose, and a loud voice—I am a school lady, a visiting lady, a reading lady, a distributing lady, I am on the local Linen Box Committee, and many general committees.

Note.—Wife of Mr. Pardiggle and like him. She makes her children charitable, much to their disgust.

PARENTS. Of pupil of Miss Wade.
　　　　　　L. D. lvii.
Elderly people; people of station, and rich.

PARENTS OF PUPIL. Nephew of.
　　　　　　L. D. lvii.
Whom they had brought up . . . he began to pay me attention.

PARIS. 　*B. H.* ii.; *B. R.* xliii.; *C. S., M. L. Leg* i.; *L. D.* xi.; *M. P., A. in E.*; *M. P., E. S.*; *M. P., I.*; *M. P., M. M.*; *M. P., N. J. B.*; *M. P., N. Y. D.*; *M. P., O. F. A.*; *M. P., T. O. H.*; *M. P., W.*; *O. M. F.* xii.; *P. F. I., G. T. F.*; *R. P., A. F.*; *R. P., L. A.*; *R. P., M. O. F. F.*; *R. P., O. o. T.*; *T. T. C., U. T.* iv.

PARIS. *Boulevarts* in.
　　　　　　U. T. xxiii.

PARIS. Cafe of. 　*M. P., N. Y. D.*

PARIS. Inns of. 　　*C. S., H. T.*
With the pretty apartment of

four pieces up one hundred and seventy-five waxed stairs—and the not-too-much-for-dinner, considering the price.

PARIS. The Moon. *M. P., R. D.*

PARISH. Our, The parish.
　　　　　S. B. B., O. P. i.
How much is conveyed in these two short words "The Parish"—with how many tales of distress and misery of broken fortune and ruined hopes are they associated.

PARK. People's, Near Birmingham.
　　　　　N. T. xxiii.

PARK. The. *L. D.* x.; *O. M. F.* xxxv.; *P. P.* xxxv.; *R. P., P. R. S.*

PARK LANE. ' *L. D.* xxvii.; *M. C.* xiii.; *N. N.* xxxii.; *R. P., O. o. T.*

PARK. Mungo. *M. P., L. A. V.* ii.

PARK THEATRE. The, New York.
　　　　　A. N. vi.

PARKER. A constable.
　　　　　R. P., D. W. I. F.

PARKER. Mrs. Johnson.
　　　　　S. B. B., O. P. vi.
President of Ladies' Bible and Prayer-Book Distribution Society.

PARKER. Pilot.
　　　　　R. P., D. W. I. F.

PARKER. The Misses Johnson, (seven).　　　*S. B. B., O. P.* vi.
Treasurers, auditors, and secretary of the Ladies' Bible and Prayer Book Distribution Society.

PARKER. Theodore. *M. P., S. B.*

PARKER. Uncle, Inhabitant of Corner House.　　*O. M. F.* v.

PARKER HOUSE. Boston.
　　　　　M. P., I. W. M.

PARKES. Phil, The Ranger. *B. R.* i.

PARKINS.　　　　*R. P., O. B.*

PARKINS. Mrs., Laundress of chambers in the Temple.
　　　　　R. P., G. o. A.

PARKINS. Porter of chambers.
　　　　　R. P., G. o. A.

PARKINS' WIFE'S SISTER.
　　　　　R. P., O. B.

PARKLE. H., A young barrister.
　　　　　U. T. xiv.

PARKS. The.　　　*G. E.* xxii.

PARKS. The, The lungs of London.
　　　　　S. B. B., Scenes xii.

PARKS. Your.　　　*M. C.* xxi.

PARKSOP BROTHER. *G. S. E.* vi.

PARLIAMENT. Houses of=The club.　　　*M. P., N. G. K.*

PARLIAMENT. Of the United Kingdom.　　*M. C.* xvii.; *R. P., O. B.*

PARLIAMENT. Three members of, Attending public meeting at London Tavern.　　*N. N.* ii.
One Irish—one Scotch—the third who was at *Crockford's* all night . . . will certainly be with us to address the meeting . . . honourable gentleman in patent boots, lemon-coloured kid-gloves, and a fur coat-collar.

PARLIAMENT STREET.
　　B. R. xliv.; *M. P., M. E.*;
　　M. P., R. T.; *R. P., O. B.*

PARLIAMENTARY CINDER HEAP. Houses of Parliament.
　　　　　H. T., R. ix.

PARLOURMAID. Mrs. Steerforth's
　　　　　D. C. xxix.
Modest little parlourmaid with blue ribbons in her cap.

PARLOUR-MAID-IN-CHIEF. The, of the Nuns' House. *E. D.* iii.

PARLOURS. Birmingham, *Clubs.*
　　　　　R. P., P. M. T. P.

PARMA. *P. F. I.*, *P. M. B.*;
U. T. xxviii.

PARMARSTOON. Grand Vizier=
Twirling Weathercock. Lord Palmerston. *M. P.*, *T. O. H.*

PARROT. In "Happy Family."
M. P., *R. H. F.*

PARRY. *M. P.*, *L. A. V.* ii.;
M. P., *P. F. D.*; *M. P.*, *V. C.*

PARSON. Miss Letitia, Pupil at
Minerva House.
S. B. B., Tales iii.

PARSONAGE HOUSE. Formerly the
Mr. Boythorn's residence.
B. H. xviii.
With a lawn in front, a bright
flower-garden at the side, with a
well-stocked orchard and kitchen
garden in the rear, enclosed by a
venerable wall. The house—was
a real old house, with settles in
the chimney of the brick-floored
kitchen, and great beams across
the ceilings.
Original : Parsonage House,
Rockingham.

PARSONS. Mr., Gabriel, A rich
sugar-baker. *S. B. B.*, Tales x.
A short, elderly gentleman, with
a gruffish voice—who mistook
rudeness for honesty, and abrupt
bluntness for an open and candid
manner.

PARSONS. Mrs. *S. Y. C.*

PARSONS. Mrs. Gabriel.
S. B. B., Tales x.

PARSONS. Two itinerant Metho-
dist. *S. B. B.*, Tales xi.

PARTIES. Engaging boats at Searle's
S. B. B., Scenes x.

PARTRIDGE. Mr. *M. P.*, *S. B.*

PARTY. A regular, at Astley's.
S. B. B., Scenes xi.
At Easter or Midsummer holidays—Pa, Ma, nine or ten children,
varying from five foot six to two
foot eleven—from fourteen years
of age to four.

PARVIS. Old Arson, Old resident of
Laureau. *S. S.*, *M. f. T. S.* ii.
"One of old Parvis's fam'ly I
reckon," said the captain, "kept a
dry goods store in New York
City, and realised a handsome
competency by burning his house
to ashes."

PASSENGER. A regular, Of omnibus. *S. B. B.*, Scenes xvi.
A little testy old man, with a
powdered head, who always sits on
the right-hand side of the door as
you enter, with his hands folded
on the top of his umbrella.

PASSENGER. Another regular, In
omnibus. *S. B. B.*, Scenes xvi.
The shabby-genteel man with
the green bag.

PASSENGER. Another regular, In
omnibus. *S. B. B.*, Scenes xvi.
The stout gentleman in the
white neckcloth, at the other
end of the vehicle.

PASSENGER. Husband of a, On the
"Screw." *M. C.* xvii.
Not altogether dead, sir, but
he's had more fevers and agues
than is quite reconcileable with
being alive—a feeble old shadow
came creeping down.

PASSENGER. In omnibus.
S. B. B., Tales xi.
A little prim, wheezing old
gentleman.

PASSENGER. On board the " Esau
Slodge." *M. C.* xxxiv.
A tall, thin gentleman—with a
carpet-cap on, and a long loose
coat of green baize, ornamented
about the pockets with black
velvet.

PASSENGER. Of stage coach.
S. B. B., Scenes xvi.
A stout man, who had a glass of rum-and-water, warm, handed in at the window at every place where we changed horses.

PASSENGER. On coach. *N. N.* v.
A hearty-looking gentleman, with a very good-humoured face, and a very fresh colour.

PASSENGER. Outside, On early coach. *S. B. B.*, Scenes xv.
One old gentleman, and something in a cloak and cap, intended to represent a military officer.

PASSENGER. Outside, On early coach. *S. B. B.*, Scenes xv.
Thin young woman, cold and peevish—is got upon the roof, by dint of a great deal of pulling and pushing—and repays it by expressing her solemn conviction that she will never be able to get down again.

PASSENGERS. Coming in by early coach. *S. B. B.*, Scenes i.
Look blue and dismal.

PASSENGERS. Going out by early coach. *S. B. B.*, Scenes i.
Stare with astonishment at the passengers who are coming in by the early coach.

PASSENGERS. Inside, In early coach. *S. B. B.*, Scenes xv.

PASSENGERS. Of an omnibus.
S. B. B., Scenes xvi.
Change as often in the course of one journey as the figures in a kaleidoscope, and though not so glittering, are far more amusing.

PASSENGERS. Outside, On early coach. *S. B. B.*, Scenes xv.
Two young men with very long hair, to which the sleet has communicated the appearance of crystallised rats' tails.

PASSENGERS. Regular, In omnibus.
S. B. B., Scenes xvi.
Always take them up at the same places, and they generally occupy the same seats.

PASSENGERS. Woman and three children aboard the "Screw."
M. C. xv.
Making the voyage by herself with these young impediments here, and going such a way at this time of the year to join her husband.—He's been away from her for two year—she's been very poor and lonely—looking forward to meeting him.

PASSNIDGE. Mr., Friend of Mr. Murdstone. *D. C.* ii.

PASTORAL GARDENS. *B. H.* xix.

PASTRYCOOK. In funereal room in Brook Street. *D. and S.* xxxi.

PAT. Mr. *M. P., N. G. K.*

PATAGONIA. *M. P., L. A. V.* i.

PATENT OFFICE. In Lincoln's Inn.
R. P., P. M. T. P.

PATENT OFFICE. The, Washington. *A. N.* viii.

PATIENT. First, Of young medical Practitioner. *S. B. B., O. P.* i.
Stretched upon the bed, closely enveloped in a linen wrapper, and covered with blankets, lay a human form stiff and motionless. The head and face, which were those of a man, were uncovered, save by a bandage, which passed over the head and under the chin . . . The throat was swollen, and a livid mark encircled it. . . . One of the men who was hanged this morning.

PATIENT. The hospital.
S. B. B., Char. vi.

PATRIARCH. Mr. Monomaniacal,
M. P., G. B.

PATRIOT. A certain. *M. C.* xxi.
Who had declared from his high place in the Legislature, that he and his friends would hang, without trial, any Abolitionist who might pay them a visit.

PATRONESSES. The lady. *S. B. B.*, Scenes xix.
Of Indigent Orphans' Friends' Benevolent Institution.

PATTEN-MAKERS. The, Worshipful Company of. *M. H. C.* i.

PATTY. Maiden sister of John. *C. S., H. H.*
Eight-and-thirty, very handsome, sensible, and engaging—a woman of immense spirit.

PAUL. Jean. *M. P., N. T.*

PAUL'S CHURCHYARD. *P. P.* xliv.
See also Doctors' Commons.

PAUL'S WORK. Canongate. *M. P., S. P.*

PAVILIONSTONE. *R. P., O. o. T.*
A little smuggling town.
Original : Folkestone, where Dickens made a rather long stay at one time. The name is a compound of Pavilion (Hotel) and (Folke) stone.

PAVILIONSTONE STATION. *R. P., O. o. T.*

PAVIOURS. Two, French-Flemish. *U. T.* xxv.

PAWKINS. Major, Husband of Mrs. Pawkins. *M. C.* xvi.
A gentleman of Pennsylvanian origin, was distinguished by a very large skull, and a great mass of yellow forehead ;—a heavy eye, and a dull, slow manner. In commercial affairs he was a bold speculator—in plainer words, he had a most distinguished genius for swindling.

PAWKINS. Mrs., Kept a boarding-house . . . was very straight, bony, and silent. *M. C.* xvi.

PAWKINS'. Major, House. *M. C.* xvi.
A rather mean-looking house with jalousie blinds to every window ; a flight of steps before the green street door ; a shining white ornament on the rails on either side like a petrified pine-apple, polished ; a little oblong plate over the knocker, whereon the name of Pawkins was engraved.

PAWNBROKER'S. Near King's Bench Prison. *S. B. B.*, Scenes xxi.
First watches and rings, then cloaks, coats, and all the more expensive articles of dress have found their way to the pawn-broker's. Dressing-cases and writing-desks, too old to pawn, but too good to keep.

PAWNBROKER'S SHOP. Customers in. *S. B. B.*, Scenes xxiii.

PAWNBROKER'S SHOP. Little boxes in. *S. B. B.*, Scenes xxiii.
Little dens, or closets, which face the counter—here the more timid or respectable portion of the crowd shroud themselves from the notice of the remainder.

PAWNBROKER'S SHOP. The. *S. B. B.*, Scenes xxii.
Situated near Drury Lane, at the corner of a court, which affords a side entrance for the accommodation of such customers as may be desirous of avoiding the observation of the passers-by, or the chance of recognition in the public street. Tradition states that the transparency in the front door, which displays at night three red balls on a blue ground, once

bore also the words "Money advanced on plate, jewels, wearing apparel, and every description of property."

PAYNE. Surgeon. *P. P.* ii.
A portly personage in a braided surtout.

Note.—The fire-eating doctor who attended Dr. Slammer in the intended duel.

PAYNTER. My enemy.
M. P., N. Y. D.

PEACE. Name of bird. *B. H.* xiv.

PEACE SOCIETY. *M. P., P. F.*; *P. P.* xiii.; *N. N.* v.

PEACOAT. A Thames policeman. *R. P., D. W. T. T.*

"PEACOCK." The, An inn.
C. S., H. T.
A coaching-house at Islington.

PEAK. Mr. *C*hester's manservant. *B. R.* xxiii.
Note.—Sir John Chester's man-servant. He adapts himself so completely to his master's standard that on Sir John's death he decamps with everything portable and sets up as a man of fashion on his own account. His career in this rôle is not a long one, however, as he is apprehended and imprisoned.

PEAKS. The, Former name of Bleak House. *B. H.* viii.

"PEAL OF BELLS." Village ale-house. *C. S., T. T. G.* i.
Original : " The White Hart," *Stevenage.*

"PEAL OF BELLS." Landlord of the. *C. S., T. T. G.* i.

PEASANT WOMAN. Owner of apartments to let. *L. D.* lvi.
Strong, cheerful—all stocking, petticoat, white cap, and ear-ring.

PEASANTS. *P. F. I.*

PEBBLESON. Nephew. *N. T.*, Act i.

PECKHAM. *D. and S.* iv. ; *M.P., E. T.* ; *M. P., W. R.* ; *U. T.* vi.

PECKSNIFF. Mr. Seth, Architect and land surveyor. *M. C.* ii.
Was a moral man ; a grave man, a man of noble sentiments, and speech. He was a most exemplary man : fuller of virtuous precepts than a copy-book. His hair just grizzled, with an iron-grey —stood bolt upright, or slightly drooped in kindred action with his heavy eyelids.—His very throat was moral. You saw a good deal of it. You looked over a very low fence of white cravat—and there it lay, a valley between two jutting heights of collar, serene and whiskerless before you.

Note.—Cousin of old Martin Chuzzlewit. He is an architect and surveyor near Salisbury, living, however, on the labours and fees of his pupils and his reputation for respectability. He calls a meeting of the family at his house, while old Martin is lying ill at "The Dragon." Martin is the rich relative from whom all have expectations. Thinking to advance his interests with the old man, Pecksniff takes young Martin into his house to learn architecture. On a hint from old Martin that this course does not please him, he turns his young kinsman out of doors. Old Martin Chuzzlewit then comes to reside with him, and gives him to understand that he will inherit the largest portion of his wealth. He simulates senility and allows himself to be dominated by Pecksniff, who fawns on him and abases himself continually. On his return from America in company with Mark Tapley, young Martin finds Pecksniff receiving encomiums on the designs for a grammar school which Martin himself drew while he was with Pecksniff. This point of the story is somewhat impossible from a professional point of view, but it adds to the interest of the narrative and shows the development of Pecksniff's character. Still acting under the impression that he is studying the grandfather's desires, he repulses Martin. Ultimately his hypocrisy is laid bare by old Martin, his daughters are left unhappy and unfortunate, while he ends his days poverty-stricken in the curse of drink.

Original : May have been suggested by Pugin, as Pecksniff's house was built by that architect. But generally believed to be Mr. S. C. Hall, at one time of the "Art Journal."

PECKSNIFF. Miss Charity, Daughter of Pecksniff.   *M. C.* ii.

Miss Pecksniff's nose—was always very red at breakfast-time. For the most part, indeed, it wore at that season of the day a scraped and frosty look, as if it had been rasped ; "Charity," said Mr. Pecksniff, "is remarkable for strong sense, and for rather a deep tone of sentiment."

Note.—The elder daughter of Pecksniff was the replica of her father. Throughout our acquaintance with her she is a hypocritical shrew. She becomes betrothed to Mr. Moddle, one of Mrs. Todger's boarders. The house is furnished, the wedding breakfast is ready, and the guests, who have been invited by Cherry to witness her triumph are waiting, when a letter is received from Mr. Moddle announcing the fact that he has run away. Cherry is last seen in company with her father living on the charity of Tom Pinch.

PECKSNIFF. Miss Mercy, Younger daughter of Mr. Pecksniff.
                    M. C. ii.

She was the most arch, and at the same time the most artless creature—she was too fresh and guileless, and too full of childlike vivacity—to wear combs in her hair, or to turn it up or to frizzle it or braid it. She wore it in a crop, a loosely flowing crop which had so many rows of curls in it, that the top row was only one curl. Moderately buxom was her shape, and quite womanly too ; but sometimes she even wore a pinafore.

Note.—" Merry " Pecksniff, although

filled with much the same falsities as her father, had some redeeming traits, or, at all events, she excites some sympathy on account of the terrible suffering she experienced after her marriage to Jonas Chuzzlewit. She enters into wedlock with him for a variety of reasons, none of which was a good one. After the wedding she sees her husband as he is, and he does not find it so very difficult a task to " break her spirit ! " The trial purifies her nature, and she is last seen leaving Mrs. Todger's boarding-house with old Martin Chuzzlewit, who has determined to befriend her.

*Original of Pecksniff's house :
"St. Mary's Grange" on the Southampton Road from Salisbury. A red-brick building built by Pugin. Or it has been suggested as on the road to Wilsford, at Amesbury, with a path to the north-west corner of the churchyard.*

PEDDLE AND POOL. Solicitors.
                    L. D. xxxvi.

PEECHER. Miss Emma, Schoolmistress.   *O. M. F.* xviii.

Small, shining, neat, methodical, and buxom—cheery-cheeked and tuneful of voice.

Note.—Mistress in the girls' department at the school in which Bradley Headstone is master of the boys. She loves Bradley, but he has no affection for her, so she sighs in secret.

PEECHER. Miss, Schoolhouse of.
                    O. M. F. xviii.

Her small official residence, with little windows like the eyes in needles, and little doors like the covers of schoolbooks—dusty little bit of garden attached.

PEEL. Mr. Frederick.
                    M. P., N. J. B. ; *M. P., C. P.*

PEEL. Sir Robert.
                    M. P., T. D. ; *M. P., E. R.*

PEEPER. New York.   *M. C.* xvi.

PEEPY. The honourable Miss.
                    R. P., O. E. W.

The beauty of her day.

PEER. The old, Another frequenter of Bellamy's. *S. B. B.*, Scenes xviii.
Old man—his peerage is of comparatively recent date—has a huge tumbler of hot punch brought him.

PEERS. M.P.'s.
S. B. B., Scenes xviii.

PEERS. House of. *M. P., G. B.*

PEERYBINGLE. Mr. John, *C*arrier.
C. B., C. o. H. i.
Lumbering, slow, honest—so rough upon the surface, but so gentle at the core.

PEERYBINGLE. Mrs., Wife of *C*arrier Peerybingle.
C. B., C. o. H. i.
Fair and young : though something of the dumpling shape.

PEERYBINGLE. Young, Infant son of carrier. *C. B., C. o. H.* ii.

PEFFER. Deceased partner of Peffer and Snagsby. *B. H.* x.
Has been recumbent this quarter of a century in the churchyard.

PEFFER AND SNAGSBY. Law stationers. *B. H.* x.

" PEGASUS'S ARMS." Public house.
H. T., S. vi.
Underneath the winged horse, upon the signboard, " The Pegasus's Arms " was inscribed in Roman letters.

Original : The inscription on the inn at which Sleary and his circus put up, has been traced to the " Malt Shovel " at the foot of Chatham Hill.

PEGG. A male crimp. *U. T.* v.
In a checked shirt, and without a coat

PEGG. Mrs., Wife of Pegg, a female crimp. *U. T.* v.
A crouching old woman, like the

picture of the Norwood gipsy in the old sixpenny dream-books.

PEGGOTTY. *C*lara, David's nurse
D. C. i
There was a red velvet footstoo in the best parlour, on which my mother had painted a nosegay The ground-work of that stoo and Peggotty's complexion ap peared to me to be one and the same thing. The stool was smooth and Peggotty was rough, but tha made no difference.

Note.—Peggotty is the homely bu kindly, good-hearted servant to Mrs Copperfield, and nurse to David. On her mistress' marriage to Murdstone she loses some of her influence, and when Mrs. Copperfield dies she is dis charged. She then marries Barkis, the carrier. Barkis is somewhat miserl in his way and leaves Peggotty, on hi death, with a fair sum. Part of thi Peggotty wants to hand over to Davi on his aunt's loss of fortune. Peggott sticks to them in the end and " alway . . . comes Peggotty, my good ol nurse . . . accustomed to do needle work at night very close to the lamp.

Original : Generally believe to have been founded on Dickens own nurse, Mary Weller, " wh afterwards married Thomas Gibson a shipwright in the (Chatham Dockyard."

PEGGOTTY. Daniel, *C*lara Peg gotty's brother. *D. C.* i
A hairy man with a very good natured face.

Note.—Brother of Peggotty, David nurse. He lives at Yarmouth in a boa converted into a house, with his ne phew Ham, his niece Emily, and Mr Gummidge. He is last seen whe David goes to Yarmouth while h mother is being married to Mr. Murd stone. Later on David visits thei again with Steerforth. The latte brings about the ruin of Little Emil and Dan'l sets forth to find her. H travels for months on his search,' n one knows where, until David mee him in London one day and learns th he has travelled over a great part of t Continent, " mostly a-foot," in h search for his poor niece. Eventually he succeeds in finding her and they emigrate to Australia, where they prosper and Emily is able in some measure to forget the earlier happenings. Dan'l returns once to England and visits David.

Original of the house : Sometimes believed to have been the " old, inverted boat, bricked up and roofed in, which revealed itself in 1879, *during the process of demolition."*

PEGGOTTY. Ham, The intended husband of Little Em'ly. *D. C.* i.

A huge, strong fellow of six feet high, broad in proportion, and round-shouldered ; but with a simpering boy's face and curly light hair.

Note.—Ham was Daniel's nephew. He is terribly upset when Emily runs away with Steerforth. When Steerforth and Emily part and the former is on his way to England the vessel is wrecked at Yarmouth. Ham attempts to rescue the passengers and endeavours to bring Steerforth to land. They are both drowned.

PEGGY.   *C. S., G. i. S.*

PEGGY. King Watkins the First's Lord Chamberlain.   *H. R.* ii.

PEGLER. Mrs., Bounderby's mother.   *H. T., G.* v.

"I have never said I was your mother. I have admired you at a distance—though his mother kept but a little village shop, he never forgot her, but pensioned me on thirty pound a year—only making the condition that I was to keep down in my own part."

PEGWELL BAY. *S. B. B.*, Tales iv.

PELL. Mr. Solomon, An attorney. *P. P.* xliii.

A fat, flabby, pale man, in a surtout, which looked green one moment and brown the next ; with a velvet collar of the same chameleon tints. His forehead was narrow, his face wide, his head large, and his nose all on one side,

as if Nature, indignant with the propensities she observed in him in his birth, had given it an angry tweak, which it had never recovered.

Note.—The rather disreputable attorney who undertook Sam Weller's "business" in confining himself in prison with Mr. Pickwick.

PELL. Mrs., A widow—deceased. *P. P.* lv.

A splendid woman, with a noble shape, and a nose formed to command and be majestic.

PELTEER.   *M. P., L. A. V.* i.

PELTIROGUS. Horatio, Supposed suitor for Kate Nickleby's hand. *N. N.* lv.

A young gentleman who might have been, at that time, about four years old, or thereabouts.

PELTIROGUSES. The, *N. N.* xlv.

PENITENTIARY. The. *S. B. B.*, Scenes x.

PENKRIDGE.   *M. P., E. S.*

PENNSYLVANIA. *A. N.* xvii. ; *M. P., P. P.*

PENREWEN. Old resident of Laureau.   *C. S., M. f.* T. *S.* ii.

PENRITH.   *C. S., W. O. G. M.*

PENSIONER. Greenwich, with an empty coat-sleeve. *U. T.* xxvii.

His coat-buttons were extremely bright, he wore his empty coat-sleeve in a graceful festoon, and he had a walking-stick in his hand that must have cost money.

PENSIONER. Mrs. G., Late Mitts. Ex-occupant of Titbull's Almshouses.   *U. T.* xxvii.

PENSIONERS. Old, Of Greenwich. *S. B. B.*, Scenes xii.

Who for the moderate charge of

a penny exhibit the mast house, the Thames and shipping, the place where the men used to hang in chains, and other interesting sights, through a telescope.

PENSON. Mrs. W., as Mrs. Noakes.
M. P., S. G.

PENTON PLACE. Pentonville.
B. H. ix.

PENTONVILLE. *L. D.* xiii.; *M. P., P. F.*; *M. P., P. P.*; *O. T.* xii.; *P. P.* ii.; *S. B. B.*, Char. iv.; *S. B. B.*, Tales xi.; *U. T.* xiv.

PEOPLE. Busy, Seeing Mark Tapley off. *M. C.* vii.

PEOPLE. Government office,
S. B. B., O. P. vii.
In light drabs, and starched cravats, little, spare, priggish men.

PEOPLE. Married, At tea gardens.
S. B. B., Scenes ix.

PEOPLE. Of the United States.
M. P., Y. M. C.

PEOPLE. On Sands at Ramsgate.
S. B. B., Tales iv.
The ladies were employed in needlework, or watch-guard making, or knitting, or reading novels; the gentlemen were reading newspapers and magazines; the children were digging holes in the sand. The nursemaids, with their youngest charges in their arms, were running in after the waves, and then running back with the waves after them.

PEOPLE. Several, Young and old.
M. C. xxxi.

PEOPLE. Shabby-genteel.
S. B. B., Char. x.
You meet them, every day, in the streets of London—they seem indigenous to the soil, and to belong as exclusively to London as its own smoke, or the dingy bricks

and mortar. This shabby gentility is as purely local as the statue at Charing Cross or the pump at Aldgate. It is worthy of remark, too, that only men are shabby-genteel—a woman is always either dirty and slovenly — or neat and respectable, however poverty-stricken in appearance.

PEOPLE'S THEATRE = Eagle Saloon. *M. P., A. P.*

PEPLOW. Husband of Mrs.
S. B. B., Scenes ii.

PEPLOW. Master, Son of Mrs. Peplow. *S. B. B.*, Scenes ii.

PEPLOW. Mrs.
S. B. B., Scenes ii.

PEPPER. Pip's "Boots."
G. E. xxvii.
Clothed him with a blue coat, canary waistcoat, white cravat, creamy breeches, and the boots already mentioned.

PEPS. Doctor Parker, Attending Mrs. Dombey. *D. and S.* i.
One of the court physicians, and a man of immense reputation for assisting at the increase of great families.

PEPYS. Mr. *M. P., L. L.*

PERCH. Mrs., Wife of Dombey's messenger. *D. and S.* xiii.

PERCH. The messenger at Dombey and Son's. *D. and S.* xiii.
Whose place was on a little bracket like a timepiece. When Perch saw Mr. Dombey come in— —or rather when he felt that he was coming, for he had usually an instinctive sense of his approach—he hurried into Mr. Dombey's room, stirred the fire, quarried fresh coals from the bowels of the coal-box, hung the newspapers to air upon the fender, put

the chair ready, and the screen in its place, and was round upon his heel on the instant of Mr. Dombey's entrance, to take his great-coat and hat, and hang them up.

PERCY. Lord Algernon.
B. R. lxvii.
Commanding Northumberland militia.

PERCY STREET.
S. B. B., Char. ix.

PERKER. Mr., of Gray's Inn., Mr. Pickwick's lawyer. *P. P.* x.
He was a little, high-dried man. with a dark, squeezed-up face, and small, restless, black eyes, that kept winking and twinkling, on each side of his little inquisitive nose, as if they were playing a perpetual game of peep-bo with that feature.
Note.—The little attorney who first appears as the election-agent of Slumkey, the "Blue" candidate in the Eatanswill election, and afterwards conducts Mr. Pickwick's side of the Bardell v. Pickwick case.
Original: Founded on Mr. Ellis of Ellis and Blackmore, where Dickens was at one time employed. Also said to have been founded on a man at Sudbury.

PERKINS. A general dealer.
C. S., H. H.

PERKINS. Mrs. *B. H.* xi.

PERKINS. Mrs. *M. C.* xix.

PERKINS. Young. *B. H.* xi.

PERKINS'S BROTHER-IN-LAW.
C. S., H. H.
A whip and harness-maker, who keeps the post office, and is under submission to a most rigorous wife of the Doubly Seceding Little Emmanuel persuasion.

PERKINS INSTITUTION and Massachusetts Asylum for the Blind at Boston. *A. N.* iii.

PERKINSOP. Mary Anne, Mrs. Lirriper's maid.
C. S., M. L. Lo. i.

PERRIN BROTHERS. Clockmakers.
C. S., N. T., Act iv.

PERSIA. *M. P., S. R.*

PERSON. Hired by Smallweed.
B. H. xxvi.
One of those extraordinary specimens of fungus that spring up spontaneously in the western streets of London.

PERSON. A roving, Member of Mr. V. Crummles' Company.
N. N. xxiii.
In a rough great-coat, who strode up and down in front of the lamps, flourishing a dress-cane, and rattling away in an undertone, with great vivacity—for the amusement of an ideal audience.

PERSONAGE. Elderly, Frequenting "The Peacock." *P. P.* xiv.
With a dirty face and a clay pipe.

PERSONAGES. Several, Eminent and distinguished. *P. P.* xlvii.

PERSONS. Another class of.
P. P. xl.
Waiting to attend summonses their employers had taken out, which it was optional to the attorney on the other side to attend or not—and whose business it was, from time to time, to cry out the opposite attorney's name; to make certain that he was not in attendance without their knowledge.

PERT. Miss Scornful, Pussy.
E. D. ii.

PERUGIA. *P. F. I., R. D.*

PESSELL AND MORTAIR. Messrs.
Mud. Pap. ii.

PET. Family, A burglar. *O. T.* xxxi.

PETER. Lord.
S. B. B., Tales viii.
An imbecile lord, for whom Mr.
Alexander Trott was mistaken.

PETERSHAM. Surrey. N. N. 1.

PETO AND BRASSEY. Messrs.
U. T. xxiv.

PETOWKER. Miss, of the Theatre
Royal, Drury Lane. N. N. xiv.
Young lady, daughter of a
theatrical fireman, who " went on"
in the pantomime, and had the
greatest turn. for the stage that
ever was known.

Note.—A friend of the Kenwigses.
Captivates Mr. Lillyvick, the collector,
and marries him. But she tires of her
husband and runs off with a half-pay
captain. Lillyvick utterly renounces
her in the presence of the assembled
Kenwigses.

PETTIFER. Tom., *Captain Jor-*
gan's Steward.
C. S., M. f. T. S. i.
"Afraid of a sunstroke in England in November, Tom, that you
wear your tropical hat, strongly
paid outside and paper-lined inside, here ? " said the captain.
A man of a certain plump neatness, with a curly whisker, and
elaborately nautical in a jacket,
and shoes, and all things correspondent.

PEW-OPENER. In church where
Paul Dombey was christened.
D. and S. v.
A wheezy little pew-opener,
afflicted with asthma—went about
the building coughing like a gram-
pus.

PEW-OPENER. Of church where
Walter and Florence are married.
D. and S. lvii.
A dusty old pew-opener, who
only keeps herself, and finds that
quite enough to do.

PEW-OPENER. The.
S. B. B., O. P. vi.

PHANTOM. Image of Redlaw,
Dead. C. B., H. M. i.

PHANTOM. Sister of, Late sister
of Redlaw. C. B., H. M. i.

PHARISEE. Rev. Temple.
M. P., G. B.

PHELPS. Dr., House of at Stratford, Connecticut. M. P., R. S. D.

PHELPS. Mr., Actor.
M. P., M. B.

" PHIB." Miss Squeers' handmaid.
N. N. xii.
The name " Phib " was used as
a patronising abbreviation.

PHIBBS. Mr., Haberdasher.
R. P., T. D. A. i.

PHIL. B. H. xxvi.
What with being scorched in an
accident at a gasworks ; and
what with being blowed out of
winder, case-filling, at the fire-
work business ; I am ugly enough
to be made a show on.
See Squod, Phil.

PHIL. Serving-man in Our School.
R. P., O. S.

PHILADELPHIA. A. N. vii. ;
M. P., I. W. M. ; M. P., P. P. ;
M. P., S. B. ; U. T. xxiii.

PHILANTHROPISTS. Body of
professing. E. D. vi.

PHILANTHROPISTS. Convened
chief. E. D. vi.
Composite Committee of Central
and District.

PHILANTHROPY. Haven of.
E. D. vi.

PHILHARMONIC SOCIETY.
M. P., M. M.

PHILLIPS. Mr. M. P., E. T.

PHILLIPS. Mr. Commissioner.
M. P., I. M.

PHILLIPS. Mr. R., as Father
Francis. M. P., N. T.

PHILLIPS. The constable.
B. R. lxi.

PHILOSEWERS. My friend.
M. P., P. M. B.

PHOEBE. Lamps' daughter.
C. S., M. J. ii.
Lay on a couch that brought
her face to a level with the window.
The couch was white, and her
simple dress or wrapper being
light blue, like the band around
her hair, she had an ethereal look,
and a fanciful appearance of
lying among clouds.

PHOEBE. Mother of, Deceased.
C. S., M. J. iii.
Who died when she (Phoebe)
was a year and two months old,
was subject to very bad fits—
she dropped the baby when "took."

PHOEBE. The biggest scholar of.
C. S., M. J. iii.
The domestic of the cottage,
had come to take active measures
in it, attended by a pail that
might have extinguished her, and
a broom three times her height.

PHUNKY. Mr., junior, barrister
for Pickwick. P. P., xxxi.
Although an infant barrister,
he was a full-grown man. He had
a very nervous manner, and a
painful hesitation in his speech;
arising from the consciousness of
being "kept down" by want of
means, or interest, or connection,
or impudence as the case might be.

Note.—The "infant" barrister of
little more than eight years' standing
—junior counsel with Serjeant Snubbin
in Mr. Pickwick's case.

PHYSICIAN. The great. L. D. lxi.

PHYSICIAN. Famous. L. D. xxi.
In attendance on Mr. Merdle.

PHYSICIAN. Daughter of a,
C. S., S. L. ii.
In an open carriage, with four
gorgeously attired servitors—in
massive gold ear-rings, and blue-
feathered hat, shaded from the sun
by two immense umbrellas of
artificial roses.

PHYSICIAN'S GUESTS. At dinner
party. L. D. lxi.

PHYSIOGNOMIST. The changer
of countenances. U. T. xxv.

PIACENZA. P. F. I., P. M. B.

PIAZZA. M. P., W. S. G.

PIAZZA. Great, in Padua.
P. F. I., A. I. D.

PIAZZA HOTEL. In Covent
Garden. D. C., xxiv.; N. U. xiii.
Original: The Tavistock in
Covent Garden.

PIAZZA. The, Parma.
P. F. I., P. M. B.

PIAZZA. The, Rome. P. F. I., R.

PIAZZO OF THE GRAND DUKE.
Florence. P. F. I., R. D.

PICCADILLY. B. R. lxvii.; C. S.,
S. L. iii.; C. S., T. G. S. i.;
D. C. xxviii.; M. P., A. P.;
M. P., N. J. B.; M. P., T. D.;
M. P., T. T.; N. N. lxiv.;
O. M. F. x.; R. P., D. W. I. F.;
S. B. B., Scenes i.

PICHLYM. A chief of the Choctaw
tribe of Indians. A. N. xii.

PICKFORD. U. T. xii.

PICKLE OF PORTICI. Mr., A
tourist. P. F. I., R. D.

PICKLES. Mr., A fishmonger.
H. R. ii.

PICKLESON. Rinaldo di Velasco.
C. S., D. M.

PICKWICK. Samuel, General chairman and founder of the Pickwick Club, and central figure of the *Pickwick Papers.* *P. P.* i.

The eloquent Pickwick, with one hand gracefully concealed behind his coat-tails, and the other waving in air, to assist his glowing declamation; his elevated position revealing those tights and gaiters, which, had they clothed an ordinary man, might have passed without observation, but which, when Pickwick " clothed them "— if we may use the expression— inspired voluntary awe and respect.

Note.—The founder of the club from which the Papers take their rise. Originally a somewhat eccentric and almost unlovable character, he develops into a genial, jolly old gentleman. The gradual change was intentional, or at all events Dickens was aware of it. We are first introduced to the General Chairman of the Pickwick Club, at a club meeting, but the fabric of the club as a vehicle for the episodes of the story is soon relinquished. The reason for this is explained in the preface to " Pickwick," but it is too lengthy for insertion here. When in London, Mr. Pickwick resided in Goswell Road, but except for the incident giving rise to the " Trial," neither the lodgings nor the landlady are essential. Most of the adventures take place in Kent, Bath, or in the various parts of London. Reference may be made to the places the Pickwickians visited and the friends and enemies they met and made. The outline of the story, so far as it is a connected story and has an outline, is this : Mr. Pickwick, accompanied by Tupman, Snodgrass, and Winkle, sets out on his travels. Their first objective is Rochester, and the Three Towns. While attending a grand review at Chatham they meet Mr. Wardle and his family. (*See* Dingley Dell, and Muggleton). Later on they set out on an expedition to Eatanswill—*which see.* The breach of promise case between Mrs. Bardell and Mr. Pickwick is the most connected theme of the book, and is the medium

for some of the best descriptions of law life and court practice of the time. The Bath expedition is of value, as it contains a small piece of corroborative evidence regarding the house in which Dickens spent the honeymoon of his marriage in 1836. The Manor House, at Chalk, is usually described as that in which the then young and little-known author spent his honeymoon and wrote some of the earlier chapters of Pickwick, but evidence, brought to light during the last two years, or thereabouts, points to a small weatherboarded cottage not far distant from the Manor House, as the place. Stated succinctly, the evidence is as follows : Witnesses in the village of Chalk testified that no young married couple stayed at the Manor House in 1836, while such an event occurred at the cottage. The Manor House was then in the occupation of a French surgeon M. Lereaux, a gentleman of means who did not take lodgers, while Mrs. Craddock, the landlady of the cottage, did " do for them." The belief, the outcome of an ignorant mixing of the character with the author, still exists in the village, that Mr. Pickwick stayed at the unpretentious cottage. Mr. Pickwick refuses to pay costs and damages in the breach of promise case, and spends some time in the Fleet Prison. Dodson and Fogg, however, commit Mrs. Bardell to the same prison on her inability to pay her costs. This moves Mr. Pickwick to pay costs of both himself and Mrs. Bardell, and so effect the release of both. He resigns his membership of the Pickwick Club, which thereafter dissolves, and retires into private life at Dulwich.

And Fifth member of Master Humphrey's Club.
M. H. C. iii.

An elderly gentleman—the sun shining on his bald head, his bland face, his bright spectacles, his fawn-coloured tights, and his black gaiters. He has a secret pride in his legs.

Original : On the Bath Road there was at one time a Pickwick House as well as a Pickwick Lodge, and the Moses Pickwick, of coach fame, was picked up as a baby on the Bath Road, by a mail-coach guard who gave him the name he became so well known by.

Other suggestions are : (1) *A Mr. Pickwick kept the " White Hart " Inn at Bath in the last decade of the eighteenth century.*

(2) *Founded, in appearance at all events, on a friend of Mr. Chapman's, named John Foster, who lived at Richmond. So far as the name is concerned, it has been derived from Moses Pickwick, a coach-owner at Bath, This is mentioned in " Pickwick Papers," but it was nevertheless a fact.*

Original of Pickwick's house at Dulwich : Stands a stone's throw from Alleyn's almshouses.

PICKWICK CLUB. The imaginary club of which Mr. Pickwick was Grand Chairman. *P. P.*

Note.—The club was the suggestion of Mr. Edward Chapman or of Mr. Seymour, and was introduced by Dickens with some reluctance. Its influence and importance become less as the narrative progresses.

PIDGER. Mr., Once a suitor of Lavinia Spenlow. *D. C.* xli.
Who played short whist and would have declared his passion, if he had not been cut short in his youth (at about sixty) by over-drinking his constitution, and overdoing an attempt to set it right again by swilling Bath water.

PIEDMONTESE. *M. P., N. J. B.*

PIEDMONTESE OFFICERS.
P. F. I., G. A. N.

PIE-SHOP IN THE BOROUGH.
Civil man in. *L. D.* lxx.

PIEMAN. A, Selling brandy-balls.
B. H. xi.

PIEMEN. *S. B. B.*, Scenes. i.
Expiating on the excellence of their pastry.

PIER. Floating, at Greenwich.
O. M. F. liv.

PIERCE. Captain, Of the " Halse-well." *R. P., T. L.* v.

PIERCE. Miss Mary, One of Captain Pierce's daughters.
R. P., T. L. v.

PIERCE. Two daughters of Captain. *R. P., T. L.* v.
On board the " Halsewell."

PIFF. Miss, Of Mugby Junction Refreshment room staff.
C. S., M. J. v.

PIG AND TINDER-BOX.
Mud. Pap. i.

PIG-FACED LADY. *N. N.* xlix.
Original : Wonderful Miss Atkinson.

PIGEON. Mr. John.
R. P., T. D. P.

PIGEON. Mr. Thomas, Tally-Ho Thompson. *R. P., T. D. P.*

PIGGLEMU BUILDINGS.
R. P., O. V.

PILGRIMS. *P. F. I., R.*

PILKINS. Mr., Family practitioner to the Dombeys. *D. and S.* i.
Who had regularly puffed the case for the last six weeks, among all his patients, friends, and acquaintances, as one to which he was in hourly expectations day and night of being summoned in conjunction with Doctor Parker Peps.

PIMIKIN AND THOMAS'S. " Out o'door." *P. P.* xx.

PIMLICO. *N. N.* xliv.

PINCH. Mr. Tom. *M. C.* ii.
An ungainly, awkward-looking man, extremely short-sighted, prematurely bald—dressed in a snuff-coloured suit of an uncouth make at the best, which, being shrunk with long wear, was twisted and

tortured into all kinds of odd shapes; but notwithstanding his attire, his clumsy figure—and a ludicrous habit of thrusting his head forward—one would not have been disposed—to consider him a bad fellow by any means.

Note.—Tom Pinch was assistant and general factotum to Pecksniff. He was devoted to his master, whom he thought harshly judged by those who discovered his hypocrisy and his meanness of character. Later on, however, he himself sees Pecksniff in his true colours, and is discharged. He goes to London. Here he receives a mysterious appointment, through Mr. Fips, to arrange the library of an unknown benefactor. The "unknown" afterwards turns out to be old Martin Chuzzlewit.

PINCH. Ruth, Tom Pinch's sister.
M. C. vi.

Was governess in a family, a lofty family; perhaps the wealthiest brass - and - copper founder's family known to mankind. . . . She had a good face; a very mild and prepossessing face; and a pretty little figure—slight and short, but remarkable for its neatness.

Note.—Ruth is governess in a brass-founder's family at Camberwell. While she is there Pecksniff and his daughters visit her, with a fitting show of condescension. This results in her dismissal, and she then keeps house for her brother Tom. Ultimately she marries John Westlock, a former pupil of Pecksniff.

PINDAR. Peter.   *M. P., S. P.*

PINK. One of boating-crew training for racing.   *S. B. B.,* Scenes x.

PIP. Mr., Theatrical Man.
M. C. xxviii.

PIP. *See* Pirrip, Philip,

PIPCHIN.   *M. P., N. Y. D.*

PIPCHIN. Mrs., Keeper of infantine boarding-house.
D. and S. viii.

Who has for some time devoted all the energies of her mind, with the greatest success, to the study and treatment of infancy, and who has been extremely well connected. This celebrated Mrs. Pipchin was a marvellously ill-favoured, ill-conditioned old lady of a stooping figure, with a mottled face, like bad marble, a hook nose and a hard grey eye, that looked as if it might have been hammered at on an anvil without sustaining any injury.

Original : Founded on Mrs Roylance, Dickens' landlady in Little College Street, Camden Town, before he moved to Lant Street, while his father was in prison.

PIPCHIN'S HUSBAND. Mrs.
D. and S. viii.

Broke his heart—in pumping water out of the Peruvian mines.

PIPER. Alexander James, Son of Mrs. Piper.   *B. H.* xi.

PIPER. Mr., Husband of Mrs. Piper.   *B. H.* xi.

A cabinet maker.

PIPER. Mrs. Anastasia.   *B. H.* xi.

PIPER. Professor.
M. C. xxxiv.

PIPER. Young.   *B. H.* xi.

PIPKIN. Mr.   *Mud. Pap.* ii.

PIPKIN. Nathaniel.   *P. P.* xvii.

Parish clerk of the little town at a considerable distance from London. A harmless, inoffensive, good-natured being, with a turned-up nose, and rather turned-in legs, a cast in his eye, and a halt in his gait, and he divided his time between the church and his school.

PIPS. Mr., Of Camberwell.
M. P., N. G. K.

PIPSON. Miss, Pupil of Miss Griffin.
C. S ., H. H.

Having light curly hair and blue eyes.

PIRATES. Captain of the.
C. S., P. o. C. E. P.
A Portuguese ; a little man with very large ear-rings under a very broad hat, and a great bright shawl twisted about his shoulders.

PIRATES. One of the.
C. S., P. o. C. E. P.
One of the Convict Englishmen, with one eye, and patch across the nose.

PIRATES. The, Crowd of.
C. S., P. o. C. E. P.
Malays, Dutch, Maltese, Greeks, Sambos, Negroes, and Convict Englishmen from the West India Islands, some Portuguese, and a few Spaniards.

PIRATE CHACE PARTY. The.
C. S., P. o. C. E. P.

PIRRIP. Family name.   G. E. i.

PIRRIP. Deceased father of Philip.
G. E. i.
A square, stout, dark man, with curly black hair.

PIRRIP. Philip, An orphan.
G. E. i.
Brought up " by hand " by his sister—apprenticed to his brother-in-law as blacksmith—then educated for " great expectations," which failed, and finally became first clerk and then partner in Clarriker and Co.

Note.—The principal character. He is introduced, as quite a little fellow, brought up " by hand "; an orphan living with his sister and her husband. His sister treats him unkindly, but as her husband suffers in the same way, Pip, as the boy was called and he become fast companions in spite of the difference between their ages. While still a child Pip meets an escaped convict in the marshes who compels him by threats to procure food and a file for him. Some time after he goes to Miss Havisham to play. He is then apprenticed to his brother-in-law. Following that he receives great assistance from an unknown benefactor through Jaggers. He receives

a large allowance at once, with future " great expectations." After this good fortune he drifts away from his early friends. By the return of Magwitch he discovers that his unknown benefactor is not Miss Havisham, as he had thought, but the convict of his early childhood who has amassed wealth in New South Wales. Pip conquers his disgust to a large extent. Magwitch is recaptured and sentenced to death. The sentence is not carried out as he dies in prison, but his wealth is forfeited to the Crown. Pip thus finds himself not only without money but heavily in debt. When he recovers from a severe illness, brought on by his devotion to Magwitch in prison, he sells everything for the benefit of his creditors, and, finding that Biddy has married Joe, accepts Herbert's offer of a clerkship in Clarriker and Co., and eventually becomes a partner in the firm. In the end he marries Estella.

PISA.   P. F. I., R. P. S.

PITCAIRN'S ISLAND. R. P., T. L. V.

PITCHER. That young, A pupil of Squeers.   N. N. vii.

PITCHLYNN.   A. N. xii.

PITT. Miss, Jane.   R. P., T. S. S.

PITT. William. M. P., F. O. E. G.
See also Mistapit.

PITTSBURG.   A. N. vii.

PLACE.   C. S., S. L. ii.

PLAINS. The.   U. T. xx.

PLAINS OF ABRAHAM. Near Montreal.   A. N. xv.

PLANTER'S HOUSE. A large hotel in St. Louis.   A. N. xii.

PLASHWATER MILL WEIR LOCK.
O. M. F. xli.
Original : Henley Lock.

PLEADER. A special, from the Temple.   P. P. xlvii.

PLORNISH. Mrs. Sally, Wife of Plornish.   L. D. xii.
A young woman made some-

what slatternly in herself and her belongings by poverty, and so dragged at by poverty and the children together, that their united forces had already dragged her face into wrinkles.

PLORNISH. Thomas, Only a plasterer.   *L. D.* ix.

A smooth-cheeked, fresh-coloured, sandy-whiskered man of thirty. Long in the legs, yielding at the knees, foolish in the face, flannel-jacketed, lime-whitened.

Note.—A small plasterer making ends meet with difficulty. He lives in Bleeding Heart Yard, and is a tenant of Mr. Casby. They are befriended by Arthur Clennam, and when he is in a debtor's prison Mr. and Mrs. Plornish visit him.

PLORNISH'S HABITATION. In Bleeding Heart Yard. *L. D.* xii.

The last house in Bleeding Heart Yard—was a large house, let off to various tenants; but Plornish ingeniously hinted that he lived in the parlour, by means of a painted hand under his name, the forefinger of which—referred all inquirers to that apartment.

PLOW AN' HARRER. *O. C. S.* xv.

"There's travellers' lodging, I know, at the Plow an' Harrer."

PLUCK. Mr., Guest of Ralph Nickleby.   *N. N.* xix.

A gentleman with a flushed face, and a flash air.

PLUMMER. Blind daughter of Caleb.   *C. B., C. o. H.* ii.

PLUMMER. Caleb, A toymaker.
                                C. B., C. o. H. i.

A little, meagre, thoughtful, dingy-faced man, who seemed to have made himself a great-coat from the sackcloth covering of some old box—upon the back of that garment, the inscription G. and T. in large capital letters.

Also the word *Glass* in bold characters.

PLUMMER. Dear boy of Caleb.
                                C. B., C. o. H. i.

PLUMMER. Mrs. Edward, Née May Fielding.   *C. B., C. o. H.* iii.

PLUNDER. Name of a bird.
                                B. H. xiv.

PLUNDERER. New York.
                                M. C. xvi.

PLYMOUTH.   *B. H.* xxxvi.

PLYMOUTH HARBOUR.
                                B. H. xiii.

PLYMOUTH SOUND. *M. P., N. E.*

PO. The.   *P. F. I., T. B. F.;*
                                R. P. D. W. T. T.

POBBS. Miss.   *M. P., T. T.*

POCKET. Fanny, Daughter of Mr. Matthew Pocket.   *G. E.* xxiii.

POCKET. Joe, Son of Mr. Matthew Pocket.   *G. E.* xxiii.

POCKET. Master Alick, Son of Matthew Pocket.   *G. E.* xxii.

POCKET. Miss Jane, Daughter of Matthew Pocket.   *G. E.* xxii.

POCKET. Mr. Herbert, "A prospective Insurer of Ships."
                                G. E. xi.

A pale young gentleman with red eyelids and light hair—in a grey suit—with his elbows, knees, wrists and heels considerably in advance of the rest of him as to development.

Note.—Son of Matthew Pocket. First introduced as the pale young gentleman at Miss Havisham's who fights Pip. When Pip comes to London he lodges in Barnard's Inn with Herbert and they become very close friends. They both spend more than they should. Pip secures a partnership in Clarriker and Co. for Herbert, unknown to him. Herbert marries Clara Barley. They go abroad for the business.

POCKET. Mr. Matthew, Miss Havisham's cousin.   *G. E.* xviii.

A very young-looking man, in spite of his perplexities, and his very grey hair.

Note.—One of Miss Havisham's relatives—not of the self-seeking kind, and father of Herbert. Pip read with him for a time. Through Pip, Miss Havisham leaves him a cool four thousand.

POCKET. Mrs. Matthew.   *G. E.* xxii.

Highly ornamental, but perfectly helpless and useless. . . . Only daughter of a certain quite accidental deceased knight.

POCKET. Sarah.   *G. E.* xi.

A little, dry, brown, corrugated old woman, with a small face that might have been made out of walnut-shells, and a large mouth like a cat's, without the whiskers.

Note.—One of Miss Havisham's fawning relatives. Left with " twenty-five pound per annum fur to buy pills."

POCKET-BREACHES. Borough of.   *O. M. F.* xx.

POCKET-BREACHES. Branch Station.   *O. M. F.* xx.

POCKET BREACHES. Market.   *O. M. F.* xx.

Some onions and bootlaces under it [the town hall] which the legal gentleman says are a market.

POCKET-BREACHES. Town Hall of.   *O. M. F.* xx.

A feeble little town hall on crutches.

PODDEES. The girl " minder."   *O. M. F.* xvi.

PODDER. Mr., A most renowned member of the All-Muggletonians.   *P. P.* vii.

PODGERS. John, A widower.   *M. H. C.* iii.

Broad, sturdy, Dutch-built, short, and' a very hard eater—a hard sleeper likewise. The people of Windsor—held that John Podgers was a man of strong sound sense—not what is called smart—but still a man of solid parts.

PODGERS. Mr.   *L. T.* i.

POD'S END.   *H. T., S.* v.

PODSNAP. Mr., In the marine insurance way.   *O. M. F.* ii.

Two little light-coloured, wiry wings, one on either side of his else bald head, looking as like his hair-brushes as his hair, dissolving view of red beads on his forehead, large allowance of crumpled shirt-collar up behind.

Note.—The hook on which much of the book is hung, but of very little importance as an integral part of the story. He is last seen giving a dinner at which Eugene's marriage is discussed and condemned by the " voice " of society as represented by all present save Lightwood and Twemlow.

PODSNAP. Mrs.   *O. M. F.* ii.

Fine woman—quantity of bone, neck and nostrils like a rocking-horse, hard featured, majestic head-dress in which Podsnap has hung golden offerings.

PODSNAP. Miss Georgiana.   *O. M. F.* xi.

An undersized damsel, with high shoulders, low spirits, chilled elbows, and a rasped surface of nose.

Note.—Podsnap's daughter. She was taken in hand by the Lammles. And was at one time in danger from their machinations.

POFFIN.   *O. M. F.* xxv.

POGRAM. Elijah, Member of Congress.   *M. C.* xxxiv.

He had straight black hair, parted up the middle of his head, and hanging down upon his coat ; a little fringe of hair upon his chin.

Note.—A member of Congress met with on Martin's travels in America.

POISSY. *R. P., M. O. F. F.*

POLCEVERA. The river.
P. F. I., G. A. N.

POLICE. Assistant Commissioner of. *R. P., D. W. I. F.*

POLICE. Thames,
R. P., D. W. I. F.

POLICE. The, An excellent force.
U. T. xxxvi.

POLICE. The detective.
R. P., T. D. P.

POLICE. The new.
S. B. B., Char. i.

POLICE COMMISSIONER.
M. P., S. F. A.

POLICE FORCE. The Liverpool.
U. T. v.

POLICE-OFFICE. *N. N.* lx.

POLICE-OFFICE.
S. B. B., Scenes xvii.

POLICE-OFFICERS. *O. T.* vi.

POLICE-OFFICERS.
S. B. B., Scenes xvii.

POLICE-OFFICERS. Two.
B. H. lvii.

POLICE STATION.
O. M. F. lxiii.

POLICE STATION. *U. T.* xxxvi.

POLICEMAN. *B. H.* xi.
With his shining hat, stiff stock, inflexible great-coat, stout belt and bracelet, and all things fitting, pursues his. lounging way with a heavy tread, beating the palms

of his white gloves one against the other.

POLICEMAN. *M. P., P. L. U.*

POLICEMAN. An accoucheur.
G. E. iv.

POLICEMAN. Occasional.
S. B. B., Scenes i.
Listlessly gazing on the deserted prospect before him.

POLICEMEN. In attendance—in London Tavern. *N. N.* ii.

POLICEMEN. Two, on duty in the Good Hippopotamus' den.
M. P., G. H.

POLICINELLI. *P. F. I., R. D.*

POLL. *D. and S.* xxviii.

POLL. A suicide. *U. T.* iii.

POLLY. Daughter of old sweet-heart of Mr. Jackson (Barbox Brothers). *C. S., M. J.* iv.

POLLY. Schoolmaster's daughter.
C. S., M. L. Lo. ii.

POLLY. Waitress at " Slap Bang."
B. H. xx.
A bouncing young female of forty.

POLREATH. David, Old resident of Laureau. *C. S. M. f. T. S.* ii

POLYGON. The. *B. H.* xliii

POLYGLON. The. *P. P.* liii

POLYPHEMUS. The, Private West India trader. *D. and S.* iv.

POLYTECHNIC INSTITUTION. In Regent Street.
M. P., A. P. ; M. P., R. S. D.

POMPEII.
P. F. I., R. D. ; U. T. xxviii

POMPEY. A negro fellow—slave
A. N. xvii

PONT ESPRIT. *L. D.* xii

POODLE.

POOL. Lo

POOL. Th

POONEY.

POOR-HOU

POOR-LAW

POOR-LAW

POPE. Al

POPE. The

POPE OF R

POPES. Th

POPLAR.

POPLAR.

Taken shape by my moth born.

POPLAR \

POPLARS. House.
A solit sadly ne of about Second— mal, and possibly too close by tree poplars

POPOLO.

POODLE. *B. H.* xii.

POOL. Lower. Below Bridge.
G. E. xlvi.

POOL. The. *S. B. B.*, Tales vii.

POONEY. Mr., *C. D. S.*
M. P., W. R.

POOR-HOUSE. The, The House.
O. M. F. xvi.

POOR-LAW COMMISSIONERS.
M. P., P. T.

POOR-LAW INSPECTOR.
M. P., P. T.

POPE. Alick=Man of Ross.
M. P., I. W. M.

POPE. The. *P. F. I., R.*

POPE OF ROME. In 1850.
M. P., L. W. O. Y.

POPES. The Palace of the.
P. F. I., L. R. G. A.

POPLAR. *M. P., C. J.;*
M. P., I. S. H. W.

POPLAR. At house in.
C. S., W. O. G. M.
Taken care of and kept ship-shape by an old lady, who was my mother's maid before I was born.

POPLAR WALK. Stamford Hill.
S. B. B., Tales ii.

POPLARS. The, The Haunted House. *C. S., H. H.*
A solitary house, standing in a sadly neglected garden—a house of about the time of George the Second—as stiff, as cold, as formal, and in as bad taste as could possibly be desired—was much too closely and heavily shadowed by trees—there were six tall poplars before the front windows.

POPOLO. Piazza del.
P. F. I., R.

POPOLO. Porta del, Rome.
P. F. I., R.

PORDAGE. Mr., *C*lerk and super-cargo of. *C. S., P. o. C. E. P.*

PORDAGE. Mr., *C*ommissioner of Silver-Store Island.
C. S., P. o. C. E. P.
A stiff-jointed, high-nosed old gentleman, without an ounce of fat on him, of a very angry temper and a very sallow complexion.

PORDAGE. Mrs., Wife of *C*ommissioner Pordage.
C. S., P. o. C. E. P.
Making allowance for difference of sex, was much the same.

PORK PIE. A spirit.
M. P., W. R.

PORKENKAM. Miss, Bosom friend of the Nupkins. *P. P.* xxv.

PORKENHAM. Mrs., Bosom friend of the Nupkins. *P. P.* xxv.

PORKENHAM. Old, Husband of Mrs. Porkenham. *P. P.* xxv.
Opposition magisterial party.

PORKIN AND SNOB. *P. P.* xl.

PORT. A spirit. *M. P., W. R.*

PORT. The, In French watering-place. *R. P., O. F. W.*

PORT HOPE. *A. N.* xv.

PORT LEOPOLD HARBOUR.
M. P., E. T.

PORT MIDDLEBAY HARBOUR.
D. C. xxxiv.

PORT NICHOLSON. Cook's Straits.
M. P., E. T.

PORT ROYAL. *C. S., P. o. C. E. P.*

PORTA CAPUANA. Church by the.
P. F. I., R. D.

PORTE ST. MARTIN. Paris.
M. P., W.

PORTER. *S. B. B.,* Scenes iii.

PORTER. *D. and S.* lv.
At the iron gate which shut the courtyard from the street.

PORTER. At Mansion House.
B. R. lxi.

PORTER. At Mugby Junction.
C. S., M. J. i.

PORTER. *C*arrying Nicholas' luggage to coach to Yorkshire.
N. N. v.
Had evidently been spending the night in a stable, and taking his breakfast at a pump.

PORTER. Head. *C. S., M. J.* iii.

PORTER. Kentucky giant.
A. N. xii.
Seven feet eight inches in his stockings.

PORTER. Miss Emma, Daughter of Mrs. Porter.
S. B. B., Tales ix.

PORTER. Mrs., Joseph, A gossip.
S. B. B., Tales ix.
The good folks of *C*lapham and its vicinity stood very much in awe of scandal and sarcasm, and thus Mrs. Porter was courted and flattered and caressed.

PORTER. The under, Of the Anglo-Bengalee Disinterested Loan and Life Assurance *C*ompany.
M. C. xxvii.

PORTER FELLOW. *L. D.* x.

PORTERS. At Gray's Inn Square.
P. P. liii.

PORTERS. Foolish Mr. *E. D.* iii.
A certain finished gentleman.

PORTERS AND WAREHOUSEMEN.
N. N. xxxvii.
Of Cheeryble Brothers.

PORTERS. Warehouse,
R. P., T. *D. P.*

PORTLAND. A suburb of Louisville. *A. N.* xii.

PORTLAND PLACE.
D. and S. iii. ; *M. P.,*
P. F. ; *O. M. F.* xlix.

PORTLAND STREET. *M. P., W. R.*;
S. B. B., Tales vii.

PORTMAN SQUARE. *M. P., C.*;
O. M. F. xi.

PORTSMOUTH.
N. N. xxii. ; *U. T.* v.

PORTSMOUTH YARD. *C. S.,*
P. o. C. E. P. ; *M. P., N. G. R.*

PORTUGAL. *P. F. I., G. A. N.*

PORTUGAL STREET. *P. P.* xliii.

PORTUGUESE CAPTAIN.
C. S., P. o. C. E. P. i.

POSILIPO. Grotto of.
P. F. I., R. D.

POSTBOY. *P. P.* l.

POSTBOY. (Of the village) The.
B. R. lxi.
A soft-hearted, good-for-nothing vagabond kind of a fellow.

POSTBOY. The. *B. H.* vi.

POSTBOYS. *P. P.* xiii.

POSTBOYS. At the " Great White Horse." *P. P.* xxiv.

POST-CHAISE. Owner of and tenant.
U. T. xxii.
A little spare man who sat breaking stones by the roadside.

POST-OFFICE. *M. P., M. E. R.*

POST-OFFICE. Bury.
P. P. xviii.

POST-OFFICE. Leith Walk, waste ground. *P. P.* xlix.
An enclosure belonging to some wheelwright, who contracted with

POTTERIES. The. *U. T.* x.

POTTERSON. Job, Ship's steward.
O. M. F. iii.

Note.—Brother of Miss Abbey Potterson. Having been steward of the ship on which John Harmon returned from Africa, he is able to identify him in John Rokesmith. It is to be inferred that Job takes over the "Six Jolly Fellowship Porters" in the future.

POTTERSON. Miss Abbey, Sole Proprietor and Manager of the "Six Jolly Fellowship Porters."
O. M. F. vi.
A tall, upright, well-favoured woman, though severe of countenance—more the air of a schoolmistress than mistress of the "Six Jolly Fellowship Porters."

Note.—The landlady of the "Six Jolly Fellowship Porters." She befriends Lizzie Hexam in her trouble when her father is accused of the murder of John Harmon. She enters casually into the book when John Rokesmith is identified at the "Porters."

POTTINGTON. *M. P., B. A.*

POUCH'S. Jo, Widow.
B. H. xxvii.

POULTRY. The. *B. R.* lxvii.

POUNCERBY. Squire. *U. T.* xi·

"POWDER." Mr. Merdles' footmen.
L. D. xxi.

POWLERS. Relations of Mrs. Sparsit. *H. T., S.* vii.
The Powlers were an ancient stock who could trace themselves so exceedingly far back that it was not surprising if they sometimes lost themselves.

PRACTITIONER. Young medical.
S. B. B., Tales vi.
Recently established in business . . . began to wonder when his first patient would appear.

PRAIRIE. La. *A. N.* xv.

PRAISER. A, A poet.
R. P., T. N. S.
Singing the praises of his chief.

PRANTA DEL MONTE.
P. F. I., R.

PRATCHETT. Mr., Husband of Mrs. Pratchett in Australia.
C. S., S. L. i.

PRATCHETT. Mrs., Head chambermaid. *C. S., S. L.* i.

PRATT. Messrs., In Bond Street.
M. P., I. M.

PRATT. Parley P., A Mormon.
U. T. xx.

PRATT'S SHOP. For sale of armour. *R. P., G. o. A.*

PRAYMIAH=The Talkative Barber.
M. P., T. O. H.
The Prime Minister.

PRECEDENT. Name of a bird.
B. H. xiv.

PRECINCTS. The. *E. D.* xiv.
Never particularly well-lighted.

PRE-GALILEO BROTHERHOOD.
M. P., O. L. N. O.

PRE-GOWER AND PRE-CHAUCER BROTHERHOOD.
M. P., O. L. N. O.

PRE - HENRY - THE - SEVENTH - BROTHERHOOD.
M. P., O. L. N. O.

PRE-NEWTONIAN BROTHERHOOD. *M. P., O. L. N. O.*

PRE-PERSPECTIVE BROTHERHOOD. *M. P., O. L. N. O.*

PRE-RAPHAEL BROTHERHOOD.
M. P., O. L. N. O.

PREMIER. *M. P., I.*

'PRENTICE KNIGHTS. Secret Society of. *B. R.* viii.

PREROGATIVE OFFICE. In Doctors' Commons.
S. B. B., Scenes viii.
A long, busy-looking place, partitioned off, on either side, into a variety of little boxes, in which a few clerks were engaged in copying or examining deeds.

PRESBYTERIAN BROTHER.
M. P., S. B.

PRESCOTT. Mr. M. P., I. C.; M. P., L. A. V. ii.

PRESIDENT. M. P., Y. M. C.

PRESIDENT. T. T. C. bk. iii. ch. vi.

PRESS-ROOM. In Newgate Prison.
S. B. B., Scenes xxv.
Immediately on your right as you enter is a building containing the press-room, day-room and cells. It (the press-room) is a long, sombre room, with two windows sunk into the stone wall, and here the wretched men are pinioned on the morning of their execution, before being removed towards the scaffold.

PRESTON.
G. S. E. iii.; M. P., O. S.

PRESTON COTTON LORDS.
M. P., O. S.

PRESTON MASTERS. M. P., O. S.

PRESTON OPERATIVES.
M. P., O. S.

PREVENTIVE STATION. Naval officer of the. R. P., O. E. W.
With that bright mixture of blue coat, buff waistcoat, black neckerchief, and gold epaulette.

PRICE. Under arrest. P. P. xl.
A coarse, vulgar young man of about thirty, with a sallow face and a harsh voice.

PRICE. 'Tilda, Friend of Miss Fanny Squeers. N. N. ix.

A miller's daughter of only eighteen, who had contracted herself to the son of a small corn-factor, residing in the nearest market town. She was pretty, and a coquette, too, in her small way.
Note.—A miller's pretty daughter. She marries John Browdie. She is a friend of Fanny Squeers, who is exceedingly jealous of her good fortune in securing a husband. Miss Price takes a great delight in furthering the "suit" of Nicholas with Miss Squeers, which exists only in Miss Squeers' imagination. 'Tilda, however, proves a good friend to Nicholas, together with her husband; and they befriend the boys of Squeers's school after the last and only "break up" of Dotheboys' Hall.

PRIEST. L. D. lv.
He was an ugly priest by torchlight; of a lowering aspect, with an overhanging brow.

PRIEST. A. B. R. lxi.
A mild old man—whose chapel was destroyed.

PRIESTS. M. P., D. V.

PRIESTS. P. F. I., T. R. P.

PRIG. Mrs., Betsey, Nurse from Bartholomew's. M. C. xxv.
"The best of creeturs, but she is otherwise engaged at night" . . . of the Gamp guild, but not so fat; and her voice was deeper, and more like a man's—she had also a beard.
Note.—Betsey Prig was a companion character to Mrs. Gamp, and, in fact, "nurse together, turn and turn about." Her character is of secondary importance, and for that reason is not so detailed. She is last seen making a violent exit from Mrs. Gamp's room after a quarrel over poor old Chuffey.

PRIME MINISTER.
M. H. C. i.; M. P., G. B.

PRIME MINISTER. M. P., W.

PRIMROSE HILL TUNNEL.
M. P., O. S.

PRINCE. English.
M. P., L. W. O. Y.

PRINCE. The. *M. P., F. O. E. G.*

PRINCE CONSORT. *M. P., T. B.*

PRINCE OF WALES.
M. P., N. E.; *M. P., T. B.*

PRINCE REGENT. The.
M. P., C. P.; *N. N.* xxxvii.

PRINCESS. Of Little Dorrit's tale
to Maggy. *L. D.* xxiv.

PRINCESS'S ARMS. In Princess's
Place. *D. and S.* vii.
Much resorted to by splendid
footmen. A sedan chair was kept
inside the railing before the Princess's Arms, but it had never
come out within the memory of
man—and on fine mornings the
top of every rail was decorated
with a pewter-pot.

PRINCESS'S CHAPEL. In Princess's Place. *D. and S.* vii.
With a tinkling bell, where
sometimes as many as five-and-
twenty people attended service
on a Sunday.

PRINCESS'S PLACE.
D. and S. vii.
It was not exactly a court, and
it was not exactly a yard, but it
was the dullest of No-Thorough-
fares, rendered anxious and haggard by distant double knocks.
The name of this retirement,
where grass grew between the
chinks in the stone pavement, was
Princess's Place.

PRINGLE. Mr., The butcher.
M. P., S. P.

PRISCILLA. Mrs. Jellyby's maidservant. *B. H.* iv.
A young woman, with a swelled
face bound up in a flannel bandage, blowing the fire of the

drawing-room. The young woman
waited (at dinner) and dropped
everything on the table wherever
it happened to go, and never
moved it again till she put it on
the stairs.

PRISON. *B. H.* lii.
A large prison, with many
courts and passages so like one another, and so uniformly paved....
In an arched room, by himself
like a cellar upstairs : with walls
so glaringly white, that they
made the massive iron window
bars and iron-bound door even
more profoundly black than they
were, we found the trooper.

PRISON PHILANTHROPIST.
M. P., M. P.

PRISONER. *M. P., S.*

PRISONER. A debtor friend of
doctor in Marshalsea.
L. D. vi
Was in the positive degree of
hoarseness, puffiness, red-faced-
ness, all fours, tobacco, dirt, and
brandy.

PRISONER. A doomed wretch
in Newgate. Two sons of, (Rioters.) *B. R.* lxiv
Heard, or fancied they heard
their father's voice—one mounted
on the shoulders of the other
tried to clamber up the face of the
high wall. At last they cleft
their way among the mob about
the door—and were seen in—yes
the fire, striving to prize it down
with crowbars.

PRISONER. A sallow, In Court of
Chancery. *B. H.* i
Has come up, in custody, for
the half-dozenth time, to make a
personal application " to purge
himself of his contempt " (a
solitary surviving executor who
has fallen into a state of con

glomeration about accounts of which it is not pretended he had ever any knowledge).

PRISONER. Condemned to death.
S. B. B., Scenes xxiv.
How restlessly he has been engaged—in forming all sorts of fantastic figures with the herbs which are strewed upon the ledge (in the dock) before him.

PRISONER. In the Fleet.
P. P. xli.
Another man evidently very drunk, who had probably been tumbled into bed by his companions, was sitting up between the sheets, warbling as much as he could recollect of a comic song, with the most intensely sentimental feeling and expression.

PRISONER. The Italian Giovanni Carlavero. *U.* T. xxviii.

PRISONERS. About to enter prison van. *S. B. B.*, Char. xii.
Boys of ten, as hardened in vice as men of fifty—a houseless vagrant going joyfully to prison as a place of food and shelter, handcuffed to a man whose prospects were ruined, character lost, and family rendered destitute by his first offence.

PRISONERS. About to enter prison van. *S. B. B.*, Char. xii.
A couple of girls, of whom the elder could not be more than sixteen, and the younger of whom had certainly not attained her fourteenth year.

PRISONERS. At Newgate in the Press-room.
S. B. B., Scenes xxv.
Three men—the fate of one of these prisoners was uncertain—the other two had nothing to expect from the mercy of the Crown. "The first man had been a soldier of the Foot Guards."

PRISONERS. Certain English.
C. S., P. o. C. E. P.

PRISONERS. In new jail at Clerkenwell. *B. R.* lxvi.

PRISONERS. The gentlemen, in Marshalsea. *L. D.* vi.

PRISONS. *C. B., C. C., S.* i.

PRISONS. Mamertine.
P. F. I., R.

PRITCHARD. Mr., As the second husband. *M. P., N. T.*

PRIVATE HOUSE. A, in Princess's Place. *D. and S.* vii.
Tenanted by a retired butler, who had married a housekeeper—at this other private house, apartments were let furnished.

PRIVY COUNCIL. *B. R.* lxvii. ;
M. P., C. P.; M. P., R. H. F.

PRIVY SEAL. Clerk of the Lord Keeper of the. *R. P., P. M. T. P.*

PRIVY SEAL. Lord Keeper of.
R. P., P. M. T. P.

PRIVY SEAL OFFICE.
R. P., P. M. T. P.

PROCESSION. Funeral to Protestant Cemetery near Italian City.
U. T. xxvi.
I. Mr. Kindheart, much abashed, on an immense grey horse.
II. A bright yellow coach and pair, driven by a coachman in bright red velvet knee-breeches and waistcoat. Both coach-doors kept open by the coffin, which was on its side within, and sticking out at each.
III. The mourner for whom the coach was intended, walking in the dust.
IV. Concealed behind a roadside well, the unintelligible upholsterer (who made the arrangements) admiring.

PROCTER. Miss Adelaide Anne.
    M. P., A. A. P.

PROCTER'S. Miss, Sister.
    M. P., A. A. P.

PROCTER. Mrs. *M. P., A. A. P.*

PROCTOR. A.   *C. S., S. P. T.* i.

PROCTORS. The, In Doctors' Com-
    mons.   *S. B. B.*, Scenes viii.
    Very self-important-looking per-
    sonages, in stiff neckcloths, and
    black gowns with white fur collars.

PRODGIT. Mrs., A MaternityNurse,
    R. P., B. M. S.
    She wore a black bonnet of
    large dimensions, and was copious
    in figure.

PROPRIETOR. Irish. *M. P., C. P.*

PROPRIETOR. Of hairdresser's es-
    tablishment.   *N. N.* lii.
    Wore very glossy hair, with a
    narrow walk straight down the
    middle, and a profusion of flat,
    circular curls on both sides.

PROPRIETOR. Proprietor of
    gambling booth.   *N. N.* l.
    A tall, fat, long-bodied man,
    buttoned up to the throat in a
    light green coat, which made his
    body look still longer than it was.
    He wore, besides, drab breeches,
    and gaiters, a white neckerchief,
    and a broad-brimmed white hat.

PROPRIETORS OF DONKEYS.
    Deputy.   *S. B. B.*, Tales iv.
    Donkey boys.

PROSECUTOR.   *M. P., W. M.*

PROSEE. Mr., eminent counsel.
    P. P. xlvii.

PROSPECT PLACE. Poplar.
    M. P., I. S. H. W.

PROSS. Miss, Miss Manette's nurse
    and attendant.   T. T. *C.* iv.
    A wild-looking woman, all of a
    red colour . . . dressed in some

extraordinary tight-fitting fashion.
. . . "I really think this must be a
man ! " was Mr. Lorry's breathless reflection.

Note.—Miss Lucie Manette's maid
and sister of Barsad. She accompanies
Lucie to Paris, and when her mistress
and her husband escape she covers
their retreat. While doing this she is
assailed by Madame Defarge, who endeavours to force her way into the
room where she believes the fugitives
are hidden. Madame Defarge draws a
pistol, but as she fires it, Miss Pross
strikes her arm and the charge kills
" The Tigress." Miss Pross locks the
room, throwns the key into the river,
and succeeds in making good her
escape, but she is rendered stone deaf.

PROSS. Solomon, --The degraded
    brother of Miss Pross.
    There never was, nor will be,
    but one man worthy of Ladybird,
    said Miss Pross, " and that was my
    brother Solomon, if he hadn't
    made a mistake in life."

Note.—Pross was the real name of
John Barsad. Brother of Miss Pross
whom he defrauds of her money. When
he enters the story he is a spy and the
principal witness against Darnay. He
is seen again a spy in Paris, and then
as a turnkey in the Conciergerie, where
he is utilized in Darnay's escape. It
is understood that he eventually suffers
death from the guillotine.

PROTESTANT ASSOCIATION. The
    Great—of England. *B. R.* xxxviii.

PROUT. Mr.   *M. P., E. T.*

PROVIS. *See* Magwitch, Abel.

PROWLER. Mr.   *M. P., B. A.*

PRUFFLE. Scientific gentleman's
    servant.   *P. P.* xxxix.

PRUSSIA.   *M. P., C. P.*

PRUSSIA. King of.
    M. P., L. A. V. ii.

PUBLEEK. Or the many-headed.
    M. P., T. O. H.; *M. P., T. O. P.*
    The Public.

PUBLIC COMPANIES.
                    D. and S. xxv.

PUBLIC HOUSE.   Just opposite
the Insolvent Court.   *P. P.* xliii.
*Original : Supposed to have been
the " Horse and Groom."*

PUBLIC HOUSE.   *D. C.* xi.
*Original :   " Red Lion,"   48,
Parliament Street.*

PUBLIC HOUSE.   A low dingy.
                    S. B. B., Scenes v.
In Seven Dials.

PUBLIC HOUSE.   An old, quiet,
decent.   *S. B. B.,* Char. v.
· A modest public house of the
old school, with a little old bar—a
snug little room with a cheerful
fire, protected by a large screen.

PUBLIC HOUSE.   Obscure, Proprietor of.   *M. C.* xiii.
In a fur cap, who was taking
down the shutters.
*Original of public house: Pro-
bably the " Fox under the Hill " in
the Adelphi.*

PUBLIC HOUSE.   Small. *O. T.* xlviii.
*Original : " Eight Bells " at the
bottom of the main street, Hatfield.*

PUBLICAN.   The.   *M. H. C.* i.

PUBLICCASH.   The Dowager Marchioness of.   *S. B. B.,* Tales i.

PUBSEY   AND   CO.   *See* Fledgeby,
Young.

PUDDING   SHOP.   Close to St.
Martin's Church.   *D. C.* xi.

PUDDING SHOP.   Good, In Strand.
                    D. C. xi.

PUFFER.   Princess,   The opium
dealer.   *E. D.* xxiii.
As ugly and withered as one of
the fantastic carvings on the
upper brackets of the stall seats.
*Original : Lascar Sal of Lime-
house.*

PUFFY.   *B. H.* xii.

PUGIN.   Mr.   *M. P., O. L. N. O.*

PUGSTYLES.   Mr., Heading a depu-
tation to Mr. Gregsbury, M.P.
                    N. N. xvi.
A plump old gentleman.

PUMBLECHOOK.   Premises of Mr.
                    G. E. viii.
In the High Street of the
market town, . . . were of a pepper-
corny and farinaceous character, as
the premises of a corn-chandler
and seedsman should be.
*Original : Identical with those of
Mr. Sapsea.*

PUMBLECHOOK.   Uncle, Joe Gargery's Uncle, a well-to-do corn-
chandler.   *G. E.* iv.
A large, hard-breathing, middle-
aged, slow man, with a mouth like
a fish, dull staring eyes, and
sandy hair standing upright as
if he had just been all but choked
and had that moment come to.

Note.—Joe Gargery's uncle.   A corn-
chandler and seedsman " Up-town."
He takes Pip to Miss Havisham and
" takes him into custody " with a sort
of proprietary right.   When Pip comes
into his money and expectations Uncle
Pumblechook abases himself.   Orlick
and others break into the shop, rob the
till, give Pumblechook " a dozen," and
stuff his mouth with " hardy annuals."
When Pip returns, Pumblechook is as
obnoxious in another way.   His humility becomes patronizing pity for Pip's
reduced circumstances—circumstances
brought on through Providence by
Pip's ingratitude to him.

PUMKINSKULL.   Prof.
                    Mud. Pap. ii.

PUMP.   Titbull's in Titbull's Almshouses.   *U. T.* xxvii.
Which stands with its back to
the thoroughfare just inside the
gate (of court of Titbull's Almshouses), and has a conceited air of
reviewing Titbull's pensioners.

PUMP. [Trough].   *P. C.* lii.
Original : Probably erroneously identified with the pump at the "Angel" Inn, at Bury. Also, of course, traced to the horse trough of the "Marquess of Granby."

PUMP-ROOM. The.
    D. and S. xxi.

PUMP-ROOM. The Great—Bath.
    P. P. xxxv.

PUMPION. Alexander.
    M. P., W. R.

PUMPION. Widow. *M. P., W. R.*

PUNCH.   *M. P., O. S.*

PUNCH.   *M. P., R. G.*

PUNCH'S OPERA. Proprietor of.
    M. P., G. H.

PUPFORD. Assistant of Miss.
    C. S., T. T. *G.* vi.
With the Parisian accent—never conversed with a Parisian, and was never out of England—except once in the foreign waters which ebb and flow two miles off Margate.

PUPFORD. Cook of Miss.
    C. S., T. T. *G.* vi.

PUPFORD. Establishment of Miss.
    C. S., T. T. *G.* vi.
For six young ladies of tender years, is an establishment of a compact nature, an establishment in miniature, quite a pocket establishment.

PUPFORD. Housemaid of Miss.
    C. S., T. T. *G.* vi.

PUPFORD. Miss, Schoolmistress.
    C. S., T. T. *G.* vi.
When Miss Pupford and her assistant first foregathered is not known to men, or pupils. A belief would have established itself—that the two once went to school together—were it not fo the audacity of imagining Miss Pupford born without mittens— a front—a bit of gold wire among her front teeth, and little dabs o powder on her neat little face and nose.

PUPIL. Of Miss Wade's.
    L. D. lvii
A girl of fifteen who was the only daughter.

PUPIL. Of special pleader.
    P. P. xlvii
Who had written a lively bool about the law of demises, with a vast quantity of marginal note and references.

PUPKER. Sir Matthew, Chairman of United Metropolitan Improved Hot Muffin and Crumpet Baking and Punctual Delivery Company.
    N. N. ii
Had a little round head with a flaxen wig on the top of it.

PURBECK. Island of.
    R. P., T. *L. V*

PURBLIND. Mr.   *Mud. Pap.* ii

PURDAY. Captain (the old Nava officer on half pay).
    S. B. B., O. P. iv

PURSE-BEARER. The Lord Chan cellor's.   *R. P., P.M . T. P*

PUSSY=Dr. Pusey.
    M. P., A. J. B

PUTNEY. Formal, precise, com posed and quiet.   *D. C.* ix.
    L. D. xvi. ; *M. H. C.* iii.
    M. P., L. H.

PYEGRAVE. Charley, client of Miss Mowcher's.   *D. C.* xxii
In the Life Guards.

PYKE. Mr., Guest of Ralph Nickle by.   *N. N.* xix
A sharp-faced gentleman.

Q

QUACK DOCTOR. *M. P., M. M.*

QUADRANT, THE. *S. B. B.,* Char. i.

QUAKER HOSPITAL. In Philadelphia. *A. N.* vii.
Not sectarian in the great benefits it confers.

QUALE. Mr. *B. H.* iv.
With large shining knobs for temples, and his hair all brushed to the back of his head.
Note.—Friend of Mrs. Jellyby and intimately concerned with her philanthropic objects. He is also a prospective candidate for Caddy's hand, which she refuses.

QUALITY. Person of.
M. P., N. J. B.

QUANKO SAMBO. Bowler in Jingle's West Indian cricket match.
P. P. vii.

QUAPAW INDIANS. *A. N.* xvii.

QUARL. Philip, Gifts on Christmas tree. *R. P., A. C. T.*

QUARLL. Philip. *M. C.* v.

QUEBEC. *A. N.* xv. ; and *M. P., L. A. V.* ii.

QUEEN SQUARE. *B. H.* xviii. ; *P. P.,* xxxv. ; and *R. P., B. S.*

QUEEN'S PALACE. *B. R.,* lxvii. ; and *M. P., B. A.,* and *M. P., W. H.*

QUEENSTOWN.
A. N., xv. ; and *U. T.* ii.

QUEENSTOWN HARBOUR.
U. T. xxxi.

QUEER CLIENT. Prisoner in Marshalsea. *P. P.* xxi.

QUEER COMPANY. The Queer Hall of some. *U. T.* xxi.
Gives upon a churchyard.

QUEERSPECK. Prof.
Mud. Pap. i.

QUICKEAR. Of Liverpool Police Force. *U. T.* v.

QUILP. Daniel, Trent's evil spirit.
O. C. S. iii.
An elderly man of remarkably hard features and for bidding aspect, and so low in stature as to be quite a dwarf, though his head and face were large enough for the body of a giant. His eyes were restless, sly, and cunning.
Note.—Quilp was the malignant dwarf—the evil geni of the story. He lent money to Nell's grandfather and then turned them into the street. He had Sampson Brass under his thumb and compelled him to do the dirty work. He had a pretty wife whose life he made one long spell of terror. Tom Scott, his errand boy, was the only being with whom there could be said to be any sympathy. Quilp's end is a violent one : he falls from his own wharf into the river and is drowned, when attempting to escape from the police officers. Having had no time to make his will his wife inherits his property.

Quilp was said (by an American newspaper) to be a Louisvillian theatre manager. But he is also said to have been well known in the vicinity of the Thames. The river foreshore on which his body is supposed to have been cast up is Bugsby's Marsh.

QUILP. Mrs., Betsy, the dwarf's wife. *O. C. S.* iii.
" Pretty Mrs. Quilp, obedient, timid, loving Mrs. Quilp, thus her lord and master." A pretty, little, mild-spoken, blue-eyed woman.
Note.—The wife of the evil dwarf. A pretty, little, mild woman who paid for her folly in a state of constant fear of her deformed husband. She inberits his wealth and marries again.

QUILP'S BOY. *See* Scott, Tom.

QUILP'S WHARF. *O. C. S.* iv.
On the Surrey side of the river was a small, rat-infested, dreary yard. . . in which were a little

wooden counting-house . . . a few fragments of rusty anchors; several large iron rings; some piles of rotten wood ; and two or three heaps of old sheet-copper.

Original : Stood on a site close to the eastern of the southern end of the Tower Bridge, and afterwards occupied by Butler's wharf.

Original of Quilp's House : Said to have been No. 6, Tower Dock.

QUIN.   *M. P., R. S. L.*

QUINCH. Mrs., Eldest occupant of Titbull's Almshouses.
                       U. T. xxvii.

QUINION. Mr., Manager of Murdstone's wine business.   *D. C.* ii.

Note.—Quinion, the manager at Murdstone and Grinby's, is first seen at Lowestoft, before Murdstone's marriage with Mrs. Copperfield. After that he is seen as head of the warehouse, where David is placed by his stepfather. Quinion is not unkind, but the nature of the work makes it impossible for the sensitive boy to endure it. Quinion drops out of the story after David runs away from the warehouse.

QUODLE.   *B. H.* xii.

R

R. Y.   *C. S., S. L.* iv.

RABBI. Chief, Office of the.
                       U. T. ii.

RABBIT DEALERS.
                S. B. B., Scenes v.

RACHAEL. A mill hand.
                       H. T., S. x.
A quiet oval face, dark and rather delicate, irradiated by a pair of very gentle eyes, and further set off by the perfect order of her shining black hair. It was not a face in its first bloom. She was a woman of five-and-thirty years of age.

Note.—Rachael was the friend of Stephen Blackpool, although she was

unable to marry him, as his wife a dissolute woman, was alive. When Stephen is accused of the bank theft Rachael protested his innocence. When Stephen did not return, she was certain that something had befallen him, and was through her that he was discovered injured at the bottom of the old shaft

RACHAEL. Mrs., *See* Chadband Mrs.

RACHAEL. Mrs., Daughter of.
                       B. H. ii

RACHAEL. Mrs., Servant of Miss Barbary.   *B. H.* ii

RACHEL. "A negro woman slave.   *A. N.* xvi

RADCLIFFE. Mrs.
                S. B. B., Scenes xxiv

RADDLE. "Misses" (Mrs.) Bob Sawyer's landlady.   *P. P.* xxxii
A little, fierce woman.

RADDLE. Mr., Husband of Mrs Raddle.   *P. P.* xxxii
My husband sits sleeping down stairs and taking no more notice than if I was a dog in the street A base, faint-hearted, timorous wretch.

RADDLE. Mrs.   *P. P.* xlvi

RADFOOT. George, Third mate on board ship.   *O. M. F.* xxix

RADICALS. In Parliament.
                S. B. B., Scenes xviii

RADICOFANI.   *P. F. I., R. P. S*

RADLEY. Mr., Of the Adelphi Hotel.   *A. N.* i

RAGFAIR.   *L. D.* ix

RAGGED SCHOOL.   *U. T.* ii.

RAGGED SCHOOL. West Street, Saffron Hill.   *M. P., S. S. U.*

RAGGED SCHOOLS.
                M. P., C. and E.

RAGLAN. Lord. *M. P., S. F. A.*

RAGS. Name of a bird.
B. H. xiv.

RAILWAY. Northern. *C. S., H.* T.

RAILWAY ARMS. The.
D. and S. vi.

RAILWAY EATING-HOUSE. The.
D. and S. vi.

RAILWAY HAM, BEEF, AND GERMAN SAUSAGE WAREHOUSE.
M. P., U. N.

RAILWAY HAT AND TRAVELLING CAP DEPOT—HAIRCUTTING SALOON—IRONMONGERY, NAIL AND TOOL WAREHOUSE— BAKERY—OYSTER ROOMS AND GENERAL SHELL-FISH SHOP— MEDICAL HALL—HOSIERY AND TRAVELLING OUTFITTING ESTABLISHMENT — RAILWAY HOTEL (late "Norwich Castle").
M. P., U. N.

RAILWAY PASSENGERS ASSURANCE COMPANY. *M. P., E. S.*

RAILWAY PIE-SHOP. *M. P., U. N.*

RAILWAY PORTER. Begging Letter Writer. *R. P., T. B. W.*

RAILWAY TAVERN. *M. P., U. N.*

RAINBIRD. Alice, A schoolgirl, aged seven. *H. R.* i.

RAINFORTH. Miss, As Lucy Benson. *M. P., V. C.*

RAIRYGANOO. Sally, One of Mrs. Lirriper's maids, still suspect of Irish extraction.
C. S., M. L. Leg. i.

RAMES. William, Second mate of the "Golden Mary."
C. S., W. o. G. M.

RAMPART. Sir Charles.
S. B. B., Tales i.
Commanding officer in volun-

teers in Mr. Tibb's unfinished tale.

RAMSEY. Mr., Client of Dobson and Fogg. *P. P.* xx.
That chap as we issued the writ against at Camberwell. A precious seedy-looking customer.

RAMSGATE. Allowed by the Tuggs's to be just the place of all others. *S. B. B.,* Tales iv.

RAMSGATE PIER.
S. B. B., Tales iv.

RANDAL. Runaway slave of J. Surgette. *A. N.* xvii.

RANDOLPH. Assumed name.
S. B. B., Scenes xiii.

RANDOM. Hon. Charles.
M. P., C. Pat.

RANELAGH. T. T. C. bk. ii, ch. xii.
Mr. Stryver inaugurated the Long Vacation with a formal proposal to take Miss Manette to Vauxhall Gardens, that failing, to Ranelagh.

RANGOON. *M. P., L. A. V.* ii.

RANK AND FILE. 130 Nobodies.
R. P., N. S.

RANKIN. Mr. *M. P., Th. Let.*

RANSON AND CO. *M. P., I.*

RAPHAEL. *M. P., O. L. N. O.*

RAPPER. A, One of a sect.
C. S., H. H.
A fellow-traveller in a coach, a goggle-eyed gentleman of a perplexed aspect.

RARX. Mr., Passenger on "Golden Mary." *C. S., W. o. G. M.*
An old gentleman, a good deal like a hawk if his eyes had been better and not so red. Not a pleasant man to look at, nor yet to talk to—a sordid and selfish character.

RATCLIFFE.   *D. and S.* xxiii. ;
O. M. F. iii. ; *O. T.* xiii. ;
U. T. xxx.
A squalid maze of streets, courts,
and alleys of miserable houses let
out in single rooms.

RATCLIFF HIGHWAY.   *R. P.*,
D. W. T. T ; *S. B. B.*, Scenes xxi.
That reservoir of dirt, drunkenness and drabs : thieves, oysters,
baked potatoes and pickled salmon.

RATS CASTLE.   *R. P., O. D.*

RAVEN. In the Happy Family.
M. P., P. F.

RAVENDER. Father of William
George.   *C. S., W. o. G. M.*

RAVENDER. William George, *Captain* of the " Golden Mary."
C. S. ; W. o. G. M.
Apprenticed to the sea when
twelve years old. Part-owner of a
smart schooner.

RAVENGLASS.   *M. P., E. S.*

RAYBROCK. Alfred, A young fisherman.   *C. S., M. f.* T. *S.* i.
Of two or three-and-twenty, in
the rough sea-dress of his craft,
with a brown face, dark curling
hair, and bright, modest eyes,
under his sou'wester hat, and
with a frank, but simple and
retiring, manner.

RAYBROCK. Father of Hugh and
Alfred.   *C. S., M. f.* T. *S.* i.
Had been a small tradesman.

RAYBROCK. Hugh, Fisherman.
C. S., M.f. T. *S.* v.
Returned from desert island,
where he was supposed to be
drowned.

RAYBROCK. Jorgan, Son of Alfred
and Kitty.   *C. S., M. f.* T. *S.* v.
A rosy little boy.

RAYBROCK.   Mrs., Draper and also
post office.   *C. S., M. f. T. S.* i.
A comely, elderly woman, short
of stature, plump of form, sparkling and dark of eye.

RAYBROCK.   Private sitting-room
of Mrs.   *C. S., M. f.* T. *S.* i.
Little, low back room—decorated
with divers plants in pots, tea-
trays, old *C*hina teapots and punch-
bowls—which was at once the
private sitting-room of the Raybrock family, and the inner cabinet of the post office.

REACH. Some, Down the river.
D. and S. xix.

READE. Mr.   *M. P., M. E. R.*

READING.   *B. H.* iii. ;   *M. P.*,
I. S. H. W. ; *M. P., P. P.*

REBBECK. Mr.   *M. P., P. T.*

RECEIVER. The, In the cause.
B. H. i.

RECKLESS GUESSER.
M. P., S. S. U.

RECORDER. For the *C*ity of London.   *M. H. C.* i.
A man of education and birth,
of the Honourable Society of the
Middle Temple, barrister-at-Law.

RECORDER OF LONDON. In 1811.
M. P., C. P.

RED. One of boating-crew training
for race.   *S. B. B.*, Scenes x.

RED LION SQUARE. *M. P., G. A.*

RED MAN. Red Indian. *A. N.* xii.

RED SEA.   *M. P., H. H.*

RED TAPE.   *M. P., R. T.*
*See also C*ircumlocution Office,
and Searli Tapa.

REDAN.   *M. P., B. A.*

REDBURN. Brother of Jack.
　　　　　　　　M. H. C. ii.
　Master Humphrey.

REDBURN. Jack, Member of Master Humphrey's Club.
　　　　　　　　M. H. C. ii.
　Master Humphrey's librarian, secretary, steward, and first minister —something of a musician, author, actor, painter, very much of a carpenter, and an extraordinary gardener. He wears a quantity of iron-grey hair. We seldom see him in any other garment than an old spectral dressing-gown, with very disproportionate pockets.

REDBURN. Younger brother of Jack. 　　　　*M. H. C.* vi.

REDFORTH. Bob, Cousin of William Tinkling. 　　　*H. R.* i.

REDFORTH. Lieut-Col. Robin.
　　　　　　　　H. R. i.

REDLAW. Mr., The haunted man.
　　　　　　　C. B., H. M. i.
　A learned man in chemistry, and a teacher.

REDMAYNE'S. 　*S. B. B.,* Tales v.

RED 'US. The.
　　　　　S. B. B., Scenes x.

REEFAWM = Light of reason. Youngest and fairest of all the Sultan's wives. 　*M. P., T. O. H.* Reform.

REFORM CLUB. 　*M. P., B. A.*

REFORM CLUB-HOUSE.
　　　　　　　R. P., B. S.

REFORM PARTY. *See* Reefawm.

REFRACTORIES. Inmates of Refractory Ward of Wapping Workhouse. 　　　　*U.T.* iii.
　Picking oakum in a small room giving on a yard. They sat in line on a form, with their backs to a window ; before them, a table, and their work. The oldest re-

fractory was, say twenty ; youngest refractory, say sixteen.

REFRESHMENT ROOM. At Mugby Junction. 　*C. S., M. J.* v.

REFRESHMENTERS. At Mugby Junction. 　*C. S., M. J.* v.
　Ockipying the only proudly independent footing on the Line.

REFUGE FOR THE DESTITUTE. New York. 　　　*A. N.* vi.

REGENCY PARK. 　*P. P.* xlv.

REGENT STREET. 　*M. P., A. P.* ;
　　M. P., P. F. ; *M. P., R. D.* ;
　　N. N. x. ; *S. B. B.,* Char. i. ;
　S. B. B., Scenes xvi. ; *U. T.* xvi.

REGENT'S CANAL. 　　*U. T.* vi.

REGENT'S PARK. 　*M. P., F. L.* ;
　　M. P., P. F. ; *U. T.* xviii.

REGIMENTAL BANDS. Of Stepney Union. 　　　*U. T.* xxix.

REGISTRAR. The, In Chancery Court. 　　　　*B. H.* i.

REGISTRAR. The, In Doctors' Commons. 　*S. B. B.,* Scenes viii.
　An individual in an armchair, and a wig.

REGISTRAR-GENERAL.
　　　　　　M. P., F. N. P.

REGONDI. Signor Giulio.
　　　　　　　M. P., M. M.

REID. Dr. 　　　*M. P., N. E.*

REIGATE. 　　　　*U. T.* xi.

REIGATE STATION. 　*R. P., A. F.*

RELATION. Poor, Of John.
　　　　　　R. P., P. R. S.
　Nobody's enemy but my own.

RELATION. Poor, Of Ralph Nickleby, senr. 　　*N. N.* i.
　To whom he (Ralph Nickleby senr.) paid a weekly allowance of three shillings and sixpence

RELATIONS. Poor, A couple of.
_P. P._ xxviii.
At wedding of Bella and Trundle.

REPORTERS. Of *C*ourt of *C*hancery.   _B. H._ i.

REPORTERS. Of the newspapers.
_B. H._ i.

REPRESENTATIVES. House of, Washington.   _A. N._ iii.
A beautiful and spacious hall, of semicircular shape, supported by handsome pillars.

" RESERVE." Detective.
_O. M. F._ iii.

RESINA.   _P. F. I., R. D._

REST. Name of bird.   _B. H._ xiv.

RESTORER.   _M. P., N. Y. D._

RETAINER. Fifth—of Veneerings.
_O. M. F._ ii.
With a mournful air.

RETAINERS OF VENEERINGS. Four.   _O. M. F._ ii.
Pigeon - breasted — in plain clothes.

RETREAT. Mr. Bounderby's.
_H. T., R._ vii.
About fifteen miles from *C*oketown.

RETREATS.   _U. T._ xxvii.
There is a tendency in these pieces of architecture to shoot upward unexpectedly.

REVEREND. The, Master of school.
_R. P., T. S. S._

REVIEWER. The, _M. P., M. E. R._

REYNOLDS. Miss, Pupil at the Nun's House.   _E. D._ ix.

RHINE. The restless inns upon the.
_C. S., H. T._; _C. S., N. T._ Act iii.;
_M. P., A. P._; _P. F. I., V. M. M._
_S. S._; _R. P., D. W. T. T._

Where your going to bed— appears to be the tocsin for everybody else's getting up—and where in the table d'hôte room—one knot of stoutish men, entirely dressed in jewels and dirt—will remain all night, clinking glasses and singing.

RHODE ISLAND.   _A. N._ vi.

RHONE. The.   _C. S., N. T._ Act iii.; _P. F. I., L. R. G. A._

RIAH. Mr.   _O. M. T._ xxii.
An old Jewish man in an ancient coat, long of skirt, and wide of pocket. A venerable man, bald and shining at the top of his head, with long grey hair flowing down at its sides and mingling with his beard.
Note.—The Jew who, as the tool of Fascination Fledgeby, acts as Pubsey and Co. While he is a noble character, he is considered "a regular Jew" when he is doing the work of his employer. He befriends Lizzie Hexam and assists her to employment at the up-river mill. He arrives at the conclusion that he is doing his race an injustice so long as he remains Pubsey and Co., and gives Fledgeby notice. After that he takes up his residence with Jenny Wren.

RIALTO. The.   _L. D._ xli.

RIBBLE. River.   _G. S. E._ v.

RICHARD I. King.   _M. P., C. C._

RICHARD II.   _B. H._ Pref.

RICHARD III. _S. B. B._, Scenes xiii.

RICHARD IV.   _P. P._ xxv.

RICHARD. Brother of one of the wrecked and drowned from the " Royal *C*harter."   _U. T._ ii.

RICHARD. Meg's sweetheart.
_C. B. C., G._ i.
A handsome, well-made, powerful youngster—with eyes that sparkled like the red-hot droppings from a furnace fire ; black hair

that curled about his swarthy temples rarely—and a smile.

RICHARD. Richard Doubledick.
C. S., S. P. T. ii.

RICHARD. Waiter at Saracen's Head. *N. N.* iv.

" RICHARDS." *See* Toodle, Mrs.

RICHARDSON. Mr. *M. P., J. G.*

RICHARDSON. Sir John.
M. P., L. A. V. i.

RICHARDSON'S. The Booth at Greenwich Fair.
S. B. B., Scenes xii.

Where you have a melodrama, a pantomine, a comic song, an overture, and some incidental music, all done in five-and-twenty minutes.

RICHMOND. Earl of.
S. B. B., Scenes xiii.

RICHMOND. *A. N.* ii.; *G. E.* xxxiii.; *O. M. F.* li.; *P. P.* lvii.; *S. B. B.,* Scenes vi.; *S. B. B.,* Scenes x.

RICHMOND. The terrace at.
P. P. lvii.

RICHMOND. (U.S.A.) *A. N.* viii.

RICHMOND HILL. *M. P., I.*

RICKITTS. Little, A pupil at the Nuns' House. *E. D.* xiii.

RIDERHOOD. Home of.
O. M. F. xxix.

In Limehouse Hole, among the riggers, and the mast, oar and block makers, and the boat-builders and the sail-lofts.

RIDERHOOD. Miss Pleasant, An unlicensed pawnbroker, and daughter of Rogue Riderhood.
O. M. F. xxix.

In her four-and-twentieth year of life—possessed of what is colloquially termed a swivel eye—

she was otherwise not positively ill-looking, though anxious, meagre, of a muddy complexion, and looking as old again as she really was.

Note.—Rogue Riderhood's daughter. She is first seen managing her father's house and acting as " an unlicensed pawnbroker " upon the smallest of small scales. Eventually she marries Mr. Venus.

RIDERHOOD. Mrs., The late.
O. M. F. xxix.

Mother of Pleasant Riderhood.

RIDERHOOD. Roger, A waterside man. *O. M. F.* vi.

With a squinting leer, who fumbled at an old sodden fur cap, formless and mangy, that looked like a furry animal, dog or cat, puppy or kitten, drowned and decaying.

Note.—A Thames " night-bird " of ill-fame. John Harmon is maltreated in the Rogue's house. The " secret " of the book is the identity of the murdered man. But Riderhood lodges an accusation of the crime against Gaffer Hexam, for the purpose of obtaining the reward offered by Mr. Boffin. The death of Hexam deprives him of this, which leaves him with a feeling of decided injury. Rogue Riderhood becomes a lock-keeper at Plashwater Weir, and discovers Bradley Headstone's attempted murder of Eugene Wrayburn. He blackmails Bradley and persecutes him until the schoolmaster turns in desperation and drowns both the Rogue and himself in the lock.

RIDING-MASTER. At Astley's.
S. B. B., Scenes xi.

None of your second-rate riding-masters—but the regular gentleman attendant on the principal riders, who always wears a military uniform with a tablecloth inside the breast of the coat, in which costume he forcibly reminds one of a fowl trussed for roasting.

RIGAUD. Late, Madame, Widow of M. Henri Barronneau. *L. D.* i.

One night Madame Rigaud and

myself were walking—on a height overhanging the sea—I remonstrated on the want of duty and devotion—Madame Rigaud retorted—I retorted—Mme. Rigaud leaped over, dashing herself to death.

RIGAUD, Monsieur.   *L. D.* i.

He had a hook nose, handsome after its kind, but too high between the eyes, by probably just as much as his eyes were too near to one another. For the rest he was large and tall in frame, had thin lips where his thick moustache showed them at all, and a quantity of dry hair, of no definable colour, in its shaggy state, but shot with red. The hand—was unusually small and plump ; would have been unusually white, but for the prison grime. When (he) laughed, a change took place in his face, which was more remarkable than prepossessing. His moustache went up under his nose, and his nose came down over his moustache in a very sinister and cruel manner. . . . " I myself was born in Belgium—call me thirty-five years of age—have been treated and respected like a gentleman everywhere."

Note.—First seen in prison on a charge of killing his wife. He escapes, however, and makes his way to England, where he is closely entangled in the story. He is a polished scoundrel living on his wits. He obtains possession of the box of papers confided to Ephraim Flintwich by his brother Jeremiah, and endeavours to extract money from Mrs. Clennam by threatening exposure. He does not succeed, however, and dies in the ruins of Mrs. Clennam's house, which falls on him.

Original : This character was named after General Rigaud at the time in England. He was a friend of Dickens, but it does not appear that he had the qualities of Dickens' villain, although the use of his name

brought about a certain coolnes. Also traced to Thomas Griffith Wainwright, the infamou murderer.

RIGAUD.   *M. P., M. E. I*

RIOTERS. Of the Gordon Riots.   *B. R.* lxii

RIOTERS. Two.   *B. R.* lxxvi
Were to die before the prison.. who had been concerned in th' attack upon it.

RIVER. The.   *S. B. B.*, Scenes x'

RIVIERA. The.   *P. F. I., G. A. N*

RIVOLI. Rue de.   *P. F. I., G. T. F. R. P., A. F.* ; *U. T.* vii

ROADS. The, within twelve mile of London.   *B. R.* i
Were at that time ill paved seldom repaired, and very badl' made.

ROBBERS. Captain of the.   *M. P., T. O. H*

ROBBERS. Forty.   *M. P., T. O. H*

ROBBINS. Mr., A bank officer   *A. N.* xvii

ROBBS.   *M. P., T. T*

ROBEMAKER. Two daughters of   *B. H.* x
Combing their curls.

ROBERT. Uncle, Husband of Aun Jane, guest at Christmas family party.   *S. B. B., Char.* ii

ROBERTS.   *M. P., O. L. N. O*

ROBERTSON. Mr. Peter.   *M. P., S. P*

ROBIN. Cecil.   *M. P., P. M. B*

ROBIN HOOD. A toy.   *R. P., A. C. T*

ROBINS. Mr. Auctioneer.   *S. B. B., Tales* i

ROBINSON
Miss W

ROBINSON

ROBINSON
Louise.

ROBINSON
D. C. v.

ROBINSON
Christm

ROBINSON

ROCHEST
D. C. x

The
proud f
streets
lake, a
S.. c'

ROCHEST

Full
and tin
faces
a quee
over th
red-bric
trees i
as if i
peeked

ROCHES

A wonderfully quaint row of red-brick tenements. They had odd little porches over the doors, like sounding-boards over old pulpits.

See also Minor Canon Corner.

ROCHESTER. The old gates of the city of.   *C. S., S. P.* T. iii.

ROCHESTER. Strood, etc.
                              P. P. ii.
The principal productions of these towns appear to be soldiers, sailors, Jews, chalk, shrimps, officers, and dockyard men.

ROCHESTER BRIDGE.   *P. P.* ii.

ROCHESTER CASTLE.   *P. P.* ii.
                      C. S., S. P. T. i.
Frowning walls—tottering arches dark nooks—crumbling staircases.

ROCHESTER CATHEDRAL.
        C. S., S P. T. i. ; *P. P.* ii.
Earthy smell—little Saxon doors —confessionals like money-takers' boxes at theatres.

ROCKINGHAM. Lord.
                      B. R. lxvii.

ROCKINGHAM. Marquis of.
                M. P., A. in E.

ROCKY MOUNTAINS.   *M. P.,*
        T. O. P. ; *O. M. F.* viii.

RODOLPH. Mr. Jennings, vocal and musical friend of Journeyman Painters.   *S. B. B.,* Char. viii.

RODOLPH. Mrs. Jennings, musical friend of journeyman painter.
                S. B. B., Char. viii.

ROE. Richard.   *M. P., L. E. J.*

ROE FAMILY. The only female member of the.   *B. H.* xx.

ROEBUCK. Mr.
    M. P., T. *B.*; *M. P.*, T. T.

ROGERS. Friend of Mrs. Nickleby.
    N. N. xxxvii.
A lady in our neighbourhood when we lived near Dawlish.

ROGERS. Johnny, Workhouse inmate.   *R. P.*, *W. I. A.*

ROGERS. Mr.   *M. P.*, *F. L.*

ROGERS. Mr., A policeman.
    R. P., *D. W. I. F.*

ROGERS. Mr., The parlour orator.
    S. B. B., *C*har. v.
A stoutish man of about forty, whose short, stiff, black hair curled closely round a broad, high forehead, and a face to which something besides water and exercise had communicated a rather inflamed appearance.

ROGERS. Mr., Third mate of the "Halsewell."   *R. P.*, T. *L. V.*

ROGERS. Mrs., Mrs. Raddles, lodger.   *P. P.* xlvi.

ROGUE. A.   *C. S.*, *S. P.* T. i.

ROKER. Mr. Tom, Gentleman who had accompanied Mr. Pickwick into the prison.   *P. P.* xli.

ROKESMITH. *See* Harmon John.

ROKESMITH. Mrs., John. *See* Wilfer, Bella.

ROLLAND. Partner of Defresnier et cie.   *C. S.*, *N. T.* Act ii.

ROLLS YARD.   *B. H.* x.

ROMAN BATH. In one of the streets out of the Strand.
    D. C. vi.

ROMANA CAMPAGNA.
    P. F. I., *R. P. S.*

ROMANS. Sulky.   *P. F. I.*, *R.*

ROME. *B. H.* Pref.; *L. D.* xlvi; *P. F. I.*, *R.*; *P. F. I.*, *R. P. S.*; *R. P.*, *L. A.*; *U. T.*

ROME. *C*atacombs of.
    P. F. I.,

ROMER. Mr. R., As first husband
    M. P., *N.*

ROMILLY. Lawyer. *M. P.*, *C.*

ROMILLY. Sir Samuel.
    B. R. Pr.

RONCIGLIONE. *P. F. I.*, *R. P.*

ROOD LANE. London.
    M. P., *E.*

ROOKERY. At Blundestone, Suffolk, David's birthplace.
    D. C.

*Original : There is some dou*bt *about the Rookery, both Blundesto*ne *Rectory and Blundestone Hall havi*ng *been identified. The evidence a*p*pears to be in favour of the forme*r

ROOKERY. The.
    S. B. B., Scenes xx
That classical spot adjoining the Brewery at the bottom of Tottenham *C*ourt Road. The filthy and miserable appearance of this part of London can hardly be imagined by those who have not witnessed it. Wretched houses with broken windows patched with rags and paper : every room let to a different family, and in some instance to two or even three—fruit and "sweet stuff" manufacturers the cellars, barbers and red-herring vendors in the front parlour cobblers in the back; a bird fancier in the first floor, three families on the second, starvation in the attics, Irishmen in the passage, a musician in the front kitchen, a charwoman with five hungry children in the back—filth everywhere.

"ROOMS." Master of the.
R. P., O. E. W.
Wears knee-breeches.

ROOMS. The Assembly Rooms.
R. P., O. E. W.
Original: At Broadstairs.

ROPE-WALK. Old Green Copper.
G. E. xlvi.

ROSA. A dark-eyed, dark-haired, sly village beauty. B. H. vii.

Note.—A maid whom Mrs. Rouncewell takes young to train. Watt Rouncewell falls in love with her, but there are difficulties. Eventually, however, Rosa leaves for a year's polishing in Germany before marrying Watt.

ROSA. Father of. E. D. ix.
Died brokenhearted on first anniversary of that (the accidental drowning of his wife) hard day.

ROSA. Mother of. E. D. ix.
A pretty little creature—brought home in her father's arms, drowned.

ROSA VILLA. Clapham Rise.
S. B. B., Tales ix.
In occupation of Mr. Gattleton —usually so neat and tidy, was regularly turned out o' windows in preparation for private theatricals.

ROSE. M. P., V. C.

ROSE. Enemy of Col. Potter.
A. N. xvii.

ROSE. Oliver Twist's aunt.
O. T. li.

ROSES AND DIAMONDS. Jemmy.
C. S., M. L. Lo. i.

ROSINA. M. P., M. N. D.

ROSS. Mr. A. N. xvii.

ROSS. Sir James. M. P., E. T.

ROSSINI. Signor. M. P., M. M.

ROTHERHITHE.
M. P., G. B. ; O. T. l.

To reach this place the visitor has to penetrate through a maze of close, narrow, and muddy streets. The cheapest and least delicate provisions are heaped in the shop ; the coarsest and commonest articles of wearing apparel dangle at the salesman's door, and stream from the house parapet and windows.

ROTHSCHILD. M. P., G. A.

ROTHSCHILDS. M. P., F. L.

ROTTEN GRAY'S INN LANE.
R. P., D. W. I. F.

ROTTINGDEAN. D. and S. viii.

ROUGE ET NOIRE. Demented woman. M. P., W. S. G.

ROUNCEWELL. An Ironmaster. Son of Sir Leicester Dedlock's housekeeper. B. H. xxvii.
A little over fifty, perhaps, of a good figure, like his mother ; has a clear voice, a broad forehead, from which his dark hair has retired, and a shrewd, though open face. A responsible-looking gentleman dressed in black, portly enough, but strong and active.

Note.—Son of Mrs. Rouncewell. He stays in England and prospers as an ironmaster. It is his son Watt who is betrothed to Rosa.

ROUNCEWELL. Children of the ironmaster. B. H. lxiii.

ROUNCEWELL. Mr. George, Ex-trooper, and shooting-gallery owner. B. H. vii.
A swarthy man of fifty ; well made and good looking ; with crisp dark hair, bright eyes, and a broad chest. His sinewy and powerful hands, as sunburnt as his face, have evidently been used to a pretty rough life.

Note.—Rouncewell is first seen as the keeper of a shooting range. It transpires that he is the son of the Dedlock's housekeeper. Eventually he becomes a companion-servant to Sir Leicester Dedlock.

ROUNCEWELL. Mr., Husband of Mrs. Rouncewell.   *B. H.* vii.

Died some time before the decease of the pretty fashion of pigtails.

ROUNCEWELL. Mrs., House-keeper at Chesney Wold.
          B. H. vii.

A fine old lady, handsome, stately, wonderfully neat, and has such a back and such a stomacher, that if her stays should turn out when she dies to have been a broad old-fashioned family fire-grate, nobody who knows her would have cause to be surprised.

Note.—Housekeeper at Chesney Wold. Mother of George and the iron-master. She is devoted to the Dedlock family, and when the story closes she is still seen "harder of hearing," but looking after her duties.

ROUNCEWELL. Mrs., Wife of the ironmaster.   *B. H.* lxii.

ROUNCEWELL, WATT. *B. H.* vii.

Note.—Son of the Ironmaster and grandson of Mrs. Rouncewell. He meets Rosa at Chesney Wold and falls in love with her. There are difficulties in the way. But she is eventually sent to Germany " to be polished up " as the intended wife of Watt.

ROVINGHAMS. Commission mer-chants.   *L. D.* v.

All our consignments have long been made to Rovinghams', the commission merchants and—as a check upon them, and in the stewardship of my father's re-sources, your judgment and watch-fulness have been actively exerted.

ROWDY JOURNAL. New York.
         M. C. xvi.

ROYAL ACADEMY OF ARTS.
M. P., O. L. N. O.; R. P., G. o. A.

ROYAL ACADEMY OF MUSIC.
         M. P., O. L. N. O.

ROYAL ALMACKS.   *M. C.* xxi.

ROYAL COLLEGE OF SURGEONS.
         M. P., O. L. N. O.

ROYAL EXCHANGE. *B. R.* lxvii.; *C. S., W. o. G. M.; D. and S.* iv.; *M. P., I.; M. P., W.; R. P., B. S.; U. T.* vi.

ROYAL FREE HOSPITAL. Gray's Inn Road.   *M. P., V. D.*

ROYAL GEORGE. Dover.
     T. T. C., bk. i. ch. iv.

Original: Said to have been the "King's Head Hotel."

ROYAL GEORGE. The, Hotel.
   C. B., C. o. H.; R. P., A. F.; S. B. B., Tales x.

ROYAL HÔTEL. The, Angaishee Ouse Calais.   *U. T.* xvii.

ROYAL HOTEL.   *P. P.* xxxvii.

Original: Probably the "York House Hotel," Bath, "frequently patronised by Royalty."

ROYAL HOTEL. Leamington.
         D. and S. xx.

Original: Was well known at the time " as if he [Dombey] were the proprietor "=Regent Hotel.

ROYAL ITALIAN OPERA.
         U. T. iv.

ROYAL OLD DUST BIN. Dining-rooms.   *C. S., S. L.* i.

ROYALE. Rue.   *R. P., O. o. S.*

RUDDLE. Mortgage of. *N. N.* ii.

RUDGE. Barnaby.   *B. R.* i.

His hair, of which he had a great profusion, was red, and hanging in disorder about his face and shoulders.—His dress was of green, clumsily trimmed here and there—with gaudy lace; brightest where the cloth was most worn and soiled. A pair of tawdry ruffles dangled at his wrists. He had ornamented his hat with a cluster of peacocks' feathers—girt to his side was the steel hilt of an old sword without blade or scabbard. When her son was born, he bore upon his wrist what seemed a smear of blood but half washed out.

Note.—The title-character of the story. A shrewd, kindly, but half-witted youth, with a deep knowledge of, and love for, wild life: deeply exercised in mind as to what makes the stars shine. He is watched over by his mother. His closest companion, after his raven, is Maypole Hugh, like whom he is strong and muscular. He is embroiled with the rioters, and on the suppression of the disturbances he is sentenced to death, but is pardoned, as the result of Varden's efforts on his behalf. Afterwards he settles down on the Maypole farm and improves in mind and intellect. But the wild scenes in London have had so much effect on his mind that he will never after enter London.

Original: Said to have been founded on Walter de Brisac, living at Chatham. Died 1893.

RUDGE. Mr., Steward of Reuben Harewood. *B. R.* i.

Whose body—scarcely to be recognised by his clothes and the watch and ring he wore—was found at the bottom of a piece of water in the grounds, with a deep gash in his breast where he had been stabbed with a knife.

Note.—Barnaby's father. He was formerly steward to Reuben Haredale. Mr. Haredale was murdered and Rudge fled. A dead body, so disfigured as to be unrecognisable, is discovered, and it is supposed to be that of Rudge the murderer. Later on he returns and pesters his wife in secret. It is discovered by others that he is alive, and his identity established. It is proved not only that he murdered Mr. Haredale, but also that the death of the man whose body was taken for that of Rudge himself, was due to him, and he is executed.

RUDGE. Mrs. Mary, Barnaby's mother. *B. R.* iv.

About forty—perhaps two or three years older—with a cheerful aspect, and a face that had once been pretty.

Note.—Mother of Barnaby. She watches over her son, and her whole life is devoted to keeping him away from his father and out of his clutches: and with this end in view, she is reduced to all kinds of stratagems.

RUDGE ROW. *R. P., B. S.*

RUFFIAN NUMBER ONE. *U. T.* xxxvi.

A shirking fellow of five-and-twenty, in an ill-favoured, and ill-savoured suit.

RUFFIAN, NUMBER TWO. *U. T.* xxxvi.

A burly brute of five-and-thirty, in a tall stiff hat, is a composite, as to his clothes, of betting and fighting man; is whiskered—has insolent and cruel eyes; large shoulders; strong legs, booted and tipped for kicking.

RUFFIAN. The. *U. T.* xxxvi.

Always a ruffian, always a thief.

RUFFIANISM. Preparatory schools of. *U. T.* xxxvi.

RUGBY. *M. P., E. S.; M. P., L. L.; M. P., O. S.*

RUGG. Miss Anastasia, Daughter of Rugg. *L. D.* xxv.

A lady of a little property, which she had acquired—by having her heart severely lacerated—found it necessary to proceed at law to recover damages for a breach of promise of marriage.—Had little nankeen spots, like shirt-buttons, all over her face, and whose yellow tresses were rather scrubby than luxuriant.

RUGG. Mr., Mr. Panck's landlord.
L. D. xxv.
General agent, accountant, debts recovered, had a round white visage, as if all his blushes had been drawn out of him long ago—a ragged yellow head like a worn-out hearth-broom.

Note.—Pancks' landlord. He is Arthur Clennam's professional adviser in his financial reverses.

RUIN. Name of a bird. *B. H.* xiv.
RULE OFFICE. *B. H.* x.

RULER. Gentleman, Landlord of lodging-house. *N. N.* xlvi.
Who was smoking hard in front parlour (though it was not yet noon).

RULES. The, Of the King's Bench Prison. A certain liberty adjoining the prison.
N. N. xlvi.; *S. B. B.,* Scenes xxi.
Comprising some dozen streets in which debtors who can raise money to pay large fees, from which their creditors do *not* derive any benefit, are permitted to reside by the wise provisions of the same enlightened laws, which leaves the debtor who can raise no money, to starve in jail, without the food, clothing, lodging or warmth which are provided for felons convicted of the most atrocious crimes that can disgrace humanity. There were small gardens in front—which served as pens for the dust to collect in.

RUMMUN. Prof. *Mud. Pap.* ii.
RUNAWAYS. Some five-and-forty.
B. R. xxxiii.
Varying from six years old to twelve.

RUSH. Murderer. *M. P., D. M.*
RUSSELL. Lord John.
M. P., N. E.; M. P., T. B.

RUSSELL. Mr. *M. P., B.*.
RUSSELL SQUARE.
N. N. xxxvii.; *S. B. B.,* Char.
RUSSIA. *M. P., C. P.; M. 1, N. G. K.; M. P., W.; M. 1, W. H.; U. T. v.*
RUSSIA. *C*zar of. *M. P., R. S.*.
"RUSSIA." First officer of steame.
U. T. xx
"RUSSIA." Second officer steamer. *U. T.* xx:
"RUSSIA." Third Officer steamer. *U. T.* xx:,
Posted at the stern rail with lantern.
"RUSTIC LODGE." Near Readin
M. P., I. S. H.
RUTLANDSHIRE.
C. S., M. L. Lo.
RYDE. *N. N.* xx

S

S. Mrs. *M. P., S.*.
SACKVILLE STREET. *O. M. F.*
SACRISTAN. The.
P. F. I., L. R. G.
SADDLER. The. *G. E.* vi
SADLER'S WELLS.
S. B. B., Scenes xi
SADLER'S WELLS THEATRE.
O. T. vi
SAFE. John, Engine-driver,
M. P., R..
SAFFRON HILL. *B. H.* xxvi
M. P., C. and E.; M. P., S. S. U
O. T. vi.
SAGE. *M. P., P. M.*
SAGE. Dick. *M. P., G. 1*

SAGGERS. Mrs., Eldest but one of occupants of Titbull's Almshouses.   *U. T.* xxvii.

SAILOR.   *M. P., G. F.*

SAILOR. Body of a.   *O. M. F.* iii. With two anchors and a flag and G.F.T. on his arm.

ST. AGATA.   *P. F. I., R. D.*

ST. ALBAN'S.   *B. H.* vi. ; *D. C.* xxiv. ; *M. P., F. C.* ; *O. T.* xlviii. ; *U.* T. xi.

ST. ALPHAGE.   *Canterbury.* *D. C.* xvi.

ST. ANDREW'S.   *Churchyard of.* *B. H.* x.

ST. ANDREW'S, HOLBORN. *O.* T. xxi.

ST. ANGELO.   *P. F. I., R. D.*

ST. ANGELO. Bridge of. *P. F. I., R.*

ST. ANGELO. *C*astle of. *P. F. I., R.*

ST. ANNE'S VILLAS.   *M. P., N. S.*

ST. ANTOINE. A suburb of Paris. *T. T. C.* v. *C*old, dirt, sickness, ignorance, and want, were the lords in waiting on the saintly presence.

ST. BARTHOLOMEW. Hospital of. *L. D.* xiii. ; *R. P., T. D. P.*

ST. BARTHOLOMEW. Surgeon of. *L. D.* xiii.

ST. BENEDICT.   *N. N.* vi.

SAINT BLANK'S HOSPITAL. House surgeon of.   *R. P.,* T. *D. A.* iii.

SAINT BLANK'S HOSPITAL. Secretary of.   *R. P.,* T. *D. A.* iii.

ST. BLANK'S HOSPITAL.   A student.   *R. P., T. D. A.* iii. A tallish, good-looking young man of one or two and twenty, with a light whisker.

SAINT BLANK'S HOSPITAL. Treasurer of.   *R. P.,* T. *D. A.* iii.

S. CARLINO THEATRE. *P. F. I., R. D.*

S. CARLO. Theatre of. *P. F. I., R. D.*

ST. CATHERINE'S DOCKS. *U.* T. xxviii.

ST. CLAIR. Assumed name. *S. B. B.,* Scenes xiii.

ST. CLEMENT'S CHURCH. *P. P.* xxiii. ; *S. B. B., O. P.* vii.

ST. CLEMENT'S DANES. *C. S., M. L. Lo.* i.

SANTA CROCE. Church of. *P. F. I., R. D.*

SAINT DUNSTAN. *B. R.* xl. ; *M. H. C.* iii.

ST. DUNSTAN'S.   The figures at. *M. P., G. A.*

ST. EVREMONDE. Marquis de. *T. T. C.,* bk. ii., ch. xxiv. A man of about sixty, handsomely dressed, haughty in manner, and with a face like a fine mask.

Note.—Uncle of Charles Darnay. He rides over a child and kills it in the streets of Paris. Gaspard, the father, follows him to his chateau and kills him. On the night before his murder his nephew arrives from London to visit him.

ST. EVREMONDE. Marquis. *T. T. C.* bk. iii., ch. x.

Note.—The father of Charles Darnay and twin brother of the monseigneur of the story. Dead when he is mentioned first.

ST. EVREMONDE. Marquis. *See* also Darnay, *C*harles, who succeeded his uncle, when Monsieur the Marquis was murdered.

ST. EVREMONDE. Marquise.
T. T. *C.*, Bk. iii., ch. x.

Note.—Mother of Charles Darnay. She visited Dr. Manette after he had learned the secret of her husband and his brother.

ST. GEORGE OF SOUTHWARK.
L. D. xiv.; *R. P., D. W. I. F.*

ST. GEORGE'S CHAPEL. Windsor.
M. P., C. C.; *M. P., T. D.*

SAINT GEORGE'S CHURCH.
L. D. vi.; *N. N.* xxi.; *P. P.* xxi.; *U. T.* iii.

SAINT GEORGE'S CHURCH. Clerk of. *L. D.* lxx.

ST. GEORGE'S CHURCH. Hart Street. *S. B. B.*, Tales xi.

ST. GEORGE'S FIELDS. Southwark. *B. R.*, xlviii.; *M. P., G. F.*; *M. P., S. B.*; *N. N.* xlvi.; *P. P.* xliii.; *S. B. B.* xxvii.; *U. T.* x.
Really fields at that time.

ST. GEORGE'S GALLERY.
R. P., T. N. S.

ST. GEORGE'S-IN-THE-EAST.
U. T. iii.

ST. GERMAIN.
M. P., L. A. V. i.; *P. F. I., R. D.*

ST. GILES. *B. R.* xliv.; *M. P., G. A.*; *P. F. I., A. G.*; *P. F. I., R. D.*; *R. P., D. W. I. F.*; *S. B. B.*, Scenes v.; *S. B. B.*, Scenes xxii.; *S. B. B.*, Tales xi.; *U. T.* x.

ST. GILES STATION HOUSE.
R. P., D. W. I. F.

SAN GIOVANNI DECOLLATO.
Church of. *P. F. I., R.*

ST. GIOVANNI AND ST. PAOLO.
Church of. *P. F. I., R.*

ST. GOTTHARD PASS.
C. S., N. T., Act iii.

ST. HELENA. *M. P., L. A. V.* ii.

ST. HONORÉ. Rue. *U. T.* vii.

ST. JACQUE DE LA BOUCHERIE, Tower of. *U. T.* xviii.

ST. JAMES'S. *C. S., M. L. Lo.* i.; *M. P., F. C.*; *O. M. F.* ii.; *U. T.* iii.

SAINT JAMES'. Court of.
B. H. xii.; *M. C.* xvi.

ST. JAMES'S ARMS. Chambermaid at the. *M. P., S. G.*

ST. JAMES'S ARMS. In a small town of the road to Gretna.
M. P., S. G.

ST. JAMES'S CLUB-HOUSE.
N. N. l.

ST. JAMES'S PARISH. *M. P., N. Y. D.*; *N. N.* iv.; *U. T.* xxiii.
Where bell wires are esteemed as convenient toothpicks.

ST. JAMES'S PARK. *M. C.* xiv.; *M. P., F. N. P.*; *M. P., Th. Let.*; *N. N.* xliv.; *S. B. B.*, char. i.

ST. JAMES' SQUARE. *B. R.* lxx.; *M. C.* xxvii.; *O. M. F.* ii.

ST. JAMES'S STREET. *C. S., T. G. S.* i.; *H. T., G.* iii.; *R. P., O. B.*

ST. JAMES'S THEATRE. *M. P., I. S. H. W.*; *M. P., V. C.*; *R..P., F.*

ST. JANUARIUS'S GALLERY.
M. P., T. B.

ST. JOHN'S. *A. N.* xv.

ST. JOHN'S ROAD. *O. T.* viii.

ST. JULIEN HORATION, alias Jem Larkins.
S. B. B., Scenes xii.

ST. MILDRED'S CHURCH.
B. R. lxvii.

SAINT OMER'S. *B. R.* xliii.

ST. PANCRAS. The old church burial-ground.
T. T. C., bk. ii., ch. xiv
Far off in the fields.

Note.—Cly's pseudo burial of paving stones took place here.

ST. PANCRAS BOARD OF GUARDIANS. *M. P., S. Pigs.*

ST. PANCRAS WORKHOUSE.
M. P., P. P.

ST. PAUL'S. *B. H.* xix. ; *B. R.* xxii. ; *C. S., N. T., O.* ; *D. C.* iv. ; *G. E.* xx. ; *L. D.* iii. ; *M. C,* xxxviii. ; *M. H. C.* i. ; *M. P., A. in E.* ; *M. P., C.* ; *M. P., G. A.* ; *M. P., G. B.* ; *M. P., P. A. P.* ; *M. P., P. F.* ; *M. P., T. D.* ; *M. P., R. S. D.* ; *M. P., V. and B. S.* ; *N. N.* xlv. ; *O. M. F.* xxxiv.

ST. PAUL'S CHURCHYARD. *B. R.* xxxvii. ; *C. B., C. C., S.* i. , *M. H. C.* i. ; *O. M. F.*, viii. *P. F. I., R. P. S.* ; *R. P., B. S.* ; *S. B. B.*, Scenes iii.

ST. PÉLAGIE. *R. P., O. o. S.*

ST. PETER. Church of. *L. D.* xliii. ; *M. P., V. and B. S.* *P. F. I., R.* ; *R. P., O. B.* *U. T.* ix

ST. PETER'S. Great Piazza of. *P. F. I., R.*

ST. PETERSBURG. *L. D.* xvi.

SAN PETRONIO. Church of. *P. F. I., T. B. F.*

SAN PIETRO CATHEDRAL. Mantua. *P. F. I., V. M. M. S. S*

SAN REMO. *P. F. I., G. A. N*

SALTINE. Gorge of the.
P. F. I., V. M. M. S. S.

SALVATORE, SIGNIOR. Head guide.
P. F. I., R. D.

SALWANNERS. The, The Savannah.
B. R. lxxii.

SAM. Cab-driver.   P. P. ii.

SAM. Mr. Pecksniff's hostler.
M. C. v.

SAM. Slave.   A. N. xvii.

SAMBO PILOT. Christian King
George.   C. S., P. o. C. E. P.

SAMBOS.   Natives of Silver Store
Island.   C. S., P. o. C. E. P.
Half-negro and half-Indian.

SAMPSON.   George, Sweetheart
of Bella, and afterwards of Lavinia
Wilfer.   O. M. F. iv.

Note.—A young man, a kind of pet
poodle belonging to the Wilfers. At
the opening of the story he is beginning
to become devoted to Bella, but transfers his adoration to her sister, when
she is adopted by the Boffins. It
would perhaps be better to say that,
deeming it likely that another pet
poodle in the family would be difficult
to obtain, Lavinia took him over. He
is left paying a visit to his future sister-
in-law in her " marble halls."

SAMPSON. Mr., Chief manager
of an insurance office. H. D. i.

SAMPSON'S. AUNT.   O. M. F. lv.

SANDERS. Mrs., particular acquaintance of Mrs. Bardell.   P. P. xxvi.
A big, fat, heavy-faced personage.

SANDFORD. Master Harry, Pupil
of Mr. Barlow.   U. T. xxxiii.

SANDGATE-BY-THE-SEA.
M. P., S. F. A

SANDHURST.   M. P., G. D.

SANDUSKY.   A. N. xiv.

SANGAR POINT. C. S., W. o. G. M.

SANTENSE'S. Madame.
O. M. F. xi.

SAONE. The river.
L. D. xi. ; R. P., D. W. T. T.
Like a sullied looking-glass in a
gloomy place, reflected the clouds
heavily ; and the low banks
leaned over here and there, as if
they were half-curious, and half-
afraid, to see their darkening
pictures in the water.

SAPPER. A huge-bearded.
U. T. vii.

SAPSEA. Maid of Mr.   E. D. iv.

SAPSEA. Mr. Thomas, Auctioneer.
E. D. iv.
Dresses at the Dean—has been
bowed to for the Dean—spoken
to as my Lord, under the impression that he was the Bishop—
without his chaplain.   Much
nearer sixty years of age than fifty,
with a flowing outline of stomach
—reputed to be rich.

Note.—The pompous Mayor of
Cloisterham.   An auctioneer reputed
to be rich. He may be considered
almost as one of the auxiliary char-
acters of the book, as, so far as the
story goes, he occupies a quite subsi-
diary place. When introduced he is
composing an epitaph for his wife's
tomb, as follows :
Ethelinda,
Reverential Wife of
Mr. Thomas Sapsea,
Auctioneer, valuer, estate agent, etc.,
of this city.
Whose knowledge of the world,
Though somewhat extensive,
Never brought him acquainted with
A spirit
More capable of
Looking up to him.
Stranger, pause
And ask thyself the Question,
Canst thou do likewise ?
If not,
With a blush retire.
At the last mention in the book he has
just made the acquaintance of Datchery.

Original : Compound of two
originals well known in Rochester

—a *Mr. B. and a Mr. F., who had many characteristics of the quondam Mayor of Cloisterham.*

SAPSEA. The late Mrs., Ethelinda.
           E. D. iv.

"SARACEN'S HEAD." Snow Hill.
    N. N. iii. ; *O. M. F.* xlix. ;
           U. T. iii.

"SARACEN'S HEAD." Towcester.
           P. P. li.
   " Everything clean and comfortable. Wery good little dinner, sir, they can get ready in half an hour —pair of fowls, sir, and a weal cutlet ; French beans, taturs, tart, and tidiness."

SARAH.   *P. P.* xli.

SARAH. Domestic at Westgate House.   *P. P.* xvi.

SARAH. Maid of old lady.
          S. B. B., O. P. ii.

SARAH. Seven Dials lady.
          S. B. B., Scenes v.

SARAH'S SON'S HEAD. *See* Saracen's Head.

SATIS HOUSE. The Manor House.
          G. E. viii.
   Original : Restoration House, in Crow Lane, now Maidstone Road, opposite the Vines. Charles II lodged there when it was in the possession of Sir Francis Clarke.

SAUNDERS.   *S. Y. C.*

SAUNDERS. Robt. L. *M. P., O. C.*

SAVAGE. A baby ; a waif.
          C. B., H. M. i.
   A creature more like a young wild animal than a young child—a bundle of tatters, held by a hand, in size and form almost an infant's, but in its greedy—clutch, a bald old man's—a face rounded and smoothed by some half-dozen

years, but—twisted by the exper ence of a life. Bright eyes, bi not youthful—naked feet, bea tiful in their childish delicacy- ugly in the blood and dirt th cracked upon them.

SAVAGE. The noble.
          R. P., T. N.

SAVANNAH. The.   *B. R.* lxxi

SAVILLE ROW.   *U. T.* xv

SAVILLE. Sir George.   *B. R.* lv

SAVIOUR. The.   *M. P., I. M*

SAWBONES. A couple of surgeon *See* Allen Benjamin, and Sawye Bob.

SAWYER. Bob, Very particula friend of Mr. Benjamin Alle
          P. P. xx
   Wore a pair of plaid trouser and a large double-breasted wais coat ; out of doors he carried stick with a big top. He e chewed gloves, and looked, upo the whole, something like a diss pated Robinson Crusoe.

   Note.—A medical student, frien of Benjamin Allen. He sets up a a chemist - medical - practitioner i Bristol, but in spite of many artfu dodges, does not succeed. He eventu ally passes through the Gazette an accompanies Benjamin Allen to Beng in the service of the East India Com pany.

SAWYER. Mr.   *M. R. B*

SAWYER. Visitor to Bob.
          P. P. xxxi
   Prim personage in clean line and cloth boots.

SCADDER. Mr. Zephaniah, Agen for the Eden Settlement.
          M. C. xxi
   He was a gaunt man in a hug straw hat, and a coat of gree stuff—he had no cravat, and wor his shirt-collar wide open ; so tha every time he spoke somethin

was seen to twitch and jerk up in his throat like the little hammers in a harpsichord when the notes are struck. Two grey eyes lurked deep within this agent's head, but one of them had no sight in it, and stood stockstill. Each long black hair upon his head hung down as straight as any plummet-line ; but rumpled tufts were on the arches of his eyes.

Note.—This land-agent was a typical real estate swindler. While he does not lie enough perhaps to bring him within the American law of the time, he conveys the impression that Eden is a thriving city, and sells Martin Chuzzlewit a " lot " of fifty acres. The " city " turns out to be all in the future, its present consisting of a few log huts ; the property, a morass, and the population a handful of broken settlers dying under the ravages of fever.

SCADGERS. Lady, Great-aunt of Mrs. Sparsit. *H. T., S.* vii.
An immensely fat old woman, with an inordinate appetite for butcher's meat, and a mysterious leg which had now refused to get out of bed for fourteen years.

SCALA. Santa, or Holy Staircase. *P. F. I., R.*

SCALEY. Mr., A bailiff. *N. N.* xxi.
Proprietor of a white hat, and a red neckerchief, and a broad round face, and a large head, and part of a green coat.

SCALP. An Indian chief. *A. N.* ix.

SCARBOROUGH.
D. and S. xxi. ; *H. D.* iv.

SCARLI TAPA. *M. P.,* T. *O. H.*
Red tape.

SCARLI TAPA. Son of.
M. P., T. O. H.

SCARLI TAPA. Wife of.
M. P., T. O. H.

SCAVENGERS. Theatre of the.
M. P., N. Y. D.

SCEAUX. *R. P., M. O. F. F.*

SCHLESINGER. Mr.
M. P., I. W. M.

SCHÖN. Mr., Missionary.
M. P., N. E.

SCHOOL. *O. C. S.* xxiv.

SCHOOL. *R. P., S.; S.*
Original : Generally believed to have been based on Giles School and Wellington House Academy.

SCHOOL. High, Cloisterham.
E. D. xiv.

SCHOOL. In Canterbury. *D. C.* xvi.
A grave building in a courtyard with a learned air about it.

SCHOOL. Ladies, late shop.
S. B. B., Scenes iii.

SCHOOL. Our. *R. P., O. S.*

SCHOOLBOYS. Three or four.
S. B. B., Scenes i.
On a stolen bathing expedition.

SCHOOLMASTER. *O. C. S.* xxiv.

SCHOOLMASTER. At the Tooting Farm. *M. P., P. S.*

SCHOOLMASTER. Former, of Scrooge. *C. B., C. C., S.* ii.

SCHOOLMASTER. Our.
S. B. B., O. P. i.
One of those men one occasionally hears of on whom misfortune seems to have set her mark. His talents were great ; his disposition easy, generous, and liberal. His friends profited by the one, and abused the other. He is an old man now. He had never cared for himself, the only being who had cared for him—was spared to him no longer—meek, uncomplaining and zealous.

SCHOOLS. Day, In Seven Dials.
S. B. B., Scenes v.

SCHUTZ. Mr., A passenger on the " Halsewell." *R. P., T. L. V.*

SCIENTIFIC GENTLEMAN.
P. P. xxxix.
An elderly gentleman of scientific attainments, writing a philosophical treatise. In the agonies of composition, the elderly gentleman looked sometimes at the carpet, sometimes at the ceiling, and sometimes at the wall.

SCIENTIFIC SHOEING - SMITH AND VETERINARY SURGEON.
U. xxii.

SCOTCH FELLOWS. Three or four, Guests of the Baillie. *P. P.* lxix.
Stout, bushy-eyebrowed, canny old Scotch fellows that the Baillie had got together to do honour to my uncle.

SCOTLAND. *B. R.* lxxxii. ; *M. P., A. in E.* ; *M. P., O. C.* ; *M. P., R. S.*

SCOTLAND YARD.
S. B. B., Scenes iv.

SCOTT. Miss. *M. P., S. P.*

SCOTT. Sir Walter. *M. P., M. B.* ; *M. P., S. P.*

SCOTT. Tom, Quilp's boy.
O. C. S. l.
Note.—Quilp's errand-boy. He is nearly as eccentric as Quilp himself, which may account for the affection or sympathy existing between them, in spite of Quilp's brutality to him. On Quilp's death he becomes an Italian tumbler, thus putting to effective use the accomplishment he had acquired and used for Quilp's annoyance.

SCOUTS. Hangers-on and outsiders about Doctors' Commons.
D. C. x.

SCRADGER. Mr. *M. P., W. H.*

SCREWZER. Tommy.
D. and S. lxi.
A man of an extremely bilious habit.

SCRIVENS. *M. P., C. Pat.*

SCROGGINS. Sir Giles. *M. P., W*

SCROGGINS AND PAYNE. Messr. Solicitors. *S. B. B.*, Tales vi.

SCROOGE. Counting-house of old
C. B., C. C., S. i
The door of Scrooge's counting-house was open that he migh keep his eye upon his clerk, who in a dismal little cell beyond, sort of tank, was copying letters.

SCROOGE. Ebenezer. Of Scroog and Marley. On 'change.
C. B., C. C., S. i
A squeezing, wrenching, grasping, scraping, clutching, covetou old sinner. Hard and sharp as flint—secret—and solitary as an oyster. The cold within him froze his old features, nipped his pointed nose, shrivelled his cheek, stiffened his gait ; made his eyes red, his thin lips blue, and spoke out shrewdly in his grating voice.

SCROOGE. Father of.
C. B., C. C., S. ii.

SCROOGE. Niece by marriage of.
C. B., C. C., S. iii.

SCROOGE. Ruin of school attended by. *C. B., C. C., S.* ii.

SCROOGE. Spirit of sister of.
C. B., C. C., S. ii.

SCROOGE'S CHAMBERS.
C. B., C. C., S. i.
A gloomy suite of rooms, in a lowering pile of building up a yard. It was old enough—and dreary enough, for nobody lived in it but Scrooge, the other rooms being all let out as offices.
Original : Scrooge's knocker had its original in the knocker of a house in Craven Street.

SCROOGE'S NEPHEW.
C. B., C. C., S. i.

SCROOGE'S NIECE'S SISTER.
C. B., C. C., S. iii.
The plump one with the lace tucker.

SCUTARI.
M. P., S. F. A. ; *M. P., T. T.*

SEA-CAPTAIN. *M. P., L. E. J.*

SEACOMBE. *R. P., T. L. V.*

SEALER. Deputy.
R. P., P. M. T. P.

SEAMAN. Rough. *M. P., S. W.*

SEAMAN'S BOARDING-HOUSE.
O. M. F. xxix.

SEAMAN'S HOMES. *U. T.* v.

SEAMSTRESS. Little.
T. T. C., bk. iii., ch. xiii.

SEAPORT. (Chatham.)
M. P., N. Y. D.

SEARLE'S YARD. Boating establishment. *S. B. B.*, Scenes x.

SEBASTOPOOL.
M. P., T. O. P. ; *M. P., T. T.*

SEBASTOPOL. Boulevard de.
U. T. xviii.

SECRETARY. Pickwick Club.
P. P. i.

SECRETARY TO THE POST-OFFICE. *M. P., M. E. R.*

SEDAN-CHAIR. Bearers of.
P. P. xxxvi.
One short fat chairman, and one long thin one.

SEINE. The. *R. P., D. W. T. T.*

SELF AND CRAGGS. Snitchey and Craggs. *C. B., B. o. L.* i.

SEMANDRÉ. *M. P., L. A. V.* i.

SEMINARY. National.
S. B. B., O. P. vi.

SEMINARY. Thiere's kitchen and.
R. P., D. W. I. F.

SEMPRONIUS. Mr., Son of Ganttleton. *S. B. B.*, Tales ix.

SEN' GEORGE'S CHANNEL.
D. and S. xxiii.

SENATE. The, " A dignified and decorous body."
A. N. iii. ; *M. P., Y. M. C.*

SENATOR. A certain. *M. P., W.*

SENECAS. Indians. *A. N.* xvii.

SENEGAL. *M. P., L. A. V.* ii.

SENIOR UNITED SERVICE CLUB HOUSE. *M. P., B. A.*

SENS. *C. S., M. L. Leg.* i. ;
P. F. I., G. T. F.

SENTRY. At Chatham Dockyard.
U. T. xxiv.

SEPTIMUS. Nephew of Mr. Booley,
M. P., E. T.

SERAGLIO. *C. S., H. H.*

SERAPHINA. Daughter of schoolmaster. *C. S., M. L. Lo.* ii.
Had brown hair all curling beautifully.

SERAPHINA. Lady. *L. D.* xvii.

SERGEANT. *G. E.* v.

SERGEANT. Recruiting.
B. R. xxxi.

SERGEANT. Returned from India.
U. T. viii.
A man of very intelligent countenance.

SERJAMESES STREET. St. James' Street. *U. T.* xvi.

SERJEANT-AT-ARMS.
S. B. B., Scenes xviii.

SERJEANT'S INN. *P. P.* xl.

SERJEANTS. Three. *P. C.* xxxiv.

SERVANT. *M. P., L.*

SERVANT. Another, of J.P.
     B. R. xlvii.

SERVANT. At the Warren.
     B. R. xiv.

SERVANT. In livery of old gentleman.   *S. B. B., O. P.,* v.

SERVANT. John.   *I. S. H. W.*

SERVANT. Lodger's, Of Mrs.
Raddles.   *P. P.* xlvi.

SERVANT. Miss Madeline Bray's.
     N. N. xlvi.

SERVANT. Mr. Boythorn's man.
     B. H. ix.

SERVANT. Of Catholic gentleman.
     B. R. lxi.

SERVANT. Of Mr. and Mrs. Parsons.   *S. B. B.,* Tales x.
A middle-aged female.

SERVANT. Shivering, Of passenger
by early coach.
     S. B. B., Scenes xvi.

SERVANT GIRL. *M. P., N. Y. D.*

SERVANT GIRL. Of the Wilfers.
     O. M. F. iv.

SERVANT GIRL. Of lady in distress.   *S. B. B., O. P.* v.

SERVANT GIRL. Young, Employed
by Squeers.   *N. N.* vii.

SERVANT MAID. Of Miss Havisham.   *G. E.* xxix.

SERVANTS. *S. B. B.,* Scenes i.

SERVANTS. Of all work.
     S. B. B., Scenes i.

SERVANTS. Of hotel in Brook
Street.   *L. D.* lii.

SERVANTS. Of Mr. John Jarndyce.
     B. H. xxxi.

SERVANTS. Two female, Of Mrs.
Tibbs.   *S. B. B.,* Tales i.

SESSIONS HOUSE. The. *B. R.* lxv.

SESSIONS HOUSE. Wards of.
     S. B. B. Scenes xr.
There are several (wards) n
this part of the building buta
description of one is a descr-
tion of the whole. A spacio$,
bare, whitewashed apartme$,
lighted of course, by windows lo-
ing into the interior of the prisor –
a large fire with a deal table bef.e
it—along both sides of the ro'n
ran a shelf, below it, a row f
large hooks—on each of which \s
hung the sleeping mat of a prisor',
her rug and blanket on the sl f
above.

SESSIONS HOUSE PRISON YAR).
     S. B. B., Scenes x'.
One side of this yard is rai d
off, at a considerable distance, ε d
formed into a kind of iron ca$,
about five feet ten inches in heig',
roofed at the top, and defend
in front by iron bars, from whh
the friends of the female prison s
communicate with them.

SESSIONS HOUSE PRISON YAR).
Another prisoner in.
     S. B. B., Scenes x'.
A squalid-looking woman, n
a slovenly, thick-bordered c),
with her arms muffled in a la e
red shawl.

SESSION HOUSE PRISON YAR).
A visitor in.
     S. B. B., Scenes x'.
A yellow, haggard, decrepit d
woman, in a tattered gown t t
had once been black, and e
remains of an old straw bom$,
with faded ribbons of the sa e
hue.

SESSIONS HOUSE YARD. Prison s
visitor.   *S. B. B.,* Scenes x'.
Thinly clad, and shaking wh
the cold. Barely past her ch l-
hood, it required but a glance o
discover that she was one of th e
children, born and bred in negl t

maze of streets, courts, lanes,
and alleys ? The streets and
courts dart in all directions until
they are lost in the unwholesome
vapour which hangs over the
house-tops, and renders the dirty
perspective uncertain and confined.

SEVEN HILLS.   *L. D.* li.

SEWER. New York.   *M. C.* xvi.

SEWERS. Hon. Board of Commissioners of. *M. P., L. W. O. Y.*

SEXTON.   *L. D.* xiv.

SEXTON.   *O. C. S.* xxv.

SEXTON. At church where Paul
was christened.
D. and S. v.

SEXTON. Of church where Walter
and Florence are married.
D. and S. lvii.
The shabby little old man,
ringer of the disappointed bell, is
standing in the porch, and has
put his hat in the font, for he is
quite at home there, being sexton.

SEYMOUR. Lord, Member for Totnes.   *M. P., I. W. M.*

S ABBY-GENTEEL MAN.
S. B. B., Char. x.
Clad in an old rusty and threadbare black cloth, which shines
with constant wear as if it had
been beeswaxed. The trousers
tightly strapped down, partly
for the look of the thing and partly
to keep his old shoes from slipping
off at the heels—his yellowish-
white neckerchief is carefully
pinned up, to conceal the tattered garment underneath, and
his hands are encased in the
remains of an old pair of beaver
gloves—you may set him down as
a shabby-genteel man.

SHADWELL CHURCH.   *U. T.* xx.

SHAFTESBURY. Lord. *U. T.* xvi.

SHAKER. A grim old. *A. N.* xv.

"SHAKER VILLAGE. The." *A. N.* xv.
Peopled by " shakers."

SHAKESPEARE. *A. N.* vii. ; *D. and S.* lxi. ; *E. D.* ix. ; *L. D.* xii. ; *M. P., E. S.* ; *M. P., G. D.* ; *M. P., O. F. A.* ; *M. P., P. S.* ; *M. P., R. S. L.* ; *M. P., S.* ; *M. P., R. G.* ; *M. P., W.* ; *O. M. F.* ii. ; *P. P.* xli. ; *R. P., T. B. W.* ; *R. P., T. N. S.* . *U. T.* iv;

SHALLOW FAMILY. Justices. *M. P., S. D. C.*

SHANKLIN. *O. M. F.* x.

SHARKEY. A. C., *A. N.* xvii.

SHARP. Mr., First master at Salem House. *D. C.* vi.
Mr. Mell took his meals with the boys, but Mr. Sharp dined and supped at Mr. Creakle's table. He was a limp, delicate-looking gentleman, I thought, with a good deal of nose.

SHARPER. Abandoned. *M. P., T. T. C. D.*

SHARPEYE. Of Liverpool police force. *U. T.* v.

SHAWNEES. Indians. *A. N.* xvii.

"SHED." A, near Maiden Lane. *S. B. B.,* Scenes xx.
A wooden house with windows stuffed with rags and paper, and a small yard at the side, with one dust-cart, two baskets, a few shovels, and little heaps of cinders, and fragments of china, and tiles, scattered about it.

SHEEN AND GLOSS. Mercers. *B. H.* ii.

SHEEPSKIN. Name of a bird. *B. H.* xiv.

SHEERNESS. *C. S., S. P.* T. i

SHE-GOBLIN. *P. F. I., L. R. G.*

SHELLEY. The grave of. *P. F. I.,*

SHEPHERD. Miss, A boarder the Misses Nettingall's establis ment. *D. C.* xvi
A little girl, in a spencer, wi a round face, and curly flax hair.

SHEPHERD. The, Methodistic *P. P.* xx
"A great fat chap in black, with great white face, and a smilin' av like clockwork."

SHEPHERDSON. Mr., A butch thief. *R. P., T. D.*

SHEPPERTON. *O. T.* x

SHERMAN. Captain, Command of the steamboat "Burlington." *A. N.* x

SHERRIFF. A. *M. H. C.*

SHERRIFFS. The. *D. and S.* xx

SHERRIFFS'. The. *S. B. B.,* Scenes xi

SHERRIFFS. The. *S. B. B.,* Scenes xx

SHINY WILLIAM. Deputy host at the "Bull Inn," Rochest *P. P.*

"SHIP." Landlord of the. *G. E.* l
A weakly, meditative man, wi a pale eye.

"SHIP." The. A public-house. *G. E.* l
Original : "*Ship and Lobste situated on the river wall ab half a mile below Gravesend. T fulfils the description of the "Shi accurately, even to the washi up of the dead bodies. At one ti it was celebrated as a tea gard*

couple of windows, whereof a tenth part might be of glass, the remainder being stopped up with old copy-books and paper. There were a couple of long, old, rickety desks, cut and notched, and inked, and damaged in every possible way ; two or three forms, a detached desk for Squeers ; and another for his assistant. The ceiling was supported, like that of a barn, by cross beams and rafters ; and the walls were so stained and discoloured, that it was impossible to tell whether they had ever been touched with paint or whitewash.

SHOP. Proprietor—and Co.
S. B. B., Scenes iii.
Did nothing but walk up and down the shop, and hand seats to the ladies.

SHOP. Tobacconist's.
S. B. B., Scenes iii.
Succeeded by a theatrical hair-dresser.

SHOP. Young men in.
S. B. B., Scenes iii.
Such elegant men.

SHOPBOYS. Patrons of private theatres. *S. B. B.*, Scenes xiii.
Who now and then mistake their masters' money for their own.

SHOPMAN. Mr. Pumblechook's.
G. E. viii.

SHOPMEN. *S. B. B.*, Scenes i.
Engaged in cleaning and decking the windows for the day.

SHOPS. Gin, In the rookery.
S. B. B., Scenes xxii.
All is light and brilliancy. The gay building with the fantastically ornamented parapet, the illuminated clock, the plate-glass windows surrounded by stucco rosettes, and its profusion of gaslights in richly-gilt burners, is perfectly

dazzling. A bar of French polished mahogany, elegantly carved, extends the whole width of the place.

SHOPS. Twenty.
S. B. B., Scenes iii.
Which we are quite sure have paid no taxes for the last six years.

SHORE. Jane. *R. P., A. C. T.*

SHOREDITCH.
O. T. xxi. ; *R. P., B. S.*

SHOREDITCH CHURCH.
M. P., A. P.

SHORT. One of prisoners taken by pirates. *C. S., P. o. C. E. P.*

SHORT. Trotters. "Punch" show-man. *See* Harris.

SHORTHAND WRITERS. In High Court of Chancery. *B. H.* i.

SHORT-TIMERS. School-children.
U. T. xxix.

SHOW-TRAMP. *U. T.* xi.

SHREWSBURY SCHOOL.
T. T. C. bk. ii. ; ch. iii.
The old Sydney Carton of old Shrewsbury School.

SHROPSHIRE. *D. and. S.* xxxvi.

SHYLOCK. *G. E.* xliii. ; *P. F. I., A. I. D.*

SIBTHORP. Great.
M. P., S. for. P.

SIBYL. Temple of the.
P. F. I., R.

SIDDONS. Mrs. *M. P., S. P.*

SIDNEY. Master, As Little Walter Wilding. *M. P., N. T.*

SIDNEY. Mr., As John Johnson.
M. P., S. G.

SIENA. *P. F. I., R. P. S.*

SIERRA LEONE. *M. P., N. I*

SIGHT. Goblin, Elfin creatures (the Bells. *C. B., C.*, q. ii
Leaping, flying, dropping, pou ing from the Bells without pause.

SIGNALL HILL. *C. S., P. o. C. E. I*

SIGNAL-BOX. *C. S., T. G. S.* i
There was a fire, a desk for a official book in which he had t make certain entries, a telegraphi instrument with its dial, face, an needles.

SIGNALMAN. The.
C. S., T. G. S. i
A dark sallow man, with dark beard and rather heav eyebrows.

SIGNET. Clerk of the.
R. P., P. M. T. I

SIGNET OFFICE. *R. P., P. M. T. I*

SIKES. Bill, A burglar.
O. T. xii
A stoutly-built fellow of abou five-and-thirty, in a black velve teen coat, very soiled drab breeches lace - up half - boots, and gre cotton stockings, which inclose a bulky pair of legs, with larg swelling calves. He had a brow hat on his head, and a dirt belcher handkerchief round hi neck.

Note.—Sikes with his mistres Nancy are the two figures which d most to carry out Dickens' object i writing this story of crime. Sikes i the most villainous character of th whole gang, of whom even Fagin i afraid. He is common thief, burglar and becomes a murderer. As he firs enters the story he receives the sprin kled contents of a pot of beer in hi face. The pot was thrown by Fagi at the Artful Dodger. Sikes plans t carry out a burglary at Mrs. Maylie house, and Fagin sends Oliver wit him and Toby Crackit, to craw through the window and to open th door. The scheme miscarries and Oliver is snatched from Fagin's clutches. Nancy discloses the secret to Rose Maylie, and Fagin, who discovers what he thinks is the girl's treachery, tells Sikes. The burglar beats out Nancy's brains with his pistol and club. He immediately escapes to the country. But everywhere he goes he feels himself marked, and he returns to one of the thieves' haunts, on Jacob's Island bordering on the Folly Ditch. His former friends shrink from him, however, and Charley Bates shrieks for the police from the window. Sikes seeing all other means of escape cut off, attempted to leave by the ditch. He fastened one end of his rope round the chimney stack, and was adjusting the other in a loop beneath his armpits, when he glanced up and saw, in imagination, Nancy's eyes. He staggered and lost his balance, and the noose tightened round his neck as he fell for thirty-five feet. His dog attempted to jump to him, and feel into the ditch, where he was killed.

SILENT GENTLEMAN. Interviewing Martin. *M. C.* xxii.
With glazed and fishy eyes, and only one button on his waistcoat (which was a very large metal one, and shone prodigiously) got behind the door, and stood there, like a clock, long after everybody else was gone.

SILSILEH. *M. P., E. T.*

SILVER-STORE. The Island of. *C. S., P. o. C. E. P.*

SILVER STREET. Golden Square. *N. N.* vii.

SILVERMAN. George, An orphan. *G. S. E.* i.
A worldly little devil was my mother's name for me.

SILVERSMITHS. In *Chalons*. *L. D.* xi.

SILVIA. *C. S., G. S. E.* v.

SIMKIN AND GREEN'S MANAGING CLERK. *P. P.* xx.

SIMMERY. Mr. *P. P.* lv.

SIMMONDS. Miss, In Madame Mantalini's employ. *N. N.* xviii.

SIMMONS. Mrs. Henrietta, Another of Mrs. Quilp's visitors. *O. C. S.* iv.

SIMMONS. The parish beadle. *S. B. B., O. P.* i.
Perhaps the most important member of the local administration. The dignity of his office is never impaired by the absence of efforts on his part to maintain it. On Sunday in his state-coat and cocked hat with a large-headed staff for show in his left hand, and a small cane for use in his right. . . . With the glare of the eye peculiar to beadles.

SIMMONS. William, van driver. *M. C.* xiii.
A red-faced, burly young fellow ; smart in his way, and with a good-humoured countenance—his spruce appearance was sufficiently explained by his connection with a large stage-coaching establishment.

SIMON. Negro man slave. *A. N.* xvii.

SIMON. Servant of J.P. *B. R.* xlvii.

SIMPLON. Pass. *C. S., N. T.* Act iii. ; *L. D.* xxxix. ; *P. F. I., V. M. M. S. S.*

SIMPSON. Mr., A Boarder at Mrs. Tibb's. *S. B. B.*, Tales i.
As empty-headed as the great bell of St. Paul's ; always dressed according to the caricatures published in the monthly fashions ; obtained engagement at a fashionable hairdresser's.

SIMPSON. Mr., Prisoner in the Fleet. *P. P.* xlii.
Leaning out of the window as far as he could without over-balancing himself, endeavouring, with great perseverance, to spit upon the crown of the hat of a

personal friend on the parade below.

SIMPSON. Mr. Shepherdson.
R. P., T. *D. P.*

SIMPSON. The late Mr.
S. B. B., Scenes xiv.

SIMSON. Mr., One of steam excursion party. *S. B. B.*, Tales vii.

SINBAD THE SAILOR.
M. P., *G. A.*

SING. HE, Mandarin passenger.
M. P., *C. J.*

SING. SAM, *M. P.*, *C. J.*

SING SING. Prison for the State at.
A. N. vi.

SINGER. At harmonic meeting.
S. B. B., Scenes ii.
Stout man with the small voice with brown small surtout, white stockings and shoes, is in the comic line.

SINGER. Comic.
S. B. B., Scenes xi.
The public-house chairman.

SINGERS. Four something-ean : in the costume of their country.
P. P. xv.

SINGLE GENTLEMAN. Lodger wanted by the City clerk.
S. B. B., *O. P.* vii.
Good-humoured looking gentleman of about five-and-thirty—invited friends home, who used to come at ten o'clock and begin to get happy about the small hours.

SIR SOMEBODY'S HEAD. A public-house. *S. B. B.*, Char. vii.

SISTINE CHAPEL. *P. F. I.*, *R.*

SISTER. A little. *M. P.*, *N. Y. D.*

SISTER. Of Mr. Allen's aunt.
P. P. xlviii.
Who keeps the large boarding-school just beyond the thir milestone—where there is a ver large laburnum tree and an oa gate.

SISTER. Tim Linkinwater's.
N. N. lxii
The chubby old lady.

SISTER. Twin (deceased) of Pet's
L. D. ii
Who died when we could jus see her eyes—exactly like Pet's—above the table, so she stood or tiptoe holding by it.

SISTER OF MRS. KENWIG'S.
N. N. xi
Sister of Mrs. Kenwigs—quite a beauty.

SISTERS. The Weird, Character of play. *S. B. B.*, Scenes xiii
Three uncouth-looking figures with broken clothes-props in their hands, who are drinking gin and water out of a pint pot.

SISTERS OF YORK. Five.
N. N. vi.
Tall stately figures, with dark flashing eyes and hair of jet; dignity and grace were in their every movement ; and the fame of their great beauty had spread through all the country round.

"SITTERS." Two, Passengers in four-oared galley. *G. E.* liv.

SITTINGBOURNE. *L. D.* liv.

"SIX JOLLY FELLOWSHIP-PORTERS." *O. M. F.* iii.
A tavern of dropsical appearance, had long settled down into a state of hale infirmity. In its whole constitution it had not a straight floor, and hardly a straight line, but it had outlasted many a better trimmed building. Externally it was a narrow, lopsided, wooden jumble of corpulent windows, heaped one upon the other.

SIX MILE ISLAND. *A. N.* xvii.

SKELETON. A living, Exhibited at Greenwich Fair.
S. B. B., Scenes xii.

SKETTLES. Lady, Wife of Sir Barnet. *D. and S.* xiv.

SKETTLES. Master, Prospective pupil at Dr. Blimber's.
D. and S. xiv.
Revenging himself for the studies to come, on the plum-cake.

SKETTLES. Sir Barnet, Guest of Dr. Blimber. *D. and S.* xiv.
In the House of Commons, and of whom Mr. Feeder said that when he *did* catch the speaker's eye (which he had been expected to do for three or four years) it was anticipated that he would rather touch up the radicals.

SKETTLES. Residence of.
D. and S. xxiii.
A pretty villa at Fulham, on the banks of the Thames, which was one of the most desirable residences in the world when a rowing match happened to be going past, but had its little inconveniences at other times, among which may be enumerated the occasional appearance of the river in the drawing-room, and the contemporaneous disappearance of the lawn and shrubbery.

SKEWTON. Friends of Mrs.
D. and S. xxxvi.
Guests at Dombey's housewarming.
With the same bright bloom on their complexion, and very precious necklaces on very withered necks.

SKEWTON. The Honourable Mrs., Mrs. Granger's mama.
D. and S. xxi.
Although the lady was not young, she was very blooming in the face—quite rosy—and her dress and attitude were perfectly juvenile, her age, which was about seventy—her dress would have been youthful for twenty-seven. . . . What I have ever sighed for has been to retreat to a Swiss farm, and live entirely surrounded by cows—and china.
Original : A Mrs. Campbell well known at Leamington, and locally alluded to under the name in the novel.

SKIFFINS. An accountant and agent, Miss Skiffin's brother.
G. E. xxxvii.

SKIFFINS. Miss. *G. E.* xxxvii.
Was of a wooden appearance—the cut of her dress from the waist upwards, both before and behind, made her figure very like a boy's kite—her gown a little too decidedly orange, and her gloves a little too decidedly green

SKIMPIN. Mr., Serjeant Buzfuz' junior barrister for Bardell.
P. P. xxxiv.

SKIMPOLE. Arethusa.
B. H. xliii.
"My beauty daughter—plays and sings odds and ends like her father."

SKIMPOLE. Children of Harold.
B. H. vi.

SKIMPOLE. Harold, A musical man, and an artist too.
B. H. vi. ; *M. P., L. H.*
"At least as old as I am"—but in simplicity, and freshness, and enthusiasm, and a fine inaptitude for all worldly affairs—a perfect child. A little bright creature, with a rather large head ; but a delicate face, and a sweet voice—had more the appearance of a damaged young man than a well-preserved elderly one.
*Note.—*A friend of Mr. Jarndyce, upon whom he sponges. He is with-

out principle and affects an absolute childishness about money, with the result that he is thoroughly selfish. Originally a medical man, he has not sufficient strength of character to do anything. A coolness arose between him and Mr. Jarndyce, but his later history is given in brief. He died some five years afterwards, leaving a diary and letters behind him which were published.

Original : Leigh Hunt, and so far as the diary was concerned, Haydon.

SKIMPOLE. Kitty. *B. H.* xliii.
"My comedy daughter—sings a little, but don't play."

SKIMPOLE. Laura. *B. H.* xliii.
"My sentiment daughter— plays a little, but don't sing."

SKIMPOLE. Mrs., Wife of Harold Skimpole. *B. H.* xliii.
Who had once been a beauty, but was now a delicate, high- nosed invalid, suffering under a complication of disorders.

SKIM'S. Mrs., Private hotel and commercial lodging-house.
M. P., L. T.

SKIRMISHERS. Refractories in Wapping workhouse. *U.* T. iii.

" SKYLARK." Mr. *D. C.* ii.
A very nice man, with a very large head of red hair. . . . I thought " Skylark " was his name ; and that as he lived on board ship, and hadn't a street door to put his name on, he put it on his chest instead.

SLACKBRIDGE. *H. T., R.* iv.
Chairman of United Aggregate Tribunal.

SLADDERY. Mr., Librarian.
B. H. ii.

SLAMJAM COFFEE HOUSE.
C. S., S. L. i.

SLAMMER. Dr., Surgeon to the 97th. Chatham Barracks.
P. P. ii
A little fat man, with a ring of upright black hair round his head and an extensive bald plain on the top of it. The doctor took snuff with everybody, chatted with everybody, laughed, danced. made jokes, played whist, did everything, and was everywhere at the Charity Ball, Rochester.

Note.—The surgeon of the Ninety- seventh Regiment, who feels himself affronted by Mr. Jingle in the affec- tions of a wealthy widow. Jingle is dressed in Winkle's Pickwick coat, and as Jingle refuses his name, the doctor has only the evidence of the coat to go upon. Winkle receives the doctor's chal- lenge to fight a duel, and supposes he was drunk. The affair goes as far as Winkle on the field with his eyes shut ready to fire, when Dr. Slammer of the ninety-seventh finds that Mr. Winkle is not the man. The affair was arranged, and the whole party left the field in a much more lively manner than they had proceeded to it.

Original : It is said that " Dr. Sam Piper of the provisional battalion of Chatham recognised in Dr. Slammer a caricature of him- self," and that James Lamert, Army Staff Doctor, who married Dickens' Aunt Fanny, sat for the portrait.

SLAMMONS, Mr. *See* Smike.

SLANG. Lord. *S. Y. C.*

SLAP. *M. P., M. N. D.*

" SLAP BANG." A dining-house.
B. H. xx.

SLAPPENBACHENHAUSEN. Baron.
S. B. B., Tales i.

SLASHER. Surgeon at St. Bartho- lomew's. *P. P.* xxxii.
Took a boy's leg out of the socket last week, boy ate five apples, and a ginerbread cake, exactly two minutes after it was

all over—and he'd tell his mother if they didn't begin.

SLAUGHTER. Lieutenant, Friend of *C*aptain Waters.

S. B. B., Tales iv.

SLAUGHTER. Mrs., Greengrocer, etc., of Great Twig Street.

M. P., A. N.

SLAUGHTER. Young.

M. P., A. N.

SLAUGHTER-HOUSES.

R. P., M. O. F. F.

SLEARY. Miss Josephine, Daughter of Sleary. *H. T., S.* iii.

A pretty, fair-haired girl of eighteen—tied on a horse at two years old—had made a will at twelve—expressive of her desire to be drawn to the grave by two piebald ponies.

SLEARY. Owner of a circus.

H. T., S. iii.

A stout modern statue—with one fixed eye, and one loose eye, and a voice (if it can be called so) like the efforts of a broken old pair of bellows, a flabby surface, and a muddled head which was never sober, and never drunk.

Note.—Proprietor of Sleary's Circus. He is kindly and gentle. When Tom Gradgrind's guilt is discovered, he hides the culprit, and when he is detected in his disguise, Sleary enables him to escape out of the country.

SLEEK. Dr., Of the *C*ity-free.

U. T. xix.

SLEEPY HOLLOW. *A. N.* xv.

SLEIGHT. Hannah. *M. P., P. T.*

SLIDERSKEW. Peg, Arthur Gride's servant. *N. N.* li.

A short, thin, weasen, bleareyed old woman, palsy-stricken and hideously ugly, wiping her shrivelled face upon her dirty apron.

Note.—Housekeeper to Arthur Gride, the miserly usurer. She steals his box of documents in revenge for what she thought she had suffered at his hands. Squeers makes friends with her to obtain documents relating to Madeline Bray's fortune. In the end she "went beyond the seas" and never returned.

SLIMMERY. Frank, Friend of Wilkins Flasher Esq. *P. P.* lv.

A very smart young gentleman, who wore his hat on his right whisker, and was lounging over the desk, killing flies with a ruler.

Both gentlemen had very open waistcoats and very rolling collars, —very small boots—very big rings —very little watches—very large guard - chains and symmetrical inexpressibles, and scented pockethandkerchiefs.

"SLINGO." Dealer in horses.

L. D. vii.

SLINKTON. Mr. Julius, A murderer. *H. D.* ii.

About forty or so, dark, exceedingly well dressed in black, being in mourning. His hair, which was elaborately brushed and oiled, was parted straight up the middle.

Original: *Thomas Griffiths Wainwright.*

SLITHERS. Mr., Barber.

M. H. C. i.

A very brisk, active little man, for he is, as it were, chubby all over, without being stout or unwieldy.

SLIVERSTONE. Mr. *S. Y. C.*

SLIVERSTONE. Mrs. *S. Y. C.*

SLOANE STREET. *N. N.* xxi.

SLOGGINS. *M. P., G. B.*; *M. P., N. G. K.*; and *M. P., S. F. A.*

SLOPPY. A love-child.

O. M. F. xvi.

A very long boy, with a very little head, and an open mouth

of disproportionate capacity—
parents never known—was brought
up in the House. Too much of
him longwise, too little of him
broadwise.

Note.—First introduced " turning "
[the mangle] for Betty Higden. He
had been a street child, brought up at
the workhouse and taken charge of
by Betty. He is not very bright, but
is assisted by the Boffin's and taught
woodwork. He is last seen visiting
Jenny Wren, promising to come again
and to make her several things as
specimens of his craft.

SLOTH. Mr. Wombwell's.
M. P., G. H.

SLOUT. Mr.   *O. T.* xxvii.

SLOWBOY. Maternal and paternal
parents of Tilly slowboy.
C. B., C. o. H.
Were alike unknown to fame.

SLOWBOY. Miss, Tilly Slowboy.
C. B., C. o. H. i.
Of a spare and straight shape—
insomuch that her garments appeared to be in constant danger
of sliding off these sharp pegs, her
shoulders.

SLUDBERRY. Complainant in
brawling case.
S. B. B., Scenes viii.

SLUDBERRY. Thomas.
S. B. B., Scenes viii.

SLUDGE. A murderer.
R. P., O. B.

SLUFFEN. Mr., A master sweep.
S. B. B., Scenes xx.

SLUG. Mr.   *Mud. Pap.* i.

SLUM. Mr., A military gentleman,
a poet.   *O. C. S.* xxviii.
" Ask the perfumers, ask the
blacking-makers, ask the hatters,
ask the lottery office-keepers—
ask any man among 'em what
my poetry has done for him, and
mark my words he blesses the

name of Slum. . . . Then upc
my soul and honour, ma'ar
you'll find in a certain angle (
that dreary pile, called Poet
Corner, a few smaller name
than Slum."
*Original : Believed to have bee
founded on an employé of Warren
Blacking Factory.*

SLUMKEY. The, Hon. Samuel (
Slumkey Hall.   *P. P.* xii
Blue candidate for Parliamen,
for Eatanswill, in top boots, an'
blue neckerchief, patted the babie'
on the head, kissed one of 'em.

SLUMKEY'S MAN. Agent.
P. P. xiii,

SLUMMERY. Mr.   *S. Y. C*

SLUMMINTOWKENS. Friends o
the Nupkins.   *P. P.* xxv

SLURK.   *P. P.* li
Note.—Editor of the *Eatanswil*
Independent, and on that account the
opponent of Mr. Pott.

SLY. Mr., Of " King's Arms " and
Royal Hotel.   *C. S., D. M*

SLYBOOTS. A, Mr. Krook.
B. H. xxxii.

SLYME. Chevy.   *M. C.* iv.
Perpetually round the corner.
Wrapped in an old blue camlet
cloak with a lining of faded
scarlet. His sharp features being
much pinched and nipped by
long waiting in the cold, and his
straggling red whiskers and frowzy
hair being more than usually
dishevelled from the same cause;
he certainly looked rather unwholesome and uncomfortable than
Shakespearian or Miltonic— " Too
insolent to lick the hand that fed
him in his need, yet cur enough to
bite and tear it in the dark."
Note.—A kinsman of old Martin
Chuzzlewit and, like so many of his
relatives, with an eye on the old man's

money. He engages in several occupations, but is a general failure. He is last seen as a police officer engaged in the arrest of Jonas Chuzzlewit. He says he has taken up the work to shame old Martin.

SMALDER GIRLS. The, Acquaintances of cousin Feenix. *D. and S.* xli.

SMALLCHECK. Sam Weller's name for gamekeeper. *P. P.* xix.
A half-booted leather-leggined boy.

SMALLWEED. Judith, Twin sister of Bartholomew Smallweed. *B. H.* xxi.
Never owned a doll—never played at any game.

SMALLWEED. Joshua, Grandfather Smallweed. *B. H.* xxi.
"He's a leech in his disposition, he's a screw and a vice in his actions, a snake in his twistings, and a lobster in his claws."

Note.—Relation of Krook. A discounter of bills, etc. He endeavours to blackmail Sir Leicester Dedlock, and finds a will in old Kroeks' papers relating to the Jarndyce case which he disposes of to Bucket for Mr. Jarndyce.

SMALLWEED. Mrs., senior, grandmother of Bartholomew Smallweed. *B. H.* xxi.
An eternal disposition to fall asleep over the fire, and into it.

Note.—Of little more importance in the story than as a foil to show off the eccentricities of her husband, old grandfather Smallweed.

SMALLWEED. Young Bartholomew, clerk in Kenge and Carboy's. *B. H.* xx.
He is something under fifteen, and an old limb of the law. A town made article of small stature and weazen features ; but may be perceived from a considerable distance by means of his very tall hat.

Note.—Smallweed's grandson and

sister of Judy. Friend of Mr. Guppy. They fall out to some extent over the letters which Lady Dedlock wants destroyed.

SMANGLE. Mr. Prisoner in the Fleet. *P. P.* xli.
An admirable specimen of a class of gentry which never can be seen in full perfection but in such places. A tall fellow, with an olive complexion, long dark hair, and very thick bushy whiskers meeting under his chin. He wore no neckerchief—on his head he wore one of the common eighteenpenny French skull caps, with a gawdy tassel dangling therefrom, very happily in keeping with a common fustian coat. His legs, which were long, were afflicted with weakness . . . graced a pair of Oxford mixture trousers.

SMANKER. John, One of a select company of Bath footmen. *P. P.* xxvii.

Note.—Bantam's footman who introduced Sam Weller to the select company of Bath footmen in the small parlour of the greengrocer's shop.

SMART. Tom, Friend of Bagman's uncle. Of the great commercial house of Bilson and Slum. *P. P.* xiv.
Tom sometimes had an unpleasant knack of swearing.

Note.—Introduced in the "Bagman's Story." Prevents the marriage of Jinkins with the landlady of the inn by marrying her himself.

SMIF. Putnam. *M. C.* xxii.

SMIFSER. Suitor of Mrs. Nickleby. *N. N.* xli.

SMIGGERS. Joseph, Esq. Perpetual Vice-President of the Pickwick Club *P. P.* i.

SMIKE. Mother of. *N. N.* ix.
Secret marriage—the result of

this private marriage was a son. The child was put out to nurse, a long way off ; his mother never saw him but once or twice, and then by stealth.

SMIKE. Squeers' boy, An orphan pupil. *N. N.* vii.

A tall, lean boy with a lantern in his hand. Although he could not have been less than eighteen or; nineteen years old, and was tall for that age, he wore a skeleton suit, such as is usually put upon very little boys, and which, though most absurdly short in the arms and legs, was quite wide enough for his attenuated frame. He was lame.

Note.—First met with at Squeers' school in Yorkshire, a poor drudge half-witted through cruelty and privation. Nicholas feels compassion for him, and when, after an escape and recapture, Squeers proceeds to flog him, Nicholas interferes. Nicholas leaves Dotheboys' Hall and travels towards London ; on the way he finds Smike and is persuaded to take him. They reach London, but leave it again for Portsmouth where Smike becomes a fellow member of Crummles' theatrical company with Nicholas. Away from the reign of terror at Squeers, Smike, though simple, is willing and devoted. They return to London, and Smike is again captured by Squeers, but he escapes with the assistance of John Browdie and returns to Nicholas, who refuses to give him up. His early hardships have undermined his constitution and broken his spirit ; and though the latter might mend, the former was past it and he dies. It transpires that Smike was the son of Ralph Nickleby. Brooker, at one time clerk to Ralph, had placed the boy in Squeers' hands, and told the father he was dead. The regret and remorse had something to do with Ralph s death at his own hands.

SMITH.   *M. P., C.*

SMITH. Adam, A young Gradgrind.
    H. T., S. v.

SMITH. Captain Aaron.
    N. P., P. F.

SMITH. Fixem.
    S. B. B., O. P. ·

SMITH. Job. *M. P., N. G. I*

SMITH. Joe, The prophet.
    U. T. x;

SMITH. Miss, As Fanny Wilson
  M. P., S. G. ; *M. P., V. C*

SMITH. Mr. *Mud. Pap.* i

SMITH. Mr. *S. B. B.,* Scenes xix

SMITH. Mr. Albert.
    M. P., L. A. V. ii

SMITH. Mr., A clerk.
    S. B. B., Char. i

A tall, thin, pale person, in a black coat, scanty grey trousers little pinched-up gaiters, and brown beaver gloves. He had an umbrella in his hand—not fe use, for the day was fine—but evidently, because he always carried one to the office in the morning.

SMITH. Mr., *C. F.,* as Jean Marie.
    M. P., N. T.

SMITH. Mr., Our new member.
    S. B. B., Scenes xviii.

SMITH. Mr. Samuel, Salesman in linen-draper's, in silk department.
    S. B. B., Tales v.
Alias Horatio Sparkins.

SMITH. Sydney. *M. P., M. E. R.* ;
    M. P., S. D. C.

SMITH. T. Southwood.
  M. P., O. C. ; *M. P., R. T.*

SMITH AND ELDER. Messrs., of Cornhill. *M. P., L. H.*

SMITH, PAYNE AND SMITH.
 M. P., G. A. ; *M. P., I.* ; *U. T.*
    xxi.

SMITH SQUARE.   *O. M. F.* xviii.

SMITHERS. Miss, A lady boarder at Westgate House.   *P. P.* xvi.

SMITHERS. Miss Emily, Pupil at Minerva House.
S. B. B. Tales iii.
The belle of the house.

SMITHERS. Mr.   *M. P., F. C.*

SMITHERS. Robert, A clerk in the City.   *S. B. B., C*har. xi.
Generally appeared in public in a surtout and shoes—a rough blue coat with wooden buttons, made upon the fireman's principle, a low crowned flower-pot-saucer-shaped hat.

SMITHERS AND PRICE'S.   *C*han-cery.   *P. P.* xx.

SMITHFIELD MARKET.   *B. R.* xviii.; *G. E.* xx.; *L. D.* xiii.; *M. P., L. T.*; *N. N.* iv.; *O. T.* xvi.; *R. P. M. O. F. F.*; *R. P., T. D. P.*; *U. T.* xxxiv.
It was market morning. The ground was covered, nearly ankle deep, with filth and mire; a thick steam perpetually rising from the reeking bodies of the cattle, and mingling with the fog, which seemed to rest upon the chimney-tops, hung heavily above. Countrymen, butchers, drovers, boys, thieves, idlers, and vagabonds of every low grade were mingled together in a mass.

SMITHICK AND WATERSBY. Merchant house. Of Liverpool.
C. S., W. o. G. M.

SMITHIE. Miss.   *P. P.* ii.
Present at the *C*harity Ball, Rochester.

SMITHIE. Mrs.,Wife of Mr. Smithie.
P. P. ii.
Present at the *C*harity Ball, Rochester.

SMITHIE. Mr., Something in the Dockyard.   *P. P.* ii.
Present at the *C*harity Ball, Rochester.

SMITH'S BOOKSTALL. At Mugby.
C. S., M. J. v.

SMITHS. The, Guests of the Gattle-tons.   *S. B. B.,* Tales ix.

SMIVEY. *C*hicken.   *M. C.* xiii.

SMOLLETT'S GRAVE. Leghorn.
P. F. I., R. P. S.

SMORLTORK. *C*ount, A literary man.   *P. P.* xv.
A well-whiskered individual in a foreign uniform. The famous foreigner—gathering materials for his great work on England.
Original : Founded on Prince Puckler Muskau.

SMOUCH.   *P. P.* xl.
Man in the brown coat—troubled with a hoarse cough.

SMUGGINS. Mr., Another artist.
S. B. B., Scenes ii.
Sings a comic song.

SNAGGY BAR. On Ohio River.
M. P., E. T

SNAGSBY. Mr., Law stationer.
B. H. x.
A mild, bald, timid man, with a shining head and a scrubby clump of black hair, sticking out at the back—in grey shop-coat and black calico sleeves.
Note.—Law stationer in Cook's Court, Cursitor Street. He is intimately wrapped up, much against his desire, in the Dedlock mystery, and is worried by his wife, who becomes intensely jealous of his secrecy. This does a good deal of harm to the others, but when things are cleared up, her husband is exonerated in her eyes by Bucket, and she shows contrition.

SNAGSBY. Mrs., Niece of Mr. Peffer.
B. H. x.
Something too violently com-

pressed about the waist, and with a sharp nose like a sharp autumn evening.

SNAP. Betsy, Uncle *C*hill's domestic.   *R. P., P. R. S.*
A withered, hard-favoured, yellow old woman—our only domestic.

SNAPPER. Mr., Emphatic gentleman.   *M. P., O. S.*

SNAWLEY. Mr., Stepfather — or "father-in-law" of two boys, pupils of Squeers, in the oil and colour way.   *N. N.* iv.
A sleek, fat-nosed man, clad in sombre garments, and long, black gaiters, and bearing in his countenance an expression of much mortification and sanctity.

Note.—Snawley is first seen placing his two stepsons with Squeers. He is a man of a similar kidney to Squeers, and the future of the poor boys is well understood between ·them. He is employed by Ralph Nickleby to personate the father of Smike, but the scheme fails, and he laid bare the plans of the two principal schemers.

SNEVELLICCI. Miss, Member of Mr. V. Crummles' *C*ompany.   *N. N.* xxiii.
Who could do anything from a medley dance to Lady Macbeth— always played some part in blue silk knee-smalls, at her benefit— glancing from the depths of her coal-scuttle bonnet.

Note.—Miss Snevellicci was one of the leading ladies in Crummles' theatrical company. She was very much smitten with Nicholas, who did not reciprocate her feeling.

SNEVELLICCI. Mr., A member of Mr. Crummles' Company.   *N. N.* xxx.

Note.—Father of Miss Snevellicci, a member of the same Company, and much addicted to drink.

SNEWKES. Mr.   *N. N.* xiv.
Supposed to entertain honourable designs upon last lady mentioned (sister of Mrs. Kenwigs).

SNICKS. Mr., The life office secretary.   *P. P.* xlvii.

SNIFF. Mrs., Wife of Sniff. One of refreshment room staff at Mugby Junction.   *C. S., M. J.* v.
"She's the one with the small waist buckled in tight at front, and with the lace cuffs at her wrists, which she puts on the edge of the counter before her, and stands a smoothing while the public foams."

"SNIGGLE AND BLINK."   *P. P.* xl.

SNIGGS. Mr.   *Mud. Pap.*

SNIGSWORTH. Lord. Twemlow's relative.   *O. M. F.* ii.

SNIGSWORTHY PARK.   *O. M. F.* ii.

SNIPE. Honourable Wilmot, Ensign 97.   *P. P.* ii.
Great family—Snipes—very.

Note.—The "little boy with the light hair and pink eyes" at the charity ball at the "Bull inn."

SNITCHEY. Mr. A lawyer.   *C. B., B. o. L.* i.
Like a magpie, or raven, only not so sleek.

SNITCHEY. Mrs., Wife of Mr. Snitchey.   *C. B., B. o. L.* ii.
The feather of a bird of Paradise in Mrs. Snitchey's turban trembled, as if the bird were alive again.

SNITCHEY. Jonathan, Mr. Snitchey.   *C. B., B. o. L.* i.

SNITCHEY AND CRAGGS. Lawyers.   *C. B., B. o. L.* i.

SNITCHEY AND CRAGGS. Office of.   *C. B., B. o. L.* ii.

NOADY. *M. P., L. T.*

NOBB. Mr., The Honourable, Guest of Ralph Nickleby. *N. N.* xix.

A gentleman with the neck of a stork and the legs of no animal in particular.

NOBEE. Mr. *S. B. B.,* Char. iii.

NOBS. Subjects of Prince Bull. *R. P., P. B.*

NODGRASS. Augustus, Member of the Pickwick Club. *P. P.* i.

The poetic Snodgrass. . . enveloped in a mysterious blue coat with a canine-skin collar.

Note.—One of the Pickwickians, a member of the corresponding society of the club, who accompanied Mr. Pickwick. He married Emily Wardle and settled on a small farm at Dingley Dell, which they cultivated more for occupation than profit. And Mr. Snodgrass, being occasionally abstracted and melancholy, is . . . reputed a great poet among his friends and acquaintance.

Original: The name has been suggested as a variation of Snodland, a Kentish village, and has been traced also to Gabriel Snodgrass, a shipbuilder of considerable repute in Chatham, and to Bath, and the registrar's papers at Chatham.

SNOOKS." Fictitious name of correspondent leaving gift with Father of Marshalsea. *L. D.* vi.

NORE. Prof. *Mud. Pap.* i.

NORFLERER. Lady. *S. Y. C.*

NORRIDGE BOTTOM.
C. S. ; P. o. C. E. P.

NOW HILL. *B. R.* lxvii. ; *L. D.* xiii. ; *N. N.* iii. ; *O. T.* xxvi. ; *R. P., M. O. F. F.* ; *S. B. B.,* Tales xi.

NOW. Tom, Black steward of " Golden Mary."
C. S. ; W. o. G. M.

SNUBBIN. Serjeant, Barrister. *P. P.* xxxi.

A sallow-faced, sallow-complexioned man, of about five-and-forty—or as the novels say he might be fifty. His hair was thin and weak. He had that dull looking boiled eye which would have been sufficient without the additional eyeglass which dangled from a broad black riband round his neck, to warn a stranger that he was near sighted.

Note.—Snubbin was " for the plaintiff " in Bardell v. Pickwick. A counsel very much in demand and well aware of his own worth ; though abstracted, and careless of other matters.

SNUFFIM. Sir Tumley, Mrs. Wititterly's doctor. *N. N.* xxi.

SNUFFLETOFFLE. Mr.
Mud. Pap. ii.

"SNUG." A singing house. *U. T.* v.

About the room some amazing coffee - coloured pictures varnished an inch deep, and some stuffed creatures in cases.

SNUGGERY. The. *P. P.* xlii.

SNUGGERY. The, In the Marshalsea. *L. D.* vi.

SNUGGERY. Barmaid of.
L. D. viii.

SNUGGERY. Potboy of.
L. D. viii.

SNUGGERY. Waiter of.
L. D. viii.

SNUGGERY. Landlord of.
L. D. viii.

SNUGGERY. The, Tavern estalishment at the upper end of prison. *L. D.* viii.

Where the collegians had just vacated their social evening club.

SNUGGLEWOOD. A physician.
R. P., O. B.

SNUPHANUPH. The Dowager Lady. *P. P.* xxxv.

SO AND SO. Mr. and Mrs., Guests of the old lady.
S. B. B., O. P. ii.

SOBBS. *M. P.*, T. T.

SOCIAL OYSTERS. Private club. *M. P., E. T.*

SOCIEETEE. Prince, Ward of the Genie Law. *M. P., T. O. H.*

SOCIETY FOR THE PROPAGATION OF THE GOSPEL IN FOREIGN PARTS. *B. H.* xvi.

SOCIETY FOR THE SUPPRESSION OF VICE. *S. B. B.*, Tales xi.

SOCIETY OF WELLDOING.
R. P., O. F. W.
Who are active all the summer, and give the proceeds of their good works to the poor.

SOEMUP. Dr. *Mud. Pap.* ii.

SOHO. District of, London.
C. S., N. T., Act i. *M. P., G. F.*;
N. N. lxiv. ;
A curious colony of mountaineers, has long been enclosed within that small flat—district. Swiss watch - makers, Swiss silver-chasers, Swiss jewellers, Swiss importers of Swiss musical boxes, and Swiss toys of various kinds—Swiss professors of music, painting and languages. Swiss artificers—Swiss laundresses — shabby Swiss eating-houses, coffee-houses, and lodging-houses.

SOHO SQUARE. *B. H.* xxiii. ; *C. S., N. T.*, Act i. ; *M. P., N. Y. D.* ;
T. T. C., bk. ii., ch. vi.
The quiet lodgings of Dr. Manette were in a quiet street-corner not far from Soho Square.

Original: Stands in Carlisle Street.

SOLA ACQUA, *P. F. I., G. A. N.*

SOLDIER. Irish, In workhouse n Liverpool. *U. T.* vi.
The dismalest skeleton—e ghost of a soldier.

SOLDIERS. *G. E.* v.

SOLDIERS. *P. F. I., G. T.*.

SOLDIERS. Guard of, and Offi r in command of. *L. L.* i.
A stout, serviceable, pr-foundly calm man, with his dra n sword in his hand, smoking a cig.

SOLDIERS. Two, Billeted n Madame Bouclet. *C. S., S. L.* i.

SOLICITOR. *N. N.* i.

SOLICITOR-GENERAL. *U. T.* i.

SOLICITOR-GENERAL.
T. T. C., bk. ii., ch. i.

SOLICITOR-GENERAL. In 18
M. P., C. .

SOLICITOR'S BOYS. *B. H.* .

SOLICITORS. Three. *P. P.* xl .

SOLICITORS. Various, in the ca e in Chancery High Court. B. H .
Ranged in a line, in a l g matted well (but you might l k in vain for Truth at the bottom f it).

SOLOMONS. Owner of an assun d name. *S. B. B.*, Scenes x

SOLS. Mr., Toots' name for Gi , Sol, *which see.*

" SOL'S ARMS." The. *B. H.* .
Original : Identified as the d Ship Tavern " once standing at e corner of Chichester Rents."

" SOL'S ARMS." The potboy of t . *B. H.* xx

SOLVENT COURT. *P. P.* .

SOME ONE. Shadow of. *L. D.* xx .
Who had gone by long befo .
Character in Little Dorrit's t to Maggy.

SOM
SOMEB
SOMEB
SOMEB
Ralph
Wh
weight
SOMEB
in V
SOMEB
SOMEB
Guest
SOMER
M. P.
R. P.
SOMER
SOMER
M. P.
P. P.
S. B.
SON, O
ling's
Dy
SOPHIA
Pinch
A
thirte
ready
whale
had
Not
and R
has b
follow
gover
SOPHI
SOPHO
SOPHF
SOPHV

SOPHY. Daughter of, *C. S., D. M.* She can speak.

SOPHY. Husband of. *C. S., D. M.* (Also deaf and dumb.)

SOPHY. Willing, Mrs. Lirriper's maid.   *C. S., M. L. Lo.* i. Upon her knees scrubbing early and late and ever cheerful, but always smiling with a black face.

SORDUST.   *M. P., C. Pat.*

SORRENTO.   *P. F. I., R. D.*

SOUDAN.   *M. P., N. E.*

SOULS OF THE DEAD. *M. P., R. S. D.*

SOUTH COUNTRY.   *B. H.* xxiii.

SOUTH-EASTERN RAILWAY COMPANY.   *R. P., O. o.* T.

SOUTH KENSINGTON MUSEUM. *M. P., C. H.* T. ; *M. P., L.*

SOUTH SEA HOUSE. *M. P., G. A.*

SOUTH SEA ISLANDS. *R. P., D. W. I. F.*

SOUTH SQUARE. Late Holborn *Court.*   *P. P.* xxxi.

SOUTHAMPTON. *D. and S.* xxxii. ; *N. N.* xxiii.

SOUTHAMPTON BUILDINGS. *Chancery Lane. R. P., P. M. T. P.*

SOUTHAMPTON STREET. *E. D.* xxii.

SOUTHCOTE. Mrs.   *A. N.* xviii.

SOUTHCOTE. Mrs. *R. P., T. B. W.* Wife of a begging-letter writer.

SOUTHERN STATES.   *A. N.* iii.

SOUTHWARK. *B. R.* v. ; *L. D.* vi. ; *M. P., F. S.* ; *M. P., S. B.* ; *O. T.* l. ; *P. P.* xxxii. ; *R. P.*; *D. W. T. T.* ; *U. T.* ix.

SOUTHWARK BRIDGE. *O. M. F.* i. ; *R. P., D. W. T. T.*

SOVEREIGN LADY OF OUR ISLE.
M. P., T. B.

SOWERBERRY. Mr., Parochial undertaker. *O. T.* iv.
A tall, gaunt, large-jointed man, attired in a suit of threadbare black, with darned cotton stockings of the same colour, and shoes to answer. His features were not naturally intended to wear a smiling aspect, but he was in general rather given to professional jocosity.

Note.—The undertaker to whom Oliver was "apprenticed." He was somewhat kindly disposed towards the boy if only for business purposes; kindly disposed, that is, compared to most of the others who were connected with parochial authority. To satisfy his wife he is obliged to thrash Oliver severely, and this, together with the other insults and injuries, causes the boy to run away.

SOWERBERRY. Mrs., Undertaker's wife. *O. T.* iv.
A short, thin, squeezed-up woman, with a vixenish countenance.

Note.—The wife of the undertaker. She had a violent dislike to Oliver; and fed him on scraps and refuse.

Original : The name has been traced to Sowerberry in the Church Registers at Chatham.

SOWNDS. Mr., The beadle.
D. and S. xxxi.
Sitting in the sun upon the church steps—seldom does anything else, except, in cold weather, sitting by the fire.

SOWSTER. *Mud. Pap.* ii.

SPADA. PALAZZO. *P. F. I., R.*

SPÂGNA. Piazza di. *P. F. I., R.*

SPAIN. *M. P., C. P.; P. F. I., G. A. N.; U. T.* xv.

SPANIARD. A. *M. P., L. L.*

"SPANIARDS." The, At Hampstead. Tea gardens. *P. P.* xl.

SPANIARDS. Courteous, In nurse tale. *U. T.* ı.

SPANISH FRIAR. *M. P., Dr.*

SPANISH JACK. Visitor at the "Snug." *U. T.*
With curls of black hair, rin in his ears, and a knife not i from his hand if you got in trouble with him.

SPANISH MAIN. The. *R. P., O.*

SPARKE. Thomas, Fireman.
M. P., R.

SPARKINS. Horatio, Mr. Smit *S. B. B.*, Tales
Young man with the bla whiskers and the white cravat

SPARKLER. Colonel, Decease. *L. D.* x:
Mrs Merdle's first husband.

SPARKLER. T.=Dickens, Charle *M. P., N.*

SPARKLER. Mr. Edmund, Son Mrs. Merdle. *L. D.* x:
He was of a chuckle-heade high-shouldered make, with general appearance of being, n. so much a young man, as a swell boy. Monomaniacal in offerin marriage to all manner of und sirable young ladies, and in r marking of every successive you lady to whom he tendered a mati monial proposal, that she was "doosed fine gal—well educat too—with no biggodd nonsen about her."

Note.—Mrs. Merdle's son by h former husband. He has an unfo tunate propensity for wanting to mar most of the girls he meets. In th way he becomes entangled with Fan Dorrit while she is a ballet danc He is extricated by his mother. B when the Dorrits come into their estat he again meets Fanny and eventual marries her.

SPEEDIE. Dr.   *L. T.* ii.

SPENLOW. Dora, Mr. Spenlow's
daughter.   *D. C.* xxvi.

A fairy, a sylph.

Note.—The daughter of Mr. Spenlow, of Spenlow and Jorkins, falls in
love with David Copperfield as David
falls in love with her. There appears
little prospect of the realization of their
hope, however, until the death of
Dora's father, leaving her with a small
inheritance to the care of his two
sisters. After this Dora becomes the
" child - wife " ; and she and David set
up house. He endeavours to teach her
how to manage the housekeeping and
other duties, but without success, and
eventually relinquishes the attempt.
It is not very long before her health
breaks down and she dies.

*Original : Said to have been
founded on Miss Beadwell. Flora
Finching, said to have been from
the same original in later life.*

SPENLOW. Misses, Maiden sisters
of Mr. Spenlow. *D. C.* xxxviii.

Who lived at Putney, and who
had not held any other than chance
communication with their brother
for many years. Dry elderly
ladies dressed in black.

SPENLOW. Mr., Attorney.
                            D. C. xxxiii.

In a black gown trimmed with
white fur. . . . A little light-
haired gentleman, with undeniable
boots, and the stiffest of white
cravats and shirt-collars. He was
buttoned up mighty trim and
tight, and must have taken a great
deal of pains with his whiskers,
which were accurately curled.
He was got up with such care, and
was so stiff, that he could hardly
bend himself ; being obliged, when
he glanced at some papers on his
desk, after sitting down in his
chair, to move his whole body,
from the bottom of his spine, like
Punch.

Note.—A partner in the firm of
Spenlow and Jorkins, proctors in
Doctors' Commons, to whom David

Copperfield is articled. He uses Jorkins' name as a convenience when anything unpleasant has to be done, notably in his refusal to cancel David's articles and refund his aunt's £1,000. He dies, and contrary to expectations, leaves only a small property.

SPENLOW AND JORKINS. Attorneys in office in Doctors' Commons. *D. C.* xxiii.

SPEZZIA. *P. F. I., R. P. S.*

SPIDER. The, *See* Drummle, Bentley.

SPIKE PARK. *P. P.* xlii.

SPIKER. Mr. Henry, Solicitor to something or somebody remotely connected with the Treasury. *D. C.* xxv.
So cold a man, that his head instead of being grey, seemed to be sprinkled with hoar-frost.

SPIKER. Mrs. Henry. *D. C.* xxv.
A very awful lady in a black velvet dress, and a great black velvet hat.

SPILLER. Portrait by, Of Pecksniff. *M. C.* xxiv.

SPINACH. Name of a bird. *B. H.* xiv.

SPINE. John, Celebrated novelist. *R. P., O. B.*

SPIRIT. An anonymous. *M. P., S. B.*

SPIRIT. The. *M. P., D. V.*

SPIRIT OF THE FORT. Boy emerging from the Fort. *U. T.* xxiv.

SPIRITS. Three. *C. B., C. C., S.* ii.

SPIRITS. First of the three. *C. B., C. C., S.* ii.
A strange figure—like a child, yet not so like a child as like an old man, viewed through some supernatural medium.

SPIRITS. The second of the three. *C. B., C. C., S.* iii
Clothed in one simple green robe, or mantle, bordered with white fur—hung so loosely—that its capacious breast was bare; Its feet—were also bare—and on its head—no other covering than a holly wreath, set here and there with shining icicles,—girded round its middle was an antique scabbard; but no sword was in it.

SPIRITS. The third of the. *C. B., C. C., S.* iv
The phantom—shrouded in a deep black garment, which concealed its head, its face, its form and left nothing of it visible save one outstretched hand. It was tall and stately.

SPITALFIELDS. *O. T.* xix.; *R. P.; M. O. F. F.; U. T.* x

SPITHEAD. *R. P., A. F.; U. T.* xv

SPITHERS. The new attorney general. *M. P., G. D*

SPODGER. Miss. *M. P., L. E. J*

SPODGER. Mr. *M. P., L. E. J*

SPODGER. Mr. B. *M. P., L. E. J*

SPOFFINS. *O. M. F.* xxv

SPOKER. Bust by, Of Pecksniff. *M. C.* xxiv

SPOTTED BABY. The, One of Magsman's troup. *C. S., G. i. S*

SPOTTLETOES. Mr., Husband of Martin Chuzzlewit's niece. *M. C.* iv
"Spottletoe married my father's brother's child, didn't he? and Mrs. Spottletoes is Chuzzlewit's own niece, isn't she," said Chevy Slyme, Esquire, who was so bald and had such big whiskers.

POTTLETOES. Mrs., Wife of Mr. Spottletoes, and niece of Martin Chuzzlewit. *M. C.* iv.

Much too slim for her years, and of a poetical constitution, was accustomed to inform her more intimate friends that the said whiskers (Mr. Spottletoes'), was the lodestar of her existence.

"SPREAD EAGLE." *M. P., E. S.*

SPRING GARDENS. *S. B. B.,* Char. ix.

SPRINGFIELD. *A. N.* v.

SPUNGING HOUSE. A lock-up-house. *S. B. B.,* Tales x.

SPRITES. On stage in Britannia. *U. T.* iv.

SPRODGKIN. Mrs. Sally, A widow. *O. M. F.* lxi.

Member of the Reverend Frank's congregation, made a point of distinguishing herself in that body by conspicuously weeping at everything, however cheering, said by the Reverend Frank.

SPROUSTON. *M. P., E. S.*

SPRUGGINS. Candidate for post of beadle, with ten small children (two of them twins), and a wife. *S. B. B., O. P.* iv.

A little thin man, in rusty black, with a long, pale face, and a countenance expressive of care and fatigue.

SPYERS. Jim, Police officer. *O. T.* xxxi.

SQUARE. The. *D. C.* xxx.

SQUARE. The. *N. N.* xxxvii.
Original: The works of the brothers Grant, the Cheeryble Brothers of the story, at Ramsbottom were called " The Square." The locale of London was probably deceptive. Although it is considered by some

to have been situated within Threadneedle Street, Cornhill, Finch Lane, and Bishopsgate.

SQUEERS. Junior, Son of Squeers. *N. N.* viii.

A striking likeness of his father, his chief amusement was to tread upon the other boys' toes.

Note.—Young Wackford followed closely in his father's footsteps and delighted to inflict his own small but ingenious tortures on the boys, besides wearing the clothes sent them.

SQUEERS. Miss Fanny, Daughter of Squeers. *N. N.* ix.

In her three-and-twentieth year —not tall like her mother, but short like her father ; from the former she inherited a voice of harsh quality ; from the latter a remarkable expression of the right eye, something akin to having none at all—her hair—it had more than a tinge of red—curled in five distinct rows—and arranged dexterously over the doubtful eye.

Note.—Fanny Squeers combined the bad qualities of both parents. She fell in love (so far as the term can be used in this way) with Nicholas, but when he rejected her advances her affection turned to hate. She was a friend of 'Tilda Price, although she was bitterly jealous of the miller's daughter.

SQUEERS. Mr. Wackford, Master of Dotheboys' Hall. *N. N.* iv.

He had but one eye—unquestionably useful—but decidedly not ornamental ; being of a greenish-grey, and in shape resembling the fanlight of a street door. The blank side of his face was much wrinkled and puckered up, which gave him a very sinister appearance, especially when he smiled. His hair was very flat and shiny, save at the ends—brushed up very stiffly from a low protruding forehead. He was about two or three and fifty—a trifle below the middle size—wore a white neckerchief with long ends, and a suit of scholastic black—his coat-sleeves a great deal too long, and his trousers a great deal too short.

Note.—Squeers was a schoolmaster of the type then prevalent in Yorkshire. He took little boys without any qualifications for educating them, partially starved them and brutally illtreated them. Unfortunately for him he engages Nicholas Nickleby as usher. When Squeers is about to flog Smike, Nicholas soundly trounces him. This enrages Squeers, who assists Ralph in his plans to ruin Nicholas. These plans fail, however, and Squeers is transported. When this happens his school is broken up with great rejoicings by the boys.

Original : Shaw, a one-eyed schoolmaster at Bowes, has been identified as the prototype of Squeers. Squeers also recalls Dirk Hatteraick in Guy Mannering.

SQUEERS. Mrs., Wife of Mr. Squeers.   *N. N.* iv.
" You will have a father in me, my dears, and a mother in Mrs. Squeers." Of a large, raw-boned figure, about half a head taller than Mr. Squeers, dressed in a dimity night - jacket ; with her hair in papers—she had also a dirty nightcap on, relieved by a yellow cotton handkerchief, which tied it under the chin.

Note.—Wife of Squeers, an able assistant in his career of cruelty.

SQUIRES. Olympia,   *U.* T. xix.
Childhood's sweetheart of the Uncommercial Traveller.

SQUOD. Phil, Custodian of George's gallery in George's absence.
                         B. H. xxi.
A little grotesque man, with a large head—is dressed something like a gunsmith, in a green baize apron and cap ; and his face and hands are dirty with gunpowder—

with a face all crushed togethei who appears, from a certain blu' and speckled appearance tha one of his cheeks presents, to hav. been blown up, in the way c business at some odd time or time —is lame, though able to mov very quickly.

Note.—A man picked out of th gutter, employed by Mr. George in hi shooting gallery, and afterwards accom panies him to Chesney Wold.

Original : Said to have bee founded on the attendant at We lington House Academy, Hampstea' Road. The name of this porter wa Phil, and he displayed some c the qualities of his namesake.

STABBER. New York.   *M. C.* xv

STABBERS'S BAND.   *M. P., A. N*

STABLES. The Honourable Bot
                         B. H. i
Who can make warm mashe with the skill of a veterinar. surgeon, and is a better shot tha. most gamekeepers.

STAFFORD.   *M. P., J. 7*

STAFFORDSHIRE. *R. P., A. P. A*

STAGE-COACH HOUSE.   An old
                         U. T. xxii

STAGG. Proprietor of cellar nea Barbican.   *B. R.* viii
Wore an old tie-wig as bare an(frowsy as a stunted hearthbroom His eyes were closed, but had the] been wide open it would have bee] easy to tell, from the attentiv. expression of his face—that h was blind.

Note.—Stagg keeps an undergroun(drinking den. It is here that Simo] Tappertit and his " United Bull-Dogs ' foregather, Deprived of sight, hi other senses become abnormally deve loped.

STAGG'S GARDENS.
                         D. and S. vi.
In a suburb, known by the in

habitants of Stagg's Gardens, by the name of Camberling Town. It was a little row of houses, with little squalid patches of ground before them, fenced off with old doors, barrel staves, scraps of tarpaulin, and dead bushes ; with bottomless tin kettles and exhausted iron fenders thrust into the gaps. Here the Stagg's gardeners trained scarlet beans, kept fowls and rabbits, erected rotten summer - houses (one was an old boat), dried clothes and smoked pipes.

TAINES. *O. M. F.* xli.

TALKER. Inspector, A detective. *R. P.*, T. *D. P.*
A shrewd, hard-headed Scotchman—in appearance not at all unlike a very cute, thoroughly trained schoolmaster.

TALKER. Mrs., A thief. *R. P.*, *D. W. I. F.*

TAMFORD. *N. N.* v.

TAMFORD HILL. *S. B. B.*, Scenes ix.

TAMFORD STREET. *R. P.*, *D. W.* T. T.

TANFIELD. *M. P., O. L. N. O.*

TANFIELD. Mr. Clarkson, *M. P., A. P.* ; *M. P., L. S.*

TANGER. Dr. *M. P., N. E.*

TANLEY. Lord. *S. B. B.*, Scenes xiii.

TANLEY. Lord, An M.P. *S. B. B.*, Scenes xviii.

TANLEY. Sir Hubert. *D. and S.* i.

TAPLE. Mr., A Dingley Deller. *P. P.* vii.

STAPLE INN. Holborn. *B. H.* x. ; *E. D.* xi.
One of the nooks, where a few smoky sparrows twitter in smoky trees, as though they called to one another " Let us play at country," and where a few feet of garden mould, and a few yards of gravel enable them to do that refreshing violence to their tiny understandings.

STAR. Eastern, East London Children's Hospital. *U. T.* xxxiv.

STARELEIGH. Mr. Justice, Judge. in Bardell v. Pickwick. *P. P.* xxxiv.
Who sat in the absence of the Chief Justice, occasioned by indisposition. So fat that he seemed all face and waistcoat. He rolled in, upon two little turned legs, and having bobbed gravely to the bar—put his legs underneath his table, and his three-cornered hat upon it.
Original : There is no doubt that Mr. Justice Stareleigh was drawn from Sir Stephen Gaselee, who although reputed a most estimable man, particularly in private life, "had made himself a legitimate object of ridicule by his explosions on the bench.

STARGAZER. Emma. *M. P., L.*

STARGAZER. Master Galileo Isaac Newton Hamstead. *M. P., L.*

STARGAZER. Mr. *M. P., L.*

STARLING. Alfred. *C. S., H. H.*
An uncommonly agreeable young fellow of eight-and-twenty.

STARLING. Mrs. *S. Y. C., L. C.*

STARTOP. *G. E.* xxiii.
He had a woman's delicacy of feature.
Note.—Friend of Pip's, boarding at Mr. Pocket's. He introduces Pip and

Herbert to the "Finches of the Grove." He is also a party in the attempted escape of Magwitch from England. The story leaves him after the overturning of the boat.

STATE HOSPITAL FOR THE INSANE. S. Boston. *A. N.* iii.

STATE HOUSE. The. *A. N.* iii.

STATE PAPER OFFICE.
M. P., W. R.

STATESMAN. Great.
M. P., L. W. O. Y.

STATION HOUSE.
S. B. B., Char. xi.

STATIONER. Eldest, Daughter of fancy. *S. B. B.*, Scenes iii.

STATIONER. Fancy, A widower.
S. B. B., Scenes iii.
Occupant of shop.

STATIONER'S HALL. *U.* T. ix.

STEADIMAN. John, Chief officer of the "Golden Mary."
C. S., W. o. G. M.
Aged thirty-two—a brisk, bright, blue-eyed fellow, a very neat figure, and rather under the middle size—a face that pleased everybody, and that all children took to.

STEAM PACKET WHARF.
S. B. B., Tales vii.

STEELE. Tom, A suicide.
R. P., D. W. T. *T.*

STEEPWAYS. Village of.
C. S., M. f. T. *S.* i.
There was no road in it, there was no wheeled vehicle in it, there was not a level yard in it. From the seabeach to the cliff top two irregular rows of white houses. The old pack-saddle—flourished here intact. Strings of pack-horses and pack-donkeys toiled slowly up the staves of the ladders, bearing fish, coal, and such other cargo as was unshipping at the pier.—The rough, sea-bleached boulders of which the pier was made, and the whiter boulders of the shore, were brown with drying nets.

STEERFORTH. James, Head boy at Salem House. *D. C.* v.
Before this boy, who was reputed to be a great scholar, and was very good-looking, and at least half a dozen years my senior, I was carried as before a magistrate.

Note.—The head pupil at Salem House when David Copperfield enters it. For certain reasons he enjoys immunity from punishment and presumes accordingly, but his engaging manners make him a prime favourite. He drops out of the story after David's leaving the school until David returns to London some years later. He visits Mr. Peggotty at Yarmouth with David, and entices Emily away. They live abroad at various places, but in the end Steerforth desires to turn her over to his valet, Littimer, and deserts her. The ship on which he returns to England is wrecked off the Yarmouth coast. Ham Peggotty endeavours unsuccessfully to attempt a rescue and meets his death. The stranger whom he swam to rescue is washed ashore, dead, and is found to be Steerforth.

Original : Has been identified as Stroughill, at No. 1, Ordnance Terrace, one of Dickens' early playfellows.

STEERFORTH. Mrs., Steerforth's mother. *D. C.* xx.
An elderly lady, with a proud carriage and a handsome face, who lived in an old brick house at Highgate on the summit of a hill.

Note.—Mrs. Steerforth, with a blind love for her son, is nevertheless eventually estranged from him ; and she is last seen broken and mentally deranged.

STELLA. Violetta, of the Italian Opera. *O. C. S.* xl

STEPFATHER. Of Neville and Helena (deceased). *E. D.* vii

STEPHENSON. Mr., Engineer.
M. P., C. C.; *M. P., S.*

STEPNEY. *M. P., C. J.*

STEPNEY FIELDS. *O. M. F.* xv.

STEPNEY PAUPER UNION.
U. T. xxix.

STEPNEY STATION. *U. T.* xxxiv.

STEVENS. Billy, Inmate of workhouse. *R. P., W. I. A. W.*

STEWARD. In *C*lifford's Inn.
P. P. xxi.
Thought he had run away; opened the door, and put a bill up.

STEWARDS. Fourteen, At Guildhall. *S. B. B.,* Scenes xix.
Each with a long wand in his hand, like the evil genius in a pantomime.

STIFFINS'S ACRE. Great Winglesbury. *S. B. B.,* Tales viii.

STIGGINS. Mr. *P. P.* xxvii.
Prim-faced, red - nosed man, with a long thin countenance, and a semi-rattlesnake sort of eye— rather sharp but decidedly bad.

Note.—The shepherd was very much addicted to pineapple rum and water. He "led" a flock of silly women, one of them Mrs. "Tony" Weller. With his humbug he so prevailed on her that she made old Weller's life miserable at home. Old Weller on one occasion makes him drunk when he has to attend a monthly meeting of the Brick Lane Branch, with results highly entertaining to Sam Weller and his father. Ultimately the shepherd is literally kicked out of the Marquis of Granby by Tony Weller.

Original : The name is found at Higham, a place Dickens knew somewhat at the time of the writing of Pickwick.

STILL-BORN BABY. A. *L. D.* xxv.

STILTSTALKING. Augustus.
L. D. xxvi.

STILTSTALKING. Lord Lancaster.
L. D. xxvi.
A grey old gentleman of dignified and sullen appearance—in a ponderous white cravat, like a stiff snow-drift. He shaded the dinner, cooled the wines, chilled the gravy, and blighted the vegetables.

STILTSTALKING. Tom, Dick or Harry. *L. D.* xxvi.

STILTSTALKING. Tudor.
L. D. xxvi.

STILTSTALKINGS. Branch of the.
L. D. x.
Who were better endowed in a sanguineous point of view than with real or personal property.

STOCK EXCHANGE. *P. P.* lv.

STOCKHOLM. Academy of.
M. P., L. L.

STOCKPORT. *M. P., O. S.*

STOCKWELL GHOST.
M. P., R. S. D.

STOKE. *R. P., A. P. A.*

STOKE NEWINGTON. *U. T.* xii.

STOKER. Mrs., As the first wife.
M. P., N. T.

STOKES. *M. P., C.*

STOKES. Mr. Martin. *M. P., V. C.*

STONE. *L. D.* xxv.

STONE. Mr. *M. P., C.*

STONE JUG. The. *O. T.* xliii.

STONE LODGE. Mr. Gradgrind's house. *H. T., S.* iii.
A great square house with a heavy portico darkening the principal windows—six windows on this side of the door—six on that —a total of twelve in this wing, a total of twelve in the other wing;

four-and-twenty carried over to the back wings.

STONEBREAKER. Owner of old post chaise. *U. T.* xxii.

STONEHENGE. *C. S.*, *T. H.* ; *U. T.* i.

STOUT. Mr., Master of workhouse. *O. T.* xxvii.

STOWELL. Rev. Hugh. *M. P.*, *P. F.*

STOWMARKET. *M. P.*, *E. C.*

STRADA BALBI. *P. F. I.*, *A. G.*

STRADA NUOVA. *P. F. I.*, *A. G.*

STRADELLA. *P. F. I.*, *P. M. B.*

STRAGGLERS. Uncouth, interviewing Martin. *M. C.* xxii.
Men of a ghostly kind, who being in, didn't know how to get out again.

STRAND. *B. H.* xix. ; *B. R.* xv. ; *C. S.*, *M. L. Lo.* i. ; *C. S.*, *S. L.* i. ; *M. C.* xlviii. ; *M. P.*, *G. A.* ; *M. P.*, *M. E. R.* ; *M. P.*, *N. E.* ; *M. P.*, *O. C.* ; *M. P.*, *R. D.* ; *M. P.*, *R. H. F.* ; *M. P.*, *T. D.* ; *N. N.* iii ; *O. C. S.* viii. ; *R. P.*, *P. M. T. P.* ; *R. P.*, *T. D. P.* ; *S. B. B.*, Char. i. ; *T. T. C.* bk. ii., ch. xiv. ; *U. T.* xxxiv.

STRAND BRIDGE. A toll-taker. *R. P.*, *D. W. T. T.*
Muffled up to the eyes in a thick shawl, and amply great-coated, and fur-capped.

STRAND LANE. *S. B. B.*, Tales vii.

STRANDENHEIM. A shopkeeper. *U. T.* vii.
He wore a velvet skull-cap, and looked usurious and rich. A large-lipped, pear - nosed old man, with white hair, and keen eyes.

STRANDENHEIM'S HOUSKEEPE *U. T.* ·
Far from young, but of comely presence—was cheer dressed, had a fan in her hand, a wore large gold earrings and large gold cross.

STRANGE GENTLEMAN. *M. P.*, *S.*

STRANGER. Ancient. *C. B.*, *C. o. H.*
Who had long white hair, go features, singularly bold and w defined for an old man, and da bright, penetrating eyes. I garb was very quaint and odd a long way behind the time. J hue was brown all over. In l hand he held a great brown clu or walking-stick ; and striki this upon the floor, it fell asund and became a chair.

STRANGER. Nobleman. *M. H. C.*

STRANGERS' GALLERY. Doc keeper of. *S. B. B.*, Scenes xvi
Tall stout man in black.

STRANGERS' GALLERY. In Hou of Commons. *M. P.*, *P. L. U* *S. B. B.*, Scenes xvi

STRANGER'S GRAVE. The, Ne York. *A. N.* v

STRANGERS. At sale of Dombey furniture. *D. and S.* li
Fluffy and snuffy stranger stare into the kitchen range, curiously as into the attic clothe press.

STRASBOURG. *C. S.*, *N. T.*, Ac iii. ; *R. P.*, *M. O. F. F.* ; *U. T.* vi

STRATFORD. Mr. *N. N.* xxvi

STRATFORD-UPON-AVON. *M. P.*, *E. S.* ; *U. T.* xi

STRAW. Sergeant, A detective *R. P.*, *T. D. P*
A little wiry sergeant.

the house : his clothes not particularly well brushed, and his hair
not particularly well combed.

Note.—Dr. Strong is the master of
the school at Canterbury to which
David Copperfield is sent by his aunt.
He is engaged on the compilation of a
monumental dictionary which might be
completed " in one thousand six hundred and forty-nine years, counting
from the Doctor's last, or sixty-second,
birthday." At the time the story
leaves him he has reached the letter
" D." His enemies endeavour to sow
discord between him and his young wife,
but without success. He relinquishes
the school, going to live at Highgate.
When Betsey Trotwood's reverse of
fortune occurs, David Copperfield goes
to Dr. Strong's to assist him.

*Original of Dr. Strong's House :
Identified as the old building at the
corner (No. I), of Lady Wootton's
green.*

*Original of Dr. Strong's School :
Probably identical with King's
School in the Cathedral Close,
Canterbury.*

STRONG. Mrs., Dr. Strong's young
wife.   *D. C.* xvi.

Note.—The young and beautiful wife
of Dr. Strong. She had been formerly
inclined towards Jack Maldon, her
cousin, but came to the conclusion that
there could be no happiness in an un-
suitable union. Jack, however, continues to make love to Mrs. Strong,
even while he is accepting the doctor's
gifts and assistance. The doctor de-
clines to mistrust his wife, and is
eventually justified, as she confesses to
him, and the cloud between them is
removed.

STRONG WIND.   *M. P., Th. Let.*

STROOD.   *P. P.* ii.
The smell which pervades the
streets must be exceedingly deli-
cious to those who are extremely
fond of smoking. The principal
productions of these towns appear
to be soldiers, sailors, Jews, chalk,
shrimps, officers, and dockyard
men.

STROUD. *See* Strood.

STRUGGLES. Mr., Player in the Dingley Dell Club. *P. P.* vii.

Note.—An All Muggleton cricketer.

Original : So far as the name is concerned, at least, this is founded on Stroughill, of Ordnance Terrace.

STRUMPINGTON. *M. P., C. P.*

STRYVER. *C. J.,* Counsel for Darnay at Old Bailey.
T. T. C., bk. ii., ch. iii.
A man of little more than thirty, but looking twenty years older than he was, stout, loud, red, bluff, and free from any drawback of delicacy.

Note.—Counsel for Charles Darnay in his trial for treason. He was the friend and employer of Sydney Carton, who "did" his cases. He finds that single life loses its attractions, and proposes to marry Lucie Manette. But he "counts his chickens" too soon, as Mr. Lorry assures him he has no chance with the young lady. Stryver thereupon faces about and makes believe that the young lady wanted him, and he had thought better of it. Stryver of the King's Bench bar passes out of the story quite casually.

STRYVER. Mrs.
T. T. C., bk. ii., ch. xxi.

STUBBS. Mrs., Mr. Percy Noaks' laundress. *S. B. B.,* Tales vii.
A dirty old woman, with an inflamed countenance.

STUCCONIA. *O. M. F.* x.

STUMPINGTON. Lord.
M. P., C. P.

STUMPS. Bill, A labouring man.
P. P. xi.
The man who was reported to have said he was responsible for the letters on the famous stone.
Original : Founded on episode in "Memoirs of a sad dog," Chatterton. Has also been suggested as having been founded on Kits' Coty House, with which Dickens was well acquainted.

STUMPY AND DEACON. *P. P.,*

STYLES. John. *M. P., P.*

STYLES' SISTER. John,
M. P., P.

SUBURBS. The.
S. B. B., Scenes

SUDBURY. *S. B. B.,* Tales

SUE. A suicide. *U. T.*

SUEZ. *M. P., E.*

SUFFOLK. *C. S., D. M.* ; *D.* xxxiv. ; *M. P., E. C.* ; *M. F. S.* ; *S. B. B.,* Tales

SUFFOLK BANTAM. Pugilist
P. P. xx

SUGAR BAKERS. German.
R. P., D. W. I.

SUITOR. Another, Ruined Chancery Court. *B. H*

SULLIWIN. Mrs. Sarah.
S. B. B., Scenes

SULLIWIN. One of boating-cr training for race.
S. B. B., Scenes

SULLY. Mr., A distinguish American artist. *A. N.*

SUMMERSON. Esther, An orph niece of Miss Barbary. *B. H.*
I was brought up, from r earliest remembrance—by my go mother.

Note.—She is the narrator of p tions of the story, and is in many w the central figure in the narrati She is introduced early into the boc and the secret of her birth is well ke This secret is that she is the illegitime daughter of Lady Dedlock and Capta Hawdon, before the former marri and became Lady Dedlock. She is that a woman is supposed to be, mode but capable, and as a result she respected and admired by all and cc sulted by many of her more intime friends. She is the particular frie of Ada Clare and of Richard Carsto

Mr. William Guppy, of Kenge and Carboy's, proposes to her, but is rejected. She is attacked by smallpox and her good looks suffer. After this Guppy is afraid he may be held to his earlier promise. John Jarndyce, the friend and employer of Esther, wishes to marry her, but she ultimately becomes the wife of Allan Woodcourt.

Original : Said to have been a ward of Charles Dickens himself.

SUMMERSON. Mother of Esther.
                                B. H. iii.

SUN STREET.   *O. T.* xxi.

SUNBURY CHURCH.   *O. T.* xxi.

SUNDERLAND. Mr., The mesmeriser.   *M. P., S. B.*

SUPERANNUATED WIDOWS.
                                B. H. viii.

SUPERINTENDENT. Mr., Of Liverpool police force.   *U. T.* v.
A tall, well-looking, well set-up man of soldierly bearing, with a cavalry air, a good chest, and a resolute, but not by any means ungentle face.

SUPERINTENDENTS.
                                M. P., H. H. W.

SUPREME COURT. At Washington.
                                A. N. iii.

SURAT.   *M. P., L. A. V.* ii.

SURFACE. Joseph. *M. P., S. for P.*

SURGEON. A.   *M. C.* xlii.

SURGEON. A, At pit-mouth.
                                H. T., G. vi.
Who brought some wine and medicines.

SURGEON. Parish.   *O. T.* i.

SURGEONS' HALL.
          B. H. xiii. ; *B. R.* lxxv.

SURGETTE. James, Plantation owner.   *A. N.* xvii.

SURINAM.   *M. P., L. A. V.* ii.

SURREY. *B. H.* xxvii. ; *B. R.* xlviii. ; *C. S., H. T.* ; *C. S., M. L. Lo.* ; *D. C.* xi. ; *G. E.* xxxiii ; *O. M. F.* i. ; *R. P.* ; *B. S.* ; *S. B. B.*, Scenes iii. ;
                                U. T. xi.

SURREY CANAL.   *U. T.* vi.

SURREY HILLS. The.
          L. D. lv. ; *U. T.* xxxv.

SURREY THEATRE. *M. P., A. P.*

SURREY ZOOLOGICAL. Keepers at.   *M. P., G. H.*

SURROGATE'S.   *D. C.* iv.

SUSAN.   *M. P., M. N. D.*

SUSAN. Mrs. Mann's domestic.
                                O. T. ii.

SUSANNAH.   *M. P., S. R.*

SUSQUEHANNA.   *A. N.* ix.

SUSSEX. Duke of.
          M. P., C. C. ; *M. P., T. D.*

SUSSEX.   *U. T.* xi.

SUSSEX COAST. *D. and S.* xvii.

SUSSEX COUNTY HOSPITAL.
                                U. T. xi.

SWALLOW. Mr.   *B. H.* iv.

SWALLOW. Owner of a chaise.
                                N. N. xiii.

SWALLOW. Rev. Single.
                                M. P., G. B.

SWALLOW STREET. *B. R.* xxxvii.

SWALLOWFLY. Our good friend,
                                M. P., G. D.

" SWAN." At Wolverhampton.
                                M. P., F. and S.

" SWAN." The, A public house.
          S. B. B., Tales ii.

SWEDEN.   *M. P., C. E.*

SWEDEN. Poor of. *M. P., L. L.*

SWEEDLEPIPE. Paul, Barber and bird-fancier. *M. C.* xxvi.

A little elderly man, with a clammy right hand, from which even rabbits and birds could not remove the smell of shaving soap —wore in his sporting character, a velveteen coat, a great deal of blue stocking, ankle boots, a neckerchief of some bright colour, and a very tall hat. Pursuing his more quiet occupation of barber, he generally subsided into an apron not over clean, a flannel jacket, and corduroy knee shorts.

Note.—Mrs. Gamp's landlord, and friend of Bailey. He was barber and bird-fancier. He leaves the story in company with Mrs. Gamp, and Bailey, whom he vows he will take into partnership.

Original : It is suggested that " Poll " was derived from Poll Green, one of Dickens' fellow-workers in the blacking factory.

SWEENEY. Mrs. A laundress of chambers. *U. T.* xiv.

In figure extremely like an old family umbrella—in figure, colour, texture and smell. The tip-top complicated abomination of stockings, skirts, bonnet, limpness, looseness, and larceny.

SWEENEY. The late Mr. *U. T.* xiv.

Was a ticket-porter of the Honourable Society of Gray's Inn.

SWEEP. A little, Afterwards a master sweep.
S. B. B., Scenes xiv.

With curly hair and white teeth. He believed "he'd been born in the vurkis, but h'd never know'd his father."

SWEEP. Little.
S. B. B., Scenes i.

Knocked and rung till his arms ache—sits patiently down on the door step.

SWEEP, CHIMNEY. *U. T.* xxxv.

SWEEPS. The, On first of May
S. B. B., Scenes xi

Got the dancing to themselve and handed it down.

SWEET WILLIAM. Travellin showman. *O. C. S.* xi

Probably as a satire upon h ugliness . . . as he had rathe deranged the natural expressio of his countenance by puttin small leaden lozenges into his ey and bringing them out at h mouth.

SWEETHEARTS. At tea garden
S. B. B., Scenes i

SWIDGER. Charley, Junior.
C. B., H. M.

Nephew of Mrs. Willia Swidger.

SWIDGER. George, Eldest son Mr. Philip. *C. B., H. M.*

SWIDGER. Mr., Senior. Fath of Mr. William Swidger.
C. B., H. M.

SWIDGER. Mr. William, Gat keeper at students' college.
C. B., H. M.

A fresh-coloured busy, man.

SWIFT. *M. P., W. S.*

SWILLENHAUSEN. Baron Von.
N. N. v

SWILLS. Little, Comic vocalist.
B. H. x

A chubby little man in a lar shirt collar, with a moist eye, an an inflamed nose.

SWINDON. *M. P., E.*

SWISS. *M. P., N. J.*

SWISS GUARD. The Pope's.
P. F. I.,

SWOSSER. *C*aptain, Of the Royal
Navy.   *B. H.* xiii.
First husband of Mrs. Badger.

SYDENHAM. Exhibition at.
M. P., N. G. K.

SYDNEY.
M. P., C.; *R. P., P. M. T. P.*

SYDNEY COLLEGE. *C*ommittee of.
M. P., C.

SYLVIA. Farmer's daughter.
G. S. E. v.

SYMONDS' INN. *C*hancery Lane.
B. H. xxxix.
A little, pale, wall-eyed, woe-
begone inn, like a large dustbin,
of two compartments and a sifter.

T

T. J. P.
*Original : Suggested as the Pre-
sident [of the Society of Ancients of
Staple Inn], James Taylor, but may
have been some other.*

TABBY. Miss Griffin's servant.
C. S., H. H.
Upon whose face there was
always more or less blacklead.

TABERNACLE CHAPEL. Finsbury.
M. P., R. S. D.

TABLE ROCK.   *A. N.* xiv.

TABLEWICK. Mrs.   *S. Y. C.*

TACKER. One of Mr. Mould's
assistants.   *M. C.* xix.
His chief mourner in fact—an
obese person, with his waistcoat
in closer connection with his legs
than is quite reconcilable with the
established ideas of grace ; with
that cast of feature which is
figuratively called a bottle-nose ;
and with a face covered all over
with pimples. . . . Who from his
great experience in the performance of funerals, would have made
an excellent pantomime actor.

A A

TACKLETON. Gruff and Tackleton.   *C. B., C. o. H.* i.
A man whose vocation had been quite misunderstood by his parents and guardians. . . . He despised all toys. . . . What he was in toys, he was in other things. He delighted in his malice to insinuate grim expressions into the faces of brown-paper farmers who drove pigs to market.—You may easily suppose, therefore, that within the great green cape—there was buttoned up to the chin, an uncommonly, pleasant fellow ; and that he was about—as agreeable a companion as ever stood in a pair of bull-headed looking boots with mahogany coloured tops. He always had one eye wide open, and one eye nearly shut.

TADGER. Brother, Member of Ebenezer Temperance Association.
            P. P. xxxiii.
A little emphatic man, with a bald head and drab shorts.

Note.—Brother ʰTadger introduced Mr. Stiggins in an inebriated state to the meeting of the Brick Lane Branch —and was knocked down the ladder.

TAILOR AND FAMILY. Of the audience in theatre. *N. N.* xxiv.

TAIT. Mr., Of Edinburgh.
            M. P., Overs.

TALA. Mungongo.   *N. T.* xxvi.

TALFOURD. Mr. Justice.
            M. P., J. T.

TALLOW CHANDLER'S COMPANY.
            M. P., M. B. V.

TALLY-HO. Thompson.
            R. P., T. D. P.

TAMAROO. Successor to Bailey at Todger's.   *M. C.* xxxii.
This ancient female had been engaged, in fulfilment of a vow, registered by Mrs. Todgers, that no more boys should darken the

commercial doors ; and she w: chiefly remarkable for a tot absence of all comprehension upc every subject whatever. She w: a perfect tomb for messages ar small parcels.

TAMBOUR-WORKER. A.
            L. D. x:
A spinster, and romantic, st, lodging in the yard.

TAMPLE. Bob.   *M. P., G. i*

TANGLE. Mr.   *B. H.*

TANK. The, *C*lerk's room : Scrooge's counting-house.
            C. B., C. C., s.

TAP. The, Inn attached to coac office.   *S. B. B.,* Scenes x:

TAPAAN ZEE.   *A. N.* x:

TAPE. A tyrannical old go mother.   *R. P., P. i*

TAPENHAM. Mr.   *M. P., C. Pa*

TAPKINS. Felix. *M. P. I. S. H.* ᵂ

TAPKINS. Miss.   *O. M. F.* xv:

TAPKINS. Miss Antonia.
            C. M. F. xv

TAPKINS. Miss Euphemia.
            O. M. F. xv

TAPKINS. Miss Frederica.
            O. M. F. xv

TAPKINS. Miss Malvina.
            O. M. F. xv

TAPKINS. Mrs.   *O. M. F.* xv

TAPLEY. Mark.   *M. C.*
A young fellow of some five six and twenty perhaps, and w dressed in such a free and fl away fashion, that the long en of his loose red neckcloth was streaming out behind him as oft as before ; and the bunch of brig winter berries in the buttonho of his velveteen coat was

visible—as if he had worn that garment wrong side foremost. " I'm a Kentish man by birth."

Note. — Hostler at the "Blue Dragon." His spirits rose in adversity, and he was always on the outlook for greater misery, so that he could be the more jolly. A whimsical, kind-hearted character. Believing that there will be some opportunity of shining under adverse circumstances he accompanies Martin Chuzzlewit to America. There he is the constant friend, although he takes the position of a servant. He nurses Martin through the fever at Eden—a place where he thinks he really can rise superior—and then takes the same complaint himself. After his second recovery they return to England; and Mark both witnesses and takes a great part in the retribution that overtakes Pecksniff. Eventually he marries Mrs. Lupin of the "Blue Dragon," and changes the name of the inn to the "Jolly Tapley."

Original : The name was one well known in Chatham.

APLIN. Mr. H., Comic singer of White Conduit.
                          S. B. B., Char. viii.

APPERTIT. Simon, Apprentice to Gabriel Garden.   *B. R.* iv.

An old-fashioned, thin-faced, sleek-haired, sharp-nosed, small-eyed little fellow, very little more than five feet high—a figure, which was well enough formed, though somewhat of the leanest, for which he entertained the highest admiration—his legs, in knee-breeches, were perfect curiosities of littleness. . . . In years just twenty, in his looks much older, and in conceit at least two hundred.

Note.—Mr. Varden's apprentice. He makes himself a duplicate key and goes out at night to meetings of the "United Bull-Dogs." The "Bull-Dogs" are a body of apprentices banded together to suppress their masters and elevate themselves to their former state—a state of independence, holidays and a participation in innumerable rows ! Sim fancies himself in love with Dolly Varden, and becomes the desperate and unscrupulous rival, so far as his

spirit permits the expansion of those qualities, of Joe Willet. On the other hand, Miggs, Mrs. Varden's servant, covets his hand and his heart. As founder and captain of the "United Bull-Dogs," Simon takes part in the Gordon Riots. During the disturbances he is shot and his legs are crushed. He is eventually discharged with two wooden legs, and set up in business as a shoe-black. His military and other customers become so numerous that he engages two assistants and marries the relict of a rag-and-bone merchant. With a due regard to the marriage vows he endeavours to enforce the obedience of his spouse ; while she, taking advantage of his infirmity, retaliates by abstracting his wooden legs.

Original : Thomas Mitton, " Dickens' solicitor as well as his schoolfellow."

TAPPERTIT. Two apprentices of Simon.   *B. R.* lxxxii.
In business as shoeblack.

TAPPERTIT. Simon, Wife of.
                          B. R. lxxxii.
Widow of an eminent bone-and-rag collector.

TAPPLETON.   Lieutenant, Dr. Slammer's friend.   *P. P.* ii.
Note.—The officer who arranged the details of Dr. Slammer's intended duel with Mr. Winkle.

TARTAR. A, Mr. Boythorn.
                          B. H. ix.

TARTAR. Chambers of Mr.
                          E. D. xxii.
His sitting-room was like the admiral's cabin, his bath-room was like a dairy, his sleeping chamber, fitted all about with lockers and drawers, was like a seedsman's shop.

TARTAR. Retired naval lieutenant.
                          E. D. xvii.
A handsome gentleman, with a young face, but with an older figure in its robustness and its breadth of shoulder ; say a man of eight-and-twenty, or at the

utmost thirty, so extremely sunburnt that the contrast between
his brown visage and the white
forehead, shaded out of doors by
his hat, and the glimpses of white
throat would have been almost
ludicrous, but for his broad temples, bright blue eyes, clustering
brown hair, and laughing teeth.

Note.—A retired lieutenant, who
has inherited a fortune and occupies
chambers close to those of Neville
Landless in Staple Inn. He only
appears towards the end of the book
and makes the acquaintance of Neville
and of Rosa Bud. It seems probable
that the author intended him to occupy
an important post in the remainder
of the story.

TARTARS. Kingdom of.
     M. P., *T. O. H.*

TARTARY.   *H. T.*, *S.* xv.

TARTARY. Emperor of. *N. N.* xli.

TARTER. Bob, First boy at school.
     R. P., *T. S. S.*

TARTER. Father of Bob.
     R. P., *T. S. S.*

TASSO'S PRISON. *P. F. I.*, *T. B. F.*

TATE. Mr. Nahum. *M. P.*, *R. S. L.*

TATERS. *C*harles. *M. P.*, *P. M. B.*

TATHAM. Mrs.
     S. B. B., Scenes xxiii.
Customer of pawnbroker, pawn-
ing clothes.

TATT. Mr.   *R. P.*, *T. D. A.* ii.

TATTLESNIVEL. A town.
     M. P., *T. B.*

TATTLESNIVELLIAN. Outraged,
     M. P., *T. B.*

TATTYCORAM. Miss Meagle's maid.
From the Foundling Hospital.
     L. D. ii.
A handsome girl with lustrous
dark hair and eyes, and very neatly
dressed.

Note.—Originally a foundling, b
at the time of the story maid or cor
panion to Minnie Meagles. She i
however, jealous and passionate. An
in the belief that she is becoming mo
independent she runs away to Mi
Wade. This is not very successful, an
she returns to her old master with tl
iron box he has been scouring Euro
for as an intercession.

TAUNTON. *C*aptain.
     C. S., *S. P. T.* i
Whose eyes—were bright, han
some dark eyes—what are calle
laughing eyes generally, and, whe
serious, rather steady than sever

TAUNTON. Miss Emily.
     S. B. B., Tales vi
Elder daughter of Mrs. Taunton

TAUNTON. Miss Sophia.
     S. B. B., Tales vi
TAUNTON. Mrs.
     S. B. B., Tales vi
A good-looking widow of fifty
with the form of a giantess, an
the mind of a child. The pursu
of pleasure, and some means
killing time, were the sole end
her existence. She doted o
her daughters, who were as frivo
lous as herself.

TAUNTON. Mrs., Mother of Ca
tain Taunton.   *C. S.*, *S. P. T.* i
A widow.

TAUNTON. Servant of Mrs.
     C. S., *S. P. T.* i

TAUNTON. Vale of.
     B. H. xxxvii. ; *N. N.* xxx

TAUNTONS. Family of.
     S. B. B., Tales vi

TAVERN.   *T. T. C.*, bk. ii., ch. i
Original: " *Ye Olde Cheshi*
Cheese."

TAVERN. A.   *M. H. C.* i

TAVERN. Waiter of. *M. H. C.* i

TAVISTOCK SQUARE. *P. P.* xxx

TAVISTOCK STREET. Cover
Garden.   *S. B. B.*, Tales

"TEMERAIRE." Page at, Youth in livery. *U. T.* xxxii.

· "TEMERAIRE." Two ladies in bar of. *U. T.* xxxii.
Who were keeping the books.

"TEMERAIRE." Waiters at. *U. T.* xxxii.
Who was not the waiter who ought to wait upon us, and who didn't.

TEMPLE. Middle. *M. H. C.* i.

TEMPLE. The. *B. H.* xix.; *B. R.* xv.; *C. S., H. T.; G. E.* xxxix.; *M. C.* xxxviii.; *O. M. F.* viii.; *P. P.* xxxi.; *R. P., B. S.; R. P., G. O. A.; S. B. B.,* Tales iv.; *T. T. C.,* bk. ii., ch. iii.; *U. T.* xiv.

TEMPLE BAR. *B. H.* i.; *B. R.* viii.; *C. S., T. G. S.* i; *L. D.,* liii.; *M. H. C.* i.; *M. P., G. A.; M. P., T. D.; M. P., W.; O. M. F.* xliv.; *R. P., P. M. T. P.*

TEMPLE CHURCH. *O. M. F.* xii.

TEMPLE GARDENS. *B. R.* xv.; *C. S., H. T.*

TEMPLE GATE. *G. E.* xlv.

"TEMPLE OF EQUALITY." Washington. *A. N.* viii.

TEMPLE OF VESTA. The. *L. D.* li.

TEMPLE STAIRS. *E. D.* xxii.; *G. E.* xlvii.

TEMPLE WATCHMEN. One of our. *C. S., H. T.*

TENANT. Solitary, Prisoner in the Fleet. *P. P.* xli.
Poring, by the light of a feeble tallow candle, over a bundle of soiled and tattered papers.

TENANT IN CLIFFORD'S INN. Top set. *P. P.* xxi.
Shut himself up in his bedroom closet, and took a dose of arsenic.

TENTERDEN. Lord. *M. P., C. P.*

TERNI. Falls of. *P. F. I., R. D.*

TERRACINA. *P. F. I., R. D.*

TESTATOR. Mysterious visitor to Mr. *U. T.* xiv.
A man who stooped—with very high shoulders, a very narrow chest, and a very red nose. He was wrapped in a long, threadbare black coat, fastened up the front with more pins than buttons.

TESTATOR. Tenant of chambers in Lyons Inn. *U. T.* xiv.

TETTERBY. Adolphus, Eldest son of Tetterby. *C. B., H. M.* ii.
Also in the newspaper line of life, being employed, by a more thriving firm than his father and Co., to vend newspapers at a railway station—and his shrill little voice—as well known as the panting of the locomotives.

TETTERBY. *C*hildren of.
C. B., H. M. ii.
Seven boys and one girl.

TETTERBY. Johnny, Second son of Tetterby. *C. B., H. M.* ii.
*C*onsiderably affected in his knees by the weight of a large baby, which he was supposed—to be hushing to sleep.

TETTERBY. Mr., A newsvendor.
C. B., H. M. ii.

TETTERBY. Mrs., Wife of Mr. Tetterby. *C. B., H. M.* ii.
The process of induction, by which Mr. Tetterby had come to the conclusion that his wife was a little woman, was his own secret. She would have made two editions of himself easily.

TETTERBY AND CO. A.,
C. B., H. M. ii.

TETTERBY'S BABY. Daughter of Tetterby. *C. B., H. M.* ii.

TEWKESBURY. At the Hop Pole. *P. P.* l.

TEXAS. *N. N.* xiv.

THACKERAY. Mr., W. M.
M. P., I. M. T.; M. P., M. E. R.

THAMES. *A. N.* ii.; *B. R.* xv.; *C. S., N. T.,* Act i.; *C. S., S. L.* iii.; *G. E.* liv.; *M. H. C.* i.; *M. P., E. T.; M. P., H. H.; O. M. F.* i.; *P. P.* xxi.; *R. P., B. S. P.; R. P., D. W. T. T.; S. B. B.,* Scenes x.; *U. T.* iii.

THAMES POLICE OFFICE.
S. B. B., Tales vii.

THAMES STREET. *B. R.* xiii.; *D. and S.* vi.; *N. N.* xi.

THANET. Isle of. *U. T.* xvi.

THATMAN. Prospective M.P.
U. T. xxx.

THAVIES INN. *B. H.* iv.

THEATRE. *C*ity.
S. B. B., Char. xi.

THEATRE. Gentlemen of the.
L. D. xx.
Some half-dozen close-shaved gentlemen, with their hats very strangely on, who were lounging about the door.
Original: Possibly the Surrey Theatre.

THEATRE. Manager of a private.
S. B. B., Scenes xiii.
He is all affability when he knows you well—or in other words, when he has pocketed your money once, and entertains confident hopes of doing so again.

HEATRE. Private.
S. B. B., Scenes xiii.
The little narrow passages beneath the stage are neither especially clean nor too brilliantly lighted ; and the absence of any flooring,. together with the damp mildewy smell which, pervades the place, does not conduce—to their comfortable appearance.

HEATRE. Proprietor of a private.
S. B. B., Scenes xiii.
May be an ex-scene painter, a low coffee-house keeper, a disappointed eighth-rate actor, a retired smuggler, or uncertificated bankrupt.

HEATRE EMPLOYÉ. L. D. xx.
A sprightly gentleman with a quantity of long black hair.

HEATRE FRANÇAIS.
M. P., W. ; R. P., T. N. S.

HEATRE OF PUPPETS. The, Or Marionetti. P. F. I., G. A. N.

HEATRE OF VARIETIES.
M. P., N. Y. D.

HEATRES. Penny, in Seven Dials.
S. B. B., Scenes v.

HEATRES. Principal patrons of private, dirty boys.
S. B. B., Scenes xiii.

HEBES. M. P., E. T.

HEOPHILE. Corporal.
C. S., S. L. ii.
Devoted to little Bebelle . . . walking with little Bebelle . . . brought his breakfast into the place, and shared it there with Bebelle. Always Corporal and always Bebelle.

HICKNESS. Mr. M. R. B.

HIEF. The. U. T. xxxvi.
Always a thief, always a ruffian.

THIRSTY WOMAN OF TUTBURY.
N. N. xlix.
Original : Ann Moore, the fasting woman of Tutbury.

THISMAN. Prospective M.P.
U. T. xxx.

THISTLEWOOD. M. P., S. for P.

THOM. Mr., Of Canterbury.
A. N. xviii.

THOMAS. Groom in Sir Leicester Dedlock's household. B. H. xl.

THOMAS. Mr. Mortimer Knag's boy. N. N. xviii.
A boy nearly half as tall as a shutter.

THOMAS. Pastrycook.
S. B. B., Tales ix.

THOMAS. Tom. C. S., S. L. iii.
" I was the real artist of Piccadilly, I was the real artist of Waterloo Road, I am the only artist of all those pavement-subjects—I do 'em and I let 'em out."

THOMAS. Waiter at " Winglebury Arms." S. B. B., Tales viii.

THOMAS. Waterman.
O. M. F. xv.

THOMPSON. Bill, Actor in Victoria Gallery.
S. B. B., Scenes ii.

THOMPSON. Daughter of.
R. P., T. D. P.

THOMPSON. Harry, Bather at Ramsgate. S. B. B., Tales iv.
Friend of Captain Waters.

THOMPSON. Julia. S. Y. G.

THOMPSON. Mr.
S. B. B., Scenes v.

THOMPSON. Mr. M. P., S. P.

THOMPSON. Mrs. S. Y. G.

THOMPSON. Mrs., Wife of Thompson. *R. P., T. D. P.*

THOMPSON. Tally Ho, Horse-stealer. *R. P., T. D. P.*

THOMPSON'S. *S. B. B., O. P.* v.

THOMPSON'S. Great room. *S. B. B.,* Scenes ix.

THOMPSON'S WIFE. *R. P., T. D. P.*

THOMSON. Owner of an assumed name. *S. B. B.,* Scenes xiii.

THOMSON. Sir John, An M.P., with the yellow gloves. *S. B. B.,* Scenes xviii.

THOMSON. T. R. H. *M. P., N. E.*

THOROUGHFARE. No, A court in City of London. *C. S., N. T.,* Act i.
A courtyard diverging from a steep, a slippery, and a winding street connecting Tower Street with the Middlesex shore of the Thames.

THOROUGHGOOD AND WHITING. Bill-printers. *R. P., B. S.*

THREADNEEDLE STREET. *C. S., D. M.; N. N.* xxxv.; *S. B. B.,* Tales ii.

THREADNEEDLE STREET. Old Lady in. *M. P., F. L.*

"THREE CRIPPLES." Landlord of *O. T.* xxvi.

"THREE JOLLY BARGEMEN." The, Public-house. *G. E.* x.
"There was a bar—with some alarmingly long chalk scores in it on the wall at the side of the door, which seemed to me to be never paid off."
Note.—The inn to which Orlick went to eat his dinner.

Original : Supposed to have been founded on the "Horseshoe and Castle," at Cooling.

THREE KINGS. Hotel of the, A Bâle. *P. F. I., V. M. M. S. &*

THREE PROVINCIAL BROTHERS Café of the, *M. P., N. Y. L*

THROSTLETOWN. Delegate from *M. P., O. &*

THROWER. A, Worker in pottery *R. P., P. A*

THRUSH. William. *M. P., P. M. B*

THUGS. *M. P., S. F. A*

THUMB. The Hon. T. Barnum *M. P., R. S. D*

THURSTON. Samuel, A young duellist, aged fifteen. *A. N.* xvii

THURTELL. Mr. *M. P., T. F*

THURTELL. Murderer. *M. P., D. M*

TIBBS. Mr., Husband of Mrs Tibbs. *S. B. B.,* Tales i
Had very short legs, but by way of indemnification, his face was peculiarly long. He was to his wife what the 0 is in 90—or some importance *with* her—nothing without her. . . . He always went out at ten o'clock in the morning, and returned at five in the afternoon, with an exceedingly dirty face.

TIBER. The. *P. F. I., R.; R. P., D. W. T. T.*

TICKET PORTER. *D. and S.* xiii
If he were not absent on a job, ran officiously before to open Mr. Dombey's office door, and hold it open, with his hat off, while he entered.

TICKIT. Grandchild of Mrs. *L. D.* xxvii

TIC

TICKIT. keeper the fa house were a

TICKLE.

TICKNOF

TICKNOF

TIDDY.

TIDDYP(

TIER-RA

TIESOLE

TIFFEY. kins' el A di stiff br were n

TIFFIN.

TIGG.) The of app termed fingers gloves, were a from boots. of a stretch conflic straps. mome der a colour was b the ch such been it was He w

Note.—Friend of Chevy Slyme. A self-reliant but impecunious knave. He enters into partnership with Crimple, and together they float the Anglo-Bengalee Disinterested Loan and Life Insurance Company—a bigger swindle than any he had previously engaged in. Learning that Jonas Chuzzlewit had made an attempt to poison his father, he uses the knowledge to compel Jonas to enter the firm, to invest his own money in it, and to persuade Pecksniff to do the same. Jonas turns at length and murders Tigg. The crime is discovered and the murderer arrested.

TIGGIN AND WELPS. In the calico and waistcoat piece line.
        P. P. xlix.
    Employer of Bagman's uncle.

" TILTED WAGON." An inn.
        E. D. xv.
    A cool establishment on the top of a hill.

TIM. Fat clerk of Cheeryble brothers.   *N. N.* xxxv.
    A fat, elderly, large-faced clerk, with silver spectacles, and a powdered head.

TIM. Tiny, Cripple son of Bob Cratchit.   *C. B., C. C., S.* iii. ;
        and *M. P., I. W. M.*
    He bore a little crutch, and had his limbs supported by an iron frame.

TIMBERED. Mr.   *Mud. Pap.* i.

TIMBERRY. Mr. Snittle, Actor.
        N. N. xlviii.
    Member of Mr. Vincent Crummles' Company.

TIMKINS. Candidate for Beadle's post.   *S. B. B., O. P.* iv.

TIMSON. Coach-owner. *U.* T. xii.

TIMSON. Uncle of Mr.
        S. B. B., Tales x.

TIMSON. The Reverend Charles.
        S. B. B, Tales x.

TINKER. A. *D. C.* xiii.
Most ferocious-looking ruffian.

TINKER. A dusky.
C. S., *T. T. G.* i.
Who had got to work upon
some villager's pot or kettle, and
was working briskly. . . . How
should such as me get on, if we *was*
particular as to weather ? There's
something good in all weathers.
If it don't happen to be good for
my work to-day, it's good for some
other man's to-day, and will come
round to me to-morrow.

TINKER. Travelling. *O. T.* xxviii.
Who had been sleeping in an
outhouse . . . on Mrs. Maylie's
premises.

TINKLER. Mr., Mr. Dorrit's valet.
L. D. xli.

TINKLING. Esq., William, A school-
boy aged eight. *H. R.*, *P.* i.

TIP. Mr. Gabblewig's " tiger."
M. P., *M. N. D.*

TIPKINS. Churchwarden.
D. C. xxix.

TIPKISSON. A constituent.
R. P., *O. H. F.*

TIPP. Another packer in Murdstone and Grinby's. *D. C.* xi.

TIPPIN. Master, Son of Mrs.
Tippin. *S. B. B.*, Tales iv.

TIPPIN. Miss, Daughter of Mrs.
Tippin. *S. B. B.*, Tales iv.

TIPPIN. Mrs., Of the London
theatres. *S. B. B.*, Tales iv.
Sings in Ramsgate Library.

TIPPIN. Mr., Husband of Mrs.
Tippin. *S. B. B.*, Tales iv.

TIPPINS. Sir Thomas. *O. M. F.* x.
Knighted in mistake for somebody else.

TIPPINS. Lady, Guest of Vene-
ings. *O. M. F.* i.
With an immense, obtuse, dr ,
oblong face, like a face in a tab-
spoon, and a dyed " Long Walk"
up the top of her head, as a co-
venient approach to the bunch
false hair behind.

Note.—Merely a " hook " in t
story. She is present at the meetin
of Society as represented by dinn s
at Veneering's and Podsnap's. She
last seen on one of these occasio
eliciting the " voice " of Society in
verdict on Wrayburn's marriage.

" TIPPINGS." A branch of t
spiritual proceedings. *M. P.*, *S.*

TIPSLARK. Suitor of Mrs. Nicklel
N. N. x.

TIPSTAFF. The. *P. P.*

TISHER. Mrs., A deferent
widow. *E. D.*
With a weak back, a chron
sigh, and a suppressed voice, w
looks after the ladies' wardrob
and leads them to infer that s
has seen better days.

TITBULL. Sampson, Founder
Titbull's Almshouses. *U. T.* x
Original : " *Reminiscent*
those almshouses on the east s
of Bayham Street, nearly oppos
to Dickens' sometime home."
Vintners' Almshouses in Mile E
Road. Also suggested as foun
on Cobham College.

TITBULL'S ALMSHOUSES. No.
U. T. xx
A tall, straight, sallow la ,
who never speaks to anybo ,
who is surrounded by a supers-
tious halo of lost wealth, who d
her household work in housemai
gloves, and who is secretly mu
deferred to ; though open
cavilled at—and it has obscur
leaked out that this old lady h
a son, grandson, nephew, or oth

fascinating as the baker himself ;
fond of mails, but more of females.

TODDLES. The boy " Minder."
O. M. F. xvi.

TODDYHIGH. Joe, Poor boy with
the Mayor. *M. H. C.* i.
Not over and above well dressed,
with sunburnt face and grey hair.

TODGERS. M., Proprietress of
commercial boarding-house.
M. C. viii.
Rather a bony and hard-featured lady, with a row of curls in
front of her head, shaped like
little barrels of beer ; and on the
top of it something made of net—
you couldn't call it a cap exactly—
which looked like a black cobweb.
She had a little basket on her arm,
and in it a bunch of keys, that
jingled as she came.

> *Note.*—Mrs. Todgers kept a boarding-
> house. So far as the fact that she is
> the landlady of a boarding-house will
> admit of it, she is kind-hearted, and
> warmly befriends Mercy Pecksniff,
> then Mrs. Jonas Chuzzlewit, after the
> suicide of her husband. She is last
> seen at Cherry Pecksniff's " wedding "
> party.

" TODGERS'S." *C*ommercial boarding house. *M. C.* x.

TOFTS. Mary. *N. N.* xviii.

TOLLMAN. The. *M. C.* v.
A crusty customer, always
smoking solitary pipes in a windsor
chair.

TOLLMAN'S CHILDREN. *M. C.* v.

TOLLMAN'S WIFE. *M. C.* v.

TOM. *M. P., S. G.*

TOM. *M. P., S. R.*

TOM. *P. P.* iv.

TOM. Another assistant of Mr.
Mould. *M. C.* xix.

TOM. Attendant at the " Leather Bottle." *P. P.* xi.

TOM. Captain, Prisoner in Newgate. *G. E.* xxxii.

TOM. Chemist's boy. *P. P.* xxxviii.
In a sober grey livery, and a gold-laced hat.

TOM. *C*lerk in general agency office. *N. N.* xvi.
A lean youth with cunning eyes, and a protruding chin.

Note.—The clerk at the registry office to which Nicholas applies for a position. He is overheard by Frank Cheeryble "insulting a young lady" and promptly punished, and in leaving the house of refreshment he leaves the story, never having been anything more than a subsidiary character.

TOM. Coachman of the Dover Mail. *T. T. C.* ii.

TOM. Detective. *S. B. B.*, Tales xii.

TOM. Driver of chaise. *S. B. B.*, Tales viii.

TOM. Driver of omnibus. *S. B. B.*, Tales xi.

TOM. Driver of train which killed the signalman, who saw the spectre. *C. S.*, T. G. S. ii.

TOM. Gardener working for Mr. Parsons. *S. B. B.*, Tales x.
In a blue apron, who let himself out to do the ornamental for half-a-crown a day, and his " keep."

TOM. Gattleton's man. *S. B. B.*, Tales ix.

TOM. Honest, An M.P. *S. B. B.*, Scenes xviii.
The smart-looking fellow in the black coat with velvet facings, and cuffs, who wears his *D'Orsay* hat so rakishly.

TOM. Kentucky, Runaway slave of J. Surgette. *A. N.* xvii.

TOM. Mr. Peggotty's brother-in-law. *D. C.* iii.
" —Dead, Mr. Peggotty ? " I hinted, after another respectful silence. " Drown dead," said Mr. Peggotty.

TOM. Mulatto. *A. N.* xvii.

TOM. One of boating-party. *S. B. B.*, Scenes x.

TOM. Tom Pettifer Ho. *C. S.*, M. f. T. S. i.

TOM. Uncle, Pawnbroker. *P. P.* xlii.

TOM. Young man in the art line. *C. S., S. L.* iii.
Of that easy disposition, that I lie abed till it's absolutely necessary to get up and earn something, and then I lie abed again until I have spent it.

TOM. Young medical practitioner's boy. *S. B. B.*, Tales vi.

TOM TEA-KETTLE. *M. P., N. E.*

TOM THUMB. General. *M. P., Th. Let.*

TOM TIDDLER'S GROUND. Ruined hermitage in. *C. S.*, T. T. *G.* i.
A dwelling-house, sufficiently substantial, all the window-glass of which—abolished, and all the windows of which were barred across with rough-split logs of trees nailed over them on the outside.

TOM-ALL-ALONE'S. A ruinous place. *B. H.* xvi.
In a black, dilapidated street— crazy houses were seized upon, when their decay was far advanced, by some bold vagrants, who, after establishing their own possession,

took to letting them out in lodgings. These tumbling tenements contain, by night, a swarm of misery. This desirable property is in *C*hancery, of course.

Original : Said to have existed " where the new part of York Street, Covent Garden, is now to be found, and the gate of the deserted graveyard was about the centre of the northern side of that new thoroughfare." Also a piece of land now occupied by the Convict Prison, Chatham, belonged to a singular character named Thomas Clark, who lived on the spot in a small cottage, who used every night as he went home to sing or shout " Tom's all alone ! Tom's all alone ! "

'OM'S COFFEE-HOUSE.
M. P., E. S.

'OM'S WIFE. *G. E.* xi.

'OMBS. Old, of Rome. *L. D.* li.

'OMBS. The, New York Prison.
A. N. vi. ; *R. P., T. D. P.*

OMKINS. The lady abbess of *V*/estgate House. *P. P.* xvi.

OMKINS. *C*harles. *M. P., S. G.*

OMKINS. A pupil at Dotheboys' Hall. *N. N.* xiii.

OMPKINS. Mr.
S. B. B., Scenes xix.

OMKINS. Mr. Alfred, Boarder at Mrs. Tibbs. *S. B. B.,* Tales i.
*C*lerk in a wine-house—a connoisseur in paintings, and had a wonderful eye for the picturesque.

OMLINSON. Mr., As a monk.
M. P., N. T.

OMLINSON. Mrs., The post-office keeper. *P. P.* ii.
Seemed, by mutual consent, to

have been chosen the leader of the trade party, at the *C*harity Ball, Rochester.

TOMMY. Little greengrocer with a chubby face. *S. B. B.,* Char. iii.

TOMMY. Waterman. *P. P.* ii.
A strange specimen of the human race, in a sack-cloth coat, and apron of the same, with a brass label and number round his neck.

TOMPION CLOCK. Pump Room, Bath. *P. P.* xxxvi.
Original : Clock by the maker of that name. Tompion was born in 1640 *and died in* 1713.

TONGA ISLANDERS. *U. T.* xxvi.

TONY. Young, Grandson of old Weller, and son of Sam.
M. H. C. iii.
A playin' with a quart pot—and smoking a bit of fire-wood and sayin' " Now I'm grandfather."

TOODLE. Mr., A stoker, Mrs. Toodle's husband.
D. and S. ii.
He was a strong, loose, round-shouldered, shuffling, shaggy fellow, on whom his clothes sat negligently ; with a good deal of hair and whisker, deepened in its natural tint, perhaps, by smoke and coal dust: hard knotty hands : and a square forehead, as coarse in grain as the bark of an oak.

TOODLE. Mrs. Polly, Foster-mother to Paul Dombey.
D. and S. ii.
Mother of five children— youngest six weeks. . . .
Original : Mrs. Hayes, née Littlefair, has been suggested as the

prototype of Polly Toodle, but apparently on insufficient grounds. Mrs. Hayes was at one time nurse in the Burnett's family.

TOODLES JUNIOR. Biler, otherwise Rob, otherwise Grinder.
D. and S. **xxii.**
A strong-built lad of fifteen, with a round red face, a round sleek head, round black eyes, round limbs, and round body, who to carry out the general rotundity of his appearance, had a round hat in his hand, without a particle of brim to it—a velveteen jacket and trousers very much the worse for wear, a particularly small red waistcoat like a gorget, an interval of blue check, and the hat before mentioned.

TOODLESES. Two, Youngest children of Mr. and Mrs. Toodles.
D. and S. ii.
Two rosiest of the apple-faced family.

TOOKE. Thomas. *M. P., O. C.*

TOOLEY STREET. *B. R.* lxvii.; *H. T., S.* iii.; *M. P., I.*; *M. P., S. Pigs.*

TOORELL. Dr. *Mud. Pap.* i.

TOOTING. *B. H.* x.; *M. P., P. T.*; *M. P., T. F.*; *M. P., V. D.*; *R. P., W. I. A. W.*

TOOTLE. Tom. *O. M. F.* vi.

TOOTLEUM-BOOTS. Mrs. Lemon's baby. *H. R.* iv.

TOOTS. Another little stranger.
D. and S. lxii.

TOOTS. Florence, Daughter of Toots. *D. and S.* lxii.

TOOTS. Mrs., *Née* Nipper, Susan. *D. and S.* lx.

TOOTS. P., Head boy at Dr. Blimber's. *D. and S.* xi.
When he began to have whiskers

he left off having brains : you Toots was, at any rate, possess of the gruffest of voices, and 1 shrillest of minds ; sticking on mental pins into his shirt, a keeping a ring in his waistco. pocket to put on his little fing by stealth, when the pupils we out walking.

TOOTS. Susan, Daughter of Too
D. and S. l1

TOOZELLEM. The Honoural Clementina. *L. D.* x1

TOPE. Mr., Chief verger and sho man of the cathedral. *E. D.*

Note.—Verger of the cathedral Cloisterham, whose grammar requi and receives correction by Mr. C1 parkle. There has long been a bill the window regarding lodgings to 1 although it has probably fallen do and never been replaced. but Datchery manages to get there, wh he can keep a watch on Jasper.

Original : Mr. William Mil He was connected with the cathed1 for seventy-five years, and died, pensioned ex-verger, at the age ninety-two.

TOPE. Mrs., Wife of the verg A comely dame. *E. D.*

TOPHANA. In the Western hanc cap. *M. P., B.*

TOPPER. Guest of the Cratchits
C. B., C. C., S. i
Had his eye on one of Scroog niece's sisters.

TOPPITT. Literary lady.
M. C. xxxi
Wore a brown wig of uncomm size.

TORIES. In Parliament.
S. B. B., Scenes xvi

TORLONIA BANK. The. *L. D.*

TORONTO.   *A. N.* xv.

TORRAZZO. The, Cremona.
                  P. F. I., V. M. M. S. S.

TORRE DEL GRECO. *P. F. I., R. D.*

TOTNES.   *M. P., N. G. K.*

TOTT. Mrs. Bell. *C. S., P. o. C. E. P.*
     Widow of a non - commissioned
officer of the Line. She had got
married and widowed at St. Vincent, with only a few months
between the two events. With a
bright pair of eyes, rather a neat
little foot and figure, and rather
a neat little turned-up nose.

TOTTENHAM   COURT   ROAD.
     B. R. xliv. ; *M. P., M. E.* ;
     M. P., M. E. R. ; *S. B. B.,*
     Scenes vii. ; *S. B. B.,* Tales v.

TOTTLE. Mr. Watkins.
                  S. B. B., Tales x.
     He was about fifty years of age ;
stood four foot six inches and
three-quarters in his socks—for
he never stood in stockings at all—
plump, clean, and rosy—had long
lived in a state of single blessed-
ness, as bachelors say, or single
cursedness, as spinsters think.

TOULON. *P. F. I., V. M. M. S. S.*

TOWCESTER.   *P. P.* li.

TOWER. Cathedral.   *E. D.* iii.
     Its hoarse rooks hovering about
—its hoarser and less distinct
rooks in the stalls far beneath.

TOWER. Leaning, Pisa.
                  P. F. I., R. P. S.

TOWER. Moorish. In Vauxhall
     Gardens.   *S. B. B.,* Scenes xiv.
     That wooden shed with a door in
the centre, and daubs of crimson
and yellow all round, like a gigantic watchcase.

TOWER. The, Of London. *B. R.*
     lxvii. ; *M. C.* xi. ; *O. M. F.* iii.
                       U. T. xxxi.
     Fortified, the drawbridges
were raised, the cannon loaded and
pointed, and two regiments of
artillery busied in strengthening
the fortress and preparing it for
defence.

TOWER. White.   *G. E.* liv.

TOWER HILL.   *O. C. S.* iii. ;
     O. M. F. xxv. ; *R. P., D. W. T. T.*

TOWER STAIRS.   *B. R.* li.

TOWER STREET.   *B. R.* xxxi. ;
                  C. S., N. T., Act i.

TOWER STREET. Church near.
                       U. T. ix.
     There was often a subtle flavour
of wine : sometimes of tea.

TOWLER. Private John, Of the
     2nd Grenadier Guards.
                       M. P., R. T.

TOWLINSON.   Manservant in
     Dombey's household.
                       D. and S. v.

TOWN. Country.   *O. C. S.* xix.
     Original : Bushey.

TOWN. High, Overlooking French
     watering-place.   *R. P., O. F. W.*
     An old walled town—on the top
of a hill.—There is a charming
walk, arched and shaded by trees
—whence you get glimpses of the
streets below, and changing views
of the other town, and of the
river, and of the hills, and of the
sea.

TOWN. Small, on the road to
     Gretna.   *M. P., S. P.*

TOWN. Small English country.
                       B. R. xlv.
     The   inhabitants   supported

themselves by the labour of their hands in plaiting, and preparing straw for those who made bonnets and other articles of dress and ornament from their material.

Original : There is little doubt that the town indicated was Luton, although it is sometimes suggested as Dunstable.

TOWN ARMS. Eatanswill.
P. P. xiii.

TOWN HALL.   G. E. xiii.
A queer place—with higher pews in it than a church—and with some shining black portraits on the walls, which my unartistic eye regarded as a composition of hardbake and sticking-plaister.

TOWN HALL. O. C. S. xxvii.

TOWN HALL. Ipswich. P. P. xxii.

TOWNSHEND. Chauney Hare,
M. P., C. H. T.

TOX. Miss, Very particular friend of Mrs. Chick. D. and S. i.
A long, lean figure wearing such a faded air, that she seemed not to have been made in what linen-drapers call " fast colours " origin-ally, and to have, little by little, washed out. Had the softest voice that ever was heard—nose, stupen-dously acquiline, had a little knob, in the very centre or keystone of the bridge, whence it tended down-wards towards her face, as in an invincible determination never to turn up at anything. Miss Tox's dress—had a certain character of angularity and scantiness — when fully dressed she wore round her neck the barrenest of lockets, representing a fishy old eye.

TOX'S HOUSE. Miss, In Princess's Place.   D. and S. vii.
A dark little house, that had

been squeezed, at some remo period of English history, into fashionable neighbourhood at t west end of the town, where stood in the shade like a po relation, looked coldly down up by mighty mansions.   Perha there never was a smaller entr and staircase, than the entry a staircase of Miss Tox's house— was the most inconvenient litl house in England, but then " what a situation." The din tenement—was her own.

TOYNBEE. Mr.   M. P., R.

TOZER. Pupil of Dr. Blimber.
D. and S. x
Whose shirt-collar curled up the lobes of his ears.

TOZER. Mrs., Mother of pupil Dr. Blimber's.   D. and S. xi

TPSCHOFFKI. Major.
C. S., G. i.

TRABB. Mr., Tailor.   G. E. xi
A prosperous bachelor.
Note.—Tailor and undertaker " Up-town." He officiates at Pip sister's funeral.

TRABB'S BOY. Shopboy to Trabl
G. E. xi
The most audacious boy in a the country side.
Note.—The tailor's errand-boy. H annoys Pip exceedingly at variou times. But is instrumental in savin Pip from Orlick.

TRACEY. Mr., Prison Governo
M. P., C. and I

TRADDLES. David's friend an old schoolmate.   D. C.
Note.—Traddles enters the scene as schoolfellow of David Copperfield Salem House. Later on when Davi returns to London from Dover he find Traddles lodging with the Micawber and looking forward to his marriag

TRAMP CHILDREN.   *U. T.* xi.
Attired in a handful of rags.

"TRAMPERS."   Lottery *Commis*-
sioners billstickers. *R. P., B. S.*

TRAMPFOOT.   Of Liverpool police
force.   *U.* T. v.

TRAMPING SAILOR.   *U.* T. xi.

TRAMPING SOLDIER.   *U.* T. xi.

TRAMPS.   *U.* T. xi.

TRAMPS. Harvest.   *U.* T. xi.

TRAMPS. Haymaking.   *U.* T. xi.

TRAMPS. Hopping.   *U.* T. xi.

TRANSCENDENTALISTS.   Sect of
philosophers.   *A. N.* iii.

TRATTORIE. Suburban,
                 P. F. I., G. A. N.

TRAVELLER.   *C. S.*, T. T. *G.* i.

TRAVELLER.   Demented, in train.
                      R. P., A. F.

TRAVELLER.   Grandfather   at
*C*hristmas party. *R. P.*, T. *C. S.*
Set out upon a journey. It was
a magic journey.

TRAVELLER.   Guest in great hotel
in Marseilles.   *L. D.* ii.
A clerical English husband in a
meek strait-waistcoat, on a wedding trip with his young wife.

TRAVELLER.   In coach with Esther
Summerson.   *B. H.* iii.

TRAVELLER.   In hotel in Marseilles.   *L. D.* ii.
A deaf old English mother,
tough in travel, with a very
decidedly grown up daughter indeed.

TRAVELLER.   In hotel in Marseilles.   *L. D.* ii.
Went sketching about the uni-
verse in the expectation of ultimately toning herself off into
the married state.

TRAVELLER. Jaded. *E. D.* i.

TRAVELLER. Mr., The traveller.
C. S., T. T. *G.* i.

TRAVELLER. Resting at "The Nutmeg Grater."
C. B., B. o. L. iii.
Attired in mourning, and cloaked and booted like a rider on horseback—an easy, well-knit figure of a man in the prime of life. His face, much browned by the sun, was shaded by a quantity of dark hair, and he wore a moustache.

TRAVELLER. Uncommercial.
U. T. i.
When I go upon my journeys, I am not usually rated at a low figure in the bill—when I come home from my journeys, I never get any commission—I am both a town traveller, and a country traveller, and am always on the road—I travel for the great house of Human Interest Brothers.

TRAVELLERS. For pleasure.
L. D. ii.
Guests in great hotel in Marseilles.

TRAVELLERS. Guests in great hotel in Marseilles. *L. D.* ii.
Merchants in the Greek and Turkey trades.

TRAVELLERS. On business.
L. D. ii.
Guests in great hotel at Marseilles.

TRAVELLERS. Six poor.
C. S., S. P. T. i.
A very decent man, with his arm in a sling, a little sailor-boy, a mere child, a shabby-genteel personage, with a dry suspicious look ; the absent buttons on his waistcoat eked out with red tape. A foreigner by birth, but an Englishman in speech, who carried his pipe in the band of his hat . . . A little widow, who had been very pretty. . . . A book pedlar

TRAVELLERS. Third party of
L. D. xxxvii
Four in number : a plethoric hungry, and silent German tutor in spectacles, on a tour with three young men, his pupils, all plethoric, hungry, and silent, and all in spectacles.

TRAVELLERS. Two, At hotel a Martigny. *L. D.* xxxix
Mrs. Merdle and Mr. Sparkler

TRAVELLERS' COFFEE-HOUSE In Coketown. *H. T., R.* vi
A nice clean house.

TRAVELLERS' TWOPENNY.
E. D. v
Original : At one time th " White Duck " public-house, late on it was named " Kitt's Lodging House," and was situated in Maid stone Road, Rochester.

" TREASURY." Guest of Mr. Merdle
L. D. xxi

TREASURY. *M. P., R. T*

TREASURY. The, Washington
A. N. viii

TREATY OF AMIENS. *A. N.* xi

TREDGEAR. John, Old resident of Laureau. *S. C., M. f.* T. *S.* ii

TREGARTHEN. Mr., Father of Kitty. *C. S., M. f.* T. *S.* ii
A Cornishman—a rather infirm man, but could scarcely be called old yet, with an agreeable face and a promising air of making the best of things.

TREMONT HOUSE. An hotel.
A. N. ii

TRENCK. Baron. *M. P., W. S. G*

TRENT. Frederick, Little Nell's brother. *O. C. S.* i

" A profligate, sir, who has forfeited every claim not only upon those who have the misfortune to be of his blood, but upon society, which knows nothing of him but his misdeeds."

Note.—Little Nell's profligate brother. He plans to marry her to his friend Dick Swiveller for the sake of the money he believes their grandfather to have. He falls in with a gang of sharpers and gamblers. Then goes abroad and continues the same course of life. His body is recognised at that hospital in Paris where the drowned are laid out to be owned.

RENT. Little Nell's grandfather.
O. C. S. i.

He was a little old man with long grey hair . . . though much altered by age, " I fancied I could recognise in his spare and slender form something of that delicate mould which I had noticed in the child."

RENT. Little Nell. The principal figure in the story. *O. C. S.* i.

"She put her hand in mine, as confidingly as if she had known me from her cradle . . . child she certainly was, although I thought it probable from what I could make out that her very small and delicate frame imparted a peculiar youthfulness to her appearance."

Note.—The heroine of the story is one of Dickens' most touching and pathetic characters. She lives with her grandfather in the Old Curiosity Shop. After they are turned out by Quilp, of whom the old man has borrowed money for gambling, Nellie and her grandfather leave London on foot, tramping through the country in an endeavour to find a refuge. They find many strange people on the road. Codlin and Short, the men with the " Punch," are perhaps the most lifelike characters of this miscellaneous collection. They get the idea that there will be some reward obtainable for information regarding the wanderers. Nellie guesses at something of the sort and managed to slip away from them. After this the travellers make the acquaintance of Mrs. Jarley, of Jarley's wax-

works. This good woman befriends them and employs Little Nell to exhibit the figures in her show to visitors. Little Nell and her grandfather are caught in a thunderstorm one evening and take refuge in a public-house, " The Valiant Soldier." Here they find three men playing cards, and the old man's dominant passion is roused. Little Nell is unable to deter him from playing, and finds him on another occasion playing with the same gang, and being persuaded to rob Mrs. Jarley. Nellie can see only one path open—" to again wander forth " ; this they do. They again meet with the poor schoolmaster, who is instrumental in obtaining a post for them in the same village as that to which he has been appointed clerk. They enter upon the quiet, peaceful life with thanksgiving, but Nellie's health has been destroyed, and she sinks and dies and is buried in the old church. The direction of Nell's flight has been much discussed, but it cannot be laid down with certainty.

Original : The death of Little Nell is said to have been founded on that of Mary Hogarth.

TRENT. Valley of the Sparkling.
R. P., A. P. A.

TRESHAM. Beatrice's husband.
C. S., M. J. iv.

TRESSEL. *S. B. B.,* Scenes xiii.

TRIMMER. Mr. *N. N.* xxxv.
Getting up a subscription for the widow and family of a man who was killed in the East India Docks this morning. "Smashed, sir, by a cask of sugar."

TRING. *M. P., E. S.*

TRINITY HOUSE. *O. M. F.* xxv.

TRINKLE. Mr., Upholsterer.
R. P., T. D. A. i.

TROTT. Alexander—mistaken for another. *S. B. B.,* Tales viii.
A young man, had highly promising whiskers, an undeniable tailor, and an insinuating address —he wanted nothing but valour, and who wants that with three thousand a year. Party to a duel

which never came off, and who was taken by force to Gretna Green in mistake for Lord Peter.

TROTTER. Job. *P. P.* xvi.

Young fellow in mulberry-coloured livery, who had a large, sallow, ugly face, very sunken eyes, and a gigantic head, from which depended a quantity of lank black hair.

Note.—Job Trotter is a curious character. An abnormal cunning is united with an unwavering devotion to Jingle, his master and companion. He first enters the story in connexion with Jingle's bogus attempt to enter the bonds of matrimony. He shares Jingle's fortunes even to a debtor's prison—the Fleet—and finally accompanies him to the West Indies.

TROTTER. Captain H. D.
M. P., N. E.

TROTTLE. *C. S., G. i. S.*

TROTWOOD. Betsey Trotwood's husband. *D. C.* xviii.

"The time was, Trot, when she believed in that man most entirely. He repaid her by breaking her fortune . . . married another woman, became an adventurer, a gambler and a cheat . . . and I believed him—I was a fool !—to be the soul of honour."

Note.—Miss Betsey Trotwood's husband occupies a mysterious position of anonymity until near the end of the book, when he dies. Although handsome and pleasing, he treats his wife cruelly, and they separate. He sinks low in the social scale, and periodically pesters Miss Betsey for money, which she, foolishly, she admits, gives him.

TROTWOOD. Betsey (*C*opperfield), god-daughter of Betsey Trotwood. *D. C.* xxxv.

TROTWOOD. Miss Betsey, David's great-aunt. *D. C.* i.

"My aunt was a tall, hard-featured lady, but by no means ill-looking. There was inflexibility

RUMAN, HANBURY AND BUX-
TON. *D. C.* xxviii.; *M. P., U. N.*

RUMBULL. *C*olonel, An artist
and member of Washington's
staff. *A. N.* viii.

RUNDLE. Mr., The future husband of Isabella Wardle. *P. P.* iv.

Note.—A curiosity in the book, as
although several times on the stage, he
has never a "speaking part." He
marries Miss Isabella Wardle quite
prosaically.

RUSTEE. Witty. *M. P., L. E. J.*

RUSTEES. Ballantyne,
M. P., S. P.

RUSTEES. Of Titbull's Almshouses. *U. T.* xxvii.

UCKETT'S TERRACE.
R. P., O. V.

UCKLE. Mr., Footman.
P. P. xxxvii.
A stoutish gentleman in a bright
crimson coat, with long tails,
vividly red breeches, and a cocked
hat.

UFNELL. Mr., School inspector.
U. T. xxix.

UGBY. Former porter of Sir
Joseph Bowley. *C. B., C.,* q. iv.
Mrs. Chickenstalker's partner
in the general line.

UGBY. Mrs., Late Chickenstalker.
C. B., C., q. iv.

UGGS. Joseph, A grocer.
S. B. B., Tales iv.
A little dark-faced man, with
shiny hair, twinkling eyes, short
legs, and a body of very considerable thickness.

UGGS. Miss Charlotte, Only
daughter of Mr. and Mrs. Tuggs.
S. B. B., Tales iv.
The form of—fast ripening into
—luxuriant plumpness.

TUGGS. Mrs., Wife of Joseph
Tuggs. *S. B. B.,* Tales iv.
The figure of the amiable Mrs.
Tuggs—if not perfectly symme-
trical, was decidedly comfortable.

TUGGS. Simon, Only son of Mr.
Tuggs. *S. B. B.,* Tales iv.
There was that elongation in his
thoughtful face, and that tendency
to weakness in his interesting legs,
which tell so forcibly of a great
mind and romantic disposition.
He usually appeared in public in
capacious shoes with black cotton
stockings—was observed to be
particularly attached to a black
glazed stock, without tie or ornament of any description.

TUILERIES. The.
M. P., R. S. D.; U. T. vii.

TULKINGHORN. Mr. *B. H.* ii.
The old gentleman is rusty to
look at . . . wears knee-breeches
tied with ribbons, and gaiters or
stockings : and reputed to have
made good thrift out of aristocratic marriage settlements.

Note.—Family lawyer of Sir Leicester
Dedlock. He is constantly appearing
and reappearing in the story, but the
chief fact is that he becomes cognisant
of some of the particulars of Lady
Dedlock's secret. He threatens to
reveal his knowledge to her husband.
As a result she leaves home and dies.
Mr. Tulkinghorn is found dead—shot ;
and Lady Dedlock and Mr. George
are suspected, but Inspector Bucket
traces the crime to Mademoiselle
Hortense, who murdered him because,
although she had obtained the information required, the lawyer played
with her and refused to give her as
much as she thought the service worth.

TULKINGHORN'S CHAMBERS.
*Original : Forster's house, No.
58, Lincoln's Inn Fields.*

TULRUMBLE. Mr. *Mud. Pap.*

TULRUMBLE. Mrs. *Mud. Pap.*

TULRUMBLE. Master. *Mud. Pap.*

"TUMBLER'S ARMS." The.
G. E. xiii.

TUNBRIDGE. R. P., A. F.

TUNGAY. Factotum at Salem
House. D. C. v.
We were surveyed when we
rang the bell by a surly face,
which I found, on the door being
opened, belonged to a stout man
with a bull-neck, a wooden leg,
overhanging temples, and his hair
cut close all round his head.

TUPMAN. Tracy, Member of the
Pickwick Club. P. P. i.
The too susceptible Tupman,
who to the wisdom and experience
of maturer years superadded the
enthusiasm and ardour of a boy,
in the most interesting and pardon-
able of human weaknesses—love.
Time and feeding had expanded
that once romantic form.
Note.—Tupman supplies the ama-
tory character of the members of the
Corresponding Society of the Pickwick
Club. Tupman is easily led into a
predicament by the machinations of
Jingle, and goes to Cobham with the
object of "hastening altogether" from
the world. The Pickwickians find
him preparing to do so by dining off
roast fowl, bacon, ale, etc. He never
proposed again, however, and finally
took lodgings at Richmond, where he
enjoys the admiration of the elderly
ladies.
*Original : Lacey Chapman,
butcher of Canterbury, and belonging to a Gravesend family. Another original is said to have existed
in a middle-aged man named
Winters, "who used to ogle the
ladies in Hyde Park."*

TUPPINTOCK'S GARDENS. Liggs
Walk, Clapham Rise. C. S., H. H.

TUPPLE. Mr., Junior clerk in
Somerset House.
S. B. B., Char. iii.
A tidy sort of young man, with
a tendency to colds and corns—

a perfect ladies' man—such
delightful companion — delightful
partner—makes one of the most
brilliant and poetical speeches that
can possibly be imagined.

TURIN. M. P., A. A. I

TURKEY. M. P., B. S. ; P. P. xxii

TURNCOCK. Attached to the
waterworks. D. C. xxviii.
M. P. W

TURNER. M. P., O. L. N. C

TURNKEY. At Marshalsea.
L. D. v
Practical Turnkey. . . . God-
father to Little Dorrit. Time went
on and the Turnkey began to fail
"When I'm off the lock for good
and all, you'll be the father of the
Marshalsea."

TURNKEY. Fleet Prison. P. P. x
Stout turnkey—sat down and
looked at him carelessly from time
to time.

TURNKEY. In Fleet Prison.
P. P. xl
A long, thin man—thrust his
hands beneath his coat-tails, and
planting himself opposite, took a
long view of him."

TURNKEY. Third, Of Fleet Prison
P. P. xl
Rather surly-looking gentleman
who had apparently been dis-
turbed at his tea—stationed himself close to Mr. Pickwick, and
resting his hands on his hips
inspected him narrowly.

TURNKEYS. The, Of Newgate.
B. R. lxxiv

TURNPIKE-KEEPER. A cobbler
U. T. xxii
Unable to get a living out o
the tolls, plied the trade of a
cobbler.

TURNPIKE-KEEPER. Children
of. U. T. xxii
Sunburnt, dusty.

TURNPIKE-KEEPER. Wife of.
U. T. xxii.
Sold ginger-beer.

TURNPIKE HO. *U. C.* xxxi.
*Original : Has been traced to
the house at Amesbury.*

TURTLE. Great, An Indian chief.
A. N. ix.

TURVEYDROP. Mother of one of
apprentices of. *B. H.* xxxviii.
The melancholy boy's mother
kept a ginger-beer shop.

TURVEYDROP. Mr. Prince, Junior.
B. H. xiv.
Christened Prince, in remembrance of the Prince Regent.
A little blue-eyed fair man of
youthful appearance, with flaxen
hair parted in the middle, and
curling at the ends all round his
head.
Note.—The son of Mr. Turveydrop.
He maintains his father. And, when
he marries Caddy Jellyby, they continue to do it together. They prosper,
however, and Caddy is last seen with
her own little carriage, working hard,
but living in a better part of the town.
*Original : There may be no
foundation for the suggestion, but
there appears to be some resemblance
between Prince Turveydrop and
Caddy Jellyby and their child and
the Burnetts. Dickens' sister Fanny
" herself a musician of considerable
acquirements," married Henry
Burnett, " an accomplished operatic
singer . . . who had taken up his
abode in Manchester as an in-
structor on music," and they had a
crippled son.*

TURVEYDROP. Mr., Senior, A
widower. *B. H.* xiv.
A very gentlemanly man indeed ;
celebrated, almost everywhere, for
his deportment . . . with a false
complexion, false teeth, false
whiskers, and a wig. He had a
fur collar—a padded breast to his

coat, which only wanted a star or a
broad blue ribbon to be complete.
Note.—Father of Prince Turveydrop.
He lived on his deportment—and his
son. He had married a little dancing-
mistress, whom he had allowed to work
herself to death ; and continued the
same course with his son. When his
son married he still lived with them
and on them. The book leaves him
exhibiting his deportment about town
in the same old way.

*Original of Dancing Academy :
Has been credited to a house in
Gower Street, and No. 143 or 145 is
suggested.*

TURVEYDROP. Mrs. *See* Jellyby,
Caddy.

TURVEYDROP'S APPRENTICES.
B. H. xxxviii.
Four—one indoor, and three
out. One melancholy boy—
waltzing alone in the empty
kitchen—only for their steps.
Two other boys—and one dirty
little limp girl in a gauzy dress,
such a precocious little girl with a
dowdy bonnet on. When our outdoor apprentices ring us up in the
mornings I am actually reminded
of the sweep.

TURVEYDROP'S DAUGHTER.
Little Esther. *B. H.* l.
A tiny old-faced mite, with a
countenance that seemed to be
scarcely anything but cap-border,
and a lean, long-fingered hand,
always clenched under its chin.

TUSCAN VILLAGES.
P. F. I., R. P. S.

TUSCANY. *M. P. C. P.; P. F. I.,
R. D.; U. T.* xxviii.

TUSCANY. Dukes of.
P. F. I., R. P. S.

TUSCULUM. Ruins of.
P. F. I., R.

TUSSAUD. Madame. *R. P., B. S.*

TUSSAUD'S WAXWORK. Madam. *M. P., I. M.*

TUTBURY. *See* Thirsty woman of Tutbury.

TWEMLOW. Melvin, First cousin of Lord Snigsworth. *O. M. F.* ii.
Grey, dry, polite, susceptible to east wind. First-gentleman-in-Europe collar and cravat, cheeks drawn in as if he had made a great effort to retire into himself some years ago, and had got so far, and never got any further.

Note.—First cousin to Lord Snigsworth, upon whose generosity he lives. He is a member of "society" as represented by the dinners of the Veneerings and the Podsnaps. He is unassuming, but because of his relationship is "in demand" with society. He is last seen at a dinner at Veneering's defending Wrayburn's marriage to Lizzie.

TWICKENHAM. *L. D.*, bk. i., Ch. xvi.

TWIGGER. Mr. *Mud. Pap.*

TWIGGER. Mrs. *Mud. Pap.*

TWINKLETON. Miss. *E. D.* iii.
Every night the moment the young ladies have retired to rest, does Miss Twinkleton smarten up her curls a little, brighten up her eyes a little, and become a sprightlier Miss Twinkleton than the young ladies have ever seen.

Note.—Mistress of the Nuns' House boarding-school. She becomes companion to Rosa Bud when the girls run away from Cloisterham to avoid Jasper's attentions, and carries out a brisk warfare with the Billickin, the landlady.

TWIST. Oliver, Born in a workhouse. *O. T.* i.
There was considerable difficulty in inducing Oliver to take upon himself the office of respiration. Oliver Twist's ninth birthday found him a pale, thin child, somewhat diminutive in stature, and decidedly small in circumference—nature or inheritance had implanted a good sturdy spirit in Oliver's breast.

Note.—The chief character of the book. He is the son of Agnes Fleming and Leeford (the elder), born and bred a "workhouse brat." He was apprenticed to Sowerby, an undertaker; but ran away to London. On the road he met the Artful Dodger who took him to Fagin. Fagin kept a thieves' school in Saffron Hill, and considered Oliver a suitable scholar. Monks, Oliver's half-brother, discovers him later and bribes Fagin to make a thief of the boy—to bring him to the foot of the gallows. This Fagin had already endeavoured to do. On the first morning out Oliver was chased, captured and falsely charged with stealing. He is sentenced to imprisonment by Fang the magistrate, but is released on the testimony of the bookseller, who saw the theft committed by the Dodger. Mr. Brownlow took him home, and, later, to show his trust in him, sent him with books and money to the bookseller. While on the errand he is recaptured by Nancy. He is then used by Sikes and Toby Crackit "in cracking the Chertsey Crib." But endeavouring to alarm the household, already alarmed, he is shot, and eventually taken care of by Mrs. Maylie. Nancy revealed enough of the secrets she has learned to enable Oliver's new friends to discover his parentage and to make Monks share the remainder of his father's fortune with him. Through Monks it is discovered that Rose Maylie is really Oliver's aunt.

Original : The name has been traced to the Salford Register for 1567, but there is no evidence that Dickens was aware of the entry, which is : " Ye xth daie of Maie, John Twiste, sonne of Oliver Twiste."

Original of Oliver's native town : Generally believed to be either Peterborough or Market Harborough, with a predominance in favour of the former.

TWO ROBINS INN. *L. T.* ii.

TYBURN. *B. R.*, Pref. ; *P. P.* xliii.

TYK
TY KON
TYLER'S

UMBREL

UMTARG

UNCLE.

Foun
he was
yard, o
burgh n
and we
warm t

UNCLE.
wit.
I ha
irresist
thing I
except
carry a
my w
uncle's.
age an
very e
writes.
"It is

UNCLE.
Blimbe
Who
aminat
on ab
innoce
wrench
purpos

UNCLE
create

Not
uncle
what
invoke

UNCLE

of his nephews and nieces : as a matter of course, therefore, an object of great importance in his own family. Always in a good temper, always talking—wore top boots on all occasions—remembered all the principal plays of Shakespeare.

UNCOMMERCIAL. Mr., The Uncommercial Traveller. *U. T.* xx.

UNCOMMERCIAL TRAVELLER'S LODGINGS. In Arcadian London. *U. T.* xvi.
My lodgings are at a hatter's— my own hatter's. The young man is a volunteer.

UNDERRY. Mr., A solicitor. *C. S., H. H.*

UNDERTAKER. *C. B., C. C., S.* i.

UNDERTAKER'S MAN. Phantom. Phantom undertaker's man in faded black. *C. B., C. C., S.* iv.

" UNION." The, Workhouse. *L. D.* xxxi. ; *C. B., C. C., S.* i.

UNION HALL. *R. P., T. D. A.* i.

UNITARIAN CHURCH. In St. Louis. *A. N.* xii.

UNITED AGGREGATE TRIBUNAL. *H. T., R.* iv.

UNITED AGGREGATE TRIBUNAL. President of. *H. T., R.* iv.

UNITED BULL DOGS. The. *B. R.* xxxvi.
Formerly the 'Prentice Knights.

UNITED KINGDOM. *M. P., N. J. B.* ; *M. P., R.* T.

UNITED PICKWICKIANS. The Pickwick *C*lub. *P. P.* i.

UNITED STATES. *A. N.* ; *B. R.* lxxii. ; *C. S., H. T.* ; *C. S., M. J.* iv. ; *H. R.* iii. ; *M. C.* xii. ; *M. P., A. in E.* ; *M. P., B. A.* ;

M. P., C. P.; M. P., F. F.;
M. P., I. C.; M. P., L. A. V. ii.;
M. P., L. H.; M. P., N. G. K.;
M. P., N. S. E.; M. P., O. F. A.;
M. P., P. P.; M. P., R. S. D.;
M. P., T. O. P.; M. P., Y. M. C.;
N. N. xviii.; P. P. liii.; R. P.,
T. D. P.; U. T. x.

UNITED STATES. Delegate from. M. P., F. F.

UNITED STATES. Inns of. C. S., H. T.

UNITED STATES BANK. Philadelphia. A. N. vii.

UNIVERSITIES. Criminal Court. U. T. xxxvi.

UNIVERSITIES. See also separate names.

UNIVERSITY. Old, In Padua. P. F. I., A. I. D.

UNKNOWNS. Attendant, At wedding. O. M. F. x.

UPPER SERVANTS' HALL. House of Commons. M. P., B. S.

UPPER SEYMOUR STREET. Portman Square. M. P., C.

UPTOWN. Scene of Pip's origin. G. E. i.

Originals : May have been Rochester, Chatham, or Gravesend. Though some of the description would apply to Rochester, undoubtedly the " atmosphere " can be identified with Gravesend.

UPWICH. Richard, Greengrocer, juryman. P. P. xxxiv.

URANUS. M. P., W.

URBINO. M. P., O. L. N. O.

USHER. At Our School. R. P., O. S.

UTAH. U. T. xi

UXBRIDGE. C. S., D. M.; D. C. xix

V

VAGRANT. Houseless. S. B. B. vii
Coiled up his chilly limbs i[n] some paved corner, to dream o[f] food and warmth.

VALE OF HEALTH. O. T. xlvii.

VALENTINE. A toy. R. P., A. C. T

VALENTINE. Private. C. S., S. L. ii
Acting as sole housemaid, valet cook-steward, and nurse in the family of Monsieur le Capitain de la Cour.

VALET. Mr. Dorrit's. L. D. xxxix

VALEXO. Rinaldo di, The gian[t] belonging to Mine. C. S., D. M. P

" VALIANT SOLDIER." By Jen[ny] Groves. Public-house and gambling den. O. C. S. xxix
Where have you come from, i[f] you don't know the " Valian[t] Soldier " as well as the Churc[h] catechism?

VALMONTONE. P. F. I., R. D

VAN DIEMEN'S LAND. C. S., W. o. G. M

VARDEN. Dolly. B. R. iii
A face lighted up by the lovelies[t] pair of sparkling eyes—the face o[f] a pretty, laughing girl, dimpled fresh, and healthful—in a smar[t] little cherry-coloured mantle, wit[h] a hood of the same drawn over he[r] head, and on the top of that hood a little straw hat, with cherry coloured ribbons, and worn th[e] merest trifle on one side—a crue[l] little muff, and a heartrendin[g] pair of shoes.

Note.—The daughter of the old locksmith resembles her father rather than her mother in disposition, and renders the old man's life much more endurable than it would otherwise be. She is the companion-friend of Miss Emma Haredale. Eventually she marries Joe Willet.

VARDEN. Gabriel, A locksmith.
B. R. ii.

A round, red-faced, sturdy yeoman, with a double chin, and a voice husky with good living, good sleeping, good humour, and good health. He was past the prime of life—bluff, hale, hearty, and in a green old age—muffled up in divers coats and handkerchiefs—one of which, passed over his crown—secured his three-cornered hat and bob-wig from blowing off his head.

Note.—The locksmith's was one of those hearty, kindly characters in the delineation of which Dickens was so successful. He was father to Dolly, master of Tim Tappertit, friend of Mr. Willet, and benefactor of many of the characters of the story. In the commencement he suffers from his wife's meagrims, but he is finally left happy and comfortable.

VARDEN. Martha, Wife of Gabriel Varden. *B. R.* ii.

A lady of what is commonly called uncertain temper—who did not want for personal attractions, being plump and buxom to look at, though, like her fair daughter, somewhat short in stature.

Note.—Mr. Varden's wife is first seen as the shrew, but she ultimately becomes a good and attentive wife.

VARDEN. Mother-in-law of.
Dead twenty years. *B. R.* iii.

VARIÉTÉS. Paris. *M. P., W.*

VARNA.
M. P., N. G. K.; M. P., S. F. A.

VATICAN. The.
L. D. xliii.; *M. P., T. O. H.*; *P. F. I.*

VAUDEVILLES. Theatre of.
M. P., N. Y. D.

VAUXHALL. *B. R.* xli.; *R. P., D. W. T. T.*

VAUXHALL BRIDGE. *C. S., S. L.* iii.; *O. M. F.* xviii.; *S. B. B.,* Scenes x.

VAUXHALL GARDENS. *M. P., R. H. F.; P. F. I., G. A. N.; S.B. B.,* Scenes xiv.; *T. T. C.* bk. ii. ch. xii.

VAUXHALL GARDENS. Visitors to. *S. B. B.,* Scenes xiv.

Gentleman, with his wife and children and mother, and wife's sister, and a host of female friends, in all the gentility of white pocket-handkerchiefs, frills, and spencers.

VECCHIO. Palazzo. *P. F. I., R. D.*

VECCHIO. Ponte. *P. F. I., R. D.*

VECK. Margaret, Toby Veck's daughter. *C. B., C.* q. i.

VECK. Toby, Porter. *C. B., C.* q. i.

A very small, spare old man. He was a very Hercules—in his good intentions. He loved to earn his money—was very poor—and couldn't well afford to part with a delight—to believe—that he was worth his salt. Toby trotted—making with his leaky shoes a crooked line of slushy footprints in the mire—blowing on his chilly hands—poorly defended from the searching cold by threadbare mufflers of grey worsted—his cane beneath his arm.

VEFOUR. Café. *M. P., N. Y. D.*

VELINO. River. *P. F. I., R. D.*

VENDALE. Master George, Partner in Wilding and Co.
C. S., N. T., Act i.

A brown-checked, handsome fellow—with a quick, determined eye and an impulsive manner.

VENDALE. Marguerite, Wife of George Vendale.

    C. S., N. T., Act iv.

VENDERS. Flat fish, oyster, and fruit.   *S. B. B.,* Scenes ii.

VENDOME PLACE.   *R. P., A. F.*

VENEERING. Mrs. Anastatia.

    O. M. F. ii.

Fair, acquiline-nosed and fingered, not so much light hair as she might have, gorgeous in raiment and jewels, enthusiastic, propitiatory, conscious that a corner of her husband's veil is over herself.

VENEERING. Mr., and Mrs., Baby of.   *O. M. F.* ii.

A bran-new baby.

VENEERING. Mr. Hamilton, Of Chicksey, Veneering and Stobbles.

    O. M. F. ii.

Forty, wavy-haired, dark, tending to corpulence, sly, mysterious, filmy—a kind of sufficiently well-looking veiled prophet, not prophesying.

Once traveller, or commission agent of Chicksey and Stobbles—signalised his accession to supreme power, by bringing into the business a quantity of plate-glass window, and French mahogany partition, and a gleaming and enormous door-plate.

Note.—As the name denotes these people were of recent manufacture and a "trifle sticky." He had been commission agent in Chicksey and Stobbles, but in time he becomes the firm. His dinners are the media for advancing the story on several occasions. He enters Parliament in a rotten borough, but eventually becomes bankrupt, and retires to Calais, where the family live on Mrs. Veneering's jewels.

VENEERING'S. House of.

    O. M. F. ii.

A bran-new house in a bran-new quarter of London.

VENEERING'S. Nurse of Mrs.

    O. M. F. x

VENGEANCE. The, A woma revolutionist.

    T. T. C., bk. ii., ch. xx

The short, rather plump wif of a starved grocer.

Note.—Friend of Madame Defarg She not only takes a leading part in th women of the Revolution, but sh enjoys intensely the executions. An she is left in the story gloating over th execution of Sydney Carton Darnay but bewailing the absence of Madam Defarge. In the "prophetic vision she is executed later on by the guillo tine.

VENICE. *L. D.* xxxix. ; *P. F. I A. I. D.* ; *R. P., D. W. T. I*

VENICE. The inns of.

    C. S., H. T

With the cry of the gondolie below.

VENNING. Mrs., Inhabitant o Silver Store Island.

    C. S., P. O. C. E. P

A handsome, elderly lady.

VENTRILOQUIST.   *U. T.* xxv

Thin and sallow, and of a weakly aspect.

VENUS. Mr., Preserver of animal and birds.   *O. M. F.* vii.

A sallow face with weak eyes surmounted by a tangle of reddish-dusty hair—no cravat on—no coat on—only a loose waistcoat over his yellow linen. His eyes are like the overtired eyes of an engraver, but he's not that ; his expression and stoop are like those of a shoemaker, but he is not that.

Note.—Friend of Silas Wegg. Silas takes Venus into his confidence and together they explore and examine the dust mounds. Venus allows Wegg to think he is with him in his scheme for blackmailing Mr. Boffin, but he early becomes disgusted with its meanness and dishonesty and reveals it to Mr. Boffin. He is a taxidermist and

VER

"art..."
with Fla...
eventua...

Origi...
been ide...
Andrew...

VERBOSIT

VERDI. S

VEREY. (

VERGER.

VERISOPH
Guest of

The ge...
of clothe...
out, and
similar...
head of

Note.—
fledglings
He coars...
Nickleby
Sir Mulbe...

VERITY.

VERMONT

VERNON,

VERONA.

VERULAM

VERULAM

VESTRIS.

VESTRY.

VESTRY-C
ney.

A she...
black, w...
consider...
in two l...

VESUVIU
P. F. I

VEICHES

"articulator" in Clerkenwell in love with Pleasant Riderhood, whom he eventually marries.

Original of Venus' house : Has been identified as No. 42, Great St. Andrew Street, Seven Dials.

VERBOSITY. Member for.
     R. P., O. H. M.

VERDI. Signor.   *M. P., M. M.*

VEREY. Café.   *M. P., N. Y. D.*

VERGER. The.   *C. S., S. P. T.* i.

VERISOPHT. Frederick Lord, Guest of Ralph Nickleby.
     N. N. xix.
The gentleman exhibited a suit of clothes, of the most superlative cut, and a pair of whiskers of similar quality, a moustache, a head of hair, and a young face.

Note.—One of Sir Mulberry Hawk's fledglings whom he designs to pluck. He quarrels with his mentor over Kate Nickleby and is killed in a duel with Sir Mulberry.

VERITY. Mr.   *G. S. E.* iv.

VERMONT.   *A. N.* iii.

VERNON, Mr.   *M. P., G. F.*

VERONA. *P. F. I., V. M. M. S. S.*

VERULAM BUILDINGS. *U. T.* xiv.

VERULAM WALL. Old.
     B. H. xliii.

VESTRIS. Madame.   *R. P., B. S.*

VESTRY. Our.   *R. P., O. V.*

VESTRY-CLERK. The, An attorney.   *S. B. B., O. P.* i.
A short, pudgy little man, in black, with a thick watch-chain of considerable length, terminating in two large seals and a key.

VESUVIUS. Mount. *D. C.* xxiii. ; *P. F. I., R. P. S.* ; *R. P., L. A.*

VETCHES. Edward.
     M. P., P. M. B.

VETERINARY COLLEGE.
     D. C. xxvii.

VETERINARY HOSPITAL.
     P. P. xxi.

VETTURINO. Half-French, half-Italian.   *P. F. I., G. A. N.*

VEVAY.   *C. S., N. T.,* Act iii.

VEVAY. The town of.
     P. F. I., V. M. M. S. S.

VHOLES. Jane.   *B. H.* xxxvii.

VHOLES. Mr., A widower—a lawyer.   *B. H.* xxxvii.
A sallow man with pinched lips that looked as if they were cold, a red eruption here and there upon his face, tall and thin, about fifty years of age, high-shouldered, and stooping. Dressed in black, black-gloved, and buttoned to the chin.

Note.—Richard Carstone's solicitor in the great Chancery suit. He does not appear to do much, and Richard is encouraged in his unfortunate pursuit of a myth.

VIA GREGORIANA. *L. D.* xlvii.

VIA SACRA. *P. F. I., R.*

VICAR GENERAL'S OFFICE.
     D. C. iv.

VICAR OF WAKEFIELD.
     M. P., F. F.

VICAR'S FAMILY.   *M. P., E. C.*

VICE CHAMBERLAIN. [Of Queen Adelaide.]   *M. P., C. C.*

VICKSBURG.   *A. N.* xvii.

VICOLI OF VIENNA. *M. P., N. G. K.*

VICTORIA. Queen of England, *M. C.* xxi. ; *M. P., C. C.* ; *M. P., E. T.* ; *M. P., G. L. A.* ; *M. P., N. E.* ; *M. P, N. G. K.* ; *M. P, O. L. N. O.* ; *M. P. T. B.* ; *R. P., P. M. T. P.*

VICTORIA GALLERY.
     S.B.B., Scenes ii.

VICTORIA THEATRE. *M. P., A. P.*
S. B. B., Scenes ii.

VICTUALLER. Mr. Licensed, Host
of the " Snug." *U. T.* v.
A sharp and watchful man—
attended to his business himself,
he said. Always on the spot.

VIDE POCHE. *C*arondelet.
A. N. xiv.

VILDSPARK. Tom, *C*ase of man-
slaughter quoted by Sam Weller.
P. P. xxxiii.

VILLAGE. An English.
M. P., V. C.

VILLAGE. Pip's home. *G. E.* i.
Original : Cooling, Kent.

VILLAGERS.
T. T. C., bk. ii., ch. viii.

VILLAGES. Swiss.
P. F. I., V. M. M. S. S.

VILLAIN. The greatest=William
Bousefield. *M. P., D. M.*

VILLE. Hôtel de. *U. T.* xviii.

VILSON. *P. P.* xxxix.

VINES. The, An open green in
Rochester. *C. S., S. P. T.* iii.

VINYARD. James R. *A. N.* xvii.
Member from Grant County.

VINING. Miss, Actress.
M. P., V. and B. S.

VINTNERS' COMPANY.
C. S., N. T., Act i.

VIRGILIANA. Piazza (Mantua).
P. F. I., V. M. M. S. S.

VIRGINIA. (U. S. A.) *A. N.* viii. ;
M. P., V. and B. S.

VIRGINIUS. *M. P., V. and B. S.*

VISCOUNT. A certain.
M. C. xxviii.

VISITOR. One other.
M. P., P. L. U.

VISITOR. To bar-parlour.
*S. B. B., C*har. iii
An elderly gentleman with a
white head and broad-brimmed
brown hat.

VISITORS. Female, At Mano
Farm. *P. P.* xxviii

VISITORS. To Martin in room o
state of National Hotel. *M. C.* xxii
One after another, dozen after
dozen, score after score—all
shaking hands with Martin. Such
varieties of hands, the thick, the
thin, the long, the short, the fat,
the lean—the hot, the cold, the
dry, the moist, the flabby—such
diversities of grasp.

VITERBO. *P. F. I., R.* ; *P. F. I.*
R. P. S.

VOIGT. Maître, Chief notary of
Neuchâtel. *C. S., N. T.*, Act iv.
Professionally and personally,
the notary was a popular citizen.
His long brown frock coat and his
black scull-cap, were among the
institutions of the place ; and he
carried a snuff-box which, in point
of size, was popularly believed to
be without parallel in Europe.

VOIGT. Maître, Room of.
C. S., N. T., Act iv.
A bright and varnished little
room, with panelled walls, like
a toy chamber. According to the
seasons of the year, roses, sun-
flowers, hollyhocks, peeped in at
the windows. A large musical
box on the chimney-piece often
trilled away—had to be stopped by
force on the entrance of a client,
and irrepressibly broke out again
the moment his back was turned.

VOLUMNIA'S MAID. *B. H.* lviii.

VOLUNTEERS. Royal East London,
B. R. xli.
Original : Said to have been the
City Volunteers.

VOTERS. With blue cockades.
P. P. xiii.

VUFFIN. Mr., Travelling showman. *O. C. S.* xix.

The proprietor of a giant, and a little lady without legs or arms.

W

WAAGEN. Dr. *M. P., P. L. U.*

WACKLES. Miss Jane. *O. C. S.* viii.

"The art of needlework, marking and samplery, by Miss Jane Wackles," at the Ladies' Seminary, Miss Jane numbered scarcely sixteen years.

WACKLES. Miss Melissa. *O. C. S.* viii.

"English grammar, composition, geography and the use of the dumb-bells, by Melissa Wackles," at the Ladies' Seminary. Miss Melissa verged on the autumnal.

WACKLES. Miss Sophia, afterwards Mrs. Chegg. *O. C. S.* vii.

"She's all my fancy painted her, sir, that's what she is."

WACKLES. Mrs. *O. C. S.* viii.

"Corporal punishment, fasting, torturing and other terrors," by Mrs. Wackles, at the Ladies' Seminary.

WADE. Miss. *L. D.* ii.

A handsome young Englishwoman, travelling quite alone, who had a proud observant face—so still and scornful, set off by the arched dark eyebrows, and the folds of dark hair. Although not an open face, there was no pretence in it.

Note.—She inveigles Tattycoram away from the Meagles and retains her by force of character. Tattycoram is very miserable, however, and runs away from her to return to the Meagles.

WAGGONER. Of Mr. Jarndyce's waggon. *B. H.* vi.

WAGGONER. The sleepy. *S. B. B.*, Scenes i.

WAGGONER'S BOY. *S. B. B.*, Scenes i.

Luxuriously stretched on the top of the fruit-baskets, forgets his curiosity to behold the wonders of London.

WAGHORN. Mr. *Mud. Pap.* i.

WAITER. *D. C.* v.

WAITER. *D. and S.* lv.

WAITER. *M. P., L. T.*

WAITER. At Bachelors' Inns at Temple Bar. *M. C.* xlv.

In white waistcoat, never surprised—a grave man, and noiseless.

WAITER. At coffee-house in Ludgate Hill. *L. D.* iii.

WAITER. At famous inn—in Salisbury. *M. C.* xii.

WAITER. At old Royal Hotel. *P. P.* l.

WAILER. At the Spaniards' tea garden. *P. P.* xlvi.

WAITER. Come of a family of waiters. *C. S., S. L.* i.

WAITER. In restaurant. *P. P.* xliv.

WAITER. Innocent young, in hotel at Greenwich. *O. M. F.* liv.

With weakish legs, as yet unversed in the wiles of waiterhood, and but too evidently of a romantic temperament—finding, by ill fortune, a piece of orange flower somewhere in the lobbies—approached—and placed it on Bella's right hand.

WAITER. Live, Of " White Horse Cellar." *P. P.* xxxv.

Which article is kept in a small kennel for washing glasses, in a corner of the compartment.

WAITER. Non-resident, Laundress' daughter's husband.
P. P. xlvii.

WAITER. Of "The Bush."
P. P. xlviii.

WAITER. Representative of waiter of tavern. *M. H. C.* ii.
A poor, lean, hungry man.

WAITERING. Father of the, Old Charles. *C. S., S. L.* i.

WAITERS. At the "Great White Horse." *P. P.* xxiv.

WAITERS. Hired. *P. P.* xv.
A dozen in the costume of their country—and very dirty costume too.

WAITERS. Two, At Guildhall.
S. B. B., Scenes xix.

WAITERS. Two, At "The Peacock." *P. P.* xiii.
"Pumpin' over the independent woters as supped there last night."

WAITING MAIDS. Of Dorrit's party. *L. D.* xxxvii.

WAITRESS. *U. T.* xxii.

WAITRESS. A, Sister of waiter.
C. S., S. L. i.

WAITS. The. *C. S., S. P. T.* iii.

WAITS. The. *R. P., A. C. T.*

WAKEFIELD. Mr., *M. P., C. P.*

WAKEFIELDS. The.
S. B. B., Tales vii.
Mr. Wakefield, Mrs. Wakefield, and Miss Wakefield of the steam excursion party.

WAKLEY. Mr. *M. P., P. T.*

WAKLEY. Mr., Late coroner.
U. T. xviii.
Nobly patient and humane.

WALCOT SQUARE. Lambeth.
B. H. lxiv.

WALDENGARVER. Mr., An actor at a small provincial theatre.
G. E. xxxi.

WALES. *C. S., M. J.* iv.; *M. P., E. S.*; *M. P., R. S.*; *U. T.* ii.

WALES. Young Prince of.
B. R. lxxviii.

WALKER. A crimp. *U. T.* v.

WALKER. Mick, Regular boy at Murdstone and Grinby's. *D. C.* xi.

WALKER. Mr.
S. B. B., Scenes xix.
Auditor of indigent Orphans Friends' Benevolent Institution.

WALKER. Mr., Prisoner in lock-up-house. *S. B. B.,* Tales x.
A horsedealer from Islington.

WALKER. Mr. H., Tailor; convert to temperance. *P. P.* xxxiii.
When in better circumstances, owns to have been in the constant habit of drinking ale and beer . . . is now out of work and penniless, has nothing but cold water to drink, and never feels thirsty.

WALKER. Mrs., At No. 5.
S. B. B., Scenes ii.

WALKER. Mrs., Convert to temperance. *P. P.* xxxiii.

WALKER. Mr. and Mrs., Children of, *P. P.* xxxiii.

WALKER. Owner of an assumed name. *S. B. B.,* Scenes xiii.

WALKER. Secret name. *N. N.* ii.

WALL STREET. New York.
A. N. vi.
The Stock Exchange and Lombard Street of New York.

WALLACE. Mr., Member for Greenock. *M. P., M. E. R.*

WALLACE. Mr. Vincent.
M. P., M. M.

WALMER. Mr., Father of Master Harry. *C. S., H. T.*
A gentleman of spirit, and good

looking, and held his head up when he walked, and had what you may call fire about him.

WALMERS. Master Harry.
C. S., H. T.

WALTER. An Indian merchant.
R. P., A. C. T.

WALTER. Edward M'Neville, Theodosius' butler.
S. B. B., Tales iii.

WALTERS. Charley, Inmate of workhouse. R. P., W. I. A. W.

WALTON. O. M. F. xli.

WALWORTH. G. E. xxiv. ; S. B. B., Tales vi. ; U. T. vi.

WALWORTH. House of patient in.
S. B. B., Tales vi.
A small low building, one storey above the ground—an old yellow curtain was closely drawn across the window upstairs, and the parlour shutters were closed, but not fastened. The house was detached from any other.

WALWORTH. Inmate of patient's house in. S. B. B., Tales vi.
A tall, ill-favoured man, with black hair, and a face (as the surgeon declared afterwards), as pale and haggard as the countenance of any dead man he ever saw.

WANDSWORTH.
C. S., D. M. ; S. B. B., Tales v.

WANT. Name of a bird. B. H. xiv.

WAPPING. B. R. liii. ; C. S., M. f. T. S. v. ; H. T., S. vi. ; M. P., G. A. ; O. M. F. xxix. ; U. T. iii.

WAPPING OLD STAIRS. U. T. iii.

WAPPING WORKHOUSE. East end of London. U. T. iii.

WAPPING WORKHOUSE. Matron of. U. T. iii.
Very bright and nimble—quick, active little figure and intelligent eyes.

WAPPING WORKHOUSE. Two aged inmates of. U. T. iii.
Sitting by the fire (in one large ward) in armchairs of distinction—were two old women—the younger of the two, just turned ninety, was deaf, but not very—in her early time she had nursed a child—now another old woman, more infirm than herself, inhabiting the very same chamber. The elder of this pair, ninety-three—was a bright-eyed old soul, really not deaf—and amazingly conversational.

WAPPING WORKHOUSE. Two inmates of ward for idiotic and Imbecile. U. T. iii.
Two old ladies in a condition of feeble dignity, which was surely the very last and lowest reduction of self-complacency, to be found in this wonderful humanity of ours.

WAPPING WORKHOUSE. Wards-woman of ward for idiotic and imbecile. U. T. iii.
An elderly able-bodied pauper-ess, with a large upper lip, and an air of repressing and saving her strength—biding her time for catching or holding somebody—a reduced member of my honourable friend Mrs. Gamp's family.

WAR HATCHET. An Indian chief.
A. N. ix.

WAR OFFICE. B. R. xxxi.

WARDEN. Of Fleet Prison.
P. P. xl.

WARDEN. Master, A detective.
S. B. B., Tales xii.

WARDEN. Mr., A client of Snitchey and Craggs. C. B., B. o. L. ii.
A man of thirty, or about that time of life, negligently dressed, and somewhat haggard in the

C C

face, but well-made, well-attired, and well-looking.

WARDEN. Wife of Michael. *Née* Marion Jeddler.
C. B., B. o. L. iii.

WARDLE. Emily, Wardle's daughter. *P. P.* iv.

Note.—Daughter of Mr. Wardle. Marries Mr. Snodgrass and settles down on a farm at Dingley Dell.

WARDLE. Isabella, Wardle's daughter. Married Mr. Trundle. *P. P.* iv.

Note.—Daughter of Mr. Wardle. Marries Mr. Trundle.

WARDLE. Mr. *P. P.* iv.
In an open barouche . . . stood a stout old gentleman, in a blue coat and bright buttons, corduroy breeches and top boots.

Note.—Wardle's is a pleasing picture of the old English yeoman farmer—jovial in spirits and substantial in body and purse. He has two daughters who are the means of affording many interesting incidents and adventures. Mr. Snodgrass marries Emily, and Isabella is wedded to Mr. Trundle. Tupman falls in love with Wardle's sister Rachel. Jingle supplants him and elopes, giving rise to the famous episode of the chase from Muggleton to London, which results in the discovery of Sam Weller. Wardle is a good friend to the Pickwickians, who visit him on occasion at the Manor Farm, Dingley Dell. Mr. Wardle and the Pickwickians meet at the grand review at Rochester. Wardle is left in the midst of Snodgrass' wedding festivities.

Original : Said to have been Mr. Spong, of Cob Tree Hall, Sandling.

WARDLE. Mrs., Mr. Wardle's mother. *P. P.* vi.
A very old lady, in a lofty cap and a faded silk gown.

Note.—Old Wardle's mother. She is deaf, but affects to be more deaf than she really is. She is seventy-three years of age.

Original : Suggested to have been Mrs. Spong, the mother of the

occupant of Cob Tree Hall in Dickens' time."

WARDLE. Miss Rachel, Wardle's sister ; a " lady of doubtful age." *P. P.* iv.
" She's a miss, she is ; and yet she ain't a miss—eh, sir, eh ? "

Note.—Mr. Wardle's sister. She displays a shrewish jealousy of her nieces. Tupman falls in love with her. But Jingle by a clever ruse transfers her affections to himself. They elope together. Pickwick and Wardle pursue them, but the chaise breaks down, and the fugitives escape. They are discovered at the White Hart Inn in the Borough in time for the marriage to be prevented. Jingle is bought off for £120, and Miss Rachel returns to Dingley Dell.

WARDOUR STREET. *M. P., I. M.*

WARDS City. *B. R.* lxvii.

WARE. *M. P., E. S.*

" WAREHOUSE. The," Of Mr. Mortimer Knag. *N. N.* xviii.
About the size of three Hackney carriages.

WARNER. Captain. *M. P., G. D.*

WARREN. An engine driver. *A. N.* iii.

WARREN. Mr. *M. P., E. T.*

WARREN. Mr.
S. B. B., Scenes v.

WARREN. The. *B. R.* i.
A large old red brick mansion, a dreary, silent building, with echoing courtyards, desolated turret chambers, and whole suites of rooms shut up and mouldering to ruin.

WARREN STREET. *M. P., M. E.*

" WARWICK. The Earl of," A pickpocket. *R. P., D. W. I. F.*

" WARWICK ARMS." An inn. *R. P., T. D. P.*

WARWICK CASTLE.
D. and S. xxvi.

WAR

WARWICK

WARWICK

WARWICK
7

WASHINGT(

WASHINGT(
ance Soci

WASHINGT(
magnifice:

WASHINGTC
more.

"WASP."]

WASTE. Na

WATCH. M:
club in Ma

Consist:
the barber
Sam.

WATCHMAK

WATCHMAN

WATCHMEN

WATERBRO
field's agen
A middl
a sore thre
shirt-collar,
black nose
pug dog.

WATERBRO
A large
large dress
which was
lady.

WATERHOU:

WARWICK LANE. *R. P., M. O. F. F.*

WARWICK STREET. *B. R.* l.

WARWICKSHIRE. *D. and S.* lviii.; *T. T. C.*, bk. ii. ch. xviii.

WASHINGTON. Negro man slave. *A. N.* xvii.

WASHINGTON. Auxiliary Temperance Societies. *A. N.* xi.

WASHINGTON. "The city of magnificent distances." *A. N.* iii.; *M. P., I. C.*

WASHINGTON MONUMENT. Baltimore. *A. N.* ix.

WASP." Passenger in train. *R. P., A. F.*

WASTE. Name of a bird. *B. H.* xiv.

WATCH. Mr. Weller's, A kitchen club in Master Humphrey's. *M. H. C.* v.
Consisting of the housekeeper, the barber and Mr. Weller and Sam.

WATCHMAKER. The. *G. E.* viii.

WATCHMAN. A. *B. R.* lxi.

WATCHMEN. Temple, One of. *C. S., H. T.*

WATERBROOK. Mr., Mr. Wickfield's agent. *D. C.* xxv.
A middle-aged gentleman with a sore throat and a good deal of shirt-collar, who only wanted a black nose to be the portrait of a pug dog.

WATERBROOK. Mrs. *D. C.* xxv.
A large lady—or who wore a large dress, I don't exactly know which was dress and which was lady.

WATERHOUSE. Pegg. *U. T.* v.

WATERING PLACE. Our English. *R. P., O. E. W.*
Sky, sea, beach, and village, lie as still before us as if they were sitting for the picture.
Original: Broadstairs.

WATERING PLACE. Our French, *R. P., O. F. W. P.*
Original: Boulogne.

WATERLILY. Hotel at Malvern. *M. P., M. D.*

WATERLOO. *A. N.* xvii.; *C. S., S. L.* iii.; *M. P., G. D.*

WATERLOO BRIDGE. *B. H.* xxi.; *M. P., G. F.*; *P. P.* xvi.; *R. P., D. W. T. T.*; *S. B. B.*, Scenes xiii.; *S. B. B.*, Tales xii.; *U. T.* x.

WATERLOO PLACE. *S. B. B.*, Scenes xv.

WATERLOO ROAD. *C. S., S. L.* iii.; *R. P., B. S.*; *R. P., D. W. T. T.*; *U. T.* xxxvi.

WATERMAN. *S. B. B.*, Scenes vii.
Dancing the "double shuffle" to keep his feet warm.

WATERMAN. With one eye. *D. and S.* xix.
Had made the captain out some mile and half off, and had been exchanging unintelligible roars with him ever since.

WATERMEN. *S. B. B.*, Scenes ii.
With dim lanterns in their hands, and large brass plates upon their breasts—retire to their watering-houses, to solace themselves with the creature comforts of pipes and purl.

WATERMEN. Thames. *U. T.* xiv.

WATERS. Captain Walter. *S. B. B.*, Tales iv.
A stoutish, military-looking gentleman in a blue surtout buttoned up to his chin, and white trousers chained down to the soles of his boots.

WATERS. Companion to a married lady.   *N. N.* xxi.

WATERS. Mrs. Captain.
    S. B. B., Tales iv.
    Black-eyed young lady.

WATERSIDE - LABOURERS. At Ratcliff.   *U. T.* xxx.
    Occupants of single rooms.

WATERTOAST GAZETTE. Two gentlemen from the.   *M. C.* xxii.
    Had come express to get the matter for an article on Martin— one took him below the waist; one above.

WATKINS. Mr., Kate Nickleby's godfather.   *N. N.* xviii.
    Said he was very sorry he couldn't repay the fifty pounds just then—should take it very unkind if we didn't buy you a silver coral and put it down to his old account.

WATKINS. The, Who kept "The Old Boar."   *N. N.* xviii.

WATKINS THE FIRST. King.
    H. R. ii.

WATKINS THE FIRST. Queen of.
    H. R. ii.

WATSONS.   *S. Y. G.*

WATT.   *M. P., S.*

WATTS. The tomb of Master Richard.   *C. S., S. P. T.* i.
    With the effigy of worthy master Richard starting out of it like a ship's figure-head.

WATTS. Worshipful Master Richard.   *C. S., S. P. T.* i.

WATTS' CHARITY.
    C. S., S. P. T.
    A clean white house, of a staid and venerable air, with an arched door, choice long low lattice windows, and a roof of three gables.
    Original: In Rochester.

WATTS' CHARITY. Daughter of matron of.   *C. S., S. P. T.* i.

WATTS' CHARITY. Matron of.
    C. S., S. P. T. i.
    A decent body, of wholesome matronly appearance — a mighty civil person.

WATTY. Mr., A bankrupt.
    P. P. xxxi.
    A rustily-clad, miserable-looking man in boots with tops, and gloves without fingers. There were traces of privation and suffering—almost of despair, in his lank and careworn countenance.
    Note.—Mr. Perker's bankrupt client; to whom his lawyer is not at home. Cf. with the chancery characters of Bleak House.

WAYFARER. Hungry.   *S. B. B.*, Scenes ii.

WEBB. Lieutenant.   *M. P., N. E.*

WEBSTER.   *M. P., O. L. N. O.*

WEBSTER. Mr.   *A. N.* xiv.

WEBSTER. Mr. Benjamin, as Joey Ladle.   *M. P., N. T.*

WEDGINGTON. Master B., Aged ten months.   *R. P., O. o. S.*

WEDGINGTON. Mr. B., An actor.
    R. P., O. o. S.

WEDGINGTON. Mrs. B., An actress.
    R. P., O. o. S.

WEDLAKE. Mary.   *M. P., F. F.*

WEEDLE. Anastasia, Emigrant.
    U. T. xx.
    With Mrs. Jobson. A pretty girl in a bright garibaldi.

WEEVLE. *See* Jobling, Tony.

WEGG. Silas.   *O. M. F.* v.
    A man with a wooden leg (had sat for some years) with his remaining foot in a basket in cold weather, picking up a living in this wise. Every morning — he stumped to the corner, carrying

chair, a clothes-horse, a pair of trestles, a board, a basket, and an umbrella, all strapped together. The board and trestles became a counter—the basket supplied the fruit and sweets he offered for sale upon it, and became a foot-warmer. The unfolded clothes-horse displayed a choice collection of half-penny ballads. All weathers saw the man at his post. When the weather was wet, he put up his umbrella over his stock-in-trade, not over himself. In front of his sale board hung a little placard, like a kettle-holder, bearing the inscription—

Errands gone
On with fi
Delity By
Ladies and Gentlemen
I remain
Your humble Servt
Silas Wegg.

Note.—Introduced as a stall-keeper in the vicinity of Cavendish Square. Mr. Boffin is attracted by the collection of ballads which flanks the fruit and gingerbread, and hires the vendor for two hours every evening to read to him. Wegg is an illiterate rascal. Being put in charge of the Bower he discovers a will later than that proved by Mr. Boffin. By this he hopes to keep the Golden Dustman's nose to the grindstone, i.e., to extract from him all or most of the money Boffin has inherited. Boffin allows him to continue under this delusion for some time, Mr. Venus having betrayed him because of the meanness of his scheme, and then greatly surprising him by showing that he was cognisant of the scheme, and proving the existence of a will still later than that discovered by Wegg. Silas, no longer a thriving " literary man with a wooden leg," then returns to selling fruit and gingerbread.

WELBECK STREET. *B. R.* lii.

WELLER. Mrs. *P. P.* xx.

" There never was a nicer woman as a widder than that 'ere second wentur of mine. All I can say on her now is, that as she was

such an uncommon pleasant widder, it's a great pity she ever changed her con-dition. She don't act as a vife. Take example by your father, my boy, and be wery careful o' widders all your life."

Note.—The buxom widow Mrs. Clarke, whom Tony Weller married. She is grossly imposed upon by the hypocritical shepherd, the Rev. Stiggins, who drinks unlimited pineapple-rum at the " Marquis of Granby," Mrs. Weller's public-house. Mrs. Weller thinks her husband a reprobate and renders his life miserable. She catches cold whilst " settin too long on the damp grass in the rain a-hearin' of a shepherd who warn't able to leave off till late at night owen to his havin' vound his-self up vith brandy and water," and dies regretting that she hasn't looked after Tony better.

WELLER. Sam. *M. H. C.* iii.; *P. P.* x.

Habited in a coarse-striped waistcoat, with black calico sleeves, and blue glass buttons; drab breeches and leggings.

Note.—Next to Pickwick, Sam Weller is the most important character in the book. He is first met with cleaning boots at the " White Hart " inn, Borough. Mr. Pickwick is very favourably impressed and engages him as his servant. Sam then accompanies the Pickwickians on their travels. He is an amusing and invaluable witness in the trial Bardell v. Pickwick. He is instrumental in discovering Jingle's machinations. When Mr. Pickwick elects to go into the Fleet Prison rather than pay costs and damages, Sam arranges for his own committal to the same prison. When Pickwick is exposing Jingle to the Mayor of Ipswich, Sam meets Mary, the housemaid, with whose charms he is very much struck. When Mr. Pickwick settles down at Dulwich, Sam refuses to leave him, but after two years Mary is promoted to the position of housekeeper to Mr. Pickwick and she and Sam are married. According to Sam himself, he was turned out on the streets at a tender age for his education, with the result that he is full of a shrewd, quaint humour. He afterwards reappeared in " Master Humphrey's Clock."

Original : Numerous sources for the name of the character have been discovered, amongst them the Archbishop's Registrar's papers at Canterbury, and a tombstone in the churchyard of St. Mary's Church, Chatham, and to another in the parish churchyard at Upper Town, Eastbourne. The character is said to have been founded on Samuel Vale of the Surrey Theatre in the character of Simon Spatterdash, in the ".Boarding House" by Beazeley. It has also been attributed to Joe Baldwin buried in Rainham Churchyard. Another prototype of Sam has been suggested in Andrew Fairservice in " Rob Roy."

WELLER. Tony, Sam Weller's father.   *M. H. C.* iii. ; *P. P.* x.

Stout, red-faced, elderly man . . . A rayther stout gen'lm'n of eight-and-fifty. His face had expanded under the influence of good living—and its bold, fleshy curves had so far extended beyond the limits originally assigned them, that unless you took a full view of his countenance in front, it was difficult to distinguish more than the extreme tip of a very rubicund nose.

Note.—As Sam is typical of London life below stairs, so his father is representative of the coachmen who were displaced by the coming of the railways. His second wife is the only one we are made acquainted with. She was a widow, and landlady of the " Marquis of Granby." Tony Weller looks upon himself as an awful example to all young men of the effects of marrying a " vidder " ; and repeatedly warns his son against women in general and widows in particular. Eventually he is compelled, by gout, to relinquish his coach. But the contents of his pocketbook have been so well invested for him by Mr. Pickwick " that he had a handsome independence to retire on."

Original : Said to have been founded on old Cholmeley (or Chumley), driver of the coach from Charing Cross to Rochester.

WELLESLEY.   Sir A., Duke o Wellington.   *M. P., T. D*

WELLINGTON. Duke of. *M. P. E. S.; M. P., E. T.; M. P. R. T.; M. P., S. F. A.; M. P T. D.; M. T., T. O. P*

WELLINGTON STREET.   *R. P., T. D. P*

WELLS, TUNBRIDGE.   *E. D.* iii

WELSH COAST.   *U. T.* xxxi

WELSH MOUNTAINS.   *C. S., W. o. G. M*

WEMMICK. Mr., Mr. Jaggers' clerk. *G. E.* xxi

A dry man, rather short in stature, with a square wooden face, whose expression seemed to have been imperfectly chipped out with a dull-edged chisel. There were some marks in it that might have been dimples—but which— were only dints. He wore at least four mourning rings, besides a brooch representing a lady and a weeping willow at a tomb with an urn on it. Several rings and seals hung at his watchchain. He had glittering eyes—small, keen and black.

Note.—Jaggers' clerk. In business he matches his master, but, like him, he is good-hearted. Wemmick holds the money for Pip, and a friendship grows up between them. Pip goes out to the Castle at Walworth, where he sees the senior Mr. Wemmick and Miss Skiffins, whom Mr. Wemmick marries.

Original : Thomas Mitton, " Dickens' solicitor as well as his schoolfellow."

WEMMICK. Mrs., *née* Skiffins. *G. E.* lv.

WEMMICK. Senr.   *G. E.* xxv

Note.—The father of Mr. John Wemmick. Known as " The aged."

WEMMICK'S HOUSE. In Walworth.   *G. E.* xxv.

A little wooden cottage in the midst of plots of garden, and the top of it was cut out and painted like a battery mounted with guns, with the queerest Gothic windows, and a Gothic door, almost too small to get in at.

WENTWORTH STREET.
R. P., D. W. I. F.

WEST. An artist.   *A. N.* vii.

WEST. Dame, The grandmother of the schoolmaster's favourite scholar.   *O. C. S.* xxv.

WEST BROMWICH.
R. P., P. M. T. P.

WEST END.   *C. S., S. L.* iv.;
N. N. xi.; *R. P., B. S.*

WEST-ENDERS.   *N. N.* xxxvii.

WEST INDIA DOCKS. *M. P., C. J.*

WEST INDIES.   *B. R.* lxxviii.;
C. S., P. o. C. E. P.; C. S., W. o. G. M.; D. and S. xiii.;
M. P., C. J.; M. P. L. T.; N. N. xxxvii.; *O. T.* xiv.; *P. C.* xxvii.; *R. P., T. S. S.; U. T.* xix.

WEST RIDING.   *N. N.* xxxv.

WEST STREET. Saffron Hill.
M. P., C. and E.; M. P., S. S. U.

WEST TWENTY-SIXTH STREET. No. 78.   *M. P., S. B.*

WESTERN ROAD.   *M. C.* xlii.

WESTERN OCEAN.
M. P., L. A. V. ii.

WESTGATE HOUSE. Establishment for young ladies. *P. P.* xvi.

Consisting of the spinster lady of the establishment, three teachers, five female servants, and thirty boarders.

Original : There is some doubt

expressed about the original of Westgate House, one theory identifies it with Southgate House at Bury. It is sometimes traced to Pageant House, Bury, and it has been suggested that Eastgate House, the Nuns' House, Rochester, is the prototype. Still further, the High School, Bury, is claimed by some Dickensians as the original.

WESTLOCK. John, Pupil of Pecksniff's.   *M. C.* ii.

A good-looking youth, newly arrived at man's estate.

Note.—John was one of those pupils of Pecksniff who found him out. He left his mentor and prospered. He was a staunch friend of Tom Pinch, and a friend of old Martin Chuzzlewit. He eventually marries Ruth, Tom's sister.

WESTMINSTER.   *B. R.* xxxviii.;
M. P., H. H.; M. P., O. C.; M. P., S. S.; N. N. xxxvii.; *O. M. F.* iii.; *R. P., G. o. A.; R. P., T. D. P.; U. T.* iii.

WESTMINSTER. Great conservator of the peace at.
S. B. B., Scenes xviii.

Stout man, with a hoarse voice, in the blue coat, queer crowned, broad-brimmed hat, white corduroy breeches, and great boots.

WESTMINSTER ABBEY.   *G. E.* xxii.; *L. D.* xv.; *O. M. F.* vi.; *U. T.* xiii.

WESTMINSTER AND BLACK-FRIARS' BRIDGES.   *L. D.* xli.

WESTMINSTER BRIDGE.   *B. R.* xlvii.; *O. M. F.* xviii.; *R. P., P. R. S.; S. B. B.,* Scenes x.; *U. T.* xiii.

WESTMINSTER BRIDGE ROAD.
M. P., M. B. V.

WESTMINSTER HALL. *B. H.* xix.; *B. R.* lxvii.; *D. C.* xxx.; *L. D.* lxi.; *M. P., M. E.; M. P., P. F.; M. P., S. of C.; O. M. F.* xxi.; *R. P., G. o. A.*

WESTMINSTER MARKET.
        M. P., O. C.

WESTMINSTER SCHOOL.
        H. T., R. vii. ; *N. N.* xvii.

WESTWOOD. Mr., Friend of Sir Mulberry Hawk.   *N. N.* l.

WHARF. A.   *D. and S.* xix.

WHARF. A, Opening on the Thames—behind the old dingy house.   *N. N.* xi.
   A picture of cold, silent decay . . . . An empty dog-kennel, some bones of animals, fragments of iron hoops, and staves of old casks, lay strewn about, but no life was stirring there.

WHARF. Spigwiffin's. *N. N.* xxvi.

WHARTON. Mr. Granville, George Silverman's pupil.   *G. S. E.* ix.

WHATELEY. Archbishop.
        M. P., P. P.

WHAT'S-HER-NAME. Mrs.
        U. T. xii.
   A lodger at greengrocer's shop in High Street, Dullborough.

WHAT'S-HIS-NAME. Pupil at Dotheboys' Hall.   *N. N.* vii.

WHEELWRIGHTS. Seeing Mark Tapley off.   *M. C.* vii.

WHELKS. Joe.   *M. P., A. P.*

WHEEZY. Prof.   *Mud. Pap.* i.

WHIFF. Miss, Of Mugby Junction. Refreshment-room staff.
        C. S., M. J. v.

WHIFFERS. Mr., Footman.
        P. P. xxxvii.
   Gentleman in orange-coloured plush.

WHIFFIN. The town crier of Eatanswill.   *P. P.* xiii.

WHIFFLER. Mr.   *S. Y. C.*

WHIFFLER. Mrs.   *S. Y.* (

WHIGS. In House of Parliamen
        S. B. B., Scenes xvi

WHILKS. Mr.   *M. C.* xi

WHIMPLE. Mrs.   *G. E.* xlv
   An elderly woman of pleasar and thriving appearance.

WHIP. The.   *B. H.* lvii

WHIPPERS-IN. M.P.'s.
        S. B. B., Scenes xvii

WHISKER. Red, One of part picnicing near Guildford. *D. C.* iv
   Pretended he could make a sala and voted himself into the charg of the wine-cellar, which he cor structed, being an ingenious beast in the hollow trunk of a tree.

WHITBY.   *D. and S.* xv

WHITE. Betsy, A female crimp.
        U. T. v

WHITE. Constable.
        R. P., D. W. I. F

WHITE. One of Mrs. Lemon's pupils.   *H. R.* iv

WHITE. One of the "Army."
        S. B. B., Scenes xiii

WHITE. Young, At gasfitter's.
        S. B. B., Char. ix

WHITE HART. Bath. *P. P.* xxxv.

WHITE HART. Borough. *P. P.* x.

WHITE HOUSE.   *A. N.* viii.

WHITEBAIT-HOUSE. Blackwall.
        M. P., C. J.

WHITECHAPEL. *B. R.* iv. ; *C. B.,* *C. C.,* s. iii. ; *M. P., F. S.* ; *M. P.,* *G. B.* ; *M. P., N. S. L.* ; *M. P.,* *T. O. P.* ; *O. T.* xix. ; *P. P.* xx. ; *R. P., B. S.* ; *R. P., D. W. T. T.* ; *R. P., M. o. F. F.* ; *U. T.* x.

WHITECHAPEL CHURCH.
        U. T. iii.

WHITECHAPEL WORKHOUSE.
        M. P., N. S. L.

WHITE CONDUIT CONCERT HALL.
S. B. B., Char. viii.

WHITE CONDUIT HOUSE.
S. B. B., Scenes xix.

WHITECROSS STREET. P. P. xl.

WHITEFRIARS. B. H. xxvii.
G. E. xliv. ; S. B. B., Tales xii.

WHITEFRIARS. See also Hanging-sword-alley.

WHITEHALL. A. N. xv. ; M. P.,
F. F. ; M. P., O. C. ; P. P. ii. ;
R. P., P. M. T. D.

WHITE HART INN. High Street,
Borough. P. P. v.
A great, rambling, queer, old place, with galleries, and passages, and staircases, wide enough and antiquated enough to furnish materials for a hundred ghost stories.

WHITE HORSE CELLAR.
B. H. iii. ; P. P. xxxv.
Starting place for coach for Bath.

WHITE HOUSE. Grogus's.
S. B. B., Tales ii.

WHITE LION. The. O. M. F. xli.

WHITE RIDING HOOD.
U. T. xxxvi.

WHITE WOMAN. M. P., W. S. S.

WHITENED SEPULCHRES. Hon.
Member for. M. P., S. S.

WHITFIELD TABERNACLE.
M. P., N. Y. D.

WHITROSE. Lady Belinda.
O. M. F. xxxv.

WHITTINGTON. M. P., M. B. V.

WHITYBROWN. Bellringer of an old City church. U. T. ix.

WICKAM. Mrs., Paul's nurse.
D. and S. viii.
Mrs. Wickam was a waiter's wife—which would seem equivalent

to being any other man's widow—whose application for an engagement—had been favourably considered, on account of the apparent impossibility of her having any followers, or any one to follow—was a meek woman, of a fair complexion, with her eyes always elevated, and her head always drooping ; who was always ready to pity herself, or to be pitied, or to pity anybody else.

WICKFIELD. Agnes, Mr. Wickfield's daughter. D. C. xv.
Her face was quite bright and happy, there was a tranquility about it, and about her—a quiet, good, calm spirit.

Note.—Agnes is David's "sister" during his schooldays at Canterbury, and his counsellor afterwards. Uriah Heep designs to marry her but fails ; and her father's name is cleared. Eventually she marries David.

Original : Said to be Miss Georgina Hogarth.

WICKFIELD. Mr., A lawyer.
D. C. xv.
A gentleman with grey hair (though not by any means an old man) and black eyebrows.

Note.—Mr. Wickfield is a Canterbury lawyer, legal adviser and friend of Betsey Trotwood. He is entirely wrapped up in his daughter Emily, but after his wife's death he loses spirits and drinks rather more port than is necessary. Uriah Heep is clerk in the office, but as Mr. Wickfield's infirmity increases he gains a greater ascendency. But his machinations are defeated and Mr. Wickfield is rescued from him.

Original of Wickfield's House : This has been identified as No. 71, St. Dunstan's Street, Canterbury ; and has been suggested as situated in Burgate Street, but there is no support for this theory.

WICKFIELD. Mrs., Agnes' dead mother. D. C. xxxi.
She married me in opposition to

her father's wish, and he re-nounced her. She prayed him to forgive her, before my Agnes came into the world. He was a very hard man, and her mother had long been dead. He repulsed her. He broke her heart.

WICKS. Mr., *C*lerk of Dodson and Fogg. *P. P.* xx.
In a brown coat, and brass buttons, inky drabs, and bluchers.

" WIDEAWAKE." *L. D.* vi.

WIDGER. Mr. Bobtail. *S. Y. C.*

WIDGER. Mrs. Bobtail. *S. Y. C.*

WIDOW. Dreary, Pew-opener.
O. M. F. x.
Whose left hand appears to be in a state of acute rheumatism, but is in fact voluntarily doubled up to act as a moneybox.

WIDOW. Landlady of inn in Marl-borough Downs. *P. P.* xiv.
Buxom . . . of somewhere about eight-and-forty or there-abouts, with a face as comfortable as the bar.

WIDOW. Next lodger of *C*ity clerk.
S. B. B., O. P. vii.

WIDOW, Son of.
S. B. B., O. P. vii.
Earned, by copying writings, and translating for booksellers. Nature had set that unearthly light in his plaintive face, which is the beacon of her worst disease.

WIDOW LADY. *C*ross.
M. P., F. F.

WIELD. Inspector *C*harley, A detective. *R. P., T. D. P.*
A middle-aged man, of a portly presence, with a large, moist, know-ing eye.

WIFE. Country manager's.
M. P., G. F.

WIFE. First. *M. P., N. T.*

WIFE. Of J.P. *B. R.* xlvi
A lady—who had the appear-ance of being delicate in health and not too happy.

WIFE. Of prisoner in the Fleet
P. P. xli

WIFE. Second. *M. P., N. T.*

WIFE. Young, Of clerical English traveller. *L. D.* ii

WIGAN. *M. P., F. S.*

WIGGS AND CO. Owners of the "Polyphemus." *D. and S.* iv.

WIGS. Name of a bird. *B. H.* xiv

WIGSBY. Mr. *Mud. Pap.* i

WIGSBY. Mr., A vestryman.
R. P., O. V.

WIGZELL. J. *M. P., U. N*

WILBURN. John. *A. N.* xvii

WILDE. Sir Thomas.
M. P., M. E. R.

" WILD BEAST SHOWS." Travel-ling menageries.
S. B. B., Scenes xii.

WILD LODGE. East Cliff.
R. P., O. o. S.

WILDERNESS. *See* Quilp's Wharf.

" WILDERNESS WALK."
R. P., O. V.

WILDING. Little Walter.
M. P., N. T.

WILDING. Mr. Walter, Of Wilding and *C*o. *C. S., N. T.,* Act i.
An innocent, open-speaking, unused-looking man, with a re-markably pink-and-white com-plexion, and a figure much too bulky for so young a man, though

of a good stature. With crispy, curling brown hair, and amiable, bright blue eyes.

WILDING. Walter, The second so-named foundling.
          C. S., N. T., Act i.

There was a question that day about naming an infant, a boy, who had just been received. We generally named them out of the Directory. One of the gentlemen who managed the hospital happened to be looking over the Register. "He noticed that the name of the baby who had been adopted (Walter Wilding) was scratched out, for the reason that the child had been removed from our care. "Here is a name to let," he said, "give it to the new foundling who has been received to-day."—You, sir, were that child.

WILDING AND CO. Mansion of.
          C. S., N. T., Act i.

It really had been a mansion in the days when merchants inhabited the *C*ity, and had a ceremonious shelter to the doorway without visible support, like the sounding board over an old pulpit. It had also a number of long, narrow strips of window, so dispersed in its grave brick front as to render it symmetrically ugly. It had also, on its roof, a cupola with a bell in it.

WILDING AND CO. Wine merchants.   *C. S., N. T.*, Act i.

WILDING'S HOUSE. *M. P., N. T.*

WILFER. Bella,   *O. M.* iv.

Note.—Left in John Harmon's will, like his other goods, to his son. She is adopted by the Boffins, and there meets the secretary, John Rokesmith. She marries him and afterwards discovers that he is the John Harmon of the will. She is the spoiled daughter of Reginald Wilfer, although in the testing she is proved to be true gold.

WILFER. Cecilia. *O. M. F.* iv.

Note.—Daughter of Reginald Wilfer and younger sister of Bella. She is jealous of her sister's good fortune. She has no respect for her mother, and has not her sister's love for their father. After Bella leaves home, Lavvy takes George Sampson "in tow."

WILFER. John.   *O. M. F.* iv.

WILFER. Mrs., Wife of R. Wilfer.
          O. M. F. iv.

A tall woman and an angular —much given to tying up her head in a pockethandkerchief knotted under the chin. This headgear, in conjunction with a pair of gloves worn within doors, she seemed to consider as at once a kind of armour against misfortune—and as a species of full dress.

WILFER. Reginald, A poor clerk.
          O. M. F. iv.

His black hat was brown, before he could afford a coat, his pantaloons were white at the seams and knees, before he could buy a pair of boots, his boots had worn out, before he could treat himself to new pantaloons.

Note.—Bella's father has several nicknames, amongst them, "The Cherub," and "Rumty." He is greatly at his wife's mercy and something of a nonentity in his home. Bella loves him and gives him several treats. He is appointed secretary in place of Rokesmith, when Rokesmith reveals himself as John Harmon.

WILKINS. *C*aptain Boldwig's sub-gardener.   *P. P.* xix.

WILKINS. Dick,
          C. B., C. C., S. ii.

WILKINS. Mrs.   *M. C.* xlix.

WILKINS. Mr. Samuel, A journeyman carpenter.
          S. B. B., Char. iv.

Below the middle size—bordering perhaps upon the dwarfish. His face was round and shining, and his hair carefully twisted into the outer corner of each eye till it formed a variety of that description of semi-curls usually known as " aggerawaters."

WILKS. Mrs. *M. C.* xix.

WILKS. Thomas Egerton.
M. P., J. S.
To . . . was confided the MS. of Grimaldi's life and adventures.

WILL. *M. P., S. G.*

WILL. Uncle, Wiliam Fern.
C. B., C., q. ii.

WILL OFFICE. *P. P.* lv.

WILLET. Joe, Son of John Willet.
B. R. i.
A broad-shouldered, strapping young fellow of twenty, whom it pleased his father still to consider a little boy, and to treat accordingly . . . enrolled among the gallant defenders of his native land. . . . I am a poor, maimed, discharged soldier.
Note.—The son of John Willet and his assistant in the "Maypole." He resents his father's treatment of him, however, and enlists in the Army. During the war in America he lost an arm at the siege of Savannah—which arm Dickens seems to be rather uncertain. He returns to England at the time of the Riots and proves of the utmost assistance to his friends. He marries Dolly Varden, and after his father's death inherits his wealth and becomes a man of great consequence in the district.

WILLET. Joe and Dolly, Children of. *B. R.* lxxxii.
A red-faced little boy, a red-faced little girl, another red-faced little boy—more small Joes, and small Dollys than could be easily counted.

WILLET. John, Landlord of the " Maypole." *B. R.* i.
A burly, large-headed man, with

a fat face, which betokened profound obstinacy and slowness of apprehension, combined with a very strong reliance upon his own merits—a pair of dull, fish-like eyes.
Note.—The honest landlord of the " Maypole " inn was so obtuse, and his density was only equalled by his obstinacy and ignorance. He regards Joe, his son, as still a boy and treats him as such. After Joe's return from the " Salwanners " he is so surprised that he never really recovers, though he is inordinately proud of his son, and still more proud of his loss of an arm—in the "Salwanners" When he dies it is found that he has left even more money than was generally supposed.

WILLET. Mrs. Joe, *Née* Varden Dolly, *which see.*

WILLIAM. *D. C.* xii.

WILLIAM. *M. P., N Y. D*

WILLIAM. Mrs., Mrs. Swidger.
C. B., H. M.

WILLIAM. One of visitors to Astley's. *S. B. B.,* Scenes x
Encouraged in his impertinence

WILLIAM. Shiny, *See* Shiny William.

WILLIAM. Sir Mulberry Hawk's groom. *N. N.* xxxii

WILLIAM. Son of the drunkard *S. B. B.,* Tales xii
A young man of about two-and-twenty, miserably clad in an old coarse jacket and trousers.

WILLIAM. Son of the widow.
S. B. B., O. P. vii

WILLIAM. Waiter. *D. C.* v
He was a twinkling-eyed, pimple-faced man, with his hair standing upright all over his head.
Note.—This was the waiter who ate David's dinner and drank David's ale.

WILLIAM. Waiter at " Blue Boar."
G. E. lviii

WILLIAM. Waiter at "Saracen's Head."					*N. N.* v.

WILLIAMS.   A constable.
					R. P., D. W. I. F.

WILLIAMS, WILLIAM.   *O. M. F.* vi.

WILLIAMSON. Mrs., Landlady of "Winglebury Arms."					*S. B. B.*, Tales viii.

WILLIAMSON.   Mr., As John, a waiter at the "St. James's Arms."
					M. P., S. G.

WILLING.   Sophy.   *C. S. M. L. Lo.*

WILLING MIND.   The.   *D. C.* iii.
   Mr. Peggotty went occasionally to a public-house called "The Willing Mind."

WILLIS.   Miss, The eldest.
					S. B. B., O. P. iii.

WILLIS. Mr., A prisoner in lock-up-house.					*S. B. B.*, Tales x.
   A young fellow of vulgar manners, dressed in the very extreme of the prevailing fashion—with a lighted cigar in his mouth.

WILLIS.   Mrs., Kate.   *S. B. B., O. P.* iii.

WILLIS.   The second Miss.
					S. B. B., O. P., iii.

WILLISES.   The four Miss.
					S. B. B., O. P. iii.
   Were far from juvenile.

WILLISES.   The two other Miss.
					S. B. B., O. P. iii.
   Used to "play duets on the piano."

WILLMORE.   Mr. Graham.
					M. P., L. E. J.

WILLY. The brother of Little Nell's friend.					*O. C. S.* lv.
   Willy went away to join the angels; but if he had known how I should miss him, he never would have left me, I am sure.

WILSON.   Police-officer.
					S. B. B., Scenes xviii.

WILSON.   Fanny.   *M. P., S. G.*

WILSON.   Mary.   *M. P., S. G.*

WILSON. Miss, Pupil at Minerva House.					*S. B. B.*, Tales iii.
   The ugliest girl in Hammersmith.

WILSON. Mr.					*M. P., F. C.*

WILSON.   Mr.   *S. B. B., Char.* iii.

WILSON.   Mr.
					S. B. B., Scenes xix.

WILSON. Mr., Friend of the Gattletons.					*S. B. B.*, Tales ix.

WILSON.   Mr., Godfather to the Kitterbells' baby.
					S. B. B., Tales xi.

WILSON.   Mrs., Godmother to the Kitterbells' baby.
					S. B. B., Tales xi.

WILSON.   Professor.   *M. P., S. P.*

WILTSHIRE.   Farm in.   *M. C.* xiii.

WILTSHIRE. Hanger on at inn down in.					*C. S., H. T.*
   A supernaturally preserved Druid I believe him to have been—with long white hair, and a filmy blue eye always looking afar off, who claimed to have been a shepherd.

WILTSHIRE.   Inn down in.
					C. S., H. T.

WILTSHIRE.   Labourer emigrant.
					U. T. xx.
   A simple, fresh-coloured farm labourer, of eight-and-thirty.

WILTSHIRE LABOURERS.
					M. P., W. L.

WILTSHIRE VILLAGE.   *M. C.* ii.
   The declining sun, struggling through the mist which had

obscured it all day looked brightly down upon a little Wiltshire village. The wet grass sparkled in the light ; the scanty patches of verdure in the hedges—took heart, and brightened up. The birds began to chirp and twitter on the naked boughs. The vane upon the tapering spire of the old church glistened from its lofty station.

WILTSHIREMAN.   *Cheeseman.*
         R. P., T. S. S.

WIMPOLE STREET.   *U. T.* xvi.

" WIN THE DAY."   *M. P., O. S.*

WINCH. Mr.   *M. P., P. T.*

WINCHESTER.
         B. H. iv. ; *N. N.* xxix.

WINDER. At last shift. *M. P., O. S.*

WINDERMERE.   *M. P., E. S.*

WINDMILL, The old, Hexam's dwelling-place.   *O. M. F.* xii.

WINDSOR.   *B. H.* iii. ; *C. S., D. M.* ; *M. C.* xxi. ; *M. H. C.* iii. ; *M. P., C. C.* ; *M. P., E. S.* ; *M. P. S. D. C.* ; *M. P., T. D.* ; *R. P., A. F.* ; *R. P., O. o. T.* ; *U.* T. x.

WINDSOR PAVILION.   *M. C.* xxi.

WINDSOR TERRACE. City Road.
         D. C. xi.
Micawber's address. His house in Windsor Terrace which was shabby like himself, but also, like himself, made all the show it could.

WINE MERCHANT'S. Courtyard in.
         M. P., N. T.

WINE VAULTS. Keepers of.
         S. B. B., Scenes xxii.

WINGLEBURY. Great, The little town of.   *S. B. B.*, Tales viii.
Is exactly forty-two miles and three-quarters from Hyde Park Corner. It has a long, straggling, quiet High Street.
Original : Rochester.

WINGLEBURY. Little.
         S. B. B., Tales vii
Down some cross-roads about two miles off—Great Winglebury

WINGLEBURY. Mayor of,
         S. B. B., Tales vii

WINGLEBURY. Post office o Great.   *S. B. B.*, Tales vii

WINGLEBURY. Town hall of Great
         S. B. B., Tales viii
Half way up (High Street) with a great black and white clock.
Original : Corn Exchange Rochester.

" WINGLEBURY ARMS." The, inn
         S. B. B., Tales viii
In the centre of the High Street opposite the small building with the big clock, is the principal inn of Great Wwinglebury—the commercial inn, posting-house, and excise office. Blue house at every election, and judges' house at every assizes. A large house with a red brick and stone front ; a pretty, spacious hall, ornamented with evergreen plants.
Original : " Undoubtedly intended for the principal hostelry " of Rochester—the Bull.

" WINGLEBURY ARMS." Four stout waiters of.   *S. B. B., Tales viii.*

" WINGLEBURY ARMS." Landlady of.   *S. B. B.*, Tales viii.

WINKLE. Mr., A wharfinger.
         P. P. l.
Note.—Mr. Winkle, Senior, the father of Nathaniel, was a wharfinger at Birmingham, was precise and business-like and naturally resented his son's marriage to Arabella Allen. Arabella herself conquers him, however, and he takes his son back to favour.

WINKLE. Nathaniel, Member of the Pickwick Club.   *P. P.* i.
In a new green shooting-coat,

plaid neckerchief, and closely-fitting drabs.

Note.—One of the members of the corresponding society of the Pickwick Club who accompanied Mr. Pickwick on his expeditions of research. Mr. Winkle's desires to be a sportsman are greater than his skill, and he has an unfortunate habit of making others think he is one, with humiliating results to himself. He is challenged to fight a duel by Dr. Slammer, although he has no knowledge of firearms. Happily the doctor discovers that Winkle is "not the man," and the event terminates happily for everyone. To Winkle was due the invention of the Pickwick Coat with the "P. C." buttons. Winkle marries Arabella Allen quietly without consulting his father, upon whom he is dependent. A reconciliation is effected, however, and Nathaniel becomes London agent for his father, discards the Pickwick coat, and "presented all the external appearance of a civilised Christian ever afterwards."

INKLE. Private residence of Mr.
P. P. l.

In a quiet, substantial-looking street, stood an old red-brick house with three steps before the door, and a brass plate upon it, bearing in fat Roman capitals the words "Mr. Winkle." The steps were very white, and the bricks were very red.

Original of house : Identified as in Easy Row, Birmingham, in close proximity to the old wharf.

INKS. *See* Deputy.

IRY TARRIER. Licensed house.
M. P., G. B.

ISBOTTLE. Mr., Boarder at Mrs. Tibbs. *S. B. B.,* Tales i.

A high tory—clerk in the Woods and Forests Office—knew the peerage by heart—had a good set of teeth and a capital tailor.

ISCONSIN. *A. N.* xvii.

ISCONSIN. Legislative Hall.
A. N. xvii.

WISEMAN. Dr. *M. P., F. F.*

WISEMAN. Master=Cardinal Wiseman. *M. P., A. J. B.*

WISEMAN. Nicholas.
M. P., L. W. O. Y.

WISK. Miss, Fiancée of Mr. Quale.
B. H. xxx.

WIT. Of counting-house of Dombey.
D. and S. li.

Reconciliation is established—between the acknowledged wit of the counting-house and an aspiring rival, with whom he has been at deadly feud for months.

WITCH. First, In Liverpool, in common lodging-house. *U. T.* v. Making "money bags."

WITCH. Second, In Liverpool, common lodging-house. *U. T.* v.

WITCH. Third, In Liverpool, in common lodging-house. *U. T.* v.

WITCHEM. Sergeant, A detective.
R. P., T. D. P.

Marked with the smallpox. . . . He might have sat for Wilkie for the soldier in the reading of the will.

WITHERDEN. Mr., Notary.
O. C. S. xiv.

Short, chubby, fresh-coloured, brisk, and pompous.

Note.—The notary to whom Abel Garland was articled : and largely instrumental in securing the downfall of Sampson Brass.

WITHERFIELD. Miss, Middle-aged lady. *P. P.* xxiv.

Mr. Pickwick had no sooner put on his spectacles than he at once recognised in the future Mrs. Magnus, the lady into whose room he had so unwarrantably intruded on the previous night.

Note.—Miss Witherfield was the lady whom Mr. Magnus came to propose to and in whose room Mr. Pickwick had the night adventure.

WITHERS. Mrs. Skewton's page. *D. and S.* xxi.
The chair (in which Mrs. Skewton was seated) having stopped, the motive power became visible in the shape of a flushed page—who seemed to have in part outgrown and in part out-pushed his strength, for when he stood upright he was tall, wan, and thin.

WITHERS'S. At Brighton. *M. P., G. D.*

WITITTERLY. Henry. *N. N.* xxi.
An important gentleman of about eight-and-thirty, of rather plebeian countenance, and with a very light head of hair.
Note.—The husband of Mrs. Witterly. He supports his wife in her affected airs and simulated delicacy without any regard for the feelings of others.

WITITTERLY. Mrs., Julia. *N. N.* xxi.
The lady had an air of sweet insipidity, and a face of engaging paleness; there was a faded look about her.
Note.—The soul-ful lady to whom Kate Nickleby acts as companion.

WIX. Mr. *R. P., D. W. I. F.*

WIZZLE. Mr., One of steam excursion party. *S. B. B.*, Tales vii.

WOBBLER. Mr., Of Secretarial Department in *C*ircumlocution Office. *L. D.* x.
Polishing a gun-barrel on his pocket-handkerchief.

WOLF. Mr., Literary character. *M. C.* xxviii.

WOLVERHAMPTON. *M. P., F. and S.; M. P., L. S.; R. P., A. C. T.*

WOMAN. *L. D.* xiv.
She was young—and neither ugly nor wicked looking. she spoke coarsely, but with no naturally coarse voice; there was even something musical in its sound

WOMAN. *C*ustomer at sp chandler's. *D. and S.*
*C*ame to ask the way to M End Turnpike.

WOMAN. Deceased husband *S. B. B., O. P.*
Died in the hospital.

WOMAN. Fat old, A nurse. *S. B. B., O. P.,*
In a cloak and nightcap, w a bundle in one hand and a p of pattens in the other.

WOMAN. In tea gardens. *S. B. B.*, Scenes

WOMAN. Miserable-looking, widow. *S. B. B., O. P.*
Represents a case of extre destitution.

WOMAN. Old. *M. P., G.*

WOMAN. Old, In Marshalsea. *L. D.* lx
Who arranged Mr. Clennam rooms in the Marshalsea.

WOMAN. Old, Mother of corp *O. T.*

WOMAN. An old, very dirty, ve wrinkled and dry. *L. D.* xxv

WOMAN. One worthy. *B. H.* xx
To assist in nursing Charley.

WOMAN. Outside the workhou *M. P., N. S.*

WOMAN. Prisoner's wife in t poor side of the Fleet. *P. P.* xl
Watering, with great solicitud the wretched stump of a dried-u withered plant, which, it was pla to see, could never send forth green leaf again; too true emblem, perhaps, of the office s had come there to discharge.

WOMEN. Old, On board Gravesend packet.   *S. B. B.*, Scenes x.

Who have brought large wicker hand-baskets with them.

WOMEN. Strong young, Applicants to General Agency Office.
           N. N. xvi.

Some half dozen strong young women, each with pattens and an umbrella.

WOOD. Mr.   *M. P., C. C.*

WOOD. In which Jonas murdered Montague.   *M. C.* xlvii.

Original: Identified by one writer as Clarendon Park.

WOOD OF BOULOGNE.
           M. P., N. Y. D.

WOOD STREET. *G. E.* xx.; *L. D.*
           xiii.

WOODCOURT. Allan, Miss Flite's physician.   *B. H.* xiv.

The kindest physician in the college.

Note.—At first a naval surgeon. But practising in London he comes in contact with Jo, the Snagsbys and others, and so occupies a rather important position, and eventually marries Esther Summerson.

WOODCOURT. Children of Allan and Esther.   *B. H.* lxvii.

WOODCOURT. Esther, *Née* Hawdon. *See* Summerson, Esther.

WOODCOURT. Mr., Deceased.
           B. H. xxx.

Served his king and country as an officer in the Royal Highlanders, and he died on the field.

WOODCOURT. Mrs., Mother of Allan Woodcourt.   *B. H.* xvii.

She was a pretty old lady, with bright black eyes, but she seemed proud.

Note.—Mother of Allan Woodcourt; a Welsh lady with the utmost reverence for her ancestry. She thinks Esther has no ancestry, but she ultimately gets to love her.

WOODENCONSE. Mr. *Mud. Pap.* i.

WOODS. Prison in the, Of the pirates. *C. S., P. o. C. E. P.*

WOODS AND FORESTS OFFICE. *M. P., R. T.*

WOODSTOCK COMMISSIONERS. *M. P., R. S. D.*

WOOL-DEALER. Son of a Warwickshire, *R. P., N. S.*

WOOLFORD. Miss, Lady equestrian, at Astley's. *S. B. B.*, Scenes xi.

WOOLWICH. *B. R.* lxvii. ; *M. P., N. E.* ; *U. T.* v.

WOOLWICH. Young, Son of the Bagnets. *B. H.* xxvii.
Got an engagement, with his father, at the theayter, to play the fife in a military piece.

WOPSLE. Mr., Church clerk. *G. E.* iv.
United to a large Roman nose, and a large and shining bald forehead, had a deep voice which he was uncommonly fond of.

Note.—Friend of Pip's sister. He lives over his great-aunt's shop, and once a quarter he examines her scholars by acting before them. He is parish clerk, but he relinquishes that and takes to the London stage, where he meets with no very brilliant success.

WORCESTER. *A. N.* v. ; *M. P., E. S.*

WORKHOUSE. Common to most towns. *O. T.* i.
In this workhouse was born the item of mortality . . . whose name is prefixed to the head of this chapter (Oliver Twist).

WORKHOUSE. Master of, in Liverpool. *U. T.* viii.

WORKHOUSE. Master of the. *S. B. B., O. P.* i.
We should think he had been an inferior sort of an attorney clerk, or else the master of national school. His income small, certainly, as the rusty blac coat and threadbare velvet colla demonstrate : but then he live free of house-rent, has a limite allowance of coals and candle He is a tall, thin, bony man, a ways wears shoes and black cotto stockings with his surtout.

WORKHOUSE. Master of, in S George's-in-the-East. *U. T.* ii

WORKHOUSE. Pauper in, in S George's-in-the-East. *U. T.* ii

WORKHOUSE. Metropolitan. *R. P., W. i. a. W*

WORKHOUSE. Refuge for th destitute. *N. N.* x

WORKMAN. A, In Dr. Blimber': *D. and S.* xiv
There was something the matte with the great clock ; and a work man on a pair of steps had take its face off, and was poking instru ments into the works by the ligh of a candle. The workman o the steps was very civil.

"WORKS." The, Of Daniel Doyc and Clennam. *L. D.* xxiii
The little counting-house re served for his (Daniel Doyce's own occupation, was a room o wood and glass at the end of a lon low workshop.

WORSHIPFUL COMPANY. Maste and wardens of. *D. and S.* lvii
Inscription about what the masters and wardens of the Wor shipful Company did in one thou sand six hundred and ninety-fou (in the church where Walter and Florence were married).

WOSKY. Mr., Attending Mrs. Bloss. *S. B. B.*, Tales i.
A little man with a red face—

dressed, o a stiff w very gool money, w invariably fancies of families h duced to.

WOZENHA keeper.
With a of bones— in pork.

WRAYBUR

In sus . . . I as consisten

Note.— wood, sin panies M and meets tracted b; why, or w makes her himself it He takes Bradley F stone, and madness. traces he followed murder however, that he i the only does not some tim left in th the face wife's se

WRAYBU brother Heir ments the fa

WRAYB father

WRAYE broth

dressed, of course, in black, with a stiff white neckerchief—had a very good practice, and plenty of money, which he had amassed by invariably humouring the worst fancies of all the females of all the families he had ever been introduced to.

VOZENHAM. Miss, Lodging-house keeper. *C. S., M. L. Lo.* i.
With a cast in the eye, and a bag of bones—her father having failed in pork.

WRAYBURN. Eugene.
O. M. F. ii.
In susceptibility to boredom . . . I assure you I am the most consistent of mankind.

Note.—Friend of Mortimer Lightwood, aimless and indolent. He accompanies Mortimer in the Harmon case and meets Lizzie Hexam. He is attracted by her, and without knowing why, or where his action will lead, he makes her acquaintance and interests himself in improving her education. He takes a delight in tormenting Bradley Headstone. To avoid Headstone, and so save Wrayburn from his madness, Lizzie leaves London. Eugene traces her, however, and is in turn followed by Bradley, who attempts to murder him. Lizzie saves Eugene, however, and although it is expected that he will die, he marries Lizzie as the only reparation he can make. He does not die, however, although it is some time before he recovers, and is left in the story determined to stand in the face of society and fight, for his wife's sake.

WRAYBURN. Eugene, Eldest brother of. *O. M. F.* xii.
Heir to the family embarrassments—we call it before company, the family estates.

WRAYBURN. Eugene, Respected father of. *O. M. F.* xii.

WRAYBURN. Eugene, Second brother of. *O. M. F.* xii.
A little pillar of the Church.

WRAYBURN. Eugene, Third brother of. *O. M. F.* xii.
Pitchforked into the navy.

WRAYBURN. Eugene, Youngest brother of. *O. M. F.* xii.
It was settled—that he should have a mechanical genius.

WRAYBURN. Mrs. Eugene, *Née* Lizzie Hexam. *Which see.*

WREN. Miss Jenny. *See Cleaver, Fanny.*

WRETCHES. Four doomed. In Newgate. *B. R.* lxiv.
Who were to suffer death—could be plainly heard—crying—that the flames would shortly reach them—and that with as much distraction—as though each had an honoured happy life before him, instead of eight-and-forty hours of miserable imprisonment, and a violent death.

WRIGHT'S. Inn "next door" to "Bull" Inn, Rochester. *P. P.* ii.
Original : Said to have been the "Crown Hotel," in High Street, although at the time there was a "Wright's."

WRITER. The begging-letter.
R. P., T. B. W.
Has been in the army, the navy, the Church, and the law.

WRYMUG. Mrs., Applicant for cook at general agency office.
N. N. xvi.
Pleasant place, Finsbury—wages twelve guineas. No tea, no sugar—serious family.

WUGSBY. Jane. *P. P.* xxxv.
The prettier and younger daughter.

WUGSBY. Mrs. Colonel, One of whist party at Assembly Rooms, Bath. *P. P.* xxxv.
Of an ancient and whist-like appearance.

WURZEL. Roger. *M. P., P. M. B.*

WYE.   *M. P., I. W. M.*

WYNFORD. Lord.   *M. P., C. P.*

X

X. Right Hon. Mr.   *M. P., R. T.*

XAVIER. Saint Francis, *Cathe*dral dedicated to in St. Louis.
                              A. N. xii.

Y

Y—. Earl.   *M. P., R. T.*

YALE COLLEGE. New Haven.
                              A. N. v.

YARD. The. *See* Chatham Dockyard.

YARMOUTH.   *D. C.* ii.
    Then there's the sea ; and the
    boats and ships ; and the fishermen ; and the beach.

YARMOUTH ROADS.   *U. T.* xvii.

YAWLER. Schoolfellow of Traddles.
                              D. C. xxvii.
    With his nose on one side . . .
A professional man who had been
to Salem House.

YAWYAWAH.   Captain of the
robbers.   *M. P., T. O. H.*

YELLOW. Another boating man.
                    S. B. B., Scenes x.

YELLOW DWARF. A toy.
                    R. P., A. C. T.

YELLOW STONE BUFFS.
                              M. P., A. P.

YORK. *C. S., H. T.*; *N. N.* vi.;
                              L. D. xxv.

YORK. (U.S.A.)   *A. N.* ix.

YORK MINSTER.   *N. N.* vi.

YORKSHIRE. *B. H.*, lx. ; *C. S.,
    H. T.* ; *G. E.* ; *H. T., R.* xi. ;
    M. P., P. F. and S. R. ; *O. M. F.*
    x. ; *R. P., A. C. T. and B. S.* ;
                              U. T. x.

YOUNG. Brigham, A Mormon.
                              U. T. xx.

YOUNG ENGLAND. *M. P., A. J. B.*

YOUTH. From a library.
                        D. and S. xii.
    A white-haired youth, in a black
calico apron.

YOUTH. Name of bird. *B. H.* xiv.

Z

" Z."   *M. P., F. N. P.*

Z——. Lord.   *M. P., R. T.*

" ZAMIEL." Passenger in train.
                              R. P., A. F.

ZOBBS.   *M. P., T. T.*

ZOOLOGICAL GARDENS. Regent's
Park. *M. P., F. of the L. and
    M. P., P. F.*; *U. T.* xxiv.

INDEX TO ORIGINALS

NOTE.—Places and characters only appear in this index when the originals have names different from those in the books.

Red Lion Inn	Angler's Inn.	Stroughill, Lucy	Lucy.
Red Lion Inn	Inn.	Stroughill, Lucy	Manette, Lucy.
Regent Hotel, Leamington	Royal Hotel.	Sudbury	Eatanswill.
Restoration House, Rochester	Satis House.	Sun Inn, Canterbury	Inn, Little.
		Surrey Theatre	Theatre.
Rigaud, Gen.	Rigaud, M.	Swan Hotel	Blue Lion.
Rochester	Abbey Town.	Swan, The	Hungerford Stairs.
Rochester	Cloisterham.		
Rochester	Mudfog.	Tavistock, Covent Garden	Piazzo Hotel.
Rochester	Our Town.	Taylor, James	T. J. P.
Rochester	Uptown.	Taylor, Mr.	Mell, Mr.
Rochester	Winglebury.	Tenterden	Muggleton.
Rochester Mystery	Drood (Edwin).	Tom's Coffee House, Russell Street	Coffee House, Noted.
Rockingham	Chesney.		
Rockingham	Parsonage House.	Tong	Village, also Church.
Rockingham Castle	Chesney Wold.	Tower Dock, No. 6	Quilp's House.
Royal Crescent, Bath	House at Bath.	Town Malling	Abbey Town.
Royal Hotel	Copps' Hotel.	Trood, Edwin	Drood, Edwin.
Roylance, Mrs.	Pipchin, Mrs.	Tubby	Harris.
Russell Court.	Churchyard.	Tubby	Short.
S. . . , John, of Broadiswood	Browdie, John.	Vale, Samuel	Weller, Sam.
		Vines, The	Monks' Vineyard.
Sadler, John	Merdle, Mr.	Vintners' Almshouses, Mile End Road	Titbull's Almshouses.
St. Alphege, Greenwich	Church.		
St. Botolph's Churchyard	Churchyard.	Wainwright, Thomas Griffiths	Chuzzlewit, Jonas.
St. Botolph's Church	Houndsditch Church.	Wainwright, Thomas Griffiths	Rigaud, M.
St. Dunstan's Church	Chimes, The.	Wainwright, T. G.	Slinkton, Julius
St. Dunstan's St., Canterbury.	Wickfield, Mr.	Ward of Chas. Dickens	Summerson, Esther.
St. Mary's Grange	Pecksniff's House.	Warren's Blacking Factory	Murdstone and Grinby.
St. Thomas' Street, Portsmouth	Crummles' Lodgings.	Watson, Hon. Mrs.	Dedlock, Lady.
Sandling	Dingley Dell.	Watson, Robert	Gashford, Mr.
Shaw	Squeers, W.	Welbeck Street, 64	Gordon's, Lord House.
Shepherd's Shore	Inn.		
Ship and Lobster	"Ship."	Weller, Mary	Mary.
Ship Tavern, Greenwich	Hotel.	Weller, Mary	Peggotty.
Shorne	Churchyard.	Wellington House Academy	Our School.
Singlewell	Dingley Dell.	Wellington House Academy	Salem House.
Snodgrass, Gabriel	Snodgrass, Augustus.	Wellington House Academy	School.
Snodland	Cloisterham Weir.	White Duck.	Travellers' Twopenny.
Snodland	Snodgrass, Augustus.	White Hart	Inn, A famous.
Sondes Arms, Rockingham	"Dedlock Arms."	White Hart, Stevenage.	"Peal of Bells."
Southgate House, Bury	Westgate House.	Wigmore Street	Mantalini's house.
Southwark Bridge	Iron Bridge.	Willis, Tom	Codlin.
Spong, Mr.	Wardle, Mr.	Winters, Mr.	Tupman Mr.
Spong, Mrs.	Wardle, Mrs.	Wood, Mrs. Somerville	Hunter Mrs. Leo
Square, The, Ramsbottom	Square, The, London.	Workhouse Girl	Marchioness.
Stevenage, Herts	County. [sey.	Wren	Cleaver, Fanny.
Strong, Miss	Trotwood, Betsey	York House Hotel, Bath	Royal Hotel.
Stroughill	Steerforth, James.	York St., Covent Garden	Tom-all-alone's.
Stroughill	Struggles.	Zoar (Strict Baptist) Chapel	Bethel Little.
Stroughill, Lucy	Green, Miss.		

Butler & Tanner, The Selwood Printing Works, Frome, and London.

Lightning Source UK Ltd.
Milton Keynes UK
UKHW010749221118
332685UK00007B/1286/P